Resolution and Determination

A Pride and Prejudice Variation

By Kate Speck

Updated January 2020

All Kate Speck books available on Kindle eBook:

Resolution and Determination: An Erotic Adventure Fiction (Rated M)

Lessons in Gratitude (Rated T)

Services of a Friend (Rated K)

The Proud and The Beast (Rated T)

Clues to a Mystery: A Pride and Prejudice Sequel; short-story (Rated T)

First Impressions of a Second Nature (Rated T)

Growing Pains (Rated T)

Growing Pains Too: A Pride and Prejudice & Persuasion Crossover (Rated T)

Teachings of His Father (Rated K)

November Twenty-Seventh (Rated M)

Murders in London (Rated T)

The Next Mrs. Darcy (Rated T)

The Adventures of Lizzy Bennet Books 1 – 3 (Rated K)

Rank and Circumstance (Rated T)

Love in the Afternoon (Rated T)

50 First Impressions (Rated T)

The Diary (Rated T)

Mr. Darcy's Deception (Rated T)

PART 1

Chapter 1

Fitzwilliam Darcy was done. He had had enough. After Caroline Bingley's pathetic attempts in ingratiating herself with him this morning and then receiving Lady Catherine's demands to marry her daughter Anne de Bourgh once again, he was sick and tired of being a gentleman: A gentleman who had to constantly watch for traps; one who could not speak his mind freely to be proper; one who could not enjoy life like his friends.

This past summer had been one of the most painful times in his life, other than losing his parents, when his baby sister almost eloped with his childhood friend-turned-enemy George Wickham. Georgiana was an innocent and thank God she still remained so, but her spirits were low and he was advised by his uncle and aunt, Lord and Lady Matlock, to give her some space to heal.

Darcy had arrived in Netherfield yesterday, exhausted but restless, and Charles' shrew of a sister was constantly asking him questions, touching his bodily person in one way or another, and would not let him be, when he only wanted some peace and quiet and perhaps a little intelligent conversation.

Darcy had been an honourable man all of his life. He was master of a massive estate and other holdings, single, and one of the most eligible bachelors in the country, and above all, lonely. He had been busy with extensive education on how to be a landowner from an early age and seeing his parents' love for each other as the prime example of a happy marriage, he never thought he would be in his place now as a twenty-seven-year-old having never experienced love.

After his parents passed, his mother first after Georgiana was born, and then his father from a lingering illness several years ago, he threw himself into working and raising his sister. He had been to plenty of ballrooms and dined with the most esteemed of nobilities but never found anyone that sparked his interest longer than the night. He had met the best that society had to offer and found them all wanting.

The ladies were vapid and empty-headed, even if beautiful with bedecked jewellery and yards of silk, since he knew they were either after his wealth or his body. He had been propositioned by married women, young widows, and even maidens, who offered endless pleasures without commitment, but he was able to resist them all. He wanted to marry for love. He wanted a wife who would treasure him as a man alone.

At breakfast this morning, all he wanted was his coffee and newspaper but Miss Bingley had the gall to wake up earlier than her wont to disrupt his peaceful hour. She asked if he slept well, if his room was to his expectations, if the coffee was hot enough, and complained about the backwater county that she was forced to reside while speaking of the grandeurs of Pemberley and how much his home needed a woman's touch. Did she not realise that she was putting down her brother for choosing Netherfield, which was her own home now, and that although larger and certainly better in Darcy's mind, Pemberley was still in the country where trees and farmlands were the main surroundings? She also insulted his mother and his sister who had decorated his mansion and made it a home. She had visited Pemberley only once and he knew she only wanted to be mistress there to access his wealth and connections.

He had excused himself as quickly as possible and wanted to ride his favourite horse around the land to enjoy the outdoors, but then his aunt's letter had arrived and had ruined his day.

While pacing the pathway in the garden in contemplation after he read the letter, Darcy could not believe the rudeness and haughtiness that his aunt's letter presented. He knew all of her repeated demands that it was his mother's favourite wish to unite Rosings and Netherfield were false, as his mother had written him a letter to specify that she wanted him to find happiness with a wife he loved. He had written proof in his mother's hand! Lady Catherine was a grasping, mercenary woman who flaunted rank with arrogance and she expected all to carry her commands as if law. Darcy shook his head, *I would rather be a poor stable-hand than be proud and obnoxious as she.* He also detested Caroline Bingley for all her pretences of being a lady when she was a tradesman' daughter with £20,000 dowry and that was her only redeeming quality.

Darcy thought of what he wanted in his future wife. Did he desire a large dowry? Miss Bingley had £20,000 while his cousin Anne had £30,000. No. He did not care for money as he had too much as it were. His properties and investments had brought in £45,000 last year alone and he had kept it a secret from all except from Richard Fitzwilliam. His cousin and co-guardian to his sister was the only one who knew his deepest wishes and Darcy had helped build up Richard's inheritance of £25,000 in return for his true friendship. Richard only stayed a colonel in the army because he desired to serve the country and to train the new recruits to make them better on the field during the war. Darcy's rumoured £10,000 a year was ridiculous but he had let it circulate, since he would find absolutely no rest should the truth be found. No, he did not need more funds.

Did he need status? His family was one of the oldest in the lands and highly respected. Although not titled, he garnered more prestige than any earl and he was master over hundreds of tenants and servants. He had connections aplenty and his uncle, the Earl of Matlock, was his biggest champion. No, he did not need or want a wife with a lineage which might require even more socialising with more time required at insipid dinners and Ballrooms.

Darcy wanted love. He wanted respect and intelligent conversation with a woman who was pleasing to look at and would have eyes only for him. He knew the ways of the world. He was still chaste, a feat in itself, considering the temptations thrown his way, but he had witnessed couples on the throes of passion and how the marriage bed worked. His cousin Richard, who had extensive experience, had shared that even though the act was immediately gratifying, it was not long-lasting and he knew Richard was secretly awed that Darcy was still a virgin. Bingley had explained in detail how pleasurable bedding a woman was and how often he needed to visit a brothel. Darcy advised Bingley against taking a mistress after a spectacular failure at courting a pretty woman with £10,000. Bingley was particularly depressed that the lady whom he had loved so deeply for two months would turn her attention to Darcy as soon as introduced and had pursued his wealthy friend, attempting to compromise Darcy in public.

Darcy wanted to take beautiful women to bed. He wanted to be a rake and flirt and visit whores. He wanted to be carefree and get drunk and gamble. But having seen Wickham first-hand at all these things, he had his family's name to protect. His sister was his top priority and he could never be so dishonourable.

But now, he was determined to change his life. He wanted to speak his mind. He did not believe that being more open would mean being dishonourable but rather, he had the wealth and status and the power to wield his opinions. He would not be so obnoxious as Lady Catherine, he hoped, but he would be frank and sincere if possible and cease the unwanted attentions of these mercenaries. He would step out of his shyness and perhaps talk to an interesting woman. He prayed there must be someone who could ignite his mind as well as his body.

—

4

Darcy gathered his thoughts and went into the Netherfield library where the shelves sat mostly empty and wrote a letter to Lady Catherine.

Madam,

I have received your most ill-mannered letter and have determined that I shall be as frank and sincere with you as you always have claimed to be.

I know for a fact that your declarations that my mother had desired my marrying your daughter is a falsehood and I have it in writing as proof of her wishes. She desired me to marry for love and never once mentioned an arrangement. Your continued demands that your daughter and I are engaged are lies and I will no longer tolerate your commands that I do so.

It is on your head if your daughter should be a permanent spinster, as you denied her a season in town and have filled her head with talks of becoming mistress of my homes.

You, madam, have forgotten that you have relied on my benevolence for the past four years of overseeing your estate on my annual visits and that without my supplementing and managing Rosings Park, you would need to retrench or likely lose your precious estate completely. As I have loaned to you £10,000 the last four years in order for you to continue to live so lavishly, I will now demand that your debt be repaid in the next twelve months.

You have exhausted my patience as I have repeatedly told you that I would not marry your sickly daughter. I have no feelings than a cordial acknowledgement of her as a cousin and your continued delusions have made her into a voiceless creature, whom I will never consider as a wife.

I have met many mercenary women and I believe you are the worst one, using the familiar connections to disparage me and spread lies. If I hear of you telling anyone of my being engaged to your daughter one more time, you will force my hand to require payment of your debt to me immediately and I will make it publicly known that I have cut ties with you.

I have written to my solicitor to make arrangements for the repayment of the debt and will also be writing to inform my uncle, your brother, that I wash my hands of you. I will ask him to take over management of Rosings and do not dare believe Richard or I will ever assist you again. Your latest letter was the last straw and I am now more determined than ever to make my own path, regardless of society's expectations and misplaced sense of duty. I owe my duty and honour to the Darcy name and I am master of my family.

I will now consider our ties to be at an end. I find it hard to forgive your follies and vices and your offences against me. You have lost my good opinion long ago and it is lost forever.

Fitzwilliam Darcy, Master of Pemberley

He sanded and dusted the letter and also wrote to his uncle Matlock and his solicitor. He saw that it was time to prepare for the Meryton assembly as he had promised Bingley he would attend and rose to dress.

I dread what I will find there but I must be more open and converse tonight, Darcy thought, *if only to keep my distance from Caroline Bingley!*

Chapter 2

The residents of Meryton were eagerly anticipating the Netherfield party, as rumours were rampant on how wealthy Mr. Bingley was and everyone wanted to see if they could capture his attention. There were several unmarried daughters who wanted to forge a connection, as Netherfield was one of the largest properties in Hertfordshire, and none were more eager than Mrs. Bennet, who had five daughters who were all out in society.

Mr. and Mrs. Bennet had a happy marriage for the first several years but after Lydia was born, Mrs. Bennet despaired from not having an heir for Longbourn and began to distance herself from her husband. They continued to drift apart until he was no longer visiting her bed and she had become a shrill and excitable woman. She constantly worried for her future and knew her husband was gravely disappointed in her and avoided spending time alone with her husband as much as possible. Her 'nerves' were legendary but she was most afraid that her husband would hate her for only providing daughters.

Mr. Bennet was disappointed when his wife withdrew from his attentions and had initially wanted to give her time and space, but she became more distant and avoided him altogether. He wanted to comfort her and love her but it was easier to retreat to his study and focus on his work. He had poured his attentions on his first three daughters who were very intelligent, and educated his second daughter, who was his favourite. Elizabeth was bright and happy as well as energetic and beautiful. His wife had preferred Jane, who was similar in looks to herself, and found it distressing to have Lizzy question her on everything around the household and run out of doors in the rain, but Mr. Bennet spent his time teaching Lizzy languages and mathematics and philosophy, and shared his library with her to further open her mind.

Mary was similar in Lizzy's looks but was quiet and shy like Jane. Where Jane showed kindness, Mary hid behind her pianoforte, and she was well read like Lizzy but preferred novels and spiritual studies. Mr. Bennet and Lizzy often strategized to bring Mary out of her shell but she had remained demure for years.

Kitty and Lydia were young and had been left to Mrs. Bennet's care and grew to be thick as thieves now at the age of seventeen and fifteen. Although Mrs. Bennet saw to their education, Mr. Bennet encouraged Jane, Lizzy, and Mary to have a hand in helping them understand propriety and how to comport themselves in society. Mrs. Bennet begged and bemoaned for all of the girls to be 'out' at fifteen and although complying with the request, Mr. Bennet ensured that they would behave properly or their allowances would be withheld if they should be silly girls.

Mr. Bennet attended the assembly waiting for Mr. Bingley's party after meeting Charles Bingley a week ago and found him to be amiable and kind. He thought he would be good for Jane, as they were similar in character, but worried that his wife would push for the acquaintance harder than Jane's wont.

He had been diligently saving for nearly twenty years, after Lizzy was born, to increase his daughters' dowries and to secure their futures in the hopes that each of his daughters would find their own contentment. When he looked into Lizzy's eyes after she was born, he did not want to fail his family by being unprepared, should he have only daughters, and he wanted to ensure his beautiful daughters would be well-provided in their adulthood. He had not told his wife until only two months ago, after Lizzy's persistence that her mother should know, that he had been able to save

—

£5,000 each for his daughters so far and was certain with Mr. Gardiner's investments, he would be able to raise it to £6,000 each for his three youngest daughters, as Jane and Lizzy would most likely marry soon.

Jane and Lizzy had had several offers of marriage already and they had turned them all down, as none of the men were deemed worthy to be their future companions. They were considered the belles of the county but truly, they were beautiful women who were coveted when they ventured to town. Jane was a quiet beauty, tall and blonde with deep blue eyes, and she had attracted a baronet, a landowner of £4,000 a year, as well as several wealthy tradesmen who wanted a pretty gentlewoman on their arms.

Lizzy, though, was the striking beauty that men were dumbfounded when meeting her. She was a brunette and petite with pure green eyes that shone like gems. She was full of intelligence and laughter but had a cutting remark should she or her family be disrespected, and she was well-read and had worked with her father and the steward on estate management and too clever for most men. She had captured the attentions of several prominent aristocrats but she would fend them off by subtly citing incompatibility. She desired to marry for love and none of the men were half-interesting enough for her to settle. She knew she had too many opinions about everything in the world and had no wish to be someone's arm decoration in public and to sit and embroider in the sitting room all day. She wanted to experience the world and to learn and have the attention of a man who would challenge her mind. The viscount and the second son of the duke were dull and she knew they desired her only for her body. They were given their wealth and status and took it for granted, and their £8,000 a year was not enough temptation for her to agree to their marriage proposals when they did not wish to hear of her views of the world. Beauty would fade and she refused to be trapped in a loveless marriage. She was determined to be a great aunt to Jane's children and teach them to play the pianoforte terribly.

~*~

The anticipation was finally over when the Bingley party entered the assembly. Instead of the rumoured twelve ladies and eight gentlemen, two ladies and three gentlemen arrived. Sir William Lucas approached the group to make introductions and soon, the music resumed.

Bingley was introduced to the Bennets and immediately asked Jane to dance. As he left to the main floor, Darcy frowned and remained behind the Hursts after the brief introductions since he was angry with Miss Bingley, when she once again presumed an intimacy that did not exist. They had been delayed in leaving Netherfield due to some poor excuse when Miss Bingley had to suddenly change her dress. Louisa Hurst rolled her eyes and they had to wait another half-hour and Darcy was furious when he realised that she had gone to change her gown to match his green waistcoat. She had been wearing a hideous orange gown earlier and had bolted upstairs to change into a putrid green dress that looked like horse hay-vomit. He was disgusted with her behaviour and was determined to end it tonight. He would not dance with her and planned to advise her that all of her schemes would not work. He was determined more than ever to be open and direct, even if it meant being brutally honest and was going to tell her so after the assembly, but she had grabbed his arm on their way into the assembly hall and had rubbed her breasts against him, and he was infuriated with her lack of propriety. By the time they had entered the hall, he was still in high dungeon and was not in the mood to be introduced or pleased.

He went to the table to get himself a drink and hoped the punch had a good amount of alcohol in it. He never drank to excess but he needed to fortify himself as he heard loud whispers of 'five thousand a year' amongst the crowd. He knew the rural townsfolk would be crass but it was not dissimilar to Derbyshire and even the London scene had been worse. He tried to shake off his foul mood but it had been too soon, even after he took several breaths to calm himself.

Bingley approached him and jovially stated, "I have never seen so many pretty girls in my life!"

Darcy scoffed. He had not noticed anyone, but then again, he was still wallowing in his rage. Jane Bennet looked pretty enough, although she disinterested him immediately. He replied, "You are dancing with the only handsome girl in the room."

Bingley laughed with glee, "Oh, yes! She is the most beautiful creature I have ever beheld. You know how I truly prefer blondes. But her sister Elizabeth is very agreeable. Quite agreeable."

Without even looking, Darcy gruffly answered, "Barely tolerable, I daresay." He was tired of this conversation already. "I will need to talk to you about your sister later, Bingley. She has finally reached my limit and I do not know if I can stay two more months at Netherfield if she continues her way. I am in a foul mood and am not pleased to be here. Go back to your partner and enjoy her smiles. You are wasting your time with me."

~*~

Elizabeth was shocked and angry to hear Mr. Darcy state that she was barely tolerable but she then heard his reason for his foul mood and sympathised with the man. He was very handsome but wore a scowl and it appeared that Mr. Bingley's sister was the reason for his irritability. She was hurt that such a handsome man found her barely tolerable but she lifted her chin and decided he was not worth her time. She walked past him and stopped to converse with Charlotte Lucas to find humour in his criticism of her appearance, but consoled by the fact that at least he thought her sister Jane handsome. She glanced at him and caught his eye but turned back quickly to Charlotte when she spoke.

Charlotte stated, "Oh, Eliza, I am sure he does not mean it. You are very pretty and I know your mother keeps telling you Jane is most beautiful but I promise you have exceeded her by far. You must know that you are such a lovely young woman, unlike me. I rarely am asked to dance and I am afraid I will be a spinster aunt and a burden to my family."

Hearing her dearest friend despair once again, Elizabeth quickly rallied, "You and I will be spinsters together. I will invite you to live with me and we shall teach our nieces to play the pianoforte and how to be impertinent. You shall never fear for your future, dear Charlotte. We have each other."

Charlotte smiled brightly with tears in her eyes. "Thank you, Eliza. You are a true friend. Shall I go and do the same with Mr. Darcy as I did with my brother?" And soon, they were laughing together.

They did not realise that they had an audience, though.

As soon as Elizabeth passed by him, Darcy felt like a cad. He was certain she had heard his comment of her being 'barely tolerable' and as he watched her from behind, he quickly realised she had a light and pleasing figure. She wore a dark green dress that was cut well and as much Caroline Bingley bemoaned the fact that these 'country bumpkins' had no style at all, Miss Elizabeth looked quite fine, at least from behind.

—

8

He stood immobile when she turned, though. He had not looked at her face at all and definitely was not thinking when he spoke those harsh words, but when she turned towards him before facing her friend, he could see that she was beautiful. Their eyes met for a split second and he felt his heart lurch; when she broke into a wide smile and he heard her laugh with Miss Lucas, he knew he was in danger. *What an arse I am! She is gorgeous!*

Darcy had met dozens and hundreds of beautiful women in town and had seen all types of figures. He had preferred blondes most of his life, as his own mother was blonde and beautiful as was his sister, and many men considered the classic beauty to be as such. But he had noticed that his eyes drew to darker-haired women more often lately. He knew he definitely preferred larger bosoms and was embarrassed that he had been drawn to such base desires, but he had kept himself in check and deterred from thinking of such physical attributes as much as possible. When Miss Elizabeth turned her face towards him, he saw a spark in her beautiful green eyes and he desired to know her. No woman had inspired his body in such a way before and her eyes appeared so intelligent, he knew he had to apologise. Since he was determined to be more open now, he swallowed his pride and walked over where she stood.

"Miss Lucas, may I request an introduction? I believe we were briefly introduced but Mr. Bingley had left to dance with Miss Bennet before more conversations could be had." Darcy humbled himself as he looked at Miss Elizabeth.

"But of course, Mr. Darcy. This is my dearest friend Miss Elizabeth Bennet of Longbourn. Eliza, this is Mr. Darcy." Charlotte replied.

"Fitzwilliam Darcy, at your service, madam. Miss Elizabeth, I must beg for your forgiveness. I believe you had heard my comment to Mr. Bingley and you must know that I was in a foul mood but it is no excuse. I behaved ungentlemanly when I stated that you were barely tolerable." Here, Darcy decided to try his first attempt at flirting. "In all honesty, I find you to be quite tolerable and wish to ask if you are available to dance the next with me." He flashed a shy smile, as he knew he must have sounded like a fool.

Elizabeth laughed and returned a broad smile. "Thank you, Mr. Darcy. Your apology is accepted and I would be happy to dance with you."

Darcy was relieved that she did not begrudge him his rude comment, as many ladies would have taken offense and might have made him suffer for it. He was also pleased that he would dance with her and displayed a big grin, making Elizabeth and Charlotte gasp in surprise. He was dashingly handsome as he flashed his dimples and his whole countenance was changed.

~*~

Darcy proffered his arm and Elizabeth took it gently as they headed to the dance floor. She was surprised by his candour and apology and looked forward to speaking with him. He appeared to be quite shy and she was curious what it was about this man that intrigued her so. She was flattered that he had immediately confessed his error and wondered of his situation, even though she had heard that he was a gentleman of some means but not much more was known about him. There was some talk of his being possibly above Mr. Bingley's consequence and he did dress very well, but she could not imagine having two of such wealthy gentlemen in her quiet country. She cared not for wealth or rank and she was determined to get to know him better and asked him for conversation, as it would be odd to be silent for the next half hour.

Darcy was entranced. Miss Elizabeth was witty and she glimmered with joy; she was the most beautiful woman he had ever met and her intelligence was unparalleled. They discussed books and she had been able to quote philosophical anecdotes that he had learned at university that most men would be unable to recall, and she laughed wholeheartedly as they spoke of the theatre and the latest musicale that she attended last spring. He could not help but smile as she glided on the dance floor so gracefully during their set together. She spoke of her mother who was desperate to marry off her daughters in concern for her own future but she laughed that she would rather settle with her sisters in a small cottage and live out her life in quiet and peace than to marry someone odious and possibly odiferous. He had never met her equal and was resolute that he should court her.

Now, would she have him, though? He had never considered anyone to refuse him. With his status and wealth, he had flocks of women seeking his attention, and this was the first and only woman, as he considered her words, who might be happier sitting in a cottage than to be married to someone she did not love. *Damn! I think I have found the perfect woman and she might not have me. I was such a fool. She is much more than tolerable. Irresistible, in fact!* Darcy thought.

He decided to gauge her response and see what she might think of him. He had thought himself quite handsome, but it was obvious that his looks and wealth would not be a factor in her affection. He had been so shy, he always envied his cousin for his charming personality. He thought of how Richard approached ladies and attempted to emulate him. As they stood on the sides of the dance floor and he offered her a glass of punch, he continued his conversation with her.

"You seem to enjoy dancing very much. You are quite light on your feet and I have never enjoyed a dance more, Miss Elizabeth."

"You are quite skilled yourself, Mr. Darcy. Do you dance often? You must have many chances to do so; I have heard Mr. Bingley speak of how much he enjoys it." Elizabeth replied.

"I do indeed attend many dances but I rarely dance. To be truthful, I never dance except when required. I believe I have been waiting for the right partner." Darcy flirted.

Elizabeth blushed, "But such skills deserve to be used more often, sir. Will you dance with your hostess Miss Bingley? She appears to be looking your way often." She teased him. She had heard what he had said about 'reaching his limit' and was curious.

"I will not dance with her. Miss Elizabeth, I know you overheard my comments." He flashed a grin. "You tease me and I will tell you. I had a terrible summer with some... bad experiences several months ago and had agreed to join Bingley for some peace and rest. His sister had not left me alone and I was at my wit's end today. She has... expectations that I cannot fulfil and I, only today, have made decisions for great changes in my... life choices. I wonder, Miss Elizabeth... I have found our conversations more pleasing than I have ever had with another woman. Would you be... May I call on you tomorrow?" He had started strong but became more timid as he began to open his heart to her at the end. He was aware there were several eyes trained at them and even Bingley was standing with his mouth gaping. His friend had never seen Darcy speak with a woman for more than a few words and he never danced and he never smiled so.

Elizabeth's heart fluttered. She had many suitors but none had thrilled her like Mr. Darcy, who was intelligent and incredibly handsome and patient. He had listened and answered her without condescension, and he appeared to be pleased when she spoke her mind, not irritated that she showed some sense in her opinions.

"I would be pleased if you would call on me, Mr. Darcy. I enjoyed our dance and conversation very much. I must return to my parents now to await my next partner." Elizabeth beamed.

"May I walk you over?" Darcy returned her smile. She nodded. As they walked to the other side of the room, he asked, "Do you have another dance available? May I have another set?"

Elizabeth was stunned at the request. He had told her that he never danced and he asked her to dance twice. "Yes, I am available for the last set."

"Thank you. I will return later." He bowed to her.

He had heard Miss Lucas' sadness of not having a dancing partner and approached her for the next set. He wanted to be near Miss Elizabeth's proximity as well.

"Miss Lucas, may I have the pleasure of dancing the next set?" Darcy gave her a soft smile, attempting to not glance at Elizabeth's direction.

Charlotte knew that Mr. Darcy was smitten with Eliza and surmised quickly that he was trying to impress her dearest friend. "Mr. Darcy, I am available. Thank you for asking. I would be happy to speak with you about some of my *dear friend's* stories." She laughed as he smiled broadly.

Elizabeth saw Mr. Darcy speaking with Charlotte and beamed when she saw them line up for the dance. *He is most considerate. I know he is dancing with Charlotte to please me. How can my heart beat like this for a man that I just met today?*

Darcy smiled a few times as Charlotte shared stories of Eliza and he attempted to be a gentleman to keep his eyes on his dancing partner but could not help himself as he looked at Elizabeth often. *She is the most beautiful creature I have ever met!*

After the dance, Darcy thanked Miss Lucas and returned to Mr. Bingley who was standing next to his sisters.

Bingley grinned stupidly at him as he saw him approach. Miss Bingley was red and fuming, and the Hursts appeared apathetic.

"So, it appears you found some pleasant company, Darcy. Are you having a good time?" Bingley asked.

Darcy's mask of indifference returned. He did not want to appear too pleased, especially in front of Caroline Bingley. He detested her right now and did not want to show any pleasure in her presence. "Yes, quite. I enjoyed dancing with Miss Elizabeth and Miss Lucas was telling me more about her friend. Miss Elizabeth is quite intriguing, Bingley. I asked to call on her tomorrow and she has accepted." He could not help but smile a little. "She is a fascinating lady. Have you much luck with your Miss Bennet?"

"Oh yes, we can call on them together tomorrow. She is a lovely creature." Bingley preened.

Caroline Bingley wanted her share of the conversation and intruded. "You danced wonderfully, Mr. Darcy. Why, I do believe the last set will be starting up soon and I am certain you wish to show how *our* sphere excel at the activity," she began to reach for his arm, fully expecting him to ask for the last dance.

He stepped back with his arms behind. "*Our* sphere, Miss Bingley? How presumptuous of you." He scoffed. "I must find my partner, pray excuse me." And he left quickly. He felt Bingley behind him as they both approached the Bennet party.

Several gasps were heard as Bingley led Jane and Darcy led Elizabeth to the floor. Bingley could not believe Darcy was dancing a second set with one lady when he had never done so before.

As they lined up, Bingley was in another shock as he saw Darcy's full smile and he actually winked at him!

Chapter 3

Darcy lay on his bed looking at the canopy above him after the wondrous night at the assembly. He had never enjoyed a country-dance more and he remembered every word that Elizabeth spoke and her looks and her sparkling eyes. It also appeared that no one in Meryton knew of his status or wealth, and Bingley spoke on the return ride that it was generally believed that Darcy was a gentleman of perhaps £2,500 a year and he had laughed at Sir William's blabbering but had not corrected the man's assumptions since Bingley was well aware of Darcy's requirement for privacy. Miss Bingley was fuming as it was evident of the attention that Elizabeth Bennet had been given and refused to talk to him and Darcy could not be more delighted that he was finally being left alone by the shrew.

A quick nightcap with Bingley determined that as long as Miss Bingley kept her claws off, Darcy would remain at Netherfield and they compared their delightful dancing partners then headed off to bed. Darcy would finally be at peace for a while and he would see Miss Elizabeth soon to request her for courtship. He was certain she was the woman he had been waiting for, and although it had been only one evening, he felt more desire for her, more consideration, and thought of their time together more than he did any other woman. He remembered her curves. From her jaws to her neck to her bounteous bosoms down to her slim waist and hips, she had inspired him like no one before.

"Argh," Darcy growled. *Damn it, I cannot believe I am hard again. That beautiful creature has bewitched me.* His bulging erection was ready to explode and he knew there was only one thing he could do. He knew how his body had reacted and what he had to do to deflate it after a certain point.

When he was about fourteen, he had inadvertently witnessed his sister's nanny in an amorous embrace with the head gardener. He did not quite understand why the man would be on top of her with his trousers down and what he was doing to her that made her make those sounds. She soon opened her legs wider on the sofa and he was able to see the man's erect penis penetrating inside her between the legs. He ran away as she screamed her pleasures and went to his father to ask what had happened and if she was being hurt.

His father told him to stay in the study while he looked into the matter, and when he returned, he had explained that they were having marital relations in a public area and they would have to be married now. His father took pains to teach Darcy about the marriage bed, how a man had fulfilled a woman and how a child was produced. He also cautioned his son about the dangers of being 'captured' by a mercenary woman and spoke of marital fidelity and avoiding temptations. His father patiently taught him about self-gratification to release the built-up tensions and to keep himself busy so that he would not dwell on sexual thoughts.

Darcy released his large manhood from his breeches. He stroked himself and could not stop thinking of Elizabeth. As he pumped wildly a few more times, he released with a loud grunt as he yelled out, "Elizabeth!" He lay panting for several moments realising that he had never before thought of a specific person while he masturbated. He had visualised women's décolletage or pretty mouth; he recalled pictures or statues that he had seen that showed a woman's figure; but never before a living and breathing person had seduced him with such desires. He saw that he had shot so hard that there were semen stains on the canopy. "Blasted!" he cursed. It was embarrassing enough that he had to release himself but he would be mortified should the maids see this mess. Grabbing a towel, he wiped himself and stood on the bed to wipe off the stains as much as possible and went to sleep with a smile on his face.

~*~

Elizabeth was lying in her bed and gossiped with Jane on what they saw during the evening to talk of their dancing partners and they sighed contentedly, as they both realised that they had one of the most pleasurable evenings of their lives. Elizabeth soon revealed Jane of Mr. Darcy's initial slight.

Shocked, Jane spoke, "Surely he cannot have meant it, Lizzy! I cannot believe anyone would believe you to be 'tolerable'! It is shocking; but you danced with him. Twice! How did that come about?"

Elizabeth replied, "He truly said it, Jane, but I have absolved him of his conduct as he confessed to me quickly that he was wrong and that he found me 'quite tolerable' and asked me to dance. We spoke of so many topics and I am glad he was not how he appeared when he first walked in. He was so amenable and he even flattered me. He was not condescending and he did not look down on me or ignore my comments but he was gentlemanly and so handsome, too. I know Mama is disappointed that he is only half as wealthy as Mr. Bingley but I believe she is pleased that I received some attention. I was afraid she would never forgive me for turning down the Duke's son but can you imagine me married to that insipid man, even if he had £8,000 a year?" She laughed. "I am truly glad that Papa has taken pains to rein in Mama more lately. Although she still has her nervous fits, she is much improved after I insisted that he tell her about our dowries. It was not fair to put her through such worries for so many years."

Although Mrs. Bennet had flittered about and was initially very upset that her husband had kept such a thing from her, she had eventually realised her own errors in keeping her distance and was proud that her husband took such care for her and their daughters' futures.

Jane and Elizabeth giggled until exhaustion took over and they fell asleep, each dreaming of their handsome suitors who would call upon them tomorrow.

~*~

Darcy woke up completely tangled. *What happened?!* He asked himself. He had been having a most wonderful dream about a particular woman with green eyes and leaning in to kiss her. He groaned as he saw the effect of the delicious fantasy on his body and decided to go for an early ride.

Xerxes was saddled and Darcy spotted a vista point that overlooked the whole neighbourhood and decided to race towards it to vent off some of his energy. He found the landscape beautiful. He always preferred the peaceful quiet of the countryside to the busy bustle of the city, and he had loved Derbyshire best but had wanted to find good in this 'backward country' as Miss Bingley called it, as he had found a woman worthy of his attentions. The townsfolk were a bit obtuse but they seemed to have good intentions and it was no different than the people of his own province.

He had looked down on people who were not of the first circles or from his own area and recognised once again his arrogance. Had he been so pompous all his life? How could he have been so like Lady Catherine and Caroline Bingley, the two females that he abhorred most in all of society? His behaviour last night, even after his resolve to change himself had been awful. He had walked into the assembly angry and scowling and had insulted a beautiful woman who did not deserve his slight. Thank God she had not been angry. He was fascinated that she would be so good-humoured to laugh off such an offense, since most ladies would have found it incredibly offensive and would have demanded an apology or publicly shamed him by crying out loudly and letting it known to everyone, to make certain he recompensed somehow for such an impolite act.

He pulled the reins to slow Xerxes when he approached the peak of the mount when he spotted a figure that resembled the woman of his dreams. He smiled and hoped that it was Elizabeth and he carefully approached and grinned like an idiot when he did indeed see Miss Elizabeth.

Dismounting, he cheered, "Good morning, Miss Bennet! How wonderful it is to see you here. I did not expect to see you until later this morning."

Elizabeth was surprised to see him here at Oakham Mount. She had dreamt about him and had woken before the household to walk and sort her thoughts. Mr. Darcy had invaded her thoughts nonstop and she worried that her heart was already his, as she had never felt such a pull towards a man before. She had met handsome and wealthy men before, those with titles and connections beyond what Mr. Darcy could offer. Although it was assumed that Mr. Darcy had about half of Bingley's wealth and he was certainly handsome, he had offended her by saying that she was 'barely tolerable' in a public place, no less, and appeared to be quite proud and difficult to please. But then he had quickly apologised and they had spoken of topics that most gentlemen would have snubbed. She could tell he was shy but not once did he talk down to her or belittle her opinions. He had smiled and encouraged her to speak on several topics and treated her as an equal. She understood quickly that he had had a terrible day that day and that he had been in a foul mood, but also could see that he was timid and unused to socialising. His attempts at flirting were terrible but endearing.

She smiled widely and responded, "I had a few things to sort out and decided to walk here early as I do every morning. I understand this is your second day here. I am surprised you found my favourite spot already."

This will be my favourite spot now! Darcy thought. "I had wanted to ride yesterday morning and if I had known I would find your favourite spot, I am certain I would have been in a better mood last evening!" *What am I doing, I am terrible at flirting!* He internally groaned.

"Well, I am glad you are having a better day today. I would be happy to share my favourite place with you." Elizabeth retorted in return. "Come and see. Beautiful, is it not?"

"Oh yes, beautiful. Most beautiful." Darcy replied quietly.

Elizabeth blushed when she understood he was not looking at the landscape but at herself. "Mr. Darcy, you must not speak so. I might think you are a rake and I wish to think you a good man, although we just met." She winked. *I cannot believe I am flirting back!*

Darcy wore another stupid grin. "Would you believe that you know me better than any woman who is not a relative? Perhaps not my history or my family but my thoughts and feelings, I have never shared so much with another living soul before. Miss Bennet, I must admit that I have been acting very out of character since meeting you."

Raising an eyebrow, Elizabeth asked, "So I have been under false pretences, sir? Perhaps you are not as charming as you seem now. Should I believe you to be arrogant and insufferable as you first appeared to be? I thought I saw through that part of you." She mocked as she smiled.

Darcy froze for a second but seeing her smile, he knew she was teasing. Oh, how he loved her. *Wait, love? I just met her last night. But she is wonderful and I must know her better.* Straightening, "Perhaps I was and still am arrogant and insufferable, but I had made a resolution to overcome those obstacles to open myself more freely only yesterday."

He smiled softly as he met her gentle eyes. He went on to explain the changes he wanted to make. He could not believe it but he talked to her of Lady Catherine's demands, the loss of his parents and difficulties raising his baby sister, Miss Bingley and other women who were chasing him, and how he wanted to find a wife who was worthy of being pleased. "I am certain I will revert to my stoic, haughty self several times but I hope you will see me as who I truly am, Miss Elizabeth. Who I want to be." He had confessed much of what was in his heart and was elated as she smiled and touched his arm.

"I thank you for sharing your difficulties with me. I am sorry that you have gone through so much. Losing your parents at such a young age and having additional responsibilities of caring for your sister cannot have been easy and I am quite proud to consider you to be a good friend already. I hope you will not be offended that I speak my mind so freely as well. I have not met any gentleman that actually listened to my opinions and find it so refreshing to not have to hold back." Elizabeth smiled brightly.

"Miss Elizabeth," Darcy stood a little closer and touched her hand that was holding his arm. "I am very pleased to hear that you consider me a friend. I know that our acquaintance has been brief but I must confess that my feelings for you have been stronger than I have ever felt and I wish to court you. I wish to know you better, to hear your thoughts on life and your wishes, and I wish for you to know me. I wish to speak my mind and for you to challenge me. Our talks yesterday and today have opened my eyes to how I want my future and I see you beside me to walk through life together. Would you... could you permit me to court you? I know it is quick but I wish to court you for the purpose of marriage." Darcy now held both of her hands and looked deeply into her eyes.

Elizabeth gasped as he spoke. *He wants to court me? Could I marry such a man? We only met yesterday but I feel a connection that I never have before. Could I already be falling in love with him? We have already spoken as if we are lifelong friends.*

Nodding, she replied, "Mr. Darcy, I must warn you that I am stubborn and have strong opinions. I never wish to be a mute wife to a man that would put me on the shelf and only use me as an arm decoration. I wish to be treated as a partner in life and request to be respected. Knowing this, if you are still willing," she paused to see him nod his head in agreement with a smile, "I would be happy to be courted by you. I would like to get to know you better."

He kissed her hands in joy and she felt warmth and tingles where his lips touched her. She continued, "I will confess to you; my parents had not been in a good marriage for many years and they are just now re-learning to get along. I had dreaded a marriage of unequal affections for many years and I had planned to never marry. Although you were initially offensive, you immediately reproached your behaviour and spoke to me as an equal. You treated me as an intelligent being. I could not consider my future with a man whom I could not respect and you have already earned it, sir."

Darcy kissed her hands. "Thank you, Miss Elizabeth. I believe we are a good match. May I walk you to your home and speak with your father?"

Pleased with the respect and care he was showing, Elizabeth smiled and nodded. They walked arm in arm with Darcy's stallion walking beside them. They continued to talk and laugh, learning more about each other.

When they approached Longbourn, Darcy kissed her hand again and requested to see Mr. Bennet.

~*~

Mr. Bennet was surprised to see Mr. Darcy so early in the morning and greeted the young man warmly into his study. He had seen the gentleman and his daughter together and noted the significance of the second dance with this reserved gentleman last night but did not expect to see him already. After hearing that by coincidence they came across each other at Oakham Mount, he asked Mr. Darcy several questions before agreeing to the courtship.

Unbeknownst to Darcy, Mr. Bennet had already been aware of who Mr. Darcy was and his standing, from his investments in London. He had heard of the rumours last night of Darcy having only £2,500 a year and laughed, as he knew that the Darcy fortune was massive and it was gossiped in London as being greater than £10,000 a year. He had invested in some of the same ventures as Mr. Darcy and although not knowing him personally, he knew of Darcy's reputation of being a stand-up gentleman, as well as his connections, and of being highly coveted as a single man of a very large fortune.

Mr. Bennet was now shocked by what Mr. Darcy had revealed about his true position and income. How could the neighbourhood have been so wrong to think Darcy was worth half of Bingley? It was the other way around; rather, Darcy's income was so significantly larger that Mr. Bingley's 5,000 a year was a pittance to Darcy's. He knew his favourite daughter was special but to draw the attention of such a great man was still astonishing.

"Mr. Darcy, I have heard of you and your reputation in town and the £10,000 a year that is gossiped about, but our neighbourhood is under the impression that your income is half of Mr. Bingley's, when it is actually that Mr. Bingley's income is half of your rumoured 10,000. But you are now telling me that your income is nearly *five times* that consequence? It is an incredible figure, sir."

Darcy laughed. "Yes, I had heard that rumour and I am glad that no one knows the truth. I have always been treated superior due to my wealth and status, and I have been exhausted of the façade of indifference and dealing with misplaced respect. Women have been chasing me for my fortune and I never felt the liberty to be myself and if the truth were known, I would have had absolutely no peace. I had made the resolution to be free from such burdens and speak my mind and then I had the blessing to meet your most wonderful daughter who touched my heart. I will tell her of my true status soon, sir. I plan to court her but I must confess I wish to make her my wife, as I have not met her equal and I feel she and I are perfect for each other already. I do not wish to rush her and I promise you that I would never do anything to hurt her or damage her reputation, but if you are agreeable, I would like to meet her in the mornings on Oakham Mount in private. I feel our conversations this morning helped us to understand each other better than any ballroom dances or drawing room visits. I truly wish to please her, sir."

Mr. Bennet could tell that the young man was already in love with his daughter. His eyes were teary, as he understood he would be losing his favourite daughter soon.

"Yes, Mr. Darcy. I will allow it. I trust that you will keep her and her reputation safe." He replied.

Darcy was relieved. He wanted to see Elizabeth and talk to her as often as possible without prying eyes and interferences. "Thank you, Mr. Bennet. I will not break your trust in me. I care for your daughter very much, sir."

"Mr. Darcy, my daughter is under the impression that you are a moderate landowner with 2,500 a year. Only a few know, but not only do my daughters now have £5,000 dowry each, they have been pursued relentlessly by gentlemen of some means for their beauty alone. The fact that Elizabeth has agreed to your courtship speaks well of her opinion of you. You may not know yet, but she refused a proposal of marriage from several gentlemen, as well as a viscount a couple of years ago and the second son of a duke recently; Lord Harold Haversham, you may know him. She found him dull and uninspiring and refused him avidly, but I see that you care for my Lizzy already and would welcome you into the family when you are ready to propose." He smiled and they shook hands.

Darcy had been stunned for a moment when he heard Lord Harold's name. He was a friend from university and had £8,000 a year. His friend was pursued heavily for his status and wealth, more than himself due to his family connections, and was considered a highly eligible bachelor. The man was not especially bright, though, and he knew that Elizabeth would not have been happy with him.

He relaxed as Mr. Bennet gave his consent and welcomed him. He would not lose his chance of winning his Elizabeth and was glad he had given up his damnable pride to pursue a woman in this corner of the country; one who had been chased by nobility! He preened, as he now had the privilege of courting that lady.

Darcy left Mr. Bennet's study and entered the sitting room where Elizabeth sat with her sister. She was so beautiful and his heart was full, knowing that he wanted to spend the rest of his life with her. He greeted Miss Bennet and kissed Elizabeth's hand and told her of her father's approval. He promised to return with Bingley later that day and departed Longbourn with a smile on his face.

Chapter 4

"I thought you got lost, Darcy! I was about to send out a search party!" Bingley greeted him as he entered Netherfield. "How do you find this country? I know none compares to Pemberley but there are several good prospects here, do you agree?"

Bingley was his jovial self and woke after a night of good rest. His sister remained in her rooms and the house was quiet and serene, and he looked forward to visiting the Bennets so he could see the beautiful Miss Bennet.

"Good morning, Bingley. Yes, I was out early and had the fortune of finding the most wonderful prospect and have made a life-changing decision today." He smirked as he saw Bingley's mouth agape again.

"What do you mean? Do you wish to move to Hertfordshire? What kind of decision could you have made?" Bingley was curious. He had never seen his long-time friend so open and engaging. Last night had been the first time in the whole of their acquaintance that he had ever danced with a lady who was not a relative or the hostess, and he had danced *twice* with the same lady! He knew Darcy's heart must had been touched, as he had never shown any attention before and Miss Elizabeth was exquisite. She had caught his eye first but then he saw Miss Bennet and he had always preferred blondes.

"Bingley, I am formally courting Miss Elizabeth Bennet. I met her by chance this morning and asked for courtship and have the approval from her father as well. I plan to get her to know me better and wish to marry her and I will not stand for anyone who interferes with my decision. By the by, Bingley, I still do need to speak to you about your sister. I was in a foul mood last night when she grabbed my arm and rubbed her chest against my arm. *That* is not the behaviour of a lady and I will no longer tolerate her presumptions. Not only did she delay our leaving by half an hour by changing her dress to match me, but she continued to touch my person as if there is an understanding between us and I would be mortified if Elizabeth saw such a thing and thought me a rake." He paced in anger. The thought of Elizabeth spurning him due to rumours of being engaged to Anne or thinking that Miss Bingley and he had an understanding would have broken his heart. "You must speak with her and get her under control. I will never marry her, even if she arranged a compromise, Bingley. I would cut her and she would be shunned in society as I find nothing pleasing about her."

Darcy took several breaths to calm himself. *What would Elizabeth do? Would she think I was being too proud?* "Bingley, I apologise for my outburst. I am not angry with you but I should have made it clearer to your sister that I am not interested in her. With your permission, I will speak to her with you in the room and explain that I am courting a most worthy lady and that she should look elsewhere for her future companion. I regret that I had not made it clear to her myself. I am not surprised that she would not listen to you and that she needs to hear it directly from me."

Bingley walked over to Darcy and tapped his shoulder. "Thank you, my friend. I see a change in you that impresses me greatly. I have talked to Caroline several times and she refuses to listen to me but she will know for certain to hear the words from you and finally end her disillusionment. Perhaps after luncheon this afternoon? I would love to visit the Bennets after you break your fast. Come, tell me how this courtship came about."

As Darcy ate, he told him about meeting Elizabeth and the conversations they had. They soon headed towards Longbourn, eagerly anticipating seeing their ladies.

~*~

Mrs. Bennet was shocked that after one evening at the assembly, Lizzy was now in courtship with Mr. Darcy. He seemed humourless and proud at first but she had noticed the smiles and sparks flying while her least favourite daughter and he danced two sets. She was confident Mr. Bingley preferred Jane and she would soon have two daughters married.

"Oh, Lizzy! I saw you dancing with Mr. Darcy last night and although he seemed a very serious young man, I am so pleased that he asked you for courtship! I am certain Mr. Bingley will ask Jane also and I shall have two daughters married this year! How wonderful! Even though Mr. Darcy is nowhere near Mr. Bingley's consequence, I am sure he will provide you such pin money and such jewels! I knew Jane was not beautiful for nothing and of course, she was able to draw the attention of the wealthier man but I am glad Mr. Darcy saw something in you as well." Mr. Bennet coughed in gentle reprimand. "Oh, I am sorry, Lizzy. I do not mean that you are worth less than Jane. You are very lovely." Mrs. Bennet blushed. She was trying to correct herself but often failed when her words left her mouth.

Turning more seriously to Elizabeth, she held her hand, "I am sorry, my child. You are a very beautiful woman and I keep begrudging you for turning down a son of a Duke and his £8,000 a year. As long as you are happy, I am very pleased that you have accepted Mr. Darcy's courtship. I hope he will make you happy and even if he has only 2,500 a year, you are very frugal and you do not care for laces and I am certain you will make the right decision." Mr. Bennet snorted at this but Elizabeth hugged her mother.

"Thank you, Mama. I believe he is a very good man and whatever happens, I appreciate that you support me and care for my happiness." Elizabeth responded.

With tears in her eyes, Mrs. Bennet returned the embrace. She was grateful that her husband had taken the time to speak with her more and now knowing that she and her daughters would be provided for, in the event that he should pass away in the near future, she felt the comfort of being secure and wanted be a good wife and mother. "I love you, Lizzy. I know I have not told you girls enough, but I love every one of you and I am still learning to think before I speak. I am proud of you, Lizzy. I do wish you to find your contentment and I know you need a strong man who can match your intelligence. And Jane, Mary, Kitty, and Lydia, I hope you know I love you all as well and that I wish you would follow your sister's example in finding your match. Do not settle for someone if they cannot make you fully happy, girls. You must find a husband whom you respect as much as I respect your father." She smiled and winked at Mr. Bennet.

All the Bennets wiped the tears in their eyes when Mrs. Hill announced their visitors. "Mr. Darcy and Mr. Bingley."

Darcy's eyes immediately sought Elizabeth as soon as he entered. *How is it possible that she has become more beautiful in the last few hours?* He greeted the family first then stood in front of Elizabeth as he reached for her hand and kissed it. They were lost in each other's gaze until they heard Lydia comment, "Aw... it is so romantic..." and Kitty began giggling. They both blushed and took a seat next to each other.

The conversation was easy and pleasant. The family congratulated them on their courtship and he spoke a little of Derbyshire in comparison to Hertfordshire. Darcy suppressed his surprise when he learned that Mrs. Bennet was a daughter of a solicitor with a brother in trade and another brother who was a solicitor but shook his head and laughed at himself as he recalled that one of his best friends was the son of a tradesman. *Will my arrogance know no end? I am infinitely glad to have met Elizabeth.*

He spoke kindly to Mrs. Bennet who was excitable but he could tell she cared for her daughters very much. He noticed Bingley in conversation with Miss Bennet and saw how interested he was in her and knew he would need to speak with Bingley, since his friend had fallen in and out of love so often and Darcy wanted to ensure his intentions were sincere. Darcy could not imagine Elizabeth's furore should his friend wound her favourite sister. Mrs. Bennet invited the gentlemen for luncheon and after agreement, he asked for a walk in the gardens.

Bingley and Miss Bennet were speaking with each other at a distance while the younger girls giggled and looked at the flowers. Darcy led Elizabeth slightly further away from the groups and spoke to her as she held his arm. "Miss Elizabeth, I have never courted anyone before so I would ask you to be patient as I fumble. Would it be acceptable if I called you by your given name in private?" With her agreement, he continued. "Elizabeth," he smiled as he said her name, "I asked your father's permission to meet with you on your early morning walks. I wanted to make sure that I had his approval, as I found our time together this morning to be most important to getting to know each other better. There are several items that I need to clarify and would like to share with you tomorrow. Is that acceptable?"

"Yes, Mr. Darcy."

"Will you not call me by my name, Elizabeth?" He looked at her longingly.

"Fitzwilliam." Elizabeth whispered shyly.

It took all of his willpower to not kiss her then. He had not had anyone calling him by his given name other than his parents or occasionally his sister and felt his connections deepen with such affection for his Elizabeth when she spoke his name. He kissed her hand quickly.

"Let us return inside as it is a bit chilly this morning." He gruffly responded to calm his heart. "Thank you, Elizabeth."

Chapter 5

After luncheon, Darcy and Bingley returned to Netherfield with the promise of visiting again the next day.

"Bingley, I suppose we need to get to the business of talking with your sister now," Darcy stated, as they were met with Miss Bingley's enthusiastic greetings as they entered the foyer.

"Yes, Darcy. It seems we must." Bingley frowned as his sister exuberantly flailed her arms and ordered the servants about. "Caroline, I must speak with you in the study. Now, if you please."

"Oh, but Charles, I dearly missed Mr. Darcy's company and you both were gone for so long and I *must* know his opinion about this mundane county and the commoners here. Mr. Darcy was the consummate gentleman, lowering himself to socialise with the general populous here, but I am certain he will agree with me that there was no beauty to be seen; only terrible manners and matrons trying to trap him in with their desperate daughters." Caroline could have never admitted to herself that she had given no consideration from the rich gentleman and had been green with envy that Mr. Darcy had danced two sets with a prettish local woman. She vowed to show him how awful these grasping women were and that *Eliza Bennet* was not worth his consideration.

"Darcy will join us as well. Let us go." Bingley was firm.

"But of course, Charles!" She fawned. She attempted to grab Darcy's arm but he was too quick and began to walk away from her, leading Bingley instead of the other way around.

Bingley closed the door behind and waited for Caroline to sit. Caroline's heart fluttered as she believed that Darcy might be finally ready to propose to her. *He must have gotten Charles' permission to address me!*

20

Caroline had chased Darcy for the past five years after he and Charles had become acquainted, and she quickly ingratiated herself into every visit to the Darcy residence and fawned and flirted for his notice. Due to Darcy's close friendship with Charles, she was certain she would become Mrs. Darcy and Charles would marry Miss Darcy, with her £30,000, and they would keep the magnificent fortune within the family. She daydreamt of spending Darcy's £10,000 a year and after visiting Pemberley once, she knew exactly which rooms she wanted to update and the top-quality furnishings that she must install there. She would demand a ball to be thrown in her honour and be a leader in London society, to laugh at those women who had spurned her and mocked her for being a daughter of a tradesman.

She fluttered her eyelashes and put on her most fawning smile as she awaited the pertinent question.

Darcy cleared his throat and began, "Miss Bingley, I appreciate your time with me today as I have something important to discuss with you. As you are aware, I spent a lot of time yesterday in a company of a young lady and have determined that I need to seek a companion for my life."

"Oh, Mr. Darcy! I knew I should not have fretted about you dancing with that *Eliza Bennet*! I am sure that harlot was trying to trap you last evening when she was blatantly flirting with you all night long. I have heard that she and her sister were considered the 'jewels of the county' but I saw nothing in her! Her teeth are tolerable but she has no beauty! I heard from my maid that her mother is a daughter of a solicitor and she has family in trade! Certainly, you would never lower yourself to her and I should not have spent one minute in worrying about the chit. I am so glad you have come to your senses and as your wife, I would update your homes and give grand parties befit..."

"CAROLINE!" Bingley yelled.

"MISS BINGLEY!" Darcy boomed.

Bingley was mortified and Darcy was red with fury. They both yelled to cease her speech but already heard her crass comments.

As Caroline shut her mouth, Darcy quickly shouted, "I will no longer tolerate your rude remarks and ridiculous behaviours. I am courting Miss *Elizabeth* Bennet and I plan to marry her. She is a true lady and I care not about her connections to trade. YOU, madam, are below her and how dare you disparage her so! I have been determined to make choices that will constitute my own happiness and it does NOT include you and if you continue to denigrate Miss Elizabeth and her family, who are all very excellent people, you should know, I have no choice but to cut you and I will have no hesitancy to do so. She is above you in every way, madam.

"Also, I will no longer tolerate your selfishness and presumptions. You have no right to grab for my arm and scowl at others in public as if you had a claim on me. I was disgusted by your behaviour when you rubbed your chest against my arm repeatedly and I find you repulsive and there is nothing about you that interests me. I would never make an offer for you and there is nothing in this world that would tempt me to take you as my wife. You have done nothing in any possible way that would have tempted me to offer for you. From the first moment I met you, your arrogance and conceit, your selfish disdain for the feelings of others, made me realise that you were the last woman in the world whom I could ever be prevailed upon to marry." Turning to Charles, "I apologise, Bingley. I will remove myself to the inn until I am able to find lodgings while I continue my courtship with Miss Elizabeth. I plan on inviting Georgiana and my cousin to meet her and I know I am no longer welcome here."

Bingley quickly replied, "No! You must stay. Caroline is the one who will be leaving. Caroline, you will be visiting our aunt in York for an unforeseeable time. Pack your trunks right now, as you will be leaving tomorrow. This is the last time you have offended me, my friend, and all of our acquaintances. You are excused." Bingley thundered.

Caroline fled in tears. Bingley turned to Darcy again, "I am sorry, Darcy. I knew she was out of control but for her to speak so was wrong. I hope you will not leave. I will ask Louisa to be hostess and you must invite Georgiana and Fitzwilliam to meet Miss Elizabeth. If you will excuse me, I will see to my sisters now."

Darcy was relieved that it was over. Caroline was as self-absorbed as expected but for her to have criticised the Bennets in such a way and to speak as if he were proposing to her, she was indeed delusional and possibly insane.

He went to his rooms to put his thoughts away from Miss Bingley and to remember Elizabeth's beauty and blushes today.

~*~

Caroline was devastated. She was so certain a proposal was coming that when Mr. Darcy spoke of courting Elizabeth Bennet and yelled at her, she was caught completely unawares. She paced the room and screeched at her maid to begin packing her belongings. Her despair became anger as she considered how dare that interloper come and swoop *her* Mr. Darcy. As she considered last evening's events, she was sure that he was only tempted by her flesh and she did not care whom he bedded as long as his fortune was hers. She was not a maiden and knew the temptations that men faced.

Caroline Bingley lost her virtue five years ago to a friend of Mr. Darcy shortly after Charles and Darcy had become friends. She met him during her one and only visit to Pemberley and he was a dashing young man who flirted with her and showered her with attention. She, being only nineteen years old, did not realise that her virtue was being taken as he kissed her and fondled her. Only when she felt pain between her legs, did she understand that her maidenhead was taken. He had been so gentle and amorous that as they rolled in the lovely fields at Pemberley, she opened her legs for him then he took her most roughly. As she screamed in pain, Mr. Wickham covered her mouth with his hand and continued to push his hard cock inside her and then pumped wildly until he moaned with his release.

Afterwards, George Wickham straightened his appearance and helped her stand. He kissed her hand and thanked her for the pleasure and she never saw him again. She walked awkwardly back to Mr. Darcy's home and thought of herself now being a true woman.

She wanted to marry the young Mr. Darcy, of course, but it was pleasurable to have Mr. Wickham's affections so she had allowed the kissing and fondling to occur. She wanted Mr. Darcy to be jealous, as she had often seen them together in town and believed them to be great friends. She only apprehended later that Mr. Darcy hated George Wickham and that she had given her virtue to the son of Pemberley's steward.

Wickham had lied to her into believing that he was a wealthy gentleman who would be given a great inheritance, and after Mr. Darcy's father passed, she saw that all ties between Darcy and Wickham were cut and Charles sternly told her to never speak his name in front of Mr. Darcy.

Caroline learned much of the marriage bed during the past five years as she had relations with several married men for invitations to the most exquisite parties, and Charles, in his drunkenness a few months ago, had inadvertently shared with her that Darcy was inexperienced in the ways of women and her brother had laughed that in one thing, he himself had more experience than the all-knowledgeable Fitzwilliam Darcy. Charles had been depressed when the most current love-of-his-life had abandoned him for Mr. Darcy and she rejoiced that Mr. Darcy had cut that snivelling harlot in public. An idea formed in her head now, and although she would have to wait, by morning, she would be engaged to Mr. Darcy.

Chapter 6

When dawn approached, Darcy quickly rose out of bed and dressed to rush Xerxes to Oakham Mount. He was pacing and frantically running his fingers through his hair when Elizabeth arrived.

Elizabeth had seen him from a distance and could tell he was agitated and wondered at the cause. He was so pleased and had smiled at her when he left after telling her that he had several things to discuss the next morning, and she had had the most pleasant dream about him during the night. She had dreamt that he kissed her and as she recalled the dream, she felt warm and tingly all over. But now, as she saw him pace, she became concerned for his well-being. *What has happened since yesterday that has him agitated so? I hope he is all right. How can I comfort him?*

In his worry, Darcy did not hear her approach. *How am I supposed to tell her what happened? Would she understand? Will she believe me?* He felt her dainty hand on his arm. He turned around quickly to find her face flushed and eyes shining brightly from the exercise. She had a small smile on her lips but her eyes showed concern.

He could not help himself as he drew her into his arms swiftly and kissed her; not a gentle and soft kiss as he had wanted his first kiss to be, but a hungry, desperate kiss. His one arm held her tightly against his chest while the other wrapped around behind her neck to keep her face as close as possible, and when he felt her arms wrap around his neck, he wrapped both of his arms around her waist to lift her up even closer to the full length of his body. His tongue entered her mouth and delved inside to taste her and their tongues danced as if to pull the other's soul from the body. As they parted for the much-needed air, they were both dizzy with passion while Darcy slowly lowered her feet back to the ground.

They looked at each other, never breaking eye contact. Darcy was mortified that he could behave so ungentlemanly and Elizabeth was blushing brightly red, as she had never expected her first kiss to be so powerful. Darcy sighed and took a breath of relief when he saw her smile, holding her closer and inhaling the soft scent of lavender from her hair. He knew he needed to calm his arousal or else he would make a complete fool of himself but it was difficult to do; she was so passionate and had once again forgiven him of his trespasses quickly and kindly. Finally, after taking several soothing breaths, he spoke.

"Elizabeth, I apologise for my behaviour. I am sorry that I acted as I had done but believe me that I do not regret it. I have never kissed a woman before and I lost myself as soon as my lips touched yours. I hope you will forgive me for taking such liberties." Darcy held her hands and kissed them one at a time.

"Fitzwilliam, I do not understand how it is that I feel so strongly for you. It was my first kiss as well and I am completely bewildered to my reaction as well but I also have no regrets. I hope you do not think me wanton for my behaviour. I never felt so for another person in my life." Elizabeth confessed. "Has something happened? I saw you pacing and was concerned for you. I am glad to offer you my ears but I do think we need to stand a bit apart. I fear with this closeness, I cannot think clearly." She teased.

Darcy leaned forward and kissed her cheek. *How sweet she is!* "Yes, I understand and thank you, my dear. I am considerably calmer now that you are here. Yes, something did happen last night and it has nothing to do with us but Miss Bingley." Darcy spoke as he led her to a large rock to sit upon. He sat next to her and continued to hold her hand. "After leaving Longbourn, Bingley and I spoke with Miss Bingley to inform her of my courtship with you. She has been one of many women chasing me for years. Ha! Do not smirk. Yes, I have had women chasing me even with my obnoxious countenance and abominable pride." He smiled and kissed her forehead. "I told her that under no circumstance would I have offered for her and she fled to her room to avoid me for the rest of the night. I was pleased and was looking forward to meeting you this morning that I neglected to lock my chambers as my usual wont.

"My valet, Wilkins, who has been with me for the past fifteen years, rushed into my bedroom as I slept in the middle of the night and I had never had him act in such a way and I was shocked. I was ready to yell but he actually put his hand over my mouth and closed the bed curtains. I had never had him or anyone else ever climb into my bed but I was certain there must have been a reason so I remained quiet only to hear my door open and close. Imagine my surprise when I could see Miss Bingley pull open the curtain and climb into my bed. Oh, Elizabeth, she was attempting to compromise me and she had the audacity to take her robe off and come under the counterpane in an inappropriate nightgown. I yelled then and told her to leave immediately but she was determined that she would now have to become Mrs. Darcy and she said that I could take you as my mistress but that I was honour-bound to marry her. Thankfully, Wilkins coughed and grabbed her and told her that he knew of her plans and that it was foiled and everyone would be made aware of her attempt at the compromise. Thank God Wilkins was there! I swear to you I never touched her and I never did anything to provoke her, Elizabeth. Please believe me that nothing would have happened even if I were alone." Darcy repeatedly kissed her hands and looked at her desperately for forgiveness.

"Oh, Fitzwilliam, of course I believe you! I know you care for me and I know you have no warm feelings for that woman whatsoever. What happened next?" Elizabeth kissed his knuckles to calm him.

Darcy hugged her tightly and sighed. "Thank you, my love. Wilkins told me later that he had heard Miss Bingley's maid talk about getting ready her sheerest nightgown and understood that she would be attempting to compromise me. He said that as he was entering my rooms from my dressing room, he could already hear her steps at the door and had to rush into my bed. He apologised profusely for invading my personal space but wanted to ensure he had proof of her attempt and that I would be safe. He lifted her and dropped her unceremoniously in her nearly naked nightgown in the middle of the hallway and boomed loudly for Mr. Bingley. I stayed in my rooms out of sight and was told that Bingley and the Hursts rushed out of their rooms to find Caroline shamefully trying to hide herself with what little clothing she had on. I could hear Wilkins shouting, 'This intruder was found in my master's room and should be disposed of quickly, sir!' I had never laughed so hard in my life and I plan on giving him a large bonus." He laughed. "Bingley installed two footmen to guard Caroline's room after ensuring that all servants' doors were locked and inaccessible. Her trunks were being packed as I left and she should be gone by the time I return but I was desperate to see you. I could not bear for you to think ill of me should you have learned of this from someone else. I love you, Elizabeth. I fell in love with you the first moment I met you."

Darcy spoke his last words looking deeply into her eyes. He knew they had not known each other long but he meant every word. He loved her. He loved her as a man loved a woman, not just as friends. She inspired his mind and body and he wanted to hold her and kiss her and make love to her, as much as he wanted to talk with her and argue with her and bring out that sparkle in her eyes when they flashed with indignation. He wanted to tease her and flirt with her and hold her and love her with all of his soul. He loved her.

"I know we began our courtship yesterday and I wish I could take you for my wife today, Elizabeth, but I will not rush you. I will propose when we are both ready and society will know that we are not rushing for some nefarious reasons, but I am in love with you, Elizabeth. Your beauty captured my soul and I will never let you go. You are the most kind and intelligent woman I ever beheld and I am honoured that I can court you. I will not keep any secrets from you and will show you all of myself, even if it is embarrassing or fearsome, but I wish for you to know me as I wish to know you. You have a generous heart and there is still much for me to learn about you but I love, I love you. I love you deeply and I will tell you often and without hesitancy that I love you. I love you, Elizabeth Bennet, with all my heart." He leaned in and kissed her lips, very gently this time.

"I love you, too, Fitzwilliam." Elizabeth replied with tears in her eyes. She felt cherished and important to this man. This handsome man, who was shy and afraid of showing his true self to others, but he was willing to peel off all of his layers to expose his weaknesses and strengths to her. He had been afraid that she would reject him; afraid that she would think he took another woman to bed, but she trusted him completely and had never crossed her mind that he would have asked for such an assignation. That Miss Bingley! Good thing she was being sent away or else she would have given her a piece of her mind!

As she heard the words that he spoke, she knew she loved him in return. Her heart had never been touched so and she desperately wanted to know more about him.

"I wish to know you better as well. Your favourite food, what museums you visited, if you prefer Bach or Beethoven. Do you bite your nails? What your moods are like on a Sunday afternoon with nothing better to do; or if you write evenly or cannot mend a pen to save your life? There is so much that I do not know about you, and yet I feel we know each other better than anyone else. I agree it is too early to speak of marriage but I will not hide my feelings, either. My courage always rises when I am faced with a challenge and I will tell you my heart as well. I am in love with you, too, Fitzwilliam Darcy." And she returned his gentle kiss.

"I wish nothing more than to kiss you as I had before, Elizabeth, but I do not wish to break the trust that your father has bestowed on me, as your honour means the most to me. Let us walk toward Longbourn and I must speak with you about the topics that I actually wanted to discuss." Darcy stood up and they descended the mount.

He explained to her about his sister's summer, how she had been close to eloping with George Wickham, who was compensated £3,000 in lieu of the clergy living at *his* request and how the rogue attempted to elope with his fifteen-year-old sister for her £30,000 dowry. Georgiana was still heartbroken, not because of her love for the man, but for the betrayal that she suffered at the hands of a man who had always shown her affection. George Wickham was not to be trusted as he gambled and drank heavily and had several illegitimate children. Darcy also confided in her that he felt somewhat responsible for Caroline Bingley's downfall, as he had known that George Wickham had imposed himself on her. Pemberley staff were very loyal and she had been witnessed having relations with Wickham on Pemberley grounds. Darcy had told his father about it but his father had advised that as a tradesman's daughter, he had not expected a better behaviour and that she would not be invited back to Pemberley again. His father had been ill and Darcy had not wanted to cause more pain but his father finally understood that George Wickham was not the jovial, innocent young man that he had wanted to believe and at the last minute, the elder Mr. Darcy did change his will, decreasing Wickham's inheritance from £10,000 to £1,000. He had hoped that the living would help him turn from his life choices to become a better person but it was not to be.

Bingley had known of Wickham's dissolute ways as well, and although he had never confronted Caroline for losing her virtue, as he avoided confrontations as much as possible, he knew that Caroline's value as a wife was severely lessened now and never pushed for her to marry anyone from that day forward.

"Fitzwilliam, I am shocked to hear of this man whom your father doted on and provide such an education. How dare he betray your family so! I would give him a piece of my mind and perhaps kick him in the shins!" And she demonstrated her kick in anger.

Darcy laughed at her gesture and he adored her. She was angry for a man who imposed on his family without ever meeting Georgiana and cried for his sister's pain. She was truly kind-hearted and caring.

Elizabeth blushed as she was caught doing something so childish but beamed brightly when she heard his hearty laugh. He was truly the most handsome man, especially when his dimples appeared.

"I wonder, though, your father must have been very generous to provide so much for your sister. I know that my father has been saving for our dowries and I was amazed when I found out how much my sisters and I would be receiving. He had saved for over twenty years and we had to be quite economical to save such an enormous amount and your father must have been very frugal to be able to provide so much for your sister's dowry as well as leave you the estate and also a living and such a large sum for his steward's son. Your mother must have been a wealthy heiress?" She innocently asked.

She was a quick study and math was her forte. She had calculated in her head what it would take for an estate of £2,500 a year to be able to save such a vast amount. She and her sisters had over £25,000 altogether, which included her mother's £5,000, but she knew the pains that her father had taken to economise for twenty years, and Darcy had spoken of a property in Ramsgate as well as a house in town and to offer £10,000 to a steward's son was unheard of. And here he was, taking a two-month holiday with Mr. Bingley while his steward took care of his estate. It did not make sense to her that he could be a master of only 2,500 a year.

"Elizabeth, you never cease to amaze me. I know you care not for my income but you have a bright mind and your intelligence on the inner workings of estate management is something that no other women would comprehend. I pray you will understand, it is something that I wanted to address with you today also. Your father explained to me that the whole of Meryton believed that I was half Bingley's consequence. Is this your understanding as well?"

Elizabeth blushed. "I know it is no one's business but it was bandied about that one of you had double the income of the other and it was naturally assumed that Mr. Bingley, who is residing in one of the largest estates in Meryton, was the wealthier one. It truly matters naught to me, but I was only concerned on how I could help you and how my dowry should be used to provide for us in the future. IF we should marry." She winked. They were quite certain that they *would* marry; it was just a matter of *when*.

Darcy stopped their steps. He drew close to her again and kissed her. Not so gentle but not as deep as their first kiss. He had vowed that he would not kiss her like that again until they were engaged but he loved her so much; he kissed her lips but pressed a little more urgently.

"I love you, Elizabeth. I love that you care for me and that you are already looking out for our future. You are intelligent and that you love me for myself is the greatest gift you could bestow upon me, only second to accepting my proposal, *eventually*." He flashed a smile. "My rumoured fortune is actually what is double of Bingley's consequence. I am rumoured to be worth 10,000 a year."

Elizabeth froze in her tracks. She was speechless for a second but caught his smile. "You are teasing me. You said 'rumoured', which means it is not true. So, we were all wrong, then. I must assume that your income to be similar to Mr. Bingley's." She laughed. "£10,000 a year would be impossible."

They resumed walking but Darcy rubbed her hand upon his arm. "My love, I am sorry to contradict you. I am not worth 5,000 a year but I hope you will not be disappointed to learn that Pemberley alone brings in about 25,000 a year and I have several other properties and investments that bring in another 20,000. Could you bring yourself to love me even if I have £45,000 a year?" He smiled.

Elizabeth stood frozen. She had turned down marriage offers from nobles and men of great consequence. Her mother thought her a fool for refusing a man of £8,000 a year but Fitzwilliam was *extremely* wealthy. She had laughed that £10,000 would be too much but when he said 45, she could not imagine the pressures from society and the loneliness he must have suffered being chased by women who wanted him for his fortune. Women like Miss Bingley, who attempted to sink her claws into *her* Fitzwilliam. She now understood why he felt so trapped and referred to himself as being a prey. To humble himself and ask the obscure Lizzy Bennet of Longbourn to courtship, she felt the honour.

Darcy saw the emotions on her face that appeared. It went from shock to sadness and he was not sure what to expect. His feelings for her were still so new and he feared that she might reject him. He always thought that his massive fortune would have any woman jumping at the opportunity, should he choose one to bestow his slight attention. Any woman except this one. His Elizabeth Bennet, who would kick him off his high horse should he be an arrogant ass; this little country miss with little connections hidden away like a diamond in the rough, who was the handsomest woman of his acquaintance, just might refuse him and his enormous fortune.

"Fitzwilliam, I... I cannot..." Elizabeth sputtered.

Darcy's heart dropped. He frantically uttered, "Please do not reject me. I will give all of my fortune away if you will have me if I were of lesser consequence. I can sign off the other properties to Richard and Georgiana can have Pemberley. I never thought I would wish I were poorer. I have a cottage that is about the size of Netherfield should you wish... I cannot imagine losing you... I care not for anything else..."

His rambling was stopped when Elizabeth grabbed his head with both of her hands and kissed him fully on the mouth. She did not kiss him gently but she held onto him tightly and initiated the kiss as he had first done and soon their tongues were fighting to take charge, as their bodies left no gaps in between. They parted slowly and their foreheads touched. Without losing connection, Darcy humbly asked, "Marry me?"

Elizabeth could not speak words but nodded her agreement. He laughed loudly and grabbed her by the waist and swung her around in joy. Squeals of laughter escaped Elizabeth's chest as well. He tenderly lowered her down again and kissed her softly but his tongue licking her lush lips and reverently tasting her.

"Fitzwilliam," Elizabeth began as they resumed their walking and she began to regain her wit. "I never imagined that I would marry. I pray that you believe me when I tell you that I am not marrying you for your wealth. I cannot imagine such a sum and no wonder you had been so troubled when we first met; that you would give up everything for me touches my heart. I truly love you and wish you to know that I am not mercenary."

"I certainly believe you. You thought me to be worth 2,500 and you loved me. I was torn that you would end our courtship just now. You looked so troubled and I had never wished to be poor in my life but I am glad you would deign to marry a wealthy man, even if it is slightly grander than what you are used to."

"I cannot imagine half of such a sum and I will stop thinking about it. You cannot change the blessing given to you and I am certain you and your father have done much to work steadily to provide for your tenants. I will just think of the rumoured 10,000, which is still an outrageous amount and will give it no further thought, my love. I worried for you and how you must have been chased for your '10,000 a year' and how lonely you must have been. My heart ached for you that you could not find a woman to love you for yourself, Fitzwilliam, but I am glad that you waited for me, and I do think we should have a long engagement. We have kissed several times today and I do not wish to upset my father with my recklessness. I am afraid that kissing you has definitely brought out emotions and desires that I have never felt before." Elizabeth blushed as she spoke of her desires. She was an innocent but had seen farm animals mating and read enough books to know what to expect. It was a dangerous path for a couple to venture and she knew she was far too tempted to feel Fitzwilliam's strong arms around her and a firmness that protruded from his trousers when he held her tight.

"I agree with you. I feared that I was rushing you and I know I have hurried you to an engagement but my heart is soaring that you are now my fiancée. I will speak with your father and explain but I would like to be able to kiss you again. Perhaps we can agree on three times a day?" He laughed, "But I promise we will both remain chaste for our wedding night. I am an innocent like you, Elizabeth, and I will honour my vows and we will experience everything together after we are married."

"Thank you, my love. You are truly wonderful. I know most men have extensive education and I am surprised that you have not been taught in such a way. I am glad I will be your first."

"And my last, my love. I will cherish you all my days." Darcy kissed her hand.

"And I, you, my love. I will accept your terms, sir. Three kisses a day. And you have run out for today, sir!" Her laughter tinkled in the air. "What say you to a six-month engagement?"

Darcy paled at the thought. He was barely able to keep his passion in check now after two days, and six months seemed like an eternity.

Elizabeth laughed to see his expression. She felt he was a passionate man and she delighted in his kisses and being held tightly. She quickly added, "But I enjoy our kisses too much to wait so long. Perhaps a two-month engagement? We still have much to learn about each other. I still do not know your favourite food!"

Darcy nodded in agreement and beamed his brightest smile. They arrived at Longbourn as they continued to laugh and speak of food and theatre and books.

Chapter 7

Mr. Bennet watched them as the couple walked towards the house and he could see clear as day that there was something different about their relationship already. They had been in courtship for one full day but he could tell his daughter's heart belonged to Darcy as she looked up to him with adoration and his hand was holding hers. When he heard a knock on his study, he knew they must have already reached an agreement.

"Come in, Mr. Darcy. I am at my leisure." He greeted the young man and smiled. "So, you have come for her hand? You do realise you have been courting her one day and knew of her existence only two?"

Darcy stood still, suddenly afraid that consent might be withheld. *Damn fool! Of course, I am the proud fool who thought her father would leap at the chance of his daughter marrying 45,000 a year! No, he loves Elizabeth so much that he would be the only man in England to deny me such a request. But she loves me! He smiled. She loves me and she agreed to marry me. I will show her every day how much I care for her. I will never stop courting her.*

Clearing his throat, Darcy replied, "Mr. Bennet, sir, I know that my acquaintance with Miss Elizabeth has been brief and I know that we only began courting yesterday but I truly love her and she has agreed to marry me. We know that it has come upon us both suddenly and we would like to have a two-month engagement before we marry, but we are both committed to each other, sir. I have shared with her the truth of my fortune and I had to convince her, beg her to take a wealthy suitor and she was finally convinced that she could live with me. I ask you to give us your consent to marry. I will care for her until my dying days, Mr. Bennet. I love her very much."

"When I spoke to you yesterday, young man, I meant what I said. I welcome you to the family and would be proud to call you son." They shook hands. "Two months is a good idea. You must get to know each other better and find out how to resolve your differences, since I certainly do not wish your affections to fade, but I have a feeling my Lizzy will keep you on your toes, Mr. Darcy. I would also like to make sure there is not a scandal that follows. Lizzy will go to London and you must be seen together in society. I do not wish for anyone to believe that she is a fortune seeker and you must make sure that you do your part in showing your preference for her, Mr. Darcy."

"Please call me Darcy, sir. Yes, I will definitely prove to everyone that I am the one relentlessly pursuing her. Miss Elizabeth is a remarkable woman, sir. I cannot imagine a better wife." Darcy grinned.

"She will certainly be a challenge at times but she has a kind heart and will be good for you. I am impressed with the respect that you have shown my Lizzy and I hope you will always think of her above your own needs." He paused for a moment, "Darcy, now that you will be part of the family, will you tell me a little of Mr. Bingley? I saw that his interest in my Jane was quite pronounced and I worry that there may be something else beside his jovial personality. Without breaking confidences, can you tell me if your friend is considering Jane and if I should allow such a courtship?" Mr. Bennet spoke seriously.

"I have not had a chance to speak to him about Miss Bennet, sir. I, too, noticed his deep interest and as I care so much for Elizabeth's happiness, I had wished to ask him as well. To be truthful, I have seen him in and out of love often. Most recently there was a woman that he pursued with intent of marriage but as soon as that woman met me, her attentions quickly changed and I had to cut her in public. Also, I must inform you of last night's events." Darcy told him what had happened with Caroline Bingley and emphasised that absolutely nothing had happened.

He continued, "Bingley is a good man. He is kind-hearted but still young and is learning the ways of society. He is wealthy and is a good friend of mine, so he is accepted into the first circles by some, and yet he is still shunned by others because he is the son of a tradesman. He is between worlds right now and is learning what he still wants but he would benefit from steady affections of a gentleman's daughter and I believe Miss Bennet is someone who could make him into a great man. She seems to have the patience and gentleness that matches his personality well, but I know also that Bingley is a man of the world. He is... experienced in things... that I am not yet until... the wedding... and I do not know how Miss Bennet will view such a thing. I know Miss Elizabeth was surprised at my innocence but I have had too many burdens to carry to indulge myself in those activities, which I am eternally grateful to have not yet experienced." Darcy was positively flushed in embarrassment but he wanted to be honest with his future father in law.

Mr. Bennet was also surprised at the young man's innocence and respected that he would be experiencing his carnal desires only after the wedding. Although Darcy was a shy young man, Mr. Bennet could see that he was honest and appreciated that he was vowing to protect his daughter's chastity until after the wedding.

"Thank you for your honesty, Darcy. Your father would be proud of you and I am proud to have you for my future son. If you would please speak with Mr. Bingley and if you are satisfied with his intentions, I will be also. I do not mean to shift the responsibilities to you; I fully expect Mr. Bingley to be an honourable, respectful gentleman and come to me when he is ready. I would like to make sure he knows of my expectations and I do trust your judgment. Again, welcome to the family, Darcy."

Chapter 8

"Bingley! Is she gone?" Darcy asked as soon as he entered Bingley's study.

"Yes, as unpleasant as it was, she has left and will not be returning. I am having my solicitor turn over her dowry and she will finally be independent on her next birthday. I am done with her. Oh my, Darcy. You are usually so taciturn and unpleasant but you are positively beaming right now." Bingley asked with curiosity.

Darcy quickly put on his mask. "You are to congratulate me. I am getting married." Darcy spoke with no emotions.

Bingley did not move. He halted for a moment and then laughed loudly, "You are jesting! You, who had never looked at a woman twice and just began to court Miss Elizabeth yesterday, cannot be engaged already. Her father would never have allowed such a thing! Haha!"

Darcy smiled broadly and showed his dimples. "I am in earnest, Charles. I am marrying my Elizabeth and she will be my wife in two months. I told her I could not live without her and she has accepted me. Her father gave consent, as we are not rushing into marriage and has heartily accepted me into the family but knows I will adore her for the rest of my life. I would like to write to Georgiana and request her, as well as Richard, to join me next month. We shall be married on the First of December and I would like for you to stand up with me."

"Congratulations, Darcy! I am astonished that Mr. Bennet has agreed after such a short courtship. Do you think I would be as successful with Miss Bennet?" Bingley's mind was already drifting to his desires. He had found Miss Bennet quite beautiful and she had sparked all kinds of wild imaginations last night as he lay in bed.

"Bingley, I have been given Mr. Bennet's approval to interview you about her, since I will become Jane Bennet's brother and I wish to know your intentions. I do not want to see her disappointed and it would hurt my Elizabeth should you treat her sister unkindly. I already know you are interested in her but do you wish for something deeper than one night's entertainment? She is a gentleman's daughter and will elevate your status, no matter what venom your sister has been spewing." Darcy inquired.

Bingley stumbled for a moment. He had thought of her often the past two days; she was so beautiful and genteel, and he *had* been quite entertained by her last night as had spent a full quarter hour pleasuring himself, thinking of her shy smiles and wondering what treasures lay beneath her modest dress. He was reminded of one of the courtesans that he enjoyed when last in town and he dwelled on those thoughts until he exploded soon after. Jane Bennet was beautiful and he was certain she would welcome his attentions but did he want more than his temporary pleasure? *I really did not think about it but I do not know her. I was heartbroken when Miss Sarah abandoned me. Could I feel more for Jane Bennet and would she keep my interest for longer than two months?*

Finally, he spoke. "Darcy, I do not know her well enough but I feel that she is a very kind lady and I would like to know her better. I spent time with her during two sets at the assembly and yesterday when we called. I cannot believe you are engaged to her sister within the same time I have known Miss Bennet, but I am not ready for any commitment, as you are well aware, and I promise to treat her carefully. I believe I will call on her a few more times and curb my enthusiasm and take my time to know her better. You know that I was severely affected when Miss Sarah abandoned me after meeting you. I do not resent you, my friend, but it was a sore point that will take some time to recover. I thought she truly loved me but she ended up being a mercenary wench and I did not see it coming." He sighed. "You should be aware; I believe I was affected with her more than Miss Smythe or Miss Denton because we were so intimately involved. She is the only lady that was not a hired woman that I slept with, Darcy. After I told her how much I loved her and wanted her in my life, I took her to my bed and made love to her like I would a wife. She was a maiden, I am afraid." He paused. "In our rush to consummate, I never did ask the question and she never answered. I am thankful that I was not bound to her, though. It was incredulous when you had returned to town the next day and she practically threw herself at you at dinner, and I am certain she would have broken our engagement if it existed so that she could trap you."

Darcy chuckled. "Yes, I could not believe that she had the audacity to sit next to me and kept inching closer. She was nearly on my lap until your sister dragged her away from me. That was the one time I was glad Miss Bingley was in attendance!" They laughed together. "She had decided that I was a bigger catch and jumped into my arms, believing that I would catch her. The foolish woman must have had a large bruise on her bottom for days." They were laughing with tears in their eyes now.

Bingley jumped in, "How in the world did she think you would capture her when she jumped down five stairs before getting into the carriage?! Your face was priceless when you jumped back instead of holding your arm out!" They burst out laughing louder than ever. "Well, after you failed to catch her and she heard your tongue lashing, all outside on Mayfair Street with several witnesses, her season was over and she was quickly exiled to her relatives in the North; Newcastle, I heard. Her older sister was mortified as everyone laughed and it was her fourth season. I think Miss Fleming finally married a tradesman last month but Miss Sarah will not be able to show her face for a while." Sobering a little, he continued, "I am glad I heard no word of her being with child. It was a narrow escape, Darcy. I hope to never go through that again."

Darcy finished his breakfast and rose. "I am glad you will take things slowly, Bingley. I hope you find someone who will love you for the man you are as Elizabeth loves me. I have some letters to write to inform my sister and my cousin to my news and I would like to invite them here after our return from town. Thank you for hosting my family and me. I know I do not say it enough, but I value our friendship very much, Charles."

Feeling emotional but attempting to be manly, Bingley held out his hand and shook Darcy's but he could not contain his joy. He hugged his friend and tapped him on the shoulder. "Me too, Darcy. Me too."

~*~

Louisa Hurst was in a quandary. She felt relief and peace now that her sister was shipped off to her spinster aunt in York but wondered if she was betraying Caroline in some way by staying at Netherfield and being hostess for Charles. Mr. Darcy had promptly had her kicked out of the house in disgrace after she attempted to compromise him and Louisa cried and tried to change Charles' mind into letting her stay or at least all of them leaving to return to town, but he refused to budge and she had never seen Mr. Hurst so angry.

Mr. Hurst had never liked Caroline and was glad to see her ejected from the estate. When he and Louisa first married, Caroline had been quite jealous that he had been pursuing the older sister instead and Louisa was quite gratified that she had been chosen first. Mr. Hurst had paid her a lot of attention and he was quite handsome. Their first months of marriage had been a happy one but then she had a miscarriage and everything had begun to fall apart. She did not want him in bed with her and he began to drink. Caroline lived with them and they eventually stayed with Charles most of the time, while Mr. Hurst became more distant and did not care for anything but his wine.

Caroline always bickered and complained and criticised Louisa's husband for being a drunken fool but he had not been like that always. Truly, he had become disengaged after Caroline started living with them.

Louisa's eyes widened as she suddenly understood that after her miscarriage, she had invited Caroline to visit their townhouse to comfort her and she had never left since. Mr. Hurst began to drink, he never visited her bed since, and they had become strangers. Charles was often visiting friends or going to house parties so more often than not, and the three siblings resided at the Hurst townhouse and Caroline had been constantly interfering in her marriage.

Louisa burned red as she realised that Caroline's venom had spread and she had begun to think meanly of her own husband as well for years now. *What is wrong with me? I gave up a good man just to appease my bitter sister! She, who has done nothing for me but use me for invitations and shopping! How could I have done this to Sebastian?*

She contemplated further. After Caroline left, she actually saw Mr. Hurst smiling at tonight's dinner. He was not drunk. He drank his tea and stayed away from his evening liquor, congratulating Mr. Darcy on his engagement. And Mr. Darcy! He was fully smiling and conversed freely with Charles and Sebastian as she had never seen him do before. The change in his demeanour was incredible. He was radiating with joy and no longer the dour and stoic man that he always appeared. He was very handsome and she could see why so many women wanted him, but also knew that her sister wanted him mostly for his fortune.

Louisa was determined to speak with her husband tonight. The men had stayed later to chat and plan the week. Mr. Darcy was to return to town with the Bennets in three days so Miss Elizabeth could begin her trousseau and meet Miss Darcy. After three weeks in town, Mr. Darcy would return with Miss Darcy and Colonel Fitzwilliam who would stay at Netherfield for a fortnight. Charles had planned to return to London to release Caroline's finances and wrap up some of his other businesses and would be away for two weeks. She would stay at Netherfield with her husband alone and she knew she had to make several apologies.

"Mr. Hurst, may I enter?" She knocked on his door. She had heard him rustling in his bedroom.

"Mrs. Hurst? Of course, please come in," he stated as he opened the door for her. He looked quite shocked at seeing her at his door.

After taking their seats near the fireplace, Louisa began. "Mr. Hurst, I had some time to think about what has happened to us and I wanted to apologise. I do not know what happened to us. We started our marriage well and then after I lost the babe everything fell apart and we have never been the same. I should have been a better wife but I began to ignore you and even joined Caroline in mocking you. I am so sorry that I am such a terrible wife. You have borne so much the past three years and I am so sorry that I let Caroline come between us." She had begun to cry during her speech.

"Louisa," he drew closer to her on the couch, "I never stopped loving you." She gulped a loud cry. "I thought you were the most wonderful and kind woman and I was so happy when you accepted my proposal. We were very happy once, right?" She nodded. "After we lost the babe, you seemed so distraught and I knew having your sister by you would comfort you. I just did not expect her to stay permanently. I must tell you that I never found Caroline attractive in body or soul and I detested that you always took her side. I began to drink more so I would not have to listen to her constant complaints but I wanted to be there with you wherever you were. I sat in the drawing rooms, even if I was inebriated, just so I could be near you. I love you, Louisa. I love you, still."

Louisa jumped into his arms and cried loudly. "I love you, too, Sebastian! I am so sorry!"

After holding her and she had calmed, Mr. Hurst continued, "I must cause you some pain as I have a confession to make. Louisa, your sister is not a good person. She is a harlot and an awful shrew and I should have told you before but I was afraid you would place the blame on me. Do you recall, about two years ago when Charles had gone to that house party with Viscount Fitzwilliam?" She nodded. "Caroline was particularly bitter that the Viscount was engaged to Lady Olivia after all of her attempts to compromise him. It was one night after we had all retired for the night and I had drunk quite excessively because Caroline's complaints were so irritating because she had kept going on and on about how she should have been the future Lady Matlock and how she would pain him when she became Mrs. Darcy and so forth. Well, I passed out drunk on my bed only to awaken with your sister's mouth on my manhood, Louisa." Louisa's eyes were bulging open and she was beginning to pale. "I swear, I never invited her or did anything to encourage her. Before I knew what was happening, she had climbed on me and we... she..." Mr. Hurst could not go on. How was he to explain that in his drunkenness, he had relations with Caroline to his wife?

"Sebastian, did you... You... you slept with my sister?" Louisa could not look at her husband. She was devastated to hear that her *dear* sister had seduced her husband and that he had succumbed to her wiles.

"Louisa, I thought it was you for a moment but as soon as I realised that Caroline was sitting on top of me, I promptly pushed her off and kicked her out of my room. I did not know. I was stunned that she would stoop so low but I did not continue. I swear, I would have never touched her with a ten-foot pole. She threatened me to keep it our secret or she else would poison you with my unfaithful betrayal. I detest her, Louisa, and I began to drink even more ever since that night. And Louisa, she was not a maiden." Mr. Hurst finished.

He was disgusted with Caroline and with himself for not revealing all to his wife earlier. Instead, he had taken to drinking even more and slept in the corner after meals to avoid all conversations.

"I swear to you that I have never touched her again, even though she tried a few more times. I kept my distance from her and yet I could not part from you. I drank so I would not feel the pain of your disinterest but I still wanted to be near you. I could have insisted that we return to Summerfield but I know you wanted to be near your family and my parents detest Caroline and you still desired her near. Now that she is gone, could we not try again? Could you learn to lean on me once more?"

"Oh, Sebastian, I love you and I am sorry that I have been a terrible wife to you. I swear to you that I will try to do better. I will be cutting off Caroline from my life completely. I am so angry with her but am not upset with you. I am so proud of you and relieved that you want me. Could we lie in your bed? Could you make love to me like you had done so long ago?" Louisa responded.

Without a moment's hesitation, Mr. Hurst lifted his wife off the settee and carried her to his bed, kissing her several times and whispering his love to her. They lay in bed and his hands were all over her. He had been desperate to love his wife again and he began to rip his own clothes off and caressed his wife's luscious body. He had missed her so much and although wanting to lengthen their lovemaking, he could not stop once he began to enter Louisa's womanhood and began to thrust furiously several times until he exploded.

"Louisa, I am so sorry to take you like a brute. It has been too long and I have missed you so much." He kissed her hair, panting rapidly from his ecstasy.

"Oh, Sebastian, it was wonderful. I hope you will not think me wanton but I wish to stay with you. May I stay in your bed tonight?" Louisa smiled brightly.

"I am not going to let you go, Louisa. I will never let you go again. I want you in my bed tonight and every night. And while Charles is in town, we will stay in bed all day long. I plan on ravishing you thoroughly and it will be our second honeymoon, my love." He grinned.

Mr. Hurst vowed to make it up to his wife and to shower her with love and many gifts. He helped her take the rest of her clothes off and he cuddled up with her nude body. He began fondling her breasts and licked her nipples until he was aroused again, and after kissing her mouth deeply, entered her folds and made love to her once more.

Chapter 9

Darcy joined Elizabeth every morning on her walks for the next three days on Oakham Mount and they spoke of their past and of their future together and planned many activities in town. He would introduce her to his family and would attend several functions together to enjoy their betrothal as well as to be seen by society in order to prove their affections, and Darcy had received a reply from his uncle and aunt with hearty congratulations and shared with Elizabeth, that they had despaired of his ever marrying and his words of praising her had made them so happy. They had always supported his choices and after finding out that his fiancée had loved him even with his 2,500 a year rumour, they immediately accepted that this was a love match.

Elizabeth was once again surprised that her betrothed had such illustrious relatives. His uncle was an earl and his mother was the daughter of an earl. *How I thought him a proud, dour gentleman in a foul mood with only 2,500 a year!* She laughed at herself and told Fitzwilliam to cease surprising her with unexpected news. She was quite nervous that she would be marrying a man of such a high consequence. She did not feel worthy to be a wife of someone so great but Darcy promised that her natural uniqueness was exactly what he had wished for and unable to find in the *ton*.

Darcy kept to his word that they would limit their kisses to three times a day but as the length of such a kiss had not been negotiated, he kissed her long and hard, one kiss lasting at least ten minutes. After one such kiss, Darcy suddenly stood up from the rock that they were sitting on, dropping Elizabeth quite unceremoniously onto her bottom. He paced away from her a dozen steps and stood looking at the vista, taking several deep breaths.

Elizabeth did not know what had happened. She was enjoying his kisses immensely and as much as he insisted that it was one long kiss, they had been kissing deeply for the past two days and it had really been dozens of tongue-wrestling. He had touched her back and hips and had grazed her breast today. She had been sitting on his lap and she squirmed as she felt his hot hand against her bosom and she was suddenly flushed with heat between her legs. She had felt his firm bulge before, when he had hugged her tightly as they kissed, but this was the first time that she had been placed above him. She was not sure if she had done something wrong but she waited patiently for his return while she straightened her dishevelled hair and dress.

Darcy returned in a few short minutes and appeared quite embarrassed. He kissed her hand and helped her stand, "Let us walk back to Longbourn, my love," he stated, and they began to descend the mount.

After a few more moments, he continued, "I am so sorry that I dropped you and walked away. Please know you did nothing wrong but I was completely embarrassed. Kissing you is nothing like I have ever felt and I almost... lost myself when I touched you. I have never felt such desires as being with you but you are so enticing and I must show my respect for you and honour your chastity. I almost made a mess of myself earlier and I would not have been fit to be seen, especially by your father!!" He laughed. "I promised him that I would treat you well and we must not get ahead of ourselves. I am afraid that our private times have spoiled me and we have been engaged for only four days!"

"Well, it is a good thing that we will be in London tomorrow with *many* chaperons to keep an eye on us. I am sorry as well, Fitzwilliam. I should not have sat on your lap like that. I only meant to tease you." Elizabeth blushed. She was well aware of his body's reaction to her and she did not consider that she might be causing him discomfort.

"You are too tempting, minx!" He laughed loudly. "I am glad to be suffering for you but we must behave. I plan on parading you around town and I cannot wait for you to meet my sister. She is very excited to meet you and I hope you will love her. You two are the most important ladies in my life." He gleamed. "I never enjoyed public outings but with you on my side, I will be the happiest of men."

"I am tremendously excited, Fitzwilliam! I am eager to meet Miss Darcy as well and I hope Lord and Lady Matlock will not be displeased with me. I know you will find my

Uncle and Aunt Gardiner to be fine people. I know they are not of your usual station and I hope you will not disparage them due to their status. They are good and intelligent people. I know I am unworthy to be your wife and society will censure me for being so below you..." Elizabeth responded with less confidence. He had told her several times that he would never snub her relations in trade but she could not imagine a man of the first circles with noble relations would look kindly on marrying into such a family. The other men had sneered at her relatives and that lack of respect of her family had been one of the main reasons for her rejecting their proposals in the past.

Darcy turned her and he lifted her face with his finger on her chin to meet her eyes. "Your family will be my family and I would never spurn them, my love. Elizabeth, if I had met you before I had decided on the corrections that I had wanted to make in my life, I confess that my arrogance would not have connected myself with people in trade and I would have looked down on you. Whether you had 1,000 or 10,000, I would have considered you below me and I probably would have mocked your family with Miss Bingley. But I am certain that after meeting you and seeing your beautiful eyes shine, I would have gone off my high horse to still grovel at your feet to accept me. I was once a proud arse and you would have kicked some sense into me, I am sure. I love you, Elizabeth Bennet. Never worry that I would not love all of you and all of your connections. I love you for everything that you are and are yet to be." He kissed her hand. "I am sure you may rethink our engagement should you ever meet Lady Catherine, though! She is an awful shrew and I know you could stand up to her but I do not wish anyone the company of such a miserable woman." He jested, "She would drone on and on about preserving rank and how she is so frank and sincere, but she has lied to me almost all of my life about an engagement that never existed and I am glad to have cut her out of my life. You will never meet her and you will be trapped in marrying me without ever knowing her and my awful family side!"

They laughed together until they reached Longbourn, where Mr. Darcy visited with Mr. Bennet and played another game of chess as they had done for the past three days.

~*~

The seven Bennet family members, Mr. Darcy, and Mr. Bingley travelled to London together in two carriages. The Bennets would stay with the Gardiners for two weeks while Bingley would reside at Darcy House, and after a fortnight, Mr. Bingley and the Bennets, except for Jane and Elizabeth, would return to Hertfordshire and after another week, the eldest daughters were to return with Mr. Darcy, Miss Darcy, and Colonel Fitzwilliam.

The Gardiners welcomed the party, as the nine visitors entered the townhouse with a loud ruckus. They lived in a modest sized home near Cheapside with their four children and although initially concerned how to house seven more bodies, Mrs. Bennet had emphasised that they would appreciate their hosting the large family in their two guest rooms. Jane and Elizabeth would stay in one room and the three younger girls would share rooms with their cousins.

Madeline Gardiner was surprised that Mrs. Bennet did not mention needing her own room but carefully watched the interactions between Mr. and Mrs. Bennet and quickly surmised that they must have resumed marital relations. This was quite true; in fact, Mr. Bennet, after telling his wife of their financial situation and began to pay more attention to his family, had requested and was accepted to return to her bed. They made love several times a week and began to learn about each other again. After Darcy's request for courtship, they spoke of their dreams for their daughters and it was determined that the two younger girls were too young to be out in society and Mrs. Bennet promised to teach the girls, especially Lydia, how to comport themselves as ladies.

They feared shame and resentment, as Mr. Darcy's status would open their doors to great company and they knew the younger girls still had a lot of education to complete. They would work with Mary to be more open and would spend some of their funds to ensure she dressed in brighter colours and put down her religious books. They would teach Kitty to think for herself and lead instead of being led, and find a tutor to develop her love of art. And they vowed to discipline Lydia for her rambunctious behaviours by keeping her in the nursery until seventeen. Lydia had been most difficult, who kicked and screamed when she heard she would no longer be out, but they stood steadfast and scorned her for acting like a spoiled child, and thanked her for proving to them that she was still immature to be of marriageable age. She had sulked for two full days but when she was given the choice of staying at Longbourn with Mrs. Hill or going to London to see the sights, she relented and promised to be on her best behaviour.

Mr. Bennet had shared with his wife that Mr. Darcy was worth at least £10,000 a year and that she would not have to worry for her future. Even without Mr. Darcy's assistance, she would live comfortably with the money set aside for her and their daughters, but Mr. Darcy had taken her aside personally to reassure her that she would be most welcome at Pemberley and that he would see to it that she had a comfortable place to reside, should her husband predecease her. Darcy had heard Elizabeth explaining her mother's nerves and her worries of the entailment and wanted to assure his future mother that she would always be cared for.

Mrs. Bennet's eyes teared up as she recalled Mr. Darcy's kind words to her and she knew he loved her Lizzy very much. It had been about six weeks since her husband had visited her bed again and she had guessed very quickly that she might be with child, but she was concerned that due to her age and the possibility of yet another daughter, she wanted to wait until she felt the quickening to share her news with her husband. She could not believe that she could be pregnant at nine and thirty but dearly prayed that she would finally have an heir.

Chapter 10

Darcy was pleasantly surprised at meeting the Gardiners on Gracechurch Street and due to Elizabeth's high praise of her favourite relatives, he was predisposed to like them, but after meeting them and conversing with them, he truly enjoyed their company. He found Mr. Edward Gardiner to be an intelligent, sensible businessman with manners that would befit an earl's ballroom, and Mrs. Gardiner was immediately endeared to him, as he had recognised her within several moments of entering the foyer.

"It is a pleasure to meet you, Mrs. Gardiner. You are the former Miss Weston from Lambton! I had wondered what had happened to you!" Darcy flashed a broad smile.

Mrs. Gardiner blushed, "Yes, Mr. Darcy. Imagine my surprise when Lizzy told me that she was engaged to you. I knew you as a child and I am surprised that you remember me. I married and left Lambton over ten years ago but my mother still resides in the area, but I am sure you do not associate with her."

Darcy replied, "But hardly! Mrs. Reynolds and Mrs. Weston work together to make dresses for the orphanage and I had spoken with her several times at Pemberley when I was there last. I had heard she had a cold and was under the weather. Is she fully recovered?"

"Yes, she is well. Thank you, Mr. Darcy." Mrs. Gardiner replied gratefully.

Elizabeth sat with her mouth open as she listened to their conversation. She had known her fiancé was a great man but to hear him speak of his neighbours, for him to recognise those who were so obviously beneath him and to know what was happening with them, showed such attention, such care of his lot in life, that she was awestruck. He was a kind master, a man who was not lazy or indolent, but hard working and dedicated to his responsibilities. *He is amazing and he is mine!*

After several more minutes of tête-à-tête, it was time for Darcy and Bingley to take their leave. They would return tomorrow morning to take the ladies to Darcy House to meet Miss Darcy, to tour the house, and the ladies were to begin their shopping excursions.

Elizabeth asked her father for a moment of time with her betrothed, which was quickly granted, and she walked him to her uncle's study.

"Fitzwilliam, I wanted to thank you for your kind treatment of my family. It pleased me to no end that you greeted even the children so kindly and if I did not love you already, I would have fallen in love with you today. My eyes are opened to what a great man you are and I am in awe of you. That you should choose me to be your wife is a great honour and I wanted to tell you that I love you very, very much, Fitzwilliam." Elizabeth spoke gently as she kissed his knuckles several times.

Darcy was touched by her confession. He had not done anything to deserve such generous words but he was being himself, his true self, without his pride or prejudice of rank in the way, and she had continued to challenge and inspire him to put aside his fears and shyness; to be free to enjoy life with her at his side. He cleared his throat, "Um, Miss Bennet," he sounded serious, "I believe you have violated our agreement and I must collect your debt at this very moment."

Elizabeth's heart beat faster. She quickly saw that he was teasing and replied, "What might that be, sir? I know of no debt to you." She smiled.

He drew closer to her to rub her arms with his face an inch from hers, and he replied, "I have had only two kisses today." And he slowly leaned to touch her lips with his and kissed her reverently and gently. "I dare not ask for more, Elizabeth, but I hope you will make up for it tomorrow. I love you. My heart is completely yours and yours alone. All I have, all my connections and fortune, I would give it up in a moment if it meant having you by my side. Your family is my family and your cares are my cares. Please do not ever forget." He kissed her lightly once more and they returned to the family.

~*~

The next day, Elizabeth and Jane Bennet finally met Georgiana Darcy, who was a young woman of sixteen years of age, slightly older than Lydia, but behaved very demure and was extremely shy. Elizabeth had discerned that some of her shyness was due to her heartbreak during the summer and spoke to her gently and encouraged her to speak of music, which was Georgiana's favourite topic.

They discussed concerts and museums and Georgiana slowly opened up. Her brother's betrothed was young and vibrant, and so enthusiastic about her engagement and journeying to London, that Georgiana could not help but to laugh and be pleased for them both.

While the two ladies jovially chatted, Bingley and Jane spoke quietly as well on the side. The two had become closer while chaperoning Darcy and Elizabeth and although Bingley's attentions were far less pointed now, they were getting to know each other better and enjoyed their time together. Jane was close to falling in love with Mr. Bingley and Bingley was half in love with her already but was determined to take things slow.

Darcy watched in wonder as Georgiana's laughter rang in the air as he had not heard her laugh for several months now and knew it was only due to Elizabeth that she was returning to her old self. Even yesterday, after arriving from the Gardiners, Georgiana had greeted him but immediately burst into tears. She was thrilled for her brother to finally be engaged but feared that his wife would reject her and send her off to live someplace far away. Darcy held her and encouraged her to speak and let the tears flow out, as Elizabeth had recommended that he do. After her tears were spent, he spoke of his desire for freedom to choose his life's path and how his engagement came about, and he told her that Elizabeth already knew of Wickham's deeds and described to her how she had wanted to kick him in the shins.

He knew he was staring as Elizabeth turned to him and winked at him, and he beamed his broadest smile in appreciation of her love and care. He was then interrupted by his butler that his solicitor had arrived. He and Bingley excused themselves to the study to allow the ladies to converse and get to know each other better.

Darcy and Bingley had used the same solicitor so Bingley spoke with Mr. Henderson first to talk about releasing Caroline's dowry to her next May. That matter was settled and Bingley excused himself to return to the ladies while Darcy remained with Mr. Henderson to discuss his settlement for his upcoming marriage.

~*~

After the important matters were discussed, Mr. Henderson left and Darcy began to work on the engagement announcement.

He heard a knock and bid the guest to enter and his cousin Colonel Richard Fitzwilliam popped his head in.

"Richard! I did not expect to see you for another couple of days! How are you?" Darcy smiled.

Richard shook his hand, "I returned this morning from Dover. I was able to leave a little early after receiving your rushed letter about your engagement to a Miss Bennet from Hertfordshire, cousin! I had never seen your handwriting so uneven before and I cannot wait to meet her! I will have to return to my office soon but I was visiting my parents and heard that you had already arrived yesterday, and Darce, I just saw Georgiana and she was laughing. Laughing! Damn! I know that she was pleased with your engagement but I cannot believe such a sudden change. I heard voices so I peeked in but they did not see me. I saw Bingley and Georgiana and two very beautiful ladies. I am guessing one of them is your fiancée?" *It must be the blonde. She is just Darcy's type and I want to know more about the gorgeous brunette!*

Darcy grinned. "Yes, the ladies are my fiancée and her sister. My Elizabeth is wonderful; I cannot believe how quickly she helped Georgiana relax and I am so happy to have her here. You will love her, Richard. I will tell you all about her later. Let us go up and have you meet her now. I am done here."

"You are different, Darce. I have never seen you smile so!" Richard laughed and was very pleased for his cousin. He had known that for years that Darcy had been lonely and was losing hope of finding his soul mate. He did not know how he did it. His cousin stayed away from whoring and gambling and had worked hard to increase his fortune as well as adding to his own inheritance. He was steadfast and honourable but had become more aloof in society and had suffered much after Georgiana's summer, but here he was now, smiling like a mooncalf and engaged to a woman he loved.

Richard was surprised with himself that he was so nervous as he walked toward the music room where Darcy's guests sat. He had briefly looked into the room earlier and not wanting to be caught, he glanced quickly at Georgiana who was laughing at something that the brunette lady had said, and Richard's eyes were immediately drawn to that lady's sparkling eyes. He noted quickly the pretty blonde woman next to her but his eyes returned to the stunning woman with the green eyes.

He always had an eye for beautiful women and as a second son of an earl, he was still considered a great catch. He had a small property that was left to him by his maternal grandmother as well as Uncle Darcy's £25,000 inheritance that Darcy had worked so hard to increase to £40,000, and he knew he cut a dashing figure in his red coat. He was chased by a few heiresses and enjoyed favours from a long list of women. He had his favourite widows and visited a particular brothel often; the women seemed to line up to enjoy his attentions. His military pay kept him comfortable and he was frugal and now had nearly £45,000 in savings. He knew he could marry whomever he wanted, but like Darcy, he wanted to find that perfect woman. He wondered if that woman was sitting in Darcy House right now and could not get her out of his mind. *I wonder what her name is, if Darcy's fiancée is Elizabeth. It is not from lack of release that I feel drawn to this brunette since I had a woman only two days ago. What is it about this woman that intrigues me so? Perhaps I will become Darcy's brother by marriage if this is my perfect woman. I need to see her again. I must talk to her and get to know her.*

As they entered the sitting room, Richard's eyes immediately went to the brunette. Seeing her face fully now, she was even more beautiful than he initially saw, and her eyes sparkled with so much joie de vivre, he knew his heart was touched deeper than he had ever felt. He was disheartened, though; her vision was directed at his cousin and he could see the love in her eyes for Darcy. *Damn! Of course, she is his.* Hiding his disappointment quickly, he greeted Georgiana and Bingley, and was introduced to the ladies.

Miss Elizabeth smiled at him softly, "It is a pleasure to meet you, Colonel Fitzwilliam. Georgiana has been telling me all about you and your bravery. Is it true that you were able to defeat six Frenchmen with your bare hands or is it a *slight* exaggeration as men often embellish, when stories are repeated?" She teased.

Richard knew his heart was gone for certain then, but he gulped down his misery and timidly returned the greeting while he could not keep his eyes off of her as he kissed her hand. "I have no idea how these stories end up becoming so embellished but I will not ruin my dear cousin's stories and will keep the truth to myself." Richard finally answered as his heart thumped rapidly.

"Oh, Colonel Fitzwilliam! You are as intriguing as dear Georgiana had described you!" Her merry laughter pealed in the air and he was lost. *It was eight men and I was already wounded but Elizabeth would not be flattered by my valour. Look at how she gazes at Darcy. Blasted! How can I feel this way for a woman I just met?*

"Miss Elizabeth, will you please call me Richard? Welcome to the family." He lifted up her hand and kissed it again. *Elizabeth... My Elizabeth...* He sighed internally as his heart was breaking. It was obvious that she had eyes only for Darcy.

Darcy tapped his shoulder and beamed. "Thank you, Richard. She calls me 'Fitzwilliam' so it would be confusing to have both of us answer by the same name!"

And yet I would follow every command she gives to my death. Damnation! She is as wonderful as I imagined she would be. She smiles and teases and my heart is hers. How could this be? He nervously sat down with the group, wishing nothing but to pull her in and touch her. He had never felt so drawn to a woman before and definitely never this anxious.

He was truly happy for Darcy. His usually dour cousin was now smiling and flirting and could not help but exude his happiness while he sat with the ladies. But he felt the bitter jealousy pierce his heart and was repulsed with himself for feeling so. *Why could he not have preferred the blonde? He always liked blondes! Because, you fool, Elizabeth is incredible. See how she includes Georgiana into the conversation and makes my quiet cousin smile. She is an incredible woman and you should be happy for Darcy, you arse!* He chided himself.

He realised that his attraction to Elizabeth was not just because of her beauty, but she was everything he desired rolled into one. Her kind heart and the ability to laugh and enjoy life surpassed every requirement of his perfect woman. His past years of chasing petite brunettes, he realised his ideal, his heart's soul mate, was sitting in front of him.

Determined to please his cousins, he spoke with the party and he could not help himself but to flirt a little with the ladies. He smirked as he realised that his flirting with Miss Bennet had turned Bingley green.

Aha! So, Bingley likes Miss Bennet. Should have guessed – he always preferred fair-coloured women. She is nothing compared to Elizabeth, though. Insipid. Oh, Elizabeth... He realised he was staring at her once again and sitting silent like an idiot, so he attempted to engage her in conversation.

"So, Darcy had written me and told me that he met a wonderful lady and that he was engaged, but he had not revealed much else. I think in his excitement, he only wrote that he was getting married to a 'Miss Bennet' in two months and that he would be showing you off in town. You have one beautiful older sister. Any other siblings? Can you tell me more about your home?" Richard winked at Bingley.

Jane Bennett shyly blushed while Elizabeth beamed and told Richard of her family and Longbourn. He was surprised that a daughter of an inconsequential squire in the backwater country like Hertfordshire could capture Darcy's eye, but he also knew that once he himself was aware of her existence, he would have searched to the ends of the earth to find her again. *If only I had met her first!*

Then he redoubled his efforts to flirt with Miss Bennet. He would have his amusement even though his heart was breaking at the loss of a woman that he never had. He felt no attraction to Jane Bennet whatsoever but attempted to act his norm in front of Darcy but he could see that his cousin was distracted by Elizabeth and paid very little attention to Miss Bennet and Bingley. He hoped that no one would notice how uneasy he was when conversing with Darcy's betrothed.

Georgiana perked, "Lizzy! Shall we tour the house now? Brother, let us go now! I cannot wait to show Lizzy the library. We have been talking about the number of books at Pemberley and she is very excited to borrow a few volumes. Let us go!"

The Darcys and the Misses Bennet, as well as Bingley, left to tour the house and Richard chose to remain in the room.

~*~

Richard contemplated his cousins. He had never seen Darcy so exuberant and Georgiana had not been this animated since several Christmases ago and was shocked at the change. Elizabeth had laughed at something he said and he could not forget the sparkle in her eyes.

Elizabeth is a true gem. **Miss** *Elizabeth, you idiot.* **Miss.** *Damn it! Darcy was right. He said I would love her and little did he know I would fall head over heels for her at first glance. How did I allow myself to fall in love with her in a matter of minutes? After thirty years of my life, why did it have to be an engaged woman? Darcy's fiancée, of all people? I have never felt this way towards a woman in my life!* He thought of their conversation, her eyes, her gorgeous figure, as well as her intelligence. She was smart and beautiful: A deadly combination to his soul and body. *Damn it, I need to go to Madam Beverly's right now!*

Unwilling to remain in the house when he could feel his desire begin to expand, he wrote a quick note for Darcy and left to Madam Beverly's establishment where he asked for a petite brunette. The woman had brown eyes but he cared not. Without taking his clothing off, he unbuttoned his fall to bend her over and inserted his swollen cock inside her and began to pump from behind as quickly as possible. He thought of Elizabeth and her voluptuous bosom while he thrust into the petite woman repeatedly. Keeping his eyes closed tightly, he flipped her over and kissed the woman beneath him as if he were kissing Elizabeth, tongue diving deep into her throat and his hands through her hair and roughly grabbing her breasts. He pounded into the prostitute furiously, imagining *her* laying under him, and cried out 'Elizabeth!' loudly as he climaxed harder than ever before. *Blasted! This will not do. I cannot covet my cousin's future wife like this.* He groaned after rolling off the prostitute.

He sat on a distant chair for several minutes still fully dressed, watching the whore still panting in bed after he poured himself a drink. Having his release felt good but the reality of the woman that he just used not being Elizabeth depressed him. Richard closed his eyes and thought of Elizabeth once again, feeling his arousal return as he dreamt of her beautiful eyes. *That creature has bewitched me. I have never felt like this before. I must purge this lust from myself. It will pass. It has to pass. She is just a passing fancy.* He kept repeating to himself.

He lay back in his chair and requested the experienced woman to suck on his semi-erect penis. *Get your cock up, Colonel!* He commanded himself. He watched the doxy hungrily take his soft manhood into her mouth while trying to pump it back to life with her hand. She had been very pleased with his passion and was returning the favour. *Think of some of the pretty women I fucked. What was the name of the widow with the big teats last week? Blasted! I cannot think of a single woman who exceeds my Elizabeth. No one compares. No one will ever compare to my Elizabeth.*

He then closed his eyes and all he could think of was Elizabeth's smile and her soft red lips and he felt another huge erection coming. *If she were not Darcy's fiancée, I would have stolen her away from any other man but I cannot betray Darcy. One more time and I will be fit to be seen in public. Oh, Elizabeth, my heart. I have never wanted one woman this desperately in my life! I can only dream of touching her. Loving her. I want to make love to her more than anything I ever wanted.*

His erection returned full and he had the prostitute ride him until he came again, not realising that he had screamed out Elizabeth's name once more.

~*~

After working at his office for several hours, Richard returned to Darcy House for dinner as he had indicated on his note, and was relieved that the ladies were gone.

Georgiana had joined the ladies on their shopping expedition and Bingley had gone to the club to meet with a few of his friends and Richard found Darcy working in his study again.

"Darcy, you are closeted here yet again instead of being glued to your fiancée?" Richard jested. He knew his cousin worked harder than any other gentlemen of leisure.

"Richard! You left so suddenly. I am glad you are joining us for dinner. The ladies have been gone shopping all day but Georgiana should be returning soon. I asked Georgiana to take Elizabeth to her modiste and Aunt Susan was to meet them there. So, what did you think of her?" Darcy asked with curiosity. Darcy had noted the strange look on his cousin's face when he introduced his betrothed and it was rare for Richard to be so subdued in company, even if he had begun to flirt a bit later on.

Richard cleared his throat and answered a bit stiffly, "She is... not what I had expected. She... Your Elizabeth is a smart and sensible woman, Darcy. Since when did you prefer brunettes? I was certain you would prefer Miss Bennet, as you always preferred blondes before." *Why could you not prefer someone else? I want Elizabeth more than anything I ever wanted.* After a quick pause to settle the pain in his heart, he continued, "You are a damn lucky man, Darce. Damn lucky."

Darcy broke into a huge smile. "I know, Richard. Elizabeth is wonderful! Her sister Jane is a kind lady but I never looked at her twice. How Elizabeth has changed Georgiana in one afternoon is incomprehensible but I know I am most fortunate. With all your ravings of your dark-haired beauties, I found myself falling for her the first moment I saw her."

Richard saw the smile and as Darcy finished speaking, he could see him drift to daydream of his love. He chuckled. His cousin was a mooncalf and it was wonderful. *Me, too, Darcy. Me, too. I fell for her at first sight but I cannot be dishonourable to my favourite cousin, my best friend.* He decided that he would do everything in his power to promote the match. His cousin loved her and *she* loved his cousin.

"You are a lovesick mooncalf, Darce! Finally, I have something to tease you about! I could tell right away that she cared for you but I hope she is not after your fortune." *Though I would give her everything I own if she would have me!* "Your letter explained how you met her at the assembly and that you were going to marry her, but how did such a quick courtship and engagement come about?" Richard laughed and returned slowly to his jovial self. He was hoping he would discover some serious defects or faults about Miss Elizabeth so he could get her out of his mind and heart.

Darcy rapidly told him of his new resolution and how he had insulted her and of their quick courtship, as well as the engagement after Caroline Bingley's seduction attempt.

Richard's respect for Elizabeth grew and he questioned if he could have won her hand.

In his own arrogance, he had thought that should he have met her first, she would have been impressed by his looks and status, but to hear Darcy tell him about Haversham chasing her and her declining his attentions, and that she had loved Darcy believing that he had 2,500 a year with no connections, he knew he never had a chance, even with his connections and nearly £3,500 a year.

After Georgiana returned and during dinner, she rambled on about her outing and how many beautiful dresses were ordered, and Richard was struck with the thought that even his own mother loved Elizabeth upon meeting her. It did not matter that she was the daughter of an obscure gentleman of 2,000 a year with relatives in trade; she was kind-hearted and generous and perfect. Perfect for his cousin.

Richard also regretted bedding that whore today. In his urgency to seek relief, he had taken her twice and did not think about how a virtuous and intelligent lady like Elizabeth would view such vices. His cousin probably barely kissed her hand and she was sure to love Darcy for his innocence. He could not imagine Elizabeth tolerating Darcy visiting whores or dallying with widows. If Elizabeth were his own fiancée, Richard could not imagine needing to go anywhere else, but there was no way in hell that she would have approved his visits with other women.

If Darcy can do it, I can do it, too. I will be more respectful towards women as a whole sex, not just the ones that are rich or have status, and I must stop visiting prostitutes. I am determined to be a better man. I hope to God that I can find a worthy lady like my Elizabeth someday.

~*~

Elizabeth was exhausted after all of the fabulous day she had with her future family. As she lay in bed with Jane snoring lightly next to her, she reminisced about the day's events. It had been a very busy day, meeting the shy Georgiana and Fitzwilliam's dashing cousin, the Colonel, and touring Darcy House and seeing her future residence. Her fiancé's home was warm and welcoming and she did not expect it to be so large and richly furnished, but it was comfortable and she knew it would be a happy home. Lady Matlock was very pleasant and she was obvious to show her approval of the engagement to the other patrons of Madam Sutherland's busy shop. She had looked at yards and yards of fabric and could not believe that Lady Matlock demanded that she order three-dozen dresses as well as many accoutrements to outfit her trousseau. She was surprised that an account had already been set up for her, and although she pressed for a third of the number of dresses, Lady Matlock was insistent that she must look and dress the part of Mrs. Darcy. Her Fitzwilliam had already made sure all of the bills would go to him and when she told her father about the arrangement, he did not appear surprised at all. Her father soon confessed that Darcy had insisted upon taking up the burden as she would soon be his wife and that he was taking such a treasure away from the family, that he felt he must compensate a fraction of what he was gaining from the betrothal. Her father had also told her that he had planned to use the funds to dress her sisters so they would be fit for public outings and she could not deny her sisters the luxury.

What she recalled the most was when during the tour, Bingley had taken Jane and Georgiana to the ballroom while she and Fitzwilliam had remained in the library a little longer to pick some volumes for her leisure.

"Elizabeth, are you pleased with the townhouse?" Darcy asked as he kissed her hands.

"Oh, Fitzwilliam! How could I not be? There is no one who could believe your home to be wanting." Elizabeth exclaimed.

"*Our* home, my love. Your opinion is worth more than anyone else's, although I can tell you that Miss Bingley constantly bemoaned that it needed a woman's touch." They laughed. "I am desperate for your kiss. May I?"

"I believe I am overdue, my love." Elizabeth teased.

Darcy drew her closely and wrapped her in his arms. He leaned in and kissed her gently but deeply. He had missed her so much and their tongues met and danced wildly as he held her close. After several moments, Darcy took a few breaths and spoke.

"You had better return to your sister. I will need a few moments, my love, but I will join you shortly. Just head down the stairs and you will find them." He turned to face the window to stare out to calm his arousal.

Elizabeth knew why he needed a moment, since his arousal was more pronounced than ever and she knew that after their vows were made, she would be able to finally discover what lay beneath. After kissing his cheek one more time, she trailed downstairs and looked at the ballroom and Darcy joined them a few minutes later.

She loved his kisses. They had seven more weeks to go and it would be torturous but worth the wait. They were getting to know each other better and she looked forward to being seen in public on his arm. They were to see each other tomorrow and she fell asleep, eagerly counting down the hours until she could see him again.

Chapter 11

The next three weeks flew quickly, as the newly engaged couple enjoyed their formal outings together. Darcy was seen everywhere with his beloved and the official engagement was published in the papers, and many gawked at the ever-elusive Mr. Darcy's betrothed and found her to be beautiful and charming. Disappointed single ladies and matrons looked for a non-existent flaw, while tempted men of varying ages wondered if they could pluck the lovely English rose from under Darcy's nose.

When the Darcy carriage arrived at the theatre, there was a hushed anticipation as all gathered to see who this mysterious lady was. Darcy exited first and there was a gasp as the crowd noticed a wide smile on his face. Mr. Darcy had been consistent at every public outing he ever attended as he was always dour and stoic. Until now. He wore a large smile this night and he laughed as he handed out a young lady. Her small glove was seen in his hand as his laughter rang in the air, and many ladies fanned their faces as they witnessed the most handsome face of the mysterious Mr. Darcy. The crowd gasped when a petite brunette exited the carriage and her eyes twinkled as she returned Darcy's laughter with a beautiful smile of her own.

The whispers became louder as Darcy drew her close and placed her hand on his arm. The affection between them was evident and several hearts broke at seeing the attachment.

Many had hoped that he had been trapped into marrying a country nobody and yearned for a break in the engagement but the couple had an obvious affection for each other and none could deny that they were happy to be seen together. Mr. Darcy looked immaculate as ever in his long black suit and the lady on his arm was wearing Madam Sutherland's masterpiece, a gorgeous ivory silk dress, with a simple garnet cross.

Mr. Bingley exited with another beauty, who was dressed in an impressive blue dress, as well as the gallant Colonel Fitzwilliam with the young Miss Darcy. Two older couples joined the party and they all greeted Lord and Lady Matlock near the stairwell. All in attendance now knew that this engagement had been vouched by the family, as it was a public declaration that this Miss Elizabeth Bennet was now under Matlock's protection and any defamation or slander would not be tolerated.

Many opera glasses were trained on Darcy's box until the lights were out and it was obvious that they had a love match as more hearts broke when Darcy kissed Elizabeth's hand.

The theatre outing was one of the first places they were seen together during the weeks. They were seen at the museum, numerous art galleries, at Hyde Park where they were actually seen at fashionable hours, and at several balls.

Darcy had been infamous for standing about at balls; he was typically expressionless or appeared angry, unwilling to socialise with most and dancing only once or twice the required number, usually the hostess or married sisters of his friends. He rarely danced with older, unmarried ladies and never with young ones. At the past four balls, though, Darcy danced three dances with his fiancée, one with Miss Bennet, one with Miss Mary, and one with his cousin, Lady Iris Fitzwilliam, the daughter of Lord and Lady Matlock who was allowed to dance with her family only. He had never danced more in his life and he had never had a better time at a ball with Elizabeth now by his side.

There were several situations where the catty rivals attempted to gossip and spread ill-news of Miss Bennet but Colonel Fitzwilliam had heard some of the women who tried to besmudge her reputation and quickly came to her defence at one of the parties.

"Ladies, I just heard you speak of my future cousin and I must correct you. It is true that their engagement came about quickly but I assure you, Miss Bennet had nothing to do with it. It was Darcy who threw himself at her feet for mercy and had to beg her to marry him. I am certain you *ladies* have no idea what it means to be chased, so I will leave it to you to see who else you can attempt to entrap in his stead. It would be wise to remember that I am protective of my family's honour and that I know your secrets and will not tolerate any slander against Miss Elizabeth Bennet." Richard threatened.

He was disgusted with these women who tried to spread false rumours, as he had bedded several of them and knew they were far from the virginal and genteel women that they attempted to emulate. *I dare you to speak ill of my Elizabeth again! I will ruin you and expose you for the whores that you are!* Richard thought to himself. His love for Elizabeth had grown more now and he would defend her with his life.

As Richard returned to his group and shared what he had learned with Darcy and Elizabeth, he made sure to point out the harlots and laugh at them, knowing full well that they were watching. Elizabeth was under his protection and he would make sure everyone knew of it.

Word began to circulate that Miss Elizabeth Bennet was certainly under Matlock's protection and the ever-honourable Colonel Fitzwilliam took a personal interest in protecting his favourite cousin and his betrothed's honour. As a war hero and the son of the most prominent of earls, all who knew him had no doubt that he would cut off the tongue of anyone who spoke ill of the Darcys and those who considered to denounce the future Mrs. Darcy kept their mouths shut in fear of their lives.

~*~

Lady Catherine sat fuming on her throne at Rosings Park. She had received Darcy's letter three weeks ago and did not think twice about it. His empty threats meant nothing to her, as she was certain Darcy would never displace his beloved mother's sister, and Rosings was hers!

The sacrifices she had made to be Sir Lewis' wife had cost her dearly. She had wanted Pemberley but the handsome George Darcy was impossible to compromise and had chosen her younger sister to marry instead of herself. She had been four and twenty and he had the gall to choose her eighteen-year-old sister and swooped her off to the grand estate during her first season, while she herself had been on the market for six years.

She then met Sir Lewis de Bourgh at a dinner party and knew he was her only escape from her unmarried state. He was wealthy and kind but was also five and fifty and rather large. His first wife had died two years ago and he had been on the prowl for a young wife so she gulped her disgust and flirted with the old man, publicly acting as if they were on intimate terms. When he had walked out to the balcony for some air, she followed him and met him there alone. As Sir Lewis was not a very intelligent man and he did not think of impropriety as she greeted him in private, he spoke of menial things, finding her not particularly charming but only young and wealthy, and he was caught unawares when she began to kiss him and he returned the kiss. She grabbed his hands and placed them on her lacking bosoms and held them tightly and began to scream at the top of her lungs.

As several people rushed out, Sir Lewis was standing unmoving with his hands on the young woman's breasts and he was immediately *requested* to marry Lady Catherine by the Earl of Matlock. She married him by special license as was due to her rank as an earl's daughter and installed herself at Rosings Park a week later.

Although revolted, she had to ensure that she consummated the marriage and attempted to seduce her now husband. He had been angry at being trapped by this hoyden who thought herself above others and could not understand how he could have let her ensnare him so, but he knew it was done and hoped for an heir. His first wife, who was twenty years younger than he, had been lovely but had suffered several miscarriages and the last one had been fatal. Lady Catherine was thirty years younger and he hoped to get her with child soon.

Lady Catherine had hoped that after the wedding night, she would be able to kick him out of her bed for good, but she was mistaken. Not only was Sir Lewis quite enthusiastic in bed, but he was very virile for such an old man and wanted to mate with her several times a night and was unrelenting with his demands.

After Anne was born, he still desired a male heir and he increased his frequency, making Lady Catherine most miserable for many more months during her short marriage.

Her husband died two years after the wedding after becoming ill with influenza, but not before infecting Anne. Lady Catherine had been six months pregnant and was also affected. Anne survived but was consistently weak afterwards and Lady Catherine had lost the babe when he was delivered stillborn a month later. She resented her husband for putting her through such an ordeal and became an even worse tyrant, firing all her staff and hiring only sycophants who would flatter her and obey blindly. She coddled Anne to the point of illness and she ruled with an iron grip, overspending and buying everything she desired with Sir Lewis' money.

~*~

Now, as she read the engagement announcement and the gossip columns about her nephew and his fiancée, Lady Catherine burned with anger that her plans to take over Pemberley had been ruined. She wanted one thing and only one thing from her insipid daughter: To be Darcy's wife so she could access Pemberley and use its massive wealth, so she could live at Rosings to keep herself comfortable. She cared not for her daughter's happiness or wishes, since she was born to be used for her gains and Lady Catherine had concocted a plan to insist upon Darcy marrying Anne after her *dear* sister died.

"Mr. Collins! You are late!" She yelled at her toady parson. "What was the name of that family, the property that you are going to inherit? Come, come! Branson? Bedford?"

Mr. Collins was huffing and puffing as he had run with much haste from Hunsford to Rosings and could not speak. He was gasping for air as he replied, "Be-nne-t, Long-bou-rne, La-dy Ca-the-rine..."

"Bloody hell!" Lady Catherine cursed under her breath. She had thought the name sounded familiar when she read the announcement, as her stupid parson had blabbed on and on about the entailment and future inheritance of Longbourn and being the only heir to a Mr. Bennet. It seemed that her nephew had connected himself to a poor family of obscure origins with a little cottage with Mr. Collins as heir. What a small world, indeed.

"Mr. Collins! I demand that you travel to London with Anne and myself. I must address my nephew Darcy, as it appears he is engaged to your cousin and I must put an end to such a scheme. It is ridiculous and he must break it off immediately and do his duty to his family. You will marry this Elizabeth Bennet and offer an olive branch to your family to heal the wounds. Who better for this hussy to marry than the man who will save them from the hedgerows? You need a wife and it is the perfect solution. We leave tomorrow morning. Go home and pack!" Lady Catherine waved her hand dismissing him.

~*~

Mr. Collins had just caught his breath but as he was excused, he quickly departed, trying to figure out how he would get Mr. Bennet's daughter to marry him. He had wanted a pretty wife that would allow him to take her anytime he wanted so he would not live in sin. He had a serious weakness for the female body since he had a taste of several prostitutes during seminary school, and although absolutely repentant afterwards, he kept returning to the town whore to satisfy his carnal needs. He hoped this Elizabeth Bennet was tolerable enough to bed, although he did not care as long as she had a nice body. Thinking about having sexual relations aroused him and although it had only been two days since his last visit, Dolores was tantalising that he wanted her again.

After returning to Hunsford, he told his servant to pack up his things for travel to London and he got on his buggy to visit Dolores, who was about two miles away.

Seeing that there was no red ribbon on the doorknob, he knocked and the sensual lady answered. "Why, Mr. Collins! Back again so soon? I thought we had our appointment next week. Have you missed me already?" She smiled. "Please enter."

He was an easy coin and she enjoyed his attentions, as his manhood was a nice size, but he always finished too quickly. After about five minutes of moaning and groaning, he would release and she could still charge him double what she usually charged the other men. Having a man of the cloth was especially exciting for her.

Her husband had been a vicar who had difficulty getting aroused, as he considered his erection to be a sin. He died in a carriage accident after visiting his patroness and had left her only this small cottage. She had thought she could escape such a life but after residing in London for a year as a governess, she hit terrible luck after falling in love with a scoundrel and had to return to Kent to be the town whore to survive. Mr. Collins had been instituted at her husband's post after three other rectors had quit the position due to the horrid Lady Catherine's high demands, and Mr. Collins was the most idiotic man she had ever met, but she was good at keeping his secret and was paid well for her services.

Mr. Collins hurried into the cottage and began to tear his clothes off while she hung the red ribbon on the doorknob and began to slide off her dress and knew he would be very quick today. She walked over to her dresser and prepared her concoction for birth control. She discreetly inserted the sponge inside her vagina and lay on the bed to think of something more interesting for the next few minutes while Mr. Collins would be wheezing over her.

He was completely naked and climbed into bed with her to quickly begin to pump himself in and out of her. Within minutes, he grunted loudly as he released his seed inside her.

Panting as if he had been exercising for an hour, he rolled his sweaty body off of her and thanked her. After resting to lower his heart rate that took longer than the sexual act itself, he stood to dress and pay her and commented, "Dolores, I will be going to London and should return in a few days. I will see you next week. I believe I need to increase our meeting to twice weekly instead of weekly since I cannot stop thinking about you, Dolores. You are fantastic, my dear. I must warn you, though, I may be married soon and if my wife does not satisfy me, I will continue to visit you. If she does work out, I will return to give you a proper farewell, my dear. Goodbye." Mr. Collins bowed and left.

Dolores burst out laughing after she saw that he had gone far enough. *I have no idea who is going to marry that idiot but good luck to his future! Oh, I wish my dear George was in my bed instead. He had such a good body but sadly enough, I have to open my legs to these common cocks who know nothing about pleasing a woman.*

And she went about cleaning herself for the next client.

Chapter 12

Lady Catherine arrived at her brother's home tired and anxious. Lord Henry Matlock had a strong personality that was necessary for him to preside over Parliament and he was a respected leader with honour and a strong sense of duty, and she was counting on that family obligation to her to convince him to force Darcy marry Anne. She completely discarded his threats of repaying Darcy the debt that was owed and believed that she could make her demands known and carried out as due to her rank.

She was furious as she was asked to wait in the sitting room by the butler, since that useless servant should have led her straight to her brother's study. She yelled, "Do you know who I AM?! I demand that you take me to my brother's study NOW!"

The butler plainly answered, "Lady Catherine, I have been instructed by Lady Matlock to escort you to the sitting room." And he stood steadfast without budging, blocking her path to the study.

Disgruntled, "I shall speak to my brother about your insolence and you will be let go without a reference!" She stomped to the sitting room with Anne, Mrs. Jenkinson, and Mr. Collins in tow.

Several minutes later, Lady Matlock gracefully entered. "Ah, Catherine, and I see you brought your entourage. Anne, my dear, how are you? Good to see you again, Mrs. Jenkinson." She ignored Mr. Collins.

Anne meekly responded, "Hello, Aunt Susan." Anne had always liked Lady Matlock. She spoke kindly and was very proper, unlike her own mother, who was crass and bitter everyday of her life. Anne hated living at Rosings and she despised Mr. Collins. Mrs. Jenkinson, her companion, was very nice and kept her informed of the town gossips and it was known to a few that Mr. Collins liked to use the town prostitute, the former vicar's wife, every week. He was supposed to be a man of God but he was a bootlicker and stupid and definitely not a good clergyman. Although Anne was exhausted, she was glad to be in London. With Mrs. Jenkinson and Aunt Susan's help, she was desperately hoping that she could escape her tyrant mother and perhaps live with her uncle and aunt instead.

She could not understand why her mother was pushing so hard for her cousin's marriage to her. Fitzwilliam was very handsome but he was stiff and unfriendly and she infinitely preferred Richard's company but she thought neither of them as a husband. Anne did not want to get married at all since she was always sickly and became easily tired, but she had tried to educate herself by reading more away from her mother's eyes.

Mother always told me I was destined to be the Mistress of Pemberley but I do not know how to even manage Rosings. She is delusional if she thinks I would be a good wife to anyone, especially after all of her complaints of the 'wifely duties'! I have no beauty, no skills, and I cannot even embroider. I know myself enough that I am unfit to be anyone's companion, much less mistress of a grand estate that is five times the size of Rosings Park. I am so glad Fitzwilliam is engaged. I hope Miss Bennet can stand up to Mother. She is on a war-path!

Immediately, Anne twitched and shrunk in fear as she heard her mother's booming voice. "NO! I will not be calm, Susan! You DARE insult the daughter of an earl by making me wait here? WHERE is my brother?"

Lady Susan laughed in Lady Catherine's face. "Catherine, you are good for a laugh, that is for certain. You dare insult me, the WIFE of an earl? While you may have had the luck of being born into the family, I was CHOSEN to be a countess. Your ill manners will no longer be tolerated and you will remain here until his *Lordship* is ready to see you. Come, Anne, Mrs. Jenkinson. I will walk with you to your rooms." She gave a stern look to the two footmen and left with Anne on her arm.

Lady Catherine attempted to follow them but the footmen blocked her way. "You DARE block my path?" She screeched.

One footman spoke very curtly, "Yes, ma'am," and did not budge. Resigned, Lady Catherine sat in the largest chair, while Mr. Collins sat mutely, awed at Lady Susan and comprehending that Lady Catherine was indeed below the Countess.

~*~

Lady Matlock spoke quietly as she led Anne to her room. "You look very tired, Anne. How are you feeling?"

She was very concerned, as she had never seen Anne look so pale before. She had recently convinced her husband that they must get their timid niece away from the grips of that harridan of a woman, and with Darcy's assistance last week, they had finally formulated a way to get Anne out of Rosings and she was surprised that Anne and Catherine had arrived when they did. It was now only a matter of convincing Anne to take the next steps.

Anne was touched by the concern she saw in her aunt's eyes and immediately broke into tears. "Oh, Aunt Susan! It is terrible. Mother refuses to let me see a doctor and she says that whatever that grovelling apothecary says is good enough and will not cease in her demands for me to become Darcy's wife. After she read the engagement announcement, she told me that it is my duty to get into my cousin's bed so that Miss Bennet would break off the engagement and Darcy would be honour-bound to marry me. I am afraid she has something terrible planned." She poured out her heart.

Lady Matlock rubbed her back as Anne cried on her shoulder, settling her on the couch in front of the fireplace. She felt terribly for the lonely young woman but reddened with anger that Catherine would devise a way to break her nephew's engagement.

Lady Matlock had met Elizabeth and truly enjoyed her company. Miss Bennet did not cower to her due to her rank but was open and honest and she could immediately see why Darcy had proposed to her. Her nephew had been so lonely and desolate for years after his father's death and upon hearing that Lizzy had loved him when she thought him poor, she was immediately inclined to love her future niece.

She had actively promoted the match in public and had spent the past three weeks in getting to know her, and seeing Darcy and Lizzy in love with each other had been a balm to her heart. She owed much to Darcy for providing financial security to Richard as well and loved him like a third son.

Anne continued, "Oh, aunt! Mr. Collins is apparently the heir to Miss Elizabeth Bennet's family and Mother told him to take Miss Elizabeth as his wife under *any* circumstances. She said something about an olive branch and I pretended to be asleep but heard her order him to compromise her and ruin her so she could not be Mrs. Darcy. Oh, she is so awful!" She wailed even louder.

"Anne, I have to send an express to Darcy so he is aware of what is happening. But before I go, please tell me, what do you want with your life? What is your wish? Now that you are here, your uncle and I have been working on a way to get you away from your mother but the choice is yours." Lady Matlock asked.

"I wish to never see Mother again if at all possible. I wish to be able to make my own choices and do the things that I want to do. I have no money and no place to go, aunt. It is not possible; I will never be away from her." She cried quietly. "I do not wish to marry. I do not wish to be a wife or belong to someone else. I want to be independent and be healthy and eat what I want and meet new people. Oh, aunt, it is impossible."

Lady Matlock hugged her tighter, "No, Anne, it is not impossible. I will tell you all later but we will do as you wish. Your uncle and I will take care of you and you will be independent. Do you trust us?" She smiled, pulling herself down to look at Anne.

Seeing her aunt's confidence, Anne smiled slightly. She had hope. "Yes, Aunt Susan. Thank you for giving me hope. I appreciate you more than you will ever know."

Lady Matlock left Anne to Mrs. Jenkinson's care so she could rest. She sought her husband in his study immediately and told her briefly of Catherine's belligerence and Anne's wishes. Together, they would face Lady Catherine.

~*~

Lady Catherine was surprised when Lord and Lady Matlock walked together, arm-in-arm with a smile on their faces. She had expected that Susan would have poisoned her brother by now and he would be walking in angry but she did not expect them to both appear pleasant.

"Henry! WHAT is the MEANING of this?! Your rude wife has kept me waiting here for half an hour and probably only just told you about my being here. I TOLD you she was not of our sphere. She brings nothing but shame to our family!" She spewed.

"SILENCE! Catherine, we have been married for thirty-five years and there is nothing that you could do to change my mind about my beautiful wife. You are as ridiculous as ever and we have several things to discuss so you will keep your mouth closed. Now, first and foremost, Darcy will no longer manage Rosings and has informed me that you owe him £10,000. I have spoken with him a few days ago and we have determined that you will repay him by the end of the year out of your remaining dowry, AND," he spoke quickly as Lady Catherine began to splutter, "Anne will be given control over Rosings immediately. Your lies have gone on long enough. Anne should have been given her inheritance after she turned five and twenty but you kept her in such poor health that we did not think she would be able. We now know that Anne wishes to be independent and Albert and I will work with the steward to manage the estate. My son has wanted to practice what he has been learning from Darcy in any case and you will be moved to the dower house upon your return."

"You will NOT displace me of MY home, Henry! You have no right!" Lady Catherine yelled.

She was shocked to hear that she would be made to pay £10,000 out of her remaining funds, as that was nearly all she had left, and to move into the dower house was ridiculous. That shack only had five bedrooms and could accommodate two or three servants. To leave the grandeur of Rosings Park would never happen while she was alive!

"I have every right as the head of the family, Catherine," Lord Matlock boomed. He was sick and tired of his arrogant sister. "I am your closest relation and am an earl and you will show respect due to me. And whatever you are planning for Darcy, put it out of your mind, woman. You will never be able to separate him from his betrothed. I demand that you remove yourself to your rooms and take your meal there tonight. You are to leave first thing in the morning so do not bother unpacking. Anne will remain here." Turning to Mr. Collins, he said, "I will bestow my condescension to you; you may remain here for one night. I know that Anne will not be able to release you from the parish right now but I know of your perfidies and will be writing to the Archbishop to have you defrocked! Leave my presence now!" *The fool! I must keep them here until Darcy receives the express!*

Lady Catherine huffed and walked out of the room with the housekeeper leading her to her rooms, while Mr. Collins was directed to his room by the butler on the opposite wing.

Lord and Lady Matlock sat and took several breaths, content that this was finally done and that they could look forward to helping Anne become the rightful owner of Rosings.

An express had already been sent to Darcy to inform him of Lady Catherine's arrival as well as Anne's comments regarding Mr. Collins, the heir-presumed to Longbourn. Darcy had already worked out a plan for Lord Matlock and they intended to follow it to the letter.

~*~

Lady Catherine sat fuming and she was determined to get out of this situation. It was ridiculous that she would be forced to move to the dower house and even more ridiculous that Darcy would get her £10,000. She would have to talk some sense into him and make sure the ridiculous engagement was broken.

If there was an ugly public break, Darcy would have no choice but to marry Anne to cover his shame and it would be easy to bend Anne to her will as she had always done. Anne would move to Pemberley and she would reign at Rosings as it was meant to be. She would have access to Darcy's fortune and he would have to support his new mother and protect his own assets by infusing more money into the estate. She would be able to live grander than before.

An idea formed in her head. Instead of returning to Rosings, she would go to Darcy House. She should have gone there straight today but Mrs. Jenkinson kept pestering her that Anne was not feeling well. Tomorrow, she would get inside the house, get Anne installed in the Mistress' rooms and after talking some sense into her nephew, she would ensure that Anne was in his bed. This Miss Bennet woman would surely break off the engagement hearing that he had another woman, but even if she did not, Mr. Collins would travel to Hertfordshire and convince those conniving Bennets to take his generous offer of marriage to Elizabeth Bennet so they would not be thrown out of the home when the sickly Mr. Bennet died. Mr. Collins would be instructed to take his future wife by force if necessary and the Bennets would have no choice but to make them marry.

She smiled for the first time today, as she was certain her plan would work in her favour.

~*~

Mr. Collins had spoken to Lady Catherine about the little that he knew of the Bennets. His father had been in love with Mr. Bennet's sister and desired to marry her but she had married a Mr. John Downton who was a modest gentleman with 3,000 a year.

Elizabeth Downton died along with her babe in childbirth and Mr. Collins the elder rejoiced when hearing of her demise. He had never gotten over the fact that he was refused and after attempting to compromise her but being caught by her brother, Mr. Bennet, he received several blows to his face and abdomen and all connections between the Collinses and Bennets were severed.

The younger Mr. Collins had only heard of an irreconcilable argument between the families and that the Bennets were at fault for the insult. His parents had married, unbeknownst to him, after his father had thoroughly compromised his mother who had a £5,000 dowry by forcing himself on her in her own bed, and they had both perished in a carriage accident five years ago.

Mr. Collins lay in bed reviewing all that he had seen and heard today. He was certain Lady Catherine was a superior woman of rank but now hearing that Miss de Bourgh was the rightful Mistress of Rosings Park, he was determined to win her favour, although he knew not how. He would return to Hunsford tomorrow and planned to find ways to ingratiate himself with Miss Anne.

Dolores, he thought, *I will return earlier than expected. I cannot wait to see her again. It feels so good to have her.* He began to stroke himself as he thought of Dolores. He stroked faster and climaxed immediately.

I wonder if I have time to visit a brothel in London. There must be so many to choose from here. He fell asleep quickly as he dreamt of the multitudes of buxom ladies in waiting for his virile body to pleasure them.

Chapter 13

Darcy and Elizabeth had been seeing each other daily, either at public outings, at balls and dinners, or in the quiet of the drawing room with chaperons. They had rarely any time alone in London, as their days were filled with so many appointments.

The final Banns were read in Meryton and they had one more month to go. Darcy had asked for the Banns to be read as quickly as possible since he did not want any impediments in making Elizabeth his wife. In his wisdom, he knew Lady Catherine would vehemently interfere somehow, and wanted to have everything ready, even obtaining a special license during the first week in London. In town, there were many who congratulated Darcy of his upcoming marriage and some, who were viciously jealous but kept their opinions to themselves.

Darcy sat in the Netherfield library, where he had been given complete privacy to work on his businesses, staring into the wall as he contemplated his next action. He had a candid conversation with Richard on how to control his passions and his cousin had shared with him that it had been a month since he himself had used a woman. Richard had confided in him that using a woman for carnal needs might be enjoyable for the few seconds it took to release, but that Darcy was most fortunate to have a wife and that it would be worth the wait. Darcy had been remembering kissing Elizabeth this morning, having resumed their morning meetings on Oakham Mount, fantasizing about taking her to his bed, and was about to drop the fall of his breeches when there was a knock at the door. Grunting, he sat up and bid the intruder to enter.

There was an express from his Uncle Henry and he was initially concerned that something might have happened to his cousin Albert or Aunt Susan, since Georgiana and Richard were here with him and safe.

As he perused through the letter, he became angry that Lady Catherine would once again invade his peace and bring such misery to everyone within her reach. He had vowed to cut her off directly and would need to deliberate with Elizabeth on how to prepare for her attack. He asked Richard to join him and requested their horses be saddled up.

On the way to Longbourn, Darcy shared the letter with his cousin and Richard fumed in rage. They had arrived in Hertfordshire yesterday and Richard had enjoyed meeting some of the townsfolk and the serene setting the country offered. After witnessing the devastation of the war, any peace offered by the quiet country was welcome. He was to take a two-week holiday, return to town, then come back for the wedding. He enjoyed seeing Elizabeth's home and meeting her parents this afternoon and found Hertfordshire enchanting, as it had belonged to her. The past three weeks he spent almost daily in Cousin Lizzy's company had been cathartic.

Richard thought of his time with Elizabeth and how she was so genial and kind. She asked him to call her 'Lizzy' and he loved hearing his name from her lips. He always called her 'Elizabeth' in his heart, though and he had fallen in love with her and knew she would be forever in his heart. He had never met her equal in beauty and benevolence, and she was far more intelligent than the common females of society. She was witty and charming and he longed to be in the space where she was.

Internally, he knew he was falling deeper in love with Elizabeth Bennet every day, but for all appearances otherwise, he was jovial and charming and flirted with Miss Jane to fluster Bingley. He wanted Bingley to make up his mind about the beautiful Jane Bennet and it was his way to push him along. It was obvious that Miss Jane was in love with Bingley but the man seemed to be taking his time to show his preference, which was a first. Bingley had always been in and out of love quickly and Richard was fascinated that Bingley was being hesitant, but after Darcy explained to him about Miss Sarah Fleming and how Darcy had cautioned Bingley to really know his mind, Richard decided to back off to allow Bingley to pursue Miss Jane on his own terms.

Richard Fitzwilliam's heart tore every time he was in Elizabeth's presence but he was like a moth drawn to flame. He could not be away from her long, as seeing her quenched his thirst, but it also caused pain, as her eyes were only for Darcy. *If I had only met her first, she might have preferred me!* But he knew he would never find out and he could do naught but continue in his suffering. He would rather suffer in her presence than to be parted from her, though. He felt alive when she was near.

He was extremely angry with Lady Catherine. She was meddling in affairs that were not hers and was about to disrupt them in the worst way possible. It was nearing dinnertime but they rushed into Longbourn to speak with Mr. Bennet and Elizabeth.

Darcy spoke to Mr. Hill. "I have very important business with Mr. Bennet, Hill. Could you please ask Miss Elizabeth to join us as well?" as he was led to the study.

"What brings you here so late, gentlemen? Our dinner engagement was for tomorrow, not tonight." Mr. Bennet jested. Seeing the flustered look on both men, he said, "What has happened? What has disconcerted you both so?" He asked as he offered them seats and handed them a glass of brandy each.

Just then, Elizabeth entered the study. "I was asked to join? Fitzwilliam! Richard! What are you doing here? I did not expect to see you until tomorrow. Is all well? Is Georgiana well?" She asked.

Darcy smiled as he stood. *Of course, she thinks of Georgiana. How I love her.*

Richard smiled as he stood. *I love hearing my name from her lips. Stop it, man! She thinks you only as a cousin, idiot!*

Darcy answered first. "Yes, my dear. We are all well; but I have an express from my uncle that I need to share. Will you take a seat?" He continued, "My uncle wrote to me that he received unexpected visitors from Rosings this morning. Lady Catherine arrived without any notice with my cousin Anne and her companion as well as a Mr. Collins in tow at his townhouse and demanded his attention right away. Aunt Susan was able to separate Anne from her mother and was told that not only did Lady Catherine have a nefarious plan to have Anne compromise me, but that she had instructed Mr. Collins to take Elizabeth in *any* way possible to make her his wife." He gave a look to Mr. Bennet. "There was something about an olive branch and Mr. Collins being heir to Longbourn. Do you know this man, Mr. Bennet?" Darcy asked.

Mr. Bennet was red with fury. *How dare that son of a jackass agree to such a scheme!* "Yes, I know Mr. Collins. He is a distant cousin who is the heir-presumptive to Longbourn, as I have no sons. His father is a man of low morals who attempted to compromise my sister. He had remained bitter to the end that my sister chose the better man and I am certain he had poisoned his son into believing that all the wrongdoing is on my side. What do you know of their plans?"

"We will most likely receive a visit from them on the morrow." Darcy stood as he paced. "He must not meet or see Elizabeth at all. If he takes after his father and follows what Lady Catherine orders him to do, Elizabeth will be in danger, even if she is in a public place. I believe Lady Catherine is convinced that once Elizabeth is ruined, I will not want her and to save my family's honour, would marry my cousin Anne." Turning to Elizabeth and kneeling at her chair, he held her hand. "It would never happen, my love. Even if something were to happen, I would never turn away from you." He kissed her hand. He did not care if her father or his cousin was in the room. He saw the look of terror on her face and wanted to comfort her.

Richard thought the same. *I would marry her in a heartbeat, no matter what. I am going to kill Lady Catherine and this idiot Mr. Collins if they touch her. I swear Lady Catherine will never get near my Elizabeth.*

"I understand, Fitzwilliam. I know you will protect me." She cleared her throat. "Ahem. So, what will we do? What is our strategy?" She smiled but was still serious.

I love her so much. She is so brave. Darcy thought. He stood and paced while running his hand through his hair. "Well, we will hit her where it hurts. My uncle will be evicting her from Rosings immediately and setting her up in the dower house. How much comfort she will receive is up to her. The steward there is actually a man that I set up and is loyal to Lord Matlock and me and will ensure that she is given incompetent servants, IF she is given more than one, and her living status will be awful. My solicitor will demand her £10,000 debt to me to be repaid immediately instead of year-end. She will be left nearly penniless, having all her power and status taken away from her, unless she accepts my choice and begs for forgiveness. We must keep Elizabeth out of sight, though, and will need to protect her. I wish to see no harm come to her."

Darcy stopped pacing and turned to Mr. Bennet. "Sir, may I have a moment of privacy with Elizabeth? I would like her input on an idea I have before I present it to you."

Mr. Bennet smiled. Darcy had proven to be a respectable and intelligent young man and he was extremely pleased to gain him for a son, and it had nothing to do with his fortune or status but the way he treated his favourite daughter with care and honour, which was what had impressed him the most. Darcy was involved in the wedding planning to find what would please Lizzy, but more than agreeing with everything around him, his thoughts were methodical and planned and not impulsive. He had become more open with the family but always considered Lizzy's feelings and opinions first. Not many men could tolerate sitting for hours listening to Mrs. Bennet's talk of lace and flowers, but Darcy endured it all to please Lizzy. Mr. Bennet had guessed that they must have shared several kisses but the way they acted around each other, he knew they had not done much more; they were still shy and blushing frequently when they touched. He trusted Darcy.

"Yes, you may take her to the dining room to talk. You should not be bothered there for the next quarter hour. Colonel Fitzwilliam and I will catch up on his father's letter." He excused them to some private time.

~*~

Leading Elizabeth to the dining room, Darcy held her hand close to him as he wrapped his arms around her. "My love, I had been dreaming of our kisses when I was rudely interrupted and I rushed over to see you. Are you well?" He was worried for her when he had mentioned Mr. Collins 'taking her in any way possible'. It was subtly implied that the villain might resort to a public compromise or worse, forcing himself on Elizabeth to get his way. His uncle had indicated that Mr. Collins was known to visit the Kent prostitute often and he had been in the process of getting the parson defrocked for his immoral sins.

"I am well, Fitzwilliam. I am glad you are here and that you have shared with me what you heard. If you had it kept it from me, I would have been more afraid and angry but I know you will protect me." She replied as she hugged him tightly. She trusted Darcy and loved him so much and could not believe this was happening now. They had another month until the wedding and all she wanted to do was stay in his loving arms as his wife.

Darcy kissed her hair and remained holding her close. "I wanted to talk to you about a plan that I had. I know that I had rushed you to court me and then to marry me but I wondered... Would you be agreeable to our marrying tomorrow morning?"

Elizabeth gasped and looked up, releasing her hold around his waist. "Tomorrow?!"

"Yes, my love. We know we love each other and we are committed to loving each other for all eternity. I have found that the more I find out about you, the more there is to love. I cannot imagine that I will ever stop and it will take a lifetime to know you until I am satisfied. Will you marry me tomorrow? The Banns have been read and I even have the special license. We just need Reverend Bertram to perform the ceremony and I do not need anything else. We can have a small breakfast, return to Darcy House for a fortnight, then come back to Hertfordshire to have a celebration party." Seeing her hesitancy, he quickly added, "This was just an idea that sprung, my love. I do not wish to rush you but your being my wife will keep you safer than as my fiancée. Elizabeth, I desperately wish to marry you but I will stand by any decision you make. I did want to know your mind before I brought it up to your father. I care for your choices and will honour it."

Elizabeth looked at him adoringly. She had just been thinking of wanting to marry him earlier rather than waiting another full month but she had been wary of the wedding night. Her thoughts had gone straight to the marriage bed and she did not know what to expect.

Blushing, Elizabeth responded, "I never cared for a large wedding. With your help, we have been able to somewhat curtail my mother's grandiose plans for next month. I honestly want a simple wedding with you and the preacher and my close family and friends. I care not for a big wedding breakfast or the church filled with flowers. I just want you. Yes, I will marry you tomorrow. I wish to be your wife tomorrow." She blushed even deeper, "My hesitancy was not because I was worried about marrying you, Fitzwilliam; rather it had to do with the wedding night."

Darcy drew her into his arms again and kissed her tenderly. She could immediately feel the hard bulge against her abdomen and revelled in the wonder that was to come.

"I love you, Elizabeth. After you give me a moment, we will return to your father." And he went to the window to stare outside.

Elizabeth giggled to herself as she fanned her face with her hands. *I cannot believe I will marry him tomorrow! I hope Papa agrees.*

Darcy soon turned and held her hand as they returned to the study.

~*~

Richard had explained to Mr. Bennet about Mr. Collins' immoral behaviours and that he would lose his patronage at Hunsford in the near future. They discussed the possibility of displacing him and breaking the entail as well. Mr. Bennet had researched and sought legal assistance but there was no way around it as far as he knew, as he had to have a son. They discussed how they could keep Lizzy safe for a month and whether she should return to London or stay in Hertfordshire.

Richard was adamant that she would be safer at Matlock House under his parents' and his own care, with Darcy only two blocks away, while Mr. Bennet insisted she remain at home under his own care, even if it meant being imprisoned within their own house for a month.

Darcy and Elizabeth walked in as the two gentlemen were debating and Elizabeth cleared her throat. "Ahem, gentlemen, I hope you have not been making decisions for me. Father? Richard?" She lifted one eyebrow.

Mr. Bennet burst out laughing while Richard looked away bashfully.

God! What I would do to have her chastise me like a wife. Richard thought. *I love her so much. How in the world am I going to get over her?*

Darcy laughed and Elizabeth continued, "Papa, I hope you will understand that my dear betrothed was seeking my approval of a crazy idea of his and I have agreed with him. Papa, we wish to be married in the morning." She confirmed.

"Morning? As in, tomorrow morning?!" Mr. Bennet was astonished.

"Yes, Papa. Tomorrow morning. Once I am Mrs. Darcy, Lady Catherine will have no basis that Fitzwilliam would marry her daughter and Mr. Collins cannot attack me. He would be hung to attack the wife of the illustrious Mr. Darcy." She winked at Richard who was sitting with his mouth gaping.

Mr. Bennet was silent for several minutes. It was the perfect solution. Lady Catherine would lose her grounds of the non-existent engagement that was 'formed while they were in their cradles' and Mr. Collins would be promptly escorted off the property. Lizzy would be under Darcy's protection and safe. He eyed his daughter and future son and saw that they were not rushing in order to satisfy their carnal desires; there was no urgency for the union due to lack of patience. They truly loved each other and wanted to begin their lives together soon.

Tears came to his eyes. *I thought I would have another month with her but it appears I am wrong. I would not have let her go to anyone less worthy. Darcy is a good man.*

Clearing his throat, he finally spoke, "I am..." he paused for effect, "...in agreement. I will need to inform your mother of the change in date and I am certain she will be calling for her salts. Lizzy, I charge you with sorting out the details but you shall be married tomorrow morning. I will have Hill deliver my letter," he sat down to scribble the request to the parson, "to Reverend Bertram right now that he perform the services at ten o'clock tomorrow morning, sharp." He finished writing the letter as Richard and Darcy were shaking each other's hand and planning their next steps. Mr. Bennet rang the bell and asked Mr. Hill to have one of the stable boys deliver the letter right away.

"Gentlemen, I would ask you to stay for dinner but it appears Lizzy has a long night ahead of her. She will need to prepare to be a bride tomorrow!" They all laughed cheerfully. "I shall see you both tomorrow. Please send word if you hear anything else in the meanwhile. Good evening."

Darcy kissed Elizabeth's hand once more as they walked out behind Richard and Mr. Bennet was heading to Mrs. Bennet's room. "I love you, Elizabeth. I promise to cherish you every day and give you all of myself."

"I love you, Fitzwilliam. I will treasure being cherished by you and I promise not to raise your ire too often." She kissed him on the cheek and returned inside.

~*~

Mr. Bennet knocked on his wife's door. She was dressing for dinner and looked as beautiful as ever. His heart was full to see his wife in her dressing room and pleased that she had not been sleeping in her bed for the past two months. They had slept together every night and he recognised the slight changes in her body. He had never forgotten her body and how wonderful it was to have her in his bed. He had been tempted to find relief while they were living separate lives for so long, but he could never go through with bedding another woman.

"Mr. Bennet, I heard Mr. Darcy had arrived. Shall he be staying for dinner?" Mrs. Bennet asked.

"No, Mrs. Bennet, he and the Colonel have already left. Fanny, I must ask... are you... will we be parents again?" He asked as he stood behind her dressing mirror.

"How did... oh, Thomas, of course you would know. You often knew earlier than I did with our girls. Yes, I am certain I am with child. I have not felt the quickening yet and hesitated to share with you as I am so much older and it may not stay, but I believe we are expecting our sixth child. I hope it will be a boy, Thomas. I truly pray for a boy, but I will not hold it against the babe if it should be another beautiful daughter. You have provided so well for us and with Lizzy marrying Mr. Darcy, I will not worry. Mr. Darcy has been so kind and he truly loves her and has promised to provide for our family. We are so blessed, Mr. Bennet." She waved her handkerchief from old habit. It was shared that the settlement papers that Mr. Bennet signed contained details of one of his properties that would be available to her and Mr. Darcy had settled £25,000 on Lizzy, as well as an additional £25,000 to protect the Bennets should Mr. Bennet pass before the other daughters married. It was an incredulous amount but they would all be safeguarded and Mrs. Bennet would not be thrown into the hedgerows.

"Fanny, I am proud of you. No matter what, you must promise to take care of yourself and our child. We are truly blessed, but I wished to speak with you about Lizzy. You know that Mr. Darcy loves her so much. He wants to care for her and keep her safe always." His wife nodded and smiled. "There is a situation, do not worry, my dear, nothing terrible. A situation has arisen with Lady Catherine and to take preventive measures, Lizzy and Darcy will be marrying tomorrow morning."

"Tomorrow morning?!" Mrs. Bennet screeched. Mr. Bennet gave her a look.

Mrs. Bennet took a few calming breaths and spoke more quietly, "Thomas, do you believe that they *should* be married tomorrow morning? There is no other *rush* for the marriage to happen quickly?"

Mrs. Bennet was concerned that perhaps Lizzy was with child and they *needed* to marry immediately. Mr. Darcy always seemed so proper, though, but she knew his passions ran deep.

Mr. Bennet chuckled. "No, Fanny. They are as proper as ever and there will not be an early babe. Let me tell you what I learned when the gentlemen came in unexpectedly."

He proceeded to tell his wife about Lady Catherine and her long-time demands as well as Mr. Collins and the possible compromise.

"Oh, Thomas, we must keep Lizzy safe!" Mrs. Bennet exclaimed after her husband explained the situation. "I am certain Lizzy cares nothing about the flowers and the wedding breakfast. THE WEDDING BREAKFAST! I must go to Hill now and make the arrangements. Hill! Hill!" She became frantic.

Mr. Bennet reached out and pulled his wife into his arms gently. "Fanny, remember; you must care for our babe and not become over-excited. Everything will be all right."

When Mrs. Hill rushed up to answer Mrs. Bennet's loud shrieking, which had not been heard for over two months, she found the master and mistress of Longbourn in a tight embrace, kissing as if they were newlyweds. She smiled and closed the door quietly.

Chapter 14

Darcy paced in front of the church the next morning while waiting for the wedding party to arrive. The ceremony was to start at ten o'clock but he had arrived an hour early to await his future wife. He was not fearful or nervous but utterly impatient to become a married man.

After returning from Longbourn last night, he spoke with Georgiana first and then with Bingley and the Hursts of the changes in the wedding date. They were all thrilled that the wedding would take place soon and as they dined, they made plans for the trip back to London for Georgiana and Richard. Georgiana and Louisa Hurst left after the meal to look at what they would wear to the wedding and to order white soup to set a date for a celebratory ball in two weeks. Mrs. Hurst had become much friendlier and had taken Georgiana under her wings and promised to help Mrs. Bennet with the wedding breakfast, then they excitedly left to see to the details.

The gentlemen sat in the drawing room and savoured their port and Mr. Hurst wholeheartedly congratulated Darcy on his good fortune of finding such a gem. They talked very briefly of Caroline Bingley who was installed in York with their spinster aunt and laughed at her letter, where she complained that she had much preferred the backwater country of Hertfordshire than the cold harsh winter of York.

Bingley shared that he asked Jane Bennet for courtship and that it was accepted, and the men congratulated him and had another glass to celebrate. Bingley was certain that Jane Bennet was the woman he wanted to marry, but he wanted to take things slow and appreciate the lady before jumping in and regretting it later.

As they drank a little more, Bingley, who could never handle much alcohol in his life, became more inebriated and confessed that he did not know what love was until he met Jane and that all the women he bedded could not compare to the feeling of ecstasy when Jane had allowed him to kiss her lips. He blabbered on about her lips then began to describe the swelling of her chest and Darcy quickly shut him up by giving him another sip of drink and Mr. Hurst escorted him to his rooms.

Richard and Darcy laughed loudly and joked about the man not being able to tolerate his liquor. Darcy had not been drinking much, as his thoughts continuously drifted to Elizabeth and the anticipation of her becoming his wife finally, and the long list of items that needed to be prepared for the next day, but he noticed that Richard was pouring himself another glass, his sixth for the evening. He was surprised that his cousin looked quite sullen at times. He had tried to cover it with jokes and laughing with the group but Darcy had noticed several times that Richard's mind would drift and he would have a sorrowful look. Richard also had quit drinking to excess for the past ten years, so Darcy became concerned when he gulped down the next glass.

"Richard, now that we are alone, is there something you would like to share with me? Can I offer you my assistance on anything that you might be troubled with? You know that you have been my best friend and confidante all of my life and you can rely on me to assist you with anything." Darcy probed.

Richard closed his eyes and relaxed, leaning back on the couch, as he felt the heat of the port slide down. "Oh, Darcy, if you only knew my pain... My heart is not my own. I am meditating on the pleasures of a pair of fine eyes of the most beautiful woman I know." He continued to daydream.

Richard is in love? With whom? When did this happen? Darcy thought. *I did not notice him paying any particular attention to a woman and he spoke of no one in town; well, perhaps Jane, but she is not his type and he was truly happy for Bingley. I know it is* not Georgiana; he treats her as he always has and she is still a child. He has not even danced with anyone at balls lately except with family. Wait. Richard was not unaffected by Elizabeth, though. I noticed his reaction when first meeting her and he is definitely quieter than his norm around Elizabeth. Good God! He is in love with my fiancée!

He watched Richard very carefully. He saw a small smile appear as Richard kept his eyes closed. Is he dreaming about my Elizabeth? Blasted, is he getting an arousal? Damn it, he is hard for my future wife! What do I do? I certainly cannot blame him. She is EXACTLY his type. Every woman he ever chased, Elizabeth is all of his preferences rolled into one. Richard probably fell in love at first sight. How did I miss this? I should have realised that no one but a few of us call him by his given name and he had asked it of Elizabeth the first day. I thought he was doing so to avoid confusion but now I am certain he desired her from the beginning. He must be in love with Elizabeth!

As Darcy was contemplating such thoughts in his own head, Richard was imagining Elizabeth in a sheer nightgown.

"Do you think this will do for my wedding night, Richard?" She asked.

"It will have to do, although I prefer you completely undressed, Elizabeth. I do not mind anything you wear."

In his fantasy, he grabbed her waist with one hand and licked her neck as he caressed her beautiful breast with the other.

Richard snapped his eyes open. Oh, hell! Darcy is right here and here I am, dreaming of bedding his wife to be. Damn it. He saw me getting hard. He is going to kill me and I deserve it.

"Ahem. Darcy. I think I was falling asleep. I should head up to my rooms." Richard scrambled to stand, trying to cover his erection. It was deflating fast but not quickly enough. Darcy had every right to beat him to a pulp and he deserved to receive every punch. He could not look his cousin in the eyes.

Darcy spoke very quietly. "Are you in love with Elizabeth?" His words came out slowly and ominously.

He knows! Blast it!! Richard braced himself.

After some time, he finally answered, "Yes, Darce. I love her. I fell in love with her the first moment I saw her. I have not been able to touch another woman since meeting her." He added quickly, "But she loves you. She treats me like a cousin and a friend and that will be all. It will never be more and I would never betray you. You have been my best friend all of my life and I would not break that trust."

As Darcy walked closer to him, Richard finally lifted his eyes to meet his cousin's. He had spoken the truth. He would love Elizabeth until his dying day but he also loved his cousin. He would never do anything to hurt either of them.

Darcy put his hand on Richard's shoulder. "Richard, I love Elizabeth with all of my heart and I know the pull that she has on me. If you love her a fraction of how I love her, I know it is an impossible task to stop. I trust that you will love her from afar. I cannot have you dishonour her or show her any disrespect as a woman *and* as my wife, but I also know I cannot ask you to stop loving her. It would be easier to stop breathing than to stop loving her. She is my life, Richard."

"I understand, Darcy. I will never do anything to hurt either of you. I am so pleased that you have found her and she is so perfect for you. I know that I will overcome this but I also know that it will take time. I vow to protect both you and Elizabeth. I promise you that." Richard confessed.

Darcy smiled slightly. "Thank you, cousin." He tapped his back. "Let us retire now. I am getting married in the morning!"

~*~

Darcy looked around to see Richard making a joke with Bingley and he smiled. His cousin was truly a good man and he wondered if he had been his proud obnoxious self and Elizabeth had met the dashing Colonel Fitzwilliam first, would her heart have been touched? Would she have preferred the jolly charms of the handsome son of an earl in his red uniform who would have flattered her and flirted with her? Darcy knew women loved Richard's attentions and that Richard had been successful in seducing many beautiful women. Although his cousin had always bemoaned that second sons had to marry an heiress or someone with status, Darcy knew Richard did not need to marry for money and he would have desired Elizabeth above all other women. Richard would have been relentless and would have been successful at winning Elizabeth if he had met her first. *And all I did was call her 'barely tolerable' and insult her!* Darcy recalled. It was only a month ago but he was a different man then. *But she will be mine today. No, she does not belong to me. I belong to her. She has had me from the beginning and she will never lose me.*

He saw the church pews fill up. Several notes had been sent quickly to some of the close families that the wedding date had been moved up requesting their attendance the next morning. He had met quite a few of them during the first week but he knew they were here for Elizabeth. She had touched her neighbours' hearts in one way or another as she cared for the ill, visited the tenants, and spent so much time to embroider little patterns for the orphans' dresses. They were gentlefolk and servants alike, who were here to wish her the best; she was a wonder and she would be a good Mistress of Pemberley. He nodded to Charlotte Lucas who was Elizabeth's dear friend. She knew of his insults but had also forgiven him. Elizabeth had told him that Charlotte had punched her brother in the nose years ago when he had insulted her by calling her 'Dizzy Lizzy' and might have done the same to himself had he not apologised.

Although a very private person, Darcy was no longer afraid to open himself up to judgment. He guarded what was his fiercely but if the truth were something that was more worthy than his own pride of privacy, he would now share it. Thus, to put any rumours aside for the rushed wedding date, he had spoken with Sir William Lucas that they were expecting some trouble with Lady Catherine de Bourgh, patroness to Mr. Bennet's cousin, whom Longbourn was entailed to, and that they wanted to keep Elizabeth safe by putting her under Darcy's protection. Not much more details were given but word spread quickly that Mr. Darcy and Elizabeth were marrying due to the crazy, hateful woman who would use her rank and power to wreak havoc and that Mr. Collins might be dangerous as well. Conjectures were made but all the evil was placed on Lady Catherine and her minion Mr. Collins, with none of the blame on the Darcy or the Bennets.

Darcy breathed a sigh of relief as he heard some of the Bennet ladies enter the church. Mrs. Bennet winked at Darcy as she took her seat, and Mary, Kitty, and Lydia giggled as they waved to him and sat down. Mary and Kitty had become closer as they bloomed into womanhood. Mary looked fetching in her pale blue dress and Kitty was not as silly, as she attempted to emulate Mary's quiet strength. Lydia had the most significant change, as she was dressed more befitting a fifteen-year-old in comparison to the assembly when her chest might have fallen out of her dress, and she had become more demure as Jane had taken her under her wing. She was still lively but completely age-appropriate in public now.

Finally, the doors opened and he saw his Elizabeth: The most beautiful woman he had ever seen and her smile was for him. He did not notice what she wore; he only saw her eyes that were trained on his face and nothing else. He knew that she loved him with her whole heart and there was not a single person in the room who would have doubted it. Mr. Darcy smiled with his full dimples showing and the ceremony began as the couple held each other's hands.

~*~

After the registry was signed and witnessed, they were loaded onto the open carriage for the short ride to Longbourn. Darcy had kissed Elizabeth after the pronouncement of 'man and wife' was made in front of God and witnesses but he wanted a private moment to kiss her again.

"May I kiss you again, Mrs. Darcy? I believe you are still in debt for two more." Darcy teased.

"Oh, Mr. Darcy, you plan on kissing me only twice more today?" Elizabeth teased back.

Immediately, his lip was on her. He knew he should not get too excited but he reverently kissed her lips and licked them gently, wanting to taste her and inhale her scent. "Please promise me we will not have to stay long after breakfast. I plan on kissing you in private and not stop." Darcy begged.

Elizabeth beamed. "That is a deal. Since we are now married, we will kiss and not stop; only break for three meals." Her melodic laughter tinkled in the air. Darcy grinned broadly and kissed her once more, this time delving his tongue inside her as he held her cheek.

"Impertinent minx! I cannot wait for tonight." Darcy whispered in her ear.

"Fitzwilliam, it will take us about four hours to Darcy House, will it not?" He nodded. "By my calculation, we should arrive in London about four in the afternoon. I certainly hope you will not make me wait until *dark* to truly become your wife." Her eyes twinkled as she whispered in return, just as they arrived at Longbourn.

Darcy gulped. *She wishes me to take her to bed as soon as we arrive home? Good God. I am so hard right now. I need a moment. Think of something else, you fool.*

Elizabeth sat patiently knowing Darcy needed a moment. It was cruel of her but she loved seeing this passionate side of him. She turned her face away from him to give him time to settle but not before seeing his huge protrusion on his trousers. *What wonder lies there? I cannot wait to see it. Mama told me to trust him and I know he will be gentle with me.* She continued to pretend that she was fixing her hat and her cape.

"Ahem. I am ready, Elizabeth. Thank you for giving me a minute. Shall we enter?" Darcy handed her down and they greeted their friends and family and began the celebration.

~*~

The wedding breakfast in its simplicity was exactly what Elizabeth had hoped for. There was not enough time to prepare the number of dishes that Mrs. Bennet had originally intended but with Mrs. Hurst and Lady Lucas' help, it was still considered a great success.

Mrs. Bennet hugged her daughter proudly. "Congratulations, Lizzy, you caught yourself a wonderful husband. I should say, rather, he caught you!"

Mr. Bennet hugged her next, "I could not have given you away to a man less worthy. See you in two weeks, daughter. I love you. Take care of her, son." He shook Darcy's hand.

Elizabeth bid farewell to her sisters and Charlotte and other dear friends. She hugged Georgiana and kissed her cheek. "See you in a week. In her express letter this morning, Aunt Susan insisted on a wedding ball so we will attend and your brother will allow you to dance two sets."

She winked and Georgiana giggled in glee and answered, "Have a safe travel home, sister."

Elizabeth turned to Richard and smiled. She leaned forward to kiss his cheek, "Thank you for your support, dear Richard. I am glad you were able to attend on behalf of your parents. I know they are disappointed, knowing that it was such a rushed business, but their displeasure is all for Lady Catherine." She laughed. She felt Darcy's hand on her back and turned around with a bright smile, "Husband, shall we depart now?"

Darcy returned her smile and replied, "Yes, dear wife. It is time." He shook hands with Richard and gave him a look and they departed, eventually making it to the carriage amongst the many well-wishers.

Richard stood behind. He could not move after Elizabeth had kissed his cheek and where her lips had been burned. He had inhaled her scent and he flushed with desire but there was nothing to be done. *How is it possible to be so in love with a woman after a month? All I wanted to do was to grab her and make love to her just now. I vowed him my trust and I will not fail. Damn lucky Darcy.*

After calming himself, he escorted Georgiana to Netherfield after they said their goodbyes. They would leave for London in an hour and his baby cousin would stay at Matlock House with Anne.

Chapter 15

Lady Catherine rushed Mr. Collins, "Hurry, hurry, good god, man!"

Mr. Collins panted behind her, trying to keep up. *How is such an old lady so fast?!* He thought to himself.

As they climbed up the stairs to Darcy House, Mr. Collins was immediately impressed at the façade of the large home. It was the largest house on the street and it was obvious that Mr. Darcy must have a large fortune and from the sound of things yesterday, Lady Catherine had a massive debt owed to him.

He was beginning to rethink the wisdom of doing what Lady Catherine was telling him. She had dragged him out of bed early in the morning when he just wanted to sleep in the most comfortable bed he had slept on, and instead of heading back to Rosings, she took off a couple of blocks to Mr. Darcy's enormous home. She ran up the stairs and made him rush up and he was already sweating.

Lady Catherine impatiently knocked on the door with her cane. The door-knocker was down to indicate that no one was home but she knocked loudly several more times and eventually the butler answered.

"Lady Catherine," the butler answered sluggishly, as he had been expecting her. "The master is not at home, madam."

"Come, come. Where is he? Is he hiding in his study, AFRAID to show his face?" She screeched.

The butler slowly answered, "He is not at home, madam."

"Well, where IS he, damn it!" She cared not that she was making a scene and cursing. Several passers-by stopped to watch the scene. "I DEMAND to know where he is! Do you not know who I AM?!"

Mr. Mason coughed to cover his laugh. She was even more ridiculous today than ever. "I know who you are, madam. He is not here. Good day, madam." And he promptly shut the door on her face before she could get her foot in the door.

Flabbergasted, Lady Catherine turned around to see that there were half-dozen spectators and was mortified at being caught. "Come, Mr. Collins. We must go to Hertfordshire. We will visit your relatives and see your birth right and find your precious future wife. If Darcy is not here, he must be there."

~*~

They travelled the next four hours and knocked at the front door of Longbourn. Mrs. Hill opened the door.

Lady Catherine demanded, "I must see to the owner of this cottage immediately!"

Mrs. Hill had been expecting someone to arrive and was unsurprised by the offensive lady. They had just finished cleaning up after the wedding breakfast and Mr. and Mrs. Bennet placed themselves in the drawing room when they heard the grand carriage in the driveway. "And who may you be?" She asked.

"I am Lady Catherine de Bourgh and this is Mr. Collins, your future master! I demand to be taken to Mr. Bennet. If you cannot follow such simple orders, I am certain Mr. Collins will immediately dismiss you when he is master!" She belched.

Smirking slightly, "Follow me, if you please." And she announced the visitors to Mr. and Mrs. Bennet.

All the girls had gone to Netherfield after the wedding breakfast, as they expected an intrusion in Longbourn and Mr. and Mrs. Bennet had wished to avoid their daughters' presence when Lady Catherine arrived. Now that Bingley was officially courting Jane, Mary had volunteered to chaperon them while Mrs. Hurst continued her lessons with Kitty and Lydia. Mrs. Hurst had been meeting with the girls for a week to teach them about society manners and what to expect during their season.

The grand lady entered the room with her nose up in the air. "I am Lady Catherine de Bourgh, daughter of the former Earl of Matlock and wife of the late Baronet Lewis de Bourgh. This is Mr. William Collins, your heir. You shall introduce yourselves." She spat.

Suppressing the urge to laugh at her face, Mr. Bennet stood and answered, "I am Thomas Bennet and this is Francis Bennet. What brings you to our humble abode, milady?" Mrs. Bennet could not hold in a snort but quickly covered it with a cough.

Lady Catherine was actually surprised that Mr. Bennet was still young and appeared to be very healthy. The way Mr. Collins had spoken, she had expected an old, frail man close to his deathbed. "Mr. Collins, speak words." She wanted Mr. Collins to start the conversation with these peasants while she assessed the estate. It was much smaller than Rosings but the home seemed comfortable and colourful; the furnishings were outdated but functional, and it was above what she had expected Mr. Collins' inheritance to be.

Mr. Collins began, "My dear cousin Mr. Bennet, I am so pleased to meet you at last. I know that my father's wishes were for me to never contact you whilst you live but I am here with my grand patroness, Lady Catherine, to offer you an olive branch so that our houses will be once again reunited and reconciled from the silly feud that had taken place over twenty years ago.

"As your heir, I know how afraid you must be that once you leave this world that your wife and your dear daughters will be left destitute, and as your nearest relative, I will make my offer to marry your second daughter Elizabeth. I see that Mrs. Bennet is still quite beautiful and would assume that Miss Elizabeth should be tolerable enough to tempt me. I understand you have five daughters and my dear cousin Elizabeth, I am certain, will be most honoured to accept my offer, as her lot must be so small that she would have no other choices before her, and she would never receive such an offer from another.

"I understand you are under the delusion that my grand patroness Lady Catherine's nephew, a Mr. Darcy, had engaged himself to Miss Elizabeth but I assure you that it has been a great error that will be resolved as soon as possible. Once Miss Elizabeth is wedded to me, I assure you that I would be quite up to the challenge to retire from the rectory and reside at Longbourn so that I will learn to be a great master of this estate.

"Of course, I will be residing in the master's bedroom and my dearest wife should take the mistress' bedroom, and I am certain the dower house can be set up to house the both of you until the end of your days here in this world. I am also assured that my dear wife would be pleased with my attentions and we shall have many children fill the house, as I plan on ensuring that my wife will provide several healthy male children, even if her mother was unsuccessful at each attempt. I will make sure that I fill my wife's belly with my seed frequently to ensure that her duty is done..."

Mr. Bennet was initially entertained but as the ridiculous man went on and began to talk of marital relations with his favourite daughter, he stood and boomed, "MR. COLLINS!" His talks were unfit for public ears, least of all the parents of the woman that he wanted to take, whom he had never met in his life. He was rude and uncouth and completely idiotic.

Mr. Bennet had never been a physical man in his life but the insults of his home, himself, his dearest wife, and then his daughter had reached the point of no return and he punched Mr. Collins squarely on the jaw. He might have been almost fifty but he was certainly not weak.

Mr. Collins was completely knocked out, sprawled on the floor of the drawing room. When Mr. Hill entered, hearing his master's yell, and Mr. Bennet quickly ordered him, "Remove that garbage out of this house and never let him enter again. It will be over my dead body!" He turned to the lady standing stationary, "Now, Lady Catherine, I demand that you leave as well. If you do not wish to walk out of here, I will have you carried out, as deserving as it is for one of your rank. My daughter, Mrs. Darcy, is where she belongs – with her husband. Now, please leave!" Mr. Bennet calmly addressed her ladyship.

Lady was once again flummoxed. Not only did Mr. Bennet strike Mr. Collins onto his back, knocking him unconscious, but he had told her that Darcy was already married and demanded her to be quickly removed.

She grabbed her cane and stomped out of Longbourn, kicking Mr. Collins, who was waking up next to her carriage to hurry and get into the vehicle. She left most displeased and refused to acknowledge such savages.

Lady Catherine commanded her driver to return to Rosings but he subserviently told her that the horses were exhausted from the travel already and they would not make it back to Rosings immediately. They left Longbourn property quickly but slowed down when they reached Meryton for the horses to be refreshed before heading further.

~*~

It was another two hours before the horses were ready. Lady Catherine and Mr. Collins took a room at the Inn to rest first but they continuously received looks of displeasure from the inhabitants as they ordered luncheon.

Lady Catherine complained loudly that the meal was unfit for human consumption and roared loudly, "Do you not know who I am? I am Lady Catherine de Bourgh and you shall treat me with the respect owed to my rank. I demand better food to be brought out!"

The owner of the inn, hearing the commotion neared the table. "Milady, is this Mr. Collins, the future heir of Longbourn?" He asked quietly.

"Ah, finally someone who understands the distinction of rank. Yes, I am the daughter of an earl and he is Mr. Collins." She answered proudly.

The innkeeper stood taller and replied, "Madam, I am sorry to tell you that we are out of food. I insist that you pay for your room and the food *Mr. Collins* is eating and leave my establishment immediately."

The whisperings grew louder and the two travellers were receiving dirty looks from every corner of the room.

Not understanding what was happening but to avoid further disputes, she quickly placed several coins and stood. As they were exiting, she could hear the whispers of:

"Shrew!"

"The nerve of that woman. Mr. Darcy was correct."

"That odious Mr. Collins!"

"She has her nose stuck on the ceiling. What a horrid harridan!"

The insults kept coming and they hurried to the carriage and left the small village swiftly. It appeared that their reputation was already well-known, although Lady Catherine could not imagine Darcy speaking of any private matters to these commoners.

Lady Catherine continued to belittle Mr. Collins after she commanded her driver to travel to Rosings at a rapid pace.

~*~

Misfortune was their lot, as the carriage was pushed too hard for two days in a row and the wheel broke. They had nearly overturned but the driver was competent and was able to stop the vehicle from crashing. There was an inn near the accident, fortuitously, and Lady Catherine and Mr. Collins were forced to take up lodgings for two days, delaying their return to Kent.

Chapter 16

The Darcys arrived at Darcy House a little before four o'clock. Their carriage was well-sprung and the roads were fine on this beautiful November day.

Although attempting to restrain themselves, Darcy and Elizabeth had kissed several times which escalated to the point of Elizabeth's skirt being raised to her thighs and Darcy's linen-shirt pulled out from his breeches. They had touched each other over their clothing and Darcy had to literally jump off from his wife and press down his manhood to prevent it from exploding in his pants. He had kissed Elizabeth deeper than he had ever before and he had grazed her breasts. But when his hands drifted under her skirt and he touched the skin on her thigh above her stockings, he had almost exploded.

Elizabeth was equally affected. She had felt such heat between her legs when he caressed her breasts over her dress, she moaned and pulled out her husband's shirt to feel his muscular chest. When he touched her thigh and jumped off to take a seat on the other side of the carriage, she knew he must have been close to losing control. She watched him while he stared out the window and fixed her appearances, as her hairpin was loose in several places and her dress was tangled and wrinkled. She smiled as she saw her handsome husband struggle to calm his arousal. His hand was literally covering and pressing down the protrusion between his legs. *I feel sorry for men who have such a pronounced effect when they are aroused. At least women are all covered up and nothing really sticks out.* She laughed and saw Darcy's eyes meet hers, then he smiled and returned to his seat next to her.

"And what is so funny, Mrs. Darcy? Seeing your husband struggle so is amusing to you?" Darcy quipped. He loved her joie de vivre and her talent for finding humour in ridiculous situations. Here he was, trying to push down his arousal while she was glowing and more beautiful than ever.

"I find my husband to be very handsome and so tempting. I was just thinking that I feel sorry for the male symptom of arousal when women do not have the same problem. Shall we talk about the weather or politics or philosophy to distract ourselves?" She grinned.

Darcy laughed. "I think perhaps we should have stayed closer to Longbourn. We still have another three hours to go!"

"Well, let us converse. What did you think of the breakfast? You were genial to my neighbours and I do not think I have seen you smile so much in a large group." Elizabeth kissed his cheek.

Darcy held her close. "It has been the best day of my life so far. And, ahem, we have much more to experience."

"Fitzwilliam! You must take your mind off that. Three hours to go!" Elizabeth whined.

Darcy laughed loudly. "Yes, my love." He kissed her temple. "Bingley was certainly happy to see Jane. I thought he would drop to his knees and propose as soon as he saw her at church."

"Oh, yes; Jane is so happy. Mr. Bingley is making his intentions more obvious and Jane has been in love with him for a while already. I hope they marry. They are perfect for each other."

"Like we are perfect together." Darcy kissed her hand.

"Georgiana and Richard seemed to be very happy for us as well. But, my love, you gave Richard a look when we were leaving, I just remembered. What was that about? I was going to ask you but I had forgotten." Elizabeth innocently asked.

She has no idea. Good lord, what do I tell her? Darcy thought. *I cannot lie to her!*

Darcy gently rubbed her hand. "I was giving him a silent warning, Elizabeth. You kissed his cheek and he was not taking it well." *He would have carried you off to Scotland if you kissed him on the lips!*

"Oh, no! Did I offend him? Was he angry with me? Does he have a lady friend that I will make jealous? He has been a true friend to us both and I am sorry to put him in such an awkward place." Elizabeth was worried that she could distress a good man who had always been generous.

Darcy sighed. "No, my love. He does not have a lady friend. He stopped seeing *all* of his 'lady friends' a month ago." *How do I say it?*

"Oh? Why did he do that? I thought him quite dashing in his uniform and figured he would have numerous lady friends to entertain him. He is quite handsome and a flirt, you know." Elizabeth teased.

Good lord, she truly has no idea. Darcy replied, "He stopped visiting all of his friends after he met you. He is in love with you."

Elizabeth sat silent. It took a moment but she retorted, "You are jesting with me, Fitzwilliam. Be kind to your cousin! Be kind to your new wife, husband!" She smiled but seeing him still grim, she added, "You are in earnest?" He nodded.

She was silent for a full five minutes before she continued. Darcy did not know what she was thinking. *I know she loves me; there is nothing to be afraid of. But is she thinking of her life with Richard? Would he have made her a better husband? I will show her how much I love her. I will never stop courting her and I hope she will never regret me. It is no wonder she had a slew of suitors. How arrogant I was, believing that women would flock to me should I just show one just a little attention, and Elizabeth would have kicked my shin for being an arse. She is truly special and I love her so much.*

Finally, Elizabeth spoke. "Fitzwilliam, I have been cataloguing every conversation I had with Richard and I would have never guessed that he could be in love with me. He had never shown me any specific attention nor have I ever encouraged him. We attended numerous functions with him and he joined us in our outings, I know, and I danced a few times with him at the balls in London, but I cannot recall if I said anything or did anything improper. He talked to Jane more than myself and even though we got along so well and I enjoyed his company, I cannot recall if I gave him any idea of welcoming his attentions. Please believe me that I did not mean to ask for his notice. I... I hope I did not... I feel awful if he is suffering but I could never feel even a fraction for him what I feel for you. I think of him only as a good friend, like a brother..." She began to cry.

"My love, you are the most wonderful woman I have ever met and we are perfect for each other, do you not agree? Men are bound to love you because of your beauty and spirit and kind heart. Richard and I have spoken and he will love you but from afar. I trust him as I trust you and I hope you will continue to be his friend. He is lonely, as much as he flirts, and I knew he had given up visiting women a month ago but I did not know until last night why." He kissed her temple. "He was quite drunk and he slipped but I had figured out what he was about and he confessed it to me. He and I always had similar tastes in women; although I was typically turned by blondes and he, always brunettes. I should have realised that he would find you most attractive but I was quite distracted by a certain siren and did not ponder on it." He laughed.

"So perhaps there was some truth when you had first found me 'barely tolerable' when we first met?" Her eyes twinkled. "I believe Jane to be the most beautiful blonde in all of England and I know you thought her handsome. Were you jealous of Mr. Bingley?"

"You minx!" He laughed. He loved how she was able to rebound so quickly with her teasing manners. He kissed her lips tenderly. "I was lost the moment our eyes met. I have never looked at a woman twice before meeting you and will never look at another for as long as I live. You are my soulmate, Elizabeth. I am yours and yours alone."

"And I, you, my love." She returned his kiss. Several moments later she asked, "Will Richard be well?"

Darcy sighed. "Yes, he will be. I thought about myself in his shoes. If Richard had found you first and I should have met you after you were engaged to him, I would not be able to stop loving you even if it broke my heart. If you had truly loved him, you would not be turned by my wealth or status or however many carriages or jewels I could promise you, but you would be steadfast to your husband and I would have had to love you from afar. I have told him as well; I could no better stop breathing than to stop loving you. I feel his pain but I know he would act as I would. He will respect our vows and care for us and he will never betray us. He is a good man but he is still a man, Elizabeth. He will not impose himself on you and will be a gentleman, my love, but he will desire you still. I wanted to share this with you because you have a way of disconcerting me so easily and I know you have no idea what effect you have on men. You are so beautiful and charming and I know you will continue to break hearts but you are mine!" He kissed her lips. "My wife!" He pressed her lips harder, diving his tongue inside her mouth and kissing her passionately as if to claim her. He released her soon and said, "All mine." And he held her tightly on his chest.

Elizabeth giggled at his possessiveness. She was distraught that her actions may have been seen as encouragement to Richard but her husband assured her that it was her natural way. *I will have to restrain myself. Oh, Lizzy! Do not disrespect your husband or bring shame to your family by being a hoyden!* She still did enjoy having her husband hold her and teased, "So, Fitzwilliam... Tell me about these blonde goddesses that turned your head. I have not forgotten that minor detail that you grazed over so quickly."

"Minx!" He laughed heartily. He told her about the Grecian Venus that was a Miss Jasmine when he was all of seven years old, as well as another young beauty that he could not recall the name of when he was ten, and of course her own aunt Gardiner, the former Miss Weston, whom he had been infatuated with at the age of twelve. Elizabeth giggled at Darcy's description of some of the girls wanting to kiss him and his running away to hide behind his mother's skirts. He had always been shy and even if he had an eye for beautiful women, he had never acted on it and always hid in the corner of the room or stared out the window.

Elizabeth confessed to a spectacular crush she had when she was eleven to a Mr. Ramsbottom who was three and twenty who ended up marrying the blacksmith's daughter when they were found in a scandalous position and her relief at seeing him balding and quite round a few years later, which had displaced all of the fondness she ever felt. "I guess I always had a thing for older men, husband." She laughed.

They continued to speak of their memories and what they wanted to do while in town. Darcy had originally planned to take her to Ramsgate but the house was being leased and would not be available for another month yet. They would spend the fortnight in London to stay a considerable time alone in their bed, then attend the Matlock Ball next week. He planned to treat her to a few outings and show her off as well.

As the hours passed, they slept in each other's arms, as neither had slept much the night before, and soon, they arrived at Darcy House.

~*~

"Welcome to Darcy House, Mrs. Darcy!" Her husband gleamed. Elizabeth was handed down the carriage and smiled as she saw her permanent home. It was the largest on the block with the exterior façade that could match the King's palace. It was opulent but not overly extravagant. It was comfortable and she saw her husband's taste expressed outside and inside.

All twenty servants were lined up to greet the new mistress and she smiled at each of them. Several, but not all of them, had met Mrs. Darcy on her previous visits and word had spread quickly that the Master married Miss Bennet earlier than expected due to Lady Catherine's interferences. Mr. Mason quietly informed Mr. Darcy that Lady Catherine had condescended to call this morning but was quickly refused. Darcy thanked him for barring her from the home as planned and turned to Elizabeth in a broad smile. He would focus on his wife now and punish Lady Catherine later.

Darcy led Elizabeth through the foyer and held her hand. "Dearest, please tell me what you would like to do. I do not wish to rush you and if you would like to rest before a light repast or relax in the library, I will do whatever you like. But if amenable, I wish to take you to your rooms and resume our previous activity."

"I would like nothing more, Mr. Darcy." She returned the smile.

As soon as the door was closed, Darcy wrapped his arms around his wife. "Mrs. Darcy, is your room to your satisfaction?"

"Why, yes, Mr. Darcy. It is exactly as I remember when I was here two days ago, sir." She quipped. "If I may ask though, Fitzwilliam, I would like to bathe and have Hannah unpack. I wish to put on something more comfortable and will meet you in your rooms in an hour?" She raised her brow. Her mother and Aunt Gardiner had chosen some scandalous nightgowns for her to wear and she wanted to show it off to her dear husband.

Darcy gulped and nodded. "Yes, my love. Baths have already been ordered. I am glad you wish to be in my rooms. Shall I ask dinner to be sent up later?" She nodded. "I love you, Mrs. Darcy." He kissed her gently but deeply.

She melted in his arms again. Now being alone in her bedroom, she wanted nothing but to rip off their clothes and experience the marriage bed, but she wanted to wash and truly enjoy the consummation without rushing. She could feel his protrusion again and was excited to finally see what lay under.

"I love you, husband. Now off with you." She laughed.

Chapter 17

Darcy entered his bedroom through the adjoining door and took several breaths. He could hear his valet in the dressing room and the servants filling up the bathtub. He quickly undressed completely and looked down at his massive erection. He had been masturbating often and was embarrassed that he could not contain his excitement better ever since meeting Elizabeth, and it had been a daily ritual to relieve his morning arousal and then to finish the day with another tug. He had not relieved himself this morning due to his anxiety over the ceremony and preparing for the day, and he was dearly paying the price now, as his penis was constantly hard.

As he slipped into his bath and washed, he determined that he would most likely explode on sight when Elizabeth entered his room so he decided to take his release now. If he should not be able to get it up for a while, he would pleasure her first as he always intended. He had read and been taught about how a woman could achieve her release by using his tongue and fingers and wanted to make sure his wife would experience bliss as he would.

He took his long cock into his hand and rubbed it in the warm water. He stroked himself several times and thought of their kisses. He recalled the feel of her bosom in his hand and how soft her thighs were and immediately released. It was such a strong feeling that he had to roll his eyes around several times to be able to see straight.

He dried himself and dressed in a simple nightshirt and breeches after contemplating waiting for her naked in his bed, but laughed at himself for his thoughts. He would certainly scare her away, especially if there was a large tent around his groin when she lifted up the sheets.

~*~

Elizabeth bathed and cleaned herself. Her mother and Aunt Gardiner had told her some of what to expect and had advised her to clean herself well, especially her womanhood, and to wear one of the nightgowns that they had chosen together. They took turns telling her that his phallus would enter her womanhood and as Mr. Darcy loved her very much, she should relax and enjoy his attentions. There was concern that the first time would bring some discomfort but it would improve afterwards. She did not understand the looks that they were giving each other, but her mother and aunt told her that whatever happened in the marriage bed was private and that there was nothing shameful about the way a husband loved his wife. Elizabeth trusted Fitzwilliam and knew her husband would care for her.

She chose the sheer dark green nightgown and robe, leaving her hair down. Fitzwilliam had never seen her with her hair fully down so she wondered if he would be pleased by it. She remembered his kisses in the carriage and smiled as she anticipated many more kisses.

~*~

Darcy heard a knock on his door from their shared sitting room. He quickly hopped and opened the door to find Elizabeth standing in her green robe. Her hair was long and silky and it was the most beautiful sight he had ever seen. Her eyes were sparkling, matching her dress and he could not help himself as he grabbed her waist and leaned to kiss her. He gently licked her lips and breathed in her lavender bathwater scent. He could immediately feel his arousal return and was glad he had released just now or else he would have exploded by now.

"Will you not let me enter your room, husband?" She teased. They were still standing at the door-frame.

"But of course, my love." Darcy grinned. "I was too excited to see you. You are beautiful, Elizabeth." He led her toward the bed, "I am not going to mince words or be shy to drag it out, Elizabeth. I want you in my bed and I wish to make you my wife now. I do not wish to sit and partake in food and make conversation. I want to kiss you and make love to you." He kissed her deeply. His hands rubbed her back and descended toward her buttocks. "May I make you mine?" He asked after they broke for air.

Elizabeth stepped back a little and unwrapped her robe, exposing her sheer nightgown. "Take me to your bed, Fitzwilliam. Make me your wife."

He took her hand and kissed it and helped her climb onto the bed. She lay in the middle and watched her husband take his breeches off first. The protrusion of his manhood tented his shirt forward and she waited with bated breath to see what lay beneath. She had seen paintings and statues and had changed nappies on her baby cousins but had never seen a grown man's parts. Her eyes widened as he pulled his shirt over his head and she could see a long limb that looked like a very thick twig. It was reddish with a mushroom-like bulb at the tip and she had been told it would go between her legs but could not understand how it would fit.

Darcy saw Elizabeth eyeing his arousal cautiously. He had been surprised that he achieved another erection only minutes after his last release but Elizabeth was beautiful and he was eager to join with her. He saw that she was contemplating his manhood and he had never been so bared before another human being before but he did not want to withhold anything from her. He climbed into bed with her and lay next to her, covering himself up to his waist.

"Have I frightened you, my dear? Am I such a ghastly sight to behold?" He teased.

Elizabeth smiled shyly, "You are definitely a sight to behold but you are magnificent. Your chest and arms are very muscular and you are indeed very handsome, dear husband." Her eyes drew lower below the counterpane, "I have been wondering how you will fit inside me. Your... equipment... is as long as my forearm..."

Darcy laughed heartily. "My love, I am certain my 'equipment' will fit well inside you. We will keep practicing until we get it right."

He kissed her as his hands slid down to her breast. The sheer fabric was not hiding anything and he could see her dark nipples under the silky cloth and as he caressed her breast, her nipple hardened. He placed his body over hers, resting his weight on his knees as he straddled her legs. He kissed her deeply, their tongues once again dancing together, and he trailed his kisses down her neck and the swell of her bosoms. He slowly slid her gown down to expose her breasts and he kissed them and a loud moan escaped her throat as his tongue flickered on her hard nipple and he turned to the other breast and did the same.

He continued lower as his tongue trailed down to her navel. He slid her dress completely off of her, pulling it down and coaxing her legs to open. He repositioned

73

himself between her legs and breathed in her womanly scent. He looked up for approval and with her smile, he touched her legs and opened them wider. His hand gently swept over her dark curls and he touched her womanhood. She was wet with desire and as he parted her folds with his fingers, he rubbed her small protrusion with his thumb. He had read that women found pleasure in gently being touched there but he wanted to do more. As he inserted his finger inside her cave, he bent down and kissed her clitoris. A loud moan escaped from her again and he began to lick and flicker his tongue like he had done with her nipples. He continued to slide his finger in and out of her womanhood and he could feel the tight space dripping with her juices as she began to move her hips. He continued to finger her and tongue her and heard her yelp her ecstasy as her core tightened.

Darcy felt her relax around his finger and lifted up his body. After wiping his face with the sheet, he continued to caress her perfect round breasts as he rubbed his erection against her wet folds.

"Are you well, my love? Was that pleasurable?" He asked tentatively. He wanted to make sure she was not uncomfortable.

"Oh, Fitzwilliam! I have never felt such a thing before. What have you done to me, sir?" She was attempting to focus her eyes onto his face.

"I believe you have experienced your first climax." He grinned. "I had wanted to do that for you and it appears I was successful. I have heard that not all women enjoy the marriage bed but there are some things that the man could do to improve the experience."

"Oh, my love. That was an amazing feeling. I cannot wait to experience it again." Elizabeth flushed. She was embarrassed to be laying completely naked in daylight but she wanted to give everything to her husband.

"My love, I would like to enter you now. It may be uncomfortable but I am having difficulty restraining myself." Darcy confessed.

"Please, Fitzwilliam, make me your wife." Elizabeth begged.

He kissed her on the mouth while positioning his erection at the entrance of her vagina. Slowly and carefully, he pushed in the tip. She was very tight but quite slippery from her earlier orgasm and he slid in a little further and heard her gasp. He stopped himself where he was. "Are you well?" He asked.

"Yes, it feels very full but not painful. Like stretching but it does not hurt. I believe you are indeed quite large, my love."

"I am sorry, my love. Please relax if you can and I will continue. Oh, Elizabeth, this is the most exquisite feeling of my life!" Darcy thought he was going to explode but he would endure it to slowly enter her completely. He wanted to just pound into her hard but she needed to adjust to accommodate to his size. He knew he was a large man – everything was big on his overgrown body – but the last thing he wanted was to cause pain to his wife.

He felt her muscles relax a bit and he continued to inch himself forward and soon, he was in as far as he could go and sighed deeply. He held her tightly as he took a moment to be wrapped inside her, as it was the most wonderful feeling he had ever felt. He began to gently rock back and forth, sliding out a little to push himself back inside her. He kissed her throat and sucked on her tongue, returning his attentions to her breasts again as well. Her moans returned soon and grew louder as he began to thrust a bit harder.

He was once again glad that he had masturbated in the bathtub, as he would not have made it that far without it. He pumped another dozen times and groaned loudly as he released his seed deep inside her. He continued to lay over her as he shifted his weight to his arms and knees as his cock continued to throb inside her. They were panting for air and revelling in ecstasy as they continued to kiss and touch each other.

Elizabeth was pleased with her husband's lovemaking. There was truly no pain, just immense pleasure, and he had taken such care to make her his wife. She whispered, "I love you," and kissed his lips gently.

Darcy had never imagined that having sexual relations would feel so good; but he knew that it had been truly special because they loved each other and had waited for this day together. He returned the kiss and soon the kisses became heated again.

His penis had been inside her all along after his climax and he was surprised that as their kisses became more fervent, his erection was immediately returning. *How is this possible? I already came twice in the last half hour and I am getting hard again?* He had never seen his body react so, but then again, he had never made love to Elizabeth before.

Darcy slowly rocked his hips and soon, he was pumping his hard cock into his wife, this time harder and faster. Elizabeth had opened her legs fully now and he found it easier to fill her up to the hilt. As he rocked her body, she began to lift up her hips to meet his thrust and he heard her whisper, 'more'. He knew she was able to take his body now and began to plunge hard, as he had initially wanted to do. He bounced on her body and rammed his erection into her furiously and he heard her scream out her pleasures again and released his seeds deep inside her once more.

"Oh, my love, I am sorry for being a brute." Darcy apologised after they caught their breath and he rolled off of her to hold her tightly against his chest. He could not believe he had taken her twice in a row. He had meant to love her gently and perhaps once more later tonight but he had been overcome by desire and had imposed himself on her a second time. He was afraid that she would promptly kick him out of her bed and desperately wished for her to stay with him all night, every night, even if only for sleeping.

Elizabeth reached for his face and touched his cheek. "I love you. I loved being pleasured by you and our uniting was so powerful and passionate, I was able to reach another climax. I would not have you apologise for what I thoroughly enjoyed, Fitzwilliam." She raised her flirtatious eyebrow. "I hope we will repeat the exercise again, my love."

Darcy chuckled. "I love you, too. I never thought it would be so enjoyable." He kissed her temple. "Wait here; I will return." And he got up and walked into his dressing room.

He returned with a warm damp cloth and carefully wiped her nether regions.

"Fitzwilliam, you do not need to do that. I will take the cloth." Elizabeth argued.

Darcy continued to wipe her womanhood and down her legs. "I am happy to be at your service, my dear wife. I have made you bleed a little. I am so sorry. You are not in pain?" He was concerned. He had not realised that she had bled. He had wiped himself very quickly before returning to minister to his wife and felt like a cad for hurting her so. He was frustrated that he had enjoyed consummation so much to the point that he was getting aroused again while he wiped and caressed her.

Elizabeth, who, by now could quickly discern her husband's emotions on his face, sat up and kissed his face tenderly several times. "My dear husband, there was no pain, not even discomfort. Just a fullness and contentment and delight in joining with you. Perhaps we could partake our meal and talk? I wish to stay with you."

It was exactly what Darcy wished to hear. "Yes, let us eat! I cannot starve my wife on our wedding day!" He laughed as he stood to search for her nightgown and picked up her robe for her. He put his nightshirt on as well as his breeches. "I wish to stay with you all day and all night. Will you stay the night with me? Will you stay every night with me?"

"Yes, my love. I wish to never be parted from you from this day forward. Should you like to continue in your bed or my bed? As we started our married life in yours, I have no preference." Elizabeth teased.

"Well, perhaps we shall take turns. Your mattress is new and unused. We could test it out together." Darcy smirked, as he fixed a plate of food for his wife.

"I do not understand society's expectation of maintaining separate bedrooms all the time for married couples. So many spend their day apart from each other and they do not even spend the night together. I suspect some couples could go for days without seeing each other at all!" Elizabeth exclaimed.

Darcy replied, "I am certain those couples do not wish to see each other, perhaps only congregate to beget an heir or two. But we shall never be apart whenever possible. I wish to sleep with you every night."

Elizabeth blushed, "But what of my courses, Fitzwilliam? I cannot imagine you would want me during my monthlies." She was mortified to talk of this but after what they had experienced together, she wanted to share all of her concerns. "I saw your reaction to a little blood just now and my courses are more severe and I would not be available to you."

"My love, I panicked because I thought I had injured you. The sight of blood does not bother me. I just want to hold you and keep you close, Elizabeth. I will not impose on you for my needs but I still feel awful that I took you twice. I did not think it possible." Darcy blushed as well. *Thank god she is so understanding. It is so strange to talk to a woman about this.*

As Elizabeth finished chewing her food, she contemplated his statement. *What does he mean not possible? I was warned that my husband would want me a second time but is it not common?*

"Fitzwilliam, I do not understand what is not possible? I am so uneducated in this topic but would like to understand. My mother and aunt told me that you may want me a second time and is that not what happened?" Elizabeth asked.

Damn! She is so innocent and honest. She is artless and beautiful and charming and so delicious. And her bosoms are so luscious. I can see her pointy nipple through her robe. Good god, I am hard again.

Darcy arose to his feet, seeing that she was done with her meal. He took her hand as she stood up and he walked her over to the settee by the fireplace. He sat next to her and held her closely. He considered how he would explain his body and decided to be straightforward and honest.

"Elizabeth, you know that I had no experience before I met you." She nodded. "Since I was a teen, my body did react to a pretty face or the sight of bosoms and I had often had to use my hand to relieve my erections. Do you know what that means?" She shook her head. *Dear god, she is so innocent. I love her.*

Clearing his throat, "Um, it means that when I am aroused so much, either I need to wait a while for it to dissipate by focusing on something else or if am at a point where I need to release my seed, like I did when I released inside you twice, I would use my hand to rub my manhood until the semen comes out. That helps me not be so aroused." *This is mortifying.* "I used my hand to masturbate, only a few times a month to keep myself in check, but after I met you, I found myself masturbating twice daily; once in the morning and another at bedtime. It would be hours apart and I was under control most of the time. I did not masturbate this morning because I was frantically trying to get to the church on time and you saw my reaction in the carriage," they laughed together.

"My love, when we arrived, I was about to lose control and I masturbated in my bath shortly before you arrived at my door. I was surprised that I was so aroused and when we joined for the first time; that was the first time that I had experienced an arousal so soon after already releasing. Usually it is hours before it happens again. My reaction to joining you was so pleasurable that the unthinkable happened and my arousal did not deflate after spending and we consummated again. That I had released three times in half an hour is what is impossible but it did happen." He coloured in embarrassment. It was mortifying but he had been truthful.

Elizabeth grinned as she understood the effect that she had on her husband's body. He had pleasured her so well and that she should bring him such pleasures, and so often, made her incandescently happy. She wanted to see if she could arouse him again.

"Fitzwilliam, will you be earnest with me?" She asked seductively. She rose slowly to stand in front of him. "Do you find me attractive?" She asked as she pulled down her robe off one shoulder.

He gulped, "Yes." *She is a seductress! So beautiful!* He could not keep his eyes off of her.

"And are you enjoying being married to me, husband?" She pulled down the robe off the other shoulder, and it slid off, as she stood completely naked in front of him.

His hands were immediately on her waist as he drew her closer. His mouth was on her breast and he desperately rubbed his hands on her back and her buttocks. He choked out a "yes" before returning his mouth to her nipple.

She leaned closer and straddled him, placing her legs on either side of him. She could feel his hard protrusion again. *Success!* She congratulated herself. She leaned him back against the settee arm and began to pull his shirt off of him. She caressed his chest with her soft hands and leaned forward to lick his nipple as he groaned noisily. Seeing his head back and eyes closed, she kissed his neck and continued to caress his chest downward until her hand was at the waistband. She touched his arousal over his breeches lovingly and heard a loud moan after a gasp. She unbuttoned him and tentatively reached inside to touch his arousal. He was definitely hard.

She looked up to his face to see him intensely staring at her, his eyes dark with passion and flooded with lust. She gently stroked his erection. It was softer than silk but firm and hard under the skin. She rubbed it up and down as she had felt his manhood move in her hand and Darcy moaned louder than before and felt herself wet with desire and wanted him inside her again. As she continued to pump him, she propped up to kiss him and as he frantically tongued her mouth, she sat up straighter and sat on his cock, impaling herself with one swift penetration.

Darcy released her mouth and let out a yell. "Elizabeth!" He grabbed her by her buttocks and began to move her whole body up and down. She moaned and positioned her legs and helped him by moving up and down as if riding a horse. He felt so good and he was so deep inside her. She began to moan louder as he began to pump from under her as well. She let out another yelp and climaxed then she collapsed onto his chest and held him tightly as he grabbed her by the waist and continued to thrust into her. She regained her senses and kissed his neck and his mouth was back on hers as his tongue was diving into her mouth while he continued his thrusts. He lifted her up, keeping himself still inside her and put her down onto her back on the settee as he continued to drill into her. She let out another cry, as it was so pleasurable and climaxed again. He pumped roughly and hard until he groaned loudly and released. He crouched over her, panting with his head buried on her neck and she could feel the sweat drip off his body.

Elizabeth had thoroughly enjoyed the animalistic coupling and could not believe that she had been so wanton but she loved his body and she loved being connected to him.

Darcy was dizzy. His eyes would not focus and he felt as if he would die of happiness. He had never been so pleasured in his life and when his wife began to ride him, he had completely lost his mind. *She is the best thing that has happened to me. I can die a happy man now.*

After several more breaths, he sat up, taking his wife up with him, and cradled her onto his lap. His manhood had finally deflated and he kissed her reverently and softly.

"I love you. That was incredible. Are you well, my love?" He asked tenderly.

She smiled brightly, "I am well. That was wonderful. I think it gets better each time. I hope you do not mind that your wife is so wanton."

"Well, Mrs. Darcy, I prefer all my wives to be so. In fact, it is a requirement." He joked.

"Hey! You only have one wife! How many do you plan on getting?" Elizabeth whined playfully.

"I do not think I can handle more than one, my love." He kissed her hair. "You are all I need and all I will ever want. Allow me to carry you to the bed," he commented while he slid down his breeches completely off, "and we can rest. We can use a nap after such an activity."

He carried her to lay her down on the bed and climbed in. They were both completely nude and they liked it that way. They quickly fell asleep after their stomachs and desires were satiated, only to awaken to touch each other and kiss to fall asleep again. They made love twice more that night and Elizabeth was correct. It did get better each time.

Chapter 18

Wickham threw down the day's paper angrily. He had just read Darcy's wedding announcement.

Fucking Darcy! He has all the luck. I have not heard of any 'Bennets' before but I would bet she is some pretty thing. Maybe I should get a taste. That arrogant bastard needs to be brought down a notch. I will need to change my plans to visit Kent. Damn him! I had hoped he would be marrying that dull cousin of his and I was going to visit Dolores. Well, it does not matter who. I was going to put my seed deep inside his wife, whether it was going to be Anne or someone else and perhaps I will actually enjoy bedding the new Mrs. Darcy!

"George, are you paying attention?" A voice came from beneath. "What are you doing?"

"I am so sorry, my dear. Something caught my attention for a moment but I am back. Keep sucking my cock, Sarah. It feels really good." Wickham laid back as he enjoyed this slut's mouth on him. His erection grew as he thought of taking Mrs. Darcy by force and how he would drill into her until she was thoroughly ruined. Darcy would suffer to have his wife soiled and would not touch her again. That prig probably cannot get it up anyways. Darcy probably likes it up his bumhole. Never looked at a woman twice. He would blackmail them to keep it hushed, making it like Mrs. Darcy was the one that seduced him and maybe get her with child. Ah, to have his own child become heir to Pemberley would be sweet revenge.

"Ride my cock, Sarah. I want you again. Oh, yes, my dear. You feel so good." He let her ride him for a while but he was desperate to take her hard. He pushed her to her back and began to drill into her. "Do you think I am making the baby dizzy when I fuck you like this?" He pounded into her. With a few more pumps, he released inside her then rolled off of her.

He looked at his wife who was sweating and panting. She looked a little like Georgiana Darcy. Even though Sarah was considered a whore for being pregnant out of wedlock, she was pretty enough and was certainly enthusiastic in bed. She liked to take him into her mouth and opened her legs whenever he wanted her and was eternally grateful for him to have married her when she was six months pregnant with Bingley's bastard.

Wickham had laughed in glee when he found her here in Newcastle. He had been looking for some opportunities after the fiasco with Georgiana and had heard of the public cut that Darcy delivered to this stupid chit after she attempted to compromise him in public, as there were talks of Bingley having pursued her right before. When he met her a month ago, she was obviously pregnant but was trying to hide it and he flirted with her and charmed her and acted like she did not look pregnant at all, and when she confessed that she was carrying Bingley's child but she could not return to town, as her family had cut her off and exiled her here with her distant relatives, he sympathised with her and told her how horrid Darcy was and revealed his awful mistreatment of himself.

Wickham had already known of her dowry and after confessing that due to Darcy's abuse, he was left desolate and had difficulty finding work, but that he had desperately wanted to marry for love, which he believed he had finally found, she told him of her £10,000 and told him that her family would love to see her finally married. He paid her a lot of attention and bedded her a week after meeting her. She was naïve and such an easy target and was pleasing to the eyes. Bingley did always have a knack for finding a pretty lady.

He thought of what he could do once the baby was born. If she died and the baby died, he would lose access to her funds. They were leasing a small house and it was comfortable enough but Wickham certainly wanted more. His wife's dowry was tightly wrapped up and he had access only to the interest of £500 a year for the first three years and it was certainly not enough but he had no plans to keep her for three years.

If his wife and babe survived the childbirth, he would blackmail Bingley, who might be married to some wealthy heiress by then, and squeeze some funds out of him. He would keep bedding Sarah and get her with child as often as possible and perhaps she might die in one of the births. If one babe survived, that child would inherit her money and he would be able to use it as he saw fit as the father. If he got desperate enough after a year or two, he thought of ways for her to have an 'accident' so he could get his hands on her money.

For now, he planned on enjoying her pretty face and all her favours until he found ways to hurt Darcy for ruining his plans with Georgiana. He mostly enjoyed fifteen or sixteen-year-old virgins but he enjoyed sticking his cock into any woman. He truly missed Dolores' talents at getting him off but Sarah and her big belly would do for now.

~*~

The Darcys spent a blissful week in bed, experimenting and practicing their lovemaking constantly. Darcy could not believe what his body was capable of but Elizabeth had constantly pushed his limits. He had relations with his wife five times on their wedding day, not including the masturbation, and by the end of the week, he had counted seven in one day. She had been seductive, playful, and curious, and they had tried different positions, different locations throughout the house as long as the doors could be locked, and at various times of the day. He had enjoyed morning sex the most, as he was ready to go after several hours of sleep, and she had enjoyed night sex, where she could relax and fall asleep in his arms. They made the compromise that they would have relations at least twice daily so they were both satisfied.

They knew that after the week of complete isolation, they would have to merge into the public eye. Lady Matlock's Ball was tonight and they would have to be seen.

Darcy had to take care to not leave love-marks on her beautiful skin, as her dress would be quite revealing of their married status. He cared not and would have been proud to show her off but she snipped at him that it was not fair and that she wanted to represent herself well as Mrs. Darcy.

They planned out the rest of the week and decided on the theatre and a musicale with Georgiana before returning to Longbourn. They would stay three nights in Hertfordshire and travel to Pemberley where they could begin their lives as Master and Mistress there.

~*~

Colonel Richard Fitzwilliam stood in the back of the ballroom as the guests started flowing in slowly. He was glad he did not have to stand in the receiving line with his parents and brother and his wife and being a second son definitely had its advantages. He smiled as he saw many fine ladies' eyes trained on him, inspecting his figure and waving their fans at him while waiting to be asked to dance, as gossip was widespread that the dashing Colonel was finally desiring to marry.

He had been in town for a week to continue his holiday and he was to have one more week before returning to duty. His schedule had been very busy and it was difficult to take time off whenever he wanted, and he had originally planned on spending two weeks in Hertfordshire to finally relax, but with Darcy's sudden wedding, he returned to London with Georgiana and her companion Mrs. Annesley and had spent the past week accompanying his mother to three parties and getting to know Anne better away from her mother's intrusions.

He danced with numerous women at the balls this past week, all with similar attributes as Elizabeth, and had spoken with more ladies to get to know their minds than he had ever in the past. He had only flirted to seduce women to bed and had cared only for what was between her legs and never what was between her ears before, but now it had all changed. He desired to find one single woman that could inspire him to finally tame him into marriage. He danced nearly every dance, all the ladies petite and brunette, of course, to find that one person who could spark his heart as Elizabeth had done, but he found it extremely difficult to not compare every woman to Elizabeth's intelligence and kindness and found them all wanting. He now understood how Darcy found the ladies of the *ton* so vapid and uninspiring.

Darcy had explained to him that he had asked Bingley to stand up with him since he did not know if Richard would be able to attend or not due to his schedule when originally planned. Richard had been relieved that he did not have to stand up with Darcy, as he might have carried off the bride to prevent the wedding.

I wonder what she will be wearing tonight. I am sure they have had a pleasant honeymoon. I long to see her, even if I cannot be close to her. A week without her has been too long. How am I to go on when she leaves for Pemberley? It will be an eternity until I can see her again. Blasted! She is married and there is nothing to be done. I must overcome this! I must!

He was determined to find himself a woman to settle down with. There must be someone that he could tolerate well enough, and he no longer cared for money or status or even outward beauty. He only wanted to find a wife that could touch his heart enough to take the pain away but he knew it to be an impossibility. Richard's heart had found its perfect mate and he knew there was no one but Elizabeth for him.

His eyes turned to the door when the room's volume increased, as he knew the Darcys would arrive soon. As the guests of honour, they were to arrive later than the others and it was time. He saw the doors open and there were applauses from the crowd as Mr. and Mrs. Darcy entered the ballroom. His heart lurched when he saw her. She was more beautiful than ever. Her deep burgundy dress was cut to flatter her figure and she wore the famous Darcy Rubies around her neck, and her hair was shiny and perfectly coiffed but more than anything else, she had a glow about her that exuded happiness. She truly looked happy and he was happy for her. *My Elizabeth. I missed her so much. She is a balm to my soul. I will love her from afar but I will never stop loving her.*

Richard looked at Darcy and saw a wide grin on his face as well. He was radiating joy as well, more than he had ever seen on his stoic cousin. *She was THAT good, eh? But of course, she was. How could she not be?* He felt pain in his chest as he longed to hold her and taste her love but swallowed down his emotions and put on a smile as they approached him.

"Richard! It is good to see you again. Where is Georgiana?" Darcy asked, as they shook hands.

"Darcy, Cousin Lizzy," he nodded, avoiding looking at her for more than a split second while his heart fluttered. "Georgiana had a slight mishap with her dress. She and Iris should be heading down soon. Ah, here they are."

Richard's sister had taken Georgiana to help mend the small loose thread. Georgiana saw her brother and new sister and rushed over as gracefully as possible and held their hands.

"Brother! Lizzy! You both look so well! I am so glad to see you. Thank you for allowing me to dance tonight, brother. Congratulations on your marriage again!" She was speaking fast and energetically and it pleased Darcy to no end. He greeted Iris, who was seventeen and would have her first season in the spring. She had been the unplanned baby that brought joy to the Matlocks in their advanced age.

As Georgiana and Iris spoke with Darcy, Elizabeth turned to Richard. "Hello, Richard," she spoke quietly.

She had forgotten that he would be here and she did not know what to do; she wanted to continue to be a friend but was afraid to cause him any pain. She had found his company so pleasant before, being able to talk to him like an older brother and tease him, and he had been always friendly and protective of her from the beginning. They had been great friends and Elizabeth thought she must be thick-headed, not realising that he loved her from the beginning, but she had only thought of him as a kind cousin who must have wanted to spend time with Mr. Darcy. She realised that no one outside the family called Richard by his given name but he had requested it at their first meeting, while his brother's wife still called him 'Colonel' after several years of marriage. She should have seen it but had been too distracted with being presented to the public as Mr. Darcy's fiancée. From the way that Fitzwilliam had put it, Richard had been severely affected and was hurting and there was nothing to be done.

"How are you?" She attempted to be cheerful but kept the distance a bit further than her norm.

"Well, Lizzy, ahem, I am well. Everything has been wonderful." He wanted to sound jolly but he had choked on his words. He had wanted nothing more than to grab hold of her and kiss her senselessly but also that knew Darcy would murder him and his family would be disgraced.

Elizabeth unconsciously leaned forward and touched his arm. "Truly?"

Richard looked down at her hand where she touched him. It burned as if on fire. She noticed the movement and immediately took her hand away.

Damn it! She knows. She knows I am in love with her and is sympathising with me. Her kindness knows no bounds. Man up, Richard! You must conquer this.

Richard quickly took her gloved hand and kissed it, tenderly gripping it. "I am well. I will be well, Lizzy. You look happy. I am happy for you." He gave her a full smile, looking into her gorgeous eyes. The joy of having her near was worth the pain in his heart. "Has Darcy been treating you well?"

Elizabeth softly smiled in relief, seeing his pleased face. "Oh, yes. He has been kind. I could not have asked for a better husband." She gazed adoringly at her husband who had now finished his conversation with the young ladies. Darcy's eyebrows furrowed for a moment then his smile returned.

Darcy reached behind her and touched her back. "I am glad to hear you say that, Mrs. Darcy. Although I can attest to the fact that I could not have asked for a better wife."

The girls sighed and told each other how romantic he was, while Richard laughed. "It is good to see you still a mooncalf with your wife, Darce. Congratulations again. May I have your permission, sir, for the third set with Mrs. Darcy?"

"Hey, are you not supposed to ask the lady? But then again, I belong to you now, husband, so I will defer to your excellent mind to decide for me." Elizabeth jested. *I do not know how Fitzwilliam will feel but I trust him. I trust Richard as well. He is doing his duty as my cousin. He has always been like a brother to me and I value his friendship.*

Darcy smiled. *I trust Richard with my life and I must trust him with my most valuable treasure.* "Milady, I would never have claimed to *own* you but if you wish for me to decide for you, I would be happy to consent for my dearest cousin to dance with my greatest treasure." He kissed her hand. "As you wish, Elizabeth." He whispered and smiled.

He is the best of men. Elizabeth looked at him fondly. "I would be happy to accept, Cousin Richard."

Richard heard the warning and the trust as Darcy spoke. *Dear god, they are perfect for each other.*

"Thank you, Cousins. I see there are several of your friends here to greet you, Darce." He bowed, "Mrs. Darcy." And he walked to his parents on the other side of the room to compose his thoughts better. His heart continued to ache while he stood near her and he had to walk away. He suppressed his desires and spoke with his family and several of his acquaintances.

The Darcys addressed scores of guests and received sincere felicitations. These were all peers and close friends of Darcy and had genuinely welcomed them. The strings soon began to play to indicate that the first set was about to commence and Darcy led Elizabeth as the guests of honour and began their dance.

"I love you, Mrs. Darcy." He whispered as he passed her.

"I love you, Mr. Darcy." She replied at the next step.

Those in attendance could see their happiness radiating from the couple and it was obvious that it was a love match. Some were curious if she might have symptoms of pregnancy and seeing only a very slim waist and flat stomach, it left no doubt that they had married for love.

～*～

The second dance, Darcy danced with Georgiana while Elizabeth danced with the Earl. For the third dance, Darcy handed Elizabeth to Richard and he left them to escort Lady Matlock to the floor.

Richard had danced the first with his sister and the second with his mother. He was anxious for the third and when Darcy had handed his wife to him and winked at him, he knew Darcy was entrusting him with his greatest asset.

The Colonel looked handsome in his uniform and numerous ladies' eyes were on him. He had been a flirt and had charmed several women present here to their beds before, but for three months now, he had been completely disengaged, even if he had danced ever so many dances at the last three balls. Several married women knew he had gone to Dover for a month and expected him to return to their beds after his return but he had ignored them completely and did not even acknowledge them in public. He appeared to cease trifling with all women completely and spoke more restrained and asked questions that were unlike his previous flirtations. He never danced more than once with the ladies during last week's parties and he had ceased visiting his usual women since the beginning of summer. He was more stoic than ever and appeared quite serious and stayed close to his family members tonight.

Rumour was rampant that now that Mr. Darcy was married, the Colonel was searching for a wife as well and many single ladies were hoping it was true. Colonel Fitzwilliam was a fine specimen of a man, finally exceeding Mr. Darcy's status, as he remained a bachelor still.

Richard's heart beat wildly when he held Elizabeth's hand. As they lined up to dance, he tried not to stare at her but could not help himself. She would often be looking at Darcy and his mother, and he heard her laugh as his father had stepped on his sister's toes for the second time. Hearing her laughter had brought so much peace to his heart so he felt himself relax more. *No, I would never impose on her. I love her and I would protect her fiercely but only on Darcy's behalf.*

He connected eyes with Darcy and winked at him. He saw Darcy's tiny smile and knew all was well.

Seeing the exchange, Elizabeth raised her eyebrow and spoke to Richard. "Shall we have some conversation? We cannot be silent for half an hour, Cousin Richard."

"Cousin Lizzy, do you always talk as a rule when dancing?" Richard asked, his heart fluttering at her attentions.

She laughed melodically. "Why, yes, Richard, especially of books and philosophy!"

Richard grinned broader than he had in weeks. *I love hearing her laughter. I would give everything to make her happy.*

They spoke of poetry and theatre as they had done several times before and enjoyed the dance together. Richard laughed loudly several times and the eligible ladies thought him so handsome but he remained focused only on his dancing partner. When the set ended, he walked her to Darcy on his arm and passed her back to her husband after kissing her hand.

"Thank you, Mrs. Darcy. Thank you, Darcy." He said with a small smile. *She is a treasure. My heart will never be my own again.*

"You are welcome, Richard." Darcy replied. Turning to his wife, "Would you like some punch, my dear?" She nodded.

They walked over to the punch table and conversed with several more people. Soon, it was the supper set and the guests of honour happily danced again.

There was a speech by Uncle Matlock, as well as the Viscount who told an embarrassing story about his stoic cousin and everyone cheered during Supper.

The Darcys danced several more sets; Elizabeth with some of Darcy's close friends, Darcy, with the wives of his friends.

The last dance was to be a waltz and the newlyweds had anticipated it greatly. They had practiced a few times but had not yet finished a set, as their private dance had always resulted in a round of lovemaking at home, but they were ready tonight. As it was still a new dance and so intimate, only a dozen or so married couples stood to dance.

"I am so glad I am married, Mrs. Darcy. I love holding you this close on the dance floor." Darcy whispered as the dance began.

"Oh, Fitzwilliam, I feel like we are floating on clouds. I love this dance. We must practice again when we return home." Elizabeth replied archly.

"Yes, we must, Elizabeth. That we must." He grinned.

Richard watched them from a dark corner of the Ballroom. He had rarely danced tonight except the first few with his family members. He could not even consider spending a set with anyone else. *Elizabeth, she is perfect. Perfect for me. What am I going to do?* He felt as if he was drowning again and she was his only lifeline.

Unable to watch any further, he quietly hurried to his room so he could recall touching her hand and holding her waist during their dance. He knew he would never be able to smell lavender again without thinking of her.

The Matlock Ball had been deemed a success and as the party departed, the Darcys arranged for theatre and musicale outings with Georgiana before travelling to Hertfordshire and returned home to practice their waltz in private.

Chapter 19

Caroline Bingley sat completely disinterested with nothing to do in the cold, desolate county of Yorkshire. Her spinster aunt was droning on and on about the newest calf born to the Winstons and the town gossip about the baker's daughter being large with child so soon after her wedding the smithy's son. *I wish I were back in London. Only six more months and I will get my dowry. I will set up a large home with the furnishings that I want and make it grander than Louisa's home. God, I miss a good cock. I have not had a man for three months! Right before Mr. Darcy arrived at Netherfield, that footman, John, he pleasured me quite well.* She was aroused as she remembered the young muscular man that she had paid to indulge her. She had given him a whole sterling pound to get him into her room for the night and she had kept her legs open the whole night and he did not disappoint as he gave it to her three times.

She was daydreaming about getting Mr. Darcy to bend to her will, which had been a frequent fantasy of hers, when she heard her aunt utter, 'Darcy'. She snapped to attention to figure out what her crazy aunt had been saying but she had already moved on something about the cost of eggs.

"Aunt, what was it that you were saying about Mr. Darcy? Did you receive a letter from Charles recently?" She rudely interrupted her.

"Oh, yes! Did you not hear me mention it? You must pay attention, Caroline. It is no wonder you are still single and nearly on the shelf. It is not ladylike to not listen when someone is spea..."

"Aunt! What did he say?" She interrupted again.

"About what, dear?" Her aunt was confused.

"About Mr. Darcy!" *Damn senile fool!*

Aunt Bingley smiled. "Oh, yes. Charles said that he had Mr. and Mrs. Darcy at Netherfield and Louisa threw a grand party and that it was a tremendous success. It seems Mr. Darcy is very happy with his choice of wife and will be taking the Bennets to his estate for Christmas. They must be there by now. It is only ten more days until Christmas. Oh, and they think Louisa is with child. How wonderful that must be. She had wanted a child after her loss and it is about time. Louisa seems happy and she told me about the newest candles that use beeswax but it does not melt too quickly and promised to send me a few on her next correspondence. I always thought having too many candles was wasteful but if this one last longer, I say it is worth the price. I saw the most beautiful muslin at the shop the other day and that was at a good price..." She began to speak of other things.

Caroline sat in shock. *Mr. Darcy is already married? To that chit Eliza Bennet?* She grumbled while she thought of those odious Bennets going to Pemberley while she was stuck here in the backwater country, freezing her buttocks off. *I should have been Mistress of Pemberley! How dare that harlot take my rightful place!* And what was it about Louisa? Expecting? *But Mr. Hurst had not touched her for years! He had a good cock. I enjoyed sampling it and it fit so well inside me but he had the gall to kick me out of his room. He should have enjoyed himself. I cannot wait for May. I will show them all! I will get myself a husband who is above Mr. Darcy.*

She contemplated her future and her grand return to London. All of her connections were through Charles and even then, she had to get on her knees or open her legs to get the majority of her invitations. *Perhaps I will seduce Mr. Darcy and become his mistress. He will shower me with his fortune and gifts after he experiences what true bliss feels like. Eliza could not offer what I can and I am certain he must be weary of her by now. Yes, I want Mr. Darcy and his delectable body.*

~*~

Pemberley was the most beautiful place Elizabeth had ever seen. It was perfectly serene and she could not have imagined a better place where nature had done more, or where natural beauty had been so little counteracted by an awkward taste, that she stood in awe at the vista where her husband had stopped to show her their home. She whispered, "Of all this I am mistress."

Darcy hugged her from behind. "Yes, my love. Everything I have is yours. Do not be afraid. You have shown yourself to be a capable mistress of Darcy House and I have every confidence that with your kind heart and caring nature, you will rise to the challenge. Please do not feel pressured; Mrs. Reynolds has been managing so long that there is no rush."

Elizabeth turned and kissed his cheek. "You know my courage always rises with your attempts to intimidate me, sir. Lead on! Challenge accepted!" She laughed sweetly.

~*~

The three Darcys spent the next two weeks together, planning for the Bennets' trip to Pemberley before Christmas, and Darcy returned to his business correspondences and worked with his steward while Elizabeth eagerly learned the workings of the grand mansion.

Georgiana helped where she could but she had allowed Mrs. Reynolds to manage the household for so long that she felt inept in helping Elizabeth. After Elizabeth set up some time to learn together to prepare for her future as a mistress of her own home, Georgiana returned to her music and studies with Mrs. Annesley.

Mrs. Reynolds was a godsend. Elizabeth saw her as a motherly figure to the Darcy orphans and immediately loved her. Mrs. Reynolds was very knowledgeable and had been fiercely protective over the Darcy children for years and when she saw the love between the master and the new mistress, she immediately pledged her loyalty to Mistress Lizzy and loved her as well.

She took her time to teach the new mistress of the workings of the grand house as well as some of the key tenants who assisted with various tasks at Pemberley. They talked of how to barter with the wives to ensure food would always be on everyone's tables, as well as who needed more attention due to illnesses or losses in the tenant families.

Elizabeth met her Aunt Gardiner's mother and joined their efforts to dress the orphans and discussed ways to set up a school for young girls so they could learn to read and do simple math. The new Mrs. Darcy believed strongly that no woman, rich or poor, should be left to fend for themselves and educating them on how to read and sew and learn the tasks to be a good worker would prevent them from selling their bodies or being abused, should they face destitution. She worked hard to see to the needs of the tenants as well and made visits to meet the women and children and gained their respect quickly.

Darcy was immeasurably proud of his wife. There were few women whom he believed could ever have fit into his mother's shoes, but here was Elizabeth, within a month of arriving, who had not only inspired the loyalty of every single one of the hundreds of servants and tenants and their families, but went above his mother by meeting with neighbourhood ladies and getting their pledges to start a school for girls in the new year. She was not only intelligent and kind, but she truly cared for her responsibilities and desired to do everything within her power to serve the community.

He could not have asked for a better mistress of his homes and his bed.

Chapter 20

The Bennets had the jolliest of Christmases in years. Pemberley was decorated with hollies and ribbons and gifts were exchanged and stories were told. Each found a piece of heaven at Pemberley and Mr. Bennet enjoyed the library, Mrs. Bennet praised the furnishings and the grandeur of the home but also appreciated its simplicity, and the girls reunited and spent hours looking through Georgiana's closet and gossiping. Jane and Elizabeth spent time catching up and sharing stories of their beloveds.

Mrs. Bennet also announced that she was expecting and the full house roared with excitement. They had hoped for her health and safety and there were tears in everyone's eyes when she spoke truthfully when she expressed that whether boy or girl, she would love the child unconditionally as it was a blessing and a reminder of Mr. and Mrs. Bennet's reconciliation after so many years.

After a month of holiday, the Bennets returned to the serenity of Hertfordshire, where the Darcys would visit next month for Bingley and Jane's wedding. The Darcys resumed their quiet lives, once again returning to their routines yet each blissfully happy with their small family.

~*~

Richard Fitzwilliam sat at his parent's home in London. His parents had removed to Matlock last week and he sat alone at the townhouse as he wrapped up his businesses at the camp. He usually celebrated with his friends with a group of merry women, or with the Darcys if he could manage time off, but this year, he had no desire to be with anyone at all. He had received his usual bottle of the finest Scotch from Darcy as his Christmas gift, but this time, there was a note and a small book with it. He stared at Elizabeth's elegant handwriting that wished him a Happy Christmas. The book was a small volume of poetry that they had discussed several times, and he would treasure anything of hers but this was so special, his heart broke that she was not near. He desperately desired to visit a brothel to expunge his frustrations but he knew he would not be able to touch anyone who was not his beloved.

He wrote a dozen letters to confess his love to Elizabeth and how desperately he wanted her, only to burn each of the letters in the fire to destroy any evidence of his heart's deepest desire. After nearly half of the bottle of Scotch was gone, he slept deeply, only to dream of *her* being his own beloved wife once again.

~*~

Lady Catherine sat bitterly on her chair. She was alone and Christmas was anything but jolly. After finally fixing the wheel in Hertfordshire, she had returned to Rosings to find that she was barred entrance. Barred from her own home! It was ridiculous. After the steward finally arrived and told her firmly that her belongings had already been moved to the dower house and she would find her correspondences there, she haughtily entered the carriage and promptly left.

When she arrived at the meagre cottage, she became furious once again. There were only two servants to serve her and none of her belongings were in their useful places. After barking orders for changes to move some of the furniture around, she went to the small room that appeared to be a sitting room. It was facing full south and it would bring the sun all day long and it would be too hot and bright and she hated it.

She saw her correspondences and looked for the letter from her brother. It was on top, his seal proudly facing up. She ripped it open to read:

Catherine,

I hope you enjoyed your travel to Hertfordshire, as it will be the last time you will be able to travel anywhere of your choice. We know all about your visit to Longbourn and your disgrace at being ejected from the property as well as your humiliation at the Meryton Inn. Your rude manners did you no favours, sister. You will never be able to show your face there again, as you and Mr. Collins have been noted to be villains and will never be welcomed there. I am certain Mr. Collins, IF he should inherit Longbourn, will be quickly out-casted and be disliked by all the villagers.

Darcy is furious with you and has demanded that his solicitor collect the debt immediately. Your dowry is now left with £1,000 due to your excessive spending habits these past years. You should still be able to live out the rest of your life with the amount as long as you are frugal, but I know you will use it all up with your demands for the life that you have thrown away. Anne will not be providing you anything. She has asked that Richard take over management of Rosings Park on her behalf and Richard will not be a friend to you. He was angrier than Darcy for your threats and your schemes against Mrs. Darcy and plans on bringing you more misery than you ever thought, should you deign to leave your house. If you apologise and beg for mercy to Darcy, Richard might be amenable to providing you an additional servant or two, but the choice is up to you.

Mr. Collins should be receiving his own letter from the Archbishop in the next month so do not believe he will be a friend to you either. You are on your own.

I shall be more than happy to lend you an ear should you grovel and apologise for all of your misdeeds, although I doubt you are capable of such reflection. Under no circumstances are you to approach Darcy and his wife. I am certain that Richard will make sure of it; but if you dare attempt to bring any trouble for Darcy, he has threatened to put you in Bedlam where you belong.

Lady Catherine had sat stunned. After a full hour of not having a clue as to what to do next, she returned to her bedroom to find that nothing had been moved. She shrieked for her housekeeper and when she gradually appeared, she asked, "WHY has none of the furniture been moved as I commanded?!"

The housekeeper politely answered, "It was either moving your furniture or fixing your luncheon. Which do you wish? Do you wish to starve? I cannot move the furniture alone as is and you would have to hire some folks to do that for you anyways. Your meal is ready for you downstairs, Lady Catherine."

Lady Catherine yelled, "I will not have insolence in my house! You are fired! Leave!"

The housekeeper laughed in her face. "Certainly, I can leave. The Mistress of Rosings is paying my salary and I can just return there should I choose. But," she paused, "I am being paid extra to be here and I like the additional income. You do not pay my wages and you have no right to fire me but I can leave anytime I wish. Do not think that there is a slew of servants willing to come here, though. If I leave, you will have to clean and cook on your own. The manservant is the same. He is here to chop wood and do some of the manual work but we do not work for you and you cannot order us about. Excuse me." She bowed and left.

Lady Catherine sat stunned for another quarter hour until her stomach began to growl. She had not eaten for several hours and conceded to the fact that she *would* starve to death if the housekeeper did not remain.

She ate the mediocre meal and contemplated if there was anything left to do than to live out her miserable days in this hellhole.

~*~

Several days after returning to Hunsford, Mr. Collins received a very important letter from the Archbishop. He was afraid to open it so it sat still on his desk. He had tried to ingratiate himself with the new Mistress of Rosings Park after hearing that Lady Catherine had been quickly ejected from the mansion, but Miss de Bourgh had remained in London with Lord Matlock and he did not know what to do. He tried to appease the steward to gain his favour but he was harsh and determined to kick him off the property.

Mr. Collins knew that he could not be fired from his position, as it was a life-term instalment, but he felt that there was something ominous that was going to happen. *I should have never listened to Lady Catherine! She has brought me nothing but trouble.*

He visited Dolores immediately to take his mind off that letter. After huffing and puffing for less than three minutes, he rolled over and asked Dolores some questions. "My dear, do you like being here? Do you enjoy being a prostitute?"

Dolores had lain still, as he was usually in a hurry to leave but he seemed to need a little more than a quick fix this time. She was surprised when he asked her the questions. "Mr. Collins, of course I do not *enjoy* making my living this way, but I do not have many choices. My husband left me poor and I had to survive somehow. I do enjoy the act, though. You are a reverend, Mr. Collins, and you enjoy bedding me, is that correct?" He nodded. "My husband did not. He was dull and stale and refused to touch me. If I could have a way to live without bedding multiple men a day but still be able to get *some* satisfaction, it would be the best of both worlds, but it could never be."

"Marry me. I am in trouble and will need to leave Kent. I believe I am being defrocked, as Lady Catherine's brother reported my visits with you to the Archbishop. Come with me, Dolores. I have some money from my mother and eventually I will inherit Longbourn. You can be the mistress there and become a gentlewoman. Although it might take years and years for me to inherit a large estate, as my cousin Bennet appears to be quite healthy, I can provide for you and we can lease or purchase a small house and be together. Will you marry me, Dolores Younge?"

He was naked from the waist down but he knelt by the bed and proposed. He was ridiculous but endearing.

Mrs. Younge was sick and tired of being the town whore. Mr. Collins was quick but filled her well and he may have smelled but she could teach him to wash more often. The other servants and merchants and even some gentlemen and landowners had been awful, though. They lay over her, grunting and biting her breasts and some had even put it in her anus. Some were violent while others were cheap and always paid less than owed. A way to get out of this life as well as have Mr. Collins to bed was exactly what she wanted. She would need to spend some time teaching him to pleasure her but the prospects were good.

She replied, "Mr. Collins, I will have some requests from you later but I do accept. As long as you are willing to have me, knowing what I am, I would be happy to be your wife."

"Oh, Dolores, you have made me so happy. I will make the arrangements today and will return to you tomorrow. We may leave as early as ten o'clock tomorrow morning, my love! Pack your bags!" And he excitedly jumped as he dressed and left.

Dolores cleaned herself and smiled, as she had hope for the first time since marrying the awful Mr. Younge who had brought nothing but sorrow. She had a chance to start over and would do her best to be a good wife to Mr. Collins.

~*~

When Mr. Collins arrived home, he opened the letter from the Archbishop and it was exactly as he had thought. He would no longer be an ordained reverend and he had lost his status as a man of God. He quickly looked around to see what he could take. He gathered some of his memorabilia and his clothing. His valuables were placed in his trunks and he hid some of the tithe offering that he had been skimming during the past six months into his pocket. There were a few pieces of vase and useless decoration that could fetch a few coins that were packed away as well. He would leave all of his seminary books, as they were useless to him now.

He packed his letters and arranged for travel in his chaise to the inn an hour away and they would change horses and continue to Surrey where his parents' cottage was still there. It was not as comfortable as Hunsford but they would use his funds to fix it up and perhaps expand it gradually. His small parcel of land had brought an income of £500 a year at one time but his father had argued with his few tenants and the land was now a wasteland.

He suddenly recalled that his father was not a good man. He had his land that he could have worked but complained about the Bennets throughout his life and he had treated his mother poorly.

Why did I forget that my father beat my mother? I had completely forgotten about it.

———

Mother always cried or looked sullen and Father was always inebriated. He had a good thing and he threw it away. Well, I will not be like him. I will treat my wife well!

Mr. Collins met his fiancée the next day and quietly packed up their belongings and they were never seen again in Kent.

Chapter 21

The idyllic months at Pemberley flew by.

Darcy and Elizabeth had returned to Hertfordshire last month for Jane and Bingley's wedding, who had chosen St. Valentine's Day to be wed, and Mrs. Bennet went to much more trouble for this unrushed wedding. The chapel had been filled with flowers and the wedding breakfast was ostentatious with more courses than necessary, but Darcy and Elizabeth held hands as they shared with each other that they had infinitely preferred their small, simple wedding.

Mrs. Bennet was progressing well with her pregnancy and was due to deliver in June. Mr. Bennet fussed over her and brought her plates and carried drinks for her and all who saw him act this way for the first time laughed and was pleased to see him care for her in such a kind manner.

Darcy and Elizabeth farewelled her family with the promise to see them in June after the London Season since Mrs. Bennet would be delivering around that time. Elizabeth kissed Jane and winked to wish her luck on her wedding night, as she had spoken to Jane of the many pleasures of the marriage bed and to trust her husband. They would see each other for the Season in April and the Bingleys would be Darcys' guests again in August.

After returning to Pemberley, both of the Darcys were busy with their many responsibilities and spring was soon upon them. Spring plantings would begin and Darcy felt as if he were trapped in his study for the past month, seeing to tenant needs and meeting with the steward, as well as continuing his correspondences for his other properties and investments. The parson at Kympton had retired and the appropriate candidate was offered the position today. While on a quick break between appointments, he looked out the window to see the beautiful scene that he had often gazed during the past years after he became master.

Pemberley was the most beautiful place in the world to him and it would shine its best in spring and summer. He was eager to show Elizabeth the beautiful landscape that could only be traversed on horseback or walking, and excitedly anticipated picnicking and making love to his wife out of doors. Darcy felt his manhood stiffen at the thought of his wife.

They had loved each other at least daily since the wedding day. He could not get enough of her and she had initiated many of their lovemaking and he thought himself the luckiest man in the world. While they had been continuously uniting during the first week of marriage, it had become custom to engage twice daily for the past several weeks and they had continued the practice throughout their trip to Hertfordshire. They had engaged in lovemaking in the carriage and although failing at their attempts at remaining quiet, they had both enjoyed it immensely. Even during her courses, he lay with her to hold her and she would help him release using her hands and she was infinitely generous. But the past week had been different. She was exhausted by dinnertime and was sleeping by the time he joined her in bed, and she had been ill in the mornings. He was severely concerned that she was driving herself to sickness by overworking and taking too much on herself.

Elizabeth had become an exemplary mistress. She had arranged a few dinners with the neighbours and although there were some who were initially apprehensive of this unknown miss taking over the charges of the massive properties, she was quickly won over by most. There would always be some who were jealous and resentful that Mr. Darcy overlooked them or their daughters, but they paid them no attention.

They were to attend the Spring Equinox Ball at the nearest neighbour's mansion tomorrow night. It was still twenty miles away so they would travel this evening and stay two nights at Chatsworth and return the morning after the party. *I hope she will be well. Perhaps a little time away is warranted since she has been working too hard. Oh, how I miss her. Perhaps we can have a private party tonight. Has it been that long?*

He looked down and saw his bulge. *Damn! I am hard again. I had to masturbate again this morning and thinking about Elizabeth is not helping. My appointment is in ten minutes. Good god! Think of something else, man!*

Darcy thought of the plans they had made for the next several months. They would travel to London to join the Season for a few weeks, travel to Rosings for a month, then visit the Bennets during Mrs. Bennet's confinement. The Bingleys and Gardiners would be spending August here, then they would begin their property tours in September, starting with the two in Scotland, one in York, travelling south to Manchester, then return in time for Christmas. He planned on taking her to Ramsgate and Bath next year.

He thought of Bingley and his ravings of his wonderful wife made him chuckle. He had proposed marriage to Jane Bennet in December before the Bennets came here for Christmas and they were married in February. Bingley seemed to have completely gotten over Miss Sarah Fleming and Darcy knew Bingley was very compatible with Jane, who was of a very similar character as his friend. *She smiles too much. She is nothing to my Elizabeth.*

Darcy would see Richard tonight as well. The Honourable Mr. Richard Fitzwilliam. How funny that sounded. The past four months had brought him many changes, as Richard had finally retired from military service to manage Rosings. Their cousin Anne had successfully overtaken Rosings and all the legal paperwork had been completed when she was struck with another bout of illness. She had initially appeared to become healthier under the care of the best doctors and Lord and Lady Matlock took her to a few outings. Anne had told them that she was having the best time of her life but the harsh winter had its effect and she caught another cold and was ill again.

Richard had begun to manage Rosings and proved to be a fast learner but he had many questions and consulted with Darcy through letters. A new parson, a Mr. Brown, and his wife were installed, after Mr. Collins fled with Mrs. Younge, the wife of the previous vicar who had colluded with Wickham in his plan to elope with Georgiana, and he had been a significant improvement for the parish. Anne had decided that if her health continued to fail, she did not want to chance her mother taking back the estate so she had designated Richard as her heir. Rosings brought in £6,000 a year and would be a massive undertaking as master and he had begged for Darcy to join him in June. His uncle and aunt had taken Anne to Matlock and Richard had just joined them right after spring planting in Kent had completed.

Darcy wondered if Richard was still in love with Elizabeth. If he had loved her as he did his own wife, it would certainly be so, but now that Richard was master of a great estate and was free to marry for love, who would he choose? There was not a single person who could compare with Elizabeth in his mind. A nagging thought lingered in the back of Darcy's mind. *He would choose a twin of Elizabeth if such a woman* existed. *I am sure he would marry Elizabeth in a heartbeat should I die early. I would hope Elizabeth is cared for, if I should pass before her. What would I do if she passed before me?*

Ceasing his morbid thoughts immediately, he shook his head and sat at his desk again. *No, man. Do not think of such things. Back to work!*

There was a knock on the door at that exact moment and Darcy resumed focusing his attention back to the business at hand.

~*~

Elizabeth lay in bed with a cold towel on her forehead. Hannah saw to her needs and closed the drapes after helping her wash out her mouth for the eighth time.

"Ugggghhhh... Hannah, why am I so ill? I ate everything the same as everyone else and only I appear to be sick. This is the third morning in a row..." She whined. She hated feeling ill. She had always been healthy and colds and stomach ailments had been rare and short in the past.

Hannah, her personal maid, had another mistress before Mrs. Darcy and after her previous employer died during her third childbirth, she had been staying with her mother for the past two months, who was the under-cook at Pemberley, before being chosen to serve the new mistress. She had seen the signs of pregnancy with her previous mistress several times before and knew that her new mistress was not aware.

"Mistress Darcy, I wanted to remind you that you have not had your courses for two months now. I believe you are with child." She shyly spoke out.

Elizabeth abruptly sat up, dropping the wet towel onto her lap. "What?! I did not realise. I had been so busy, I lost count. Could it be true? I am carrying Fitzwilliam's child?" Her eyes immediately watered. She could not believe that a life might be growing inside her. "But what can I expect next? Do we have books in the library about this? Who can help me with my answers? My mother and aunt are too far away, Hannah. Do you think Mrs. Reynolds will help me?" She rambled on.

Hannah giggled, "Yes, ma'am. I am sure Mrs. Reynolds can help you. She has had six children of her own. I will call for her now." She stood up and went downstairs.

Elizabeth laid back and closed her eyes. *Of course, I am with child. It makes sense now. After all the lovemaking, I should not be surprised. Stupid girl! I should have counted the days better. I hope Fitzwilliam will be pleased. We had so many plans to travel and see the properties but we will have to adjust our schedules if I am truly with child. Oh, please, Lord, let me be with child.*

Elizabeth wanted to provide Fitzwilliam with an heir. She wanted to do her duty and prove that she was a good wife, not because of expectations but to show proof of their love. She knew he had wanted a large family, as having grown up as an only child and then having a sister who was twelve years younger had been very lonely for him. They would start a family together and Elizabeth could not be more excited.

Mrs. Reynolds arrived and she asked questions and had answers to what she did not even know to ask. Mrs. Reynolds loved the young mistress like family and was very excited to have another Darcy join the family. They discussed signs and what to eat and what might be avoided and Mrs. Reynolds also answered her timid question, that marital relations during pregnancy was absolutely appropriate but as she got bigger, she would need to find ways to be more comfortable.

Elizabeth flushed in embarrassment but was pleased to hear that she could continue to love her husband. They had decided to wait for the quickening before Elizabeth told Darcy, as it was common for babes to be lost in the first few months.

This saddened Elizabeth but she agreed that her husband would worry endlessly as he had already done this past week, and that once the pregnancy was confirmed, she would tell him. She did not wish to worry him should she lose the babe early on.

Mrs. Reynolds was kind and patient, advising Mrs. Darcy that it was common and it would not be her fault should the baby not stay. She emphasised eating healthy and continuing her walks as long as she felt well. Mrs. Reynolds had gone through several midwives and understood what truly helped and what was old wives' tales that was completely idiotic. She vowed to help her through it and asked the mistress to let her know right away should certain food be offensive.

Elizabeth hugged her tightly and thanked her. With tears in her eyes, Mrs. Reynolds congratulated her and left to order her some tea and toast.

Elizabeth was determined to take things easier. It mattered not whether the menu was perfect or the flowers matching throughout the house. If the maids were arguing or the table decoration was not quite right, it did not matter. Mrs. Reynolds would assist as she had done before Elizabeth arrived, and all would be well and she would focus on taking care of the precious babe growing inside her.

She smiled as she anticipated her husband's reaction and hoped she would feel the quickening soon. It would be another few weeks but it would be worth the wait.

Elizabeth asked Hannah to begin packing for Chatsworth and after eating a bit of toast and tea, she slept, dreaming of the child and their happy family together.

Chapter 22

George Wickham lay in bed looking up at the canopy. He was frustrated and tired of his life. His dear wife had the gall to survive the pregnancy and birth a healthy, wailing daughter. The stupid chit instantly loved that baby with the wild red hair and that brat bastard would not stop crying for hours at times. It had been only two weeks since the birth and Sarah was giving all of her attention to the crying baby and he was not to have relations for yet another month.

Lacking the funds to gamble and find good entertainment, he walked over to the little cottage and paid a coin to use the town prostitute. This backwoods town of Newcastle was good for one thing. Due to its isolation, many 'ladies' were sent here in shame, like his wife, and some had no choice but to sell their bodies. With the militia assigned here last year, there were quite a number of voluptuous women selling themselves and now that the soldiers had decamped, they were even cheaper and easier.

He looked down as Millie was sucking on him again. He loved having his cock in a woman's mouth. "Oh, yes, Millie. Deep down. That feels good."

She bobbed her head up and down several times then rose. "George, how are you going to survive another month? You had better come visit me a few times a week. I will give you a discount since your cock is so good to me." And she began to ride him.

"Yes, Millie, I will come to you and come in you again and again. Oh, ride me. I want to come now." And she sat on him to ride him and soon he grunted his release. He pushed her onto her back and kissed her deeply, sticking his tongue inside her mouth. "You are delicious, my dear. I will see you next week."

He dressed and began to walk home. It was March and still freezing cold and he wondered what Georgiana was doing. He had been thinking of her more often as of late and continued his daydreams of taking her as his wife to get his hands on her dowry. The £30,000 sitting around was too tempting for him to cease coveting it. His wife was good for keeping him comfortable enough right now though and he thought to keep her on the side and the money that he was able to get from her dowry to eat and be sheltered until he could find a way to elope with Georgiana and get his hands on the dowry. He would insist on living with Georgiana at Pemberley and perhaps return to Newcastle to visit Sarah for a while. Having two wives would not be so bad – how hard could it be? He would have two women to take anytime he wanted and perhaps living in Pemberley, he could seduce the new Mrs. Darcy as well. Getting all three women with child gave him another erection.

It would be like having my own harem of beautiful women at my disposal. All the money and drinks and cunt anytime I want one. That is the way!

He entered the front door with a large protrusion in his breeches. He yelled, "Sarah! Wife! Where are you?

Sarah came rushing downstairs to shush him. "George! I just got the baby to go to sleep. You must be quiet!"

Wickham smiled and pulled her into his chest. He whispered, "Come here, wife. I know we cannot make love but I want you. Get on your knees for me and pull your breasts out."

Sarah was pleased, as her husband had not been affectionate for several weeks now and he had a look of lust in his eyes. She knelt in front of him as he unbuttoned his breeches and yanked out his large cock.

"Open your mouth," he ordered, as he was stroking himself rapidly. "I want to come in your mouth. Keep it open wide. Wider, my little slut." He continued stroking with his hand while pumping his cock in and out of her mouth, and when he was close, he placed the tip of his erection on her lower lip and grunted his release, shooting his seed to the back of her throat.

Sarah licked her lips and swallowed his semen. "Mmm. Delicious, my love." She flirted. She loved seeing him so passionate.

My little whore! Yes, I will enjoy having several women at my beck and call. He helped her stand and kissed her cheek. "Thank you, Mrs. Wickham." He led her to the couch, "I am glad the baby is sleeping. I hope you will not mind, but I just received some correspondences and will need to go to Derbyshire tomorrow. It seems my former childhood friend is in need of a clergyman and he may offer the position to me now. I believe he realises the error of not obeying his father's wishes and is regretting his earlier slight. But my love, Mr. Darcy knows you and will not accept you as my wife. If I do get the position, I would want to keep you here and would return to visit you as often as possible. It would not be a conventional marriage but I would need to live there for the parish most of the time." He rubbed her back as she began to cry.

"I do not wish for you to leave me here alone! I would rarely see you and I could not visit you there. Mr. Darcy hates me and if he knew you married me, he will not give you the living. Could you not get a different position?" She cried.

"My dear, if we had access to your dowry already, we would be set up but we cannot use it for three more years. Your father made sure that the iron-clause could not be broken. I need to work, my love. I am wasting away here and as much as I love our family," he lied, "I need to keep myself busy and be able to provide for us. We would have to work hard for less than three years, dearest, and then we can be together again after we access your dowry. I will be frugal and save all of my income and we will have the funds to live in a larger house and have more servants and," he kissed her, "more children to raise. What say you? May I please accept the position?" He looked pathetically into her eyes.

Resigned, she nodded. "Yes, my love. I know you are doing this for the good of our family. I will do my best to raise little Wendy and I hope you will write to me often and let me know how soon you will return. I am so proud of you, my husband." She kissed him.

"Thank you, my love. I will need to start packing and you need to take a rest. Thank you for being a good wife." He walked her to her room.

Wickham was prodigiously proud of the plan that he had concocted on his return from Millie's. He still had some friends left in Lambton who kept him apprised of some of Darcy's business and when he had heard that the living was once again available, he thought it a perfect opportunity to get himself near Pemberley so he could spy on the family. Darcy would be busy with spring planting and that prig would assuredly be too busy to keep a close eye on his wife and sister. With the new clergyman assignment, Darcy would be interviewing candidates and be more out of the way.

He would travel to Lambton tomorrow after a quick visit with Millie. He would not find a cheap whore in Lambton and wanted another round to fortify himself before he could get himself into Georgiana and Mrs. Darcy.

~*~

Darcy and Elizabeth rode in the carriage for the two-hour journey to Chatsworth and Darcy was excited to see his wife so animated. She had been ill again this morning and he had worried for her but she appeared to be well now and was enthusiastically asking questions about the people who would be attending the ball and what the Duke of Derbyshire was like, as she had not met so many illustrious persons before marrying Darcy.

He laughed and told her tidbits of the people he knew and explained that the Duke and Duchess were lifelong friends of his father's and that the Marquess was his university friend. He teased her that she would have been Marchioness if she had accepted Lord Harold and if his older brother died without issue and how her life would have been so different. She laughed heartily that she would have never agreed and she would most likely be living with Charlotte in a small cottage in Meryton.

Darcy kissed his wife tenderly. He knew he had won a great treasure when she agreed to marry him. Even after five months of marriage, he felt stronger for her every day.

They soon arrived at the majestic Chatsworth House and Elizabeth gawked outside the window.

"It is magnificent, Fitzwilliam. It is quite grand and the property appears beautiful. Shall we update our home to take Chatsworth for a kind of a model?" She giggled. "To be truthful, I love Pemberley. All of the grandeur here does not make it a home and my home is wherever you are, my love."

Darcy was touched and kissed his wife gently again. *I love her so much.*

"I am glad you love Pemberley as I do. Chatsworth is magnificent but it is too manicured and formal." Darcy stated.

"I agree. Pemberley is handsome and natural with no artifice. Just like its master." She kissed him on the cheek.

They saw that the Fitzwilliams had already arrived and the families greeted each other after meeting the Duke and Duchess. *My husband was right; they are wonderful people. I am glad I do not have to worry about their acceptance.* Elizabeth thought. They greeted the other guests warmly before retiring to rest before dinner.

~*~

Richard Fitzwilliam thought he was prepared. He had finally retired from over a decade of military service and was living a gentleman's life now. He had moved into Rosings Park two months ago after the new year and had kept himself very busy. He had tried to not think of Elizabeth but his mind would not allow it and he dreamt of her every night. He had surprised himself that he would feel so strongly for a woman like this, and he realised he had never been in love before. He had not bedded a woman for six months and had valiantly resisted the urge to use a whore to satisfy his cravings. He could not even think of touching another woman when Elizabeth was so centred in his heart. As the distance and time away from Elizabeth increased, he had suppressed his heart enough to think of her only every hour.

When he saw her descend the carriage, handed down by her husband, his heart skipped a beat. *She is more beautiful than I remember. One hundred thirty-two days I have been away from her. All I want to do is see her and be near her. What I would give to hold her and kiss her. How will I survive the next three weeks? Why did I agree to go to Pemberley after this ball? Because you need Darcy's help, you fool.*

After the Darcys greeted the hosts and his parents, Darcy and Elizabeth walked over and greeted him. "Richard, I am so pleased to see you!" Darcy smiled and embraced him.

Elizabeth smiled brightly at him and curtsied, "Cousin Richard! You have cut your hair. Did you save your ponytail? You look very handsome, I dare say."

He could not stop himself. He reached for her hand and kissed it, inhaling her scent. "Cousin Lizzy," he replied after a moment and slowly let go of her hand. *She thinks me handsome! Stop it, man. She is ever generous.* "Darcy, Lizzy, it is good to see you. Yes, thank you, Lizzy. I did save my hair to remind me of my former career." He smiled. "I hope you are ready to dance your feet off tomorrow! It is going to be some party!" He enthusiastically retorted as they walked toward their rooms.

Elizabeth laughed merrily and teased him. "I am afraid I will be standing on the side without a dancing partner, as I know so few people here!"

"Well, we cannot have that! May I claim the second, milady?" Richard winked. *God, I love her. I would dance every dance with her for the rest of my life if I could.*

"Certainly, sir. Thank you for your willingness to dance with me." Elizabeth beamed.

Richard watched the couple walk to their rooms arm in arm and rubbed his coat pocket where he carried the small poetry volume. The pain in his heart was back as he watched her form. *How can my heart feel this way for my cousin's wife? What is there to be done? God, I need a woman.*

He retreated to his rooms quickly to contemplate how in the world he was going to get over her once again and to suppress his physical desires after being in Elizabeth's company.

Chapter 23

Dinner at Chatsworth was wonderful. Several other guests from prestigious families arrived and intelligent conversations flowed throughout the evening. The Darcys were congratulated by many of his father's closest acquaintances and his own friends from University, and at the separation after dinner, the men discussed investments and estate management while the women gossiped and spoke of household matters. There were several women near Elizabeth's age and they became fast friends. Elizabeth had few acquaintances near Pemberley and was pleased to meet well-mannered and intelligent women whom she could befriend.

While the separation had not been long, Elizabeth felt overheated. She knew it must be her pregnancy affecting her and desired some fresh air. She asked the Duchess to be excused and began to walk towards her rooms, hoping that laying down for a few minutes would refresh her.

As she walked down the hallway, she saw that Richard was standing near the balcony door facing outside. He, with his haircut and gentlemen's clothing, looked so much like Fitzwilliam when her handsome husband would often stare out the window that she giggled loudly.

Hearing her laughter, Richard quickly turned. *I know that laughter anywhere.*

"Lizzy, what are you doing out here?" He immediately noticed that she looked pale. "Are you well?" He reached for her hand and placed it on his arm.

"Richard, I am suddenly feeling poor and wish to lay down for a while." Elizabeth responded weakly as they continued to walk towards her rooms. They turned the corner and were near her door when Elizabeth collapsed.

Richard caught her in his arms and lowered her to the floor. "Elizabeth!" He gasped. She was very pale and unconscious. He held her in one arm as he wiped the sweat from her forehead and caressed her cheek then he placed his fingers on her lip and could feel her breaths. He tenderly ran his finger against her soft lips and whispered, "My love."

He did not know what was wrong with her but he loved her with all his heart and desperately desired to kiss her. But he cared more for her comfort and his heart broke at seeing his beloved in his arms like this. He lifted her up as tears pooled in his eyes and rushed her to her room, gently laying her down as he felt her stir. Suddenly, he was pulled away from her and punched across his jaw.

~*~

Darcy had been laughing merrily with his friends when he saw Richard head out. He knew that Richard was still struggling with his feelings for Elizabeth but was determined to trust him to love her from afar since he trusted in his wife's love and was enjoying the evening immensely. Elizabeth had been very excited to arrive here and be reunited with his family, as well as to meet several friendly ladies. He had hoped that she would have the energy to accept his attentions tonight. It had been over a week since they last had relations and he was aching to be joined with her.

He wanted to see her so he looked at the Duke to see if they could return to the ladies, and the Duke quickly saw that the young man, who was so in love with his wife, desired her company. They stood and entered the drawing room and Darcy's eyes immediately scoured for the sight of his wife but she was not there. The Duchess saw his furrowed brows and quietly told him she had gone to rest a few minutes ago.

Concerned that she was ill again, he bowed and swiftly sprinted to their rooms, only to find Richard bowing over her in bed with his face near her neck. He was enraged that they were having an assignation right under his nose! Without a second thought, he grabbed his cousin and threw a solid punch across his face.

"WHAT THE HELL ARE YOU DOING, RICHARD?! How dare you betray me like this? I trusted you!" He looked at Elizabeth, whose eyes were wide open in shock. "And Elizabeth! Have you been denying me this past week so you could save yourself for him? Is that why you were so excited to come here? Had you both been planning this behind my back?" He bitterly accused.

Immediately, Elizabeth was in tears. *How can he accuse me so? I do not know what happened. How did I get to be on my bed?*

Then she was angry. She had never been so furious in her life. Her husband was accusing Richard of doing something and she had no idea what had happened. She recalled walking in the hallway with Richard helping her to her room, then nothing. *I must have fainted. This pregnancy caused me to faint and my husband is accusing me.* She took several calming breaths and slowly sat up while she watched her husband standing with his fists closed, ready to attack Richard again.

Richard sat on the floor dumbfounded, not knowing what to do. He had intended to place her on the bed and call for Darcy immediately. He knew that he had touched Elizabeth's face and held her closer than he should have, but he had no intention of harming her or doing anything inappropriate. He had been too concerned for her wellbeing that imposing on her further was the last thing on his mind but he knew Darcy's anger. He was fiercely possessive of what was his and had always been. Elizabeth was Darcy's greatest treasure and for all appearances, it might have looked as if Richard was making love to his wife. He deserved to be struck for lusting over his wife for so long but he knew he was innocent of any actual actions. *I have never seen him so angry in all of the years. What do I say to him?* He remained sitting on the ground. If he stood, Darcy would hit him again and his guilt over loving Elizabeth would not allow him to fight back.

Elizabeth stood from the bed slowly, making sure that she was no longer dizzy. She saw that the bedroom door was open and thought that surely someone must have heard Darcy shouting. To prevent unwanted ears, she gracefully walked over and closed the door.

She had never seen her husband so angry before but knew this had to be cleared up directly. Richard had cared for her and had always been a gentleman and she could not accuse him of any wrongdoing before hearing what had actually happened.

She was slightly afraid of the man before her. His eyes were raging with fury and his breathing coarse and uneven. He looked like a bull ready to charge and strike anyone in his way. She had not thought about his physique and how strong he was. He had been nothing but gentle and kind to her during the entirety of their acquaintance but he was also a tall, muscular man who was protective and insecure. Knowing that she was the first and only woman that he had ever loved, she understood the jealousy and betrayal eating away at his mind. She saw the muscles on his arms bulge and twitch and became quite aroused at the sight. *He is mine. A fool right now, but my fool.*

Quietly, she stepped in front of him. *He will not injure me. Be brave, Lizzy!* She lightly touched his powerful arm and asked, "Fitzwilliam, please look at me, my love."

His eyes were trained on Richard but slowly lowered to meet her eyes. His breathing was still ragged but he had calmed slightly.

"My dear husband, I do not know what you saw but I assure you it was innocent. I had felt unwell and Cousin Richard only escorted me to my rooms when I fainted." She decided to tell him what she knew. He had to know. "I believe I am carrying our child. I fainted because I am pregnant, Fitzwilliam. I only recognised it this morning."

Darcy's eyes grew wide at hearing her speech. *A child? Our child? My Elizabeth is carrying our child?* He was speechless. The joy that sprung in his heart was immediate. *That is why she has been ill?* He saw Richard stand up in the corner of his eye. *Oh, no! What have I done?*

Elizabeth noted his excitement and then despair in his eyes. She was getting to know his moods quite well.

Darcy stepped back and plopped onto the nearest chair and buried his face in his hands and began to despair. He sat angry with himself, reflecting on his behaviour of lashing out at the two people he loved. He had felt such joy while he spoke with his friends during the reunion, bragging about his marriage and his wonderful wife, and felt such rage when he thought his best friend was imposing on his wife. And then to hear that she was pregnant but realising of what he had accused them both brought more shame than he had ever experienced. *Will Elizabeth ever forgive me? My abominable pride! I wanted to keep what belonged to me and accused them both most unjustly. Richard needs to beat me until I am black and blue. I deserve no better.*

He felt Elizabeth touch his hands to pull them away from his face. He raised his head to find her grab his hand and wrap it around her as she sat on his lap.

"Husband, we have a long night ahead of us to talk, but I think we owe it to Richard to hear him out. Will you do so now?" She softly asked. She eyed Richard to take a seat across from them.

Darcy lifted his head toward Richard and his eyes pleaded for kindness. He hoped Richard would tell him the truth and that nothing really happened.

Richard had wanted to escape and get on his horse back to Matlock, no matter the hour. He could not stand to be in this room where Darcy believed to have been betrayed. But he owed it to them to know what had happened since Elizabeth would not know when she was unconscious. He had been shocked to hear that Elizabeth was with child but it should not have been a surprise. From the way they looked at each other so often, he was certain they had frequent relations and to hear Darcy say that he had been one week without, he knew he himself would die without her touch for so long if she were his own wife.

Clearing his throat, "Darcy, I left the dining room to get some air, as you saw, and I was standing by the balcony door when I saw El... Lizzy exit the drawing room. She looked very pale and was moving slowly to her rooms so I offered my arm to escort her. She collapsed and I caught her, Darcy. After checking that she was still breathing, I carried her here to her room. My intent was to put her on the bed and call for you immediately but you had entered as I was laying her down and although it may have... appeared that I... was not behaving gentlemanly, I swear to you that my intention was to ensure her safety and get you straight-away. I swear to you, Darcy, nothing happened. I... I may have wanted... Even if I wanted to, I could not dishonour her nor you."

Darcy kissed his wife's temple and stood up. He walked the short distance to Richard and stood in front of him. Richard stood as well now, uncertain if he would receive another punch or a hug.

"Richard, I apologise from the bottom of my heart. I trusted you all of my life and should have trusted you again but in my arrogance and jealousy, I jumped to a conclusion that was false and I have wounded you. I know you have loved her for nearly as long as I have loved her and you are an honourable man. I am constantly worried that Elizabeth will finally figure out what a wretched creature I am and regret her choice. Please forgive me for not trusting you, Richard. I do not wish to lose your friendship and I know Elizabeth cares for you as well." Darcy pleaded. Other than Elizabeth and Georgiana, Richard was one of the most important allies in his life and he had meant every word. He had always feared that Elizabeth would regret him. All the wealth and status in the world would not impress her and here, he had shown his worst. He would have a lot of grovelling to do. To his wife and to his cousin.

Richard grabbed his cousin and hugged him tightly. They had grown up together, laughing and fighting like brothers, but always knew that they would watch out for each other. He knew that Darcy had been very lonely for so long and after finding Elizabeth, he had made a great concession to allow him to love her and still be a part of their lives. He was a good man and worthy of Elizabeth's love.

"As long as you do not hit me again, Darce, there is nothing to forgive. I promise, I swear to you, I will protect you both with my life and never lose your trust." Richard vowed.

The three had tears in their eyes at the reconciliation and Richard cleared his throat and continued, "Well, I believe you have some tongue-lashing coming your way, Darcy. I will leave you to it." He tapped Darcy's shoulder.

He walked to Elizabeth, who was now standing, and he could not help himself as she smiled softly at him. He leaned forward and kissed her cheek. He revelled at the closeness as he inhaled her scent. "Eli... Lizzy, I congratulate you. Please take good care of yourself and only faint when your husband is nearby." He returned her smile softly.

Elizabeth lifted her hand to gently caress Richard's jaw where Darcy had struck, then embraced him. "Thank you for your care, Richard." *If I could choose an older brother, Richard would be my first choice. He is so kind to me.* He was such a dear friend and she felt awful that her husband had violently struck him. She had known Richard had treated her with the utmost respect and care, and she loved him like a brother.

Richard's heart quivered as she wrapped her arms around his waist and he held her around his arms for several precious seconds. *I love her so much. She is affectionate without guile and I do not know how I will live without her.*

"Good night, dearest." Richard whispered, and quickly left.

~*~

Darcy paced to the window while Richard was speaking with Elizabeth as he wanted to give them a moment of privacy as a part of his apology. He had felt like a cad and did not know how much grovelling would be enough. He thought of purchasing her the largest diamond ring he could find or building her another conservatory to plant her favourite fruits or bringing the most exclusive modiste from London to make her a new closet of dresses. No, she would not be impressed by that. She was a woman worthy of pleasing and he had done the exact opposite. He had accused her of holding her favours for a week so she could carry out an affair with his dearest cousin; he had yelled at her for being excited to come to Chatsworth when he had begged her for the excursion so he could meet his friends; he had been utterly unfair and completely unjust.

After hearing the door close, he turned to see Elizabeth sitting on the chair where he had been. He gulped down his pride and ran to her, falling at her feet with his head on her lap.

"Elizabeth, my love. I... I have no excuse. I cannot believe what I said to you. I am so sorry. So, so very sorry, my love. I do not deserve you. I love you so much and I know you love me but I constantly fear that you would regret me and fear that I will return to my old stiff self and you would no longer want me. You are so beautiful and perfect for me and have made my life so good and I do not know what I would do if you left me. You do not care about fortune or the large house or my connections and when I saw Richard over you, I was overcome with jealousy that I went insane for a moment. He is a good man and I worried that you would prefer him over me and I did not even realise that you were ill tonight. I am so sorry, Elizabeth..." He buried his teary face on her lap.

Elizabeth stroked his hair. He had rambled on but she had heard his fears. How he could still be so insecure after five months, she could not believe, but then quickly comprehended that both of his parents had died early and he had to take so much on his shoulders to manage his massive responsibilities. He cared for his sister like a father and his childhood friend Wickham had betrayed him by attempting to elope with Georgiana. His own aunt had plagued him towards an unhappy reunion and the women of society had been relentless in their chase. Some of her new friends tonight had shared how much her husband had been pursued.

He had only two gentlemen, one of whom was Mr. Bingley, who was too busy courting Jane, and then Richard, who was his closest friend but saw as a threat. *I like Richard but I do not love him like a husband. How do I make Fitzwilliam understand how much I love him?*

"Fitzwilliam, would you please answer truthfully for me? Would you ever come to regret me?" She asked delicately.

His head sprung up and he yelled, "NO! Never! I love you, Elizabeth. You are the best thing in my life."

Elizabeth tenderly caressed his cheek with one hand. "I love you, too. I love you as you love me and I think I might be in danger of my loving you too much. I have never felt such a pull, such affection and care from another human being before and I had thought I had gone insane to accept your courtship after one evening but when I accepted your proposal only the day after, I knew I loved you too much to not be your wife. As certain you are that you would never regret me, please believe me when I tell you that I would never regret you. You are my life, Fitzwilliam, and none other will ever take your place."

Elizabeth shrieked as he stood up quickly and lifted her up and kissed her fervently. His lips were reassurances of his eternal love, his tongue vowing to trust her, and his hands were all over her, promising to protect her and keep her safe. He lifted her up and carried her to the bed and laid her down gently. He kissed her lips and drew down to her abdomen and kissed it.

"Hello, my child. I do not know you yet but I love you. I will try my best to be a good father to you. I will make mistakes and be a complete arse at times but I promise to care for you and love your mother deeply and teach you to be a good person." He kissed again.

Elizabeth cried at the tenderness. He was truly the best of men.

As he lay next to her and saw her tears, he wiped them with his thumbs and kissed her lips again. "I love you, Elizabeth. I am sorry to make you cry. I hope you will forgive me." His voice broke.

"These are tears of joy, my love. There is nothing to forgive. I will tell you every day how much I love you and we will argue and get angry with each other but we will kiss and make love and learn from each other. Is that a deal?" She smiled. "I would like to kiss and make love since we already argued. What say you, sir?"

Darcy was immediately over her and began to kiss her neck but suddenly stopped. "But you are with child. Are we not supposed to cease relations? How am I going to live without joining with you for the next... how many months, Elizabeth?"

She laughed jovially. "Mrs. Reynolds expects late September. And no, we do not have to cease relations. I asked her the same as well. We may love each other for as long as we are comfortable. I am certain we might have to join in some undignified positions but as long as you do not tell anyone, I am willing to bear it." She laughed again.

"Minx! I will not waste one minute of delaying your wishes, madam." And he kissed her passionately while he lifted up her skirts.

She could feel the instant hardness against her womanhood and after helping him expose herself and he was promptly inside her, she moaned out loudly. *It has been too long. He feels so good inside me.*

Darcy was careful to not put too much pressure on her but he could not hold back and began to thrust hard and fast. Truly, one week had been too long. He moaned as her hands massaged his hair and he whispered, "I love you," before releasing his seed.

Darcy lay panting next to her after immediately removing his weight off of her. "How is it possible that I had waited twenty-seven years without having sexual relations, quite peacefully, mind you, and after marrying you, I cannot go for a week without exploding like this? That was probably the worst performance of my life! I came too quick!!" He chuckled.

Elizabeth giggled at this. "I do not think it was so bad. You did what you needed to get done, sir. I certainly hope I can entertain you again later!" Quieter, she said, "I am sorry that I had been so unavailable to you, Fitzwilliam. It was not intentional and certainly no nefarious motive behind it. I had been exhaust..."

Darcy quickly quieted her with a kiss. "No, my love. I should have been more patient. I never wish for you to oblige me out of duty. I love you. I enjoy your body but I respect you too much to take what I need for my selfishness. I would have taken you while you slept if I did not care but it is for both of us. I love making love with you, not *at* you." He kissed her again. His kiss grew deeper. "It appears I am needing a second serving. With your permission, milady?"

Elizabeth's laughter tinkled in the air. "Granted, kind sir."

And he lay on top of her and entered again, this time making love to her slowly and reverently until she achieved her climax twice before spending.

He helped her undress afterwards and they climbed under the counterpane. They held each other tightly and slept, awaking to make love once more during the night.

~*~

After leaving the Darcys, Richard walked to the drawing room, just in case the argument was heard. He was thankful that the footmen who were usually stationed around the bedrooms were busy with the task of setting up for the next day's ball, as a large party was expected and all hands were needed to prepare for the guests. He looked at himself in the mirror and saw that his jaw was turning an ugly red. His skin tingled but he knew it was from Elizabeth's touch rather than Darcy's assault. He felt no pain; rather he felt pleasure from where her fingers grazed him. *I would take a hundred strikes if only to have her touch me again.* He sighed.

He knew the bruise would be forming darker and he would have to come up with some story. Who knew his cousin could still pack such a punch? But the fury in Darcy's eyes was obvious. *He would have killed me with his bare hands if he caught me doing something worse. And with his anger, he would have succeeded no matter how much I fought back.*

He shuddered at the thought. He had always been the stronger one as he was two years older than Darcy, but he had seen the smallest of soldiers fend for their lives on the battlefield and such a rage was deadly.

Richard entered the drawing room and told his parents that Elizabeth had taken ill and that he had been assisting Darcy. His parents looked at his jaw wondering if the boys had been fighting but he quickly told the group that Elizabeth had fainted and, in his rush to open the door for Darcy, he had run into the door face first. They laughed as he told them of his stumbling attempts to be of service to his cousins and with all the reported valour on the battlefield, he had panicked and was a fumbling idiot when a lady needed him.

He did not care that he was making a fool of himself and was pleased that they all believed him. He excused himself soon after, telling them that he had better put some cold cloth on his jaw so he would be presentable tomorrow and not look like he was some ruffian in a tavern fight, and retired to his rooms.

His bedroom was placed two doors down from Elizabeth's and only out of curiosity, he paused near her door to see if he could hear her tongue-lashing. He grinned knowing that Elizabeth was the one and only person that Darcy would get an earful from, but Richard knew he enjoyed it. He could hear them talking, although not clearly, but when it ceased, he wondered if they were upset with each other. But soon, he heard soft moans and then the undeniable noises of the bed creaking indicating that they were having intercourse. *Damn lucky, that Darcy. She forgives too easily.* He grinned. *Of course, she does. She is generous.* He looked down. *Again?* His erection was quite pronounced by now and he retreated to his rooms quietly and pulled down his breeches to tug at it and soon found relief.

"I need a wife!" He exclaimed. "My OWN wife!" And he threw himself on the bed and slept.

~*~

The next day's events proceeded smoothly. Richard had told Darcy what explanation he gave to the guests and there was nothing to be done about it.

It was announced that it was suspected that Mrs. Darcy was with child and everyone toasted their congratulations. Richard joked a few more times about running into the door as his bruise was dark and quite evident, and Darcy patted him on the shoulder as a silent apology once again.

The ball went off without a hitch and Darcy danced nearly every set, three with his wife and the rest with his family and his friends' wives. Elizabeth danced every set and while she danced the second with Richard, she thanked him for his assistance and for his care. She reminded him that she truly appreciated their friendship and for not damaging her husband's handsome face. Richard burst out laughing and several eyes turned toward them, but they continued their banter, jesting and laughing again. When Richard returned Elizabeth to Darcy, he told him of their conversation and Darcy loudly laughed as well. Although the guests at the ball had seen Mr. Darcy smiling and more pleasant than he had ever been in public, hearing him laugh like that had confirmed that he had married for love, that his wife did not entrap him and that he was blissfully happy with her.

Lord and Lady Matlock were pleased to see the three sharing a joke. They had been concerned that Richard might be in love with Elizabeth and that he and Darcy might have gotten into a row last night, but seeing them converse and giggle like schoolboys ensured them that all was well.

After the Ball was enjoyed by all, the Darcys heartily thanked the Duke and Duchess and hugged their friends with promises of correspondences and returned to Pemberley with Richard joining them.

Chapter 24

"Richard! It is so good to see you again! Lizzy! You are back!" Georgiana flew down the stairs to greet her cousin and her sister.

"And what am I, chopped liver?" Darcy pouted in jest. It pleased him to no end to see his sister so lively and happy.

"Oh, brother, welcome back as well. I missed you!" Georgiana kissed his cheek. "Lizzy, you must tell me all about the ball! Who did you see? How are their Graces? Their daughter Isabelle is a particular friend of mine; she is in London with her companion right now and I am certain she would have been excited for the ball at her home if she were attending. Did you meet many amiable ladies?" She threw her questions at Elizabeth as she grabbed her arm and they walked inside quickly.

"Darcy, I would not recognise Georgiana if it did not happen in front of my eyes. She is so energetic and cheerful now." Richard commented in awe.

"Yes, it is all Elizabeth's doing. I could not have asked for a better wife." Turning to Richard, "I am sure you will find someone, Richard; someone who will make you happy."

"I hope so, Darce," Richard whispered quieter, "though I doubt it very much." *I know I will never love another.*

~*~

Wickham watched them from the edge of the park. He had snuck into Pemberley Park and he knew where all the hiding spots were. He could watch the front door of the mansion from behind this tree trunk and none would be the wiser. He saw the carriage arrive and was surprised to see Georgiana springing down the steps. She had grown taller and prettier. Now sixteen, she would be a fine filly to tame.

When the carriage door opened, he saw Richard exit. *Blast it, that puts a kink in my plans. He is not going to be easy to fool.* Darcy then exited. *Bastard. I hate you, Darcy, looking so smug as if he owned the place. Damn it, he does own the place. Hopefully not too long. After I marry Georgiana, I will kill him and become master of Pemberley. But wait, who is that woman?*

He saw a petite brunette exit, handed down by Darcy. *Bloody hell! Is that his new wife? She is gorgeous. Look at her smile and her eyes! She definitely has a woman's curves. Georgiana is a stick compared to her. Wow, he must be fucking her often. I would be. Damn, my cock is stiff to take her.*

Wickham eyed the four as they enthusiastically greeted each other. He hid in the shadows as they entered the house. *Hmm... How can I draw the women out of the house? I will return early in the morning. I will need to monitor their habits and see if I can get one or both of the ladies alone for my pleasures. Delicious, that Mrs. Darcy. I could suckle those breasts like a baby. Fuck! I am going to unload now.*

He stood behind the large tree trunk and masturbated right then. *Fucking Darcy! I am going to give it to your wife hard and she is going to scream for more.* The thought of getting his cock inside the beautiful brunette against her will made him more aroused and he came hard on the trunk. After buttoning up, he left to return to the small abandoned shed, located only a mile out, to plan his attack.

~*~

Richard dove into learning all he could during the next two weeks. Darcy was an astonishing master with a talent for keeping all of his businesses well organised. He was impressed with his cousin's methods and recordkeeping, as well as his fair judgment of the tenants' needs. He saw to endless correspondences diligently but also involved his steward to many of the tasks that were minor. Darcy had confessed that he had seen to all of his work and had begun to neglect his wife, which had resulted in a week of frustration and the misunderstanding at Chatsworth. Darcy was determined to let some of the oversight be managed by the people that he had hired to do so, in order that he could attend to his wife and sister and spend time with them. What good was £45,000 a year if he could not enjoy time with his family?

Elizabeth had been ill during the mornings again but she had been much improved and took frequent mid-day naps. Darcy joined her on those naps and Richard suspected that they were doing more than sleeping.

Richard had become more comfortable around Elizabeth during these few weeks. In the past, his conversation would be stilted at times or he could not get past staring at her and wishing for her attention, but now, he was able to speak more freely with her, getting to know her mind and appreciating her intelligence and knowledge. *No wonder Darcy jumped to propose. He would have been a fool to delay asking for her hand and he is no fool.*

He knew he was completely and wholeheartedly in love with Elizabeth and desired only her. Every moment spent in her presence was precious to him, and every smile, every twinkle in her eyes, he would treasure in his heart. He was grateful that she was ever gracious, talking to him as a good friend and opening herself up to him, and he knew she cared for him, as she paid attention to his likes and preferences. Being with her was as simple as breathing. Wherever she was, he wished to be also.

He had to pause to settle his desires often in her company while they conversed and she smiled or laughed at his stories, but he was determined to love her as a cousin and learn about what he wanted from a wife. He wanted Elizabeth, but he would have to settle for someone *like* Elizabeth. *I would be content to live out the rest of my life in her presence and receive her smiles,* Richard thought, as his heart continued to ache for her.

~*~

Darcy sat with Elizabeth in the drawing room, catching up on his reading while his beautiful wife rested next to him. He glanced over and smiled, as she would fall asleep repeatedly, only to startle and wake herself up several times. He kissed her cheek and asked her, "Why do you not rest in our bed, my love? Our babe needs a nap, I think."

"Oh, Fitzwilliam, I fall asleep everywhere and I already had a good nap. I think I need to stand and refresh myself." Elizabeth laughed. Darcy helped her to stand. "Oh, I believe I left my book next to my bed on the table. I would like to read with you. Would you be so kind as to ask Bill to get it for me?" Elizabeth asked, knowing that the footman was outside the door.

"I will fetch it for you, milady. I do not mind being your humble servant." Darcy answered, flashing his broad smile. "I will also bring your favourite wrap in case you would like another nap later on." He winked.

Darcy quickly stepped up the stairs and headed to his bedroom. He and Elizabeth had spent every night in the same bed and the Mistress' bedroom was used mainly as a sitting room now. As he approached his room, he heard sounds in the dressing room where Wilkins would normally work. Hearing more than one voice and the muffled sounds of a woman, he was curious to what might be happening and opened the door, only to find Wilkins and Hannah in a passionate embrace with Wilkins laying over her and his bare buttocks pumping away between her legs. Hannah was completely naked and moaning loudly, oblivious to the audience in the dressing room, but Wilkins turned his head and saw his employer staring at him.

In shock, Wilkins flew off of his lover and threw Mr. Darcy's jacket over her while he stood up to apologise.

"Mr. Darcy... I... I am so sorry... I..." Wilkins started, as he hastily pulled up his breeches.

Hannah, realising that the Master had found them in a scandalous position, let out a cry and gathered her clothes to run out to the hallway to return to the Mistress' dressing room.

Darcy tried to calm her but she ran off quickly before he could speak to her. *I will have to let Elizabeth deal with her!* He internally laughed.

Wilkins was pale and silent now. He knew he would be let go and regretted that he had such little self-control but he had been in love with Hannah for several months and they had finally succumbed to their passions today.

Darcy had turned around to give his valet a moment to dress himself and when Wilkins coughed, he turned to face him.

"So, how long have you and she...?" He asked, smiling. It was fascinating to see his usually stoic valet be completely flustered.

Wilkins answered, "This was the first and only time, sir. I... I have loved her for a very long time and I did not... we lost ourselves... I am so very sorry. I understand you will want to release me from your service..."

"Wilkins, Wilkins!" Darcy interrupted. "James, you have been with me far too long and you know me well. If this had happened before I married, I might have released you on the spot, but after meeting Mrs. Darcy and how you had saved me from Caroline Bingley's compromise, I have a better understanding of how passions run deep and I owe you a debt of gratitude. As long as it does not happen in our rooms and you are cautious, both of your positions are safe. Do you wish to marry her? I would be happy to see you settled down after all these years, my friend."

Wilkins was visibly relieved. He let out a breath he was holding and bowed to his master. "I do wish to marry her, sir. Thank you so much for your understanding and forgiveness, Mr. Darcy. You are a kind master and I should have approached you first of our situation. I will ask her to marry me today. Thank you, sir. Thank you so much."

He bowed and left the room immediately to find Hannah to propose and to let her know that their positions would be safe.

~*~

Richard had returned from riding Xerxes after luncheon and went to his rooms to change his clothing. He felt refreshed, getting some of his pent-up energy worked outside, and stepped out of his rooms to look for Elizabeth as his wont, when he noticed Hannah, wearing nothing but one of Darcy's jackets and her clothes bundled in her arms, running out of Darcy's rooms.

He closed his door to ponder what he just witnessed and opened the door a few minutes later to spy out into the hallway. He grew red when he saw Darcy exiting the room with a big smile. *Was Darcy fucking Elizabeth's maid? In their own rooms?* He knew they slept together in the same bed and mostly used Darcy's rooms.

In rage, Richard grabbed Darcy in the hallway and dragged him quickly into his own room, which was located across.

Richard threw Darcy to the ground then closed his door. His fists were tight and he wanted to kill his cousin for betraying Elizabeth.

"HOW COULD YOU, DARCY?!" Richard yelled. Darcy was dazed but as he began to stand up, Richard gripped him by the collars and shook him. Unable to contain his anger, Richard struck Darcy in the stomach. "I thought you loved her. You would put her aside for a piece of skirt?" He punched him again. "I would give *everything* to be with her and you throw it away like this? It will break her heart, you bastard!"

Darcy did not know why his cousin was beating him but he recovered enough to block the third attack that Richard was throwing and returned his own punches, striking Richard on his jaw and pushing him down and away from himself. They both plopped down gasping for air, sitting several feet away from each other, waiting to see what the other would do.

"What the hell are you speaking of, Richard? What piece of skirt? What do you think I have done?" Darcy asked between huffs of air.

"I saw Hannah come out of your room naked, Darcy. Do not try to hide it. I know what I saw. You came out several minutes later with a large grin as if anyone could ever be better than Elizabeth. How could you betray her? She loves you! I would give my life for her love and you are throwing her away!" Richard yelled. "I thought better of you, Darcy. Damn you! You do not deserve her. I hate you for hurting her."

Darcy laughed loudly. "Damn it, Richard! Do you trust me so little? Elizabeth is my life. I would never hurt her." He laughed again.

Richard sat confused when his door suddenly burst open and Elizabeth walked in with her book and wrap in her hands.

Elizabeth surveyed the men and realised they had gotten into a row once again. They were sitting on the ground apart from each other, both of their coats torn at the shoulders and still puffing for breath.

"What has happened? Why have you been fighting? I was waiting for my book and wrap but it took so long that I came up to see what happened to you, Fitzwilliam, only to find them in front of Richard's door and you gentlemen on the floor here. What happened?"

Elizabeth rushed over to Darcy, who was standing up now, groaning and holding his stomach. "Are you well? What has your brute of a cousin done to you?"

Darcy pouted. "He hit me twice. It hurts, Elizabeth." Indeed, it was painful but Darcy played for her sympathy, now understanding why Richard was so furious. He found the situation ridiculous but quickly understood that if the shoes were reversed and Richard was cheating on Elizabeth, he would have murdered him.

"Oh, you poor man." Elizabeth kissed Darcy's cheek. Turning, she fumed at Richard, "What do you have to say for yourself, Richard?" She walked over to Richard who was now standing. Seeing blood dripping out from his lips, she quickly pulled out her handkerchief from her sleeve and dabbed his mouth. "Fitzwilliam! You hurt Richard! On his jaw again, too! Oh, you poor dear. Are you all right?" She cradled Richard's face and caressed his cheek in concern as he touched her hand and took over holding the handkerchief. She pulled both men to Richard's couch and sat them down.

Elizabeth stood in front of them both and demanded, "Well, speak! Since you have a smile on your face, Mr. Darcy, I think you had better go first."

Darcy grinned even broader. "I think Richard is going to owe me a bottle of brandy after this. I was very innocent, fetching your book and wrap, when Richard grabbed me and began to beat me up. I did not do anything wrong but he was so angry." He paused to look at Richard's face. He knew he was taunting his cousin but he would have some fun. "He hit me so I had to defend myself, Elizabeth. I did nothing wrong."

Elizabeth arched her brow. She looked at Richard and asked, "And why would you suddenly attack your cousin? What had Fitzwilliam done to incur your wrath?"

Richard did not know what to say. It was not his place to speak of Darcy's infidelity nor did he wish to wound her. He was not so certain of what he saw now either, as he saw Darcy's glint of mischief in his eyes.

"I... I think you should ask Darcy. He seems to know everything going on. I... I think... I hope... it was a misunderstanding." Richard finally answered.

Elizabeth, by now, knew that her husband was playing a joke on them both. She raised her hands to her hips and tapped her foot, giving him a stare to confess it all.

Darcy laughed and stood. He grunted as his stomach did indeed hurt, but he pecked a kiss on Elizabeth's cheek and led her to sit as he told his story.

"All right, all right. I will tell all. I was fetching your book and wrap when I heard noises in my dressing room, Elizabeth, and I unfortunately stepped in to witness Wilkins and Hannah in an... intimate... situation. They are to be married and I gave them my approval to do so. Hannah had already run off and I suppose that is what Richard saw. When I came out a few minutes later after speaking with Wilkins, Richard thought *I* was having a liaison with Hannah and attacked me. Like I said, I was *completely* innocent and was beat up for no reason at all." Darcy grinned broadly again. *Richard owes me!*

Elizabeth turned to Richard, who was sitting next to her, and asked, "Why did you jump to the wrong conclusion so quickly? How could you trust your cousin so little?" She watched him closely, as he was flushed red with embarrassment. She saw his eyes finally meet hers and quickly realised that he was fighting for her honour. *Oh, now I understand. He would have killed my husband if he were indeed cheating on me. He was championing me like a brother would because he loves me. I appreciate his care for me so much! He is such a good man.*

She smiled at Richard and he returned it. She reached for his hand and raised it to her lips and kissed his knuckles.

Richard was grateful that he did not need to explain. He had been mortified that he had jumped to the wrong conclusion so quickly but he loved her with all of his heart and could not imagine spurning her for anything in the world. *God, I love her so much. She is most precious. I should have asked Darcy first but I acted irrationally and threw my blows instead. I will have to buy him a bottle of brandy!*

He watched her lips on his hand then grabbed hers and kissed it in return. All of his fury had melted as soon as she had touched his jaw earlier and her tender kiss now soothed his soul. "I apologise for jumping to the wrong conclusion. Thank you for your understanding, El... Lizzy. Darcy, you will have your bottle of brandy. I will get you two. I am sorry, cousin. I should have known better than to believe you to be dishonourable. I know you love Lizzy dearly but I was not thinking straight." He coughed. "Now, if you will excuse me, I will need to change my coat again."

Richard quickly arose and headed into his dressing room when he realised he was still holding Elizabeth's handkerchief in his hand. He thought to return it to her but he could not. It was hers and it was a precious token to him. He pocketed it into his waistcoat and asked Garrison for a new coat after washing the blood off of his face.

Darcy smiled watching the interaction. He knew Richard would do anything for Elizabeth and was pleased that she was loved and cared for. Elizabeth had told him how much she saw him like an older brother.

Elizabeth and Darcy stood and walked to their rooms, with Elizabeth promising to soothe his aches. "I think I do need that nap now, my dear husband. You should rest your weary body as well. After the tussle you just went through, perhaps I can comfort you now, completely naked." Elizabeth whispered in his ear as she stood between his legs while he sat on the edge of the bed.

"Oh, yes. I will need a lot of soothing. Richard has quite a fist on him. I could have died!" Darcy quipped. *He would have killed me if he found me with another woman. He is so protective of Elizabeth but I would be exactly the same. I would never give up my wonderful wife. She is truly the best thing in my life!*

The next morning, Richard rose at his usual time and decided to go for an early ride. He was still quite embarrassed that he fought like a schoolboy with Darcy over the misunderstanding but was glad that Darcy had not been unfaithful. He could not imagine that he would ever stop loving Elizabeth and now knew that Darcy would not either.

Since Elizabeth's pregnancy, Darcy declined to ride Xerxes but walked the park with Elizabeth. They strode out after breakfast every morning for the past two weeks and Richard had taken Xerxes to exercise him at different times of the day.

Anticipating a good ride this morning, Richard waved to Darcy and Elizabeth as he saw them near the edge of the park. He raced towards his favourite spot where they had spent their youth. It had been ages since he had been there and he had fond memories of spending the night there, watching the stars with Darcy, Albert, and Wickham. He had a bitter taste in his mouth as he remembered George Wickham but shook off the thought and rode hard and fast.

When he approached the small clearing, he smiled as he recollected climbing the large trees and fishing in the nearby pond. He truly appreciated his family. Coming upon the shed, he saw that there appeared to be a light inside. *I thought this was abandoned! Darcy said nothing about anyone living here.*

He carefully approached the shed after tying up Xerxes several yards away. It could be a simple vagrant or poachers, he did not know. As he neared the small window, he peeked inside. It was a one-room shed with two beds and a table and a fireplace. It had been used primarily for hunting and as boys, they had all crammed upon the two beds to sleep and play in there. Seeing no signs of activity, he opened the door quietly to investigate. *I wish I still had my sword!*

He entered and saw the candle still burning but no one was within. There were a few items of clothing on the bed and some morsels of bread along with pieces of dry meats. It smelled as if someone recently slept there and he saw some scattered papers on the table. He looked through them and the top ones were blank but there was writing on a few of the bottom, as if they were practicing a letter. He read a few lines and bolted out, running to Xerxes and riding toward Pemberley as if the devil himself were chasing him.

Darcy was enjoying his walk with his wife. She had been feeling better this past week and she had gifted him with an unexpected surprise this morning. They had continued to make love in the evenings, sometimes during the daytime naps, as she felt the most energetic then, but this morning, she had awoken particularly aroused and decided to awaken him in her own way.

As Darcy began to stir, he felt warmth on his manhood and his wife's hand on his morning arousal. He turned onto his back, hoping that his wife would sit on him as she had done several times but his eyes opened shockingly as he felt her mouth on his erection. He looked down to see her bent with her tongue gliding down his shaft and licking the bulb of his penis while stroking the shaft with her small hand. He had never felt so aroused in his life as he watched his wife take his long cock into his mouth and began to suck. His breathing became uneven and rushed and he thought he would faint. "El-li-za-beth... what... are... you... doing... to... me..." He barely groaned out.

She lifted her head, "I want to pleasure you, my love," she licked the tip again, "since you are so good at pleasuring me," she sucked then licked down his shaft, "I want to return the favour." And she began to bob her head up and down again.

"Ah, oh! Elizabeth! I am going to burst!" Darcy pleaded as he attempted to lift her head off his cock but she began to suck harder and he shot with a loud grunt, as he released his seed in her mouth. He panted and huffed, as he had never expected such pleasure. He had read about it and had wondered how it felt but thought that only the prostitutes would do such a thing to prevent a pregnancy. Having his wife perform the service was the second greatest gift he had ever received; second only to her marrying him.

Elizabeth rose and licked her lips. She wiped her mouth with the sheet and said, "A bit salty but not unpleasant. I think I shall enjoy doing that again for you sometime, my love."

Darcy immediately grabbed her and held her tightly. "I am willing to accept any gift you will bestow on me, my love. That was wonderful. I loved being inside you. I love you. I do not believe I can ever look at your mouth the same. Wow. Where in the world did you learn to do that?" He kissed her hair and her temples and cheeks and lips several times in reverence.

"Well, you do have a magnificent library, my love. I came across a book on the high shelves yesterday and wanted to see your reaction. I am so pleased with the result of my extensive reading!" She merrily laughed.

Now, as they walked the three-mile park track, they spoke of names for their baby and if they preferred a boy first or a girl first. Darcy had made it clear that there was no entailment and that she need not be afraid, whether they had a household full of girls or none at all. He wanted to make sure she did not feel any pressure and to only take care of herself.

As they turned the corner where several large tree trunks were placed, Elizabeth screamed as Darcy was struck from behind with a large branch. He was hit on the head and was immediately knocked out.

She felt herself being pulled and saw a dishevelled man whom she recognised immediately from a painting at Pemberley. George Wickham was on their property and had just assaulted Fitzwilliam and was now grabbing at her. She screamed at the top of her lungs again, only to have her mouth covered with his filthy hand. He drew her close to his body, her back touching his chest.

"Ah, Mrs. Darcy. George Wickham at your service. I have been waiting for two weeks to get you alone and I will make sure to take my time with you." He began to fondle her breast and trailed his hand down to her abdomen and rubbed her womanhood over her dress.

Elizabeth frantically shook her head but could not speak as her mouth was still muffled.

"I had wanted to snatch Georgiana so I could force her to elope with me but then I saw you and wanted you. Do you feel my hard cock? I am so horny for you. I am going to tie you up first and then tie up your Darcy. He can watch us fuck." He laughed villainously. "I will take you to my hideout and ravage you repeatedly until he pays me every farthing of what is owed to me. I will come back for the little prissy Georgiana later. You will never get rid of me. I will get my revenge on Darcy through his women and get rich off him as well!"

Wickham continued to laugh as he bound her hands and when she struggled, he slapped her across the cheek. Dazed, Elizabeth's head rang while he finished tying her wrists and sat her against the tree trunk. He began to bind Darcy's hands when thunderous stampings of a horse were heard and Wickham saw Colonel Fitzwilliam nearly upon him.

Wickham quickly ran to Elizabeth and stood her up, placing her in front of him to shield himself and pulled out his knife, pointing the tip towards her neck.

"WICKHAM! You treacherous bastard! Release her!!" Richard shouted. He saw Darcy on the ground on his stomach but saw his arms twitch. Darcy would awaken soon.

"Fitz! Why the fuck are you out here? I had not seen you in the mornings. I was just introducing myself to the lovely Mrs. Darcy and getting a taste. She is quite sumptuous." Wickham gloated as he licked the left side of her neck.

Richard was immediately off the horse and began to approach slowly. Wickham had his knife on her and he could not take the chance of her being harmed. He attempted to calm himself but burned with fury as he saw her reddened cheek. "Wickham, it is over. Let her go and run away. I swear to you I will not chase you today and you might find your freedom. LET HER GO!"

"I plan on taking her with me, Fitzy! I want to ravish her and show her what it feels like to be filled by a *real* man." Wickham sneered. "I want what should have been mine. Darcy will hand over Georgiana's dowry or else the same thing will happen to his *dear* sister. I will punish him until the day he dies and I will NEVER stop haunting him." He continued as if mad and rambled on. "He should have let me marry Georgiana. My wife had Bingley's bastard and she is only good for fucking and I am so sick and tired of being poor while Darcy gloats in his wealth and is happy with this pretty thing." He leaned at Elizabeth's ear, "You will be screaming as I drill into you." He dug his finger between her legs to rub her core then grabbed Elizabeth's right breast and groped it roughly. "Such nice teats."

Elizabeth could feel his erection on her buttocks. This man was mad! Her hands were still bound in front of her but her legs were free. She saw that Darcy was stirring and Richard looked frightened for her. She knew she had to get away from Wickham's grasp.

She turned head slightly to be able to look at Wickham. His eyes were red with madness. He was truly insane. She also saw the lust in his eyes and seductively spoke to the crazy man.

"Mr. Wickham, I am pleased that you are enjoying my body," she smiled, swallowing down the bile in her throat. "I am certain your manhood is significant and *quite* pleasurable." She raised her eyebrow in flirtation.

Having this beautiful woman flirt with him had been unexpected and Wickham was flattered. He lowered his knife from her neck and turned her around so he could kiss her. Suddenly, he was kneed hard in the groin and as he was falling down, his shin was kicked. He still had his knife close to her and he sliced her as he fell, cutting Elizabeth's left thigh.

Elizabeth cried out as she felt the severe pain on her leg but was able to hop away several steps where Richard caught her.

As Wickham landed on his knees after the excruciating pain in his groin, he was knocked down by Darcy who had regained his wits by now. The knife dropped to the ground and Darcy was on him, as he punched blow after blow onto Wickham's face. He held Wickham by the throat, ready to squeeze the life out of him.

Darcy yelled, "RICHARD! IS SHE WELL?" He was close to killing his childhood friend for the harm he had caused.

Richard replied, "I have her, Darcy! She is bleeding and we need to get help!" Richard was frantic as Elizabeth was cradled in his arms. She had blood pooling on her dress and it was soaking up the material quickly. Richard worriedly lifted her skirt up to her thigh to find the injury, took off his cravat and began to bind the wound after laying her on the ground gently.

Elizabeth was too concerned for her husband to care about herself. She turned her head to see Darcy on top of Wickham. He was awake and appeared to be well. She sighed a breath of relief. She felt dizzy and could feel herself losing consciousness. "Fitzwilliam..." she whispered before everything went dark.

Richard screamed, "ELIZABETH!" and quickly put more pressure on her leg. Thankfully, he had enough experience on the field to know what to do with such wounds and tied his cravat tightly.

When Richard had screamed his wife's name, Darcy had momentarily become distracted due to his concern for her and released his grip to look towards her.

Wickham chose that opportunity to strike Darcy across the face and push him off his body. He saw his knife several feet away and reached for it while Darcy flew back to attack Wickham and hit him squarely on the jaw, knocking him out completely unconscious, but Wickham had managed to stab him on his right shoulder with his knife.

Richard heard the fight and saw his dear cousin getting stabbed. He released Elizabeth and ran to Darcy to help him. Darcy stumbled back a few steps as the intense pain began to radiate down his arm and he had still been lightheaded from being hit on the head. Richard grabbed hold of his uninjured arm and steadied him and saw Wickham on the ground to give his torso a good kick before sitting Darcy down next to Elizabeth. He took off Darcy's cravat and began to bind the shoulder to stop the bleeding, leaving the knife in place to prevent the gushing of blood. He had seen that leaving the blade in, even with the risk of infection, was safer than the immediate loss of blood.

Darcy saw his beautiful wife unconscious and tears rolled down as he gently touched her bruised cheek. She was warm and still breathing. *Thank God, she is still alive. She must be well! I cannot live without her!*

While Darcy was tending to his wife, Richard quickly untied the rope from Elizabeth's wrists and began to tie up Wickham. Knotting it tighter than necessary, his blood boiled at the damage that this criminal had caused. He knew he had to get help right away and Pemberley House was two miles away from where they were.

"Darcy, I must get you help. You are both injured. What should I do?" Richard asked, knowing the answer already.

"Richard, you must take her on Xerxes and get help. You must go now! She needs a doctor immediately!" Darcy commanded.

Richard knew what he needed to do but the thought of holding Elizabeth so close for two miles concerned him. He had dreamt of embracing her and kissing her for so long that it would be impossible to keep his promise to love her from afar if he actually held her in his arms.

Richard's eyes pleaded as he replied to Darcy, "I know, Darcy, but I... How can I hold her so and not... I cannot..."

Darcy knew what he was facing. His cousin, who had been so deeply in love with Elizabeth, would have difficulty holding her without breaking his promise. Nothing else mattered now, though. He trusted Richard that he would care for her only second to himself. She must get help.

"Richard, love her and care for her as I would. I cannot hold her and ride. You must get help! She is my life, Richard. I cannot live without her. If you truly love her, take her and help her. I release you from your vow and give you full consent to whatever it takes for you to help her. I know you love her. She loves you, too, Richard, and you must save her. Go now! Get her help, please!" Darcy begged.

Richard stood and nodded with determination to get her to the house and get help. He lifted her up and carried her to the stallion and Darcy helped him with his good arm to lift her up in Richard's embrace. His heart tore as he saw her limp body and cried for her to be well.

"Giddup!" Richard yelled, as he rode slowly and carefully towards the house. They were at a bend that was sheltered by tall trees and any sounds were sure to be muffled. It would have been impossible for anyone to have heard Elizabeth's screams.

Chapter 25

Richard carried Elizabeth closely to his chest with her limp arms wrapped around his body. He could feel her breathing on his bare neck while he held onto the reins. Her legs were over his left thigh securely to prevent further injury and he felt his heart beat wildly with her proximity. He could smell her scent in her hair and her lips were a hair's breadth away.

As he carried her on the horse, he caressed her cheek where Wickham had struck her and kissed her lips gently. "Oh, Elizabeth," he kissed her again and again. "Please wake up." He tasted her tears on his lips as he licked his own and tears stung at his eyes. He dared not go any faster in fear of losing his grip and he kissed her again, this time deeper and longer. He could not stop. He loved her so much and he knew Darcy would kill him but he could not stop. He did not want to ever stop.

He kissed her cheeks and forehead and gripped her tighter. "Elizabeth, my love, please wake up." His lips were on hers again when he felt her stir. Her lips opened and began to move and even though he knew he should stop, he pressed his lips harder instead and held her now with both arms as the horse slowed down to a halt. She began to return his kiss and he poured all of his love into her, in relief that she was going to be well now. He plunged his tongue inside her mouth and her tongue joined his. He heard her moan and released her for breath. This kiss had been the most sweet, the most delicious, and yet the most painful one of his life, as he heard her whisper, "Fitzwilliam".

He knew he had crossed the boundary, imposing on his cousin's wife but he could not regret it. Their kiss was better than he had ever dreamt and he knew he should never repeat such an experience, but would treasure it for the rest of his life. He knew then, that he would never marry. His heart belonged to her fully and he could never kiss another woman as he had just kissed his Elizabeth.

"Elizabeth," he whispered, kissing her lips tenderly once more.

He looked down and saw her eyes flutter open. Her eyes were unfocused and hazy and it took several moments for her to comprehend that the man holding her was not her husband.

"Richard, what has happened? Where am I? I was just kiss..." She quickly snapped her mouth shut. She understood that Richard must have been kissing her and she had responded in return, believing that it was Fitzwilliam. She knew he loved her but she was mortified that she had responded. She did not know if she should be ashamed or angry that he had kissed her so deeply.

Richard quickly grabbed the reins and began to trot towards the house again, this time at a faster pace. "Elizabeth, I am sorry that I kissed you without your permission. I will confess it all to Darcy and I know all ties will be cut between us, but I am in love with you, Elizabeth. I will no longer hide my feelings for you. I am resolved to love you and will love you for the rest of my life but I will not impose myself on you again. You have every right to kick me but seeing you injured broke my heart and I could not stop myself when I have you in my arms like this. I am sorry, Elizabeth, but I do not regret it." Richard spoke truthfully. He would treasure their kiss for the rest of his life.

He continued, "But if you will forgive me, and if Darcy is able to forgive me, I vow to protect you and care for you. You will always know how much I love you. I will love you until my last breath, Elizabeth."

Elizabeth was touched at his confession. Richard was not only dashing and brave, but he had been the biggest supporter of her marriage to her extremely wealthy husband, championing them in London and praising them to all for months. He was handsome and garnered respect everywhere he went and she had heard stories of his heroic actions that saved numerous soldiers. To have gained the loyalty and love from such a worthy man was an honour but she knew she could not give him more.

"Richard, I do love you, as a cousin, and I forgive you. You are a good friend to me and you saved us from Wickham. I do care for you and do not wish to lose your friendship. As long as you do not kiss me like that again, I wish for you to be in our lives." Elizabeth honestly responded as she leaned into his embrace.

Richard had a wide grin on his face. *She is ever so generous. Darcy was right. She will still grant me friendship and her love, even if just as a cousin.*

"Thank you, Elizabeth. Hold on to me tight. I need to get you home faster. I could not rush before, as I could barely hold on to you but now, you can help me. Are you well? Is your leg very painful?" He asked with concern.

"Yes, it hurts very much and I think I fainted due to my pregnancy compounded by the pain. Where is Fitzwilliam? Why is he not taking me home?" Elizabeth asked in confusion.

Richard gulped. He realised that she did not know about Darcy being stabbed. *What do I tell her? Damn it! She is holding on to me tightly and I am aroused. I truly have no scruples.* Clearing his throat and deciding to be honest, he spoke. "Darcy was stabbed by Wickham," he saw the panic in her eyes and quickly continued, "but he is well. I bound his wound and tied up the villain. I intend to get help and Wickham will be hung for his crimes. He was concerned for you and gave me leave to carry you home." He hugged her tighter. "He will be well. You must be well. He is so worried for you. I promise to get you home and return to him to ease your mind, Elizabeth." He saw her relax with the news.

Elizabeth was in pain but too many thoughts were running through her brain to pay any mind. She held on to Richard tightly so she could help him get her home quickly. Xerxes was galloping swiftly but they were still another mile away. She worried for her husband. She prayed that he would be all right and that his wound was minor. She could feel Richard's protrusion on her bottom but ignored it since she knew he could not help it, as Fitzwilliam had told her that after a certain point, it had required manual release unless enough time was given with distraction. She could feel Richard's breath on her ear and was comforted that he was knowledgeable and proficient in such an insane situation. She closed her eyes and loosened her grip in exhaustion.

"Elizabeth? Elizabeth!" She heard Richard calling her name.

She moaned but replied softly, "I am here. I am so tired."

He held her tightly again and spoke, "You must stay awake. Do not sleep. You must keep alert. We are almost there, Elizabeth."

She tried to shake her head to stay awake but continued to feel drowsy and dizzy. "I am so dizzy. Mmm... You never called me 'Elizabeth' before, Richard."

He kissed her cheek and lowered her head, shifting her legs so they were more elevated. He needed to get more blood to her head. "Because I fell in love with Elizabeth when we were first introduced. I will call you as my heart has called you from the beginning and you will know that I love you every time I call your name. Stay awake, Elizabeth. We are nearly there." He kissed her cheek again.

Very soon, he arrived at Pemberley and began to yell at the servants who saw the rider approach with a woman in his arms. Richard shouted orders for the surgeon to be fetched, that Mrs. Darcy and Mr. Darcy were injured by Wickham, and that the magistrate needed to be called. He still held on to Elizabeth while two servants helped lower her down and once on the ground, he carried her quickly to her bed, hollering for the maids to see to her needs. He lowered her gently and kissed her on her forehead and whispered, "I will see to Darcy now, Elizabeth. Be well. I love you," and quickly departed.

~*~

Darcy sat leaning against the large tree trunk watching Richard leave with Elizabeth tightly embraced in his arms. He had just released his most valuable treasure to the man who was desperately in love with her. He chuckled to himself and shook his head. *Elizabeth may be my wife but I do not own her. I love her with my life and would die for her. I know she loves me and I am willing to allow Richard to love her. She deserves all the love she receives and he will not take more than she can give and I know her heart lies with mine.*

Seeing the passionate look in Richard's eyes, he knew Richard was afraid to hold her so close. He laughed. *He has never been afraid of anything in his life and my slip of a wife probably frightens him to death! I am sure he will steal a few kisses. I cannot blame him. He is a good man and will love her till his dying breath. She is ever generous and deserves his love and respect. He will be good to her and care for her as much as I. Please be well, Elizabeth. Please be well, my unborn child.*

He saw Wickham's unconscious body begin to stir. All of his anger returned but he was too weak to stand. He watched him begin to move and jolt into consciousness and Darcy laughed, as Wickham struggled to free himself. Richard had bound his wrists and ankles together behind his back and there was no way to get free. It was like seeing a sheep or pig before slaughter.

He spoke with a slur. "Darcy! I think you broke my jaw! Damn you! Release me, you arsehole! If only Richard had not arrived when he did, I would be fucking your wife right now. That bitch also kicked me in the bollocks. I am going to kill her after I have her, do you hear me? I want my money, you bloody bastard! Your father loved me and you spoiled everything. I should have had Georgiana and I should have had her money. I should be living at Pemberley!" Wickham began to rant. He was so angry at being wounded and bound that he began spewing off everything that came to his mind.

Darcy was furious at hearing his words and wanted to stand up to kick his face in, but he began to listen to what the criminal had planned. *If I am careful, I may find out all of his plans so I can have him prosecuted and hanged!* He suppressed a chuckle in hearing that Elizabeth had kicked his manhood. *She is a fighter!*

"So, your plan was to assault my wife? What then, Wickham? I would still love her and care for her. I would never abandon her." He waited.

Wickham smirked. "I would have had you watch us fuck and then take her to my hideout. Oh, Darcy, she is a delicious thing. Smelled so good. I would have ravaged her for hours and she would have loved it. She would have screamed her pleasures with my cock drilling inside her. Such nice teats on her, Darcy!"

Darcy's blood was boiling but Wickham could do no harm to her now so he sat and remained silent.

Wickham continued, "I was going to snatch Georgiana and after I filled her with my seed, I was going to elope with her to get my hands on her dowry, but once I saw your gorgeous piece of skirt, all I wanted was to tup her. I watched you both for two weeks and I finally acted today. I would have succeeded if only damn Richard had not interfered!"

Darcy was once again grateful for his cousin. Not only had he interrupted Wickham from forcing himself on Elizabeth, he had bound their wounds and had taken Elizabeth to safety. *I pray you are well, Elizabeth.*

Wickham, clueless to Darcy's thoughts, had thought his expression as pain and continued to goad him.

"Blackmailing you would have been easy. Maybe get your wife with my child and he would be heir. That would be fantastic! You can give me funds to keep quiet and I can blackmail Bingley, too! Hahaha!"

Bingley? What does Bingley have to do with this? Did he plan on hurting Jane? Darcy asked himself.

Wickham was quite addle-brained from the beatings earlier and it did not register that he was revealing all of his plans. "My wife had Bingley's bastard and she actually loves that devil child! Oh, I could be rolling in piles of money from you and Bingley and Georgiana's dowry! Oh, to have my choice of women, that is the life..."

Darcy was horrified. *Bingley had a bastard? With Sarah Fleming? Wickham is married to that mercenary woman? Wait, he wanted to elope with Georgiana as well. Bigamy? He has lost his mind!*

Darcy was incensed beyond belief. Not only was this scoundrel about to force himself on his wife, he wanted to do the same to his sister and commit bigamy to access her dowry as well as blackmail Bingley and himself? He slowly stood, taking care to not jolt the knife that was still protruding from his shoulder. He wanted to kick Wickham until he died.

A loud roar of horses and a carriage was heard nearby just then. Darcy saw his carriage as well as a dozen men heading his way, led by his cousin. He breathed a sigh of relief. *He got her to safety.*

Soon, Richard jumped off Xerxes and tucked his shoulder under Darcy's left arm, grabbing his waist and walking him towards the carriage. "Darcy, I am glad you are well. We must get you to the surgeon. Elizabeth is well. She is being seen to as we speak." Richard quickly informed him.

Darcy sighed loudly. "Thank you, Richard. I knew you would not let me down. My shoulder hurts like the devil but my heart is rejoicing." Darcy softly smiled, patting his cousin's shoulder.

Richard felt the guilt of kissing his cousin's wife but swallowed it down for now. The priority was to care for Darcy.

"Come, come. Let us go." After closing the door quickly, he tapped on the roof and the horses lurched forward.

As Richard was tending to his wound with more cloth strips that had been prepared, Darcy began to get dizzy. He closed his eyes and thought of his Elizabeth. He dreamt of the baby that she would hold in her arms and smiled, and then there was only blackness.

~*~

Darcy opened his eyes slowly. There was a blinding light and he could hear voices but could not understand what had happened. He had awful pain in his right shoulder and his head hurt. His eyes would not focus but his hearing began to sharpen and he could discern Elizabeth's voice. *Elizabeth! Am I dead and in heaven? No, I must be alive. Elizabeth has to be alive.*

He croaked, "El..." His throat was so dry, he could not speak. Immediately he heard the most beautiful sound in his life.

"Fitzwilliam. I am here, my love. I am here. Open your eyes, Fitzwilliam." Elizabeth coaxed.

As he opened his eyes, he saw her beautiful green eyes. She was lying next to him, holding his arm. "Elizabeth," he moved his lips again. And he was being smothered by kisses on his lips, cheeks, forehead, nose, temple, and lips again.

"My love, you had been lost to us for four days. Welcome back, my dearest husband. Welcome back. Richard is going to sit you up for some water." Elizabeth gave him small sips from a cup.

He looked around and saw Richard grinning. "Hello, Darce! Welcome back to the land of the living!"

"Richard, Elizabeth, I was out for four days?" Darcy was astounded.

Elizabeth smiled but there were tears in her eyes. "Yes, my love. I feared for you but after your fever abated, I knew you would return to me. I love you, Fitzwilliam. Please do not scare me like that again!" She kissed him several more times.

Richard spoke, "Elizabeth, I will fetch the doctor to examine him. You are all right there?"

"Thank you, Richard. Yes, I am exactly where I wish to be," Elizabeth answered.

Richard left the room to call for the doctor, who had been residing in the guestroom to oversee his patient morning and night. He also wanted to give the couple some privacy.

Darcy saw that his right arm was in a sling and immobile but wrapped his left arm around Elizabeth and held her tightly. He buried his face in her hair and inhaled her scent. He was home.

Elizabeth cried in her relief and hugged his chest tightly without touching his arm. "Are you in pain, my love? The doctor will be here shortly. We were both wounded but we will be well now. All is well."

"And the babe?" Darcy asked. His stomach tightened as he had hoped the baby had not been lost.

"Everything is well. I felt the quickening yesterday. Our child is well." She kissed his cheek. "I have rarely left your side and Richard has been keeping me company. Georgiana was here but she just went to rest. I will call for her later but I just want to stay with you for now. I love you so much."

Soon, the doctor entered. Mr. Henderson had been the family doctor for decades and although now elderly, he was the most proficient doctor in the entire county. He explained that his cousin saved his life by keeping the knife in and wrapping the wound tightly, as purging it from his body would have resulted in massive blood loss. He had been able to extract the knife with Richard putting pressure on it as he stitched up the deep wound without much blood loss. Slight infection had set in and Darcy had been feverish but it had finally broken this morning after the constant attention from the servants and Mrs. Darcy, using cold towels to reduce the fever. He looked proudly at Mr. Fitzwilliam and tapped his shoulder. "If we could always have such level-headed young men during emergencies, we might see a better survival rate."

Richard lowered his eyes in embarrassment at the praise while Elizabeth beamed.

Darcy spoke, "Thank you, Richard. I am in your debt. But what about you, Elizabeth? Are you well? Your leg – is it all right?"

Mr. Henderson answered on her behalf. "Mrs. Darcy suffered a deep cut and it was quite painful. We believe she fainted due to the tremendous pain she suddenly experienced as well as being in her condition," he nodded to her, "but the stitches are in place and as long as she takes care to not pop them out with too much activity, they should come out in a week. There was no infection, mercifully, and she will have a scar but it should heal well." Mr. Henderson smiled, "Mr. Darcy, your wife is a terrible patient who likes to complain, but she is being compliant for the sake of your unborn child." He winked at Elizabeth. "She has promised that as long as she was allowed to care for you, she would not use her leg. Sir, I will return tomorrow to check on you but please feel free to fetch me should you have any needs."

He gave instructions to remain in bed until tomorrow when they could assess if he could slowly stand up and to eat soft food. "Madam," he bowed to Elizabeth, "Sir." He tapped Richard on his shoulder and took his leave.

Word quickly spread that the master was awake and recovering and Darcy's valet entered to see if he had any needs. Darcy had desperately wanted a shave and to change his nightshirt. He knew he must have sweated copiously during his fever and wanted to clean his teeth.

"Elizabeth, I would like Wilkins to wash me and give me a shave. Would you please return with Georgiana in... an hour?" Darcy asked. "Richard, please remain with me." He wanted to ask about Wickham and what else might have happened during his illness. Mr. Wilkins left to prepare for Darcy's ablutions.

"Yes, my love. I will call for Georgiana but Richard must deliver me first. I love you." She kissed him on the cheek.

Richard then walked over to Elizabeth's side of the bed and lifted her up with his strong arms and Elizabeth quickly wrapped her arms around his neck. After nodding at Darcy, he carried her quickly to her bedroom.

Darcy watched as they appeared very familiar with the exercise. *I forgot about her leg. Have they been... No, I will not think of such. Elizabeth loves me.* He told himself several times. But the intimacy that he had just witnessed told him that there was more and he would find out. *Richard loves her, you fool. And he saved both of our lives. If she accepts him, I must bear it. I would do anything to have her with me. I will not be a jealous fool.*

Richard soon returned. "Elizabeth is being tended by Hannah and Mrs. Reynolds. You scared me to death, Darce! I am so glad you are well."

Although he had not meant to, Darcy's words came out pointed. "But you would have had my wife if I had died. And since when have you started calling her 'Elizabeth'?" He had noticed the change.

Darcy is still sharp as ever. I will not lie to him. Richard answered, "Darcy, if you had died, yes, I would have married her in a heartbeat. I love her with all of my heart and I will love her until I die. But I care for you, too, cousin. I truly wish the best for the both of you and I could never wish for harm to either of you. Elizabeth is very special and she deserves every happiness and her being happy makes me happy. Her happiness is with you and always will be."

He paused to see Darcy's reaction. He did not appear angry. "I must confess that when I held her, I could not help it and I kissed her while she was unconscious. I am so sorry, Darcy. I kissed her several times." *A dozen times and I cannot mention the tongue.* He shook his head. "I was weak when I held her close to me and was terribly afraid for her. But then she woke up and threatened me to never do it again." He smiled. "She forgave me and I hope you will forgive me. I told her that I would call her Elizabeth from now, as my heart always had called her as such. I love her and I will not impose on her again but will no longer hide my feelings from her. I wish for her to know that I love her and will always love her." Running his fingers through his hair, he continued, "I tried to cover my feelings by calling her 'Cousin Lizzy' before and acting distant but I cannot, I will not hide from it. The thought of almost losing her broke my heart. If I can be in the same place where she is, if I can have her friendship and see her smiles, I can die a happy man."

Darcy remained quiet for several minutes. It had been exactly as he expected. His cousin had kissed his wife and he could see the guilt, but also the determination to love her and show his love to her. He knew that he himself would give anything just to hold a piece of her heart and it was obvious that Elizabeth had permitted Richard to do so. His cousin, whom he respected above all other men, who was instrumental in keeping both of them from further harm, who loved Elizabeth with his life, who would ask for friendship and perhaps a slice of affection from his ever-generous wife, would be a valuable ally for the rest of their lives. He and Elizabeth needed him; his friendship, his love, his care.

Richard panicked when Darcy remained silent for so long. He did not wish to leave. He had originally planned to return to Kent next week but with Wickham's attack, he had wanted to stay and assist; not only to be in Elizabeth's companionship but also to be of service to the both of them. He never wished to leave her side but he knew that if Darcy broke their friendship, he would never see them again. Never see *her* again. How could any husband accept the man who coveted his wife?

Richard spoke while Darcy was still silent. "Darcy, I told Elizabeth this; I am sorry that I kissed her but I do not regret it. She is a balm to my soul and I will never love another. I will never marry and will love her for the rest of my life but by your silence, I know that I must disgust you for coveting your wife. I would never betray you and I would only revel in what she allows me, her friendship, her conversation, perhaps a peck on the cheek for birthdays or what not, but I shall leave Pemberley immediately. I hope you will forgive me someday and that we are able to reconcile in the future."

He had unshed tears in his eyes and turned to walk out of Darcy's life forever. *I would rather die than never see Elizabeth again. How am I supposed to go back to Rosings to be alone for the rest of my life?* His heart broke.

"Richard! Please do not leave. I had been meditating on the pleasures of a pair of fine eyes of the most beautiful woman I know," he repeated what Richard had said of Elizabeth, "and the bravery and loyalty of the finest man I know. Richard, I had already guessed that you could not avoid that temptation. You would not have been allowed so much should Elizabeth have been awake, and I also know that you would not force any dishonour. I know you love her. You love her as deeply as I love her and I am most fortunate to be her husband. Whatever she will gift, you are required to receive it, cousin. She has the most generous heart and would not wish to lose your friendship. If she forgave you, I forgive you. Most wholeheartedly."

Richard coughed and quickly wiped his eyes. He was immensely relieved and gladdened that he could stay longer. He would do anything to be near his dearest Elizabeth. "You are a good man, Darcy. Thank you. Thank you, my dearest cousin." He shook Darcy's left hand.

"Richard, my debt to you for saving Elizabeth is greater than everything I own. She is the most precious thing in my life." Darcy confessed. "She deserves both of our love and we need you in our lives, cousin."

Mr. Wilkins returned and began to wash Darcy as Richard took a seat beside the bed.

Chapter 26

"So tell me about Wickham. What happened before I woke up and after I got into the carriage?" Darcy asked while his valet was washing his face and helping him brush his teeth.

Richard began. "Once you were safely transported to Pemberley, Wickham was apprehended by six of your men. Something was not right with his head, Darcy. Either your punches had him completely addled or he has gone insane. While you were knocked unconscious, he prattled about Georgiana and Elizabeth. Oh, and something about Bingley and his wife having Bingley's bastard. I do not understand what he meant by it. He had been quite disturbed that I had interrupted his revenge, and Darcy, he touched Elizabeth. I do not know if she will share with you but you must comfort her. I believe she has been having nightmares about it. He licked her neck. He also... groped her chest and fondled between..." He lowered his eyes to the groin area so Darcy would understand. Wilkins was still working on Darcy and he could keep the secrets, but Richard began to rage, remembering the sight of Wickham touching her against her will. He stood and paced to calm himself. He saw Darcy's eyes burn with anger and his one hand gripping a tight fist.

He continued, "I could see that the bastard was rubbing himself on her but Elizabeth outwitted him by asking him if he was enjoying himself with that arched brow of hers." He chuckled, "He was no match for her. He lowered his knife on her throat and she promptly kneed his cock and kicked his shin." *What a woman!* "Unfortunately, that jackass sliced her thigh and that was when you began attacking him. He is suffering in jail right now. Your men brought him and locked him up in the cellar. He did resist and your men had to 'calm him'. I believe he is missing several of his teeth and he has a broken nose as well as two broken ribs," *from where I kicked him!* He paused to turn to Darcy. "You were fearsome, Darcy. I believe you broke his jaw with your strikes and he has a deep bruise from your hand holding his throat. I have never seen you so angry. Not even compared to that night in Chatsworth." He subconsciously rubbed his jaw. "I hope you will never be that angry with me." He met Darcy's eyes in thanks for his forgiveness.

Darcy took several breaths. "Wilkins, you may continue shaving me. I promise to stop shaking." He leaned back. "Thank you, Richard. Seeing Wickham hold Elizabeth threw me into a rage and if you had told me that she had die... that she was not well, I would have squeezed the life out of him. I wish to see him hanged."

Soon, Wilkins completed his tasks and left the room to clean up the supplies.

"Richard," Darcy spoke quietly, "I allowed Wickham to continue his ramblings while I waited for assistance and he told me that he had intended to elope with Georgiana after forcing himself on her. But he saw Elizabeth and decided she was more worthy of his attentions. He had planned to rape her with me witnessing the act and then to take her to his hideout to ravage her more. He would have blackmailed me to keep the disgrace a secret and still tried to go for Georgiana. He said he wanted to impregnate Elizabeth so the heir to Pemberley would be his." He was beyond furious and wished he could stand and pace. He watched Richard's reaction as he turned red and walked in front of the fireplace. He took several more breaths, reminding himself that all this was prevented and that his family was safe.

A moment later, Darcy continued, "Bingley had relations with Sarah Fleming. He took a maiden, Richard." He saw Richard's disgusted face since it was most ungentlemanly to take a virgin before a betrothal. "She was sent off to Newcastle in disgrace and Bingley had thought the union did not result in a child but it appears he was wrong. Elizabeth will be devastated on behalf of Jane. I believe Wickham married Sarah Fleming and abandoned her there to pursue Georgiana and take his revenge on me with Elizabeth. If he had eloped with Georgiana, his marriage would have been invalid as he is already married. He would have committed bigamy. He cannot harm our family again, Richard. We must see him punished!" Darcy emphatically pronounced.

"As you wish, Darcy. I will speak with the magistrate and ensure the pertinent details are surfaced. We will keep the private details to ourselves unless absolutely necessary. You will not be able to write, Darce. I had hoped... I hope you will allow me to stay at Pemberley until you are fully recovered to be of service to you. I would like to ensure that... that Elizabeth will be well. I have heard her crying and whimpering in her sleep during the night while she lay here with you. You must comfort her and hopefully her nightmares will end soon, but damn Wickham must be tried and punished for this to end." Richard worried.

"Thank you, Richard. You have learned much and I know you will be able to manage the businesses well. My steward and staff are at your disposal. Thank you for your help with everything. Again, I am in your debt several times over. I appreciate you more than you know, cousin. You saved my wife from an unthinkable violence and I would have died if she were injured further. I meant what I said. We will love her together and she will know that she will be loved and cared for always." Darcy was teary-eyed. He was distraught for Elizabeth's nightmares but also thankful that she would rally again. With Richard at their side, they would recover.

A soft knock was at the door. Both men quickly wiped their faces and bid enter.

Georgiana arrived and rushed to Darcy's side and hugged him from his uninjured side. "I was so worried about you, brother! I am so glad you will be well!" She cried.

"Yes, my sweet sister, I will be well. I am sorry to have worried you so. Everything will be well." He kissed her temple.

Richard cleared his throat, "Ahem. Shall I see if Elizabeth is ready to return?" Darcy nodded and he left through the adjoining door.

Georgiana exclaimed, "Lizzy has been so worried about you. She rarely left your side, but then she cannot leave alone so she might not have had a choice." She joked. She was so relieved to see her brother clean and smiling and looking healthier. "Richard has had to carry her everywhere and insisted that he needed the exercise as he had been out of the military too long and was getting too weak. Lizzy has to keep her leg straight and cannot put any weight on it. She has been stir-crazy but Richard and I have been telling her stories of your youth, well, Richard more than me, but she has been more relaxed now and laughing. Richard is so kind. He read for you and Lizzy while you slept and has made sure I was taking care of myself as well. He worked with your steward and wrote to Uncle and Aunt and has been managing everything wonderfully. He is so fiercely protective of us. He truly loves us."

Georgiana rambled on about the household staff and how she had seen Wickham dragged into the jail cart. She did not appear to have been affected by the experience but was mainly concerned about her brother and her dearest sister recovering.

Richard is a good man. Elizabeth is very fortunate to have so many people love her. But it is not hard to love her; it is a privilege to love her. Darcy thought as he smiled at his excited sister.

~*~

Richard entered Elizabeth's room after knocking on the door. It had become a familiar routine for him to carry her from room to room, even if she spent most of her time in Darcy's bed, but when she had a need for privacy or needed to change her dresses, he would carry her to her bedroom and after Hannah and Mrs. Reynolds assisted her, he would carry her back to Darcy's bed.

He had taken her to the library to pick out reading materials as well as to Georgiana's room when his poor cousin burst into tears on the first day. Elizabeth had wanted to comfort her and ensure that everything would be well. She had become very comfortable in his arms and he wished he could carry her everywhere for the rest of his life.

Elizabeth was reclined on the bed and smiled brightly as he entered. *My love, my Elizabeth. She is so beautiful.* Richard had been aroused often in her presence but had been able to suppress his desires better since their precious kiss. She inspired him beyond his control but in the face of her possible death and with Darcy's injury, his concerns for them overshadowed any physical desires and he was satisfied with holding her and being in her vicinity.

He had watched Elizabeth sleep with Darcy since the first night. Her face looked so peaceful and she had constantly reached out her hand to ensure herself that Darcy was lying next to her. When her nightmares began that night, he stayed the whole night, sleeping on the chair next to the bed to awaken to her cries and soothed her, wiping away her sweat and kissing her cheek and hair, and reminded her that it was just a dream. She would whisper, "Thank you, Richard," and return to hugging Darcy and falling asleep.

He had kissed her several times on the cheek since the day of her injury and he could not have been happier. After he laid her down onto the bed, he would kiss her cheek each time and take his leave until needed again. Having her close was a gift and she had smiled brilliantly, embraced him, and had not chastised him. His heart always fluttered at her touch and it had been more than enough to satiate his craving of her.

He knew he would need to obtain a mistress, though. His carnal desires were too strong and painful that he could not go much longer without bedding a woman, and as he would never marry, he opted to search for a mistress who would see to his needs with discretion and satisfy his needs; perhaps one who could provide companionable conversation when he was not using her, and one who would not mind being called by a different name while he lay with her for his relief. Richard had a significant reputation amongst the *ton's* widows as a remarkable lover. He truly cared not for anyone else's satisfaction but given his tremendous skills, women had flocked to his notice in the past.

Once he met Elizabeth and gave up bedding all of his lady friends, many had cried and begged for his attentions again but he ceased looking at their directions completely. He thought of a couple of ladies from his prior acquaintance who might be agreeable to such an arrangement and planned on visiting them when he was in London and hoped one of them would be agreeable. He did not want to be entrapped in a loveless marriage and he certainly did not want to visit whores or be a rake ever again.

As he entered the room, he saw Elizabeth lying on her bed with Hannah fixing her hair. She beamed her biggest smile at him. *My love. She is so beautiful.*

"Hannah, will you please request some food to be delivered? Mr. Henderson has left instructions on what is best for Mr. Darcy. Luncheon for three may be sent up early as well, if Cook is agreeable. I would like to eat with my husband. Thank you."

Hannah quickly rose and left to run the errands.

With both the master and the mistress being injured, Mr. Fitzwilliam had become the stand-in Master and no one blinked an eye at the impropriety of leaving Mrs. Darcy alone with Mr. Fitzwilliam or his carrying her around the rooms. All the servants were grateful for Mr. Fitzwilliam's leadership and management and the care that he had poured onto Mr. and Mrs. Darcy. When they found out that Mr. Fitzwilliam had rescued Mrs. Darcy from further harm and saved Mr. Darcy from bleeding to death, their loyalty was complete.

Richard approached Elizabeth's bed. "Georgiana has arrived. Shall I take you over, milady?" He returned her smile.

"Thank you, Richard. It would be greatly appreciated." Elizabeth happily replied.

"As you wish, Elizabeth." He sighed in contentment as he held her in his arms.

Elizabeth quickly wrapped her arms around his neck and caressed his cheek with one hand and Richard's heart thumped at her touch. She turned his face toward hers and kissed his lips gently.

Richard froze, as she had never kissed him on the lips of her own volition. She whispered, "Thank you, Richard. Thank you for everything. You have been my rock and I appreciate you so much." And she cuddled her head into his neck.

Richard breathed in her scent and smiled. "I love you, Elizabeth. I would do anything for you." He had not repeated his sentiments since that day on Xerxes. His heart felt free, saying the words of love out loud to her once again.

She smiled, "I know. I love you like a brother, nonetheless, I love you."

Richard's mirth rumbled in his chest. "That is all I ask for, my love." And he carried her to Darcy and gently set her down to sit up next to her husband.

The four family members enjoyed their luncheon and afterwards, Georgiana returned to her daily schedule and Richard saw to the businesses that needed his attention while Darcy and Elizabeth conversed in private. Darcy would tell her about Bingley's illegitimate daughter and what would happen to Wickham.

Chapter 27

Bingley and Jane married in February and after spending a wonderful month in Bath for their honeymoon, they returned to Netherfield to start their lives together. Bingley had worried for Jane on their wedding night and hoped that Elizabeth would have shared some confidences on what to expect. He had sexual intercourse with many courtesans and with Sarah Fleming but it had been several weeks, since he proposed to Jane in December, that he had lain with anyone. He took his last opportunity when he was in London to obtain the settlement papers to visit his favourite brothel and took his weeks of pent up desires out on the buxom blonde for two days, but he had vowed to be faithful to Jane after the wedding.

Sarah Fleming had been a maiden when he took her virtue and he had felt such guilt into committing the ungentlemanly act, that part of his despair had been due to his bedding a virgin before marriage. She had flirted and seduced him, begging him to make her a woman and when he relented by taking her to his bed, he had slept with her through the night and after the initial breaking of her maidenhead and releasing inside her deeply, he had taken her twice more during the night. He had loved being the first one to penetrate her but had been relieved that no child had resulted and that he did not have to marry her.

Jane was very shy in comparison. He did not wish to hurt her as he recalled that he had taken Sarah quite roughly. Darcy had advised ways to help Jane relax, perhaps a glass of wine, and shared a book that taught a man how to pleasure a woman.

Damn! I should have studied that book more carefully. I was so busy courting and preparing for the wedding that I did not read it. Bingley thought on his wedding night. There was nothing to be done now; he would bed his wife and try to teach her to relax. Sarah had been completely naked and eager to open her legs but Jane was demure and had a modest nightgown on. He kissed her and raised her dress up and slid himself between her legs. When Bingley finally entered his wife's womanhood, he felt the tightness of the virgin flesh and revelled in it. *There is definitely something to be said about taking a virgin. This is the best feeling in the world. She is finally my wife.*

Initially, Bingley had desired to sleep together most of the nights for easier access to his wife, except during her courses and illnesses, but after the first week of their honeymoon, he took to sleeping in his own rooms after intercourse, taking his husbandly rights two or three times a week in her bed. Jane had not slept well and he felt guilty that he was constantly disturbing her with his demands.

Now that it was April, spring was blooming around them and they eagerly anticipated attending the Season together in two weeks. He would show off his beautiful bride and attend the Matlock Ball for Lady Iris' Coming Out and reunite with Darcy and Lizzy.

Bingley had tried a new position to take his pleasures last night and was still basking in its glory, as he sat in his study to work on his correspondences when he saw a letter addressed from Pemberley. Expecting communication from Darcy, he smiled and opened it to read:

Bingley –

Please read this in privacy, as it contains several shocking news and is unfit for others.

I must inform you that I am writing on behalf of Darcy, as he is unable to use his right hand. Darcy and Mrs. Darcy were attacked last week by George Wickham on Pemberley grounds and his plan had been to assault my cousin Georgiana as well as Elizabeth to revenge himself for his perceived slight of being denied the clerical living. He had been hiding out in an abandoned shed for two weeks to monitor their activities and had written out blackmail letters to be sent to Darcy should his abduction have been successful.

Darcy valiantly fought the criminal and Elizabeth was able to subdue the villain by using her knee. Darcy was stabbed in the right shoulder while Elizabeth sustained a deep cut to her left leg.

The scoundrel has been captured and will be hanged in two days. There was plenty of proof in his own writing as well as eyewitnesses and his own stupid confessions. I wish him straight to hell.

Bingley, he had a blackmail letter for you and also spoke of how he had married Sarah Fleming for her dowry but because of the legal requirements of being married to her for three years before full access, he had become desperate enough to commit bigamy in order to obtain Miss Darcy's dowry and abandoned his wife in Newcastle. He has also told us that the former Miss Fleming had your issue and that your daughter is alive and well. She was born only last month.

I do not know how you will share this with your wife but Elizabeth is distraught on her behalf. Darcy has told her all, as he keeps no secrets from her, but advised her to give you time to come clear.

Due to their injuries, our plans to return to London will be delayed and we four will arrive in May instead of this month.

I have asked Mother to delay my sister's ball a further two weeks so Darcy and Mrs. Darcy would have a chance to dance together after their recovery.

If you do not speak with your wife by the time we see you in London, be assured that Mrs. Darcy will not hesitate to inform her sister.

Sincerely,

Richard Fitzwilliam

Bingley's whole body shook as he read Fitzwilliam's letter. *Sarah had my child? Why did she not tell me? Damn it, how am I going to tell Jane?*

Jane had been an exemplary wife and the best mistress that he could have asked for. Life with Sarah as his wife would have been vastly different. He did enjoy that night with her, as she was different than the whores that he had used before, but he knew she was a grasping, greedy woman who only looked for status and wealth. That mercenary woman had always wanted flowers and gifts and to see and be seen. She would have never enjoyed the quiet country life and would have constantly demanded for grand parties and extravagant dinners. He was certain she would have flown through his income quickly.

Jane was prudent and kind and serene. She never showed unhappiness nor did she ever complain. It did not take much effort to see her smile and she seemed pleased with whatever he did. Even when he was busy with his businesses or late to dinner, she never complained and was the complete opposite of his sister Caroline. During the months they were in courtship, they had agreed upon nearly everything and although he knew she suppressed most of her emotions, she had been a peace-loving, calm woman, and he hated conflict.

I wonder if this will be the straw that breaks the camel's back. I almost wish to see her emotional but not for this reason. What have I done? I have made the biggest mistake of my life by bedding Sarah.

Bingley spent the next two hours pacing and pulling his hair, trying to figure out how to approach this problem. *What needs to be done with the baby? Sarah had married the criminal Wickham so I would no longer be responsible but Wickham would be, no, had been hanged yesterday, after he had abandoned his wife and my child. My child! MY daughter.*

He desperately wanted to speak with Darcy and a letter would not do. He needed Darcy's advice and authority. He had always looked to Darcy for advice and this was the biggest crisis that he had ever faced.

He sent an express to Darcy with wishes for their health and recovery and asked that he and Jane be welcomed for a visit. They would seek lodgings at the Lambton Inn if inconvenient but wished to stay near them to assist in any way possible. He sent the letter by express and rushed to tell Jane of the attack and to begin packing to leave the next day.

He would tell Jane of his illegitimate daughter after talking with Darcy.

~*~

Darcy lay in his bed with his wife. Although he was still weak, he tested his legs and made sure everything worked and was confident he would be allowed to leave his bed in the morning. He cuddled his wife with his left arm and held her tightly. They talked for hours of the events, their worries and fears, their unborn child, Richard's kiss and his commitment to support them through their recovery, and everything else they could think of, and finally fell asleep.

During the night, he heard her stir and begin to kick her legs. He was concerned that she would injure her leg further and he sat up slightly to soothe her. He saw that she was having a nightmare as Richard had warned him, and he kissed her lips and gently whispered words of love to her.

Elizabeth was re-living the attack and Wickham's evil laugh rang in her nightmare once again, being grabbed by his filthy hands and touched where only her husband had touched her, and she was kicking her legs at him and struggled to get free. But this time, she saw her dear husband valiantly fight the rogue, knocking him down on the ground. She saw Darcy's muscles bulge and his arms looked so strong. She felt her heart flutter at his magnificence. He was a beautiful man and exuded masculinity that awakened her desire for his body. She whispered, "Mr. Darcy," as she felt kisses on her face and her breast being gently caressed.

Darcy had been concerned for her and had begun to kiss her face and lifted his body to get on his knees so he could touch her with his left hand. She was sweating and thrashing and his hand sought to comfort her as he rubbed her cheek and neck and he caressed her breast. He had noticed that her bosom had grown larger and could not help touch them. It had been too long since his last release and he felt himself aroused immediately. She appeared to settle with his tender caresses and his heart soared as he heard her whisper, "Mr. Darcy". *She is dreaming of me! I love her so much. She loves me and she knows my touch.* He smiled as he continued to kiss her neck and breasts, taking turns at licking her nipples. *I hope she never has another nightmare but I will certainly comfort her every time.* "I love you, Elizabeth." He whispered in her ear.

Elizabeth opened her eyes to see her husband kiss her cheek and sighed. "I love you, Fitzwilliam."

Darcy returned to her lips and kissed her deeply. Elizabeth savoured in the love that her husband was showing her and returned the kiss fiercely. His tongue and lips were so sweet. She thanked God that her husband had returned to her.

"Elizabeth, I know we cannot have relations, with my arm and your leg in this way, but I desperately need to release. Will you please help me?" Darcy begged.

She smiled brightly and reached down for his manhood and stroked it. It did not take long for Darcy to release and he came hard onto her nightgown.

"I am sorry for the mess. It has definitely been too long." Darcy panted.

"I am pleased to be of help, my love. Perhaps tomorrow, after the doctor clears you, we might try some undignified positions." She giggled.

"Minx! You are too tempting. I love you. I am so glad you are well. I know you were having a nightmare but you seemed to relax when I kissed you." Darcy kissed her temple.

"I was seeing the attack and was afraid but then now that you returned to me, I recalled how strong you were and how you saved me, Fitzwilliam. You were so muscular and I was aroused because I wanted your body. Waking up with your hand on my breast was quite sensual and I am so relieved that you are well now." She cried, but she smiled quickly and continued, "We will both be well. We are stronger than before. We are stronger together, my love."

"Yes, we are, my love. Yes, we are." Darcy replied.

They fell asleep together shortly and peacefully.

Chapter 28

The Bingleys arrived at Pemberley six days later.

Darcy was cleared to ambulate, and with Richard's help, both Darcy and Elizabeth were able to leave the bedroom and soon return to their normal routine with a few restrictions. Darcy would need to keep his arm in the sling for three more weeks and he quickly became accustomed to seeing his wife in his cousin's arms to be carried everywhere, as she wanted to stay with Darcy at all times. He knew Richard loved holding her and snickered seeing his cousin's blissful face whenever Elizabeth smiled at him with happiness. Elizabeth finally had her stitches removed and although not too far yet, she delighted in being able to walk around her home on Darcy or Richard's arm.

Jane hugged her sister dearly and cried in relief as she saw that her sister was indeed well after Charles had told her of Wickham's attack. As they sat to discuss the event, the Bingleys found that Wickham was quickly found guilty and hanged. Darcy was comforted knowing that he would never harm his family again.

Jane and Elizabeth and Georgiana talked happily of Elizabeth's pregnancy and the plans in London and what they would do. They jovially spoke of friends and sisters and gossiped while the men excused themselves to Darcy's study.

"Thank you for having us, Darcy, and congratulations on Lizzy's pregnancy! I am pleased to see that you and Lizzy are recovering well." Bingley began. "That hateful Wickham could have killed you both." He paused. "I had to rush over to ask you for your advice on what to do about Sarah, ahem, Mrs. Wickham. I was stunned, am still dazed that I have a child, Darcy. I never thought I would have to face such a nightmare." He put his head into his hands. "I do not know what to tell Jane, but I know she will be heartbroken."

"Bingley, you must tell her the truth. I know she will be hurt but she will forgive you. How you tell her will be the key." Darcy answered.

"And you must allow her to be angry with you," Richard suggested. "She must be allowed to vent so it can burn off faster. If she festers on it for a long time, it will become infinitely worse."

Richard had had plenty of arguments with angry women, especially those he had slept with and refused to marry. He had to receive a few hits and let those women know that it had never been part of the offer and that it had been a night of passion and nothing more. Once the women fumed and cried, they had become congenial and he had slept with almost all of them a few more times. Those women had known deep down that he would have never offered marriage as they were the ones that had initiated the trysts in the first place.

"And what do I do about the child? Do I just give Sarah some money to care for the babe? Do I bring my bastard child into my home with my wife, or do I even acknowledge her? I never should have dropped my breeches, damn it!" Bingley took a swig of the scotch. He was confused and angry with himself.

Darcy calmly replied, "Bingley, I suggest you use my detective, Mr. O'Connor, to investigate the situation. You must find out if what Wickham has said was the truth and what Mrs. Wickham wants from you. If she had wanted you to know, she would have contacted you somehow. If she was ashamed or shunned but was fortunate enough to find herself a husband while pregnant, she may be able to find another who would not mind the babe or at least waiting for her dowry. We must have more information before you panic. But you must tell Jane soon."

"I understand. I will use your man. Thank you. I will tell Jane tonight. I hope she forgives me." Bingley conceded.

After writing a letter to Mr. O'Connor for a meeting the next day, they went their separate ways to rest before dinner.

~*~

Dinner was wonderful. Elizabeth was excited to have Jane at Pemberley and Jane was in awe of the grandeur of the house since it had been the most magnificent home that she had ever seen or visited. The men heartily laughed and recollected some of their earlier memories and Bingley promised Jane to show her some of his favourite haunts in the Pemberley wilderness.

Richard flirted a bit with Jane, just to rattle Bingley as was his custom, and when he bid goodnight to the ladies, he kissed Georgiana and Elizabeth on their cheeks and then Jane's hand with a wink. Jane blushed with the attention and acknowledged that he was extremely handsome and she enjoyed being treated like a part of the family.

Elizabeth and Darcy retired to their rooms and quickly began to make love. Even before the stitches came out, they had found positions that allowed for the union and now that Elizabeth was fully recovered, their lovemaking was fast and furious as well as numerous. Elizabeth's pregnancy cravings were not of the edible kind but the carnal kind, where she had wanted Darcy's attentions several times a day.

Richard shook his head and chuckled, as he watched the couple run off together. He knew they would be naked and in bed within minutes, if they got that far, and laughed that Elizabeth was so insatiable. She had become more and more comfortable with Richard's attentions and she truly treated him like a brother and teased him, and also allowed him to kiss her cheek and hand often.

He lay in his bed with a smile on his face, happy that he was near her and that she was pleased with his care. It was indeed a pleasure to love her now that she knew of his feelings, and he felt more peace and satisfaction in his life than ever before. He continued his daily exercise of riding and fencing slowly with Darcy, who was recovering quickly, as well as learning about estate management, feeling more confident that he would be a decent master of Rosings, and was actually thankful that his station was smaller than Darcy's, with his immense responsibilities that he would never desire for himself. He continued to dream of kissing Elizabeth and holding her in his arms, and it had been enough. He wanted to bed a woman to satiate his needs but he was content with Elizabeth's platonic love.

~*~

Bingley led Jane to their adjoining rooms. Although they had relations regularly, Bingley had been returning to his own rooms afterwards after a week of marriage, after he found out that she had slept poorly due to his loud snoring. Bingley wanted to lay with Jane tonight but he also knew he would be promptly kicked out after the conversation that needed to occur. He had avoided visiting her since he received

Richard Fitzwilliam's letter. *Be a man, damn it! Confess to her and get it over with. If she is furious, you deserve it!* He thought to himself.

"Jane, may I join you in your room so we can converse? I have something of import to tell you." Bingley asked.

"But of course, Charles. I would be happy to receive you. Please, come and take a seat." Jane replied. Her husband had been withdrawn for the past three days and she knew he had enjoyed taking his pleasures several times a week, so she was surprised at his recent reluctance. "What is it that you wish to tell me?"

Bingley sat on the couch but quickly stood to pace by the fireplace. Running his hand through his hair, he paced back and forth until he finally spoke without meeting Jane's eyes.

"Jane, my love, I have some terrible news that I must confess. When I found out about Wickham injuring Darcy and Lizzy, I also found out that Wickham had planned on blackmailing me. Now that he is dead, we are safe," he added seeing Jane's wide eyes, "but the blackmail was due to my child, my illegitimate child being born to his wife. I know I had spoken to you about the woman that I courted before meeting you. Yes, the one that tried to compromise Darcy. She married Wickham while she was pregnant and she delivered a daughter last month." He stopped to see how Jane was handling the news. She sat silent, staring into the fireplace. She did not speak a word. He continued, "I did not know that she was pregnant, Jane, and had been relieved that nothing had resulted from our union. I was shocked when I heard the news."

Jane asked, "Are you certain it is yours? Could she not have had someone else's?"

Bingley sat and buried his head in shame. "No, she had not slept with anyone else before and after meeting me as far as I know. She only married Wickham after becoming pregnant and the timing is correct. I... She... she was a maiden when I lay with her."

Jane was silent. He had hoped that she would scream and yell and cry but when he looked at her, she sat stoically and calmly, serene as ever without a hint of disturbance. She finally spoke, "Charles, I would like to be alone now. I will see you in the morning. Good night."

Never having liked conflicts, Bingley kissed her lips, which did not return the affection, and went to his rooms. He was determined to give her some time to process what had been told to her.

Jane lay in her bed and attempted to think of anything else than what Charles had just shared with her. She felt the betrayal and dishonour of being married to a man who had not only fathered a child with another woman, but that woman had not been his mistress or a prostitute but a maiden whom he had devotedly courted for two months. She shook her head to cease her thoughts and slept fitfully.

~*~

Jane awoke earlier than usual and feeling restless, she decided to go for a walk in Pemberley's picturesque gardens. She inhaled the scent of the blooms and thought of the beauty of Pemberley. She sighed as she remembered that Elizabeth had shared with her the wonders of the marriage bed and how she had so many questions, and how they had fumbled about when they first united, as her husband had no experience either.

Darcy would never have to worry about fathering a bastard! How dare Charles betray me? She bitterly thought. *I did not know that he had taken another maiden before me. I knew he was experienced, as he himself had told me, but he never mentioned that he slept with that woman he desperately chased and loved!* She began to weep on the park bench.

~*~

Richard had risen early as his custom to ride Xerxes. Darcy and Elizabeth had resumed their walks, not heading out so far as to where Wickham had assaulted them, and he consistently rode while they walked, if only to monitor them from afar to satisfy his own need to protect them. He had just returned from his ride and was feeling refreshed when he heard loud sobs from the garden, which was located near the stable.

He followed the sounds and found Jane Bingley sprawled across the bench in tears. *Bingley must have told her. I should not interfere but I cannot leave her out here alone. Where the hell is her husband?*

He approached the bench carefully and asked, "Mrs. Bingley, are you well? Is there anything I can get for you? I know it is early but perhaps a glass of wine?"

Jane abruptly sat up and wiped her tears away. She saw the attractive man standing several feet away from her. *He is very handsome. Colonel Fitz... no, Mr. Fitzwilliam is probably experienced but too honourable to bed maidens.* More tears rolled out.

"I have had some terrible news and I wanted to find some peace out here. Charles had..." She paused to look at his face. *He knows! He and Darcy already know and they were likely the ones to tell him.* She thought. "You know already, do you not?" She asked. "About Charles' child?"

He nodded. "Yes; yes, I do." He did not know what else to say.

"Will you please sit with me? I have some questions." Jane spoke quietly.

"I would be happy to answer your questions but we should return inside. We can have Elizabeth sit with us or at least in a more public place within." Richard saw the impropriety and was anxious about being out here alone in the secluded garden with another man's wife. He had not been alone with any woman for months other than Elizabeth and he did not wish for any misunderstanding to occur. The staff had treated him like another Darcy and being with Elizabeth had never been an issue, but this was not Elizabeth and certainly no woman that he had entertained in his thoughts.

"Yes, of course." Jane stood. She reached for his arm but seeing Mr. Fitzwilliam's handsome face and tall frame, she wanted to know what having another man's attentions would be like. In a rebellion against all propriety that she had ever thought capable, she threw her arms around his neck and embraced him.

Richard caught her from reflex, not knowing if she was fainting or injured but when he realised that her lips were on his chin and she was pulling his head down with her hands, he let go immediately and began to step back.

"WHAT THE FUCK ARE YOU DOING WITH MY WIFE?!" he heard someone yell. *Bingley, damn it. Not again. I will not be attacked for something I did not do. I might have deserved to get hit by Darcy but Bingley has no right.*

He saw Bingley approach with his fist in the air to hit his face and quickly dodged

Bingley's punch. Grabbing Bingley's wrists and bending it behind his back and pushing his body against the hedgerow, Richard tersely shouted, "I have done nothing, Bingley. Calm yourself, man. I do not wish to fight you."

As Richard held him, Bingley struggled to free himself to attack him again and Elizabeth and Darcy arrived at the scene after hearing the commotion. Jane looked at Elizabeth and ran off inside to her rooms in tears. Unable to run after her and seeing the men wrestling, with Richard obviously winning, Elizabeth cleared her throat.

"Ahem, gentlemen. What is happening here? Richard, let him go please." She requested. *Richard is so much taller and stronger than Charles. What in the world is Charles thinking?*

"Elizabeth, he is angry and is ready to hit me for something I did not do. I will fight back if he tries to hit me again and I do not wish to injure him." Richard confidently answered.

"How dare you touch my wife, you bastard?" Bingley was still angry and belligerent, trying to break free and fight.

Darcy stepped in. "Richard, take Elizabeth inside. She will need to see to her sister. I will trade places with you." He grabbed hold of Bingley as Richard slowly let go and quickly led Elizabeth inside on his arm.

Darcy watched his wife leave and released Bingley. He blocked the way as Bingley began to dash to follow Richard. "Bingley! Get a hold of yourself! Explain what has happened!"

Bingley paced in anger then plopped down. After huffing and puffing for several moments, he continued. "Your rake of a cousin was trying to impose on my wife. MY WIFE, Darcy! He had been flirting with her for months and it looked like he finally got her alone here to seduce her. I will kill him! He must have been in love with my wife, that bastard! How could he do this to me?" He was shouting and crying.

Darcy shook his head and rolled his eyes. *Bingley, you fool! Richard cares nothing for Jane and he would never touch her. If you only knew who he truly loved.*

"Bingley, please tell me what you saw. Were they embracing? Where were his hands? Was he kissing Jane?" Darcy asked to make him see some sense.

Bingley paused for several moments. "I saw Jane's arms around his neck and her lips on his chin. Richard's hands... his hands were raised next to his head and he was... damn it! He was stepping backwards away from her. Blasted! How can Jane betray me like this? She must have thrown herself at him and he was not participating!" He stood again and paced. "I told her about Sarah last night and she had no emotion at all. She did not yell or cry, and this morning, she was throwing herself at another man. What am I going to do?"

Darcy took a seat next to him. "I will advise you to be considerate, Charles. You must talk to her and if you still love her, you must be constant and show her how much. She may have been only desperate for attention or perhaps hearing that you had fathered a child with a woman that you had relentlessly pursued in the past caused her to want to experience what it is to be with another. I do not know the workings of your wife's mind but I know that if it were Elizabeth, I would try to understand what happened first and then knowing I was in the wrong, grovel and accept whatever punishment she saw fit. Her needing assurance from another man was to see if she was still seen as a worthy woman and also to punish you." He paused to make sure

Bingley was listening. "And do not blame Richard. It could have been any bachelor that was available and Richard is innocent, I am certain. He would never impose on your wife. With whatever flirting he might have done, he is deeply in love with a lady and he would never arrange an assignation with another man's wife."

Bingley wiped his face with his hands. "I know, Darcy. I know it is truly my fault. I was angry with myself and this situation was the perfect excuse to blame someone else. Thank you, Darcy. I will go to Jane in a moment."

Darcy left him to break his fast. Elizabeth would be most likely attempting to talk with her sister through the door and Bingley would be grovelling if he were allowed into his wife's room. *I hope Richard is not too angry with Bingley and join me for breakfast. What a mess!*

~*~

Richard walked with Elizabeth on his arm inside the house. He was still shaking slightly from the rush of being attacked but having Elizabeth near had been effective in calming him quickly.

"Elizabeth, you must know that I did not do anything. I know Jane is your quiet sister but she threw herself onto me. I swear I did not encourage it." Richard desperately hoped she would understand, as he rubbed her hand on his arm.

"Richard, Jane has never acted improperly in her entire life. Have you been trifling with her? To seduce her to your bed? I never saw her give you any encouragement and you were always flirting with her from the beginning." Elizabeth fumed. "How could you?!"

Richard was beyond angry at her words. Not only was he completely innocent, but how could she believe that he had wanted Jane Bingley in his bed? He only had eyes for Elizabeth!

He quickly pulled her into the nearest room, which was the library. He closed the door behind him and grabbed Elizabeth by both arms. He growled at her in anger, "Damn it, Elizabeth! How could you ever believe I would try to seduce your sister? How dare you forget how much I love you?"

He drew her against his body tightly and kissed her lips, holding her waist and neck and delving his tongue inside her mouth with all the passion and anger he felt until he ran out of air in his lungs. He pulled himself apart from her and released her, breathing heavily in anger and disappointment, as he cradled both of her cheeks with his hands and gently kissed her lips several times in a row. Touching her forehead with his, he softened his tone and said, "I am desperately in love with you, Elizabeth. I want nothing more than to be in your presence and perhaps kiss you a few times and have you smile at me. That has been and will be enough for me, my love. I would give up *everything* just to be with you, but I never wish you to believe that I would dishonour you by imposing on your sister or anyone else you know. I plan on taking on a mistress to be able to satisfy my carnal needs, but I will love you until my dying day and no one else. I will never marry and I will spend the rest of my life loving you. Always you. Only you. I love you, Elizabeth. I love you with all my heart and soul." He kissed her lips tenderly again several times and slowly released her.

He had not meant to kiss her so fiercely again. They had been so companionable and it had been perfect, but it broke his heart that she had thought he could be changeable after so much had happened between them. Even more than Darcy, she was his most treasured confidante and friend, and he would do anything for her happiness. He was willing to give up everything he owned for her and would die for her. He had not asked for much, but for Elizabeth to believe him a rake and a seducer made him indignant. He watched her eyes for her reaction. He expected her to slap him across the cheek for kissing her like that again and he would take any beating she would give him, but he could not live, without her knowing that he was innocent of Bingley's charges and he never wanted her to doubt his love.

Richard was tremendously relieved when he saw her smile and her small hand reached his cheek to pull his face down.

She kissed him lightly on his lips twice. "Thank you for your care, Richard. I am sorry for the accusation. I was not thinking clearly. Since you have done something that you should not have and I have wronged you as well, could we forgive each other and call it even?" She arched her brow.

Richard grinned. *How does she do it? She burns me and throws me into rage one moment and can calm me and make me the happiest of men in the next.* "Yes, Elizabeth, if your generous heart can forgive me, I forgive you fully." He leaned in and kissed her cheek. "There is no one for me but you, Elizabeth. You have my whole heart. I truly love you, you know."

She placed her hand into his hand. "Yes, I know. I love you like a brother, nonetheless, I love you." She smiled.

"That is all I ask, my love." Richard answered once again.

They walked towards Jane's room and after kissing Elizabeth's hand, he left her there to sort out the situation. *What a mess! I want no part of it!*

~*~

Richard headed down to the breakfast room and began to plate his food when Darcy entered.

"Is Elizabeth well?" Darcy asked. He was certain Richard received an earful.

Richard laughed loudly. "Yes, after the tongue-lashing she gave me, I had to clear up the misunderstanding and thankfully she understands what happened. I left her in front of Mrs. Bingley's door. I swear I did not instigate anything, Darce. Jane Bingley threw herself at me and I was trying to get away from her. If Bingley only knew..."

Darcy chuckled. "I know. Bingley finally sorted it out. I did have to tell him that you were deeply in love with another woman." Seeing his eyes widen, he quickly added, "I did not say whom. I think that information is only for the three of us, do you not agree? You must be more careful with Jane, though. I am certain it has to do with the illegitimate child. For Bingley to have fathered a bastard... I do not know if she will accept it but unless she files for divorce, she must live with his past. There is nothing else to be done."

Richard and Darcy soon spoke of estate business and when Elizabeth joined them and told them that Bingley had arrived to take her place, they spoke of packing up for their trip and what places they wanted to visit whilst in town. Soon, they parted to return to their duties.

Chapter 29

Bingley had been allowed to Jane's rooms after Elizabeth was able to console and chastise her sister for a few minutes. Elizabeth was stern with her older sister, knowing exactly what happened and what had caused such calamity. She had told Jane that she was acting like Lydia, throwing away her old toy for a shiny one when she did not get her way, and yelled at Jane that she had not acted the lady with Richard, who not only could have fought back but would have beaten Charles to a pulp. Richard was taller by nearly half a foot and with his military training, he could have killed Charles with his bare hands. Jane was very afraid at the thought and acknowledged her mistake.

Elizabeth then sat down and held Jane as she cried, and then firmly expressed to her sister that she needed to speak with Charles and although she might be very angry, he had been a man, a man with faults, and he had made this mistake before ever meeting her. Elizabeth emphasised that either Jane forgive him and support him through what was probably a very difficult time for him as well, or their marriage would be a loveless one where they would simply be living separate lives. The choice was up to Jane.

After Bingley bid to enter and Jane had agreed, Elizabeth opened the door for her sister's husband and left them to converse.

Bingley paced in front of her not knowing how to start. Seeing Jane holding onto another man in such a way had rattled him to the core. Jane had been an innocent and he had taken his pleasures frequently but she had known no other. Initially, he had been certain that he was wronged and his wife was at fault, but then again, he was the one that had the child out of wedlock and it had been with a maiden. He felt like a cad. She had only reacted as she did because she felt undervalued. She was not perfect. She had made a mistake. He had been wrong to put her on a pedestal where she was supposed to be his perfect wife, perfect gentlewoman, and a perfect human being.

He began, "Jane, I know I have wronged you and I sincerely apologise that I have made such a mistake. I did not think clearly and had lain with a woman that was not my wife and I had kicked myself for falling for such a shallow mercenary woman and congratulated myself for avoiding an entanglement. When I first met you at the Meryton assembly, I was immediately attracted to you and when Darcy began to court and became engaged to Lizzy quickly, I had contemplated asking you for courtship as well. But it was emphasised to me that due to my past rush to fall quickly in and out of love, that I should begin very slowly with you. After weeks of calling on you and then courting you, I knew I loved you beyond anyone else. Even during our engagement, I kept enough distance until I knew that we were perfect for each other." He paused to gauge her emotions. Finding a slight smile on her face, he continued. "I know that we are still perfect for each other but we are not perfect beings. Jane, I love you dearly and I wish you had spoken to me before you sought the attention of another man. It angered me and broke my heart to see you in another's arms, but I imagine you had been thinking of me with other women, as you already know that there have been many, and perhaps you wanted to experience what it would be like to be with another? Is that true?" She nodded as she cried.

He took her hand and kissed it. "If you can bear to forgive me and if you can love me for the faulty man that I am, I wish to be more open with each other and understand how we feel. I wish for you to yell at me and become angry with me instead of burying your emotions. I see Lizzy snipping at Darcy and he grins like a fool even when chastised, and I had thought it childish or that they did not love each other enough, but I now understand that they are miles and miles ahead of us because they are so open. Could we... would you be willing to try?" Bingley pleaded.

"Yes, Charles. I am so sorry for betraying you. I myself felt betrayed and I honestly do not know why I acted in such an awful way. You had been distant these past weeks and I felt lonely and I was hurt but instead of talking to you, I kept quiet and I thought it would just pass. I was wrong, my love. I love you and to think of you with another woman, a maiden, had angered me to the point of insanity. Those things that you had done were before meeting me and there is no way to change it. I hope you will forgive me. I never meant to hurt you." She paused. "Oh! What must Mr. Fitzwilliam think? I only thought that he might show me a little attention and I acted so unladylike. I can never show myself to his face again. I have never done such a thing before in my life! I am so ashamed, Charles." She began to wail.

He rubbed her back. "I will have to beg for his forgiveness as well. He would have killed me and you would have been a widow." She laughed at this. "He is VERY strong!" He teased to lighten the mood. "We will apologise together, my love. Let us go down together to break our fast and we will grovel at Fitzwilliam's feet and apologise to the Darcys as well. We have been terrible guests!" They both laughed together now. He continued, "I am determined to be more careful and to think of us and look to our future. I would like for you to go with me to Newcastle. I am hiring an investigator but it would be prudent for us to see what it is like ourselves, and we can stay in an inn and make noisy love all night long. What say you?" He flashed his smile. "You would not need to meet her but we can decide together what to do about the baby and we will be together to plan our future together."

"Charles, thank you for considering my opinions. You are well within your rights to do as you wish but I appreciate that you wish for us to decide together. I would like to go to Newcastle with you." Jane softly told her husband.

Bingley lifted her up and lowered her back down gently into his lap. He kissed her, "I am so very sorry, Jane. I love you, Mrs. Bingley."

Jane wrapped her arms around and returned his kiss. "I love you, Mr. Bingley. Please believe me when I say that I love you and only you."

They held each other for several moments longer and walked arm in arm down the stairs, where they found Darcy and Richard in the study and gave their most heartfelt apologies and also found Lizzy to do the same.

The Bingleys left the next morning to Newcastle with the investigator, and the Darcys and Richard breathed a sigh of relief as their lives resumed in normalcy.

~*~

The Bingleys travelled to Newcastle and took residence at the inn for three nights. It had been difficult to convey their apologies to Richard Fitzwilliam but they swallowed their pride and emphatically apologised for the inconvenience and the false accusations. Bingley had thanked Richard for restraining him and not fighting back and the men laughed and Richard bowed to Jane Bingley and apologised in return for his previous behaviour of trying to make Bingley jealous. He wanted to make it clear that he had not had any feelings for her whatsoever.

Bingley wanted to make it up to her and made love to her several times the first night in Newcastle to reassure her of his love and they spent the entirety of the next day in bed in the nude. They ordered food to be delivered in and conversed for hours. They wanted to enjoy themselves for the day while waiting for Mr. O'Connor to make the initial investigation and would meet him the day after.

Mr. O'Connor was proficient and researched Mrs. Wickham's situation quickly but discretely.

"I have found all I could on Mrs. Wickham, Mr. Bingley. I have written out some of the pertinent details but it appears that she married Mr. Wickham when she was about six months pregnant. She has been cut off entirely from her family but there is a legal clause that prevents access to her dowry of £10,000 until the marriage reaches its third anniversary. She lives in a moderate home with two servants and most of the neighbours know that she was with child before the wedding but suspects that Mr. Wickham was the father of the babe. The child is known to have bright red hair," he nodded to Bingley who had red hair, "but Mrs. Wickham has streaks of red as well so no one has questioned it. Mr. Wickham was well known to several prostitutes, especially a "Millie" who had been hired often to see to his needs, especially after the birth of the child seven weeks ago. Any questions so far?" He asked.

"Yes, does she know what happened to Wickham?" Bingley asked.

He replied, "Ah, that is my next report. No, sir, she does not know that he has been hanged. It is believed that Mr. Wickham had told his wife that he was being offered the clergy living at Kympton and that due to Mr. Darcy's prejudice against her from London, that she would not be welcome there as his wife. She believes that her husband will receive the living and they will live apart, except for short visits, until the clause on her dowry ends, when he would be able to quit and use her money to live in more comfort. She has had one letter from him that stated the interview had gone very well and he expected to get what was due to him soon. She is not aware of anything else afterwards."

Jane asked, "And the babe, what is her name? Are they having any difficulties?" She wanted to know if Bingley's daughter was healthy and safe. She felt awful for the woman who had been lied to and abandoned by her husband and now widowed. She knew Charles would never abandon her even if he had made mistakes in the past.

"The baby girl is named Wendolyn Wickham and she is a healthy lass. They are struggling financially. There were several debts that were found which Mrs. Wickham had not been aware of, but they have an income of £500 a year and she has promised to clear up the amount as soon as she hears from her husband. He left a debt of £900; almost double their annual income, which had been racked up during the past four months. I do also have there," he pointed to the paper in Bingley's hand, "the address where Mrs. Wickham had been sending her correspondences to her husband. It appears there is a friend in Lambton who has been passing the letters and providing pertinent information to Mr. Wickham in the past. That is all I have on the situation, sir." Mr. O'Connor concluded.

"Thank you very much for your thorough investigation. If you should like to rest and take some time off, I will speak with my wife and come to our decisions by dinnertime. We shall see you at dinner downstairs, Mr. O'Connor." Bingley stated. He shook his hands and the investigator left.

~*~

Jane was in tears as soon as the man left. "Charles, how could a man abandon his wife like so? And to leave £900 debt for her to sort! He lied and attacked Darcy and my sister and was going to force himself on sweet Georgiana. Was this man truly evil or insane?"

"I believe both, Jane. Now that he is dead, he will not hurt any of us ever again but Mrs. Wickham is left in a bad situation. What do we do? What do you believe we should do?" Bingley asked. He had thoughts of what he had wanted to do but would not make a move without his wife's agreement.

Jane replied, "I believe we need to compensate her for the child. If she was not pregnant, she might not have married Wickham. He still might have seduced her but she would not have been so desperate. Without the child, she could remarry or perhaps find support from her family for the damage Wickham has caused, but she will now need to care for her daughter."

Bingley agreed. "How much? I had initially thought £2,000 but now hearing the story in full, I was thinking £3,000. I am so sorry," he stated when he saw the shock in Jane's face at such an amount, "but she will need to pay off the debt and still save for the child. I know it is a large amount." *It is my responsibility to ensure that they are safe. I will not be responsible for someone becoming destitute and selling her body, especially the mother of my child.*

"It is a large amount but I agree with you. As long as your financial situation allows it, I think it a good idea. I know your generosity is not due to your loving her still, Charles. You are a good man." Jane placed her head on his shoulder and sighed. "Charles, I do not think... I do not dare bring the child into our home. Even if Mrs. Wickham is willing and desiring to give her to you, I cannot have the child with us. As everyone knows that I had not been pregnant and she has your red hair, everyone will quickly realise that she is your issue, no matter what excuse we give, and it will bring shame to not only our family, but to my parents, my sisters, and especially the Darcys, as they are connected to us now. I cannot bear it for our family and I have no wish to ever meet her or her mother. Am I being cruel?"

"No, Jane. I understand. I had wanted to meet the babe but I agree with you that it is not a good idea. We will advise Mr. O'Connor of our decision and leave it to him to make the arrangements. He will share the news about Wickham and his evil deeds and let her know of the account that I will set up so she can access the immediate funds needed to repay the debt. The rest will be put in a trust for my... her daughter. Thank you, Jane. You are a sensible woman and generous but I understand why you do not wish to meet them." He kissed her temple.

The Bingleys met with Mr. O'Connor and shared their decisions that evening.

~*~

Sarah Wickham had never been so surprised when an older gentleman requested an audience with her regarding pertinent information regarding her husband.

She had been shocked to learn of Wickham's debts two weeks after he had left to Derbyshire. Wickham had been able to ward off his debtors by repaying them small amounts of the debt and constantly reassuring them that he was about to be offered a very important position and promised to repay them soon. Sarah was certain there must have been a mistake and had written to her husband five times in the past two weeks without a response.

When Mr. O'Connor told her of Wickham's attempts at kidnapping and extortion and that he had been given the death penalty after being found guilty, she fainted.

With the assistance of her maid and Mr. O'Connor, she lay on the couch to hear the rest of the news.

Mr. O'Connor clearly detailed to her that Mr. Darcy had never offered the clergy living to Wickham, as he had installed a new parson before Wickham had ever left Newcastle, and that Mrs. Darcy was Mr. Bingley's wife's sister. Wickham had confessed to his plans to use Wendolyn Wickham to blackmail Mr. Bingley as well, after harming both Mr. and Mrs. Darcy with a knife and threatening to harm Miss

Darcy to obtain her dowry.

He continued that Mr. and Mrs. Bingley desired to see no harm come to Mrs. Wickham and her child, and that £3,000 had been established in the bank for the £900 debt to be cleared as soon as possible and the rest would be put into a trust for Wendolyn.

Sarah cried copiously, in despair as well as in relief, that she would not be left destitute with debt collectors chasing her. She was eternally grateful for Mr. and Mrs. Bingley for not shunning her or ignoring her situation and promised the investigator that she would keep the true parentage a secret for all of her days.

~*~

The Bingleys returned to Pemberley and soon, the time was upon them to leave for London with the Darcys and Fitzwilliam.

Chapter 30

Richard Fitzwilliam looked around the group. He had gone to his club upon his return to London to seek out news about obtaining a mistress. He was desperate to find a woman who could inspire him enough to find relief.

Last night, at a friend's dinner party, Richard saw the two widows whom he had thought might be amenable to take one on as a mistress but hearing that those women had bedded more than a dozen of his acquaintances in the past few months disgusted him.

He found nothing pleasing about them, as they had little in common with Elizabeth, and they were certainly too stupid for anything more than a night's pleasure. He wanted someone who could carry on an intelligent conversation and had not been used by so many men and could not believe he ever got between their legs. *What did I ever see in them? They are so stupid and insipid. No one comes close to my Elizabeth!*

His friends from University had told him of tonight's dinner party that would have some of the more prestigious acquaintances where several men would bring their mistresses. These parties tended to be held when an exchange of opportunities were sought and he had hoped to see what his options were.

Richard saw several gentlemen he recognised, including Lord Harold Haversham, whom he recalled had chased Elizabeth. There was a petite woman on his arm that looked vaguely familiar but he could not place where he might have seen her before. He smirked at the second son of a Duke. *You thought you could win Elizabeth? You are not half the man Darcy is and she would have never been happy with you.*

"Haversham! How long has it been since I saw you last? At least four, five years? How have you been?" He asked his old mate.

"Fitzwilliam! You are looking well! How is it that you are in such a good shape, even after retiring from the military? Congratulations on your new inheritance. We second sons must stick together! Please allow me to introduce my lady friend, Miss Abigail Harrington. Abby, this is the former Colonel Richard Fitzwilliam who is now the prosperous master to Rosings Park in Kent." Turning back to Richard, Lord Harold asked, "How is your cousin Miss Anne? I heard she had been ill."

Richard bowed to Miss Harrington, noticing that there was a glint of recognition in her eyes. He turned back to his friend and answered, "She is doing better. She had been quite ill and there was a scare that we might lose her, but she was able to recover enough to enjoy some dinner parties and outings with my brother, his wife, and my sister. She is in London to enjoy the Season but remains too weak for much of the activities." He tapped him on the shoulder and spoke quieter, a little away from Miss Harrington, "I heard you got married, Haversham. Is she your mistress? She looks familiar."

Lord Harold laughed. Turning to Miss Harrington he said, "My dear, I would like to converse with Fitzwilliam here for a while. Would you be a dear and visit with your sister? Thank you, my dear." He tapped on Richard's shoulder, "Let us go to the library for a while. I need to catch you up!"

They walked towards the library and closed the door. Lord Harold started. "You know I am not proud of it, bringing my mistress here and all, but she actually had been my mistress for nearly four years. Abby is quite sharp and witty and I enjoy her attentions immensely but I released her from my services last September after I got married. Lady Haversham is a fine lady and she demanded that I no longer bed another woman until she was able to beget an heir." He poured himself some brandy and also handed a glass to Richard. "Fine brandy Davis has here. Damn fine. Well, to continue, I fell in love with a woman last spring, a Miss Ben... Never mind. Well, I pursued her like a madman but she would not have me and after despairing for a while in the arms of Abigail, I married Catherine and that was that. Abigail went to stay with her sister for a while but after my wife got with child, I begged her to come back into my service and although I am sleeping with her again, she wishes to retire in the country somewhere. She is nearing thirty and she has been diligent to save up to live a quiet life some place far from London. She reminds me a little of Miss Ben... the other lady that I loved a while ago." He paused. "Blasted, I just realised that Miss Be... that other lady is Darcy's..." He whispered but Richard heard every word.

You loved my Elizabeth? But you had a mistress the whole time of her acquaintance, you arse! You only lusted after her. Thank God Elizabeth did not choose him. Richard thought to himself.

"Well, I saw the look in your eyes, Fitz. If you are looking to take someone on, she would be good to you. She is very beautiful and quite talented, I must say. I brought her here as a last favour so she could see if there was a patron who would not mind an older lady friend to assist with her retirement. Your estate at Rosings would be perfect. If you have a place close enough, your future wife would never need to know." Lord Harold winked.

"I will never marry." Richard blurted out quickly. "I would like to call on Miss Harrington tomorrow, if she is amenable. I do not know where I recognise her but she is pretty enough. Thank you, Haversham." *She will do. She is about Elizabeth's height with large enough bosoms. As long as she is discreet, she will be acceptable.*

They shook hands and returned to the drawing room.

Richard approached Miss Harrington and asked to call on her at her townhouse the next day and it was agreed. He kissed her hand and studied her figure. *Yes, I think I can get it up for her. She is a bit heavier but her figure is somewhat similar to Elizabeth's right now.* He laughed to himself, *Elizabeth's pregnancy is causing her to be more plump and thicker around the middle but her breasts, wow! Magnificent!* He smiled and shook his head, realising that he was thinking about Elizabeth once again.

He turned to a few of his friends and conversed with them when he noticed Miss Harrington being approached by Madam Beverly. The two women, standing next to each other, looked quite alike, which Richard had not noticed before. *Sisters! Blasted,*

Miss Harrington is Madam Beverly's sister. That is how I recognise her. Damn it. I screwed her after first meeting my Elizabeth and I did not even realise who she was today. I am such a cad. What is the chance that she was my last intercourse when I was desperate for Elizabeth? God, I want Elizabeth.

~*~

"My love, are you well? You have been so tired lately." Darcy tenderly asked his wife.

"Oh, Fitzwilliam! I have more than four months more to go but I am already the size of a cow! The dresses are helping cover up the pregnancy but I will be unfit to be seen in public in the next month! I am so large..." Elizabeth had tears in her eyes. She had been growing large quickly and looked about seven months pregnant instead of five. She had not been overeating and she had continued her walks and she could not understand why she was growing so quickly.

"But my love, I love your body. You carry our child within you and I am so pleased with your constant attentions and you are wonderful. As long as you are healthy, I care not how large you grow. Elizabeth, your breasts, they are so large and bounteous. I love watching them bounce when you walk." He kissed them lightly as her breasts were tender. "I love that I would sit in my study and you rush in to demand that I make love to you in the middle of the day. I love lying in bed and you want me relentlessly. I love you so much. After Iris' Coming Out Ball, we will be at Rosings for three weeks and we will not have prying eyes there. We can relax and you will enjoy the gardens there." Turning her to have her back against his chest, "Elizabeth, I need to be inside you. Feel how hard I am for you again. You are so beautiful. I cannot get enough of you."

"Oh, Fitzwilliam. Thank you, my dear husband. I love you. Make love to me now. I have not had you for at least three hours by my count." She giggled. She felt his massive arousal against her buttocks and was immediately wet to take him. They had made love three times already but they were insatiable.

He slid his long cock slowly from behind and massaged her clitoris with his fingers. Darcy kissed her neck and gently caressed her engorged breasts. He loved her so much and loved being joined together. He pumped harder as he rubbed her bundle of nerves and felt her tighten around him with a loud moan and he climaxed with her. "I love you, Elizabeth," Darcy whispered.

"I love you, Fitzwilliam." Elizabeth replied.

They lay joined together and slept peacefully through the night.

~*~

Richard entered the townhouse anxiously the next day. He knew she had recognised him immediately upon introductions but how was he to explain that he had no idea who Miss Harrington was after bedding her twice almost eight months ago? He felt sheepish that he had slept with so many women that they all blurred together. Even those whom he knew he bedded, he could not recollect when or where he had lain with them.

Miss Harrington sat in the sitting room awaiting his visit. After instructing the maid for the tea service, she spoke to Richard. "Mr. Fitzwilliam. How nice to see you again. How have you been these past... seven months?" Her eyes sparkled.

"Well; I am well." He paused. "I apologise for not recognising you, Miss Harrington. I was not quite myself that day but I have no excuse."

"Please do not fret. I remembered you because you had shown more passion in the hour that we spent together than other men that I had been with. I was visiting my sister that day when you had requested my attributes and thought myself very fortunate to have been at the right place at the right time." She smiled. "I have not told anyone about our previous acquaintance. My sister remembered you as her customer but no one knows of our knowing each other." She added.

"Thank you for that, Miss Harrington." He calmed. "Haversham has told me that you had been in his service for four years until his recent marriage. I am finding myself in need of a service that you have provided in the past without a commitment of marriage and I have a cottage near my estate to which you can retire. I understand this townhouse is yours to keep as well. I would like to offer you a contract."

"Mr. Fitzwilliam, you are still young and very handsome. I wonder why you are not seeking a wife. I would like to understand your situation, sir. Of course, I will keep everything in confidence. I am nearing thirty and am surprised that you are not seeking to contract with a younger woman." Miss Harrington was honest. She did not want to be used for several months to be released again. She wanted something more permanent but knew she could not marry and needed to save two to three hundred pounds more before she could retire. Most men had sought courtesans of sixteen to twenty-five or so in age and she had been fortunate to capture Lord Harold for four years when she was five and twenty.

Richard sighed, "I do believe you deserve the truth. I am deeply in love with a woman who is already married. I met her the same day that I met you and had been thinking of her while I... was with you. I have decided that I would never marry and had not visited with anyone since I sought your service. I do not wish for any emotional entanglements, as my heart is completely hers, but I still have strong carnal needs and I wish to hire you for that service alone. We would not be seen in public and I would require absolute secrecy. I wish for companionship and perhaps some intelligent conversations, but other than the time that I would spend in your bed, we would not be socialising. I can provide you a place of lodging as well as an annual stipend. You may make arrangements with me to visit with your family or friends as you wish and when I am not in Kent or London, you will be able to travel and do as you wish while I am gone. I would require that you do not entertain any other patrons. Our arrangement would not be of a short duration. As you wish to retire in the next few years, I foresee our arrangement lasting the next five years or so if we are both content."

He stood to stare out the window after he finished speaking. *It is a cold arrangement and I hope she will agree. Even as I lay with her, I would not be able to get Elizabeth out of my mind. My heart will belong to only one woman for the rest of my life.* He thought to himself.

Miss Harrington finished her tea and arose. The arrangement was exactly as she had wanted. After being a prostitute and mistress for half of her life, she was exhausted of being at the whim of men and Mr. Fitzwilliam had offered choices and comfort as well as clear expectations of the arrangement. She walked over to the window and reached for his arm. "Come, Mr. Fitzwilliam." And she led him to her bedroom.

After closing the door, she began to take off her dress. She had expected a liaison so she had dressed in a simple morning dress. She stood in her chemise and reached for his face. He leaned down and she attempted to kiss him but he turned his face and she kissed his cheek. His hands did wrap around her and brought her closer to his body. As she kissed his neck and ran her fingers through his hair, she could feel a soft protrusion against her. She helped him take his coat off and began to unbutton his trousers. He did not resist. His large manhood sprung out and she gently stroked it to arouse it, while kissing his neck again.

She walked him over to the bed and had him sit while she helped him take off the rest of his clothes. She was quite impressed with his physique. He had pounced on her fully clothed last time and although she had appreciated his large erection before, she had not seen him fully nude and she was eager to have him again, as he had a magnificent body. Abigail pulled him and they lay down together, all the while she stroked his manhood and kissed his chest.

Richard was struggling with himself as Miss Harrington seduced him. He could see her large breasts and as she stroked his long cock, he was becoming more aroused but not enough for penetration. He felt as if he were betraying Elizabeth. *Oh, if only I could have married Elizabeth. No, she would not have had me. She knows that I need a woman. Why can I not get it up? I have used so many women before but now, I only want one woman; the only one I cannot have. Damn it! Why do I feel as if I am being unfaithful to my heart? All I wanted to do was to plunge myself into a woman for months and now, my body only wants her. Oh, Elizabeth, if only I could find my release with you.*

He lay in bed with his eyes closed, thinking of Elizabeth. He felt Miss Harrington climb onto his body as she continued her kisses on his body. He could not kiss this woman on the lips. His lips would belong only to Elizabeth as she had allowed. He smelled Abigail's hair and it smelled of roses. Although a pretty scent, he desired to smell lavender like Elizabeth. He spoke quietly with his eyes still closed, "Would you be willing to change your scent to lavender?"

"As you wish. I will have lavender for you next time. Mr. Fitzwilliam, may I call you Richard?" Abigail asked.

Richard frowned as he opened his eyes. "I am sorry, but please do not address me by my given name. Only a few call me by that. You may call me 'Fitzwilliam' or 'Colonel' or even 'Fitz' if you would like." He honestly answered. He had never wanted anyone else but family to call him by his given name since he was very young.

Only my closest family, and of course my Elizabeth can call me Richard. I hate it when anyone else names me so intimately. I have never let any of the women I bedded call me by name as they only had my cock. Only Elizabeth has my heart, as would my wife. Oh, my Elizabeth, my wife. She can call me anything and I would bow to her every demand. He realised he was thinking of his beloved once again and smiled while he shook his head and closed his eyes.

"That is not a problem, Mr. Fitzwilliam. May I ask, are you in love with a woman named Elizabeth?" Abigail enquired.

Richard's eyes sprung open widely and grabbed her by both arms. "How do you know that name? What have you been told?!" *Shit!* His heart beat fast in a panic that someone would know about his love for Elizabeth. He was concerned for Elizabeth and Darcy. He did not want any rumours about his personal life.

"I assure you there are no rumours or gossips, Mr. Fitzwilliam. I only recalled you had spoken her name when we joined last. I swear I heard nothing else." She tried to assure him. Abigail was frightened for a moment that he might injure her. She had plenty of men in the past who had beaten her and took her by force, and he was a tall, very muscular man.

Richard let her arms go immediately and breathed a sigh of relief. Looking at the naked woman sitting on his groin, he quickly apologised. "I am very sorry, Abigail. I had not thought I spoke her name. Yes, it is Elizabeth." His semi-erection had quickly deflated with the shock. "Always Elizabeth," he whispered and closed his eyes again. *Only Elizabeth. God, I miss her.*

Abigail saw the pain in his eyes before he closed them. "Mr. Fitzwilliam, you can dream of her and I will pleasure you. Tell me what you love about her." She whispered as she returned to kissing his neck and coaxing another arousal with her hand.

"She is the most beautiful creature my eyes ever beheld. When she smiles, the whole room lights up. She makes me smile even when I am in the foulest of moods and calms me when I am angry enough to murder someone. Her eyes twinkle when she speaks and she has perfect round breasts." He kept speaking about Elizabeth with his eyes closed and dreamt of her kisses and his arousal bulged in full very quickly.

Abigail lifted her body to line up his cock with her opening and slowly sat on it. Richard stopped talking and began to moan loudly as she slowly rode him. His penis was thick and long and it had been one of the largest she had had before, but she knew he would not last long as his moans grew louder.

Richard felt her muscles wrap around his hungry manhood and as it was massaged and stroked deep inside her, he grunted, "Elizabeth!" and released his seed within a few minutes. He had imagined his love sitting on him and he wanted to fill her, but he knew he could never have her.

He opened his eyes to see Abigail panting and sweating above him and he smiled. *This could work.* He felt the pressure of keeping his desires to himself melt away and Abigail did not mind, but rather encouraged his fantasies.

Abigail lay down next to Richard panting. His erection had felt so good and she was eager to have him again. He had taken her twice last time and she wondered if he would do so again. She thought of her other lovers and laughed as she remembered that Lord Harold had often called her 'Miss Bennet' or 'Lizzy' as he released. She wondered if it was the same woman. *This Elizabeth must be quite a woman to have a Lord and this handsome gentleman both in love with her.*

Richard heard her chuckle and asked, "What is so funny? I hope my performance was not that shameful."

"No, no, sir! You are absolutely one of the best I ever had. I was curious," she carefully asked, "is your Elizabeth possibly a Miss Bennet or Lizzy?"

"Blasted! How in the world do you know that? Have I said those names as well?" Richard was mortified. Not only did this woman know of Elizabeth, but to have blurted out her maiden name was unforgivable. *Darcy is going to kill me!*

"No, I... I have to admit that you are the second man to desire an Elizabeth in bed. Lord Harold often called out her name." She quickly added, "I certainly do not mind but she must be a fearsome woman to attract two such worthy suitors. You said she is married?"

Richard took another breath. "That arrogant arse thought he could win my Elizabeth but she would not have him." He laughed, "She is too intelligent for him and would never have accepted him for all his wealth and rank. She is formidable but most generous and to be near her is enough for me. Abigail, I will require your absolute confidence on this. I will have the contract delivered next week." She nodded. "My Elizabeth is my cousin's wife. She is Mrs. Fitzwilliam Darcy of Pemberley."

She opened her mouth in surprise. There was not a woman in town who did not know of Mr. Darcy. He had been the most eligible bachelor in society for years and had been untouchable. His wealth was outrageous and although rumoured at 10,000 a year, it was easily understood that it must be over £20,000. He had never dallied, never visited, or even flirted with a woman. Gossip had been rampant that he might lean toward the male preference but then he had gotten himself married to a woman of unknown origins and had been seen in town smiling and laughing in public with his new wife last fall. *A fearsome woman indeed!* Abigail thought.

Richard continued, "I met her right after Darcy became engaged to her and I knew my heart was lost. I am certain I could not have won her even if she had been free, but my love grew against my will and I will never love another." He paused to make sure she understood him. "I am satisfied with using your body as a surrogate lover as long as you are content with this arrangement. It will never be more, Abigail, is that agreeable with you?" She nodded. "I cannot kiss you as my lips belong to Elizabeth. I would never dishonour her and seduce her to bed me; she dearly loves my cousin, but I have kissed her lips and cannot bear to touch another so."

"I understand, sir. I am in awe of your love for this woman. I know I will probably never meet her but I see that she has your heart completely and I am agreeable. You offer me a life of peace and comfort and I will offer you my body to bring you pleasure and completion. I am unable to bear children so you may continue to release inside me as well." Abigail smiled.

Richard was comforted knowing that he would not father a bastard. "How long have you known you cannot have children?" He asked, as he lay back and stared at the canopy above him.

Abigail honestly answered, "I have had two miscarriages early into my profession. I am ashamed to say that I have been sleeping with men since I was fifteen. I ran away from home when a man seduced me into eloping with him and after he took me several times, he promptly sold me to a brothel. After my sister's husband died, my sister found her own occupation and happened to come across me at her friend's brothel. She took me out but I continued the lifestyle, as I enjoyed having men's attentions. I had two patrons who impregnated me but I lost the babe and after the second loss, the doctor told me that I would not be able to have children again. That was over ten years ago and I have not had my courses since then."

"I am glad you have been able to heal, though, Abigail. I am sorry for the pain you had gone through. I had used women in the past and cared not about anything else than my own satisfaction but I will promise you that I will not harm you and should you require some time away from me, just let me know. I will never take you against your will." Richard held her hand for several moments. *I vowed to respect women of all stations and I will be considerate. Oh, Elizabeth, how you have changed my world. I must see her soon. I need to be with my Elizabeth!*

He stood to dress. "I will take my leave now to work with my solicitor to make the arrangements. I will be in London for the next two weeks and will send you the contract and the address of the cottage in Kent. I hope you will be pleased with it. I wish to visit you fortnightly in Kent. Is that agreeable?" She nodded. *I dare not use her more often. Although I enjoy the release, I need just enough to get by and will not use her more often than that.* "Thank you for your time and the arrangements. I hope it will bring you contentment." He bowed and left. *I must see Elizabeth. I miss her so much.*

Abigail lay in bed with happiness that she had not known. She had been quite anxious to retire from this business and Mr. Fitzwilliam was the answer to all her wishes and he had a glorious body and was incredibly handsome as well. Although she had enjoyed coupling with him and looked forward to another session, once every fortnight would be satisfactory. She rose to dress to prepare for her move to Kent and to go shopping for some lavender perfume.

Chapter 31

Elizabeth had been asleep in the library when she heard the door close.

She had been having a most wonderful dream about the baby and her husband had been feeding her strawberries. She startled then yawned widely and looked up to see Richard staring at her.

"Richard! I have not seen you for a couple of days now. How have you been? Is it near dinnertime yet? Come, sit and talk with me. Do you think Cook will have strawberries for dessert?" She smiled. Strawberries sounded so good.

Richard lifted her up as she squealed in laughter and sat her upon his lap. He had missed her so much and his heart overflowed with love for her after hearing his name from her lips. He cradled her in his arms and held her close as she leaned her head on his shoulder. He smelled her hair and kissed her head. *Lavender!* He recalled the first time he met Elizabeth and how desperate he had been to touch her. He had taken Abigail that day out of desperation, and here he was today, using Abigail once again, but this time allowed to hold his beloved in his arms. He sighed in contentment and smiled.

"You are happy. I am glad to see you smile." Elizabeth commented as she lifted her eyes to meet his.

"Of course, I am happy. I have you in my arms and I cannot imagine more happiness than right now. I missed you, Elizabeth." He gently kissed her lips several times. "How are you? How is my favourite boy or girl in there?" He caressed her abdomen and held her tighter. *Oh, my heart, she is the most beautiful creature in the world.*

"I am so large, Richard! Fitzwilliam says he does not mind but I must look like a cow! How am I to show my face to your sister's ball tomorrow?" She cried on his shoulder. "I cannot see my feet and my back is so sore. I keep falling asleep everywhere and I am unfit for decent society." She wailed louder.

He chuckled. She had become more and more irrational and although Darcy was afraid of her mood swings, Richard had found it very amusing. *Poor Darcy! She has never been so unreasonable.* He kissed her hair and rubbed her back, holding her tightly.

"My love, your pregnancy is progressing well and Darcy told me that the doctors are confident that you and the babe are healthy. Darcy is a damn large chap so your baby is probably overgrown like his father. You are beautiful, Elizabeth. Do not fret so. Darcy loves your body and he told me he drools every time he sees you grow larger." *As do I!* He kissed her cheek and forehead several times, as he inhaled her scent. "You will always be most beautiful to us. I love you." He kissed her lips gently again, holding her firmly against his body as he was aching to love her closer. "Do not forget." *I cannot believe I am aroused again having her in my arms. She has my heart wrapped around her little finger.* He sighed contently.

Instead of being comforted, she wailed even louder. "I am not worthy to be loved by anyone!" She sobbed until he could feel his shoulder dampen.

He did not know what else to do. *Where the hell is Darcy?!*

Just then, the library door opened and Darcy entered. Richard gulped, as he still had Elizabeth on his lap as he tightly embraced her. *I hope he does not kill me for holding her so!*

Darcy walked swiftly over to them and lifted Elizabeth up from Richard and winked. Richard smiled in relief. *Hopefully he knows what to do with her! The poor thing is so tired from being so uncomfortable.*

Darcy whispered, "Thank you, Richard," then carried her to return her to their bed. He saw that she was distressed and was crying heavily on his cousin's shoulder but was rather relieved that Richard had been there to comfort her, as he had been busy for the past hour with the steward.

Richard could not suppress his mirth when Elizabeth wrapped her arms around Darcy and could hear her say, "Can we have strawberries, husband?"

~*~

Darcy returned in a few minutes and sat with Richard. "Good lord, your shoulder is still wet. She must have cried rivers." They laughed. "She is sleeping. After I promised her we could have strawberries for dessert, she said she wanted to fill the conservatory at Pemberley with strawberries and began to snore. Whew... I love her to death and this is certainly such an experience but I hope you never go through this with your wife!"

Richard chuckled. "Well, watching Elizabeth through this is enough for me. You know I will never marry. I have found myself a mistress, though, Darcy. I just finished visiting my solicitor and he is drawing up the contract. She is Miss Abigail Harrington and understands all of my criteria. By the by, she was Haversham's mistress for four years. He was using her while he was courting Elizabeth."

Darcy's eyes grew wide. "That rake! Thank goodness Elizabeth saw straight through him. Will you be happy with her? Is she enough to satisfy...?" Darcy watched Richard carefully. He had seen Richard's hand on her abdomen and his lips on Elizabeth's hair and he knew that his wife would not have sat on his lap like so. But Richard had been comforting her and caring for her and she had needed him. Darcy was no longer jealous of Richard's need to physically connect with Elizabeth and he had been completely appropriate in public company. He wondered if having a mistress would be enough for Richard. He knew he himself would continue to burn for Elizabeth's touch.

"I used her today and I believe it will work, Darce. It does not quench the desire but enough to keep me sane. Darcy," he paused to look into Darcy's eyes, "I know that you know I kiss Elizabeth too often. I honestly cannot stop myself and I am sorry for it; I have never needed to be so close to anyone before. I feel empty when I am not with her. She is so precious to me, cousin. I hope you will forgive me." *I only need Elizabeth. She is the only one who can quench my passion.*

Darcy smiled. Richard had become very open and honest with his feelings for Elizabeth and he appreciated it. He would rather know the truth than for Richard to hide himself away or infringe upon Elizabeth in secret. *As much as he loves her, he knows his boundaries and still respects me. Good man.*

"Richard, until the day she slaps you across the face, you will receive as she gives. I cannot believe that I am saying this, but if I had to share my Elizabeth with anyone, I am glad it is you. You are an honourable man and you truly love her with all of your heart. You are like a brother to me and I appreciate that you care for her so deeply. I cannot imagine if she had Haversham's attentions. I would choke the life out of him!" They laughed loudly. "I hope you will be satisfied with having Miss Harrington in bed. I have been without Elizabeth for," Darcy looked at his pocket watch, "three hours and ten minutes and I am restless to have her again. I do not know how you did it for nearly eight months!"

Richard chuckled at this. "I do not know how you spent seven and twenty years without it!"

"Well, after I married and once the box was open, it will never close again." They snickered in amusement. "Let us go fence. Maybe the exercise will help me burn off some energy until my lady calls for me to do my duty with her!"

~*~

Elizabeth was very pleased with seeing the strawberries for dessert but after two bites, declared them unpleasant and requested a lemon tart. The gentlemen rolled their eyes and giggled like schoolgirls when Elizabeth's head was turned.

~*~

Lady Iris Fitzwilliam's Coming Out Ball was hailed as the event of the Season. It had been one of the last balls of the quarter, as Lady Matlock had delayed it two weeks due to the Darcys' injuries, and the general consensus was that the best had been saved for last.

The Darcys were still a novelty as their marriage was so new and it was quite apparent that she was with child now but as this was a family ball, it was deemed appropriate that she attend. The Darcys danced two sets as well as the waltz at the end of the evening.

Richard Fitzwilliam, who now carried the title of being the most eligible bachelor, remained congenial and smiled handsomely while he greeted many eligible ladies and flirted a bit, but he, once again, only danced with his mother, Mrs. Darcy, his sister, and Miss Darcy, who was allowed dancing only with family members, avoiding the other single ladies completely and staying close to his family most of the time.

Many hearts were broken, as he appeared to be no longer interested in the marriage market.

The ball was heralded as a great success and several suitors lined up to call on Lady Iris the next day, with Richard's arms crossed and frowns deterring any inappropriate behaviours from gentlemen callers.

~*~

Caroline Bingley sat fuming. *I should have been there!* She read the newspaper's gossip column for the fourth time to hear more about Mr. Darcy. There was only a small blurb about how beautiful Mrs. Darcy looked and if they might be expecting an addition to the family. *That harlot is having my Mr. Darcy's baby? I should be having his baby! I should be gifted with jewels! I should have been at the ball!*

Caroline had just returned to London after finally gaining her financial independence. She had spewed her venom at Charles and Louisa endlessly through letters while at

York and was now completely cut off by her family. She vowed to never return to Yorkshire also and burned her bridges with her aunt as well.

After finding the best townhouse that her money could lease, she purchased extravagant furnishings and ordered three dozen new dresses. She spent her money as if there was no tomorrow, in order to gain favours and appear affluent to her acquaintances.

She still had some friends who invited her to events and she quickly gave away her favours to gain a few more prestigious ones. It was most unfortunate that Lady Fitzwilliam's ball was above her friends' access.

She planned on getting near Mr. Darcy as soon as possible and believed him to be staying in London for the rest of the Season and that she would find a way to get into his bed. She was certain that once he saw her in her most seductive nightgown and smelled her concoction of musk, rose, and pumpkin perfume, that he would fall desperately in love with her and make her his mistress.

She smirked, *Especially if that whore is pregnant and fat like a cow!* She rubbed her hands in glee.

Chapter 32

It was now June. The Darcys would stay at Rosings for three weeks then remove to Netherfield until Mrs. Bennet delivered, and then return to Pemberley to await Elizabeth's confinement. They would have family visit in August and Elizabeth was especially looking forward to having the Gardiners there. Although they had seen them often, either dining at Gracechurch Street or entertaining them at her own home, Mrs. Gardiner was more a mother to her than her own.

Mrs. Bennet would be unable to join them, as it would be too soon to travel, but the Darcys were to host the Gardiners, the Bingleys, and of course Richard.

Richard had originally planned to remain at Rosings after the Darcys visited but seeing Elizabeth's moods and her growing so large so quickly, he was very concerned for her and wanted to be near. He had heard of enough women dying at childbirth and he loathed to be apart from her, not knowing how she would be faring for weeks or months, if Darcy could write to him even that often. Spending the past two months with her had been the best days of his life and he could not imagine life without her now.

He had never thought living with a woman would be so pleasurable but Elizabeth was perfect. They argued about politics and philosophy at times; they laughed about the social rules that changed with the monarchy that were inconsistent and idiotic; and they debated religion and morals as well as prejudices based on rank and sex. He could talk to her about anything and respected her views, even when they did not agree. His beloved knew his food preferences and exactly how he liked his tea, which no one had ever taken the time to discover, chastised him like a wife when he used foul language like a sailor, and teased him and laughed with him as no one else had ever done before.

Elizabeth had a way of discerning if he were not telling the truth and he could hold no secrets from her, including his visits with his mistress, but she had never judged him. Richard had opened himself up to her as he had not done with anyone else and felt contentment beyond all expectations. He felt protective of her and vowed to do everything in his power to make her happy.

Richard spoke to Darcy in his study in private. "Darce, I know that I had planned on staying here for the summer to join you in August at Pemberley but I am fearful of Elizabeth's condition. She is larger than expected and is constantly uncomfortable. I do not mean to put more fear into you or disrespect your abilities as her husband, Darcy, but I could not, I cannot face a world without her in it. I beg of you, I wish to join you to Hertfordshire and then return to Pemberley with you." He wiped a tear, "I cannot be so far from her, even for a month or two, not knowing what might happen." He paused to settle his emotions and whispered, "One hundred thirty-two."

Darcy asked, "What is one hundred thirty-two?" He heard the pain in his whisper.

Richard sighed, "One hundred thirty-two days: Days away from her, days without her. They were the longest days of my life not being near her. Not being in the same house, not seeing her, not hearing her laughter, not knowing when I would be with her again. I do not know if I can go through it again. I need to be near her, cousin. Anywhere she is, I wish to be." *I love her so much. I would die without her.*

Darcy watched his cousin carefully. *If I ever doubted his love for my Elizabeth, this is now proof that he truly loves her as dearly as I. He has expressed the same as I have been feeling. He would have made her a wonderful husband but selfishly, I am grateful to hold that office.* He carefully considered the options before him and came to a decision.

"Richard, you know that you are most welcome at Pemberley. I still owe you a debt of gratitude for saving our lives." He paused. "I have a proposition for you. As you are aware, we three, you, I, and Elizabeth, have quite an unconventional relationship. While Elizabeth loves you like a brother, I also know that she wants you in her life. She loves me dearly and requires no other, but your love for her helps her stand even stronger. I believe that knowing you would give your life for her, I have not become a jealous fool when you hold her and even kiss her, but I am even more confident in her love for me as she demands my attentions and requires *me* to hold and kiss her." He paused again.

"Richard, I would die if something were to happen to Elizabeth and I was miles and counties away. I understand your reluctance to part from her and sympathise with you completely. We believe that she is carrying twins." He saw Richard's shock on his face. "While a single birth is still dangerous, twins are even more so and I fear for her every day. But I will not allow my fears from ever stop loving her and I can only pray and care for her through this course. She does need you, cousin; we both need you. As much as I wish, I cannot be with her every minute of the day and I know she is comforted by your presence. She feels safe with both of us and her nightmare returns at times as she fears for her own and the lives of the babes that she carries. My proposition is that you will stay with us for as long as you wish.

"Working with you at Pemberley and here at Rosings, I realise that your help has been vital to me. You have done a tremendous job in supporting my businesses and know the inner workings as much as I. My properties and investments are vast and I would not have succeeded without your help these past weeks. You can manage your estate from a distance, perhaps lease it if you would like, or if you wish, we will live at Pemberley together for several months and travel back to Rosings together for several months a year. In London as well, you can continue to stay with us at Darcy House as custom. I plan on touring my properties next year and it would be a good experience for you, to see the other estates and see how they are managed. As long as we are careful, no one will question that you are part of the Darcy family. What say you?" Darcy asked.

Richard stood and hugged Darcy. Darcy was surprised at the sudden affection but knew that Richard was very pleased.

"Thank you, Darcy, thank you. That is exactly what I wished. You may never get rid of me." Richard tapped Darcy's back and grinned. "I promise to work hard." *I will do everything to prove my worth!*

"What about your Miss Harrington? What are your plans with her?" Darcy asked. "She cannot come to Pemberley. You do not wish for Elizabeth to meet her, do you?"

Richard looked stricken. "Why would I ever wish to do that? I would never bring her here and I would never entertain her at Pemberley! I set her up at the cottage that once belonged to Mrs. Younge. After she abandoned it, I was able to finally track down where she had gone by hiring a detective to track Mr. Collins. It appears that Mr. Collins had enough funds to fix up his parents' old house and they are living comfortably there. I asked for the purchase of the cottage and put the house under Abigail's name and she will reside there for the rest of her life if she should wish. I have only visited her twice, Darcy, and we have an arrangement for fortnightly while I reside at Rosings, as I do not wish to use her too often. Should I go to London, I might ask to remove herself to London to avail herself to me there, but otherwise I will go on with my life as usual. I am only keeping her for my carnal needs, but truly, if Elizabeth commands me so, I will not visit her again." He paced a bit. *I only need my Elizabeth.*

"Darcy, you referred to our situation as unconventional and while I agree with that term, I see it as being something of such rarity and special that I cannot see it as immoral. Although I might be coveting your wife in a sense, it is not to steal her away from you or to commit adultery. She will keep her vows to you and I would never take more. I respect you too much to cross that line. I have kissed her several times and enjoyed it, but I would not ask for more, Darcy. I do not know why or how, but that is enough for me. I only wish to be near her. I am frankly in awe that you are acceptable to my affections and love for her. I do believe that if the situation were reversed and you loved my wife in the same way, I would understand as well. I thank you for your patience and understanding, Darcy. You are truly a good man."

"I will need to speak with Elizabeth and obtain her opinion as well. If she is hesitant or does not wish to have you in her life daily, I must do as my lady commands. We have two more weeks here and we will make the best of it if you are not to join us to Netherfield, but I will also give you time to convince her as well. She tells me everything, Richard. She loves you." Darcy smiled.

"Like a brother," Richard grinned, "and that is all I ask."

~*~

Darcy left to find his wife sitting in the drawing room and embroidering. She was adding patterns to the baby gown. She had just finished her meeting with the housekeeper and was an exemplary surrogate mistress of Rosings. *Oh, how I love her. She is the best thing in my life.*

He sat with her and told her of his discussions with Richard and Elizabeth immediately agreed that it was a good idea. "I was afraid to leave him all alone here in this big house, Fitzwilliam. For all his professing of being well on his own, I know he will be lonely. But, my love, are you agreeable with that decision? You know he... he kisses me and embraces me often and I do not feel... I am not attracted to him in such a way but I do not wish to injure you. If you do not wish for his presence, I will do as you wish. Am I awful that I do not reprimand him? Should I begin to keep my distance? Am I wrong to care for him and enjoy his company? Am I dishonouring you?" She began to tear up.

Darcy rubbed her back gently and smiled. *She has such a generous heart but she is still such an innocent.*

"Elizabeth, when Richard kisses you or embraces you, do you wish for him to take you to his bed?" She rapidly shook her head in the negative. "And does Richard ever ask you to do anything to him? To touch him or for permission to touch you elsewhere?" Again, she shook her head. "I believe that he lives to be near you and he might steal a few kisses from you, but he truly loves you and he loves me like a brother. He would never dishonour you and he would not wound me by asking for more than what you give him. Should the day arrive that you wish to share his bed, I hope to God that you will tell me first so I can fight for you. But if you should truly wish it, I would not be in your way." He stopped to quieten his emotions. *I never wish her to be with anyone else but I would accept her desires. I love her too much to keep Richard's love from her if she wanted him in her bed. Richard is the one person in the world with whom I could share my dearest wife.*

"Fitzwilliam, I have not thought of him in such a way and I will never leave you. I care for him and love him like a brother and wish for his happiness. I know that he has resumed visiting a lady friend and I am happy for him that he could move on. I wish for him to find love and marry and have his own children, but whether you like it or not, you are stuck with me, Mr. Darcy. You might become angry with me and huff off to ride your stallion but I will be waiting for you to return and will crawl into your bed and beg you to make love to me. If I ever find another woman in your bed, I will scratch her eyes out and kick her in the shins like I did with Wickham. I will never let you go, do you hear me?" She grabbed both of his cheeks with her soft hands and held his face in front of her eyes.

Darcy laughed wildly then kissed her fiercely. "I love you, my wife." He laughed again, "I awoke in time to see you kick Wickham in the shins and although not until much later, I recalled that you had wanted to kick him after I told you about Georgiana. HAHAHA! What a sight! You are truly a wonder." He kissed her again. "I will have you speak with Richard of our decision. He will be relieved, my love. He is truly concerned for your wellbeing. Promise me that you will rest afterwards. You must take care of yourself and our babies." He kissed her belly and whispered words of love to their unborn children.

"I will, my love. Send him in at his leisure." Elizabeth replied. "Thank you, husband."

~*~

Darcy went to Richard's study with a stern face. He wanted to trick his cousin as he had done a few times in his youth. He knew it was cruel but it would be short-lived and Elizabeth had been too generous with him already.

"Richard," he said stoically, "we have come to a decision. Elizabeth wishes to speak with you."

"Is she agreeable? Will she allow me to stay with you?" He asked like an orphaned child.

Darcy just shook his head, acting as if she had denied it. "I will not say, cousin. You shall go to her now while I stay here." He looked grimly at Richard.

Richard's heart broke. If Elizabeth did not wish it, he would not press, but he had to know. She was like air to him and his life looked bleak without her near. He quietly left his study, not seeing Darcy sniggering behind his back.

You fool! You want to be in her life so badly that you did not consider her feelings. She may be sick of you, always grabbing her to kiss her and holding her so tight. Dear god, what do I do without her?

Resigned, he entered the sitting room and saw Elizabeth lying back with her eyes closed and feet lifted on a footstool. *She is wonderful and I cannot imagine my life without her. I cannot face her now. I need to get out of here!* He turned to leave. All he wanted to do was to get on his horse and ride until he jumped off the cliffs over the ocean. He took a step forward then heard her speak.

"Richard, where are you going? Why are you leaving me already?" Elizabeth asked with her eyes closed.

Wanting nothing but to escape but unable to resist being away from her longer than necessary, he walked towards her and sat on the chair across from her.

He answered her, "I am here. I will always be here." *Alone, miserable, and unable to breathe.*

Elizabeth stirred and began to sit up but she had reclined too much and needed help to avoid appearing too disgraceful. Seeing her struggle, Richard immediately got up and sat next to her to assist.

"Thank you, Richard, I am beyond large already. What would I do without you?" she smiled brightly.

Richard could not return the smile. His heart was breaking. *Please tell me you need me. Please tell me you want me close. Do not leave me!*

"Richard, what is wrong? Did Fitzwilliam not give you an idea of our decision?" She lifted her hand and caressed his cheek and saw the unshed tears. He cupped his hand over hers to lift it and kiss her palm. "That Mr. Darcy! I see what he has done." She smiled and hugged Richard, laying her head next to his heart. "We wish you to be with us always. You are a Fitzwilliam and Fitzwilliam is a Fitzwilliam and we will be together." She laughed at her own joke. "Richard, I love you like a brother, but nonetheless, I love you." She stayed in his embrace, listening to his wild heartbeats.

Richard was elated. She would allow him to stay. He would not have to live out the rest of his miserable life alone in this grand mansion with all the ostentatious furnishings. He would be part of their family and God willing, live to see her babies and be a good uncle to them. Rather, her children would be his own. He would love anything and everything she loved. He hugged her tightly and kissed her hair and temple several times. "I love you, too. I love you so much, Elizabeth. Thank you for agreeing to let me be a part of your life."

He helped her sit upright and then to standing. He held her by both cheeks and kissed her lips tenderly several times. "Thank you, my dear. You must go and rest now. I am going to go beat your husband for putting me through this but I promise not to damage his handsome face." He winked and she giggled.

He walked her to her room so she could take a nap and returned to the study.

Seeing Darcy at the desk overseeing some paperwork, he boomed, "DARCY!" and gave him his most furious look. Darcy looked up and saw the face that had beaten him up several times in their youth.

Oh, shit! He stood and began to look for a way out of the room.

Richard rushed over to the desk and Darcy flew to the other direction but Richard was too fast. He grabbed hold of Darcy's torso and pushed him down to the floor and sat on his chest. He lifted his hand as if to throw a punch but quickly lowered it to help Darcy stand up, his laughter roaring loudly in the air.

As Darcy stood, Richard hugged him tightly and tapped his back firmly. "I am glad I can still catch up to you. Thank you, brother. Thank you."

Relieved that his little joke had not resulted in loss of teeth, mostly his own, Darcy joined his laughter. He left Richard to work while he rested with his dear wife and perhaps make love to her again. It had been hours since he had provided his services to her.

~*~

All of the businesses were seen to while they remained at Rosings and they prepared to leave for Hertfordshire. Richard visited Abigail and told her of his plans.

"Abigail, I will be traveling to Mrs. Darcy's sister's home and then to Pemberley. Our schedules are not yet firm but the plan is to await Mrs. Darcy's confinement as she is due in September, and if all goes well, to return to Rosings for Christmastime. Her parents are located closer to here and I offered to host a Christmas party in December with a large crowd, as she will be hostessing her family and my family will also attend. I thought you might wish to travel for the next six months. I have brought you extra funds for your pleasure. As long as you abide by our contract, I wish for you to enjoy yourself." He concluded. He would be leaving the next day and would not see her for six months but he was of no mind to bed anyone and knew he would rally. All he wanted was to be near Elizabeth and he would sacrifice everything else.

"Oh, Thank you, Mr. Fitzwilliam. You have been and continue to be very generous. I have a distant aunt in Ireland and have wished to visit her. Now, I will be able to take my sister and see the sights as well. Thank you." She leaned in to kiss his cheek. He had been true to his word and never kissed her, even during coition, but he did not mind being kissed on the cheek.

She led him to her bed and undressed as he shed his clothing. There was no romance or foreplay, just the deed, and she had become accustomed to it after the second time. This was the third time that she would be having relations with him as his mistress, and although mechanical, she knew he had enjoyed it. As he lay down, she knelt between his legs and stroked his cock into an erection and she saw that he immediately closed his eyes and knew that he was thinking of Elizabeth. *He must love her so much. What a shame. He could have made a woman very happy as his wife.* She thought.

As she continued her massage, his erection grew larger than ever before and he began to moan. She was surprised at the firmness of his manhood and got up to sit on him but he lifted her and placed her under him. He quickly plunged into her and held her for a moment as he breathed in her hair. She had changed her perfume to lavender and the effect had been immediate.

At the last visit, he was rapidly aroused after smelling her scent, requested fellatio, and quickly released in her mouth, quietly crying out his beloved's name, but this time, he was in control. He began to rock his body from on top of hers and soon, began to thrust into her vigorously. She was panting as he was pounding into her deeply and repeatedly, then he lifted his body to open her legs wider and she saw that his eyes were still closed but he was mumbling to himself. He leaned down to grab her breasts and began licking her nipples and gripping them roughly, as he continued his hammering into her. He buried his nose in her hair again and moaned loudly, "Oh, Elizabeth, be with me always, Elizabeth," and grunted his release loudly after pumping himself fiercely into her for another quarter hour.

She was still gasping for air when she felt him stiffen and roll off. She was covered in Richard's and her own sweat, as he had franticly exercised over her body. *He is magnificent! He is the best cock I have ever had and he just made me climax several times in a row. I had forgotten what an amazing lover he is!* Abigail thought to herself. She had never screamed her orgasms so loudly before today.

Richard had been dreaming of loving Elizabeth again. It was a recurring fantasy where he would make love to her for hours and give her all of himself. It felt so good to take a woman as hard as he used to do and he dreamt of his beloved under his burning body. He was very happy to find his release this way once again but knowing that he called out Elizabeth's name so loudly shamed him. He wondered if Abigail was affected by this. *No woman would want to be called by another name!* He thought. *But I cannot help it. My heart only belongs to Elizabeth. Laying with Abigail, I feel like I am betraying my Elizabeth somehow.*

He cleared his throat, "Ahem. I apologise, Abigail. It was damn rude of me to call out her name while I was laying with you. I shall try to not do it again, at least not so loudly, but it keeps slipping out."

Abigail softly laughed. "Oh, Mr. Fitzwilliam, I am quite envious of her. She has your love completely in her hand and I wonder if she knows it. I have never seen anyone so in love before. I am content to be used by you and do not ask for more. Please, should you wish to call me Elizabeth in bed always, I will respond to you as she. I enjoy your passion when you take me like that, sir, and I loved being fucked hard while you imagined yourself taking her. That was, by far, the best sex I have ever had."

Richard's cock twitched at her words. He would love to have intercourse while calling for Elizabeth. He smiled as Abigail's hand reached for his wet cock and pumped it back to life. She returned to her previous position, kneeling between his legs and began to suckle on his growing manhood. He watched her as she vigorously pumped it while licking the tip.

"Take me deep into your throat, Elizabeth." Just saying her name loudly like so got his penis hard quickly.

He closed his eyes, "Yes, just like that, Elizabeth. Your mouth feels so good, my love. Oh, make love to my cock with your mouth, Elizabeth. I want you so much. Oh, damn!" He thrust up into her mouth and exploded once again.

Dreaming of her made him release faster and stronger than ever. He was surprised that just thinking of Elizabeth's mouth on him resulted in releasing twice in a row like this.

He opened his eyes and was disappointed that it was not Elizabeth that had given him his release. *Why do I always feel so dissatisfied? Why do I feel like I am unfaithful to my beloved by using another woman? It is not Abigail's fault, though; it is my own weakness that I need the release.* He softly said, "Thank you, Abigail." He quickly lifted himself off the bed and dressed.

"I will see you in December. I plan on returning the first week of the month and I hope to resume our fortnightly visits if you have completed your travels by then. I have left my addresses should you need something urgently. If you should need more funds, please write to me." He bowed and departed.

He rushed to his horse and galloped quickly back to Rosings. *I need to see her. Even after releasing twice, I burn to see my beloved and be in her presence.*

Abigail looked into the envelope to see what was inside. She was shocked that Richard had not only left instructions to get in touch with him should she need something during the next six months, but also a letter from the bank for her to access £400 at her convenience, as well as banknotes of another £100.

He is truly so generous. This is almost ten years' income! I am most content in my lot. Perhaps I should permanently change my name to Elizabeth.

Chapter 33

Mrs. Bennet's voice shrilled as the Darcys and Richard arrived at Longbourn. Georgiana had arrived with them at Netherfield after they stopped quickly to transport her from London to Hertfordshire, as they would be heading straight to Pemberley afterwards. The younger girls giggled and gossiped while the Bingleys and Darcys and Richard greeted Mr. and Mrs. Bennet.

Richard had originally wanted to remain at Netherfield since he felt he had no place with the Bennets, but Elizabeth had begged him.

"Richard, please... Pleeeeeaaaazzzzeeee..." she pleaded whilst they were at Netherfield. "I love my mother but she drives me insane. I have always been her least favourite child and although she loved Pemberley and my prestigious husband, she spouted her nonsense at times and Jane has told me that she has been more illogical and confusing with her pregnancy than ever before." Darcy chuckled in agreement. "If you come with us, as a son of an earl and a master of an estate of 6,000 a year, we have a chance of her behaving herself. She might perhaps attempt to throw Mary your way, as I had neglected to put my sisters in the paths of rich men, but she will be more tolerable with your presence. Please, oh please... What can I do to convince you? Please, please, please?"

Richard laughed heartily at her pathetic attempts to beg. She was so adorable and he wanted to kiss her senseless. He raised his hands up as if in defeat. "Very well! I hope you do not fault me should I fall desperately in love with Mary and it will be all your fault for Bingley to be neglected completely for only having 5,000 a year!"

Darcy laughed out loudly as well. "I knew you could not resist long, Richard. Elizabeth will get everything her heart desires." *Richard is putty in my wife's hands. He can deny her nothing, just like me!*

Richard grinned. "So true, so true."

Just then, there was a knock at the door to the library. The servant spoke, "Mr. Darcy, Mr. Bingley wishes for your audience in his study. Mrs. Darcy, Mrs. Bingley shall join you shortly. She was indisposed this morning but is feeling better." He bowed and left.

Darcy kissed Elizabeth's lips, "I love you. Will you be all right?" She nodded. "Richard, please stay with her until Jane arrives." And he left.

They had been terrified of leaving Elizabeth alone unless she demanded it. She was quite large and uncomfortable most of the time and had difficulty sitting and standing alone. One or both of them stayed near her vicinity at all times.

After Darcy left, Richard sat next to her and embraced her, bringing her face to his chest while rubbing her back. "I will go wherever you wish me to be, my dear. If you wish for me to be a distraction for your mother, I will do so, but if she disparages you, neither Darcy nor I will stand for it. Darcy told me she had spoken harshly to you a few times at Pemberley but we will no longer tolerate it." He leaned down and kissed her on her lips. "I love you, Elizabeth. All your sisters, even your precious Jane, are nothing to you and do not believe it for a second. You are the most beautiful, the most intelligent, and the kindest woman of my acquaintance." He kissed her again, a little longer and licked her lips. "And you know I have known a lot of women!" He winked at her as he lifted his face from hers and sat back, attempting to control his ardour.

She giggled at his comment, "Yes, Richard, I know. How is your lady friend? You have not told me her name. Have you heard from her?"

Richard frowned. "I am certain she is well. I do not know where she is. She is to correspond with me only if something urgent comes up but Elizabeth, she is not really a friend. She may be my confidante but only for the physical need and I do not expect to hear from her. You are the only one to know my heart. And no, I will not tell you her name. I am ashamed that I have such an arrangement but I will not expose her to you." *I hate that she even knows of her but I cannot keep secrets from my beloved.*

"But Richard, do you not wish to marry? Have your own children someday? An heir for Rosings? I had thought you were moving on and looking for someone to love. What harm could come from my knowing her name?" Elizabeth was confused.

"ELIZABETH! How could I move on? What would I move on to? You have my heart completely. Would you ever stop loving Darcy? Do you think Darcy would ever stop loving you?!" She shook her head, still confused. Richard calmed and lowered his voice after the initial outburst. "I love you and will never find another. I will never stop loving you. Oh, my love, you are still so innocent." *I only want you. I only dream of you. I wish you to be the mother of my children.*

He turned his body to face her fully then leaned in to kiss her with his hands on her cheeks, and surprising her, he opened her mouth with his tongue and slowly pushed his tongue inside her mouth. He was so passionate for her, she returned his kiss by gently dancing with his tongue. She felt loved and cared for by Richard, even if it was not sexual for her.

He moaned as their tongues wrapped around together and slowly ended their kiss.

"Thank you, my love." He cleared his throat and parted from her slightly to give himself a moment. He was extremely aroused and even though she had consciously returned his kiss for the first time, he knew that she had not meant more than her usual generous affections. He caressed her face tenderly. "I will never marry, Elizabeth. I do not want you to know her name. I do not wish for you to ever meet her. I call her by your name when I use her and I do not think of her as anything more than a surrogate body for my release. I love you with the same passion that Darcy has for you and he will kill me should I take more, and I plan on leaving Rosings for your second son. You and Darcy are my closest family and I will ensure that all your children will be provided for as well." He leaned his forehead against hers and breathed in her scent. "The only way I would move from you is if you sent me away and I hope you will never do so. I do not wish to even imagine such heartbreak. I love you so much, Elizabeth." He kissed her gently on her lips twice and released her. "I thank you for your generous kiss, Elizabeth. If you will excuse me for a moment, I will stand by the window for a bit." He stood and quickly dashed to the windows, knowing that he would explode any moment in her proximity.

Elizabeth giggled to herself as she saw his huge protrusion and realised that he was once again acting like her husband. *Cousins! They are so similar and yet so different!*

~*~

A few minutes later, Jane opened the door to enter the library. She found Elizabeth on the couch reading a book while Mr. Fitzwilliam was looking out the window. His broad shoulders and narrow hips were very attractive, as he was one of the most handsome men she had ever met and she hoped he found her attractive as well.

Jane sighed as she realised that she truly desired Mr. Fitzwilliam's attentions. His flirting before the incident had aroused a curiosity within her that she had denied to herself and she wondered, not for the first time, what it would have been like to be pursued by him. But he had only been flirting to rankle Charles and Mr. Fitzwilliam had been easy-going and friendly but showed no real interest in her. But Charles was kind and their marriage had vastly improved and she tried to show more than her just serenity with him now. She voiced her dissatisfaction some times when he frustrated her. He corrected her gently when they argued about something and she was wrong. They had been more open in their communications and their lovemaking had become somewhat pleasurable.

Jane had discovered that she was with child and lately had been ill in the mornings. Elizabeth had shared with her own symptoms and what could help with the nausea and Jane was very pleased to have the four guests in her home. She knew she would need to grovel further for Mr. Fitzwilliam's forgiveness, as he remained very distant, but she could not blame him. She had acted most unladylike and wanton and she was still mortified at the recollection of what she attempted to do. *He is such a striking gentleman. His thighs look so strong and he truly cuts a fine figure. I wonder if he will flirt with me again. I miss it.* She stopped herself from thinking further. She knew she would need to work hard to make her marriage work and pondering on another handsome gentleman would not help her cause.

Jane spoke, "Lizzy, Mr. Fitzwilliam, how are you this morning? Did you sleep well?"

"Oh, Jane, I slept terribly but our room was certainly comfortable. I love the changes you have made to Netherfield because Caroline Bingley's tastes were awful!" Elizabeth replied.

Richard laughed. He sat distant from the sisters but joined in the conversation. "Mrs. Bingley, the room was fine and Georgiana was ecstatic about her pink room. She said Miss Kitty and Miss Lydia had helped you redecorate?" He was friendly but made sure to keep at least five feet away from Jane Bingley. He had noted the blush on her cheeks when he turned around and suspected she was still embarrassed from throwing herself at him at Pemberley. He smiled to himself, as such occurrences had been quite common and he would have taken advantage of it in the past but now, his heart was only for Elizabeth.

"Oh, yes. My sisters have been very happy to help. I was actually glad Mama was unable to assist due to her pregnancy. Her tastes are terrible, although not as bad as Caroline's." She quickly placed her hand over her mouth. "I should not have... Pardon me, Mr. Fitzwilliam. My mouth ran before my brain."

Elizabeth and Richard laughed loudly at this. Richard replied, "It is quite all right, Mrs. Bingley, but I would say that Lady Catherine has the worst taste of all and I had to request Mrs. Darcy to replace nearly every piece of furniture at Rosings!"

"Oh, Jane. I think your home looks wonderful. I am looking forward to returning to Pemberley, though, since I need to prepare the nursery. When we were there last, I only prepared for one!" She smiled brightly.

The door opened and Bingley and Darcy entered. "Shall we take our leave?" Bingley asked.

The ladies and Bingley boarded the carriage while Darcy and Richard rode their stallions.

~*~

Once they arrived and greeted one another at Longbourn, though, Richard sat fuming. He could see that Darcy was at his wit's end as well, as Mrs. Bennet rattled on and on about her pregnancy and chastised Elizabeth for gaining too much weight. She reprimanded her least favourite daughter that she must watch what she ate and make sure to starve herself so that she could return to her old figure or else Mr. Darcy would find her unattractive and she would be put aside for another woman. She was crass and rude, and although she believed herself to be whispering from the other side of the room, the gentlemen could hear her every word.

Darcy saw Elizabeth rolling her eyes and attempting to cease her mother's rants by turning her attention to something else, but she kept returning to the subject when her eyes landed on Elizabeth's thick midsection. She had also begun to tell Mary to sit up and puff out her chest more. Richard was ready to get back on his horse and return to Netherfield to avoid slapping an elderly pregnant woman as he had never been so tempted to strike a woman before.

He heard her say, "Mary, you must flaunt your assets to Mr. Fitzwilliam. He is exceedingly wealthy, even greater than our dear Bingley, and although he looks as fearsome as Mr. Darcy, he must desire a wife. It is a truth universally acknowledged that a single man of good fortune must be in want of a wife! I do not know how Lizzy landed such a grand gentleman as Mr. Darcy but if she can trap someone like him, you certainly have a chance with his rich cousin!"

Outraged, Richard stood up abruptly to confront the matron. Did she not realise that she had just insulted almost everyone in the room just now? He felt Darcy's hand on his shoulder. Darcy was raging in anger as well but he had eyed Mr. Bennet to cease his wife's ramblings, as he would no longer endure it.

Mr. Bennet saw that his old wife had returned with full force and stood up. She had been behaving much better and even at Pemberley, although she had slipped a few times, it had not been this bad. He knew his son in law and Mr. Fitzwilliam had been severely offended and they were ready to take Lizzy to bolt out the door. Even Bingley looked upset at the offences laid against his friends as well as himself.

"Mrs. Bennet, you will cease speaking!" Mr. Bennet boomed. Mrs. Bennet sat with her mouth gaping in shock. He had been so kind and catering to her needs these past months that she had forgotten that he could be commanding and frightening at times. He sat down next to his wife. *Thank God Miss Darcy was not here as well. She would be another Darcy to be offended and the insult would be complete.* Georgiana, Kitty, and Lydia were upstairs comparing drawings and dresses.

Mr. Bennet continued, "Mrs. Bennet, do you not comprehend that you have offended everyone in this room?"

Mrs. Bennet cried, "But I have not! I only spoke the truth and you know the truth is always preferred. I could not have been unkind. How have I offended?"

"Well, first and foremost, our dear Lizzy, who is carrying twins, as you have conveniently forgotten, is still slight and tiny overall. She carries her weight where the babes are and as you wish for the truth, you are quite large, even for someone who is due any day now. If you do not desire for me to push you aside in the future, perhaps you should starve yourself?" Seeing the horror in her face with the possibility of her food being taken away, he continued, "And you forget that our Darcy is from one of the most prominent families in all of England. He chose her, he loved her, and he proposed to her within two days of meeting her. If you believe that he is a man with faults for choosing Lizzy, then you underestimate his love for her."

Darcy stood and walked to stand behind Elizabeth, rubbing her shoulder and handing her a handkerchief while she wiped her tears. Richard followed and stood next to Darcy. Bingley also stood behind Jane.

Mr. Bennet, seeing the gentlemen united against his wife, continued, "And Mary is a wonderful young lady and you know that she is being courted by our new parson. She will make a fine wife should he make an offer and you were pleased with it until Mr. Fitzwilliam entered our home today. Darcy's cousin is fiercely protective of all the Darcys and I am certain he will make sure that none of us are ever invited into decent society ever again. My dear, you also offended Jane and Bingley by referring to Charles' income being smaller than the other gentlemen's, when you were once so proud that Jane had captured the wealthier man's attentions before we were made aware of Darcy's income." He paused to ensure his wife was following his speech. "I understand that you are pregnant and uncomfortable and I am grateful to you for carrying our sixth child, but I refuse to be indolent ever again and must take you to task. Now, what do you have to say to our daughters and guests?"

Mrs. Bennet cried copiously by now but she replied, "I am truly sorry and I apologise for offending you. I have been trying, truly, but I do not think before I speak and I just spewed out whatever was coming to my mind. It has been a long time since our house was so full and I became too excited. I hope you will all forgive me for my arrogance and ill-manners. Lizzy, I am sorry, child. You have done so well and I am very happy for you. I can see that Mr. Darcy loves you very much and I should not have said such cruel things to you. Jane, Charles, I sincerely apologise to you as well. I had been bitter about not being able to go to your home every day and to give you my opinions about how to furnish the house, and was jealous that Mary, Kitty, and Lydia had their say but I did not. I know I should let your home be yours and I am sorry for constantly interfering. Mary, I am sorry that I was not happy for you. I know that Mr. Bertram is a good man and I am certain you will be a most excellent wife to him someday."

Wiping her tears, she turned to Richard. "Mr. Fitzwilliam, I do apologise. You are certainly one of the handsomest men of our acquaintance along with your cousin, and I only thought of how wonderful it would be to have you join our family. I do not know how it is possible to have two such handsome men in the same family. You and Mr. Darcy look very well and I am certain any woman who has your attentions will be worthy. I sincerely apologise."

Richard was a bit flattered to hear Elizabeth's mother pronounce him so handsome. *Elizabeth is definitely worthy!* He laughed internally, *Elizabeth is the most fortunate, according to her own mother's words, as she has Darcy's and my love unconditionally.* He looked to Darcy who was smirking. *Ha! Darcy is thinking the same. She gave birth to my Elizabeth and I must respect her for at least that much.*

He walked over to Mrs. Bennet and bowed over her hand. "Thank you, madam. Your apology is fully accepted." And returned to stand next to Darcy.

The others soon chimed in and accepted her apology and Mr. Bennet helped her stand and insisted on taking a rest upstairs.

The remainder of the visit went well, with the promise that they would return the next day.

~*~

Darcy rubbed Elizabeth's large belly while lying naked in each other's arms that night. He loved her so much and they had made love twice already. Her carnal appetite was still great and he had enjoyed her attentions tremendously, especially when she wanted to suckle on his manhood and taste his seed. After releasing in her mouth, she grew his erection again using her mouth and he plunged into her from behind and climaxed a second time.

As they basked in the afterglow, Darcy had told Elizabeth what Bingley wanted him to know about Mrs. Wickham. "Bingley received a letter from Sarah Wickham. She thanked him profusely for providing for their daughter and promised that she would keep her father's identity a secret. She was able to pay off Wickham's debts and has begged her parents' forgiveness as well. Her family had cut her off due to her reluctance to own up to her downfall but this experience had helped her realise how wrong she had been. She will be residing near her older brother and will continue to care for the child and stated that there were several childhood friends who had desired her attentions in the past and she might be able to find herself a new husband soon. It appears Bingley will get out of this without too much damage to his name. He also told me that Jane has become more open and they have been getting along better."

"I am relieved. I knew tensions were high. They are so good for each other." Elizabeth was comforted.

They also discussed the event at Longbourn. "My love, I thought Richard was ready to strike your mother when she continued her ramblings about your figure and my finding you unattractive to you and then her pushing Mary at him. I was angry but I had expected such, as I have known your mother longer. The only reason he was able to hold back and not run out was because he wanted to protect us. I thought his blood veins would pop from his head!" They laughed. Her mother had been ridiculous today but they were thankful that Mr. Bennet reined her back in, even if it was a little late.

"I am glad he forgave her and I was very happy that he joined us. He is so good to us. Even though we were all thoroughly insulted, having him there did divert *some* of the attention from me." Elizabeth responded.

"Yes, my love. I agree. He would do anything for you. Now, are you ready for another session? I was thinking if you could get onto your knees and hands, I might love you from behind." Darcy grinned.

And they made love once again, their moans filling the air in their room.

~*~

Richard lay on his bed and stroked himself as he remembered Elizabeth's kiss in the library. *I will never kiss another. How sweet her mouth tasted.* It was the first time, except on Xerxes when she thought him to be Darcy, that she had returned his kiss. *I love her more than ever before. I cannot imagine my life without her now, never tasting her or holding her.* He pumped harder as he imagined loving her and caressing her face. "Oh, Elizabeth! I love you!" He grunted as he came into a cloth that he had prepared.

Now that they were back in Netherfield, he knew he would have to use his hand every few days like he had done before, but he did not mind. Having had Abigail three times in the past few weeks had been a good relief but there was always a nagging guilt in the back of his mind each time he used her. He knew he would never have Elizabeth but to use a woman to call out his beloved's name bothered him, as if he was being unfaithful to his heart. He was satisfied to use his own hand to purge himself of the need rather than to touch someone who was not Elizabeth.

He thought of the things that Mrs. Bennet said and began to feel his blood boil but quickly attempted to squash it. She was a woman of mean understanding all her life and it would take years to correct her behaviours. He acknowledged that Mr. Bennet had done well to correct her and teach her so far and he was once again awed that Elizabeth could come from such a woman and as he had learned, Mr. Bennet had been indolent before she married Darcy. *How did Darcy take to the task of having such in-laws? I wonder if I would have been able to bear it if I met her and her crass parents first. Would I have spurned my Elizabeth, seeking an heiress or someone with a better pedigree?* He knew he would have, but he would never give her up now and having fallen so deeply in love with her, he would have given everything to marry her, but knowing how he was before he changed his ways, knowing society's expectations, he had not been the same man only eight months ago, when he was considered a poor colonel with a bleak future. He would have sought a woman with at least £20,000 or a daughter of at least a baronet or someone with connections that he had thought he needed.

Damn lucky Darcy! I only need Elizabeth. My cousin made the best decision of his life by marrying her and his choice taught my heart to find love as well. Damn lucky. He smiled. *I am glad Elizabeth was pleased with me for forgiving her mother. I truly love it when she kisses me on her own volition. Oh, Elizabeth, I would do anything to make you happy.* He thought, and holding onto Elizabeth's handkerchief once again, he slept peacefully.

Chapter 34

The next morning, one of the servants rushed over to knock at Netherfield at about eight in the morning. Richard had gone for an early ride so he was not there, but Jane and Bingley were given a note from Longbourn that Mrs. Bennet had gone into labour during the night and the birth was impending at any moment. Jane dressed quickly and while Charles was getting the carriage prepared, she went to Lizzy's room and knocked. Hearing no answer, she quietly opened the door. The bed curtains were closed so she walked over to the side where her sister had typically slept and opened the curtains hesitantly. Lizzy had told her that she and her husband never slept apart and she did not wish to intrude on their privacy but she needed to tell her about Mama.

She opened the curtain slightly to find Lizzy on the other side facing the edge of the bed and she was quite shocked to see Mr. Darcy cupping her sister's breast with one hand while the other arm was under her neck. She could see that they were both naked and the sheets were tangled. Elizabeth was always hot now and she had kicked off the sheets and Mr. Darcy was covered only up to his buttocks. She could see the musculature of his broad shoulders that narrowed at the waist and the smooth bulges of his buttocks. She felt heat between her legs and quickly shut the curtains. *My goodness! I am aroused by everything I see! I am so wanton and I am lusting after Mr. Fitzwilliam and now Darcy! Lizzy is most fortunate. He is a fine specimen; that is for sure.*

Shaking her head, she walked to the other side of the bed and gently tapped Lizzy's hand. She stirred and slowly opened her eyes. As Lizzy shifted her weight slightly, Darcy moved as well and lay on his back. Jane could now see his muscular, bared chest, down to the dark hairs below his navel. *Good lord! His body is magnificent. No wonder Lizzy is constantly on him!* She averted her eyes quickly and spoke. "Lizzy, I just received word that Mama went into labour last night and the babe is arriving any moment now. Shall you dress and join me to Longbourn?"

She saw from the corner of her eye that Mr. Darcy awoke, and as she spoke, he pulled the sheets up to cover Lizzy and himself. *I shall never be able to look him in the eyes again.*

Elizabeth propped up and thanked her sister. "I shall join you in ten minutes, Jane. I wish to be there for Mama and to see what to expect as well. Thank you."

Jane quickly left the room, blushing brightly. *Why am I so wanton?!*

When the Bingleys and the Darcys arrived at Longbourn, the sisters could hear their mother's screams. Darcy walked Elizabeth up to the door and returned downstairs to sit with Mr. Bennet and Bingley. The men were to sit and wait with their brandy while the women took care of the screeching woman.

Elizabeth quickly surveyed her surroundings. She had purchased several books to learn about the birthing process and studied all she could. She had also spoken and written to Aunt Gardiner in order to understand what to expect. The midwife was already there and she had been the same midwife that had delivered Kitty and Lydia and she was very knowledgeable. Jane was more afraid but with Lizzy ordering her about, she complied and learned as well.

~*~

The gentlemen sat with their drink glasses. Richard had arrived with Georgiana after receiving the note Darcy had left behind to explain where they had gone. Georgiana immediately went to sit with the three younger girls, as they had all become thick as thieves.

Darcy paced by the window while Elizabeth was upstairs assisting, convinced that she was doing more than she should be. He heard the screams and wondered if he would be able to sit downstairs like this when it was Elizabeth's turn. He would want to be with her but it was frowned upon for husbands to be present at the birthing and it was just not done. But he could not imagine leaving her alone to suffer. *I will be with her. The midwife in Derbyshire is a kind woman. I must have her see my reasons!*

Mr. Bennet kept drinking and Richard noted that after he had arrived, Mr. Bennet was already reaching for his third glass.

He stood and held his cup away from him. "Sir, do you know how many glasses of brandy you consumed?" He shook his head. "Bingley, do you know how many glasses he has had so far?" Bingley also did not know. Richard spoke to Mr. Bennet. "Sir, I understand that you are anxious but I saw you consume two glasses already and this would be your third. I arrived at least an hour later so it is possible you had more. You are looking quite inebriated and you should be alert and awake to meet your new-born child, do you not agree?"

Mr. Bennet smiled, "Ah, yes. My new-born child. You are a good man, Fitzwilliam. I think my wife was right. You would make a good husband for one of my daughters. Can I interest you in one of them?"

Darcy chortled. *He is already like Elizabeth's husband! My poor wife has to suffer with two anxious lovers.*

Richard coloured. *I already am like a husband to Elizabeth, except for the marriage bed rights. I leave that to Darcy.* He smiled when he saw Darcy wink at him. "No, sir. Not at all. I will order some coffee." He went to pull the bell. When the maid arrived, he asked for coffee for everyone and sipped at it once it arrived. *I wonder how Elizabeth is doing. With Darcy and me both here downstairs, no one will stop her if she is ridiculous enough to put too much upon herself. I wish one of us were with her. I do not know how we will be able to handle this when she goes into labour. I must convince Darcy to remain with her while she births. Damn society's expectations! He must stay with her and care for her.*

After another hour, a knock came at the door. Jane entered and advised her father to meet his newest child. He dashed out of there and once he was distant enough, she revealed that the heir of Longbourn had been born and that mother and child were doing well. They all cheered and the men took a swig of their beverage.

Darcy asked how Elizabeth was doing and Jane told him that she was well and although Lizzy had tried to do more, she had stopped her and ensured him that Elizabeth was sitting and resting through most of the ordeal. Darcy was curious why Jane was having difficulty meeting his eyes but he wanted to see his wife so he rushed upstairs.

Richard sat for a moment and not desiring to be in the Bingleys' company, he excused himself and joined the girls in the drawing room while still worrying for Elizabeth.

Jane hugged Charles as soon as they were alone. "Oh, Charles, the miracle of birth is a wondrous thing. It was dreadfully messy and there was so much screaming, but to see my baby brother take his first breath was the most beautiful experience I could have imagined. I cannot wait until February for the arrival of our own child."

Charles kissed his wife and smiled. "Yes, I cannot wait also. I love you. Are you certain you did not put too much upon yourself?"

"Oh, no. Lizzy was the general in there, asking so many questions and advising what she had read. I hope her birthing will go well. I was rather stupid and did not know what to do. I have so much to learn." She softly sighed.

"We have time, my love. We will study it together and while Lizzy is here for another week, perhaps you can talk with her often and learn from her as well; and from your Aunt Gardiner also. We will purchase the books we need and ask for help. We should never be afraid to ask for help. I am certain the massive library at Pemberley must have a journal or two to help us." He kissed her tenderly.

"Charles, I want you. I am aching for you. I do not know what is wrong with me but I am constantly desirous to be filled. I know it has been only two days since our last union but could we excuse ourselves to return to Netherfield? I wish for nothing but to lay naked in bed and make love with you." She was sitting on his lap and could feel his hard bulge. She squirmed in her seat and Bingley moaned.

"If you can ask Hill to prepare the carriage, we will return now. I just need a moment, Jane. Wow, I am liking this side of you, my love." Bingley commented.

While Jane ordered the carriage to be readied, Bingley spoke with Richard in the drawing room. "Fitz, Jane is not feeling well and would like to return to Netherfield. I trust you brought Darcy's carriage?" Richard nodded. "Thank you."

Richard replied, "But of course. Take care of your wife. We will be well and will return after luncheon." He noted quickly that Bingley had a bit of a bulge in his breeches. He grinned as he recalled that Darcy had told him of Elizabeth's insatiable period beginning in her early pregnancy stage. *Aha! He wants to fuck his wife!* "Bingley, perhaps we will return a little after luncheon. We will see you at dinner; actually, do not bother meeting any of us and you should care for your wife, however long it might take." He winked as he stood to help guard the girls from seeing Bingley's erection.

Damn! He is going to really enjoy his life now. If she is anything like my Elizabeth, they will be in bed until he is cross-eyed. He smirked. *But I highly doubt it. Jane Bingley does not have an ounce of the passion that my Elizabeth has. She is truly the best woman I have ever known. I hope she is well. I wish I could see her right now.*

He returned to his seat and continued his conversations with the young ladies, finally relaxing when Darcy returned with Elizabeth on his arm.

~*~

The rest of the week passed pleasantly, with Mrs. Bennet recovering slowly but fully, and the new heir of Longbourn was healthy and wailed loudly to assure everyone that he would grow strong. The sisters doted on him and Mr. Bennet beamed proudly, sending off letters to his family and friends.

Richard had shared with Mr. Bennet that he had discovered the whereabouts of Mr. Collins after he fled with the town prostitute and marrying her. Mr. Bennet promptly wrote to him that the entailment was now ended and Longbourn would now be passed onto Master Samuel Bennet. Several days later, Mr. Bennet received a letter from a very humble Mr. Collins who congratulated him and also profusely apologised for the inappropriate arrival and his ill-mannered speech regarding his family and his daughter. He told Mr. Bennet that he had been working hard on his father's old land and that he and his wife were also expecting a scion of their humble little family and that perhaps someday, the young masters would be able to meet and perchance become friends.

Mrs. Bennet apologised profusely again and promised she would continue to improve herself. She was beaming with her son and proudly announced him the handsomest boy in the county and all forgave her of such pride, as they knew how thrilled the Bennets were with finally having an heir.

Elizabeth was also able to take time to explain to her sister what to expect during her early stage of pregnancy. Jane was shocked when Elizabeth shared that her cravings were constant and that Darcy was glad to accommodate her multiple times a day. Jane had guessed perhaps three times but her jaw dropped when Elizabeth had said 'six'. *I cannot believe how virile Mr. Darcy is! And how wanton of Elizabeth! They are a good match. I could never...*

With the promise of a reunion in August with the Bingleys and Christmas with everyone at Rosings, the Darcys and Richard departed to return home to Pemberley.

Chapter 35

Charlotte Lucas was in a quandary. She had a very pleasant time with Eliza after she arrived at Netherfield, as her dearest friend was gigantic and she was very happy for her. It was very obvious that Mr. Darcy was glimmering with glee and only had eyes for his wife.

Initially, after Eliza quickly got herself engaged to Mr. Darcy, Charlotte had wondered if there was some foul play, since Eliza had dodged a dozen suitors and was not interested in marriage. She had always wanted to marry for love and becoming engaged to a man that she met only two days before had not made sense to Charlotte. There was concern that perhaps Mr. Darcy had compromised Eliza but seeing her dear friend so happy and he so proper had alleviated her worries.

After the rushed wedding a month later, Charlotte was lonely. She had desired to find a husband and Eliza had always promised that her future would be together to live as spinsters and to teach Jane's children to play the pianoforte, albeit terribly. Now, Eliza was mistress of a grand estate in the north, married to a man of at least £10,000 a year.

Charlotte was thrilled and was truly happy for Eliza and seeing her contentment with her husband had brought much comfort, but she was still uncertain of her own future. Eliza had written many times before to invite her to Derbyshire again and again but now, they were able to talk in detail of Pemberley and of her awful attack in April. She invited her to Pemberley once again and this time, arrangements were made for Jane and Charles to bring her in August to join the merry party.

Charlotte had found Miss Darcy a very pleasant young lady who was coming out of her shell, and with Kitty and Lydia's influence, she had become livelier than before the wedding.

Charlotte had met Richard Fitzwilliam only at the wedding and with all the festivities, she had not paid any attention to him at the time. She had been watching Mr. Darcy more often than not to ensure herself that he truly loved her dearest friend.

She had bumped into the dashing former colonel at Netherfield after the men had returned from riding when she turned the corner while bringing Eliza's book from the library. Her hand had touched Mr. Fitzwilliam's firm chest and she blushed profusely while he apologised, bowed, and left. She watched him thoughtfully at dinner and found him extremely handsome. His hair was changed since the wedding and he looked finer than any man she had seen anywhere. He was a little taller and more muscular compared to Mr. Darcy, who was also incredibly handsome, and when Mr. Fitzwilliam smiled, he was absolutely striking. She could not get him out of her mind. Her fingers tingled where she touched his masculine chest and she had never before wished more than now to see what lay beneath his clothes. Her heart fluttered nonstop when he spoke with her and Eliza when both Mr. Darcy and he sat near them in the drawing room.

Mr. Fitzwilliam was about thirty years in age with £6,000 a year, and had been a decorated colonel as well as a son of an Earl. Another man could not compare with such wealth and rank and prestige. He was by far the most prominent bachelor after Mr. Darcy that Charlotte had come across, and the townsfolk of Meryton gossiped that if Elizabeth Bennet could capture such a man as Mr. Darcy, it could be possible that another young woman could capture Mr. Fitzwilliam.

Her own mother had instructed her on how to gain his attentions, as they had known that he would be residing at Pemberley in August, to the point of compromising herself. She dreaded meeting him again so that she did not embarrass herself, but desperately desired to see his handsome face at the same time.

Oh, how wanton I am! I just hope I do not embarrass myself. I know I am reaching too high but my heart flutters every time I think of him! Oh, Eliza, I hope you can find me a good husband. I truly want only security and comfort.

~*~

Pemberley was home. It was the perfect, peaceful heaven that the four family members enjoyed and life was routine and happy. Georgiana continued her studies and practiced on the pianoforte every day and Elizabeth had arranged for some of her new friends from the Spring Equinox Ball to visit her.

Those ladies also brought their unmarried sisters, unfortunately, mostly due to their mothers pressing for an introduction to meet Mr. Fitzwilliam. Word had gotten around quickly that a most-eligible bachelor was residing at Pemberley and any method of an introduction was an advantage. Each matron was certain her own daughter would catch his eye and some of the young ladies absolutely lusted over Mr. Fitzwilliam and attempted to capture his attention, while other more sensible ones concentrated on befriending Miss Darcy, and Georgiana was extremely pleased to have gained several friends nearer to her age.

Richard avoided meeting the women as much as possible but was congenial whenever he was present. There were a few women whom he had seduced to his bed before, but he avoided them and gave them a frown whenever they attempted to capture his attentions, hoping that Elizabeth did not notice the interaction. To the other pretty younger women, he flashed his smiles often and the ladies almost swooned at the sight. He could spot from the crowd of women who were virtuous and who were not, and it thrilled him that he was capable of bedding every single one of them due to his eligibility as a suitor as well as his prowess as a rake. He knew full well that he was drawing their eyes and was flattered by all the arts and allurements the women attempted to throw his way and he laughed internally, seeing a room full of beautiful women but loving only one. Darcy had seen his face and they winked at each other.

Darcy had sat with his wife at every visit she received. He usually dreaded socialising but he had not wanted to leave her alone in case she needed him. The women sighed and ogled at Darcy also but he did not pay them any mind, keeping his focus on his wife alone. He loved his wife so much that he was willing to suffer this for her.

There were four or five women who would arrive together at visiting hours, as Elizabeth had arranged for a large gathering all at once during the day instead of several hours throughout the day. She had been so tired sporadically but had the most energy in the late mornings.

Darcy was extremely worried for her. The doctors had assured them that she was progressing well and the babies' heartbeats were strong, but Elizabeth was so petite and had grown so large that she had difficulty waddling and they had begun to limit her walking to the gardens. He or Richard had to help her sit up or stand constantly, and she still had two more months to go. Darcy was thankful once again for Richard's presence. He had been the steady support they needed, comforting them both from their worries. He had become an excellent master, managing Rosings as well as helping Darcy with many of his businesses while he was taking care of Elizabeth. His own steward followed him like a master and they had worked out a system to leave notes or instructions for each other so no details were left out. They ran the businesses in a symbiotic relationship and it was working out better than ever expected.

Darcy converted the Mistress' study for Richard's use and placed another desk in his own for Elizabeth. Richard had his choice of his own study or Darcy's or even Elizabeth's desk but the three were often in the same room to discuss and make plans.

Damn you, Richard! Darcy smirked. *He gets to leave but I am still stuck here listening to this nonsense. Elizabeth is so intelligent but some of these ladies need to cease talking about lace! I cannot blame him, though. I wish I could leave but will stay with my dearest wife. I cannot wait until the Gardiners, Jane and Bingley, and Miss Lucas arrive. The ladies could stay with Elizabeth and come fetch me should my wife need me. Two more weeks!*

~*~

August arrived, and with it, the Bingleys and Charlotte Lucas. The Gardiners would arrive the next day and the house was jumping with activity.

Elizabeth had written out her lists of tasks and she often referred to her pad of papers as she kept forgetting details. She had cried and was an emotional mess at times and both Darcy and Richard had to take care that she did not become irritated or frustrated, as she would laugh and cry within the same minute. She complained that Darcy's silent chewing bothered her and then immediately wanted him to eat more because it made her happy to see him enjoy his food. She yelled at Richard and told him to stop being so tall and then asked him to help her sit up and thanked him for being so strong.

Charlotte was amazed at the size of the mansion and could not believe that Eliza was mistress of all this. She wondered at the grandeur but the home was not ostentatious, as it was beautiful in its simplicity yet tastefully decorated furnishings. And she blushed when the incredibly handsome Mr. Fitzwilliam greeted her but quickly turned her attentions to Mr. and Mrs. Darcy.

Jane also flushed when she saw Mr. Fitzwilliam. With the summer sun, his skin was darker and he looked even more striking. She turned to her brother Darcy and coloured again. She remembered his naked torso and saw that he was also better-looking than ever. *How is it possible to have two such handsome men in one household?* She wondered. She did find her husband handsome enough but these two men were far above any other she had ever met. She hoped that her body's reaction was from her pregnancy and that it would fade in time.

The party enjoyed dinner together and was excited to see the Gardiners the next day.

~*~

The Gardiners arrived with their four children. The house was flowing with a number of guests not seen since the previous Mistress' days and the staff enjoyed having children in the household immensely, and after the children were settled in the nursery, the women sat together while the men decided to go fishing.

"Lizzy! You are looking so well! You are enormous but it is as expected for carrying twins. How are you feeling?" Aunt Gardiner asked.

"Oh, aunt, I am so hot all the time and my back aches. I cannot move the way I wish and I have not seen my feet in months. I have another month and a half to go and I am anxious to get these babes out of me!" Elizabeth laughed.

"Even if you were carrying one babe, you would be feeling the same. You are doing a marvelous job. I understand you have limited your walks?" Aunt Gardiner asked.

"Yes, I am walking inside and only to the gardens if I wish to go out of doors.

Fitzwilliam and Richard are both adamant that I have one of them walk with me as I would not give up my walks. They are so worried for me and I am such trouble." Elizabeth teared up.

"But it is because they care for you so much. Mr. Fitzwilliam owns Rosings, does he not? I am surprised he can be away from his home for so long." Aunt Gardiner was curious. She had known that he would be at Pemberley but had heard that he had travelled with the Darcys to Netherfield before arriving here. She wondered if there was an understanding with Miss Darcy but did not notice anything different in their relationship since London and he was friendly as ever with all of the ladies. She did note the blush in Charlotte's cheeks.

Georgiana cheerfully answered, "Oh, but he will stay with us always since my brother and Lizzy practically adopted him! Richard told me that he was too lonely to live in a big house alone and wanted to live with us. My brother and he had always been as close as brothers and after he saved my brother and Lizzy's lives, he is fiercely protective of all of us. He rarely leaves Lizzy's side unless Brother is with her out of concern. It is so nice to have him with us. He tells us stories and makes us laugh when he teases Brother mercilessly." She grinned.

"I understand. I am glad you have so much help, Lizzy." Aunt Gardiner replied. She looked at Charlotte and noticed that she had been intently listening. Keeping her eye on her, she said, "Perhaps when he finally finds a wife, he will not be so lonely in his grand house." She saw Charlotte's blush. *Ah, so Charlotte fancies him. I will have to see how he feels about her.*

The ladies continued their conversations and soon retired to rest.

The party gathered together for dinner and it was loud and energetic. Elizabeth had prepared a wonderful meal and the group talked excitedly of the picnic to be held tomorrow as well as the splendour of the property and shared stories of each other growing up.

Aunt Gardiner kept a watchful eye on the company. It was very obvious that Mr. Darcy was deeply in love with his wife and could not help himself to sit next to her and touch her hand or rub her back. Lizzy would often lean on him and look up to meet his eyes adoringly. She also saw Mr. Fitzwilliam's congenial attention to the rest of the party and he was quite handsome as he flashed his smiles often. She did note the worry in his eyes whenever his eyes turned to Lizzy and it appeared as Georgiana had said. He must truly love his family and had legitimate concerns, as Lizzy was very heavy with child and appeared weary.

She saw no distinction for Charlotte, unfortunately. Although affable to everyone, Mr. Fitzwilliam kept his distance from the only unattached woman other than his own cousin, but she thought it strange that he had maintained the furthest distance from the ever-serene Jane. He did not make eye contact with her at all and was very formal with her.

~*~

The next morning, Aunt Gardiner was able to find some private time with Lizzy before the others joined them in the drawing room. The men had decided to go for a ride and Uncle Gardiner had agreed to ride on the slowest mare but would enjoy the company. They had all gotten along famously.

"Lizzy, I wanted to ask you about Mr. Fitzwilliam." She started.

Elizabeth was curious as to what her observant Aunt had noticed. Richard had been a proper gentleman and was amiable to her family and friend. He had kissed her hand in view of her aunt last night when he bid everyone good night but it had been appropriate. "Of course, aunt. What do you wish to know?"

"I noticed that while he has been as genial as ever, when we met in London he was quite a bit of a flirt, especially with Jane, but last night, he was very formal with her and maintained his distance. Was he in love with your sister? Is he disappointed that she married Charles?" She asked.

Elizabeth sighed. Her aunt did not know about Jane's 'misbehaviour' and would need to know. She did not want anyone to think Richard had been in love with Jane. "Oh, aunt, you know that in April, after Fitzwilliam and I were attacked, Charles and Jane rushed here to comfort me. Well, what has not been shared, and you must not tell anyone, aunt, was that Charles and Jane argued over something that happened before they were married and Jane felt betrayed. In her despair, she threw herself into Richard's arms and tried to kiss him. Charles found them together and they had a row, but Charles quickly found out that Richard was innocent and they are now friends again." She looked at her aunt whose mouth was agape. "Richard has been a proper gentleman but refuses to be within five feet of her, and definitely never alone. He knows she will not do such a thing again, as Jane loves Charles very much and their marriage has grown stronger since then, but he does not want anyone to have the wrong idea." Elizabeth explained.

"I understand. I believe Charlotte might be in love with him. Do you think she has a chance? He must be in want of a wife." Aunt Gardiner asked.

Elizabeth shook her head. "I hope he will eventually find a good wife but I know that he is in love with someone and he refuses to look elsewhere. I tried to convince him but he gets upset so we do not talk about it." She sighed. *I am so undeserving of his love. He sacrifices too much to be a part of our family.* "I hope you will not mention it, aunt. He does not wish for anyone to know."

"I will not say a word. I am the epitome of secrecy, you know this!" She smiled. "But this woman, is she not attainable? Is something wrong with her?"

"She can never marry him, aunt, and he can never marry her. Richard says he is content with his situation but I have doubts." Elizabeth answered truthfully.

"Oh, poor Charlotte. I hope she will get over her crush. I had never seen her affected by anyone before. But he does cut a dashing figure." Aunt Gardiner commented.

"Yes, yes, he does. I do plan on introducing her to our new parson Mr. Tinsley. He is two and thirty and intelligent and very kind. He is sensible and handsome and I believe they will be a good match. I hope you will help me, aunt. I have invited him to dinner in two nights." Elizabeth excitedly declared.

"That is a wonderful idea, Lizzy!" Aunt Gardiner beamed.

The men returned and the other ladies soon joined them in the drawing room and they spoke happily together. The group separated for a quick rest, as they would head out for a picnic in a few hours.

~*~

Elizabeth waddled slowly on Richard's arm to her room. Her husband wanted to discuss some investment opportunities with Uncle Gardiner and Bingley and asked

Richard to walk with Elizabeth so she could rest and to return afterwards and he would fill him in.

Elizabeth was slower than ever but insisted she be mobile. She could not imagine being cooped up in her bedroom and knew that that was the expectation after the delivery, but she had read that women who moved and ambulated after the birth recovered faster. Her plan was to care for herself and the babes but not remain in the dark room in bed for a full month.

"Are you well, Elizabeth? You look very tired today. Shall I carry you?" Richard asked in concern. It had been days since he had been alone with her and although they were constantly in company, he had missed her.

"I am tired but I will be well, Richard. I am glad you are with me." She leaned against him.

Richard smiled. He loved having her close and he could smell the lavender scent from her hair as he kissed her head. "I will always be with you, my love."

"Oh, Richard." And she was quiet.

He leaned down to see that she was silently crying. Since they were almost at her door, he walked her several more steps and after walking through the door, he closed the door behind them and lifted her up. She was large with child but still light in his strong arms. He carried her to the bed and gently laid her down on her side to face him, kneeling at the side of the bed. He caressed her cheeks and wiped her tears.

"Whatever is wrong, dearest? Are you uncomfortable? Shall I get Darcy?" Richard asked in worry.

She began to cry harder. His heart broke to see her in distress. *I do not know what to do. Do I get Darcy? Do I stay with her?*

"Please tell me what is wrong, my love. It tears my heart to see you so sad." He kissed her hands repeatedly and rubbed her hand against his cheek while wiping her tears with his handkerchief.

"Oh, Richard, I was talking to my aunt this morning and she asked about you. I thought she might have seen your care for me but she asked about your bachelorhood and I told her that you were in love with someone and not interested in anyone else." He nodded in agreement as he continued to caress her hand. "I thought about your sacrifice to be here with us and the love that you pour onto all three of us. I do not deserve you. You should be finding someone to love and marry and have your own children but you sacrificed everything, even living in your own home, to be with me. How could you love me so?" She cried again.

Richard knew that she already knew the answer, as they had spoken of this before. He also knew that she needed reassurances and it was from her loving him that she had wanted the best for him. The pregnancy had made her emotional more than usual and he would console her as best as he could.

He kissed her hands again. "My love, my Elizabeth, I never expected my station. I had no idea that I would ever own such a property and become my own master. Darcy had helped me grow my inheritance and I always thought I would either marry an heiress for her money or connections, or be resigned to retire quietly in my small cottage that my grandmother left me. I thought I would serve in the military until I was grey or if I were ever sent back to the continent, perhaps not come back alive. I had never expected to fall in love and had used, I am ashamed to say, many women for my own pleasures, never thinking about the consequences.

"After I met you, my life had changed so much to the point that I do not recognise the man I was before. Your marrying Darcy had resulted in Anne finding freedom and leaving Rosings to me, and my meeting you had opened my heart to feel as I had never felt before. I do not regret knowing what love is and I will always be a one-woman man. My heart will never belong to anyone else and should I marry a woman for companionship and for an heir, I would be living a lie. I know it may not make sense to anyone else but we three, you, Darcy, and myself, have a love for each other that is unique and honest. I am grateful to Darcy that he comprehends my feelings for you and for him to allow me to love you would be impossible for every other man. He loves you with the depth of love that is eternal and I understand him because I feel the same. That you allow me to love you and love me, as a brother, I know, in return, is more than I had ever anticipated."

He kissed her cheek and wiped her tears again. "You deserve every happiness and you deserve the love that is freely given to you. Whether you wish it or not, I will not, I cannot stop loving you, Elizabeth. You own my heart and nothing will change it. Should you wish me to leave," he paused to see her shake her head, "I would still love you but live in misery and die a slow death. Do you recall when I had to punish Darcy for his joke?" She laughed. Darcy had told her how fearful he was of Richard's anger when he had acted as if Elizabeth had not wanted him to live together. "When I first thought you did not want me in your life, I felt such bleakness that I wished to jump into the ocean. I could not imagine being parted from you. I have faced enemies and death in the battlefields without fear but nothing scares me more than losing you, not being near you." He kissed her lips gently but long. He was surprised when he felt her tongue against his lips and he suckled her, tasting her deeply then gliding his tongue over her lips as he ended their soft kiss. "You are the love of my life, Elizabeth. I will love you until the end of my days."

She wrapped her arms around his neck tightly. "Thank you, Richard. I appreciate you so much. I love you."

He stood up and kissed her cheek. "Rest, my love. Darcy will be with you as soon as his business is complete." And he left her to nap.

He stood on the other side of her door and sighed. *She loves me. Could she ever love me as I love her? Dear God, please let her be well. I fear for her life. Should she perish during childbirth, I do not know how I would survive. I would only live to be of use to Darcy but I cannot imagine life without her.*

He hurried downstairs to join Darcy in the study and the men were concluding.

After Bingley and Gardiner left to rest with their wives, Darcy asked in concern, "You took a while. Is she well?" He was worried for Elizabeth. She had been having more discomfort and although she told him that having intercourse was the only thing to help her relax, it took longer for her to achieve her climax and she had become severely depressed lately.

"She was crying and I had to console her. She told me that she did not deserve my love and that I was sacrificing too much for her." He sat and ran his hands through his hair. "She gets extremely sad and I worry for her so much, Darcy. You must reassure her as well. She must know that I would give up everything for her. As long as you will have me, even if I had to live in the garden shed, I cannot be without her." He begged. "Will you go to her now? You must comfort her."

174

"I will. Thank you, Richard. I agree that you have made sacrifices but I would do the same." Darcy was relieved. She was just feeling emotional and feeling unworthy and it would pass. "You may stay in your current rooms." He smiled. "Thank you for reassuring Elizabeth. She has been fragile and I had hoped having her family here would help but she is still in a delicate place. We will love her together and she will have no doubt of her value, Richard. If anyone deserves to have the complete dedication of two men, it is she."

Darcy left quickly to join his wife who was sleeping peacefully. Divesting his coat and cravat, he quickly joined her and held her as she reached for his hand in her sleep and began to snore lightly.

~*~

The picnic was a success. The weather was perfect and the food delicious and they played croquet, lawn bowling, and bocce. The children ran around the grounds and laughed merrily and Georgiana was praised for her plans, as Elizabeth had insisted that she host the picnic. Elizabeth used her pregnancy as an excuse but they had all known that she wanted Georgiana to learn more of hostess duties and develop her skills managing the household. She would be coming out next year and needed to continue her education.

~*~

Darcy had reassured his wife that night while lying face to face in bed. "My love, do you believe that I love you with all my heart?" She nodded rapidly. "I know you had asked about your worthiness after you married me and I had to convince you of your immeasurable value. Richard feels the same about you and I told him also, that if anyone deserved to be loved by two men who love you wholeheartedly, it is you. You do believe that Richard and I are a good catch, do you not?" He smirked. She nodded again and smiled. "Well, as a grandson of an earl and a superior gentleman of 45,000 a year, I demand that you obey your husband and master and accept the love that is given to you. Richard is a son of an earl and a gentleman of great wealth as well. You must obey your superiors and put your feeble mind to rest in all this nonsense about your lack of worthiness." He teased.

Her eyebrows lifted and she feigned shock. She crossed her arms in fake anger then suddenly pinched him on his arms and sides. Darcy chuckled and began to tickle her in return and they laughed loudly. He caressed her cheeks and kissed her tenderly. "I love you with all my heart. I am honoured to be your husband and I am eternally grateful that you agreed to be my wife. No matter what happens, I will love you for all eternity. Richard loves you and because of my deep love for you, I understand his need to be with you. He is a good man, and just like me, he is willing to give up everything for you. Accept my love, accept his love, and know that you are worthy of being loved and adored." He kissed her deeply as she moaned. "Turn around and let me love you again."

They began their dance in their well-practiced position and soon slept peacefully.

~*~

Two days later, Elizabeth excitedly awaited the dinner with Mr. Tinsley. She had noticed that Charlotte looked to Richard often and blushed in his presence but Elizabeth sighed as she understood that although her friend would have been a good wife to him and he would make an excellent husband to anyone, his heart would not falter and he would remain steadfast in his love.

Strategizing with her aunt, Elizabeth had thought of ways to get Charlotte to notice Mr. Tinsley. He was a kind man and would be a good husband to her.

At the dinner, she made certain to seat Charlotte close to the parson and as far from Richard as possible.

Richard sat at her right as always, with Georgiana next to him and Charlotte at Fitzwilliam's left, while Mr. Tinsley was across from Charlotte on her husband's right as the guest of honour. Georgiana and Mr. Gardiner would block Charlotte's view of Richard and she would concentrate on the man in front of her. Her aunt would initiate conversations, as she would be sitting across her as well. She also told her husband and asked for his assistance with Mr. Tinsley. *Who would have thought I would become such a matchmaker?!* Elizabeth laughed to herself.

The dinner was splendid. All enjoyed the food and the company and she was happy to see that Charlotte and Mr. Tinsley got along famously as she had expected. Aunt Gardiner winked at her and Elizabeth covered her giggles. Richard gave her a look and she whispered 'later'. Richard had no idea that he had been scrutinised by her dearest friend, but she would tell him of her plans to recruit him into the scheme as well.

When they stood after the meal, Richard walked Elizabeth to the drawing room while the rest of the men stayed for their after-dinner port.

"What was that about, young lady?" He quietly asked.

"I am no longer a young lady but an old married woman with nothing better to do than play matchmaker." She giggled. "I am trying to match Charlotte." She raised her eyebrow in mirth. *I do not think Richard ever looked at Charlotte twice! Dear man, he truly loves me so much.*

He laughed out loudly. "You just turned one and twenty last month. Old woman, my arse!" He was elated to see her feeling better. *I love to see her smile. I would do anything for her happiness.*

She tapped his arm in false shock. "Language!" Then she giggled.

Richard quickly kissed her hand before leaving her in the drawing room.

Elizabeth asked Charlotte to sit close to her and Aunt Gardiner joined. The ladies spoke of the dinner and while Jane and Georgiana were occupied talking about preparing for the nursery, Elizabeth asked Charlotte.

"You seemed to get along with Mr. Tinsley well. How did you find him?"

"Oh, Eliza, he is very amiable. I found that we have very similar tastes and I was pleasantly surprised with his attentions. He is very handsome, although not as much..." she paused and blushed. "But I hope to get to know him better."

~*~

The gentlemen chatted while they drank their beverage. Darcy was surprised when Mr. Tinsley introduced the topic that he himself was trying to bring up.

"Mr. Darcy, I understand Miss Lucas is from Hertfordshire where Mrs. Darcy grew up. I wondered, sir, if you would permit me to call on her while she remains here. She told me that she would be here for another six weeks or so, through Mrs. Darcy's confinement?" He asked.

Darcy smiled. "Yes, I am pleased to hear that you enjoyed her company. You may request Miss Lucas for permission. As my wife's dearest friend, I assure you that she is a fine lady as I trust in my wife's judgment implicitly!" He laughed.

When the men arrived at the drawing room, Elizabeth could see that Charlotte's eyes were immediately drawn to Mr. Tinsley. Darcy sat next to her and held her hand and quietly whispered to her that Mr. Tinsley had requested to call on Miss Lucas and she smiled brightly.

Success! That is one-for-one! She stopped. *Oh my, I am becoming like my mother! What have I become?* She giggled.

She was joyous for her friend. If everything went well, Charlotte could marry Mr. Tinsley and remain close to her in Derbyshire!

Chapter 36

Caroline sat fuming. The man lying in her bed was snoring loudly and had no intention of leaving. She tried to wake him up before and he had rolled over and nearly suffocated her by climbing on top of her.

He had promised her an invitation to Lady Matlock's Ball in December and she would have to continue to favour him until then. It was now only the second week of August. *At least he is not fat and smelly. He is a decent lover.*

Caroline had been devastated when she found out that Mr. Darcy had left promptly after Lady Iris' Coming Out Ball. She had obtained an invitation to Lord Smythe's infamous ball, which was always the last party of the Season, and when she arrived in her best dress, looking ever so perfect, she asked Lady Matlock when she was expecting the Darcys and had been told that they had returned to the country.

The man snorted himself awake. Caroline tapped him quickly. "Lord Harold, you must leave. Your wife is expecting you for dinner in two hours and you cannot stay here!"

"Oh, Caro. She is so fat with child, as long as her food is sitting in front of her, she will not even notice my absence. Come back over here. I want you to suck on me." And he pulled her down and pushed her head between his legs.

Caroline rolled her eyes. *Men and their oral pleasures. Why do they like it so much? I will never understand.* And she began to do her duty until he was erect enough and he commanded her to ride him. As he began to climax, she jumped off so his seed would spill onto his stomach. *I will not get pregnant by this fool. I only want Mr. Darcy's seed.*

She promptly kicked him out of her bed before he could fall asleep again and went about to clean herself, since she was to have dinner with an earl that night. *Perhaps I will be a countess! One bird in hand is better than two in the bush. I will enjoy my liaisons with Mr. Darcy after my rank opens doors to his peers!*

~*~

The days passed peacefully and Charlotte and Mr. Tinsley began to see each other often. After a couple of weeks of calling, the parson asked for courtship and it was readily accepted.

Georgiana had become more comfortable playing hostess and had worked hard with Mrs. Reynolds to ensure meals were planned and activities planned. Elizabeth had been more tired and was often resting in her rooms and Elizabeth was very pleased for her sister Mary who wrote to her that she was engaged and would be married mid-September. Due to her confinement, Elizabeth would not be able to attend but she and Darcy sent a generous gift to the new Mr. and Mrs. Bertram.

It was now the end of August. It was expected that Elizabeth would deliver around the last week of September and she still had at least a month to go. She was larger than ever and irritable from being overheated. She was drained from her aches and constantly needing to use the water closet, although Elizabeth was grateful that all of their homes had been modernised with water closets. Wealth definitely had its perks.

Elizabeth was most comfortable in the evenings. She had not been eating much for the past few days and Darcy and Richard had constantly pushed food and drinks on her, and she laughed at their pathetic attempts but appreciated them as well. Her pains had become more frequent and as she knew it was too early, she had not told anyone that she was experiencing more cramping. *I must be hungry. I slept so poorly and even the short rests did not help. The only thing that helps is to have my Fitzwilliam inside me. Oh, his body comforts me so much.*

As the group sat for dinner and the courses were served, Elizabeth attempted to eat as much as possible. She actually felt hungry and everything was delicious. She ate and laughed heartily but could still feel the cramping every half hour or so.

After dessert was served, Elizabeth stood with Richard's assistance when she felt a long, sharp pain in her abdomen. It was a blinding pain and she groaned loudly, and then doubled over and began to fall.

Richard held Elizabeth's arm to help her stand when she suddenly yelped and leaned forward. He quickly grabbed her and lowered her to the ground. "Elizabeth!" he yelled. She was grimacing in pain and her dress was wet. He kept his eyes on her and yelled, "Darcy! Elizabeth needs you!" He yelled for the footman to call for the midwife. His strong arms lifted her up so he could carry her to her room.

Darcy helped him stand and took her into his own arms. "Thank you, Richard. Oh, my love. I believe it must be time." He kissed her forehead. He quickly left to place his wife into her room and saw that Hannah prepared her clothes. He stayed with Elizabeth and kissed her tenderly as she began to labour in earnest.

~*~

Georgiana was in tears but Charlotte comforted her, telling her that all would be well, while Mrs. Gardiner and Jane joined Elizabeth for the birthing process.

The men retreated to the study where Richard poured everyone a drink and stood by the window to look out into the darkness. *Oh, my love. Please be well.* All of his fears during the past months rushed in. *She must be well. Darcy must stay with her.* He suddenly realised that he had not talked to Darcy about his staying with her. *I hope he will stay with her. If he returns, I will order him back to her side.* He continued to stare out.

Bingley had heard Mrs. Bennet screaming during her labour and thanked God that the doors at Pemberley were much thicker. He thought of Jane and what she would be going through in less than six months. He was terrified but they had been studying together to learn more about what to expect and he thought of how far they had come since April, on that terrible day when the floodgates had opened.

Mr. Gardiner excused himself to check on his children and Bingley resumed his contemplation about last April. Jane had been so different then. Although he had fallen in love with her serene countenance and quiet manners, he preferred it when she would speak her mind and show a little more passion.

Looking over to Fitzwilliam by the window, he recalled that Darcy had told him about his being in love with a woman already.

While they had the time and privacy, Bingley decided to ask him about her. "Fitzwilliam, I just recalled that Darcy had told me something about you back in April. Do you recall that day I was angry with you before I knew you were completely innocent?" He began sheepishly. He still felt such guilt for accusing his long-time friend as well as making a fool of himself, believing that he could take on the former colonel. Richard turned and nodded and took a seat by the fireplace. "Well, Darcy had told me that you would have never imposed on Jane because you were deeply in love with a woman. Who is she? Why have you not asked for her hand? You are certainly in a position where anyone, except for Darcy perhaps, would envy."

Richard looked into the fire. *What do I say? How do I explain myself without breaking confidences?* After several moments, he responded. "I, yes, I have been in love with a woman for a very long time but I will never be able to marry her." He paused. *But she is my wife in my heart. Oh, Elizabeth, are you well?* He continued a minute later. "I will never marry anyone else and I will be content with my memories of her. My heart belongs to her and only her, and I will never find anyone else worthier. I do not wish to speak of her, Bingley; it pains me to think of her." *She must be in so much pain right now. My dearest Elizabeth.* He stood again and returned to the window.

Bingley sat awestruck. Fitzwilliam had spoken four or five sentences of his love and it appeared to be stronger than what he himself had ever felt. He did not know if that lady was deceased or living in the Americas or married off, but the level of love that his friend had spoken of was significant. The only other person who loved so deeply was Darcy with Elizabeth.

Would I have been able to continue to love Jane if she had died or was married to someone else? He already knew the answer. He would be despairing but after the appropriate time, he would most likely look for another wife or visit with courtesans. His misery over Sarah Fleming had lasted exactly five days while he hired six or seven whores for two days straight to drown in his sorrows. He had found another pretty face that he chased for a month, considering taking her as a mistress before Darcy advised against it, and then moved to Netherfield, only to chase Jane Bennet and marry her. He watched Fitzwilliam. He knew his friend was a man of honour and although he had been quite a flirt and a rake in the past, there was definitely a change in him. He did not dally with anyone and did not even dance with other women at balls. They had visited brothels together in the past, since it was something that Darcy did not participate in, and had even talked of their conquests several times but that was all before he had gone to Dover. While Bingley had continued to use prostitutes up until his marriage, Fitzwilliam had told him he had sworn off loose women back in October. *How did I miss it? He has definitely changed since last year. The woman he loves must be from Dover. He certainly is not visiting whorehouses or sleeping around. He has been seen with no one other than his family for a year!*

"Fitz, I will not ask about her again but I am in awe of your resolve. I do not know if I could love my Jane the way you love this woman and except with Darcy, I am shocked at such a dedication. It must be a family thing. You had not been so in the past, but you are becoming more and more like your cousin. I wish you every happiness, my friend." Bingley spoke earnestly.

Richard turned and shook Bingley's hand. "Thank you, Bingley. Who said I was not happy? I am about to become an uncle!" He smiled. He was still worried but tried to become cheerful. *Elizabeth will be well. She must.*

"Would Darcy's children not be your cousins?" Bingley innocently asked.

Richard burst out laughing. "Technically, yes, but I have been adopted by the Darcys as a brother so I will be an uncle." He continued to laugh. *I am very eager to see my nephews or nieces. Perhaps one of each! My Elizabeth's children will be beautiful.*

~*~

After Darcy carried her to her bed, Elizabeth grunted her pain and tried to take several breaths. She had read that she had to take many breaths so the babies could continue to get air from her. Her husband had stayed with her as he had promised and was wiping the sweat off her brows and patting her hair. Aunt Gardiner, Jane, and Mrs. Reynolds were busy preparing the towels and hot water and soon, the midwife arrived.

Seeing Mr. Darcy in the room, the midwife asked if he wished to remain or return downstairs. This midwife had delivered Georgiana sixteen years ago and had seen Mr. Darcy the Senior's devastation when his wife had passed. She knew that the current Mrs. Darcy was expecting twins and she had begun labouring earlier than expected and saw the worry in Mr. Darcy's eyes. She knew he would be comforted to remain with his wife should he choose, as long as he was not disruptive during the process.

Darcy was adamant that he wished to stay and be of assistance. He helped with repositioning and cradled his wife and comforted her with each pain.

After asking the questions of how long she had been having pains, Elizabeth confessed that she had been having pain since about one in the afternoon. Darcy was upset, as he had not known.

"How could you not share this with me? We might have been preparing earlier and tried to keep you comfortable." He was hurt that she had kept her pains a secret.

"I have been having pains on and off for the past month, Fitzwilliam. I did not know that it was the beginning of labour!" She snipped. "I was hungry for the first time in days and I enjoyed dinner. Is that so wrong?!"

Mrs. Meyers, the midwife, laughed. "Oh, sir, I think having a hearty dinner was a good idea. This is her first delivery so I am not surprised that she did not know, no matter how studious she has been throughout the pregnancy." She winked.

Darcy smiled a little. "Of course, you take her side." He winked in return. He really liked Mrs. Meyers. She would deliver all their children if possible.

Elizabeth panted. "Oh, my love, it hurts so much. I am sorry I did not tell you. I love you so much, Fitzwilliam." She cried.

Darcy continued to wipe her brow and whispered words of comfort to her while massaging her arms and legs and kissing her forehead and cheeks frequently.

After one spectacular labour, Elizabeth grabbed Darcy's cravat and yanked his head down forcefully. While he was choking, she yelled, "YOU DID THIS TO ME! I AM NEVER LETTING YOU NEAR ME AGAIN!" And she cried out in pain again.

Mrs. Meyers chuckled. "That is my cue. I believe it is time to push, Mrs. Darcy."

Aunt Gardiner was laughing as well. "Lizzy, Lizzy, my dear, you must let go of his cravat. Your husband is turning blue." She gently rubbed Elizabeth's arms.

Elizabeth immediately let go. "Oh, my love. I am so sorry. I did not mean it. I love you. I love you so much. I want to have a dozen babies with you. I did not mean it."

The ladies laughed as Darcy's face returned to a normal colour and he did not know if he would ever put her through this again. Rather, if he would ever put himself through this again.

"Push, Mrs. Darcy!" Mrs. Meyers ordered.

Chapter 37

After another three hours or so, Mrs. Gardiner and Jane entered the study and told the gentlemen that mother and babes were healthy and safe. They toasted in celebration and cheered.

Richard plopped down onto the nearest chair. *She is well. They are well. Thank you, Lord!* He breathed in relief. He was anxious to see her for himself and was extremely glad that Darcy had stayed with her.

Aunt Gardiner walked over to him and tapped him on his shoulder. "They asked to see you, Mr. Fitzwilliam."

Immediately, he stood and ran out the door.

Aunt Gardiner laughed. "Well, he was anxious to get out of here! He will be very pleased to meet the newest Darcys." She revealed the gender to the men now.

Mr. Gardiner chuckled. "He has been pacing around as if he were the father. That young man sure has a lot of love for his cousins and will make a fine husband to a lucky woman someday."

Bingley commented, "Oh, but he says he will never marry. I spoke with him when we had a bit of privacy. Apparently, he is deeply in love with a woman and he is determined to hold on to that love for the rest of his life. I think she may be dead, from the sound of it. I do not know who she was but he loves her fiercely and I was overwhelmed with the level of his commitment." He kissed his wife's hand. "I hope to be like that for you, my love."

The couples smiled at each other and retired to their own rooms.

~*~

Richard was anxious. Nephews or Nieces? Would they look like Darcy or Elizabeth? Perhaps take after the Fitzwilliam side? He truly wished and hoped that Elizabeth was well.

He knocked tentatively and was bid to enter. He slowly opened the door to see Elizabeth in the middle of the bed with Darcy sitting next to her in bed. She looked as beautiful as ever but now was glowing in happiness. He was so proud of her, he beamed.

She held two tiny bundles in her arms.

Darcy called, "Richard, come, come. Join us. Uncle Richard, say hello to Bennet

Alexander Darcy and Richard Fitzwilliam Darcy. The future masters of Pemberley and Rosings."

Richard's eyes teared up and he coughed to cover a sniffle. They were beautiful. His nephews. He loved that he was considered their uncle. 'Cousin' seemed too distant with the love that he carried for Elizabeth. And they had given him the privilege of naming the second son after him. His name. The future master of Rosings. He resolved to love his namesake like a son and he could not be prouder of Elizabeth.

He wiped a tear while he remained standing next to the bed.

Darcy spoke, "Richard, you have my permission to sit next to us. I will hold Bennet, my dear, and Richard can hold little Richie." He grinned.

Hesitantly, Richard sat next to Elizabeth in bed. He had never sat with her in bed like this and he felt a bit awkward but he wanted to meet the babes. Elizabeth lifted her second child and helped Richard hold him.

He looked down and saw the bluest eyes staring back at him. He knew he had given his heart completely to Elizabeth but as he saw the baby in his arms, he knew his heart had grown and loved this child fully as well. He also sat up to see Bennet. Same face. His heart inflated once again. He kissed both babes on the forehead and cried a little more.

Darcy rejoiced seeing Richard's reaction. He had done the same and had fallen in love with his children immediately. He knew Richard would be a valiant protector to the boys as he had been to Elizabeth and himself. "Are we not the proudest of fathers, Richard?"

Richard startled at this. Seeing his puzzled brows, Darcy added, "You will be their godfather, will you not? You are like a husband to Elizabeth and you will be a father figure to them. You will be a constant in their lives, besides Elizabeth and myself. You will love them as you would love your own children, Richard. Will you accept?" He smiled.

Wiping his tears with one hand while still carrying the baby, he replied, "It would be an honour. Thank you, Darcy. Thank you, my dearest Elizabeth." *My godsons; my sons. My dearest Elizabeth's precious sons.*

Elizabeth and Darcy were wiping their own tears as well. Clearing his throat, Darcy handed Bennet back to Elizabeth and kissed her lips several times. "I will fetch Georgiana. We will return in, ten minutes?" He winked at Richard.

Good man. He is giving me ten minutes alone with his wife.

When the door closed, Richard immediately held Elizabeth in his arms. They looked at the babies back and forth and smiled. "I am so proud of you, Elizabeth. You are well?" She nodded. "Our babies are beautiful, my love. You are beautiful."

She raised her face towards him and kissed him on the lips. "You are such a proud father, Richard. I hope you did not worry too much for me." She smiled as she leaned into his embrace.

"I paced and drank and worried like a husband. I have been worrying like a husband for months! I am so relieved that you are well, Elizabeth. I love you so much and I love our babies very much. I will be a good godfather to them both and I promise you I will protect them with my life. You and Darcy are the best things in my life and now I have two more Darcys to love. Thank you, my love." He leaned in and kissed her gently and deeply. Her mouth opened and she received his love and returned the kiss, entwining her tongue around his.

"Richard, we have a very unconventional relationship but we will always know that we love each other. Our children will know your love and I cannot think of a more gallant protector for Bennet and Richie." Elizabeth leaned into his chest. "I still do not think I deserve it, but will accept your unconditional love fully. I love you, Richard, I think *more* than a brother but nonetheless, I love you."

Richard's heart soared as he heard her words. He whispered to her, "I love you with all of my heart and I will cherish you all of my days, my dearest Elizabeth."

They sat cooing at the babies for a moment longer and Darcy returned with Georgiana.

It was late at night now so after Georgiana met and visited the babies for a while, she and Richard retired to their rooms.

Two maids took the babies to their rooms after Elizabeth fed them, and she kissed Darcy tenderly for being the best of husbands, the best of friends, and the best of men. The wet nurse was to be called in the morning, as Elizabeth was confident that she could handle the feedings for one night on her own and slept restfully, waking only twice during the night.

~*~

The next weeks flew and the babies grew healthy and strong every day. The Gardiners thoroughly enjoyed their visit to Pemberley and the Gardiner children ogled the babies trying to figure out which was which. Jane and Bingley anxiously awaited their own bundle of joy and Charlotte was thrilled for her dear friend.

Mr. Tinsley proposed and Charlotte promptly accepted. She thanked Eliza several times for inviting her to Pemberley and looked forward to relocating to Derbyshire, and the Bingleys and Charlotte returned to Hertfordshire with Mr. Tinsley, who would formally request Charlotte's hand and meet her parents. The Gardiners left to return to Gracechurch Street and they planned on a reunion at Rosings for Christmas.

The Gardiners were honoured to receive the invitation for Christmas, as it was surprising that Mr. Fitzwilliam would host the Bennets, the Darcys, as well as the Fitzwilliams. It would be an honour to sit at the same table with the Earl and Countess of Matlock as well as the Viscount and Viscountess. Mr. Fitzwilliam insisted that there was no longer a distinction of rank at Rosings, as long as there were good friends and good conversations to celebrate the season.

The staff would often see the two babes being carried by their master and their surrogate master. Darcy and Richard would walk out with the boys and show them flowers and talk to them about the future and laugh together as they reminisced about their own childhood.

Elizabeth was extremely proud of her sons and was determined to get out of bed. She began to recover quickly and Mrs. Meyers agreed with her that opening the drapes and letting fresh air in and walking as early as possible was a good idea. She had seen too many healthy, genteel ladies who sat still in the dark for a full month either recover slowly or die after the birth.

Elizabeth began to walk within the house and was able to get to the gardens after the first week. She continued to feed her sons as often as possible but relinquished the duties to the wet nurse during the nights.

October arrived and the babies were baptised, formally announcing Richard Fitzwilliam as godfather to both and they celebrated with a grand dinner.

~*~

Elizabeth lay in a seductive nightgown and she was nervous. It had been six weeks since they last had relations and she knew she was still plump in a few places and her bosoms were overflowing. She felt nervous that her husband would no longer find her attractive.

Darcy walked into his room nervously. It had been an eternity since he had been able to be wrapped within her folds and he was afraid he would burst as soon as he entered her. He was embarrassed at the thought of being such an inept lover and had wished he had taken a release before joining her. Her bosoms had been so tempting that he found himself jealous while his sons fed from them.

He entered his room and found his wife already in bed and covered. *I hope she will enjoy my attentions.* He climbed in and lifted the covers. *Good lord! She is gorgeous. Damn it, I am going to explode in seconds and embarrass myself.*

"Elizabeth, are you well?" Darcy asked, suddenly realising how quiet she had been.

Elizabeth gulped, "Yes, husband. I... I am well. I am just anxious for tonight."

They had spent every night together; while pregnant and immediately after the delivery. He had noted her bodily changes and he was constantly aroused but he had attempted to hide it from her so she would not be embarrassed. It had been the longest that he had gone without coition, as she had required his attention at least twice daily during the pregnancy, sometimes up to six, and he had been in heaven. He had to resort to masturbating several mornings so he could think straight, but he constantly desired his wife. He knew he was nervous from finally being allowed to plunge himself into her but could not understand why she would be nervous.

"Elizabeth, I must confess that I am nervous as well. It has been six weeks and I am desperate to have you. I worry that I will embarrass myself by exploding like a teenage boy but I do not understand why you would be anxious. My love, are you still uncomfortable? I love you and do not wish to injure you. I would be most selfish to demand of you if you are not ready." He spoke gently.

Elizabeth was teary. "Oh, Fitzwilliam! I am so flabby and my breasts leak. I am hideous!" She began to wail.

Darcy chuckled. Her emotions had not quite returned to normal yet but it was getting there. "My love, I believe you to be the most beautiful creature in the world. You are so tempting... I am so aroused for you that I cannot help myself from wanting you all the time. I love your body, Elizabeth. Your flab, as you call it, is a sign where my babies were safely kept and you are not chubby at all; just softer and very womanly. Your breast, good lord! They get me so aroused. I cannot stop looking at them and if you leak, I will lick them clean for you. How jealous I have been when Bennet and Richie are suckling on them. My love, I want your body desperately, even more than I have ever before."

Darcy began to kiss her tenderly and it grew deep and strong. He caressed her breasts gently and bent down to lick each, suckling a little to taste her milk. He fingered her folds and as her legs opened, his cock ached to be inside her.

He slowly slid his massive arousal and let out a loud moan. "Ooohhh, Elizabeth, you are my home. I am finally home now." She felt so good. Her womanhood was hot and moist and he could not control his thrusts. He tried to think about something else. *Work! What about that letter that I have to write? Babies! They are so adorable even when they cry. Oh, they cry when they are hungry and Elizabeth feeds them with her magnificent breasts! Damn it! Breasts!* He grunted loudly and uncontrollably as he came deep inside her. *Damn it! I lasted all of two minutes.*

Panting as his manhood throbbed and he continued to lay over his wife, he apologised. "Oh, Elizabeth, I was afraid I was going to embarrass myself and I did. I was trying to last longer but I think that was not even two minutes. I am sorry. I will rally again shortly and will try to pleasure you." He buried his face in her hair in shame.

Elizabeth giggled. "No, my love. It is exactly what I needed. I love seeing you lose control. Does my body truly excite you that much?"

"Oh, Elizabeth, more than you will ever know. I have been dying for you these past six weeks. I love you so much and it was worth the wait. You have provided me with two healthy sons and I find you infinitely more desirable now." He kissed her deeply as he fondled her breasts lightly. He had kept his penis inside her and it began to grow again. He smirked after releasing her mouth. "It is back already! Do you feel that, my love?" He twitched his cock and Elizabeth giggled. "I love you." And he began to pump her again, this time thoroughly pleasing her. After she climaxed for the third time, he released again and they fell asleep wrapped up in each other's arms.

~*~

Richard woke early and rode his horse, Cyrus. Darcy had gifted him the best stallion he had, second only to Xerxes, and he loved riding this beast. He had been too concerned for Elizabeth lately that he had not travelled very far from Pemberley House, and after the birth, he had been working or playing with the babies. Georgiana had been a doting aunt and they often attempted to decide which was more handsome. As they looked exactly the same, they laughed at their own antics.

Richie had a little birthmark behind one ear so that was the most distinctive way of not getting them confused, but Bennet was always kept in yellow while Richie was kept in green.

Richard laughed at the thought of his godsons. He was honoured to be part of this family, part of their love, and to have so many to love now. Although he had grown up with an older brother and a very young sister later on, he had been the closest with Darcy. After joining the military, he had often felt lonely, even with a large group of his own men under his command, and he had not felt this bliss, this peace until Darcy and Elizabeth had accepted him into their lives.

He had not thought too much about his carnal desires recently. With all the craziness, his own relief had not been a priority, but knowing that Darcy and Elizabeth would be resuming relations after the infant baptism, his needs had returned in full force last night. He wondered what Elizabeth would be wearing and he had become too aroused to not relieve himself. He had not touched himself in more than a fortnight and he was not surprised by the force of the release.

He enjoyed his ride on the stallion thoroughly, returning to the site of the abandoned shed which had been destroyed and cleared completely now, and he rode to where

Darcy and Elizabeth had been attacked. He gave a prayer of thanks that he was able to arrive in time and hoped that Darcy would soon bring Elizabeth here in order for her to heal. He knew that fear of a place or experience would impede a full recovery and now that she would be able to resume her long walks, he wanted her to enjoy and love Pemberley in full measures.

He entered the foyer and saw that Elizabeth was just entering the breakfast room. He wanted to greet her but he had sweated copiously today due to the hard ride. *I will just pop my head in quickly.*

"Good morning, Elizabeth! Are you well?" *Darcy did not take you like a beast, did he?* He smirked. *No, I am sure he was good to you.* He thought to himself as she smiled brightly at him.

"Good morning, Richard! Did you have a nice long ride?" She asked, as she walked closer to him and kissed his cheek.

"Yes, it was a good ride. It has been a while since I sweated so much." He replied as he kissed her cheek.

Elizabeth leaned in further and sniffed him. "Oh, very sweaty. So attractive, though." She nipped his earlobe with her teeth playfully.

Good lord! He pushed her against the wall and attacked her mouth. He grabbed her head with one hand while the other grabbed her waist and he delved his tongue deep inside her, sucking the air out of her lungs as he breathed in her scent. She once again returned his kiss and moaned while she began to caress his chest under his waistcoat with her soft hands. He broke the kiss just as abruptly when he realised that he almost released in his breeches when she touched him. He saw her face turned upward and lips bruised from his rough kiss. She was so beautiful. He knew that Elizabeth had become more open and had returned his kisses more freely but she could not give more. *Maybe someday? No, I cannot receive it even if she offers it.*

She snapped her eyes open. "Richard! I... that was... Oh, dear. I was thinking of Fitzwilliam..." She flushed red. She had enjoyed uniting with her husband so much that she had been constantly dreaming of him.

Richard grinned broadly. "I know, Elizabeth. I know you were thinking of Darcy. I cannot help myself from kissing you as you are so tempting." He tried to hide his arousal with his hands. It was not the first time she had seen the bulge and he was certain it would not be the last, but he was embarrassed nonetheless.

Elizabeth giggled. "Fitzwilliam said the same thing but I did not truly believe him."

"Minx! You are a gorgeous woman, Elizabeth Darcy. Now you must excuse me so I can wash up and take care of this!" He uncovered his hands to show her his bulge. He leaned in to kiss her gently on her lips. "I love you, dearest. You are beautiful and you are far too tempting. Remember that you are thoroughly and sincerely loved." He kissed her once more, licking her lower lip, and promptly left.

He heard her giggle and begin to hum a song. *She is happy. So, so lovely. Blasted! I cannot believe I almost came in my breeches. I need a cold bath! It will be good to use Abigail at Kent soon. Hopefully having a regular release should prevent this, but then again, Elizabeth has always inspired me more than anyone else. Damn it, how do I get this down before my valet sees me?*

Chapter 38

Darcy was immensely proud of his wife and his growing family. The twins were growing fast and even hearing their cries brought a smile to his face. For their first anniversary, Darcy unwrapped the painting that he had commissioned while they were in London and proudly hung Elizabeth's portrait in the grand hallway of Pemberley. She would now be a legacy, to be heralded as the best mistress of Pemberley for generations to come.

He also presented her with a beautiful phaeton that she could use when she made her tenant visits, along with two beautiful foals.

Elizabeth gifted her dear husband with a new leather journal, which she had written on the first pages a poem that she composed, declaring her love to the man of her dreams. Darcy beamed and was pleased to no end, as they had recently argued about poetry being the food of love and Elizabeth had argued that it was, only if it was already a fine, stout, healthy love.

Cook was told by Mrs. Reynolds that the master and mistress were to celebrate their first anniversary several weeks ago, so she presented the couple with three bottles of new orange wine that she had been saving for just the special occasion.

Darcy and Elizabeth opened one of the bottles on their anniversary night and enjoyed it greatly. It was sweet and although Elizabeth did not indulge in wine very often, she especially liked this flavour and how it made her feel so relaxed. The Darcys made love several times during the night and fell deeper in love.

~*~

Several evenings later, Darcy and Elizabeth shared one of the orange wine bottles with Richard after dinner. Georgiana was not feeling well so she had retired early, and the three sat, talking of some of the gossip that they had heard in town, when Mr. Jameson, the butler, interrupted Darcy due to an urgent servant issue with the magistrate.

"Do you wish for me to join you?" Richard asked. He was curious what could be so urgent this late in the evening.

"No, no. Please stay with Elizabeth and enjoy the wine. I know Elizabeth loves this particular one and she would not wish to be left alone." Darcy answered. "I shall return shortly."

Richard nodded and remained seated next to Elizabeth, who was taking several sips of the delicious wine.

After Darcy departed, Richard asked Elizabeth of any news with her family. Elizabeth eagerly shared the latest about her baby brother, Jane's pregnancy, and Charlotte's engagement, and Richard listened and conversed with her happily about his family's news as well.

Richard lifted the wine bottle to refill his glass a little more when he realised that it was empty. He looked to Elizabeth and saw that she was finishing off the last drop of Darcy's glass and her own was already empty.

"Elizabeth, do you know that you drank almost the entire bottle? Are you well?" Richard asked in concern. He knew she had never drank more than one glass before.

Elizabeth giggled. "Did I truly? I have never drank so much wine before, Richard, but it was so delicious! Should I ask for another bottle? Would you like some more?"

Richard could tell that she was becoming intoxicated. He smiled as she giggled. *She is so adorable. I will walk her to her room so she can go to sleep.* "Come, Elizabeth. Let me escort you to your rooms. You will need to go to sleep, my love." He began to rise to assist her but instead of standing up with him, Elizabeth leaned against him and laid her head on his shoulder.

"I am tired, Richard. Hold me." Elizabeth whined, as she moved closer to him and wrapped her arms around his body.

Richard stiffened at the closeness. She raised her legs up onto his thighs and was practically sitting on his lap now and he tenderly wrapped his arms around her and smelled her hair. He had not held her this close for weeks and he was extremely aroused.

He could not help himself and he kissed her hair and forehead. She lifted her face and he kissed her, tasting the wine on her lips and she returned his kiss by opening her mouth and licking his lips. He delved his tongue inside her mouth and began to kiss her deeply, wishing more than anything to take her fully, as his arousal expanded larger than ever.

Elizabeth moaned, "You kiss so well, Richard. Fitzwilliam said I am a good kisser. Do you think I am a good kisser?" She slurred her words.

Damn it, she is inebriated and she does not know what she is doing. I want her so much! She will not remember any of this most likely. If only I could... Richard thought to himself. "Yes, my love. You are an excellent kisser and I live for your kisses." Richard replied honestly.

"Mmmm. I am so glad." Elizabeth sleepily replied. "I love kissing." She proceeded to kiss him eagerly again, with her hands in his hair and then lowered her lips, pulling his cravat down, to lick his ear and neck.

Richard was ready to explode. Not only was she seducing him beyond his control, he had dreamt of having her for so long that it was too overwhelming to hold back.

He quickly sprung out his massive erection from his breeches and pulled out Elizabeth's handkerchief that he always carried. He wrapped it around the tip of his manhood and began to kiss Elizabeth furiously, holding her tightly with his left arm while his right hand pumped his arousal. Within seconds, he lifted his face off of Elizabeth's lips and grunted loudly as he ejaculated into the cloth. *Oh my god! That was the biggest release of my life!* He was dizzy with such a forceful release but was embarrassed that Elizabeth might find it offensive.

Richard looked down to Elizabeth and found her softly snoring on his shoulder. He laughed quietly, seeing her peaceful face, her lips swollen and reddened with his ardent kisses, and he pocketed the soggy handkerchief and buttoned his breeches with one hand while he still held her. He saw that her dress had shifted and one of her breasts was almost falling out, so he changed her position to correct her posture.

As Richard moved Elizabeth slightly, she mumbled, "Take me to bed, Fitzwilliam."

Richard sighed with satisfaction. *I love her so much. She calls out for her husband and she loves him, but I know she cares for me as well. I would never impose on her and I would never be so ungentlemanly to take what does not belong to me. Oh, she has so much passion in her little body. I will never stop loving her. Having her in my arms is a dream and it is enough for me. I will honour her vows.*

He sat for several moments, trying to figure out what to do. He could carry her upstairs to her room but there were many servants still about and it would appear odd for him to be taking the unconscious Mistress to her bed. He certainly could not leave her here alone, and he did not know when Darcy would return.

Thankfully, the door opened and Darcy entered.

Darcy walked in and saw that Elizabeth was out cold and snoring, but it was obvious that she had wrapped herself around Richard and his cousin was holding her while she slept. Seeing the relief on Richard's face, he smiled softly and sat across from them.

"So, what is going on, Richard?" Darcy asked nonchalantly.

Richard gulped. "Well, after you left, Elizabeth and I were talking and I did not realise how much wine she was drinking, and the next thing I know, she drank the entire bottle by herself and finished off your glass. I swear I did not do anything to encourage it. She climbed on me and then fell asleep."

Darcy smiled tenderly, "And did you have a good release? Did you enjoy her kisses?"

Richard turned completely red. "How?!" He quietly hissed. "How could you tell that I... and that she kissed me?"

Darcy chuckled softly as to not awaken his wife. "Richard, I can see her lips swollen and she is still moving her lips as if she is kissing. Also, you missed a spot. I see a wet spot on your breeches and you still have not deflated completely. I know what she does to me, cousin. I can only imagine how much she must tempt you but I hope you have not taken advantage of her in her state."

He stood and walked to the bar and poured himself a drink. After gulping down the first glass, he poured himself another and one for Richard.

He continued after handing Richard his glass. "I am saddened that Elizabeth would pounce on you as soon as I leave you two alone. I love her so much, Richard, and as much as I wish I could be generous, I am hurt that she sought your attentions. I know she loves you. She is falling in love with you and I do not blame her. You are good to her and you would have been a good husband to her. I worry that I am not enough for her. I worry that I will lose her love, Richard." He swallowed the last bit of his drink. "What if she does not want me? What do I do if she stops loving me?"

Richard smiled sympathetically at Darcy. *The poor sod. He does not know how much she loves him!* "Darcy, I will confess that when she began to climb on me and kiss me, I completely lost control and began to kiss her. I enjoy kissing her more than breathing. She did declare that she enjoyed kissing me and that you had told her she was a good kisser. I could not contain myself and burst while I kissed her but her last words to me before she fell asleep was, 'Take me to bed, Fitzwilliam.' She was thinking of you and dreaming of you." Richard paused to see that Darcy's eyes were wide in surprise. "She loves you more than anything in life and I could never take more than I have been given. I know that she cares for me but it is nothing compared to her love for you, Darcy. I love her but I will honour her vows to you. I will never stop loving her and she will never stop loving you. If she will love me a little, I am content. I know she was intoxicated and confused me with you and I am grateful for every intimacy I have with her, but I am not stupid to think that she wants me instead. She wants you and she will always want you."

Darcy smiled broadly now. "Thank you, Richard. Your honesty and reassurances bring peace to my heart and I truly appreciate it. Our marriage is still so new and I am discovering that I love her more every day. I meant what I said before, Richard. If I had to share her love with anyone, I am glad it is you. Thank you for honouring her. You could have taken anything you wanted in her incapacitated state but you were a gentleman and I am grateful." Darcy put his glass down. "I think the servant issue had depressed me. The under-gardener, Jonas, the one with the young wife, caught Mrs. Jonas in bed with Mr. Smithson, the blacksmith, and they had a row. Blood was spilled and they had vowed to kill each other, but all the blame is being placed on the wife, of course. She is being called an adulterer and a whore when the husband neglected her and visited prostitutes instead of tending to his wife. It was a matter of time until she was tempted and now, she will be under her husband's thumb even further. I will need Elizabeth's help to see what can be done with the wife but both men are in jail a couple of nights to cool off for now.

"I do not condone adultery but I do not accept neglect, either. We three have a very unusual love for each other and I do not know if it is morally correct, but I love her, you love her, and she loves us both. I will give her all of my love until my last breath and I hope to God that she will continue to love me." Darcy finished.

Richard was quiet for several moments then he spoke. "I feel the same way, Darcy. I will love her until my last breath and I can only wish for her love to grow for me. She loves you, Darcy, and she will always choose you first. I know that I am a trespasser in your marriage but I am forever grateful that you have allowed me to love her. I promise you that I will never dishonour her. and I vow to you that I will never take more than what you and Elizabeth gift me. Being in her presence, being able to see her every day has been more blessing than I ever expected and I can only hope to be near her always. I was truly relieved that you had arrived. I did not know what to do with her." Richard smiled.

Darcy stood. "Well, I will take her to bed and we will sort this out in the morning. She will have such a headache." They laughed. He bent to take her into his arms and Richard shifted her and helped Darcy lift her.

As Elizabeth moved from one man to the other, she wrapped her arms around Darcy's neck and mumbled, "I love you, Fitzwilliam," and quickly began to snore again.

Darcy beamed. He cradled his precious wife in his arms and kissed her forehead. He looked to his dear cousin and smiled, "Thank you, Richard. Thank you for being so good to both of us." He carried her to bed where he promptly fell asleep holding her in his arms with a smile on his face.

Richard grinned as he watched his beloved off to bed. *She is precious. I am thankful for her love and her kisses and I honour her vows to Darcy. They are perfect for each other.*

He rushed to his rooms to clean himself. *I cannot believe I exploded like that. Thank God she fell asleep and did not see.* He recalled her kisses and he was fully aroused again. *One more time.* He lay back and pumped himself until he released, dreaming of loving her once again.

~*~

Elizabeth woke with a groan. *What happened? Why does my head hurt so much?*

Just then, Darcy entered the bedroom and began to open the drapes quickly. "Good morning, my love! Rise and shine!"

190

Elizabeth moaned loudly. "It is too bright! What happened, Fitzwilliam? What time is it?"

Darcy chuckled. "It is past eleven o'clock, Mrs. Darcy. You have slept the morning away." He sat next to her and caressed her face. "You are suffering from your first overindulgence. Here, I have a drink for you. You must drink the whole thing. It will help your headache." He laughed again.

"Oh, Fitzwilliam. I remember talking with Richard in the drawing room and I am waking up here. What did I do?" Elizabeth croaked.

"You decided to enjoy the entire bottle of the orange wine by yourself. Apparently, you decided to make love to Richard and fell asleep in his arms before I returned to the drawing room." Darcy teased.

Elizabeth froze in shock. She began to splutter, "I... I... Fitzwilliam, I swear I did not mean to do anything. I... Did I really...?" She could not believe that she could do something dishonourable and to hear that she threw herself at Richard mortified her. She began to cry when Darcy embraced her and soothed her.

"I am sorry, my love, I only meant to tease. Nothing happened. Nothing happened with Richard. He knew you were inebriated and you only kissed him. Nothing else happened." Darcy repeated.

"Oh, Fitzwilliam. I do not remember anything. I cannot believe I could have drank so much. I am so sorry. Something could have happened if Richard was not so honourable and it is all my fault." She continued to cry.

Darcy met her eyes and kissed her lips. "My love, we would have never let you drink so much if we knew what would have happened, and we will certainly never do so again. You will only be allowed more than one glass if you are with Richard and me from now on." He laughed. "Richard and I had a good talk last night while you were sleeping and I think it was long overdue. He loves you with the same passion that I have for you and I had felt that I might be losing you to him, but he honours our vows and you said four words that comforted me beyond all hopes."

"What did I say, my love?" Elizabeth asked curiously.

"You said, 'I love you, Fitzwilliam.' After you were in Richard's arms, after kissing him fervently, while I lifted you up to carry you to our bed, you called my name. I know you love me and I am comforted that you will always choose me. I love you so much, Elizabeth, and I was trying to not become jealous of your love for Richard but seeing you in his arms and your desiring him had wounded me. But when you spoke my name, when I realised that you still loved me more, I am now comfortable with Richard's love for you and your love for Richard. I will share you as long as you always stay with me. If you will have me, I will never neglect you and will love you till my last days." Darcy held her tightly.

"I love you, Fitzwilliam. No one compares to you and I will never leave you. I am relieved that nothing more happened. I know it would not have been Richard's fault but our relationship would have been ruined and I am glad he was honourable. I love you so much, Fitzwilliam. I am so sorry." Elizabeth cuddled into his embrace.

"I love you, Elizabeth. Richard loves you dearly and I appreciate our cousin so much. He comforted me with my insecurities and his care for you is commendable. I do have an issue that I need your help on when you are ready." Darcy told her about the situation with Mrs. Jonas and what could be done.

"Oh, what a sad situation. I never believed that the wife should carry all of the burdens of an affair. It takes a lot for a wife to turn from her husband. Once my head clears, I will see what I can do. It is unfortunate that women are blamed for everything. That drink you gave me was awful but it is helping and I will need to apologise to Richard as well. Oh, what a mess. I apologise again, dear husband." Elizabeth kissed his cheek.

Darcy laughed. "Do not dwell upon it a minute longer. I will collect your debts later, my love." He winked. "Please take your time to refresh yourself and I will see you for luncheon. I know you will wish for some time with Richard. I love you. I love you with all my heart." He kissed her cheek and departed.

~*~

Once Elizabeth felt clear-headed enough, she walked down the stairs and to the dining room. Both men stood as she entered and she took her place but she could not look at Richard in the eyes and ate silently. Darcy did most of the talking, as Richard did not speak much, either, and after the meal was finished, Darcy escorted Elizabeth to his study.

"Join us, Richard." Darcy commanded. He scoffed internally. *Not only do I share my wife with my cousin, I now have to be an intermediary when they cannot speak with each other! Ridiculous, but I do care for them both very much!* "Elizabeth, I will see you in a half hour?" He winked and left them alone in his study.

Richard nervously began. "Are you well, Elizabeth?" Images of her kissing him passionately and her loose breast flooded his mind once again, making him wonder if he would ever be able to look her in the eyes again. *I am getting aroused again. Oh, Elizabeth, what you do to me!*

Elizabeth's face had been turned away from him but when he heard her stifling a sob, he immediately flew to her side and hugged her, rubbing her back until she calmed.

After a few moments, Elizabeth finally spoke. "I am so ashamed, Richard. I never drank so much before and I had no idea that I would be so wanton. Fitzwilliam forgave me but I cannot believe that I acted so unladylike and I am mortified that I behaved so badly. He told me that I... that I climbed on you and..."

Richard smiled. *She is so wonderful. So innocent and so, so lovely.*

He lifted her face to his and kissed her gently. "My love, I enjoyed your kisses last night more than anything else in my life, but I also knew that you were not yourself. One day, I hope, I sincerely hope, that you will kiss me like that again of your own volition, but I certainly do not regret last night. Having you in my arms and your seducing me was the most exciting feeling in my life and I returned your kiss most urgently but nothing more happened. I wish for you to know that you will always be safe with me. I will guard your body and your honour with my life and even if you were completely naked and begging for me," he pressed his arousal against her, "I desire you more than anything else in life but I will protect you from yourself because I love you. I love you with my soul. I live for your kisses but I know what I am allowed. I will always be here for you and keep you safe." He kissed her lips again, deeper but short.

Elizabeth wiped her tears. "Thank you for your care, Richard. You are so good to me. I do love you. Fitzwilliam knows that I love you more and he assured me that he is comfortable with our love. Our relationship is unusual but we have so much love for each other, I cannot imagine not having you with us now. I appreciate you more than you will ever know." She hugged him tightly. After a moment, she let him go and stood a little bit from him, knowing that his protrusion had not yet deflated. "Now, since you have so much experience with loose women," she winked, "help me with Mrs. Jonas and what I should do." She smiled.

Richard and Elizabeth discussed the situation and when Darcy entered later, they deliberated several options and returned to their daily businesses.

Chapter 39

Mrs. Jonas was eternally grateful when Mrs. Darcy visited her. She had already been shunned by several of her neighbours for being an adulterer and had cried copiously, not knowing what to do next. Mrs. Darcy was understanding and patient and she told her of her relationship with her husband of less than two years.

Elizabeth was shocked when she met Mrs. Jonas, who was not yet seventeen years old. She had expected an older woman with loose morals who was careless with her vows, but to hear that her husband had beat and raped her on her fifteenth birthday and that she was forced to marry him when she had been in love with Mr. Smithson since she was twelve years old, it broke her heart. The physical abuse had continued and she could see the blackened eye right now from the most recent beating, as well as several fading green and yellow bruises on her arms and chin. *I have to save her. Her husband will auction her off as an adulterer or continue to abuse her to make the rest of her life wretched. If he is a miserable, angry drunk, he might even kill her!*

"Mrs. Jonas, I know that your choices are limited and I do not condone adultery. I value the sanctity of marriage first and foremost in my own life, but understanding your situation better, I wish to help you. As the wife of your husband's employer, my hands are tied but I can connect you with someone who can assist you. If you are agreeable, you will need to remove yourself from this country and leave your husband. You will have to leave your family and everything you know." Elizabeth offered.

Mrs. Jonas cried. "Please call me Agnes, Mrs. Darcy. My parents both died last year. They were miserable that I had to marry that awful man but they saw no other way. They knew that I loved Matthew but he was poor and it was before he got his employment as a blacksmith. They got sick and they despaired that they would be leaving me like this but what could be done? I have no family left. I have no money and no wealthy relatives to take me. Where can I go? What can I do?" She cried harder.

Elizabeth consoled her. "Agnes, I will have a woman visit you later today. Your husband and Mr. Smithson will be released tomorrow and you must be gone quickly. You must not speak of my helping you and you will have to forget all you know here, but I will try to arrange for Mr. Smithson to join you eventually but it will take time. Are you in agreement, Agnes?"

Agnes sobbed. "Anything, Mrs. Darcy. You are saving my life. I was ready to run away but did not know where to go. I had planned on going to London to hide myself but I also know that I would have to become a prostitute to survive. I was willing to bear it rather than stay here with my husband. Thank you for saving my life. I am ready to go now. I am already packed."

As Elizabeth stood at the front door to take her leave, she spoke loudly, knowing that several neighbours were watching. "I am sorry to hear of your situation, Mrs. Jonas. I know women have very little rights but it is terrible that your husband, who forced himself on you to marry you, has the right to do whatever he wishes with you. It is unfair but you must pay the price for marrying that wretched man. I will certainly pray for your soul." She winked discreetly and whispered, "God bless you. Goodbye, Agnes." And she left.

~*~

Several hours later, the nosy neighbours saw Mrs. Weston and a cloaked maid knock on Mrs. Jonas' door. After Mrs. Darcy's visit, the neighbouring women had become more sympathetic to Mrs. Jonas' situation and realised that once again, women were put down first without any blame on the men and news spread quickly that although Mrs. Darcy did not condone her sins, she showed mercy and that Mrs. Jonas was indeed a poor soul whose husband had forced himself on her to have her. The neighbours thought little when Mrs. Weston left with the cloaked maid a quarter hour later and ceased paying attention to Mrs. Jonas' door.

~*~

Agnes was tremendously relieved when she finally reached her destination. She had used Hannah's cloak to leave her home with Mrs. Weston and had left with no more than a small bag that could be concealed under the large cape. Mrs. Darcy had graciously provided ten pounds and arranged for a hackney to take her to the post station. After days of journeying on the post, she knocked timidly at the door of the grand house. She handed the letter that she had carried for the past four days next to her heart to the housekeeper. As it was freezing cold, the housekeeper bid her to enter and after reading the letter, she finally spoke.

"Hello, Agnes. I am Mrs. Cleveland. Mrs. Darcy shared a little bit of your story with me and I want you to know that you will be safe here. I have not met Mrs. Darcy in person but have heard good things about her and I can tell that she has a good heart. We will protect you and you will always have a place here. As long as you are willing to work hard, you may stay here as a maid. Let me show you to your room. Welcome to Kieran Hall." She concluded.

Agnes was grateful and worked hard at the house. She was in further shock when her beloved, Matthew, arrived at the door a month later. He relayed the news that Mr. Jonas had died from drinking too much after he was fired from his position for colluding with the evil George Wickham earlier this year and ended up face down during a rainstorm. He also informed her that Mr. Fitzwilliam was able to locate a position for him to be a blacksmith nearby and he proposed marriage right away. She gladly accepted and Mrs. Cleveland arranged her residence so she could live with her new husband after the New Year.

Chapter 40

Since the babies had arrived a month earlier, they changed their plans of travel. Instead of heading straight to Rosings for Christmas, they decided to spend a fortnight in London during the first two weeks of December, attend Lady Matlock's famous Christmas Ball, then head to Rosings mid-December where they would spend the next three weeks. They planned on going to Ramsgate and Bath for a month each, travel to Hertfordshire for Jane's confinement, then return to London for Georgiana's first season.

So, during the last week of November, a large entourage of Mr. and Mrs. Darcy, Richard, Georgiana, the babies, their wet nurse, their two nannies and a slew of servants, that included Wilkins, his wife Hannah, and Richard's valet, Garrison, left for London.

It took four days instead of the usual three with the babies needing frequent rest, but everyone took turns caring for them and Darcy and Richard immediately walked them and rocked them during breaks.

Georgiana laughed and commented that Richard made a great father and Elizabeth heartily agreed but also added that her husband was still the best. She looked adoringly at Darcy after the babes were returned to their nannies and the men re-entered the carriage. "I love you, Fitzwilliam," she whispered. Her eyes shone with affection and he kissed her hands.

"I love you, Elizabeth." Darcy returned.

Richard and Georgiana giggled seeing their affections. Richard coughed.

"I love you, too, Richard. I love you, Georgiana." Elizabeth laughed.

"I love you, Elizabeth." Georgiana happily chimed.

Richard gulped. He had never said the words to her in front of Darcy and Georgiana. He knew his emotions would betray him and Darcy would punch him if he revealed his love in front of Georgiana so he coughed again. "Thank you, Elizabeth." And smiled at her and winked.

Darcy laughed and changed the subject. They spoke merrily of their plans and which outings would be interesting.

~*~

The first few days of their return were spent on many businesses. Darcy and Richard closeted themselves in the study for hours while the ladies went shopping, as Elizabeth needed to purchase a few new dresses with her changed figure and to modify her current dresses.

Darcy loved her for being so frugal even when they had nearly endless income when most women would have thrown out their whole closet for a new wardrobe with his money. He randomly thought of Caroline Bingley. She had been the most mercenary woman he had ever met and he detested her. After her attempt to compromise him in his own bed and Wilkins had foiled her plans, he hoped he never saw her again. He knew Bingley and his sister Louisa had cut all of their connections with her but he had an ominous feeling that she might be up to no good. Darcy was aware that Bingley had released her dowry to her and there was no way that a grasping woman like that would sit idly in York with her spinster aunt. It was rather likely that she would be back in London.

He worried for his wife and sons. He did not wish for any harm to come to them and Georgiana would also be affected should Caroline Bingley attempt to crash at her ball or try to ingratiate herself with his sister.

He shuddered at the thought of seeing that revolting woman again and wrote to his London investigator to find out the whereabouts of Miss Bingley. He vowed to protect his family at all cost and also wrote to Bingley to see if he was aware of her latest activities. He discussed his strategy with Richard when he returned from visiting with his parents.

Richard was severely concerned for Elizabeth as well. Darcy had told him about Miss Bingley's attempted compromise and what caused the rushed proposal, and Richard did not want Caroline Bingley within a hundred yards of his precious Elizabeth.

Richard told Darcy that Anne was once again very ill and it did not look good this time. Darcy had last seen his cousin Anne two Easters ago and decided that he would consult Elizabeth and let her decide if they should visit her the next day. Anne had been generous to will Rosings to Richard and he had never cared for her more than as a cousin but had withdrawn from her company due to her mother's demands. Darcy had hoped that she would recover but was grateful that his wife was nothing like her.

~*~

Elizabeth immediately agreed that she wished to meet Anne. Richard sent a note to his parents of Darcys' wishes to visit Anne and they agreed that next day afternoon would work.

They decided to walk the two blocks and brought the babies for Lord and Lady Matlock to visit with Bennet and Richie again. Darcy and Richard beamed at the praises of the boys and after a quarter hour, they knocked on Anne's door. Once they entered, they greeted Anne and Elizabeth and the boys were introduced to Anne, who remained lying on the bed.

The boys were soon hoisted away by the nannies and they returned to Darcy House while the adults visited. Anne greeted Elizabeth kindly. "Cousin Darcy, I am delighted to see you smile. I do not believe I have ever seen you so happy before. Mrs. Darcy, I am very pleased to meet you at last. Fitz has been praising you to the skies and I understand why. Your sons are beautiful. Congratulations on your marriage and the safe delivery." She softly spoke.

"Will you call me 'Lizzy' and may I call you 'Anne'?" Elizabeth requested. Anne smiled and nodded. "Thank you, Anne. I am very pleased to meet you. I have not had the fortune to meet your mother yet but have heard wonderful things about you."

Anne and Richard snickered while Darcy smiled slightly.

"You are very kind, Lizzy, and very beautiful. I am so glad that you married Cousin Darcy. You look very happy together. What are your plans for Christmas?" Anne asked.

Elizabeth told her about the two weeks in London and to move to her home at Rosings to enjoy the splendour there. She talked about the loveliness of the Rosings Gardens and Anne was very pleased that her new cousin had enjoyed the property. Soon, she grew tired. Elizabeth saw that Anne needed to rest and excused herself so she could return home.

Anne thanked her for the visit, "It was so very nice meeting you, Cousin Lizzy. I hope to see you again before your trip to Rosings. Fitz, will you stay for a moment?"

Richard agreed. He rose to walk to the door to open it and told Darcy that he would return on his own to Darcy House. He returned to take a seat next to the bed and asked, "Are you well, Anne? Did you wish to speak of Rosings?"

Anne paused for a moment. She kept her eyes on his and asked gently, "How long have you loved her?"

Richard spluttered. "Wha? Who? Of whom are you speaking, Anne?" His heart beat furiously. *I did not say anything or do anything. How?*

Anne smiled faintly. "I watched all three of you most carefully. When you entered, I saw the way you looked at Lizzy and I could tell. I have never seen you look at anyone like that, Fitz, and you looked at her the same way Darcy looked at her. Just because I am always silent does not mean I am ignorant. I am more observant than most anyone and I could see right away that you were in love with her. You had so many good things to say about her and although they are all true, I now understand why you were always eager to speak of her. Does she know?"

Richard sighed. He knew Anne was dying and it was no use hiding it from her. "Yes, I am most ardently and desperately in love with her. And yes, she knows." He did not know what else to say without spilling out his whole heart.

"But she is so happy with Cousin Darcy! How can you stand it? Are you not miserable in the presence of a woman who does not love you?" Anne asked curiously.

He smiled tenderly. "She loves Darcy with a devotion like I have never seen, but she loves me like a brother and it is enough for me. Anne, Darcy knows I love her and has allowed me to love her. I may not be her husband and I will never take her to my bed, but I love her so much that breathing the same air as she is enough to sustain me. I will never stop loving her."

"I am envious of her, Fitz. She has the love of the two of the best men I know. I might not know many men, but I have met quite a few, especially of late, and my mother had repeatedly told me how Darcy was the best. I never realised how handsome Darcy was until I saw him smile today. I would never have made him smile like that if I were his wife. I already know you to be generous and honourable." She rested for a few minutes.

Richard had thought she might have fallen asleep but then she continued. "I know I am dying, cousin. Aunt Susan wanted to be honest with me so I can wrap up my affairs. I appreciate your mother so much. Thank you for taking good care of Rosings. Am I correct in that you will wish to leave Rosings to Richie?" He nodded. "Bring your solicitor tomorrow and I will include an addendum in my will to ensure it will be valid." She laughed. "Mother will have her dreams come true of uniting Pemberley and Rosings."

Richard laughed. He kissed Anne's forehead. "Rest, Anne. I will see you tomorrow."

As he closed the door, he could see that Anne was already asleep and he took a deep breath to steady himself. It was difficult to see anyone suffering, especially a poor soul that had been so abused and neglected by her own mother. He vowed once again to be the best godfather to his godsons and the best uncle to any other children Darcy and Elizabeth would have.

He smiled to himself and shook his head. *Of course, Anne noticed! I will have to be more careful but thank God everyone knows that I love her already and that we are a close-knit family together.*

He farewelled his parents with the promise to return the next day and rushed to Darcy House to see his heart's desire once again.

Chapter 41

"Mr. Darcy." The man shook Darcy's hand.

"Mr. O'Connor, how are you, sir?" Darcy asked. "How is your brother Mr. O'Connor?" He smiled. The elder brother had been of great service in Derbyshire many times and Bingley had found him to be a very respectful and detailed private detective. This investigator was his younger brother whom Darcy also had used many times in the past for business needs.

"Well, sir. Thank you. I have the report that you requested on a Miss Caroline Bingley. Is this an appropriate time to discuss it, Mr. Darcy?" He asked.

"Yes, it shall be good to hear you now. Please take a seat and I will call for my cousin." Darcy opened the door and instructed the footman to request Richard's audience. It had been Richard's turn to sit with Elizabeth and Georgiana, who were practicing their curtsey with his mother.

Darcy returned to his desk and was looking at the report on paper when Richard knocked and entered.

"Mr. O'Connor, you remember my cousin, Richard Fitzwilliam." The men shook hands. "Please proceed now." Darcy requested.

"Yes, sir. I began investigating Miss Bingley last week as per your request and have concluded everything today. Miss Bingley is the twenty-five-year-old sister of Charles Bingley, who is your close associate and brother by law now. She was exiled to York with her elderly aunt who remains unmarried and had spent nearly eight months there until she turned five and twenty, receiving her dowry of £20,000. She arrived in London in May this year and has spent over £4,000 to lease a townhouse located on Grosvenor Square at double the going price and purchased extravagant furnishings. It was noted that she had a shopping expedition to the modiste that resulted in the purchase of over four dozen dresses at once."

I am not surprised. Elizabeth is a treasure! Darcy thought.

"It was also found that she has had a steady stream of men calling on her," Darcy's brows raised in surprise, "ranging from stable boys to military men to the second son of a duke."

Ah, that makes more sense, Darcy thought.

Mr. O'Connor continued, "The visits were during all times of the day and the servants had gossiped that she spent more time entertaining men in her bed than out at times. It was also noted that after one man left, another would enter soon thereafter." He cleared his throat. "It does not appear that she is a mistress to any of the gentlemen or selling her body; rather, she obtains favours and invitations to parties and dinners this way. She is no lady." He coloured. She was worse than a whore to him, as she did not need the money to survive in such a way. "It is known that her greatest achievement is Lord Harold Haversham." Mr. O'Connor added.

"Haversham!" Both Darcy and Richard shouted.

They exchanged looks, as they knew he had chased Elizabeth and was denied. Also, Richard had previously told Darcy about that rake's former mistress, currently his own, how he had screamed Elizabeth's name during his climaxes.

Darcy spoke again. "Apologies. Please continue."

"It has been found that Lady Haversham is with child and is due to deliver in February. Lord Harold has been spending time with several courtesans since he released his long-term mistress, a Miss Abigail Harrington. Miss Harrington has since retired to the country and has not been seen since and I believe all ties to Lord Harold have been severed. Lord Harold visits several exclusive courtesans as well as Miss Bingley and is reported to be searching for a new mistress with very specific criterions and has not been able to find one to satisfy him.

"There has been gossip that Miss Bingley is looking to become a mistress to a prominent gentleman, I believe that is you, Mr. Darcy, after her pursuit of the earl, Lord Devon, who had inherited the title a year ago had failed. Lord Devon is recently married to the former Miss Wentington, daughter of General Wentington. It is known that Miss Bingley attempted to seek his attentions back in May when she received an invitation to dine with Viscount Carlisle, now Lord Devon, who was already engaged unbeknownst to her, and attempted to flirt severely but failed to capture his attentions. Unknown to the public is that she dressed like a servant and snuck into the house to enter his bedroom and lay in wait to compromise him, but Viscount Carlisle spent the night with his fiancée and did not return to his home until she was found by his valet in the morning after she had fallen asleep. She scurried out in a hurry and it was not made public, as the viscount did not wish for General Wentington know that he had been having relations with his daughter prior to the wedding. The servants were willing to share the information for some coins and as the viscount had not demanded secrecy, they shared as much as they were aware.

"It is speculated that Miss Bingley is planning to attend Lady Matlock's Christmas Ball using Lord Harold's invitation and might attempt to compromise either yourself, Mr. Darcy, or Lord Devon, although she probably does not know that Lord Devon has already departed to his country home and will not attend the Christmas Ball this year with his new wife. I do not have more information on anything else, unfortunately." He concluded.

"Thank you, Mr. O'Connor. You have been most thorough. The ball is in three days and we will need to be vigilant. I refuse to allow that woman to disrupt my wife's happiness. Good day, sir." Darcy replied.

After Mr. O'Connor departed, he turned to Richard. "What do you think we need to do? How much of this do we need to tell Elizabeth?"

Richard contemplated while looking into the fireplace. *If I could only get my hands around that whore's neck, I would squeeze it tightly! But Elizabeth would not want me to be a murderer. I am certain Darcy is thinking the same.* "Since when have we been able to keep any secrets from Elizabeth? Darcy, it is most likely that Caroline Bingley will plan the same mode of attack. It seems that she only knows how to sneak in to get into a man's bed. I believe that she will attend Mother's party and flirt and try to get in your good graces. I am also certain that she is aware of my situation by now and I will do my part in trying to garner her attention. She might find the prospect of being a wife better than a mistress to you or Devon." He paused as he planned his attack. He had been one of the best war strategists and his intelligence would serve them well now. "I know that Haversham might also try something with Elizabeth. He had never been so disappointed and although he is congenial to you and me, his obsession with Elizabeth might cause him to falter. You must keep him away from Elizabeth and I will keep Miss Bingley away."

They discussed several options on what to do with her and selected the best choice. Richard continued, "Haversham knows that I am keeping Abigail. I do not want that information public but I am willing to bear it should it be made known. It might explain why I am not searching for a wife but I do not wish for Elizabeth to be exposed to her; it matters naught. We will protect our family, Darce."

"I agree with your plan, Richard. We will squash this interloper and she will be done in society." Darcy concluded.

The men departed to seek Elizabeth and the twins. They missed them and cherished every moment together.

~*~

Elizabeth was surprised when Darcy informed her of Mr. O'Connor's report in private. She had not thought about Caroline Bingley in months and burned with anger for all the wrath that this harridan brought to her husband.

"Fitzwilliam, she is a heartless, calculating harlot who only cares for connections and status. I wish to see her fall and for the truth to be revealed but I do not wish for her to harm our family, my love. Will Richard be able to do as you both planned? I would think he would rather throw her off the balcony!" Elizabeth frowned.

Darcy replied, "She is the most mercenary woman I have ever met and I have already written to Bingley that she will be publicly disgraced and will most likely be shipped off to the colonies if she does anything criminal. I am certain he will agree with whatever punishment fits. It is well known now that their ties are cut and will not affect Bingley or Jane, my love. Richard will be well. He is willing to suffer anything for us and will be glad to take her down. Now, lay back and relax so I can pleasure you."

He placed his head between her legs and pleasured her for a full quarter hour before taking his own.

Chapter 42

The Christmas Ball was one of the most elite parties of the season. It was held mid-December so many prestigious members of the *ton* could attend before needing to join their own families for Christmas, whether in London or in their country homes.

Matlock House was glowing with hundreds of soft candles and beautiful decorations and Lord and Lady Matlock stood in the receiving line to greet their guests. Viscount and Viscountess also stood for the greeting while Richard smirked at them, once again glad to be the second son. He stood with the Darcys and attempted to keep his eyes off of Elizabeth but could not help himself when they kept returning to her figure.

He remembered his misery one year ago, after Darcy had taken his new bride off to Pemberley and he was searching for a wife. He had danced with dozens of ladies and had been broken-hearted that he could not get Elizabeth out of his mind. Now, standing next to her, close enough to inhale her scent and hear her laughter, his heart was at peace and he knew he would give up everything to be near her always.

Richard softly commented to Elizabeth while looking out into the crowd while Darcy was speaking with an acquaintance, "You are very beautiful tonight, Elizabeth; that green dress is exquisite. I had thought burgundy was the best colour on you but I was wrong. I love seeing you glowing in such splendour."

Elizabeth smiled. "Thank you, Richard. I believe the Darcy Emeralds are what is glowing."

He whispered, "No, my love. It is all you. So beautiful." He sighed. He only wished this evening to be over. He wanted to hold Elizabeth and kiss her a few times and return to Rosings in two days. Abigail should have returned by now and he needed to take her a few times to purge his body of his carnal needs.

He saw Elizabeth stiffen suddenly and followed her eyes to see Caroline Bingley on Haversham's arm. *That cad brought his whore here?* He had thought that Caroline would be arriving separately but they had the gall to show up together. Everyone knew that Haversham had worsened after his marriage and he was often seen visiting whorehouses and carrying on affairs, but for that married man to arrive with the daughter of a tradesman who had slept with a dozen men into this room was a disgrace.

Richard tapped Darcy and pointed at the newly arrived couple with his chin. Their eyes met and knew it was time to begin the show.

~*~

Caroline was thrilled to enter on Lord Harold Haversham's arm. She had been favouring him since May and the seven months of performing all kinds of devious acts had finally paid off.

She had been angry when she finally discovered that Lord Harold had proposed marriage to Eliza Bennet, of all people, two years ago and that she had flatly turned him down. But she continued to bed him and rolled her eyes as he screamed out 'Lizzy' as he lay over her. She vowed to get her revenge by getting into Mr. Darcy's bed and have his child. She was distraught when she had found that Eliza had not only had an heir but had provided a spare as well. *If only she died in childbirth! But perhaps I can give Mr. Darcy a beautiful daughter in my spitting image. He can exile his hoyden of a wife to Scotland and I can be mistress to all of his magnificent properties!* She daydreamt of Mr. Darcy while Lord Harold continued his thrusts from behind as she lay on her stomach.

She heard the grunting that she had recognised as his finale and yelled, "Do not come inside me, you fool!"

He startled and pulled out. "Damn it, Caro. I want to just come inside you. You have been using birth control. What is the big deal?"

"It is not fool-proof and I cannot chance getting with child, Harry. Just come on the sheets as usual." Caroline bitterly replied.

"I have a better idea, Caro. Relax your cheeks," he said as he wiggled her buttocks. He fingered her vagina and his cock was already well lubricated from her climax. He separated her cheeks below and rubbed his cock between the fold.

Caroline smiled and relaxed. He had been a good lover and she had been quite pleased with his skills. Suddenly, she felt a sharp, ripping pain in her anus, as her lover inserted his large erection swiftly and sodomised her. She screamed and flailed her arms to get him off her but he moaned loudly.

"Get off me, you brute! What the hell are you doing?" She screamed again, "It hurts so much, get out of my hole!"

Lord Harold was a large man, more than double Caroline's size. He leaned forward and grabbed her breasts and continued his grunts as he fully penetrated her up to the hilt and continued his thrusting. "Oh, fuck, Caro. This is the best feeling I ever had on my cock." He pumped harder. "Oh, god, oh, god, oh, FUCK!" And he released long and hard inside her anus.

After his throbbing cock calmed, he pulled out his deflated manhood slowly. Looking down, he commented, "Oh, Caro. I have made you bleed. You have been deflowered, my dear. Wow, that was amazing."

Caroline was crying from the pain and kicked him off. "You are an arse, Harry. How dare you take me so roughly?" She quickly rose to wipe and tend to her pain. When she returned, Lord Harold was lying in the middle of the bed, still completely naked and stroking his erection with his hand.

"Get out of my house, Harry! I never want to see you again!" Caroline cried. She had not been too damaged and the cooling cloth had helped soothe the discomfort.

"Oh, Caro. Come here and let me have you one more time. My dear, do not desert me now. I have enjoyed our liaisons too much for seven months to let you go now and after buggering you just now, I will do anything to do it again. It was not even very messy and I want to do that all the time. I got hard again thinking about being inside your behind and releasing my seed. Oh, Caro. What can I do to convince you to let me back in there again?" He begged.

Caroline smirked. He had always had the upper hand in their relationship where she had to beg for his favours into parties and balls. She seductively crawled into bed and gently stroked his cock. "Well, Harry, I know you have been seeking a mistress and I think you should stop. Until my situation is settled, I want to be publicly seen with you so I can attend all of the functions. I wish to enter the Christmas Ball tonight on your arm and I would love for you to fund my shopping excursions. I desperately need more dresses that befits my status as your lover. What say you, Harry?" He looked a little hesitant. She knew he was looking for someone that looked more like Eliza Bennet. "I will let you in my butt again right now?" She pouted.

He pushed her onto her back and opened her legs wide open. He slowly inserted his erection inside her anus after spitting between her legs and lubricating her. He was slower this time and Caroline could feel herself getting aroused as she rubbed her clitoris while he plunged into her, and soon relaxed and climaxed. Watching Caro touch herself and reaching her ecstasy, Lord Harold began to thrust harder until the headboard was thumping against the wall and he released inside her once again.

He grunted and lay over her. Panting loudly, he moaned, "You have a deal, Caro. It is a deal."

~*~

Now, as Caroline entered the ballroom proudly as a peacock and flashing her smile to publicly announce that she was being kept by Lord Harold, she looked around and stuck her nose up in the air at those *peasants* who did not have a Lord on their arms. She arrogantly greeted the Matlocks and entered the ballroom. She was pleased to see Mr. Darcy's back, as he was conversing with another gentleman next to him, also his back to her, and she pulled on her lover's arm so she could head toward that direction.

Caroline Bingley received a huge shock when they approached the group, though, when the two gentlemen parted to show with whom they were speaking. Mrs. Darcy was in splendour with her perfect hair, sparkling eyes, and the most beautiful dress that Miss Bingley had ever seen. The emeralds around her neck were the largest and clearest that she had observed and she was slim at the waist with a décolletage that she knew most men would drool over. *Damn that wench! I would have never believed she delivered twins three months ago!* She could not speak for several moments as she stood with her mouth agape.

Lord Harold immediately approached Elizabeth, dropping Caroline's arm. *My god! She is more beautiful than I remember!* He attempted to reach for her hand to kiss it. He wanted to grab her and carry her off to a room to ravage her but he was quickly blocked by Darcy and Richard.

Darcy grabbed both his shoulders and flashed his false smile. "Haversham! How good it is to see you. I have not seen you in five years?" Releasing him but ensuring that he was keeping his distance from his wife, he continued, "I believe you know my wife, the former Miss Elizabeth Bennet."

Elizabeth quickly curtsied and stood tall. Her protectors would guard her with their lives.

Darcy completely ignored Miss Bingley and did not even look her way. "Richard, we will be getting some refreshments. Please excuse us." Darcy took Elizabeth's hand and kissed it then they both walked away from this group. They were stopped by a few acquaintances and were close enough to overhear Richard's conversation.

Richard saw that Haversham intended to chase after Elizabeth but swiftly grabbed his hand and shook it. "Haversham! It is good to see you. How have you been? May I be introduced to your friend?" He grinned his most fawning smile.

Caroline was surprised that he had not recognised her. They had met several times; dinner at Darcy House, at a few parties, and had even spent two weeks at Pemberley all those years ago. *I must be so changed that he does not remember me. I knew this orange dress was worth every penny! That modiste was so stupid to advise against it. How beautiful I must be in his eyes!* Caroline beamed.

Lord Harold looked behind him, his eyes trailing the love of his life, but turned back to face his friend. "Fitzwilliam, this is Miss Caroline Bingley, my new mistress. Caro, this is Mr. Richard Fitzwilliam. He is Lord Matlock's second son and master to Rosings Park. Say, how is Abby? Have you been enjoying her often? Did I not tell you she is very good?" He smirked.

Richard was disgusted. It was crass of Haversham to bring his new mistress here and to bring up the topic of his old mistress. He gave a frown to Haversham at the mention of Abigail but quickly turned to Miss Bingley and kissed her hand softly. "Miss Bingley! I had not recognised you; my sincere apologies. You have changed much since I saw you last." *You have turned into a whore! How revolting!* He thought but maintained his smile and flirted outwardly.

Caroline blushed at the compliment. She had heard that he had inherited Rosings and was now master of 6,000 a year, even higher than her own brother, but had not realised he was so dashing and handsome. Her eyes had been focused on Mr. Darcy for so long that Mr. Fitzwilliam had not been on her range while he had been a poor soldier.

She flirted and grabbed his arm. "Oh, Mr. Fitzwilliam! It is of no concern. I am *so* pleased to see you again." She saw that Lord Harold was still looking at Eliza Bennet's direction and she fumed. She looked up to see Richard smiling and she drew her chest closer to rub her breasts against his arm. "You look very well, sir, indeed well." She leaned closer to his ear. "Kind sir, perhaps we can get some punch? Shall you like to dance with me?" She fluttered her lashes. "Perhaps we can retire to your rooms to get some rest between sets. I might be Lord Harold's mistress but I am not locked in and would *love* to favour you with some of my talents."

She quickly concocted a plan to seduce Mr. Fitzwilliam. He was a bachelor and he would be a perfect husband, as he had wealth, was the son of an earl who could potentially become an earl himself should his brother die, and SO good-looking. He had connections and she would often dine with Mr. Darcy as well. The more she could be in Mr. Darcy's company, he would eventually realise his mistake with that little wife of his, who was probably a dull body in bed. *To have this fine man in my bed and to seduce Mr. Darcy! Oh, to have both of them be head over heels in love with me would be something!*

Richard could see the calculating look in Caroline's eyes. *She is truly a whore! I feel ill. I want to have her kicked out in shame, but damn it, it would not be enough. All of her follies must be exposed.*

He swallowed down his disgust and smiled, "Miss Bingley, I am not residing here but at Darcy House. I cannot do anything here at my parents' home..." he let the words hang. "Would you be available for the third set?" She nodded. "Thank you. Now, if you will excuse me, I must speak with my parents. I will leave you in Haversham's excellent care."

He bowed over her hand again for dramatic effect and left for his mother's side.

Caroline smacked Haversham's arm and hissed. "What the hell is wrong with you? Stop ogling that ridiculous woman. She is nothing but a grasping shrew and is not worth your notice!"

Lord Harold's eyes grew wide open and several moments later, he burst out laughing. "Shrew? Shrew? That is the pot calling the kettle black! She is the handsomest woman of my acquaintance and likely the most intriguing lady in all of England!" He said loudly enough for several guests to overhear.

Caroline turned red. "Quiet, Harold. The music is beginning. Take me onto the floor now!"

~*~

Richard had asked Miss Bingley for a set to keep up the ruse and she was immensely pleased to stand with him. When he took her to the floor for their set, she had her nose up in the air so high, Richard could not understand how she could even see, and his face remained grim as ever during the entire set.

Caroline delighted in the attentions that were given to her while she danced with Mr. Fitzwilliam. He was truly a fine specimen; he was equal to Mr. Darcy's handsomeness with similar height and slim figure. His shoulders were broad and leg muscles were strong. He would be delightful to take to her bed.

She heard the whispers around her.

'He has not danced with anyone all year!'

'I thought he was not in the market for a wife!'

'He looks so much like his cousin Mr. Darcy. How handsome!'

What she did not hear, though, were the whispers of guests mocking her for being Haversham's whore and that the former colonel must have a nefarious reason for seeking her out. There was nothing pleasing about Caroline Bingley's countenance, manners, or status that would draw out the most eligible bachelor in all of England.

Caroline knew what she needed to do. She would kick Harold out of her life for good so she could quickly become Mrs. Fitzwilliam. No one would remember that she was a mistress and it did not matter, since she would be daughter to Lord Matlock, the most prominent of earls. She knew Mr. Fitzwilliam was experienced. He had been quite a flirt and his liaisons were legendary amongst widows and courtesans. *Who the hell is*

Abby? It must be his mistress. No wonder he was not interested in marriage. Until now! She soared. *Until he met me! I do not care who he beds, as I plan on getting Mr. Darcy's cock inside me later. This arrangement works out best for both of us!*

After the dance, Haversham grabbed Caroline's arm to pull her outside of the ballroom for privacy, but she resisted and he dragged her out, many guests witnessing their argument. Yelling could be heard through the heavy doors and it was not surprising that they did not return. Gossip was rampant that Miss Bingley was dumping her lover for Mr. Fitzwilliam, or that Lord Harold was dropping Miss Bingley from his service due to her excessive flirting. They all did question what Mr. Fitzwilliam saw in her, as she had no beauty and no fashion, and the gossipers were surprised to see Mr. Fitzwilliam once again standing with his cousins and laughing loudly. Either he did not see the woman he showed interest leave, or he did not care for her one bit. They all agreed that it must be the latter.

~*~

Richard was desperate to kiss Elizabeth. He wanted to wash away the unpleasant taste in his mouth from touching Caroline Bingley's hand and dancing with her. After the ball was over and farewelling Lord and Lady Matlock, the trio boarded their carriage for the very short ride to Darcy House.

As soon as they entered, Richard reached across for Elizabeth's hands and kissed them repeatedly. Elizabeth giggled and Darcy's laughter rumbled loudly.

"That bad, Richard? I thought your performance was spot on!" Darcy chuckled.

"Oh, you have no idea. I thought I was going to be sick on the dance floor. Did you see how ridiculous she looked? I am glad we irritated Haversham enough to make them leave early." They all laughed.

Elizabeth commented, "Lord Harold was so ridiculous, trying to follow us around like a lost puppy. Do you believe their relationship is finished?"

"I have no doubt. He will be publicly scrutinised for bringing his low-born mistress to the grand ball while his wife is in confinement and he looked angry enough to cut her loose. He will certainly do so if Miss Bingley does what we suspect tonight. Haversham will not be able to show his face in proper company for a while and I understand his wife is controlling and a shrew. He married her for her money and she has a tight rein over his spending, which I am certain will be reduced significantly." Darcy answered.

Richard spoke. "I believe his father will disinherit him as well. I have heard rumours that his bad behaviours have caused such wrath that the Duke is unwilling to accept him at the family home. I will need a fortifying drink to prepare for tonight. Not too many, so I do not accidentally sleep with her, God forbid!" They laughed.

They exited their carriage and retired for the night.

Chapter 43

Caroline knew Darcy House well. She had been there several times and she spent no little time studying the furnishings, the room layout, the floor plan, and how she would redecorate every inch of that magnificent house. She knew the servants as well, especially those she wanted to dismiss, and how the household functioned. She was grateful that little change had occurred since the new Mrs. Darcy had arrived. *Of course, that little slut knows nothing about how to maintain a household as grand as this!*

She stealthily snuck in through the servant's door with the morning deliveries without being seen and kept herself hidden. After her embarrassment at the ball after Lord Harold had dragged her out, she bitterly accused him of being jealous of the attentions from Mr. Fitzwilliam and he had slapped her hard across the cheek, reminding her that she was a glorified whore and that he was done with her. He taunted her that having sex with her, even buggering her, was not worth the mortification of having such a stupid woman in public with himself. She vowed that she would show him up by getting herself engaged to the illustrious son of an earl and went home to change her clothes. The ball had ended about four o'clock in the morning as usual and she knew the household would be sleeping in late, except for the morning servants. It was not difficult to obtain clothes for her disguise and she planned on getting into Mr. Fitzwilliam's bed for a liaison this morning and become engaged by the time he was done ravaging her.

Caroline had known where the Master and Mistress rooms were located as well as Georgiana's but there were seven other bedrooms on the same floor. She knew he had to be located in the family wing, as he was always a favourite of Mr. Darcy's.

As she hid behind some delivery crates, she heard a maid speak loudly, "No, no! That goes to Master Richard's room. The one next to the Mistress' rooms. They moved him to the bigger room, remember?"

Caroline Bingley smiled broadly knowing exactly which room Mr. Fitzwilliam was located. She looked around and when the servants left to their tasks, she snuck up the stairs and slowly entered the largest room next to the Mistress' room.

The bedroom was very dark with the fire burning quite low, so she had to wait several minutes until her eyes could adjust. She could see the outline of the bed and quietly walked towards it while divesting her clothes to reveal a very scanty nightgown. She gently opened the bed curtains and climbed into the bed, expecting Mr. Fitzwilliam's welcoming arms, but shrieked as the bed curtains fully opened on both sides and there were two men behind the drapes. For a quick second, she thought Mr. Fitzwilliam was having an assignation with a man until she heard the second man's voice.

"Miss Bingley! Your old trick was anticipated. You truly are a harlot! Your pathetic attempts to entrap this fine gentleman is also foiled." Mr. Wilkins grabbed her arm and began to drag her off the bed and towards the door.

Caroline screamed at the top of her lungs. She began yelling, "But he invited me! He wanted me to come here! Mr. Fitzwilliam! Please tell him! Tell this brute that you invited me to your bed."

Richard stood and lit several candles. He was still fully dressed and red with anger. "I did no such thing, Miss Bingley! I would never have the likes of you in my house and certainly not in my bed!"

She continued to flail her legs and screeched, "You did! You said you could not have me at your parents' house and wanted me to favour you here tonight! You want to take me to bed and marry me! I am to be your wife!"

They were in the hallway now, with several servants who had heard the scream watching the scene. The same servants who had been coached to look for Miss Bingley's trespassing and to verbally inform her of the location of Richard's room also stood watching, with their arms crossed and frowns on their faces to see the woman's pathetic behaviour. Darcy and Elizabeth were also standing near. Georgiana was staying with Iris at Matlock after she enjoyed the ball, having danced with only family members.

Darcy laughed loudly. "You thought he would marry you? Be tied to the likes of you? That is golden!"

Richard was not so amused. "You are the last woman in the world whom I could ever be prevailed to marry. From the first moment of my being in the same room with you, you only caused disapprobation and I avoided you like the plague. There is nothing pleasing about you. You have no beauty, no virtue, no intelligence; nothing about you interests me whatsoever. I detest you, Caroline Bingley. You are a whore and you are ruined."

Mr. Wilkins coughed. "Mr. Darcy, once again this intruder was found where she was not invited and should be disposed of quickly." Darcy chuckled, recalling his words from her first attempt. "What shall we do with her, sir?"

Darcy smiled and pointed to two of his footmen. "Take her to the cellar and lock her in there until the constable arrives." He threw her clothes at her. "She trespassed my house with the intent of burglary and I will have her arrested."

Caroline screamed then fainted.

When she awoke, she was in the dark cellar alone and began to shiver and she banged on the door but no one would open the door. She gathered her clothing to put it on and cried until the constable arrived.

~*~

Darcy dismissed the servants and tapped Richard on his back. "It is over. She will be arrested and we will have to go to court, but all the evidence is here. She will be disgraced and out of our lives forever after I write to the constable. Comfort Elizabeth. She has been worried for you." He kissed his wife and walked down the stairs.

Richard held her hand and kissed it. He walked her to Darcy's room and entered it quickly after seeing that they were alone. After closing the door, he hugged her tightly. "It is well, my love. She will not bother us again."

She smiled and held him snugly around the waist. "I am glad Wilkins was able to provide his invaluable service again. I cannot believe the gall of that shrew. I am glad you are well, I was so worried."

He kissed her hair. She was truly wonderful. "Elizabeth, that *person* is the most awful human being that I have ever met and I need to erase the terrible event out of my mind and replace it with something more pleasant. May I kiss you?" His last deep kiss was several weeks ago when she had been inebriated. He revelled in the closeness right now while she was fully awake and participatory.

"Of course, Richard. I am happy to have you in my arms." Elizabeth smiled.

She raised her face upward while still holding on to his waist. He lifted both of her arms to wrap them around his neck and held on to her waist, pulling her in until his body was completely flushed against hers. She was wearing her nightgown with a robe over and he could feel her soft skin without her stays. He was already aroused and wanted to taste her desperately and leaned down to kiss her tenderly, increasing his pressure until he met her tongue and caressed it with his own, and he could not help himself as he dove more into her mouth and she moaned in passion. He held her tighter against his body and delved his tongue deeper than ever before. He thought he would burst so he lightened his pressure then slowly ended their kiss. *I love her so much. Having her in my arms is the greatest pleasure I have ever known.* He thought to himself.

"So sweet. Thank you, my love, I treasure your affections. I will return to my rooms and Darcy will return shortly." He kissed her quickly once more and departed.

~*~

The original plan was to return to Rosings by the sixteenth of December and the Fitzwilliams, Bennets, Bingleys, and Gardiners were to join on the nineteenth, but several letters were written to explain the delay and it was all agreed upon to unite at Rosings on the twenty-third instead.

After the constable arrived, Caroline Bingley was quickly arrested. The staff had spread the word, on their master's order, to ensure there were many witnesses seeing the trespasser being dragged out from the front door. It was obvious that a woman was wearing a manservant's clothing and whispers began as the Darcy servants told the onlookers that it was Caroline Bingley, a tradesman's daughter and mistress to several men, as of late, Lord Harold Haversham.

Gossip spread quickly and Lord Harold arrived at Darcy House that afternoon, begging for mercy in this unfortunate circumstance. Lord and Lady Matlock were also in attendance and he pleaded for forgiveness for bringing his mistress to their ball and for making such a scene. His wife had cut off his allowance and was outraged at the humiliation and she demanded he remove himself to their country home and under no circumstances was he to establish another mistress for the rest of his life. He also knew that his father, the Duke, would disinherit him when he found out and desperately asked for Darcy's help in reducing his public disgrace. His father had already ceased his allowance due to his other bad behaviours and he had been at the mercy of his wife.

After arrangements were made to meet the next day, the rest of the party laughed at the idiotic man after he left. He deserved to be humiliated but they knew he was rather stupid but not malicious.

Darcy kissed Elizabeth's hand. "Thank God you did not accept his suit. Although I am certain he would have loved having you as his wife, he is quite ridiculous!" They all laughed in merriment.

~*~

In two days, Darcy, Elizabeth, and Richard sat in the courtroom as Miss Bingley was being tried for her crimes. She looked exhausted but was able to obtain a barrister for her defence using her money. She wore a bright orange dress, bedecked with jewellery to show off her wealth and status.

The prosecutor began with the charges of trespassing and burglary with intent of bodily harm.

The barrister accepted the charges and pleaded innocence on behalf of his client.

The barrister was allowed to question Caroline for her testimony next. She represented herself as a poor victim who had been thoroughly humiliated by the rake who must have changed his mind after inviting her to his bed. She cried and wiped her false tears as she portrayed her life as serene and virtuous while waiting for her dream husband. She had been tricked into believing that Mr. Fitzwilliam was going to offer for her and that the whole ballroom saw their attachment and had commented on the upcoming proposal.

Then Darcy gave testimony on the events at the house that early morning and that Miss Bingley had not been staying at Darcy House and that she had been specifically barred from entering all of the Darcy properties. The prosecutor shared the information leading up to her coming to bed scantily dressed, with the intent to harm Mr. Fitzwilliam in body and in reputation.

Caroline screeched and insisted that Mr. Fitzwilliam had invited her into the home and to his bed, to which he only sat still and shook his head.

Surprisingly, Lord Harold took the stand next. Caroline was shocked that he was here and did not know what he would admit and nearly fainted when he betrayed her. Lord Harold explained that he had been seduced by Caroline Bingley and had been having sexual relations with her for the past seven months. He reported that the relationship was of mutual benefit, where he opened doors for exclusive parties and dinners with the first circles and that she would open her legs for him, sometimes several times daily in her appreciation. He also explained that she begged him and performed deviant acts in return for making her his mistress. She had formally been his mistress for only one day before he ended the relationship after she had flirted severely with Mr. Fitzwilliam.

The barrister asked Lord Harold if he witnessed any interest from Mr. Fitzwilliam's part, to which it was answered "no". Haversham also explained that Caroline Bingley had not been a maiden when he first lay with her and that more often than not, he would wait in the drawing room while another man finished with her and there would be a different man waiting after he was done at times.

The prosecutor asked if he had ever seen any monies exchange or if he had ever given money to Miss Bingley, to which he answered, "No, although she did demand new dresses." The audience gasped, as they understood that she had been giving out her services freely to about a dozen men, without a contract or payment.

Richard finally took the stand to answer the questions. He told the judge and jury that he never agreed to any type of assignation and that he had danced with her to find out what her intentions were regarding his cousin, whom she had attempted to compromise in the past. He also told the public that there was another peer that she had attempted the same, and he himself was at least the third attempt at compromising. He had explicitly told Miss Bingley that he was not interested in any private time with her during the ball at his parents' home. He also shared documentation, effectively ending all enquiries regarding his marriage prospects, that he had no intentions to ever marry, that all of his wealth would be inherited by Richard Fitzwilliam Darcy.

He also submitted a notarised copy of Anne Fitzwilliam de Bourgh's will, the legal owner of Rosings Park, which stipulated that should her named heir be unable or unwilling to inherit Rosings Park, that the estate would be inherited by Richard Fitzwilliam Darcy, to be managed by Fitzwilliam Darcy until he was of age.

The court deliberated for one hour and Caroline Bingley was found guilty of all charges. She did faint again when the sentence of seven-years transport to Australia and compensations of £5,000 each to Mr. Darcy and Mr. Fitzwilliam were handed down.

She wailed as she was dragged away and the Darcys and Richard hoped to never see her again.

Chapter 44

The merry family travelled to Rosings and breathed a sigh of relief from the hustle and bustle of the busy town scenes. They were able to relax and planned on enjoying their time together with the large party arriving in a few days. Darcy and Elizabeth played with their sons while Richard excused himself.

He rode on Cyrus and trotted to Abigail's cottage. He soon knocked on the door and his mistress opened it with a bright smile on her face. It felt a bit awkward to be in her presence again after being apart for months but he knew he was there to satisfy a need. He asked her how her trip went.

"It was wonderful, Mr. Fitzwilliam. Thank you so much for your generosity. I understand you were in London these past three weeks and I read about the trial. It had been one of the most exciting news in ages."

He chuckled. "I am certain it was. Usually these kinds of events are hushed up and not publicised but my cousin and I were determined to get rid of that interloper for good. She was shipped off two days ago. Good riddance."

"And has your time with your Elizabeth been satisfactory?" Abigail asked. She was curious if he still held strong feelings for her or if it had faded over time as was common. She had her answer before he even opened his mouth.

Richard closed his eyes and smiled. Every thought of Elizabeth made his heart soar. His beautiful Elizabeth who freely hugged him and laughed with him, who worried for his well-being, and nagged at times like a wife. Before he could answer, he felt Abigail sitting astride on his lap. He opened his eyes to see her arms wrapped around his neck and she began to kiss his neck. He closed his eyes again to smell the lavender in her hair and became aroused, as he dreamt of Elizabeth.

His hands lifted up her skirt and caressed her buttocks and thighs. He felt her hands unbutton the falls of his trousers and she began to caress his erection. He grabbed her buttocks and lifted her up, impaling her with his huge phallus and bounced her up and down to take her deeply.

"Oh, Elizabeth. Just like that. Yes, my love. You feel so good. It has been too long. I want you so much, Elizabeth." He whispered as he climaxed. He did not last long but it felt so good.

He laid his head back on the couch as Abigail was still grinding herself against his semi-erect cock. *I guess she missed me, too!* Richard smirked. Having a woman did feel better than using his own hand.

"Thank you, Abigail. It was quick but pleasurable." Richard commented, as he lifted her up and began to correct his clothes. "I am glad you enjoyed your trip. I will see you on the Thirty-first." He bowed and left.

After he trotted away some distance, he thought of the reunion. He knew she had been disappointed since he had had her for all of two minutes and instead of staying for another session, he had quickly departed. But he had no desire to stay in bed with her and frolic around today. He had his release and did not care for hers. This arrangement would only work if Abigail remembered that she was only a surrogate body while he dreamt of Elizabeth.

He had thought he would need to pounce on his mistress for several days straight after his delicious kiss with Elizabeth after the baptism, but when Elizabeth had begun to return his kisses consistently, he could not imagine anything more satisfying and her deep kisses had quenched his desires. No one else could compare and he felt guilty even now, after finding his release with Abigail that lasted only a few minutes. He wanted Elizabeth. He wanted *only* Elizabeth and no one else would do. *I know I have no choice but I feel as if I am being unfaithful to Elizabeth. I need to see her. Now!*

He rushed back to Rosings, desperate to be near her again. *How can I be away from her for an hour and be this eager? I hope she is not closeted away with Darcy. They might be gone for hours!* He entered his home and looked around. Rosings had looked quite different after Elizabeth had put her touch into it; all the ostentatious furnishings had been replaced with simple, elegant items; chairs that were actually comfortable, tables that were now useful. He sped his way to the drawing room where he saw her sitting and embroidering.

Home.

He was home. Wherever she was, it was home.

Richard entered with a smile and greeted Darcy and Elizabeth and talked happily of the upcoming celebrations.

~*~

On the appointed day, the guests arrived and the house became louder and merrier. Rosings Park had never seen so much joy in decades and never so full as it housed twenty adults and three babies. Mary had also travelled with her new husband and everyone congratulated them on their happy union.

Anne was able to travel with Lord and Lady Matlock but due to her illness, would remain in her rooms most of the time. The family members, whether by blood or marriage, came to visit and sit with her often and Anne was thrilled to have so many new and interesting people to know.

The women soon retired to rest until dinnertime while Darcy hosted the men in the study, sharing a glass of French cognac that Uncle Gardiner was able to get his hands on.

Chapter 45

Richard yelled at Elizabeth, "NO! You cannot ask it of me and I will not do it!"

Elizabeth walked over to the window huffing with her arms crossed. "But why will you not try? I know that she has caused so much trouble but I do not understand why you will not even give it a chance! You are so stubborn!!"

"Blasted, woman! I am bloody trying to save you from her! I am doing it for your best interest, damn it! Why can you not just do as I say instead of arguing with me?!" Richard yelled again and paced.

He turned and saw that Elizabeth's shoulders were shaking and she was frantically wiping the tears from her eyes. He suddenly felt like the world's biggest cad. *Blasted, I made her cry! Not only should I beat myself up, but Darcy is going to kill me.*

He plopped down on the chair closest to her and rubbed his face vigorously. The guests were here one day and he and Elizabeth were having the worst argument they had ever had.

Their first fight.

He was thankful Darcy was entertaining the family on the other side of the house.

After he took over management of Rosings, he redecorated several rooms, most importantly the Master and Mistress suites. He had originally established himself in the Master bedroom but he knew the Mistress room would remain empty as long as he was there, so he ordered for a new Master suite to be built on the other side of the Mistress' room after the Darcys accepted him into their lives. He gave Darcy and Elizabeth the old suites and he took the new one, which had a discreet door that led to the Mistress' room. He converted the Mistress' room as a sitting room for the three to chat comfortably in privacy. They were in that very room as they argued.

Elizabeth turned and approached him. She angrily glared at him and spoke with a dangerous tone. "Watch your language with me, Richard Fitzwilliam. I am not some subservient wife for you to rant and rave at."

"You are NOT my wife!" Richard snipped. *If only!* Then he looked up at her face and saw the devastation on her face. *Fuck!*

He jumped up and immediately ran after her as she had turned and was marching towards her bedroom. He rushed in front of her and grabbed her tightly around her waist and lifted her up into his arms. He buried his face in her hair and kissed her head and neck while he whispered, "I am sorry. I am so sorry. Sorry. Sorry." He repeated his apology over and over again until he felt her body relax slightly. He lowered her to the ground to catch her eyes. He could see the despair there and felt his heart crush again. *Bloody fool I am!*

He drew her into his chest and rubbed her back and waited for her to speak.

"I know I am not your wife, Richard. Perhaps you should marry that mistress of yours and get one instead of hanging around me all the time. I know I nag at you like I do to Fitzwilliam and I am sorry. I have gotten so used to acting like a wife to both of you, I forget that only Fitzwilliam deserves that awful side of actually having a wife." Elizabeth cried.

Richard's heart broke at her tears once again. "Oh, my dear Elizabeth, you ARE my wife. You are the mistress of my heart and I love that you nag at me. I love that you treat Darcy and me the same way as a wife does. You have all of my heart and you are my wife in my mind and soul. Darcy often jokes that you have two husbands to worry about and I know that is the truth. I am your surrogate husband and I worry for you and I love you as a husband does. I am so, so sorry. So very sorry for yelling at you and cursing like a sailor. Please forgive me, my wife. I love you, my dearest wife. Forgive me, please." He begged.

He felt her relax further in his arms. He buried his head in the crook of her neck and kissed it, trailing up to kiss behind her ear and jaw and chin, then finally her lips. He kissed her mouth and suckled on her tongue. He kissed her deeper than he had ever done and she graciously returned it. He could not stop himself. He kissed her with all the passion he had for her. He had not kissed her very long before, as he was afraid of losing control when she had begun to return his kisses, but dreading losing her, fearing never having her in his arms again, he kissed long and hard, with more hunger than he had ever possessed in his entire life. After several successions of the most ardent of kisses, he released her and placed his forehead on hers. "My Elizabeth. My wife. My dearest wife." He whispered.

After his heartbeat was no longer thumping in his ears, he gently kissed her on the lips and walked her over to the couch. Instead of allowing her to take her own seat, he pulled her down to his lap after sitting down first. As she squeaked and sat, he grabbed her waist and held her tightly.

"I am not letting you go. Never." He whispered. "I love you. Please do not leave me. I would die without you. Please stay with me." He was close to tears, despairing of life without her, without her in his arms.

Elizabeth was surprised at the level of passion that Richard was presenting today. He had kissed her deeply before but it was nothing compared to now. He was an incredible lover and she was flushed with desire, as he made love to her mouth with his ardent kisses but she knew she could not give him more. It reminded her of her first passionate kiss with Fitzwilliam and before his proposal. She smiled at the recollection and realised that once again, these cousins had more in common than they knew.

She was extremely hurt at Richard's words and after so many months of his loving her and kissing her, she had become too comfortable with him to chastise him as his closest confidante. He was so much like Fitzwilliam, having had power and freedom to make his own choices for his life, that without someone to call him on his pride or arrogance, he would become unbearable and she did not want that for him. She loved him and wanted him to be the best master and the best of men. Fitzwilliam had also been the same way at times and although they argued, her dearest husband had been quick to listen to her and treat her as an equal. *My husband is truly the best of men. Haha, I suppose my FIRST husband. Oh, dear Richard...*

"Richard, I am sitting on... you are..." Elizabeth did not know what to do. She had sat on his lap before and had felt or seen his bulge but it was massive right now and never so close to her entrance. Without any clothing, he would be inside her.

"Please do not leave me. Stay with me. I am so sorry. You are my wife. You are my first and only wife in my heart. Let me hold you. Please." Richard implored. He would never do more but it was comforting to have her so close. His heart was ripping at the thought of losing her. Not being near her.

Elizabeth sighed. He was so insecure. She knew that it was because she could never be his true wife. Her heart truly belonged to her husband and knew that the act of making love was what had brought them close and that intimacy between husband and wife was something that she could not have with Richard. Even when he kissed her, when he kissed her deeply and made love to her mouth, her love was still with Fitzwilliam and she would never break her vows to her husband.

She loved Richard but it was something between brotherly and husbandly. If she had met him before Fitzwilliam, she might have been perfectly content with Richard as a husband, but after knowing her husband and falling so deeply in love with him, none other could take his place. Richard was a close second, though. She had seen flashes of Fitzwilliam in him and they were both the handsomest men in all of England.

She caressed his hair tenderly. "Richard, I would not abandon you. I just needed some time to cool off. I might leave you to gather my wits but I would return. Do you hear me?" She tried to reassure him. He eagerly nodded but still held her tightly. She breathed and relaxed as he began to deflate from under her. "I am often wrong. I am still so young and innocent of the things that go on in the world and lord knows I might begin to have flutterings in my heart and act silly like my mother someday," he scoffed, "but I do try to be kind and to understand the views of others. I am afraid that if someone does not take you to task to see a different view of things when appropriate, you will become proud and arrogant, believing that everyone should fall at your feet and obey your commands." He opened his mouth to argue but she put her finger on his lips. "As your surrogate *wife*, I ask that you discuss it with me and talk it out, instead of shutting me out and forcing your will. I would like to be treated as an equal. Can I request that of you?"

Richard nodded with her finger still on his lips. He held her wrist and kissed her fingers, her wrist, and inside of her palm and rubbed her palm on his cheek.

"I will do anything and everything you ask. I promise to do a better job of listening. I am sorry, Elizabeth. I had been determined to never let her near you and I am so used to giving commands that I failed to listen to you. I guess I have become quite arrogant. I was touted as the most eligible bachelor and I let it get to my head. I do not know how Darcy does it. Being a Master is not all that is advertised to be." Richard sighed as he buried his face on her neck.

"Richard, I do not wish for you to blindly do everything I ask. You have responsibilities that you were not raised with, while Fitzwilliam knew exactly what he would be. You are doing very well and I am immensely proud of you. Rosings could not have asked for a better Master and I know Fitzwilliam is appreciative of all your assistance with his businesses. I would like for you to be open to listen more; even those with lower ranks may have intelligence to offer. Like my Uncle Gardiner; you like him, do you not?" Elizabeth asked.

"Of course! He is one of the most intelligent and sensible men I have ever met." Richard answered.

"Well, he is a tradesman and would never ever have shared the table with your parents if it were not for you. You have made that happen and I love you for it." Richard grinned and kissed her hand. "Please remember that there are others who may have an opinion worthy of listening to before you make your decision. Will you consider what I ask? Will you talk to her and see what she says? We must be the generous neighbour and open the door first, Richard." Elizabeth concluded.

"Oh, my love. I will do as you wish. Not because I am blindly following your orders but because I respect your opinions, and also because I love the hell out of you." He kissed her deeply again and ran his tongue along her lips. "Forgive me for angering you so. I truly love you with all my heart, my wife."

"I love you, too, husband." Elizabeth replied.

Richard beamed and stood. "You must rest. Shall I fetch Darcy for you?" She nodded. He tenderly kissed her lips once again and left.

~*~

Richard entered the study. His father was snoring on the couch and Bingley and Mr. Gardiner were debating the politics of mechanization of farming equipment. Darcy looked up and his eyes pointed towards the mistress' study, which had been converted to Darcy's study. Like Pemberley, they had made adjustments to bring a second desk in the other study for Elizabeth's enjoyment so she could sit with her husband whenever she wished.

After closing the door to the study, Darcy asked, "That took a while. Is all well? You do not usually take so long." He was curious that he was meeting privately with Elizabeth for so long. His jealousy spiked for a moment as he realised a lot could happen in that length of time but he wanted to trust them both before he jumped to conclusions.

Richard sighed. He could not meet Darcy's eyes.

The longer he was silent, the more nervous Darcy became. *Am I losing Elizabeth? Has she chosen him over me? I must have answers before I lose my mind.*

Elizabeth had asked Fitzwilliam to spend some time to convince Richard to invite Lady Catherine to Christmas Eve dinner. She had argued that as a mother, she should be given the honour to see her daughter since Anne had reached a critical point and would not live long, and Anne had agreed to Elizabeth's advice. Darcy had been hesitant but listening to her arguments and understanding her ever-generous heart, especially now as a mother herself, he agreed that if Richard was agreeable, he would support it. It should not have taken so long since he was certain Richard would do whatever Elizabeth wished.

Darcy coughed and Richard startled.

Richard had been thinking about Elizabeth's tears and his ungentlemanlike conduct of yelling at her and cursing. *I was such a brute to Elizabeth. I will never forgive myself for making her cry. How do I make it up to her?* He turned and met Darcy's eyes. The guilt of making Darcy's beloved wife cry tore at his heart. "Darcy, brother. I am sorry. I..." He had difficulty continuing. After clearing his throat, he spoke. "Elizabeth and I had a terrible row. I had never been so angry with her and I lost my head..."

Darcy ran to clutch Richard by his coat with both hands. "Did you injure her? DID.YOU.HURT.MY.WIFE?" He snarled. He was ready to murder his dearest cousin. *You said you loved her! If you laid a finger on her...*

Richard fervently shook his head. "No! I would never! I love her with my life! How could you think such a thing of me, Darcy?"

Darcy did not care to listen to his speech. He threw him down to the chair and ran to see his wife.

He burst in through his bedroom to see Elizabeth lying on the bed, who jumped up when the doorknob loudly thumped against the wall.

"AHH!" she screamed. "Fitzwilliam! Whatever is the matter? You gave me a fright!"

Seeing that she was not crying or damaged in any way, he sighed and closed the door gently. "I am sorry, my love. You and Richard were ensconced up here for so long, I worried. My love, he did not injure you, did he?"

"No, never!" Elizabeth drew him in as he climbed into bed with her and held her.

"Elizabeth, I... I was jealous that you might be up here enjoying his favours. I know that he kisses you passionately and you enjoy it and I know that it is difficult to resist..." Darcy could not finish. He did not want to know the truth if she had decided on Richard and yet he did not want to be lied to, either.

Elizabeth sensed his insecurity right away. He had given so much to allow Richard to love her but it would still be difficult to imagine a wife having a liaison with another man, no matter how worthy that other man might have been. She smiled. She liked that he was so protective of her. As much as Richard loved her and she loved him more than as a brother, no one would take the place of her beloved Fitzwilliam.

Elizabeth reached up and kissed his lips tenderly. "You are truly the best of men. Thank you for being honest with me instead of bottling it up or avoiding it. If you had not come to me right away, it would fester inside you and it would have made everything worse from now on. Why did you think he injured me?"

"He said that he was angry with you and lost his head. He could not go on." Darcy sighed. "I jumped to the conclusion, as much as I had wished not to, that he must have hurt you or possibly attempted to force himself on you. Did he grab you? Did he try to...?" Darcy looked into her eyes with fear.

"Oh, that man. My love, I must confess that he did grab me, no, no! Not in any harmful way. He always grabs me, you know. He grabs my waist and pulls me and hugs me. I have shared with you that he kisses my mouth and he... certainly enjoys... he gets aroused." She blurted out. She would not lie to her husband. "He kisses me deeply like you kiss me but he has never touched anywhere else and has never asked for more. He is a perfect gentleman most of the time but he does kiss me often. I allow it but will stop him should you wish. I feel like he needs the affections, though, and he is so happy when he does kiss me and I am comforted by it as well. I know he cares for me and I enjoy being able to comfort him when he is troubled. I constantly think of you, though. I find myself needing you and desiring you." Seeing Darcy's smile, she continued. "He yelled at me and used some language and I cried. I think he feels guilty for making me cry. I promise you that he did not injure me. If he tried something, my knee would be between his legs!"

They laughed.

Darcy kissed her. "Your kisses are so sweet, I cannot imagine my life without them."

Elizabeth pressed her kiss deeper and reached for his tongue with hers. "Oh, my love. Will you make love to me now? I know we do not have much time... EEEK!!" She squealed as he lifted her up and climbed on her, lifting her dress and tickling her with his kisses all over her neck and chest.

She laughed gleefully and began to moan as soon as his arousal was inside her.

They were not seen until dinnertime.

Chapter 46

"Richard, a word, please." Darcy commanded in his Master of Pemberley voice. The gentlemen were enjoying their port in the dining room while the ladies chatted in the drawing room. Richard grimly stood and followed him.

Lord Matlock commented, "Those boys. I think they are fighting over something. Like brothers, they are. More than you, Albert! Darcy looked fine during dinner, smiling and flirting with his wife, but Richard looked like he was going to the gallows. Like when his favourite toy got taken away. I wonder what they are arguing about. It was probably Richard's fault." He laughed. "Darcy can do no wrong."

"I believe it! He has been the epitome of the word 'Perfect' but I am certain it is because my Lizzy has a short leash on him!" Mr. Bennet added.

Bingley quickly agreed that Darcy was as perfect as a man could be and the gentlemen laughed. They spoke of other things while waiting for the Master of Rosings to return.

~*~

"Darcy." Richard stood near the window of his study. He still felt guilty about making

216

Elizabeth cry but angry that Darcy had accused him of hurting her. *I would never hurt her. I might have made her cry but how can Darcy think me capable of hitting a woman?*

"Richard, I owe you an apology. I jumped to the wrong conclusion once again and initially I had worried that you and Elizabeth might be having an assignation upstairs when you were both gone so long, but then when you said that you were angry with her, I lost *my* mind thinking that you had injured her. Elizabeth had explained to me that you were harsh and she cried, but you talked it over and have worked it out. I am sorry. Will you accept my apology?" Darcy asked.

Richard took a moment and comprehended he would murder anyone who would dare to harm his Elizabeth, even if it were Darcy himself. He was fiercely protective of his beloved and knew Darcy was the same and they both loved her with every fibre of their being. He smiled and shook Darcy's hand. "All is forgiven. I was hurt that you thought me capable of raising my hand to a woman, but if I did not know the full story, I would be vehemently protective of Elizabeth as well. I love her with my life, Darce. I would rather die than to cause her harm. You already know that I would not hesitate to beat you if you wounded Elizabeth." He shook his head. "We are pathetic, are we not? In love with the same woman and constantly jumping to wrong conclusions?"

"I believe she has more difficult time with us. We are so arrogant and have such strong opinions all the time that sometimes I have to stop myself to see the world through her eyes. She is so kind and sees things that no other would see. A wife's view is a precious thing." Darcy replied, pouring Richard and himself a drink and taking a seat.

Richard took a sip and spoke. "I angered her by refusing to listen to her and I knew I was wrong but I was an obnoxious arse and she called me on it. I should have listened better but I yelled and cursed instead, making her cry. I had never felt so hopeless than when she turned her back to me. I cannot live without her, brother. I know that I am not her husband but I have always thought of her as my wife. Darcy," Richard turned to face him to make sure to meet his eyes, "I love her so much and I cannot bury my need to physically connect with her, but she loves you beyond any love she might carry for me. I am sorry that I take advantage of her generosity but I need her. I have never needed anything more in my life. I would have never believed I could be so dependent on a woman's touch but to be near her is a dream. Even the thought of life without her puts me in a dark place and if she were to banish me from her side, I do not believe I could live half a life. I still have nightmares from the war, Darce, but it is nothing to the despondency that I feel when I remember life without her. She makes me feel alive and happy and I cannot be without her. Elizabeth's affections are the greatest gift I have ever experienced and I hope you will forgive me." Richard confessed.

Darcy chuckled. "Elizabeth shared with me her thoughts on it. She told me that she allows it because it seems to give you assurances. She told me that she does think of me when she kisses you, but you have not asked for more and she enjoys your attentions. Again, until she slaps your face, you may accept the gift she gives you. I trust you and I know you are honourable. You *are* like a husband to her and she agrees that she is wife to us both, except for the marriage bed with you."

Richard smiled. They were both so generous. "I cannot thank you enough, Darcy. You are sharing your greatest treasure and I will cherish it for the rest of my life." He paused for a moment. "Darcy, in exchange for my forgiving you for jumping to the wrong conclusion," he winked, "would you allow... may I give Elizabeth my grandmother's ring?"

Darcy smiled. He was the only one besides Richard that knew the history of his grandmother's ring and even Aunt Susan had not known. "I could not imagine it on anyone else, Richard. I feel the same way with my mother's ring on Elizabeth. Permission granted."

"Thank you, brother. Thank you for accepting me into your family. My heart is full because of you and Elizabeth." Richard coughed to cover his emotions. "Let us get back to the ladies!" He joyfully shouted.

When they returned, the other gentlemen knew all was well by the grins on both young men. They returned to the ladies and all chatted cheerfully, eagerly anticipating Christmas Eve.

~*~

Lady Catherine sat in awe as she looked around the large gathering of people in her former home. She had not recognised her own house with the furnishings completely changed and it looked quite similar to Pemberley's tastes, appearing grand but comfortable, but she refused to acknowledge it.

Lady Catherine was allowed a brief introduction to Mrs. Darcy but Darcy and Richard guarded Elizabeth fiercely and kept Lady Catherine away from her at all times otherwise. She had been shocked that Mrs. Darcy was a beautiful, spirited woman who was charming and graceful as well as obviously intelligent. Anne was in no way comparable to the woman that Darcy had chosen as his wife.

She was allowed to visit Anne who sat with Richard, who spoke more firmly than ever and told her that she forgave her. Anne told her that she would never be allowed to return to Rosings as it now belonged to Richard and Darcy's second son, but that if she could behave herself, she might be allowed to be invited for dinners for Easter. Lady Catherine was stopped from saying anything in return as Richard told her that she was here to listen and not speak, as agreed upon.

After returning to the drawing room, she attempted to take charge of the situation as her wont. "Who decorated this place? It is far too plain."

Richard calmly answered, "Mrs. Darcy has been instrumental in making Rosings a comfortable home, madam." *You will not disparage my Elizabeth, you old hag. She is the best thing in my life.*

Lady Catherine huffed, "What does she know of anything? Who is she to make such changes to my home?"

Richard leaned in to her and growled threateningly, "You will not insult my family in *my* home. The only reason you are here at all is due to Mrs. Darcy. You have made your visit with Anne; you are welcome to return to *your* home at any time."

Lady Catherine gulped. Richard had always been the scariest of the nephews. With his military background, he took his charges very seriously and he had actually killed enemies in the past. *I have been eating mediocre food by myself for too long. This meal looks delicious!*

The twenty diners, including Lady Catherine, relished the meal and cheered Mrs. Darcy for her excellent planning. Richard sat proudly and looked across the long table where his beloved sat at the mistress' place. Richard sat at the head of the table as Master and Elizabeth on the other side as the hostess with Darcy at her right and he could not be prouder of his *wife* than right now.

~*~

The next day, on Christmas morning, Elizabeth was awakened to the sensation of her husband kissing her shoulder and fondling her breasts. They had made love last night but had fallen asleep quickly and had slept long.

"Happy Christmas, my love," Darcy whispered.

"Happy Christmas, Fitzwilliam." Elizabeth answered, as she moaned when his fingers rubbed her clitoris.

"My first gift, Mrs. Darcy." Darcy cradled her from behind as he continued to caress her breasts and fingered her folds, inserting his long fingers inside her while thumbing her aroused nub. Her moans grew louder and louder until she climaxed. He pulled her onto her back and climbed on her. He inserted his massive erection slowly inside her and moaned as he filled her.

He pumped into her slowly, increasing his speed then slowing down. He drew her large firm breasts into his mouth and suckled some milk out of her and soon, Elizabeth screamed her climax again and Darcy released with a loud grunt.

"Oh, that was fantastic, husband!" Elizabeth panted. "But should that not count as my gift to you as well?" she teased.

"Minx! Yes, we will call it even. One gift for you and one for me." Darcy laughed. He leaned over to the nightstand next to his bed and drew out a velvet box. "I requisitioned this from London while we were there, my love. I hope you will like it."

The box was overlaid with green velvet and she opened it carefully to find a small watch that had been custom designed with a pin so she could wear it on her dress. It was gold with a beautiful filigree design and encased with emeralds and diamonds alternating as hour markers.

Elizabeth's eyes were teary with happiness. "Oh, Fitzwilliam, it is the most beautiful watch I have ever seen. How can you be so thoughtful?"

Darcy drew her into his arms, "I love you. Happy Christmas." He smiled.

Last year, he had given her a beautiful necklace with an enormous diamond centre and he had been true to his vow to court his wife continuously. Having Richard's affections as competition had been a good reminder for him to never cease wooing his beloved by showering her with flowers and gifts, especially after the near-death experience with Wickham. His beloved had given him a rare first volume of Wordsworth, which he absolutely loved.

"Oh, dear, I am afraid that we have been married too long, Mr. Darcy." Elizabeth teased. Darcy lifted a quizzical brow. "Here is my gift to you, my love."

She handed him a box, which was also green velvet and slightly larger than her gift. She smiled as he opened it.

Darcy was touched as he gazed at it. It was a gold pocket watch, engraved in the back with a triangle and a heart within the triangle. Inside, there was an inscription that read, 'For FD, All my love, ED'.

His eyes moistened as well and felt completely loved by this woman. He wondered at the meaning of the triangle. Elizabeth leaned and answered before he could ask.

"My love, I hope you will not mind it, but I commissioned two watches. One for you and one for Richard. His does not have the same inscription, of course, because you have all of me and you have my dedication and my commitment to be the best wife to you. The triangle is to represent our unique relationship. I have told you that I feel like I have two husbands and our love is truly special to me. If you do not wish, though, I will not give it to him. I will leave the decision to you. I will honour you and respect your wishes."

Darcy beamed. He loved hearing words of love from Elizabeth. After making love to her so pleasurably, he revelled in her kindness. *Richard will love this!* He thought. "Milady, I would, by no means, suspend any pleasure of yours. I know he will love it. I will treasure this always. It is perfect, Elizabeth."

He kissed her again. "I know Richard has a gift for you as well. He has asked for my permission and I have given it, my love. I hope you will accept it. No, I will not tell you what it is." He smiled. "You are so impatient! Like a little child!" He tickled her and they both laughed.

~*~

The Darcys knew the morning would be an exciting one, especially when the children would be given their gifts.

There were four Gardiner children and three babies, the two Darcys and one Bennet. The Bingleys were expecting and Viscount Fitzwilliam announced that the Viscountess was expecting also during dinner last night. The family was rapidly growing and it was a warm and happy time.

They dressed for the day and walked to the Mistress' room to meet Richard as custom where Richard had been nervously waiting for Elizabeth to present the ring. Darcy had agreed for some time for the exchange of gifts and kissed his wife's hand to head down to breakfast. He smiled broadly at Richard before he left.

"Good morning, Richard! Happy Christmas!" Elizabeth cheerfully greeted. She walked over and gave him a peck on his cheek.

Richard smiled nervously. "Good morning, my love. Happy Christmas. Would you take a seat?" They both sat. Richard continued to fidget and rubbed his waistcoat pocket several times.

Elizabeth was curious of his strange demeanour. They had met in this sitting room and shared breakfasts or nightcaps many times. She wondered if it had to do with the gift that he was going to present to her. She was now truly interested in what he had in mind.

Richard sat next to her and then stood and paced. *Get it done, man!* He chided himself. Taking a deep breath, he returned to her side but knelt with one knee at her feet instead.

"Elizabeth Darcy, you are the love of my life and as soon as I first saw you, my heart no longer belonged to me. It only beats for you and I am committed to dedicate the rest of my life to love you and bring you happiness. I am, by far, imperfect, but you make me a better man and my love only grows when I am in your presence. Will you do me the great honour of being the mistress of my heart, my surrogate wife, the companion of my life always? Would you wear this ring for me, to be a sign of my love for you, so that every time you look down upon your hand, you will know that you are cherished and have my full heart?"

He presented a small gold ring, delicately crafted with intertwined vines. It was not bedecked or expensive, but it appeared an antique and Elizabeth knew there must be a story behind this simple but beautiful ring.

Elizabeth was touched. He did not ask for her love. He did not ask for any promises or favours or desire to be more than what they were now. She cried and smiled as she nodded. *He is such a dear, dear man.*

He grinned and slid the ring on her slim ring finger on her right hand. *She will always know I love her. My wife.*

He took his seat next to her again and smiled as she was looking at the ring while wiping her tears. He handed her his handkerchief and held her around her shoulders. He kissed her reverently. "My wife; my heart," he whispered. *I am so pleased by her reaction. Oh, how I love her.*

"Richard, will you tell me the story behind this ring? It appears an heirloom." Elizabeth asked.

"Ah, yes, of course. This ring belonged to my maternal grandmother. Even my mother does not know this as my grandmother had told me this story when she gave me the ring as well as my inheritance of my cottage. My grandmother had actually been engaged before my grandfather and she had been deeply in love with this other man. He was a lowly gentleman who loved her desperately for years before he had the courage to propose to her. My grandmother was the daughter of a duke and he knew she was out of his league but after years of pursuing her and courting her, they were finally engaged to be married. My grandmother had told me that she had fallen in love with him at first sight and her heart was no longer hers, but unfortunately he perished in an accident two weeks before the wedding. She was devastated and had no desire to live afterwards, but she told me that having this ring, the memory of his love for her, helped her to survive and allow her heart to love. She confessed that she never did find another to love so deeply but was content with my grandfather's love for her and they married three years later.

"She told me to find someone to love and never settle for less. She said that the woman who wears this ring must have my full heart and be worthy of my love and that every time she looks upon it, it will give her the comfort of knowing that she is wholly and devotedly loved. I never thought I would ever give this ring to anyone until I met you. I knew it belonged on your hand always, Elizabeth." Richard finished.

"Oh, Richard, it is beautiful. I shall treasure it always. I shall look upon both hands and always know that I am loved by two most worthy men." She reverently kissed him on the lips.

Richard radiated happiness. She had the most generous heart.

Elizabeth asked, "May I give my gift to you?"

"Of course. I would be happy to receive whatever you give me, although your presence and acceptance of my love is more than enough, Elizabeth." Richard replied. He never expected any gift from her; just being near her was more than enough. Last Christmas, he had been miserable without her and the poetry volume from Elizabeth was the only thing that had gotten him through his endless melancholy.

He saw the small green velvet box that she fetched from her room and wondered what it could be. He hesitantly held it and felt the softness of the box. *If there is a rock inside, I will carry it for the rest of my life. Anything that Elizabeth gives me is a treasure.* He smiled, as he felt for his poetry book that she had given him last year in his coat pocket.

He was surprised to open it and see a very expensive and masculine pocket watch inside. It was something that he had never expected and he had an old watch that he carried. He and Darcy had always joked that expensive timepieces were for dandies who wanted to flaunt their wealth, as they had never met a married woman who cared to gift such a costly item for a husband, spending their pin money on themselves instead. Darcy had carried his father's and he had carried one that was dented from the war when he was on the continent.

His eyes teared. This was probably the most considerate gift that he had ever received. Other than Elizabeth's love and kisses and the poetry book that he always carried, he could not recall a more sentimental or valuable item in his possession, especially since this was from his beloved. It mattered not the cost; everything from her was priceless but this was beyond his every expectation. He turned it around and saw the decoration on the back with a triangle and heart within. He knew exactly what it was. It was the love and dedication that the three of them, Darcy, Elizabeth, and himself, had for each other and that they were solid and eternal together. He looked up and smiled at Elizabeth who was beaming. He looked back at the watch and opened it and found an inscription within: *With love.*

His heart soared. He turned to Elizabeth and kissed her lips gently several times. "My love, thank you. I will treasure it always. This is the best gift that I have ever been given, other than your kisses, of course. I truly love you. Thank you, Elizabeth. I will carry it with me and like your ring, every time I look at this will remind me of you and our love. It is perfect."

He kissed her hands and put his precious gift into his pocket. He kissed his grandmother's ring, now Elizabeth's ring, and put her hand on his arm to walk to the breakfast room.

~*~

Darcy smiled and pulled the chair out for Elizabeth. The Gardiners and Mr. Bennet were already eating and he stood next to Richard while gathering his wife's breakfast and elbowed him. Richard was very quiet and he guessed his cousin was emotional from Elizabeth's gift. He met Richard's eyes and pulled out his pocket watch to show it to his cousin and Richard smiled brightly and showed him his own. Darcy tapped him on his back and they continued to plate their food.

Richard quietly whispered, "Thank you, brother. She is the most incredible woman. Thank you."

Darcy replied, "You are most welcome, brother."

~*~

The cheerful family gathered in the drawing room later, the children sang while the Yule Log was brought out and stories were told. Gifts were exchanged and all agreed that God has been very good to all of them and that this was one of the best Christmases yet.

Chapter 47

The next several days were spent in pleasant company and they anticipated the New Year Ball. It would be the first time a ball was being held at Rosings Park, as Lady

Catherine had never celebrated any of the holidays, and dozens of neighbours were invited to attend.

The ladies gathered to plan and decorate furiously while the gentlemen went shooting or riding. A chess tournament was held for the men and the younger girls giggled as they dreamt of dancing the night away. Georgiana and Lydia would be allowed to dance with family members only and Kitty dreamt of finding her prince now that she was officially out.

Elizabeth had several errands to run. She had not grown up in Kent so she knew very little of what was available here since she had visited the town of Bromwell on her last trip but had not spent much time at the shops except at the modiste's. She and the girls giggled as they anticipated shopping for trinkets or laces to add to their dresses and they separated so the younger girls could look for sweets for the Gardiner children while Jane and Elizabeth, along with Jane's maid, headed to the seamstress. Jane had grown larger in the past two weeks and needed some larger adjustments made to her dresses.

When they entered the establishment, there were several other women inside, either being fitted or shopping for fabric. The owner rushed to Elizabeth when she entered. "Mrs. Darcy! How good of you to visit. Is there anything I can do for you?"

Elizabeth noted a woman near her gasp. She had not noticed anyone familiar when she entered, so she was curious how this stranger might know her, but she turned to the owner and replied, "Mrs. Nelson, it is wonderful to see you again. I have brought my sister Mrs. Bingley to have some of her dresses adjusted." She answered.

Mrs. Nelson could see Jane's width and knew exactly what needed to be done. "Of course, ma'am. Mrs. Bingley, a pleasure to assist you. Will you follow me, please? Mrs. Darcy, while I get your sister measured and look at her dresses, would you like to sit here or join us in the back room? I can have tea served right away as well."

"I will sit here. I am also expecting my aunt to arrive soon. My other sisters are shopping with her. Thank you." Elizabeth replied.

Taking her seat, she looked around and watched the woman who had gasped at her name. She was a beautiful petite woman, appeared to be about thirty years old, with slightly wide hips and large bosoms. She was dressed moderately, not high but a lady, and appeared to have a pleasant, genteel face with bright eyes. She attempted to recall if she recognised her but could not remember so she paid no further mind and found a fashion magazine to read. As she reached for the periodical, she saw her right hand and Richard's ring. She looked to her left and saw Fitzwilliam's. She suddenly felt warm, feeling the love from both sides. *I am so thankful for my men!*

She began to peruse through the reading materials when she heard, "Abigail? Have you made your purchases?"

Elizabeth looked up to see the same petite woman answer softly, "Yes, Penelope. I am ready to go."

As 'Abigail' reached for the door, their eyes met. The stranger dipped her head softly at her and departed.

Elizabeth pondered if she was acquainted with an Abigail. Perhaps someone's sister? She had met so many people in London and in Kent that it was all a blur.

Suddenly, she recalled Lord Harold speaking with Richard at the Christmas Ball and asking about 'Abby'. *Could that be? I know his mistress is here in Kent.* She looked down at her right hand. *I know he loves me but he lays with her. She has known him intimately when we will never be. Am I jealous? Oh, if she were Fitzwilliam's mistress, I would have scratched her eyes out.* She laughed. *She is very beautiful. I wish he did not have a mistress but I cannot give Richard more and I must accept it. I hope he is satisfied with the arrangement. I hope he will tell me if that was she.* She was burning with curiosity.

After Jane was done and thanked the seamstress for allowing her to breathe easier, all the ladies completed their shopping and returned to Rosings to rest before dinner.

~*~

Elizabeth found Richard in his study when she ventured downstairs to write a letter. She had been told that the men went for a quick fishing trip and had not expected Richard to be there. She liked Richard's study during the afternoons, as her husband's study faced full north and she found it cold sometimes.

"Richard! You are still here. I came to use your desk but I shall use my own." She smiled.

Richard smiled brightly. "I am almost done. If you will sit with me for a moment, you may take my place here." He quickly finished his sentences, sanded the letter, and sealed it. He loved Elizabeth sitting on his chair. He loved her being so comfortable in his home. Their home.

"All done. Do you need anything? Is there something I can get for you while you accomplish your task?" Richard helped her sit and kissed her cheek.

"Perhaps a glass of water? That would be wonderful." Elizabeth replied. She wrote her letter to Charlotte while Richard sat on the couch and gazed at her the whole time. As she finished, she looked up to see his eyes on her still with a small smile. "Do you not have anything better to do, Master?" She giggled.

"Nothing better at the moment, thank you." He laughed.

"Well, I am done. Thank you for the use of your desk. I will leave my letter right here for Mrs. Tinsley to be taken out with your correspondences." Elizabeth smiled and arose.

"How was your trip to Bromwell? Did you find it similar to Meryton?" Richard asked as he gathered her hand on his arm again. He began to walk her to their sitting room and hoped to steal a kiss. It had been too long since he had tasted her.

"It was a very pleasant village. I was able to find everything I needed. Mrs. Nelson was very kind in helping Jane with her predicament. Oh! I just remembered." Then she was quiet.

"Remembered what? Of what are you speaking?" Richard asked when she did not continue for another minute.

"Wait. Inside." She increased her pace and kept quiet until they reached their sitting room. After closing the door, she continued, "Richard, is your mistress named Abigail? Or Abby?"

Richard paled and then turned bright red. "How? Where did you hear that name, Elizabeth?" He growled.

"I saw a woman who was surprised when Mrs. Nelson welcomed me into her store and her friend, a 'Penelope', had called her Abigail. I just then recalled that Lord Harold had asked you about 'Abby' at the Christmas Ball. Was that her?" Elizabeth innocently asked.

Richard groaned. He could not fault Elizabeth for her curiosity. She was the most intelligent and brilliant woman he had ever known.

"Argh, Elizabeth! I wish you had not known. Did she approach you? Did she talk to you?" Richard was fuming. He wanted Elizabeth to never know her name. *What must she think of me? She now has the name and face of the woman that I use for my release!!*

"No, Richard. We saw each other and that was it. She left before I realised who she was. Please do not be upset. I was just curious. I had wanted to put a face to your lady friend. I only just recalled that her name was Ab..." Richard's lip was on hers.

He kissed her and opened her mouth and teased her tongue. He suckled deeply as he drew her closer into his embrace and held her tightly. He released her slowly as they both gasped for air.

"Please, my love," Richard's eyes pleaded. *Forget about her! I love you!*

She immediately continued, "Now that I know it, why can I not say her name? Why does it pain you for me to say 'Ab...'" His mouth was on hers again. He kissed her deeply for several minutes and slowly released her. *God, I love her so much. I am so ashamed. I wish I had never used other women.*

"I do not wish for you to ever speak her name. She is nothing to me; just a body. I am ashamed that I use her but I truly care nothing for her. My love, if you wish, I will never see her again. Please, Elizabeth, do not ever mention her again. If you see her, walk the other way. I will demand the same from her. I do not wish for you to know her, to see her, to ever think of her. I love you. I spend as few minutes as possible for my release and that is all."

He kissed her again and held her tighter. She could feel his hard erection against her abdomen and sympathised with him. She could never give herself to him and she knew he was desperate for her but never asked for more.

"Richard, I ab..." He covered her mouth again.

She giggled when he released her. Richard smiled as she laughed. "Oh, my love. I was going to say I abbb-solutely understand your situation. I will not say her name and will not acknowledge her. I will obey, Master." Richard beamed. "But I do feel awful that you are in this situation. I love you, Richard, but I cannot give you more. I cannot be a true wife to you. I will not break my vows."

Richard sighed. "And I would never ask you to. Elizabeth, should you be laying nude in your bed asking for me to love you, I might lose my mind and perform the deed, only to regret and lose the most important people in my life. I could not betray Darcy and I could not dishonour you. I should not even be kissing you but your kisses are life to me.

"I only see... *the woman*... twice a month and my last visit was after we returned from town. I am planning on seeing her again tomorrow but I feel like I am betraying you. Or betraying Darcy, because I only think of you. I have used her four times only but I always imagine loving you, Elizabeth. You already know I call her by your name and I only dream of being with you, my love. We will be leaving after Epiphany and I do not believe I will see her again for several months. It is of no great loss to me to stop seeing her. She will continue to live in Kent but I wish for you to never meet her. Should I stop seeing her? What is your wish, my love? I will do anything you command." Richard asked her desperately. *I only need you, my love.*

"Oh, Richard, I understand your predicament and I cannot fault you. I understand the need for your release and I do not judge you. As your *wife* who cannot have relations with you, I cannot tell you what to do about this situation. I do not know how I can help you but I know when you kiss me so, you have difficulty with your self-control. What can I do for you? Do I need to deny your kisses?" Elizabeth blushed. It was a strange conversation to be having but it needed to be said.

Richard gulped. *She wants to help me. How can I ask it of her?* It was one thing when she fell asleep but for her to be awake... I am so desperate for her.

After taking a few moments to calm his raging erection, Richard replied, "Please do not deny me. I cannot live without you. I have tasted the forbidden fruit and would rather die after this knowledge. Elizabeth, there is... there is a way that you can help me... I know it is not the same but..."

He paused. How would she receive his request? Would it disgust her or would she think it was too much?

"I think I would like to continue to see my... the woman... but I would also like your permission to... I do not ask you for any more than what you have given but if I am allowed to... let myself go... while I am with you..." He could not go on. He would have to show her.

He embraced her and began to kiss her fervently and began to walk her backwards so she was standing against the wall. He pressed his body tightly against hers and continued his kisses. His hands were on her neck and behind her head as his tongue was deep in her mouth. He pressed his erection against her and kept it still as she held onto his shoulders.

Elizabeth enjoyed his kisses and although she was not sure what he was about to do, he was kissing her most passionately as he had done last time, and she closed her eyes and revelled in his kisses. He was truly a fantastic lover. She found herself becoming moist between her legs as he poured out his desire for her through his mouth and returned his kisses and moaned loudly as she wrapped her arms around his neck and reached for his hair and ran it with her fingers, grabbing it tightly then stroking through it again. She felt his arms grip around her waist tightly and his hardness against her but he did not rub against her or try to lift up her skirts. Soon, he freed her mouth to kiss her neck and ear then he embraced her even closer as he grunted his release and pulsated against her groin several times.

He continued to hold her tightly as she felt his manhood throb under his trousers. He released his embrace and held her cheeks as he kissed her lips several times. "Oh, Elizabeth, my sweet Elizabeth." He continued kissing between words, "I have never felt such a rush. I know that it was ungentlemanly but such a strong release. I love you, Elizabeth. Thank you." *My god! I cannot control myself when she touches me!*

"Oh, Richard, you are such a fantastic kisser. Will it be enough, though? Will being with your *lady friend* a few times a year be enough to sustain you? I do not wish for you to suffer, Richard." Elizabeth consoled.

Richard truthfully replied, "My love, my release while you kissed me was the most powerful and amazing feeling I experienced." Richard knew he did not have much time, as his fluid was soaking through his trousers and his mess would be completely visible to her, but he continued, "Elizabeth, my love, I have had sexual relations with many women."

Elizabeth quickly asked, "How many?"

Richard laughed. "Of course, you would ask. I will not lie to you. So many that I honestly do not know, I am ashamed to say. It would range from a hundred to two hundred, should I have to guess."

Elizabeth's mouth gaped in shock. "So many! After that, how can you live with having your lady friend only four times in the past year?" Elizabeth quickly calculated that she and Fitzwilliam must have had relations at least two hundred times in the past six months, and that included the six weeks of abstinence after the babies were born!

Richard chuckled. This conversation was not going where he had wanted at all. *Damn her curious mind!* "My love, we digress. I have been managing. I have been helping myself and have sustained these past months. If I had to never release in exchange of being in the same room with you, I would still choose you. I love you. I would rather be a eunuch than violate yours and Darcy's trust. If you can help me by allowing me what I just did, even though it is messy and disgraceful, it was the best experience of my life. All the women, every one of my carnal experiences put together, paled in comparison to what I just experienced." He beamed. "Your allowing me this much is more than I had ever dreamt."

He kissed her slowly and tenderly again. He knew his erection had returned while talking of sexual acts but he would not ask for more today. "I must go and change. I am unfit to be seen. Thank you, my love. I love you, Elizabeth."

He quickly turned and sprinted to his room. He was embarrassed to have released like that but was ecstatic with how pleasurable it was to hold her so.

Elizabeth took a deep sigh. *Have we crossed the line? My feelings for Richard are growing even if not nearly as strong as I feel for Fitzwilliam. Is it possible to be in love with two men? If anyone else had caught us doing what we were doing, it would be a scandal and it would be treated equal to an affair and yet, there is so much between the three of us and we need each other. It is a secret affair but only our business. A love triangle. I must ask my husband.*

Chapter 48

Elizabeth awaited her husband in her bed. She had fallen asleep and was groggy when she flushed with desire as her womanhood was being licked. She lifted her head to look down and her dear husband was caressing her folds with his tongue and she moaned. He fingered her at her response and she thrust her hips up to get his fingers deeper inside her. She climaxed after several minutes and panted as he climbed between her legs and slid his long phallus inside her. They rocked and moaned together and as the sounds of love filled the room, they reached their finale together.

Darcy kissed her tenderly. "I have missed you so much, my love. I have not seen you for hours!" He teased.

Elizabeth held her husband tightly. He was still inside her and she lifted her arms to wrap around his neck and her legs to wrap them around his hips. "I have missed you tremendously, my love! Oh, you feel so good inside me and I cannot imagine going for days or weeks or months without having you. I love you so much!" She cried.

She held on to him as if for her dear life and initially, Darcy was pleased by her declaration but soon noticed that she was muffling a sob.

He kissed her hair and tried to see her face but she buried it in his chest and kept herself wrapped tight onto his body.

"Shhh, my love, shhh. I love you. It is well." Darcy stroked her hair. He did not know what was bothering her but his heart broke for her. Having been married for over a year, he was beginning to read her well but she had not been this emotional since nearer to the end of her pregnancy.

After several minutes when her sobs quieted, he asked, "Are you well? Did I hurt you?"

"I am not injured, Fitzwilliam. I am overwhelmed by your love. I do not deserve your love." She cried again.

He held her tightly. *What happened? She went shopping today with the ladies. Did something happen in Bromwell?*

After she calmed further, he rolled off of her petite body and held her in his arms. "My love, will you tell me what happened? Did something happen during your shopping trip? Does Richard know?"

"Fitzwilliam, my love, I do not know... I feel as if I did not do the right thing. I do not know how to feel." Elizabeth started. She would not lie to her husband. She would be honest and confess what happened and of her feelings. "I love you with so much love and passion that I am troubled that my feelings for Richard is growing." She felt Darcy stiffen. "I still do not wish for him to take me to bed, my dear husband. Rather, I think of you and how much I love our union, but I am afraid that I enjoy his kisses too much. I am scared that... I am concerned... that I allowed too much to happen today."

Darcy did not let go of her but kissed her hair. "Will you tell me what happened?" *I will not overreact. If she allowed it, I must accept it.*

"Richard has been kissing me all the time, usually the cheek or hands, but sometimes he does kiss me fervently. It has been perhaps five or six times so far. He apologises sometimes and other times, it is as if he cannot control it. I am finding that I am... I am returning the kiss and am comforted by it. I feel his love and revel in the love that he pours onto me. Today, I saw his mistress during my shopping trip and I asked him about her, and he told me that he did not want me to know her. He kissed me deeply several times and I already know that he calls out my name when he lays with her. He, he kissed me to the point of completion today. I am ashamed that I, I allowed him to lose his self-control and I encouraged it. I could imagine you and I making love and how wonderful that feels and for Richard to not have that, he suffers for months on end just to be with us, I encouraged it... and I liked it..." She could not continue. She was ashamed and worried that her husband would become angry.

Darcy sighed in relief. *Oh, my love. Is that all? If she only knew how much control it takes men.* He scoffed internally.

"Elizabeth, did he ask you to lay with him? Did he wish you to be in his bed to enter you?" Darcy asked gently. He trusted that his cousin knew his boundaries as they had discussed several times before.

"No! I told him I could not and he told me he could not. He said he would rather be a eunuch than to violate our trust. He is honourable and please do not blame him. I blame myself for allowing it. I would hate for you to believe that I betrayed you." Elizabeth begged.

Darcy turned his body and brought his head lower to meet her eyes. "Elizabeth, will you be honest with me?" She nodded. "Do you love him?"

She answered after a thought. "Yes, I love him very much. I had considered that should I have met him before meeting you and he should have proposed, I believe I would have been content with him. But it would be a contentment, not the full falling head over heels in love as I experienced with you. I love you so much that nothing else can exceed. But Fitzwilliam, I do love him."

Darcy smiled. "And will you tell me what you see on your left hand?"

"My wedding ring, of course." Elizabeth answered with curiosity.

"And on your right hand?" Darcy asked.

Elizabeth looked at her hand and comprehended what he was asking. "My other wedding ring."

Darcy laughed. "I am a jealous creature, Elizabeth, and I wish for you to be completely mine. But I love my dear cousin, who would die for us, and he loves you beyond anything else he has ever loved, including myself. I have told him that as long as you allow it, he may love you as freely as he wished. He opened his heart to you so fully that he cannot control how much love he pours out for you. The fact that he can act so proper in company astonishes me, and yet it is most likely because he has never had a true union of body with you.

"Do you recall that night when you had too much orange wine?" Darcy saw the blush on her cheeks as she nodded. "You fell asleep in his arms after kissing him and I do not know if you thought he was me or you kissed him knowing who he was, but I was distraught that I would lose you. He could have taken full advantage of you but he did not, because he loved you and admired you too much to disrespect both of us. But what you do not know is that he did find his release while he held you. He confessed to me that he could not control himself and I had seen the evidence of it when I returned. After he reaffirmed me of your love for me, I am now content to accept him as your lover who will care for you for the rest of his life.

"My love, you have two husbands. Not in a lawful way, but you have the full love of two passionate men and I am actually surprised that he had not lost his control earlier. After tasting your love, I certainly could not have lasted so long. He released his seed in his trousers while he kissed you?"

"Yes, Fitzwilliam. I allowed him to hold me tightly and he kissed me until he released. He did not rub himself on me or touch me anywhere else. He said it was the most powerful experience of his life." Elizabeth blushed again.

Darcy chuckled. "I am sure it was. Do you recall when I had to walk away from you several times to try to calm myself? I was seconds away from spending in my trousers and it was before we married. I know you love me and I appreciate that you think of me even while he kisses you, but I know he is an adept lover and you are very passionate as well. Enjoying his kisses is expected. You love him and you are so affectionate. Do you wish for him to stop? Shall I talk to him?"

"I, I do not wish to stop. I want him to experience pleasure without having marital relations with me. I was worried for him that his visits to Abigail, I found out her name, is so infrequent that I worried for his sanity. But he says he can take care of himself and it is sufficient. You do not feel that I am betraying you by allowing him to lose control?" Elizabeth asked carefully.

"My love, I expected him to have done so many times before." He laughed. "I am shocked that this is the first time. Richard has an iron will, I must say, if he lasted this long to let himself go after loving you for such a long time. I would not have made it as long." He kissed her lips. "I am so glad we are able to talk about this and I truly value your honesty." He paused.

"Elizabeth, I do not wish for you to have sexual relations with anyone but me but I understand more and more of the depth of his love for you and I know that if I were in his place, I would be dying a slow death if I could not have you. You and I have a vow to keep, a vow that belongs to you and me and not Richard. But I truly understand that he needs a release and he wants to share that release with you. I will be blunt. As long as your womanhood belongs to me, I am willing to share the rest of you with him. He will not enter you here," he rubbed her folds, "with his manhood," he inserted his fingers into her, making her moan, "but if you are willing to love him in other ways, I will allow it." He continued fingering her and began to lick her breasts. "He has had many lovers before and I know he knows the pleasures of the flesh," he suckled on her nipples, "he would enjoy your breasts," he moved to the other breast, "and your mouth, your oh so delicate mouth," he tongued her deeply, "but your vagina, your womb of my future children, it belongs to me. Do you understand?"

Elizabeth panted and yelled, "Yes!" as she climaxed with his fingers still thrusting inside her. After calming herself, "How you pleasure me so. I cannot get enough of you."

Darcy smiled. "Yes, my love. That is exactly what I wish. You may pleasure your other husband and he may excite you and make you wet between your legs, but I want you to beg *me* to take you. For only *me* to fill you and pleasure you and make you come." He climbed on her and slid his cock into her again. "For me to enjoy what belongs to me so I can love you until we are both satisfied." He pumped harder than he had done in months.

After the babes were born, he had been gentle in their lovemaking but now, he was thrusting into her with a fierceness that she had missed. She screamed again and again in pleasure and he finally climaxed with her.

They both lay panting for air for many minutes. It had been such an emotional ride for Elizabeth that she began to shiver. Darcy quickly covered her with the sheets. "Are you well? You are shivering."

"Oh, goodness, Fitzwilliam. I do not think I have climaxed that quickly and that many times in a row before. Wow. That was amazing. I love you so much. I cannot get enough of you. You are so good at what you do. I cannot believe I married a virgin who can do this to me." She giggled.

"At your service, madam. Any time, my love. I love making love with you and I know that your generous heart wants Richard to feel the love that we have. He will be more than sustained by it. He may still need to visit Miss Harrington at times but he will want you a thousand times more." Darcy kissed her temple.

"You know her! Abigail Harrington. Have you met her? What is she like? I saw her at Mrs. Nelson's shop today, Fitzwilliam. She heard my name and it appeared as if she recognised me and I was trying to figure out if I knew her but I did not recognise her.

I heard her name being called out and I recalled that Lord Harold had said something about 'Abby' when we were at Aunt Susan's ball. Richard was so upset that I knew her name now and refused to let me say her name." Elizabeth rejoined.

"I do not know her; only her name, and only that she was Haversham's mistress for four years. Yes, even while he was courting you and proposing to you, he had been keeping her. I understand Richard's reluctance for you to know her because Richard dreams only of you when he lays with her. Since he cannot and will not lay with you, he uses her body to satisfy his need of you. He does not love her and it will be nothing but a release for him. Does that bother you?" Darcy asked her.

"To be honest, it does bother me that there is someone else that he finds comfort with, but I think he needs to do it in order to meet his physical needs. She was very pretty with bright eyes; petite with large bosoms, about Richard's age, I think. Did you know that he has slept with possibly two hundred women? Is that not an incredible number? And you, just one. What a good man you are." She kissed him soundly. She was feeling better and happier and infinitely in love with her dearest husband.

"That is a large number and I am certain he has slept with many of them more than once. He has been experienced since sixteen so that is a lot of number years. It is not so uncommon, my love. I am the rarity since I was too shy and too embarrassed. I would surmise that even Bingley had at least a hundred. Should I have had a little more bravery or dishonour in my bones, it would not have been difficult to reach hundreds, given my age. Richard is two years older than I so it averages out to..."

"Once or twice a month in fourteen years." Elizabeth answered.

Darcy laughed. Her brain was first rate. "You are so intelligent, Elizabeth. So, if you double that to, let us say once or twice every fortnight, it is not a bad number, would you not say? How many times have we made love this week?"

Elizabeth laughed, "I believe we are closer to fifteen! I suppose it is not such a bad way to look at it. Richard said he arranged to visit his mistress twice a month. The poor man. I do not judge him for the number of women he had. I was more concerned that it would not be the same. I cannot imagine his releasing while kissing me would equal actual relations. He said it was better."

"He has never been in love before, my love. He used to tell me all about his conquests and I had found it fascinating that there were so many loose women who acted so proper in society. He did warn me that it was short-lasting, even with all of his gloating. He had bedded women for carnal pleasure without the emotional attachment but now, he is so attached to you that your kisses and the memory of your kisses are enough. In all the years I have known him, I have never seen him happier and you make us both so happy. Making love and having sexual relations is different, would you not agree? We could just go through the physical act of intercourse and still find release, but you and I make love and it is such a precious gift. You love me and you love Richard. We both love you as our wife and there is nothing that we would not do for you." Darcy kissed her ardently once again. "Now rest. We have only an hour until we must dress for dinner."

Chapter 49

Richard paced in his study. *I cannot believe I embarrassed myself like that today. What a mess I was. I have never released so hard in my life. What is Elizabeth going to say to me? Dare I even look her in the eyes? Perhaps I should just take my meals in my rooms tonight.* He continued to pace. *But I must see her. I need to know that she is well. It was so ungentlemanly and to be so thoughtless to lose control like that...*

He heard a knock at the door. "Enter." He called out.

Darcy entered with a stern look. He was not angry but Richard deserved some punishment for making Elizabeth miserable again, however brief it might have been.

Damn it! I hope Elizabeth is well. Darcy is going to kill me. Richard thought.

"Darce, how are you? How was the fishing?" Richard started nervously.

"Good, good. I am here to talk to you about Elizabeth, Richard. Can you tell me why she was crying in my arms today?" Darcy attempted to keep a stoic face although laughing internally at the ridiculous situation. It did not really matter since Richard was avoiding his eyes completely.

"I messed up, Darcy. I lost control. Damn it! I disgraced myself and wounded Elizabeth. I do not know how I can ever make amends. I was selfish and I, I spent in my trousers after holding on to her too tightly. Blasted! What have I done?" He paced rapidly in front of the fireplace, pulling on his hair.

He looked up to see Darcy laughing. "What, Darcy! She was not crying? Were you lying to me?" Richard boomed.

Darcy sobered. "She was crying, Richard. I was laughing because you were pacing like a mad man, but she was crying." Richard took a seat. *I am going to make him suffer a little.* "I returned from our fishing excursion and found my beautiful wife in bed asleep. I took my time pleasuring her until she awoke and made love to her, Richard. She cried after we completed and I thought I had done something wrong but it was not I, thank God. She was crying because she thought she had betrayed me by allowing you to kiss her until you released." Darcy watched Richard, as he stood then plopped down on the chair in front of him. He shook his head and smiled. *Who speaks of these things? I talk about having relations with my wife and he talks about spending himself with the same woman.*

"But she did nothing wrong, Darcy. It was all my fault. I should not have gone so far. We were talking of Abigail and my carnal needs and I explained how much pleasure I took from Elizabeth's kisses. Then I just lost it. I wanted to explode with her in my arms again and it felt so good when she returned the kiss. But I should not have. I should have controlled myself better but have so little self-control when I am near her. It was ungentlemanly and I messed up, Darce. She must regret allowing me to act so disgustingly." He stood to pace again.

Neither blames the other. They do certainly love each other and I do love them both dearly. Oh, what a tangled web. Darcy laughed. "Richard, will you sit? You are making me dizzy." Darcy requested.

"Oh, sorry, Darcy. Please tell me what to do. How can I make it up to her for losing control? I love her so much, I feel like I cannot breathe knowing that she hates me." Richard buried his face in his hands as tears rolled out.

"Richard. Richard! She does not hate you. She loves you. She loves you so much that she was miserable because she could not give you more. She will keep her vows no matter what but she wished to alleviate your discomfort and she has told me that she enjoys your attentions. She felt guilty that she should not, but I reminded her that she has two husbands."

Darcy leaned forward to tap on his shoulder. "Look at me. Look me in the eyes, Richard." He did. "I told her that her womanhood belongs to me and only me, but she is free to love you in other ways. Do you understand me? You will not bury yourself inside her womanhood. That is mine and only mine. She knows this and after I thoroughly satisfied her again, she is content with her lot of having to love two husbands. She wears my ring and she will keep her vows but she wears your ring and you will continue to love her." After seeing an understanding in his eyes, he continued, "Go slow with her. She is still innocent and having two men love her is new territory. She loves me far above you, I am certain, but she wishes to please you as well and I honour her wishes. I love her so much that I am allowing her to follow her heart. I care for you, too, brother. Your love for her is what makes me allow this. But should she feel uncomfortable, should you impose on her where you should not, I will have you arrested and hanged for molesting my wife. Do you understand me?" He threatened. "You shall never take more than what Elizabeth gives you. She is my life. As much as I share a part of her with you, she fully belongs to me."

Richard slowly nodded. He gulped, as he knew Darcy's threat was the truth. He would never take more than what Elizabeth gave and he never intended to bed her. He was relieved that she was not angry and would be willing to help him with his physical needs and he became aroused again at the thought of repeating the earlier activity but pressed it down. It was not the time.

"What are you going to do about Miss Harrington, Richard? Elizabeth is aware of her name and face." Darcy asked.

"I do not know yet. I enjoy the release but every time felt lacking. It is difficult to not imagine Eliz... but if Elizabeth is willing to... you know I only need Elizabeth. I am due to visit Abigail tomorrow. I will decide by then after I speak with Elizabeth. I might only see her only a few times a year, just for the act, but if Elizabeth does not wish it, I will never see her again." Richard paused. "Darcy, she, Elizabeth does not love me as she does you. She told me that she dreams of you even while I kiss her sometimes. But I promise you that I have never intended to do more than kissing and I would never trespass upon your vows. I would rather die than to dishonour her and betray you, brother."

Darcy smiled. "I know she loves me. I am so confident in her love and desire for me that I can talk freely about it with you. Elizabeth loves you, too. She told me that she is attracted to you and would have been content to marry you." Richard's face lit up brightly. "You would not have chosen her, Richard, with her mother the way she was, and her station and lack of dowry, and if I had been my old self before determining to change my ways, I would have met her, fallen in love with her but still insult her somehow, then crawled back to her to beg at her feet after making an arse of myself, probably spouting some nonsense about duty and expectations. I would not have let her go and I will never let her go now. Love her, Richard. Love our wife carefully and tenderly. She is most precious."

He arose to his feet. "We are late. Let us go and meet the group for dinner. They must be wondering where we are. And do not worry about Elizabeth. She is well now. She handled hearing about your two hundred lovers quite well!" He laughed loudly as Richard stood frozen with his mouth agape. He left the Master of Rosings standing in the middle of the room as he headed to the drawing room.

~*~

"Good morning, Elizabeth." Richard greeted his beloved shyly in their sitting room. He had been too embarrassed to approach her last night at dinner and afterwards had taken himself straight to his bed after feigning exhaustion. Truly, he was exhausted.

233

He had a constant arousal that he could not hide when looking at his beautiful surrogate wife, and he had to escape prying eyes.

Now, seeing her quietly on the couch enjoying her morning tea and looking so beautiful made his heart flutter. *How is it possible that after all this time, after all the kisses, my heart is still so excited to see her?* He took a seat next to her, needing to be close.

Elizabeth turned and smiled brightly. "Good morning! Hope you are feeling better." She reached up and placed the back of her hand on his forehead and caressed his cheek. "No fever, thank goodness." Then she kissed him on the lips.

Richard froze. She gave her kisses so rarely, especially on the lips, and after yesterday's embarrassment, he did not know what to think. "I am well. Quite well. Are you well, Elizabeth?" He timidly asked. He felt ominous that something was different and he did not have a clue as to what.

Elizabeth gently put down her teacup next to her and arose. Richard began to stand also but Elizabeth quickly pushed his shoulder down to remain seated. She turned herself around and straightened her dress and wrapping one arm around his neck, sat down on his lap. Wrapping the other around to embrace him, she whispered, "Good morning, husband," and began to kiss him, pressing her lips on his and suckling on his lips gently.

Richard had never been aroused so fast. He began to kiss her and he met her tongue on his lips and suckled her. She moaned and continued to wrap her tongue around his. She ended the kiss by lifting her face from his and smiled at him. "I love you," she whispered.

She kissed him once more and stood. "It is time for breakfast. I am famished!" And she merrily laughed and left the room.

Richard remained sitting, still awestruck. After several moments, he smiled and said loudly, "Minx! What am I supposed to do with this?" Looking down at his massive erection, he laughed.

I love her so much. My Elizabeth is truly a wonder.

Chapter 50

Richard left Rosings with the ladies preparing madly for the Winter Ball that evening.

Elizabeth, Mrs. Gardiner, Mrs. Bennet, his mother, Iris, his sister-in-law, Georgiana, Mrs. Bingley, as well as Mary, Kitty, and Lydia, were a force to beheld. The mansion shone like never before and he left most of the ladies fluttering about, comparing dresses and making last minute changes. The men were busy with the chess tournament that had been in place for the past three days, and it was neck-in-neck with Darcy, Lord Matlock, and Mr. Bennet tied for the winner's spot.

As always, he thought of Elizabeth. They had a chance to play with the twins before he left and even with Darcy in the room, he spoke freely.

"Elizabeth, Darcy is already aware but I plan on seeing... her... today. Will you tell me your wishes for me?" He coloured as he asked. *How does one talk to his wife about such a thing?*

"Oh, I had thought we had agreed... Fitzwilliam and I had discussed it as well and I honestly do not mind, Richard, as there are things that I cannot do for you and I do not wish to deprive you of it. You told me that visiting her a few times a year is sufficient and I trust you to make the decision for yourself. We three have a very exceptional relationship and having your... her... in the mix is understandable." She smiled.

Richard smiled in return. "Well then, I will need to go take care of some businesses downstairs. I shall leave you to enjoy some time with my godsons and will see you this evening. Oh, if I may ask, what colour dress will you be wearing?"

Darcy laughed. "I have never heard you ask about a lady's dress in my life! HAHAHA! You are a mooncalf, cousin!"

Richard coloured again. "Well, I never cared before. Although I will not be matching like you and Elizabeth, I would like to not clash."

Elizabeth giggled. "I will be in dark blue, kind sir."

Richard kissed Elizabeth's hand. "Thank you," and he left to see to his businesses.

~*~

Now as he was approaching Abigail's cottage, he was still upset that she had been identified, but by Elizabeth's story, it was only because they were at the same place at the wrong time. Abigail did not go out of her way to introduce herself or to make herself known that she was his mistress. *Elizabeth is too intelligent for her own good sometimes! Good lord, she would slap me if I said that to her.* He smiled. *She is so wonderful.*

He knocked and Abigail answered the door.

"Mr. Fitzwilliam, welcome." She greeted. "Happy Christmas. Had you a good celebration?"

"Yes, Happy Christmas. It was very pleasant. Rosings is bursting with guests and it has been wonderful." He smiled.

"I have a small gift for you. I wanted to thank you for your generosity." She handed him a box that appeared to be chocolates.

Should I have gotten something for her? No, I do not gift her like most men do with their mistresses. She knows I am only using her for my pleasures. "Thank you, Abigail. You did not need to." He opened the box and saw the row of truffles. *Good. Nothing too sentimental.* "Thank you, Abigail. I appreciate it." He placed it on the table and took a seat on the couch.

"Would you like to head to the bedroom, sir?" Abigail asked. She wanted him in her bed and hoped he would stay longer this time.

"No, I am fine here for now. I do wish to speak with you about Mrs. Darcy. I understand you saw her in Bromwell yesterday." Richard started.

Abigail gasped. *So, she did know who I was!* "Mr. Fitzwilliam, I did not approach her. I... I heard her name and knew that she was your Elizabeth and I was only surprised by it. I did notice that her eyes were on me but she did not appear to have any knowledge of me. I left soon after."

"I know. Elizabeth told me that she did not know who you were until after you left and she recollected that Haversham had spoken your name at a ball. She connected the dots and knew you were my... friend." He ran his fingers through his hair. "It is not your fault. If Haversham had not spoken of you, she would have never noticed it but she is so intelligent. Beautiful and quick." He closed her eyes thinking of Elizabeth again and their incredible kiss yesterday. "Abigail, I wish you to never approach her or be in the same vicinity as she. If you see her in town, you will depart. You will not be introduced to her, you will not speak of her to anyone, and you will never speak directly to her. Is that agreeable? I was mortified that she is aware of you and not only your name but your face now."

"But of course. She is very beautiful. I understand your love for her." Abigail softly commented.

"But she is even more beautiful on the inside, and the most generous." Richard sat up and leaned towards her chair to meet her eyes. "Abigail, are you happy here?"

"But of course, I am. After my trip I felt contentment and joy to return here to my home where I am provided for and not stepped on. I have the freedom to make friends and be known as myself, and not as a prostitute. I have joined the church choir and have volunteered to help with the orphanage. This life is something I had never expected before and I am very pleased. I am grateful to you for providing the home as well as the extra funds that you gifted to me, Mr. Fitzwilliam. One could live ten years on that much sum. You have provided more in our four times together than all of my other patrons put together." She wiped her tears. "Thank you for your kindness and for always being respectful and so gentlemanly."

"I am glad to hear it, Abigail. I must tell you that it is all Elizabeth's doing. She opened my heart to see that all women deserve respect and, in the past, I have slept with women for my pleasures to never see or even think of them again. I cared not whether she might get with child or where her next meal would come from, but meeting Elizabeth showed me that such use of a woman is wrong. That every woman is someone's daughter, someone's niece, and it matters not her station. As you have said before, my Elizabeth is a fearsome creature."

He held her hand for a moment then stood and paced. "I have made the decision to lease Rosings. I might visit in the future but it will be at least a year until my return and I wish to release you from my services. Please understand that you have been very satisfactory. I have found our... time... to be very helpful but it would not be fair for me to continue to keep you when I may be gone for a year or more." He walked back to her and kissed her hand. "Thank you for your help during my time of need. I wish you well, perhaps to find a husband for yourself?" He smiled and placed an envelope on the table next to her. "Goodbye, Abigail." And he left with the chocolates. He would give it to his housekeeper.

Abigail sat still for several minutes. She had thought he would continue his visits but it was the end. Her heart felt lighter, suddenly realising that she was no longer a kept woman but now a free woman. She was making friends here and feeling at home. The property belonged to her and she still had the £500 that he had gifted as well as her savings prior to desiring to retire.

She opened the envelope that Mr. Fitzwilliam had left and saw that there were an additional £500. He had given her £1,000 in total as well as the property and she could now be an independent woman.

She cried tears of joy and thanked God for her benefactor. Meeting Mr. Fitzwilliam had been the best thing in her life.

~*~

"May I have this dance, milady?" Richard bowed.

"It would be my pleasure, sir." Elizabeth curtsied as she smiled. She kissed her husband's cheek discreetly, with whom she had just concluded the first set, then turned to Richard. Darcy went to Georgiana to claim their dance.

Darcy and Richard had agreed beforehand that at every ball, Darcy would dance the first with his wife and Richard the second set. Darcy also claimed the supper set and the last dance. Richard claimed the set after supper, as they would always sit together.

As they lined up and began their steps, Elizabeth asked, "How was your visit with your friend, Richard? Was everything to your satisfaction?"

Richard smiled. "It went well; it was to our mutual satisfaction. How was the rest of your afternoon? Did the boys go down for their nap without problems?"

Elizabeth flushed at his answer. *What does he mean by 'mutual satisfaction'? Did he enjoy her talents that much? Did she pleasure him and he pleasure her? Why am I jealous?* She shook her head. *I must not, I cannot be jealous. It is not in our arrangement and I encouraged him to keep her.*

Richard was concerned. She did not answer his questions and she appeared overheated but just going through the dance steps automatically. "Elizabeth! Mrs. Darcy!" He called out a little loudly.

She snapped to attention but her face was still reddened and frowning. Richard eyed Darcy and he traded places with his cousin to continue his dance with Georgiana while Darcy gingerly walked Elizabeth out of the ballroom as discreetly as possible.

Richard was very concerned. She appeared to be happy and well until he talked to her. *What is wrong, my love?* He did not want to abandon Georgiana so he continued the dance but his heart was with Elizabeth.

~*~

Darcy walked her over to the punch table. "Let us get you something to drink. You are overheated."

After obtaining her a drink, he led her to Richard's study and sat her down. He felt her forehead and held her. "What happened, my love? I saw you speaking with Richard and then you were flushed. Did something happen?" He caressed her arms.

"Oh, Fitzwilliam, I do not know what is wrong with me. I cannot... should not feel so but I cannot help it." She wiped a tear. "I should not have even enquired, but I asked Richard how things went with his mistress and he said that it was of mutual satisfaction. I imagined him with that woman and became jealous. I had never felt like this before and I have no right. It is not as if I could give him more but I, I did not like... I... why am I so jealous of the woman that could give him pleasure?" She began to cry harder.

Darcy rubbed her back after handing her a handkerchief. "It is all right, my love, your feelings are natural. Elizabeth, do you recall what you said to me if you should ever find another woman in my bed? I believe you are feeling the same with Richard and although you had acknowledged that you could accept her, you love Richard and it is difficult to think of him taking his pleasures the way you and I pleasure each other. You should talk to him. He will not see her if you do not wish it. Oh, my love, having two husbands has its burdens and I believe this is one of them." She chuckled. He smiled, knowing she was feeling better. "I love you so much. Thank you for being honest with me, my dear. I know you are tremendously generous but you also have your limits. Richard loves you but for you to share him with a woman of whom you now know the name and face cannot be easy. It was easier when it was just an abstract thought, was it not?" She nodded. "You must speak with him about it, my love. He will do as you wish but we did agree that we will allow him the choice, did we not?" She nodded again.

"I love you, Fitzwilliam. I do not know how you share me with Richard. He has a piece of my heart and your willingness to allow it astounds me. I love you so much, my dearest husband." Elizabeth kissed him.

"My love, I share you because his love makes you happy. I dearly love my cousin and he loves us both. Our little family, we three, have more love for each other than most people in the world. Shall I fetch him for you? I believe the first dance is just ending and I can return to Georgina for the second." Darcy saw her nod and kissed her again and left.

~*~

Richard quickly entered his study without knocking, locking the door after him. He saw Elizabeth sitting in front of the fire and rushed over. He knelt in front of her and caressed her cheeks and saw that she had cried. He kissed her hands in worry. "What is wrong, my love? Are you feeling ill? I am so worried for you. What can I do for you?" He kissed her hands again.

"Oh, Richard! I am well. I am always well." She stood and paced, twisting Darcy's handkerchief with her hands repeatedly.

Richard sat on the chair and waited for her. He truly did not know what was bothering her and knew not what to do.

"Richard, I have a confession to make. I know we talked about it yesterday and even today..." She paused.

Richard's heart dropped. *She does not wish for me to kiss her again, to lose control... Please, I just need to be near you, Elizabeth! I cannot live without you!*

Before he could think further, she continued, "I was *jealous*! When you said that you were satisfied today, I pictured you with that *woman*," she spat out, "under you and I hated her. I was burning with anger that she touched you and that you were pleased with her attentions. What kind of terrible person am I to despise her for giving you what I cannot? You and Fitzwilliam have to share my affections and you are both so understanding but I was distraught imagining you enjoying *her*. I, I do not understand how I could be so jealous! She is so beautiful and I know how passionate you are..." She cried.

Richard immediately stood and held her. "Shhh... my love... I did not hav... use her. I am sorry that you misunderstood me. I did not lay with her, I did not do anything with her, my love." She jerked her head up and stared at him. "Elizabeth, I released her from my services. I compensated her and I let her go. I will never see her again. My visit was satisfactory because she is free, and I was satisfied with no longer keeping a woman. I felt as if I was betraying you the few times I saw her and my heart would not rest until I was faithful to you. Once my ring was placed on your finger, I could not fathom touching anyone but you. My Elizabeth, my wife."

Elizabeth choked a sob. "You let her go? For me?"

"Yes, my love. I love you and only you." Richard kissed her hair as she buried her face in his chest.

"But how will you... Will you be able to satiate..." Elizabeth could not finish as Richard's lips were on hers.

After gently kissing her and licking her lips one at a time, Richard continued, "I only need you. It was always you. I will never look to another again." He kissed her gently again.

"Oh, my love, thank you. You are so wonderful and I feel silly. I tell you one thing and then become a jealous monster the next. Women! So changeable!" Elizabeth scoffed.

Richard smiled. "No, not changeable. Lovely, intelligent, kind... my wife. You acted just as my wife should." He dried her eyes. "My Elizabeth, my wife."

Elizabeth laughed. "That is what Fitzwilliam said. How you and he are so alike."

"Well, He is a Fitzwilliam and I am a Fitzwilliam so yes, we are alike, and in love with the most wonderful woman in the world. Shall we return, my love? The set is ending."

She nodded. "Thank you, Richard. I am to dance with my father next. I know he will step on my poor toes!" Her laughter tinkled as she re-entered the ballroom.

~*~

The set had just ended and Darcy quickly approached with Georgiana on his arm. "Are you well?" He smiled, seeing her laugh with Richard.

"Oh, my love. Yes, all is well. Thank you for your assistance, dear Richard. Georgiana, shall we head to the Bennet clan? You can ask Kitty about her dance with our parson's brother, Mr. Brown!" Georgiana giggled and they both walked away.

Richard spoke first. "Thank you, Darcy. I told her I released Abigail. Even after her permission this morning, I could not fathom touching another woman ever again. I need no one else, you know. She had thought I had... she did not know and she was jealous. Why does it make me feel so good that she was jealous?" He grinned with a raised brow.

Darcy laughed heartily, turning several heads. It was still astonishing for the general populous to see Mr. Darcy jolly and pleasant in comparison to the dour gentleman he had always been. The Kent neighbours were still reeling from all the changes that had been made to Rosings.

"Because she is acting the wife. She told me that if she found a woman in my bed, she would scratch her eyes out and kick her. I am certain she felt the same with you and her. I am glad that you have made your choice. I hope you will not regret it. I could not imagine keeping a woman, even if I were never to join with Elizabeth again. I love her too much to betray her." Darcy whispered.

"I feel the same. She is the best thing in my life." Richard softly commented.

"Mine, too, Richard, mine, too." Darcy agreed.

The Winter Ball was a success and everyone toasted the new Master of Rosings and thanked the Darcys for hosting and they celebrated the New Year with champagne and kisses for their loved ones.

The Bennets, Mary and Mr. Bertram, and the Bingleys returned to Hertfordshire, and the Gardiners soon departed for London. Although it was planned for the Fitzwilliams to return to town on the third of January, Anne's condition worsened and they thought it appropriate that she be allowed to pass at Rosings to be interned at her home.

Anne de Bourgh died peacefully on Epiphany and Parson Brown performed the services, with the men attending the burial. Many neighbours visited and sent their condolences even if not knowing her personally, and many showed their respect to the former owner of Rosings.

Lady Catherine was invited but declined. Although she was saddened by her daughter's death, she was more distraught that any chance of recovering Rosings for herself had been lost now and did not wish to be seen by her neighbours.

Richard announced to his family that he would be leasing out Rosings for the next year or two as he had made plans to travel to several of Darcy's properties and he did not want it to sit empty. Everyone agreed to the idea and travel plans were made. Lord and Lady Matlock would return to London with Georgiana to continue to prepare her for her season, Viscount and Viscountess would return to Matlock, and the Darcys and Richard would spend their mourning period in Ramsgate and then travel to Bath for a fortnight before heading to Netherfield for Jane Bingley's confinement. They planned to all reunite in London for Georgiana's season before the Darcys and Richard removed to Pemberley in June.

~*~~~*~~~*~~~*~~~*~~~*~~~*~~~*~~~*~

PART 2

Chapter 1

Ramsgate was a painful memory for Darcy, as he had equated it with Georgiana's near elopement, but having his wife here now, who had never been to Ramsgate before, filled his heart with joy, as she loved the beautiful little town and was excited by everything she saw. He made love to her every night and replaced his bad memories with all the care and passion his wife shared with him.

Due to mourning customs, they kept their outings to a minimum and enjoyed playing with the twins immensely and there were many laughs as they enjoyed their intimate time together.

Darcy and Richard worked diligently to oversee their responsibilities and with Rosings out to lease and his selling off his grandmother's cottage, Richard was kept very busy. His grandmother's cottage would fetch him a handsome amount and he decided to gift the Darcys with an outing to the theatre after their mourning period ended.

Elizabeth was thrilled to see the sights and meet a few friends in the area. Ramsgate was a beautiful place and she understood why so many would come here for a holiday. She was especially thrilled when Richard met his friend at the theatre and introduced them.

"I am very glad to see you again! This is my cousin Fitzwilliam Darcy and his wife

Elizabeth Darcy." Richard began. Turning to the Darcys, "This is my good friend Captain Frederick Wentworth and his wife Anne Wentworth. How have you been?" He asked Captain Wentworth.

"Everything has been wonderful. My Anne is expecting our first child," he gleamed. "I have read of your trial in London. I was thrilled that you squashed that woman to bits! I did hear of your cousin Anne de Bourgh's passing. I am deeply sorry for your loss." Captain Wentworth offered.

Elizabeth spoke with Mrs. Wentworth and found her to be a soft-spoken and genteel woman. She liked her immediately and asked her to dinner the next night while the men were speaking. Richard kindly offered them the use of the box that he rented for the night and the Wentworths accepted.

Darcy sat next to his wife and Richard sat next to Elizabeth while Mrs. Wentworth and the captain sat behind them. They were enjoying the production immensely and Richard beamed, hearing Elizabeth's gasps and laughter during the show.

Richard was caught off-guard, though, when Elizabeth's wrap had slipped off her chair. He had seen it fall and turned to pick it up for her, when Wentworth grabbed it first and gently covered it over Elizabeth. He was surprised when Wentworth winked at him and returned his sights to the stage.

What the hell is happening? Does he have eyes for my Elizabeth? Richard thought. He tried to not dwell on it, as Wentworth had been a friend for years and had always been an upstanding man. But his jealousy grew when the men had gone to get drinks for the ladies during the first intermission.

While Darcy was ordering wines for the ladies, Wentworth whispered and asked, "So, Fitzwilliam. Tell me more about Mrs. Darcy. She is absolutely stunning. Do not get me wrong, I am happily married to my dear Anne, but one would have to be blind to ignore how gorgeous Darcy's wife is. Is she happy with her husband? I would bet she is a fantastic fuck." He smirked.

Is he bloody trying to start something with Elizabeth? Damn it! I thought him more honourable than this! Richard gruffly replied, "She is very happy. Do not get distracted by her beauty; Darcy will skin you alive if you attempt anything, Wentworth. This is my first and last warning, *friend*. If you do anything to hurt them, I will not tolerate it."

Captain Wentworth laughed at this. "Come, come, Fitzwilliam. You act like she is *your* wife. Are you in love with her? I am only joking!" He lowered his voice further. "You used to talk about beautiful wives all the time. I am just pent up. Anne does not wish to risk any dangers to the babe and I have not had her for a month now. My cock is itching for a good lay but I would not cheat on her. I love her to death and only wish she would sleep with me." He sighed. "Mrs. Darcy had twins, did she not? How did Darcy do without her for months? He seems smitten with her."

Richard relaxed a little. "Yes, he loves her and I care for their happiness so you had better not talk like that again. Mrs. Darcy is a rare woman and she inspires good in everyone. I know for a fact that Darcy and his wife were constantly on each other during the pregnancy," he saw Wentworth's eyes widen, "and the babes were fine. Eli... Mrs. Darcy invited both of you to dinner tomorrow and perhaps the ladies will have a chance to speak. I will talk to her to see if there is a gentle way to educate your wife." He saw Wentworth smile broadly. "But you must promise me to act a gentleman. No more crass military-men talk. I will not tolerate it!"

Captain Wentworth raised his hands, "I apologise. I know you are a proper gentleman now and I forgot that you had saved their lives last spring. I know you and Darcy would both kill me if I tried to seduce her, not that I would. She is beautiful, though; the most exquisite figure I have seen in a while. She is just the type of woman you chased. Are you not courting anyone? Why have you not married? Do you want me to introduce you to Anne's sister? She is an Elizabeth, too, and pretty. She is a fucking snob, but she would jump your bones." He laughed.

Richard burst out laughing. He had seen Elizabeth Elliot in London at a ball years ago and found her repulsive. She was the most obnoxious woman he had ever heard of, and definitely on the shelf now at over thirty years old. "Language!" Richard laughed. He saw Darcy approach with drinks in hand. "I would not stick that Elizabeth with a ten-foot pole!" He saw Darcy's brows furrow, hearing Elizabeth's name. Richard quickly shook his head while Wentworth was reaching for Anne's glass. "Let us return to the lovely ladies." He smiled.

Darcy nudged him as Wentworth walked ahead. "What was that about Elizabeth?" He whispered.

Richard reassured him. "We were talking about Mrs. Wentworth's sister, Elizabeth Elliot. Shrew, that one. The captain has not had sex for a month with his wife expecting, poor sod. We will need to ask our Elizabeth to fix it. Once again, our wonderful wife is desperately needed to help another soul from exploding in his breeches." They both chuckled.

During the second intermission, Richard kept a close eye on Wentworth. He saw that his friend was still flirting with Elizabeth and she was teasing him in return. Darcy was smiling and laughing as well, while Mrs. Wentworth shyly participated.

Anne Wentworth was eight and twenty and a pretty enough brunette. She had a soft-countenance and was a kind woman. *She is nothing to my Elizabeth. No wonder his eyes are wandering to my wife. I hope he is not too tempted. I know I can never control myself around her.*

He became very jealous, though, when Elizabeth laughed loudly at something Wentworth said and she laid her hand on his arm. He saw the cad rub her fingers softly and turned green with envy that she would be seeking another man's attention. *Calm yourself, man!* He told himself. *I am sure it is nothing; it has to be nothing. Damn it, Elizabeth! Why do you have to be so tempting?!*

Chapter 2

After the show, the group parted with the promise to see each other the next day, and the Darcys and Richard boarded their carriage. Richard sat with his arms crossed and attempted to not be angry but as he continued to dwell on Wentworth's comments of her beauty and the way she touched that man's arm, he became more irate by the minute.

Darcy and Elizabeth spoke excitedly of the play and the company, as they had a great time and were thrilled that they were able to enjoy themselves a little in Ramsgate. After they arrived at their Ramsgate home, which was only a short distance away, Richard requested Darcy for time with Elizabeth.

"Darcy, may I have a few minutes with Elizabeth?" Richard asked.

Darcy smirked, "I know it has been a while but must it be right now? It is late and she is tired."

Richard looked quite serious. "It is not for... that, Darcy. I need to speak to her on that delicate issue and some other things."

Darcy saw the stern face of his cousin and knew at once that he had more on his mind than his sexual release. He knew that Richard wanted to talk to Elizabeth about Wentworth's wife's pregnancy but did not know what else could be wrong. Entrusting him to fill him in later, he agreed. "Certainly, Richard. Elizabeth, I will wait up for you. Good night, Richard." And he departed, leaving the two alone in the study.

Elizabeth was curious as to Richard's serious demeanour. "What is the matter, Richard? What do you wish to speak to me about?" She sat down to await the discussion.

Richard paced instead of sitting with her. After several moments, he spoke severely. "Did you have a good time? Did you enjoy the captain's company?"

Elizabeth smiled broadly. "Oh, yes. I had a wonderful time. Thank you so much for arranging it. It was a delightful surprise, Richard." She stood and walked towards him to embrace him.

Richard saw her approach and stepped back several feet to avoid her touch, raising his hand to stop her. *I need to think clearly.* He imagined her being affectionate with Wentworth and boiled with rage now. "I saw you, Elizabeth! I SAW YOU! You were flirting with him and you enjoyed his attentions, did you not? Wentworth told me that he had not fucked for a month and he wants to get under your skirt and you ENCOURAGED it! How could you?! Do you wish him in your bed?" He fumed.

Elizabeth was shocked at his accusations. Tears rose to her eyes but she was determined to be strong and she took several breaths to calm her anger. She had noticed that the captain had flirted with her a bit but she did not think about it much until he touched her hand and she quickly realised that although Captain Wentworth was not serious, he was crossing the line with her and she had immediately put a stop to it. She had kept her distance for the rest of the evening but of course Richard had not perceived anything else.

"Oh, Richard, have you so little faith in me?" Elizabeth huffed.

Richard rushed over to her and held her arms. "I love you. I LOVE YOU! You have TWO husbands who love you and I burn for you and want you so desperately. Do you want him? Do you want to fuck him? I am dying to touch you and make love to you but seeing you with another man kills me. Watching you smiling and flirting with him in front me and Darcy, how could you?! I have not been jealous of Darcy because I have long accepted the fact that you belong to him, but for you to touch another man..."

Elizabeth quickly jumped forward and embraced him tightly. *I love him so much. How could he get jealous over the captain?* She hugged his body with both arms and held him as close as possible and remained still. She felt his breath calm and his arms around her after a long minute.

"It is not fair, Elizabeth. How am I to remain angry with you when I have you so close?" Richard finally spoke. He smelled her hair and began to kiss her temple as he caressed her back.

She raised her head to see his lips travel down as he began to kiss her jaw and neck. She felt his arousal against her as he continued to burrow into her neck, but when he tried to kiss her mouth, she pushed him away firmly and stepped back. *He needs to understand that I did not do anything to incur his wrath.*

Richard grunted in frustration. "Aargh! You are killing me, woman!" He huffed and sat down.

Elizabeth took a seat across from him. "Please listen carefully. I was NOT flirting, Richard. Fitzwilliam was with me the entire time and we both had a wonderful time. I do not know what gave you the idea that I was flirting with Captain Wentworth but as soon as I figured out that *he* was flirting with *me*, I maintained my distance from him so he does not get the wrong idea. I know nothing about his not *fucking* for a month, Richard, but his wife is lovely and it was obvious to me that they love each other very much. You saw a man who is a natural flirt, just like you, Richard, and are placing the blame onto me. I might have teased but it was harmless and I spoke to him the same as I did to his wife. Just because a handsome man spoke to me, you jumped to a conclusion that was not only erroneous but hurtful to my feelings."

"Ha! So, you *do* find him handsome?!" Richard shouted.

Elizabeth laughed with no humour in her voice. "Haha! I will not justify that with an answer. I am leaving now. You need to blow off some steam and perhaps you would like to visit one of your two hundred whores or your former mistress! Perhaps if you fuck one of them, you will think more clearly before you speak to me again. Good night." She stood up and turned away to take her leave.

Richard ran to her and grabbed her. He embraced her tightly and spoke, "Damn it, Elizabeth. You know there is only one woman I want to fuck. God! What I would give..." He held her against him as he took several deep breaths. "Do not leave me. I cannot stand to have you turn from me. I am sorry. I am sorry for the accusation and for not behaving like a gentleman." Feeling her body relax, he kissed her neck and caressed her back again. "I am sorry for the bad language as well, wife. I should have trusted you but I acted like a jealous fool instead." He kissed her lips and she had allowed it this time. He probed his tongue inside her mouth and kissed her passionately. "You are so tempting. He thought you so gorgeous and even asked me if I was in love with you. He is right. You are gorgeous and I am desperately in love with you." *Damn it! I am going to burst. I need to calm myself!*

He released her after kissing her cheek. "I am sorry, Elizabeth. You did nothing wrong and I should have been kinder to you. Wentworth told me that after his wife found out about the pregnancy, he had been barred from her bed for a month and his frustrations made me frustrated. I told him that I would ask you to perhaps bring it up with his wife at dinner tomorrow. It has been a month for me, Elizabeth. I miss you so much." He stepped away from her and walked over to the fireplace so he could control his passion.

Elizabeth sympathised with him. Her husband had been making love to her every night and she felt the guilt of not paying Richard enough attention. They had deeply kissed several times but she knew it had not been enough for him, as he was such a passionate man with a strong physical need.

"Richard, will you sit down for me?" She requested. She waited until Richard took a deep breath and sat down on the couch. She walked in front of him and set herself down onto his lap. She wrapped her arms around his neck and kissed his earlobe. "I am sorry for neglecting you, husband. I was upset that you were so quick to accuse me of having a wavering heart when you know my heart belongs to you and Fitzwilliam. I do love you very much, Richard. I wish you would love me now. Could you kiss me again?" She flirted with him.

How does she do it? I wanted to be angry with her but she calms me in seconds and completely turns the table on me. I need her desperately and she is a temptress! Richard thought as he kissed her neck and rubbed her back.

"I love you so much, Elizabeth. You are all I ever want." He obeyed quickly and began to kiss her mouth again. His arousal returned in full force and he was ready to release when Elizabeth abruptly lifted her lips off his and shifted her position. His hard cock had been rubbing against her hip but then she stood to pull her skirts up and sat astride him. He could feel her hot core against his aching erection.

She is the best thing in my life. I was an idiot to accuse her. God, this feels so good!

Richard frantically kissed her mouth and grunted and released while she gyrated her womanhood against him and made love to him. She was connected to him so closely over their clothes and it was the most sensual feeling he had ever experienced.

Richard kissed her face and neck all over as he held her in his arms. "Oh, my god! Elizabeth, that was incredible. I am sorry for everything I said to you. You are innocent and honourable and I should have never questioned you. I love you. Thank you. Thank you for loving me so much. That was unbelievable."

Elizabeth kissed him softly. "I love you. I know you share me with Fitzwilliam and I am grateful that you do not become jealous of him. You never have to fear me with a wandering eye. You and Fitzwilliam keep me quite busy and I will never tire of you two. I accept your apology and I apologise to you in return for my lack of attention to you. I know it is not the same as *fucking*, but I hope you are satiated enough."

Richard chuckled. "Language!" They both laughed. "I am more than satiated. Your love means the world to me and nothing else compares. Thank you for your love, Elizabeth. I needed you so much. My releasing with you in my arms is the greatest joy. I love you with all my heart." He kissed her tenderly and caressed her face. "It is late. I will have to run to my room to clean up this mess but I will see you for breakfast, my love. Please let Darcy know what happened and I will begin my grovelling tomorrow as soon as the sun is up." He smiled as Elizabeth giggled. He helped her to stand and pulled out his favourite handkerchief to absorb some of his wetness.

"Hey, is that my handkerchief? Where did you get it and why is it so shredded?" Elizabeth saw the small cloth.

Richard grinned. "It is what you used to wipe my mouth with when I fought with Darcy, believing that he had cheated on you with Hannah. I have used it several times and had it laundered but I keep needing it whenever I think of you. I will have to keep it safe in a box now." He stuffed it inside his breeches with a smirk. "It is my favourite token from you."

Elizabeth's laughter tinkled in the room. "Good night, husband. I will need to give you more tokens of my love. Perhaps a lock of hair next time?" She winked.

Richard walked her to her room and kissed her cheek. "Good night, wife. I love you. I love you with all my heart."

~*~

Darcy grumbled when he saw Richard at breakfast. Elizabeth was exhausted and was to join them shortly but he had wanted to speak with his cousin alone.

"Richard, you idiot. Elizabeth told me what you accused her of. Do you truly believe that she would flirt with a man like that? I was with her the entire time and she did nothing wrong and it is her natural way. She is kind and sweet and innocent and you dare accuse her? She thought she should be washing her mouth with soap after some time with you. She said she had never heard or used such terrible language until she met you. She had to tell you to go fuck one of your whores, for Christ's sake, Richard! How could you get jealous over Wentworth? He acted just like you used to. Do you not remember? You flirted ten times worse and actually took some of those loose women to bed."

Darcy huffed and paced around the dining table. "I know who you used to bed and some were married women. You dare place our dear Elizabeth in those whores' category? You still flirt, Richard. Even at Pemberley, even in London, you might not be dancing the night away but I have seen you still flirt and trifle with women. Do not blame Wentworth for being a charming sea captain when you, a gentleman, are doing the same thing. Do not dare disrespect our wife again!"

Richard immediately replied, "I am so sorry. I apologised to Elizabeth already and I apologise to you as well, Darcy. I was a jealous monster and did not think clearly and I know it is no excuse but I was pent up and did not think it through. I told her my grovelling will begin today and I will make it up to you as well. I do know that Wentworth is exactly as I had been but he is a good man. He loved his wife for a very long time before finally reconciling with her a year ago. He would not throw that away, even for Elizabeth, who did nothing and will do nothing to encourage him." Richard stood close to Darcy now. "Elizabeth loved me most kindly last night and I am definitely more clear-headed now. I know I am an idiot and I hope you will forgive me."

Darcy huffed out a deep breath. "I am glad you know you are an idiot. Yes, I forgive you. She forgave you already and we had a good laugh but I was upset on her behalf this morning. I know you have been pent up. I cannot go a day without her love and it is not fair for you to wait for a month or more. I will try to give you more time with her but it is difficult away from Pemberley or Darcy House and we must be discreet. Be kind to our wife, Richard. I will not tolerate any disrespect." Darcy put his hand out and Richard immediately shook it.

They began to break their fast when Elizabeth soon arrived and they spoke of the enjoyment of the theatre and how to prepare for their dinner with the Wentworths.

~*~

"What beautiful flowers you have here, Mrs. Darcy!" Mrs. Wentworth commented. "I have not seen so many colours of roses before. These are the most beautiful blooms I have seen and so many!"

Elizabeth beamed. "Yes, my dear *husband* purchased them as he knew I loved all the colours. I did not expect him to obtain ALL of the colours at once, but he is ever generous."

Richard smirked. *Her husband had to pay penance for being stupid but I am glad she is pleased.*

The five diners sat at dinner and the conversation was quite pleasant. Richard had pulled the captain aside and gave him a warning before being seated. "Behave yourself, Frederick. Mrs. Darcy is no pub-wench and her husband will kill you if you flirt with her. Remember, she is a lady and the only one who can help you get back in your wife's bed!"

246

Captain Wentworth conceded and agreed to behave immediately. "Thank you, Fitzwilliam. I promise to be good. I have a feeling she would put me in my place if I should not."

Richard smiled. "So true. Mrs. Darcy is known for her sharp tongue. Believe me, I hear it plenty." The gentlemen both laughed.

Captain Wentworth found Mrs. Darcy to be fascinating but behaved himself. He was itching to be intimate with his dear Anne again and although conversing happily and smiling, he restrained himself to ensure he was acting as gentlemanly as possible. He was awed at the changes that he noted in his friend as well. The former colonel was easy-going and jovial as always, but the way he carried himself and the way he spoke with Anne and the Darcys was definitely different. He could see that Mr. Fitzwilliam was a proper gentleman and very respectable.

Fitzwilliam has become more like his distinguished cousin. I forget that he is the son of an earl and can carry himself quite well. No wonder he was offended by my crass comments last night. I owe him an apology. I need to learn to be a gentleman like him now that I have retired. Wentworth thought to himself.

"So, I have heard a bit about your father, Mrs. Wentworth. I understand Sir Walter and your sister are residing in Bath? We are to travel there next week. Your husband's sister resides at Kellynch Hall?" Elizabeth asked.

Anne Wentworth softly commented. "Yes, my father is leasing a townhouse in Camden Place and after my marriage to Frederick four months ago, it has become awkward for Frederick's sister to reside in my old home, so they are looking for a new place. Kellynch Hall is a dear home to me but I am afraid it will most likely be sold off by next year. My father has not been successful at retrenching so far but I can only hope that the new owners will be good people. It is hard to think of my childhood home no longer being accessible."

"I am so sorry to hear that. Where are you residing now?" Elizabeth asked.

Captain Wentworth answered. "We will be in Ramsgate for another fortnight and then we will return to London. We hope to see you all there sometime in the future. Our hope is to find a place in Somerset where we first met and Anne's sister Mary still resides there. For now, we have a London townhouse until we find a country house for our growing family." He beamed.

Soon, the ladies departed for the separation of sexes.

Elizabeth sat next to Mrs. Wentworth. "I am so pleased to have made your acquaintance, Mrs. Wentworth. It is always a pleasure to meet Mr. Fitzwilliam's friends but I am especially happy to have met you."

"Oh, I feel the same, Mrs. Darcy. Will you call me Anne?" Mrs. Wentworth asked.

Elizabeth smiled fully. "Only if you will call me Lizzy, Anne. Thank you." She leaned closer to Anne. "I congratulate you on your pregnancy. You are now three months along?" Anne nodded. "I have twin boys; they were born in August and they bring so much joy to us all. I recall being absolutely gigantic during the pregnancy and we did not know until I was about six months along that I was carrying twins." Elizabeth laughed. "Thankfully, my husband still loved me with my huge size and never ceased to share our bed."

Elizabeth took a sip of her tea, noticing that Anne's eyes were huge when she spoke of sharing the bed. She nonchalantly continued, "I am glad we are alone and can talk about married-women things. I can see that your husband loves you very much and it must have been a love match. I have never slept apart from my dear husband and I treasure our intimacy." She sipped her tea again.

Anne spoke after several quiet moments. "Lizzy, may I ask... could you tell me if you were... intimate... during your pregnancy?" She was blushing profusely. "I had thought... I was told..."

Elizabeth smiled. "But of course; there is no harm to the child. My babes were kept quite safe and as long as Fitzwilliam was gentle to not press on me, it was quite pleasant." She leaned and touched her friend's hand. "You have a younger sister with children but no one else, am I correct?" Anne nodded. "Please feel free to ask me anything you would like. I know I am young but I would be happy to talk with you about *anything* at all, Anne. Let me ask you this; when did you discover that you were with child?"

Anne replied, "One month ago. After I had missed my courses, my maid suspected that I was with child and I consulted a midwife."

Elizabeth asked, "So you were having relations for two months prior without knowledge of your being with child? You were intimate with your husband from the beginning of your marriage, am I correct?" Anne nodded. "So just because you find yourself with child, how would further intimacies suddenly hurt your babe? I had the fortune to speak with a very motherly housekeeper with six children and I consulted many books. It is perfectly normal and healthy, even encouraged, to continue to share your bed with your husband. I would rather my husband be in my bed than to seek outside relief!"

Elizabeth saw that Anne understood her meaning clearly now and moved on to other topics. As Elizabeth would be packing and leaving in a few days for Bath, they agreed to write to each other and continue their friendship by correspondence. Elizabeth also thought it would be a great opportunity to have Captain Wentworth approach the Crofts about leasing Rosings, as Richard had been looking for candidates to reside there.

~*~

The men were drinking some port and sharing their memories. Richard told Darcy of how he met the captain seven years ago, when he and his army mates were about to be thrown out of a pub in Spain due to a mistake in the language and offending the owner's wife, and how Wentworth came to their rescue to help clear up the situation and Richard had bought his new Navy friends a round of drinks.

The captain spoke of some of his experiences at sea and how pleased that he had recently retired. He had married his wife as soon as his retirement was finalised.

"How is your wound, Fitzwilliam? A couple of years ago, in the summer, you got hurt when some arse of a new recruit threw some musket balls into the fire?" Captain Wentworth asked.

Richard scoffed. "I should have killed him after my recovery but he got twenty lashes and was sent his way. I heard he died on the continent but at least he died bravely." Turning to Darcy, he explained, "One of the musket balls heated up and bounced out of the fire and went through my hip. I had to have surgery to get it removed and was feverish for a week. Do you remember me whining and miserable at Darcy House because I refused to stay with my parents?"

Darcy laughed. "You were the biggest baby, I recall. That was before you went to Dover, after I returned to town with Georgiana, was it not? When you returned, I was engaged and you met Elizabeth."

Richard smiled softly. "Yes, it was that same time." He could not speak more. He thought of Elizabeth and how miserable he was then, falling in love with her that autumn but not being able to have her and desiring her more than anyone else he had ever met.

Captain Wentworth interrupted his thoughts, "We visited that one tart together, what was her name, Mary, Martha? The screamer."

Richard flushed red. He had many conquests and he had been proud to share countless experiences with Darcy before, but now having Elizabeth in his life, he was ashamed of every woman he had ever used.

He embarrassingly answered, "Maria. I do not recall her being worth my time. I should not have seen her but after my injury, I was trying to prove to myself that I was back to normal, I think. But I have given up that life and am trying to be a proper gentleman like Darcy. Let us not talk of that, Wentworth. I am certain your wife would not wish you to relive your glory days with loose women, and Darcy here, is too virtuous to know of what we are speaking." He winked at Darcy.

"Oh, but you must have had many adventures, Darcy!" Captain Wentworth pressed. "You are a handsome fellow. You must have had women throwing themselves at you. You look very happy with your wife now but certainly you had many enjoyments before her?"

Richard laughed while Darcy grinned. "She is my first and last, Wentworth. I will love her and only her until the day I die." Darcy proudly answered.

Richard thought to himself as he smiled, *Me, too. Only Elizabeth.*

Captain Wentworth was stunned. "How in the world?! I did not think it was possible for a man in his twenties to keep it in his breeches and it is an incredible feat. I salute you, sir. You must have some iron will. I wanted to marry my Anne when I was two and twenty but after she broke our first engagement, I threw myself into every whore I could find for a few years until I realised I needed to find a wife. I was heartbroken but I should not have used so many women. But after reuniting with my dear Anne again last year, I was so happy to finally win her back." Taking the last gulp of his drink, he looked at Darcy. "I thank you for your wife's help in speaking with Anne. I truly would not seek elsewhere but I have been desperate. I am glad we ran into you, Fitzwilliam." He grinned broadly.

Darcy replied, "Perhaps it was providence that brought us together. Elizabeth has been very pleased with Mrs. Wentworth's friendship and I hope our friendship continues to grow." He kicked Richard's leg. "This scoundrel has his good uses." They all laughed together.

Captain Wentworth's respect for Darcy and Richard grew even further, as they began to speak of estate management and several investment opportunities and how to care for the family first. He vowed to himself to care for his little family and to do everything in his power to provide for them.

~*~

The men joined the ladies a few minutes later and they entered the drawing room laughing together.

When Captain Wentworth saw his beloved wife in the drawing room, she beamed brightly and knew Mrs. Darcy had spoken with her. He smiled and sat next to Anne and kissed her hand. She squeezed his hand and whispered, "I love you, Frederick."

He knew that he would be invited back to his wife's bed and was infinitely grateful that Richard had spoken to Mrs. Darcy. He would be sure to send a bottle of champagne to his old buddy and new friends.

As they took their leave, Anne embraced Elizabeth in appreciation of their blooming friendship and promised to see each other in London in the spring. Captain Wentworth shook both Darcy and Richard's hands and bowed over Elizabeth's hand, kissing it gently and whispered, "Thank you, Mrs. Darcy. You are a true gem."

Richard watched the interaction but trusted Elizabeth. She had made friends quickly and earned their loyalty time and time again with her gentle and kind heart, and he could not begrudge her that everyone found her irresistible. He was proud of her and his heart beat wildly when she turned and smiled at him. *She is beautiful and she is mine. I love her so much.*

~*~

Richard laughed heartily when a bottle of champagne arrived the next day with a letter of gratitude from Captain Wentworth. He shared the drink and the letter with the Darcys, ensuring that Elizabeth did not have more than one glass at a time, and the trio spoke of the Crofts as potential residents at Rosings as well as planning a few more activities in Ramsgate.

They enjoyed the remainder of their days in the little seaside town, spending time with the twins and collecting happy memories.

Chapter 3

Elizabeth looked around and was fascinated by this city. She had heard and read about Bath but it was wonderful to finally be here in person. Their property was a house in Camden Place and was the largest townhouse on the block. Once again, she was amazed by the responsibilities on Fitzwilliam's shoulders, as he had to manage numerous properties and investments. Richard and her husband had been ensconced for hours on end at times in the study in Ramsgate to catch up on their correspondences, and Elizabeth hoped that they would be able to find some entertainment and rest more leisurely here.

As the carriage stopped in front of the house, Richard exited first and he was already being greeted by an acquaintance.

"Fitzwilliam! I did not know you would be in Bath! How have you been?" He heard. He turned and saw his university friend who had been a year behind him.

Darcy and Elizabeth exited the carriage and Richard turned to them. "Devon! May I introduce you? You know my cousin Darcy; this is his wife, Mrs. Elizabeth Darcy. Mrs. Darcy, this is Edmund Carlisle, Earl of Devon."

"We are acquainted. Darcy. Mrs. Darcy, it is good to see you again." Lord Devon bowed as he kissed her hand.

Elizabeth curtsied, "How have you been, sir? Congratulations on your marriage."

"Yours as well, Mrs. Darcy." Lord Devon replied. He turned and spoke with Richard. "Fitzwilliam, I know you have just arrived but I must invite you for dinner to meet my wife and her sister Grace. We are also hosting Grace's friend, Mrs. White. Here is my card. Shall you see us tomorrow night?" Richard nodded. They shook hands and Lord Devon departed.

After entering the foyer, Darcy wanted to give Elizabeth a tour. Richard wanted to ask how Elizabeth knew Devon but the servants were busy unloading and carrying their trunks and soon, the babies arrived and there was a flurry of activity. He excused himself to his usual room where he had stayed in his youth here and changed out of his clothing for a bath.

As he lay back in the tub, he relaxed and remembered every detail of his private moment with Elizabeth when he climaxed while kissing her. He stroked himself as he recalled kissing her and tasting her tongue, how he held her tightly against her lovely bosoms and his erection pressed against her hot core while she sat on him. He stroked faster and released with a grunt. It had been just as powerful to recall the memory as he touched himself each time.

It had been over a week since he had been intimate with her but every time he thought of it, his passion was still strong and fervent. He had released three times with her now and each time was even better than before. He wondered when he would have a chance to do it again since they had been busy with packing and playing with the twins the past few days.

The babies had begun to laugh and sit up and it had been a joy to spend so much time with his boys. He was pleased that Darcy and Elizabeth wanted their children in their lives more than just the once daily checks with the nannies to remain distant. Darcy and Richard were always carrying them somewhere and showing them different views and offering them a toy. Elizabeth would often find Darcy and Richard playing with the babies' toys and she laughed at them that they were still little boys.

He dressed and exited his room and walked over to the Master's room to see if they were available for an outing and he knocked but did not hear anyone within. He walked to the Mistress' room and hearing some muffled sounds, knocked, but could not tell if he was bid to enter. Having had so much freedom between the three of them at Pemberley and Rosings, he slowly opened the door a crack to check inside and he could immediately see that Darcy and Elizabeth had not heard his knock due to their current activity.

He quickly closed the door and returned to his room. He grunted and threw himself face down on the bed.

Argh! Of course, they are having sex again! Damn it. I am hard again.

He turned himself over and opened his flap to free his erection. *Blasted! I did not realise that Elizabeth did that for Darcy. Damn lucky bastard. I would give anything for her to take me like that.* He stroked himself faster as he recalled what he saw in that split second. Elizabeth was on her knees on the floor while Darcy sat reclined on the chair while her head bobbed down on his groin and making loud sloshing noises while Darcy was moaning and groaning. *Oh my god! Argh!* He came again. *Oh, Elizabeth, what you do to me.*

He straightened his clothes and headed downstairs without stopping near their rooms.

~*~

Richard was greatly enjoying himself at dinner with Devon. It had been a while since he was at a party where conversations were on military topics he enjoyed. The food was some of his favourites and he was served a superb cognac. Devon was always good for a laugh and he had been a little stiff but his wife appeared to have loosened him quite well. Being General Wentington's daughter, Lady Devon was clever and knew many histories about wars and had stories that her father had told her. Her sister, Grace, was a tall brunette of nineteen who had sparkling brown eyes and also just as intelligent. Miss Grace Wentington had come out two years ago and was quite pretty and buxom, and Lady Devon told him that her sister had several offers but that she had not found the right person yet. Miss Grace was charming and would add on to Lady Devon's stories and make the room laugh with her wit.

Mrs. Claire White was two and twenty, who was blonde and was extremely well-endowed, although on the plump side. She had been snatched up quickly after her coming out and married a colonel who unfortunately died after being called back to the continent after one year of marriage. She and Miss Grace were best of friends.

~*~

Richard returned to Camden Place late and found Elizabeth sitting alone in the library. She was intently reading and did not hear him enter and he stood silently after closing the door to admire her. She was sitting with her shoes off and feet tucked under her skirt and biting her lower lip as she frowned or raised her eyebrows according to the book's plot.

She is so beautiful. Oh, my love.

Richard approached the chair and stood in front of her and coughed.

"AH! Oh, Richard! I have been reading and I did not hear you. How are you? I have not seen much of you since we arrived." She smiled brightly, putting down her book.

He lifted her up and sat down on the couch, placing her on his lap and held her. He kissed her hair and caressed her arm. *I have missed this so much!* "I had not realised that Bath would be filled with so many acquaintances. Apparently, it is a good time to take the waters and word of my presence spread quickly. I dined with my old brigade commander last night and with Lord Devon tonight. You met him, do you recall? When we first arrived yesterday?" Richard asked.

She blushed. "Yes, I am acquainted with him."

"Oh, yes! I recall that you knew him. How did you meet? I do not remember seeing him at parties when we were in London. I believe he was either on his honeymoon or at his country home." Richard asked, as he closed his eyes and held her in his arms with his face on her neck. He trailed several kisses on her neck and décolletage and became aroused, as he relaxed while smelling her lavender scent, thinking about how he could take her to his bed and make love to her. He had enjoyed several glasses of French cognac after dinner and had drunk a bit more than his usual, although it was not more than he could handle, but he was definitely feeling more amorous than his wont.

He felt her body stiffen slightly and held her closer to his chest, lifting his head to kiss her hair. Her one hand was wrapped behind his back and the other was playing with his waistcoat buttons. *Bliss!*

"I, I know him from several years ago. Three years ago, to be exact. I met him at a ball and he asked me to dance." She paused.

"Oh, that was nice. He is a good fellow. Good dancer." Richard sleepily replied. He loved having her in his arms and wished he could sleep with her all night. Just sleep.

Elizabeth spoke again. "Yes, he was a good dancer, from what I recall. He called on me the next day and the day after that." She paused again. "He proposed to me."

Richard was smiling as he relaxed. *Called on you, yes. He would call on you. Wait, what? PROPOSE?!* He snapped to attention, startling Elizabeth as he jumped to sit upright.

"WHAT? He, Devon, proposed to you? When? Did you say three years ago? Damn it, he did not say a word!" Richard's head was spinning. *Shit! He is to come here tomorrow.* "Elizabeth, I invited him here for luncheon tomorrow, along with his wife, her sister, and her friend. I did not think you would mind and the ladies were so pleasant that I thought you would like their company. I can cancel. I will cancel." Richard stated.

"No, no! I am glad you did. I would be happy to meet them. We are both married and although initially awkward, I am certain we can be cordial. I am sorry I did not have a chance to tell you before. Fitzwilliam already knows, as I told him before we married, but there is no way you would have known. It was so long ago. It will be fine." Elizabeth confirmed.

Richard sat still. "You turned down Devon? He was probably the second most eligible bachelor after Darcy. And Haversham, too. What was wrong with Devon?" Richard asked, still in shock. *He is rich, good-looking, and intelligent. And an earl now!*

"He was too proud and condescending of my family. He did not treat me as an equal but wanted an arm piece, Richard. I could not respect him or find myself being a wife to him. I did not love him." Elizabeth honestly replied.

"I am thankful that you waited. I could not believe that Darcy courted you the day after he met you and proposed to you the day after that, but I always thought any woman would be stupid to turn him down. If he were not worthy, you would have turned him down as well, am I correct?" Richard asked cautiously.

Elizabeth laughed. "Oh, if he had been his taciturn self when I first met him, and if he had not apologised after he insulted me, I am certain he would have been the last man in the world that I would have been prevailed to marry. He was handsome but very arrogant, you know."

Richard kissed her hand. "And me? How would you have found me, should I have met you first?" He was burning with curiosity with what she would say. Darcy had mentioned what she said about him but that was after they had become friends.

"Oh, I would have found you friendly and a flirt. Dashing in that red coat of yours and absolutely charming, but would have seen through you quickly, I presume. I would have known that you would never offer for someone like me. You would not have wanted me for longer than to warm your bed, Richard, and you would have tired of me quickly, with all my impertinence, to move on to the next woman for a different challenge. You would have looked for an heiress with at least 50,000. Is that not the going rate for a second son of an earl? You might even be at three hundred women by now!" She teased.

Richard buried his face in her neck. He knew she had spoken the truth; the brutally honest, blunt truth, as guile or deception was not in her character. He felt the guilt of knowing that he would not have loved her enough. He would have made some effort to chase her then moved on. If he could have bedded her, he would have taken his pleasures and not have thought twice, whether he got her with child or if she loved him. He never took a maiden before, but with her, he would have made an exception. He would have taken what he wanted and moved on to the next conquest, knowing that she was not wealthy enough nor from a prestigious family. He recalled that even Frederick Wentworth married the daughter of a baronet and Anne Elliot had £10,000. Elizabeth would have been a nobody and he would have trifled with her but never considered to marry her. But his heart had been changed forever when he saw her at Darcy's townhouse and he was no longer that man. She had changed him and he cared nothing for wealth or status now. He wanted her more than anything he had ever wanted in his life. He completely loved this woman who was sitting on his lap, whose arms were around his waist, who was wearing his ring.

"I love you, Elizabeth. It is an honour and a privilege to love you and be loved by you." Richard whispered in her ear.

She smiled. She kissed his cheek and stood. "I love you, too. Well, I should be heading to bed. I will have to finish my book tomorrow. Sad to say, I had hoped to finish it tonight but *someone* needed some conversation." She teased.

Just then, the library door opened and a sleepy Darcy appeared. Still groggy, he asked, "My love, are you still reading? It is so late. Richard, I have not seen you for almost two days. You two catching up?" He approached yawning, wrapping a blanket over Elizabeth.

"Oh, yes. Richard interrupted my reading and I am still not done but I am too sleepy now to finish it. It will have to wait. I was telling him about Lord Devon and his proposals, Fitzwilliam." She smiled.

Richard jumped, "Proposals? As in more than one? Good lord!"

Elizabeth giggled. "Just three. Good night, Richard. You owe me for not allowing me to finish my book!" She gave a false scowl and left with Darcy as she giggled.

Richard walked to his room shaking his head. *Three proposals? Damn it! I am going to have to be on my guard tomorrow to see if he still has feelings for her. Only you, Elizabeth, would have turned down such prestigious suitors to fall in love with a poor man of 2,500 a year...*

Chapter 4

Luncheon was an awkward event. Elizabeth planned a wonderful meal, and although everyone was very cordial, it became almost like Shakespeare's comedy should an outsider be watching the scene.

Lord Devon was very proper and formal but as stories were shared and everyone began to relax, it was obvious that his eyes were turned to Elizabeth. Lady Devon was eyeing Darcy and Elizabeth in jealousy while Elizabeth was eyeing Mrs. White and Darcy. Richard was eyeing Devon while Miss Grace was eyeing Richard and Darcy. Darcy was surveying the whole room and looking for the nearest exit.

The guests conversed about several topics after the meal, similar to the evening before, and Richard definitely enjoyed the stories that Miss Grace was telling him now. Somehow, they were seated a little apart in the drawing room and Lady Devon and Mrs. White had doubled up their efforts to capture Darcy's attention by asking about the home and his parents and the history of some of the expensive heirlooms.

After the ladies had effectively isolated Darcy to a different room in the townhouse, Lord Devon sat next to Elizabeth and asked her about her marriage and children. She looked around and saw that it was a military-precision tactic of divide and conquer, as Darcy had been pulled out of the room to explain the large painting in the foyer and Richard's attention was captured by that flirt who was in her third season, who was constantly touching his person. She grew red when she saw that Richard was leering at that woman's décolletage after the harlot pulled her dress further down.

Elizabeth was on high alert when Lord Devon sat quite close to her with lust in his eyes and his hand inconspicuously grazed the side of her torso, very close to her breast as he leaned and breathed on her neck.

She stood up immediately and called out, "Richard!"

Richard's attention had been on Miss Grace but he stood sharply as his name was called and Lord Devon stood up as well.

Elizabeth continued, "Please excuse me. I am not feeling well. I will let my husband know and will retire to my rooms. It was a pl... My apologies for the sudden departure," and she swept out.

Richard was not certain what had happened. As he stood, he felt Miss Grace holding his arm very closely to her chest and he could see from the corner of his eye that she had pulled down her dress so far down that the edges of her nipples were visible. *Damn it! I have been blinded by her attentions and I was too distracted to keep an eye on Devon. Hell, I did not even realise Darcy was not here. It was a military strategy to isolate us and attack and I fell for it. That bloody bastard better not have harmed my Elizabeth.*

Darcy entered with the two ladies just then with a frown. *Blasted! Two against one, he never had a chance. What the hell do those ladies want with Darcy?* Richard was furious.

Richard finally spoke, "Devon. I wish you a good day. It was a pleasure seeing you again, ladies." He bowed to them each without kissing their hands.

After the party departed, Darcy turned to Richard, "What the hell happened, Richard? Were you not guarding her?"

"I do not know! I was talking to Miss Grace and then she suddenly stood up and excused herself. I did not see. Why were you not in the room?" Richard asked in frustration.

"The ladies begged me to show them the Judge's portrait and then began to corner me and flirt with me. I was trying to get away and then Elizabeth came out to say she had a headache." Darcy answered. "I must go to her. This is on YOUR head. You invited them here, Richard!" Then he rushed upstairs.

~*~

"Elizabeth, are you well?" Richard asked tentatively, as she sat in front of her fireplace. Darcy had spoken with her already and comforted her. Knowing the full story, he told Richard he had an hour with his wife to make a very thorough apology.

"I am well, Richard. I did have a headache but I feel better now. I apologise for cutting your luncheon party short." Elizabeth replied curtly, avoiding eye contact.

He sat next to her but without touching. He knew to apologise for not guarding her from Devon but she should have been angry at Devon. He did not know why she appeared upset with him.

"I am very sorry that I did not keep a better eye on you with Devon. After what you told me last night, I should have cancelled the luncheon but I thought you would be safe, with both Darcy and myself looking after you. Did he injure you? Did he say something to you?"

Elizabeth sighed. "He did not say anything but he touched my side after sitting very close to me." She sighed again and did not speak further.

"Oh, is that all? Well, I am very, very sorry for scheduling the lunch and not keeping that rake away from you, but I feel as if you are upset with me. Have I done something wrong, Elizabeth?" Richard carefully asked. *She always speaks her mind. She will rant and rave if I did something wrong. Why is she so quiet?*

After several moments, Elizabeth finally responded. "Miss Grace is very pretty, is she not? Tall and beautiful and young. Her father is the general that you admire and if you were still a colonel, she would be a great catch, am I correct?"

"Yes, but I do not care for her." Richard replied quickly.

"But you certainly enjoyed her company, Richard. As soon as she entered the house, I saw that her eyes were trained on you. You were the target for her capture and I am certain she, her sister, and her friend had a battle plan in place. Their goal was to divide and conquer, and you were so busy flirting and being flattered that you had no idea what was happening. She knew what you liked and how to speak to you as was probably coached by Lord Devon, who has known you for years. Of course, she heard about Rosings and how wealthy you are now; she knew what to say to you, how to say it, and how to capture your *undivided* attention. She will make you a good wife, Richard. She has the right lineage and £25,000, as her friend kept pointing out, and you would also be brother to an earl. Fitzwilliam told me that you always preferred brunettes and I watched you admiring her figure. She is perfect for you. Beauty, wealth, and status. Her father will ensure that you are connected with all the high-ranking officers that you esteem, and you can finally have a wife that you can actually bed." Elizabeth finished with disappointment.

"My god! This is what you think of me? That I would be so inconstant to you that I would drop you for the next pretty face that comes along? Thank you for explaining it to me so fully! You are a vain creature, Elizabeth Darcy, having had two men profess love to you all the time and a slew of men pursuing you, that if you are not the centre of attention for ONE meal, you feel neglected and wronged. I never asked you to take me to your bed. I KNOW what I am not allowed to have. I see you and Darcy making love when I cannot do so, but I gave up *everything* to be with you. I gave up all women before you were even married and I gave up my mistress because I felt like I was betraying you with her. I only ask to be in your presence and you scorn me because a pretty woman with an interesting conversation wants MY attentions for a change?!" Richard huffed.

Elizabeth stood and walked to the window. She remained quiet as she looked out but her tears rolled down slowly. *Ha! So, he does think she is pretty.* She wiped her face with her hand. *I hate being a jealous fool. Perhaps I am a vain creature, demanding his love and devotion when I cannot be his true wife. He should not be stuck with me like so. He needs to move on and find happiness and marry.*

Richard leaned his head back and massaged between his eyes. *Why am I fighting with her? Why the hell am I upset with Elizabeth? I know Miss Grace was flirting with me but I liked the attention. She smiled and teased and her décolletage was quite agreeable. I liked being desirable to someone. She was interesting to talk with and knew all the right things to say, but she could have never captured my attention for more than one meal. She is nothing to my Elizabeth. Could Elizabeth be right? She practiced her entrapment knowing how I would respond because Devon knew me so well?*

He thought for a few moments and realised that her conversations were everything that he had enjoyed; everything agreeable and calculated. *Blasted, I let my ego get in the way. Once again, I let my arrogance and pride of being such an eligible bachelor give the idea of more interest than I should ever have. I would have fallen into her trap and she could have been sitting on my lap to compromise me and I would have been stuck married to that conniving wench. Damn it! That harlot pulled down her dress so far down that I saw her nipples for god's sake! She is no lady and I was no gentleman. Why did I let her get that far? I already have a wife. Why, why could I not acknowledge by now that I am no longer a bachelor? I might not be married but I have a wife. My Elizabeth. How could I have hurt my beloved by paying too much attention to another?*

He wanted to hit himself as he thought more. *Damn it to hell! It was more than one meal. They plied me with drinks last night and I lost my focus. If Elizabeth gave half the attention to any man other than Darcy, I would murder that man.* He burned with jealousy as he imagined Elizabeth flirting and pulling down her dress to Captain Wentworth. *Blasted! My WIFE watched me ogle someone else's teats and I had the audacity to yell at HER? What the hell was I thinking? I WAS inconstant and ignored my Elizabeth. I did drop her for the next pretty face like an arse. It is all about MY behaviour and MY neglect. I neglected my WIFE. I called Miss Grace 'pretty', TWICE, to Elizabeth. Damn it! She is not so pretty; Elizabeth is so much more beautiful. Aargh! I accused her of calling Wentworth 'handsome' only last week. I hurt my beloved so and to accuse her as I did; what the hell is wrong with me? No wonder Darcy told me to beg for mercy. I made her cry again. I am an idiot, blaming her and accusing her for HER lack of understanding! How in the world am I going to make this right?*

He stood and walked behind Elizabeth and watched the streets outside with her. They both remained quiet a bit longer to settle all of their thoughts.

Elizabeth wiped her eyes. *Why do I never have a handkerchief?* Then Richard handed his to her. *I need to embroider some initials for him. These are so plain.* She thought, *No, his REAL wife should be doing that for him. Not his fake wife. I am a fake.* She returned to the fireplace but this time sat in the chair that only allowed for one. She needed a little distance.

Richard returned with her but was disappointed that she did not want to sit with him.

After several minutes, Elizabeth started, "Richard, I *am* a vain creature. I have been so spoiled by you and Fitzwilliam that I felt as if it was appropriate to say whatever I wished with you. It is not that I blurt out whatever flows into my head, but that I have been too open with you both that perhaps I should not speak so freely. I shall attempt to rein myself in so that I am more sensitive to your needs." She paused for several moments.

"Richard, I believe you should let me go. You resent that you have sacrificed so much, given up so much to be with me, and that resentment will eventually turn to anger, and someday, hate. I do not wish for you to regret what you have given up, the sacrifices you had to make, the pleasures that you had to forego. You say you only want my presence but your bitterness shows me that it will be always on your mind, that every time we argue, you will remind me at what cost you are with me. I do not want you to ever hate me, Richard, but I know it will become so." She paused again to gather her courage. *I love him but I must let him choose his own path.*

"I release you, Richard. Your head *was* turned today and you will find someone, I am certain. You are such a good man and I want you to be free to find a worthy woman, to find a *real* wife that you can fully love, to have your own children someday. You are, by far, the most eligible of bachelors and any woman will welcome your attentions. You are capable of so much love in your generous heart and I am certain there is someone perfect waiting for you." She swallowed a sob and placed his ring on the table in front of him.

Richard's heart broke to hear her speech. She had been right. Every time he was upset or frustrated, it had always been about what he had sacrificed. He always kept in his mind that he did a great deed to show her his love and that he had *earned* his place in her heart with what he gave up. What did he truly give up for her? He gave up his womanising ways. No woman ever inspired him like Elizabeth. He always stayed with Darcy when he was not at his office so he gave up no comfort. His mistress, he did not want her. He only ever wanted Elizabeth. He had meant what he said that releasing while kissing her was the greatest pleasure he had ever experienced. Having his beloved in his arms and loving her was more powerful and special than any other woman he had ever had. He had gained a family, someone else to look to make happy other than just himself. He had also gained a brother and his godsons.

His precious sons. It was an honour to hold them, to see them smiling at him, to see the joy in their eyes when he and Darcy played with them. And the pride in Elizabeth's eyes; the way she looked at him while he carried one or both of them, the love that shone through her smile; he would die a thousand deaths to see that smile.

He looked at the ring on the table. His grandmother's ring. No, Elizabeth's ring. The one that he pledged his love and dedication. The ring that he asked for nothing in return for her to wear, while he filled it with promises to dedicate the rest of his life to love her and bring her happiness. That ring was to be a sign of his endless love and that she was cherished, but he only accused her of being vain for being loved too much. She, who had been chased by worthy suitors, who was desperately in love with her husband, whose heart he had been able to crawl his way through and capture a small piece of it, and she finally loved him in return. He was a jealous fool, demanding her love and attentions only last week when he accused her of being a flirt, only to trifle with another woman today, knowing exactly what he was doing. *I am such an idiot! I am the one who cannot live without her and I simply expected her to accept my flirting with another woman? I hate myself for making my Elizabeth cry.* He was angry with himself for breaking Elizabeth's heart once again with his arrogance.

He rubbed his pocket watch. It had become a habit to always feel for it there and trace the engraving. He pulled it out and opened it. *With love.* She had given it to him with love and it was more than he had ever asked from her. He was supposed to love her from afar. He was to love her without ever receiving her love and it had been an honour when she opened her heart to him. He had been an imposter. A thief. He wanted to take more than what he was supposed to have.

Tears rolled down. He had betrayed her. He had betrayed his wife by laying with Abigail so he could call out Elizabeth's name. His mistress was a glorified prostitute, after all, and he had continued to be a rake. He thought *his* carnal needs were more important than being faithful to Elizabeth and his heart had known all along that he was betraying his beloved every time he used his mistress. He had still flirted and wanted to be flattered by women who wanted his attentions. He betrayed her with his pride, to remind her how much he gave, so she could be loved by him. He acted like a child when he could not have her affections and even demanded her love.

He was not worthy of her love. She did not need his love and there was nothing that he could give her that she did not already have.

He picked up the ring and held it tightly in his palm. He looked up to see Elizabeth's face. Her cheeks were tear-stained and she was intently looking into the fire.

He saw despair. He saw grief. But he also saw a glimmer of hope. She could have left him; she could have promptly kicked him out of her room and her home, and he would have no choice but to crawl back to Rosings and sit in that empty house all alone. No more smiles, no more hugs, no more kisses. *I cannot live without her. I would rather die.* But she had not done so. She awaited his decision.

He had confessed to her of his deep fear of her leaving him, and she had promised that she would not walk out on him again. *She holds all of my heart in her hands and yet she is infinitely kind to allow me my choice. I will always want her. I will always choose her. I cannot fathom life parted from her. She is my wife, my heart, my forever beloved. She is everything I want, the only thing I need.*

He stood to walk to her and knelt at her feet and placed his head on her lap. He felt her stiffen for a moment then relax. She stroked his hair gently. He felt his tears roll down again as he felt her love from her touch. *She is still so generous.* He hugged her legs and remained for several minutes.

"Elizabeth," he finally started, "I apologise from the bottom of my heart." He wiped his face with his hand and stood up. He dared not to be separated from her longer and he lifted her into his arms and placed her on his lap. She allowed it. *Hope.*

He took her right hand into his hands. He placed the ring back on her finger and reverently kissed it. She did not resist. "I have been an impostor, a liar. When I first placed this ring on you, I had pledged my love and asked for nothing in return. This ring was to remind you how much I love you and how much you are cherished but I failed you. I thought I loved you so much to the point of pain that all my sacrifices were proof of my love to you. You had told me that I had given up so much and I took that as a sign that I was worthy of your love because of it but I was wrong. I lost nothing but only gained. I gave up nothing for you but demanded more from you while going back on my word, my honour," he choked, "that I would honour you as my wife, long before this ring was ever on your hand.

"I betrayed you by flirting with your sister, not caring for any misunderstanding, that she thought she could throw herself at me. I betrayed you by taking a mistress so I could call out your name while I used her for my carnal needs. I should have never hired her. I should have listened to my heart and been faithful to you. I know I betrayed you even today, being flattered by a flirtatious woman and forgetting my duty to you. I had vowed to protect you with my life and as soon as my head was turned, I broke my promise to you. I cannot apologise enough of my actions with that woman. I was flattered and was a complete imbecile. She is nothing to me and was a mere distraction and with my stupid ego, I reverted to my old ways and I hate myself for it."

He took a deep breath of her scent and looked deeply into her eyes. "I have only gained when I fell in love with you. I cannot recall a single thing that I have given up now that I look back. I gained a brother who is my best friend, two beautiful children, an incredible option of living places and so many houses to choose from," she laughed, "as well as the love of the most generous and intelligent and *humble* woman of my acquaintance. You speak to me as an equal and you are my equal. You are actually my better, because you continuously make me a better person. I do not need anyone but you, and I could live the rest of my life with no one but you by my side, but I cannot live for a moment if you are not with me; next to me, in my heart, in a tiny place in your heart. I will never resent you. I have nothing to resent you for and I would thank you every day for kicking me off my high horse. I only ever wish for you to speak to me freely. I love that you hold nothing back and I hope you never will. I have nothing without you; I am always better with you.

"I apologise from the bottom of my heart and beg for your mercy. I was the one who was vain and I am an idiot; I should have never spoken to you in such a way. I was an arse and even if my head may have been turned for a few seconds, my heart is always with you. I swear she means nothing to me. She is no lady and I failed to remember that I am no longer that womanising soldier that I once was. I will keep making mistakes and be a proud dolt but I need you to help me as you continue to mould me to be a better man. I truly need no one else and will never regret you. I cannot imagine life without you, Elizabeth. I had always thought of myself as a strong man who could survive anything and then I met you. I have never needed anything or anyone in my life as I need you. Your presence, your smile, just being where you are sustains me and receiving your love has been the greatest gift in my life. It terrifies me to imagine life without you and I will grovel and plead for your forgiveness. I love you. I need you.

"Would you be able to find it in your ever-generous heart to forgive me? To allow me to put my pride aside once again, as I realise that I can no longer be an impostor but to show you my true self? Would you wear the ring," he kissed it again, "and see my love for you and my pledge to care for you for the rest of my life? You will always be my wife and I will strive to be a better husband to you every day." Richard finished and awaited her judgment. *I cannot live without you, Elizabeth. Please, my love.*

"Richard, I cannot..." Richard's heart dropped but remained silent. "I find that I love you too much that I cannot be without you. I was wounded that your head was turned. She is very beautiful and I saw you admire her and became jealous. I do not know when it happened, as I was in the middle of it before I realised, but I fell in love with you and it hurt me deeply that you looked to another. I know I have no right to ask for your commitment when I can never be a true wife to you but I do wish for the best for you. I wish for you to be happy and to be loved and to enjoy what short time we all have on earth. I wish for you to be surrounded by those who care for you and to know that you are always loved. I believe that your being with me, your being my *other* husband, and for me to love you and show you my love," she kissed him lightly on his lips and lay her head on his shoulder, "is the best for you right now. And if you should wish to take on another mistress or eventually marry someone worthy, I *must* accept it. Although I wish you for myself, I understand you have needs and I *will* accept your decision. I truly love you, I really do, and I wish for your happiness above all else." She kissed him again.

Richard revelled in the tenderest of her kisses. He returned the kiss softly and parted slowly. *She is in love with me!* His heart fluttered to hear her declaration of love. He had known she loved him but for her to confess that she was *in love* with him thrilled his heart to no end.

He gently spoke as he held her tightly, "Oh, my love. I am so desperately in love with you. You are the love of my life, Elizabeth, and you have all of me. All my heart, all my devotion, body, and soul. I am sorry to have given you doubts today and it will never happen again. Darcy keeps telling me what an idiot I am and I confess that I really am such a fool. I know that I will have to earn your trust again but please know that you are the most beautiful woman in my eyes and I will be faithful to you always, my dearest, dearest wife. I will never take a mistress and will never marry. I only need you, my Elizabeth, my wife."

Elizabeth sighed, then asked softly, "Do you think if you had never met me, you would have married her? She is beautiful and rich. You have so many women who want you."

He held both of her cheeks and looked deeply into her eyes. "No, my love. It matters naught who wants me, my heart had never wanted anyone but you. I had been waiting for my perfect woman like Darcy and there was no one who touched my heart until I met you. *You* are my perfect woman. There is none other and there will never be anyone else for me. My heart is completely yours and will never belong to anyone else. It stopped belonging to me the first instant I saw you and I had forgotten for a moment what my life was like when I could not be with you. I spent the most miserable one hundred thirty-two days of my life without you and I never want to go through that again. You are so precious to me, my love. Whether I am allowed to love you once a month or never again, I will be true to you. I forgot that I was supposed to love you from afar and you and Darcy have been generous beyond all of my wishes and I will never take your love for granted again. I am certain I will act a complete fool again and will make many mistakes, but I love you. Only you. Home is where you are, Elizabeth. Stay with me always." He held her tightly.

"Yes, my love. I will never leave you. You are in my heart." She whispered in return as she laid her head on his shoulder to revel in his embrace.

Chapter 5

Richard took his apology very seriously and gifted her with everything he could think of. If he excelled at one thing, it was grovelling and Darcy laughed at him that if the house had any more flowers, they would have to open up their own shop. Richard brought chocolates and purchased trinkets for her whenever he saw something that she would like, and saw to it that she had three sets of beautiful hats and gloves delivered to her as well. He also ordered a beautiful landau with green trimmings, her favourite colour, which she absolutely loved when she finally received it a few months later in London. Richard thanked Darcy for allowing the gifts and Darcy agreed that anything to keep Elizabeth happy was worth the effort.

The rest of their stay was spent in more public gatherings, as they attended musicales, art galleries, and plays. The trio was seen everywhere together and it became known quickly that Rosings Park was willed to the Darcys' second son and any rumours that Richard Fitzwilliam was looking for a wife was quickly squelched. He looked to no one, favoured no single ladies with a dance or flirting, and remained steadfast to the lady who owned his heart. In fact, his public image had altered so much that most believed that he and his cousin had switched personalities. The once dour Fitzwilliam Darcy smiled and laughed and greeted everyone cordially with his wife on his arm, while the once dashing and flirtatious Richard Fitzwilliam, although congenial, remained distant and stoic with all unmarried ladies, no matter their beauty or wealth or status. He would be seen smiling and kissing his cousin Mrs. Darcy's hand and friendly to his friends and other happily-married ladies, though, and it was a clear indication that he was absolutely not interested in marriage whatsoever.

~*~

When they next met Lord Devon and his family, Darcy had barely acknowledged him but did not give him the cut direct.

Richard greeted his *former* friend with a large smile at the theatre. "Devon! Just the man I wanted to see!"

He wrapped his arm around Devon's shoulders and squeezed it hard enough to leave a bruise, pulling him to the side.

Richard had dismissed Elizabeth's distress of being touched by Devon without dwelling on it at first, but later, when he finally had the sense to ask her where he had touched her and she pointed to it, he burned with rage. It had been too close to her breast and he himself, her surrogate husband, had not even touched her so intimately. Darcy had been furious but Richard convinced him to avoid a duel and that he would warn the earl.

Still smiling for the public, he hissed quietly in his ear, "I know what you tried with Mrs. Darcy. My cousin was ready to kill you but I saved your life by convincing him that I would murder you on his behalf if you ever touch Mrs. Darcy again." He squeezed Devon's shoulder once again until that rake cringed in pain. "And to try to entrap me with that unpleasant sister of yours... Tsk, tsk... Word is that she is mercenary and her suitors have not been rich enough for her tastes but I hope you convince her to find a husband before I spread the word on how she flung herself at me. I saw that slut's teats, Devon, and it was not at all impressive. I have heard rumours that she believes I will offer for her and it will never happen since she is not worth a second look to me and you will make sure to tell her that she disgusts me. I care not for my own reputation and I can ruin hers if she does not let go of this fantasy that she can become my wife.

"Devon, I have spies everywhere and I know you have been fucking Mrs. White as soon as you made your vows. Perhaps you might have had a taste of your sister-in-law as well, you bastard. I also know that you were tupping your fiancée that night, who was not yet your wife, when Caroline Bingley tried to compromise you. I am more than willing to let all these gossips flow to your father-in-law, as you know that he knows me and respects me from my services in the war. He will cut your bollocks off for tainting his family name and you would not survive the gossip. You do anything to the Darcys, you will be ruined. Do not believe it for a minute that your title will get you out of your mess. You are barely respected and I know the other earls hate you already, you pompous arse. Get out of my sight, Devon, and I will not cut you in public."

He tapped his shoulder harder than necessary and laughed loudly as he walked away.

Lord Devon paled and dragged his wife and the two other ladies to return home.

"Mr. Fitzwilliam, whatever did you say to that nice young man?" Elizabeth asked with her hand on Darcy's arm.

"Young man? He is older by eight or nine years to you!" Richard retorted.

"Oh, but I am an old married woman with two children now!" Elizabeth replied.

"Old woman, my arse." Richard whispered.

"Language!" Elizabeth's laughter tinkled in the air. "Perhaps I should wear a matron cap to prove my point?"

"NO CAPS!" Both Darcy and Richard shouted at the same time.

They all laughed merrily, the other audiences wondering what was so funny.

~*~

Elizabeth Elliot, who resided only a few doors down, finally deigned to call on Mrs. Darcy the second week of their arrival, only after hearing that the distinguished and wealthy Mr. Richard Fitzwilliam was staying with them.

"It is nice to meet you, Mrs. Darcy. I have heard wonderful things about you from my sister Anne." Elizabeth Elliot started with her nose up in the air, surveying the surroundings, seeing that the furnishings were elegant and expensive, even if not gilded and shiny.

"Oh, yes. She is a wonderful friend and I enjoyed meeting her and her husband very much in Ramsgate." Elizabeth replied.

Miss Elliot was jealous of her sister, who was not only married to a handsome and wealthy sea captain but was now with child. She huffed slightly but did not want to offend Mrs. Darcy. "Well, Anne is certainly fortunate in her choice of husband, even if she did marry so *late* in life."

Elizabeth hid her amusement behind her teacup. *And yet you are one and thirty and still unmarried. You are jealous of your sister!* "Yes, Captain Wentworth is certainly gallant. He is a very good friend to Mr. Fitzwilliam."

Miss Elliot's eyes widened brightly as Richard's name was mentioned. "Yes, I have heard much about Mr. Fitzwilliam. My father, Sir Walter Elliot, deeply wishes to meet all of you. Would you be able to join us for dinner tomorrow evening?"

Elizabeth smiled. *I know SHE wishes to meet him! I cannot snub them for Anne's sake.* "I will check with Mr. Darcy and Mr. Fitzwilliam for their availability. Mr. Fitzwilliam has been quite busy but I believe we are free."

They sat and spoke for a quarter hour and Miss Elliot departed.

~*~

"Fitzwilliam, Richard, I just met with Miss Elizabeth Elliot, Sir Walter's prized daughter, and she invited us to dine with them tomorrow evening. What say you? Are you ready to meet your future wife, Richard?" Elizabeth spoke to both men as she entered their study and sat on the couch.

Richard groaned. "Please, Elizabeth. You know there is only one Elizabeth in my heart." Darcy laughed. "I saw her years ago and she is an awful shrew. Wentworth told me she has gotten worse over the years but her father is the worst. I do not wish to shun them for Mrs. Wentworth's sake and I will agree to dine but you must keep me away from them. I might be tempted to wrap my hands around their throats and strangle them!"

Darcy laughed again. "I have heard of them as well, Elizabeth. Richard and I have been arranging for the Crofts to look at Rosings in a few weeks and rumour is that Sir Walter is a self-absorbed man who only looks at outward beauty and has spent a hundred pounds on some face cream that is supposed to make him look younger. He is critical of others and careless with his income and is about to lose his ancestral home. He is leasing the townhouse and yet spent over £2,000 to furnish it grander than it needs. He sounds like a male version of Aunt Catherine!" They all laughed heartily.

"Well, I would like to meet these folks to draw my own conclusions and I believe I will understand Anne Wentworth better after meeting them. I will send a note to agree to dinner. At the least, we will have some amusement." Elizabeth arched her brow.

Richard, sitting next to her, held her hand and kissed it seductively. "And if I find her absolutely gorgeous, will you become jealous if I flirt with her and kiss her hand like this and call her '*my* Elizabeth'?" He smirked. "Darcy and I can have our own Elizabeth each."

Darcy jumped in. "Oh, Richard, that would be fantastic. I can finally keep my wife to myself! What a relief!"

Elizabeth laughed uncontrollably for a minute then finally spoke. "I would love to see you try! Promise me you will behave." She was then quite sullen. "If you do find her attractive, you will tell me?" Her wound was still too fresh for her to feel confident.

Richard hugged her and held her tightly. "I love you. I am sorry for teasing and you must remember that there is no one for me but you. You have my heart completely, Elizabeth." He kissed her hair.

Darcy approached them and sat next to his wife. After Richard let her go, he kissed his wife's lips. "No one compares to you, Elizabeth. I told Richard what an idiot he was and he keeps sticking his foot in his large mouth. I hope you always remember how much you are loved."

Feeling comforted, Elizabeth smiled softly. She kissed Darcy's cheek. "Thank you, my love." She kissed Richard's cheek as well and rose from her seat. "Well, I will be off to write my note. Thank you, husbands," and she took her leave.

Darcy punched Richard on the shoulder. "You are still stupid."

Richard rubbed his shoulder and replied, "I know, Darce, I know. I will keep grovelling. Just keep knocking some sense into me."

Darcy smiled. "You can bet your life on it, brother. Let us return to our work."

~*~

Elizabeth was in awe as soon as she stepped into the Elliot residence. The townhouse was about half the size of theirs a few doors down, but the furnishings were gaudy and everything was gilded, from floor to ceiling. She had thought Rosings was one of the most extravagant and garish places she had seen before the remodel but this place was far worse. She suppressed her mirth as Miss Elliot fluttered when they entered.

Elizabeth introduced her husband and Richard and noted the shock on Miss Elliot's face seeing two such handsome men. *She does not know which is more handsome. They are both such fine specimen of their sex!* She laughed internally.

Sir Walter was as ridiculous as she suspected. He greeted them civilly but could not stop speaking of how he would be pleased to be seen with them anywhere and how fine all three of them looked.

Richard sat uncomfortably not knowing whether he should be friendly or solemn. For Wentworth's sake, he wanted to be kind to his friend's father and sister in law, but he found them just as absurd as he expected and knew Miss Elliot found him to be a most eligible bachelor but also saw her eyes wander to Darcy often.

He watched the lady carefully. She was a pretty woman who would have been quite a beauty ten years ago. Her bosoms were flat but with a £10,000 dowry and being the daughter of a baronet, she should have been swept up long ago but it was obvious that she was arrogant and self-absorbed, caring nothing for anyone but herself. Everything that spouted from her mouth was 'me' or 'I' and he saw that she was neglecting his Elizabeth. *I have slept with a lot of women in the past but would have never touched this one. She disgusts me. I need to put her in her place for neglecting my Elizabeth.*

"I have had the great fortune to meet your sister in Ramsgate, Miss Elliot, and she is certainly a wonderful wife to Wentworth. She was exactly as I guessed Wentworth's type to be: A genteel and kind-hearted lady and quite beautiful, too. She was glowing with happiness with her pregnancy." He knew it was a sour point for the older Miss Elliot and poked where it would hurt.

Miss Elliot scoffed. "Well, she is doing well. She is very fortunate that he came back for her after all those years. But of course, he is not really a gentleman and his fortune is only from the war. Mr. Fitzwilliam, I understand you were a former colonel. You must have been quite dashing in your uniform. Can you tell me a little more about Rosings? Surely such a grand estate must be in want of a woman's touch." She slyly flirted.

Richard was thoroughly repulsed. He could tell that she was jealous of her own sister and looked down on Wentworth. *I would have still been a colonel if not for Anne's will and she would have not looked at me twice for all my wealth and status then. Elizabeth made Rosings a comfortable home and I need no one but her.*

"Yes, I retired a little over a year ago and am learning much from my cousin. It is certainly no easy task to be a landowner, to be responsible for so much in my lot, and there is much on my shoulders to ensure my tenants are kept happy." He knew Sir Walter was a lackadaisical owner who was heavily in debt. "Rosings is a fine estate and a bulk of my 6,000 a year goes back to making the land flourish, and I am immensely relieved that I do not have a spendthrift wife who will waste all of my money to give me grey hairs!" He laughed loudly. He knew Miss Elliot's lips were shut in a thin line and Sir Walter was pretending to laugh but appeared ashamed. He continued, "It has been recently remodelled and is not only grand but very comfortable and I could not imagine it looking better than it does now. I am quite settled as I am now and even though I have had women with £25,000 or £50,000 throwing themselves at me, I am determined to be a lifelong bachelor. It would take a great woman to capture my heart." *Only my Elizabeth!*

Richard smiled as he saw Miss Elliot's disappointed face that she would not succeed in trying to capture him. *No one will ever exceed my Elizabeth, my wife. I swear if I am able, I am going to buy Kellynch Hall from this conceited arse and gift it to my wife.*

The rest of dinner was more civil and they all spoke of general topics, such as music and theatre. The Elliots attempted to show off their illustrious connection, the Dowager Viscountess Dalrymple, but shut their mouths quickly when Darcy subtly reminded them that Richard was the son of the most prominent Earl of Matlock and that he himself was the grandson of the previous earl.

The Darcys and Richard took their leave and breathed a sigh of relief that they had survived the unpleasant meal. They walked arm in arm down the street to their townhouse and as soon as they had the privacy to do so, they laughed loudly at the ridiculous family and promised each other to never become so obnoxious, even if they had all the gold in the lands.

Chapter 6

"Push, Jane, Push!" Elizabeth shouted.

When they had arrived at Netherfield, Elizabeth could see immediately that her dear sister was ready to pop. "Jane! Why did you not write to me that you were so far along? We could have come earlier." Elizabeth asked.

"Oh, Lizzy! I am trying so hard to make this baby arrive later." Jane cried. "I do not wish to share my anniversary date with my baby's birthdate!" She wailed.

Elizabeth hid her face and laughed. *Was I this ridiculous when I was pregnant? I know Mama was as well. Oh, the lot we must carry.*

"How long have you been labouring?" She asked.

"Since this morning, shortly before you arrived. Oooooohhhh!" Jane grunted. Suddenly her dress was soaking wet and the fluid was spreading on the couch.

"CHAAAARRRLLLESSS!!" Elizabeth called out. Within moments, Bingley, Darcy, and Richard rushed in. "Gentlemen, we have a baby coming. TODAY! Charles, you must take her up to the birthing room. Fitzwilliam, will you please assist? Richard, have the housekeeper send for the midwife." Elizabeth took charge.

Bingley lifted his wife up and Darcy opened the doors for him but then ended up carrying Jane on Bingley's behalf. Darcy was much stronger than his shorter friend and did not want him to drop her. Bingley thanked him and opened the mistress' bedroom door for him.

Darcy laid Jane on the bed and promptly left after kissing Elizabeth.

"Should we send a note to Longbourn?" Richard asked in the study.

Darcy burst out laughing, "Only if you wish to hear what sounds like pigs squealing throughout the house!"

Richard joined his amusement. He had forgotten how loud Mrs. Bennet was. "Good call, Darce. We will send a note after. Maybe tomorrow. Or next week." They burst out laughing again.

Bingley soon returned to the study and poured himself a drink. He paced around then poured himself another.

Darcy stood up and grabbed the decanter when he reached for it again. He shook his head and Bingley put the glass down and plopped on the chair.

"It was really difficult to hear Mrs. Bennet when she was screaming her lungs out during her labour. And then it was mostly sitting around during Lizzy's at Pemberley, but now, now that my Jane is upstairs, I do not know what to do. How the hell did you stay in the birthing room with your wife, Darcy? Jane just threatened me to never let me touch her again." Bingley exhaled.

Darcy chuckled. "Bingley, Elizabeth said the same thing to me as well. She choked my neck until I was turning blue and Mrs. Gardiner had to remind her to let me go of my cravat." Richard laughed heartily. "She will invite you to bed when it is time. You will be fine."

Darcy and Richard attempted to ease his pain by telling stories and reminiscing about the old days. It was nearly seven hours later, much after dinnertime, when Elizabeth entered with a smile. "Charles, your wife requests your presence."

Bingley dashed off to see his wife.

Darcy asked, "Boy or girl?"

Elizabeth answered, "I have a beautiful niece. She is so pretty and looks just like Jane." She embraced her husband. "May I get one, too?"

"We can certainly try, Elizabeth. Perhaps tonight?" Darcy replied with a broad grin.

"Ahem, I am still here, you know." Richard coughed. He winked. "I know you two lovebirds have lots of children to make but please give the poor woman a rest, Darcy! Our babies are not yet six months old!" He laughed. *Oh, to have a little girl to dote on, in the image of her beautiful mother.* "Well, I am off to bed. I look forward to going for a nice long ride in the morning and hope to be gone until all the visitors have left!" He laughed and retired to his rooms after kissing Elizabeth's cheek.

"Oh! Visitors! I must send a note to Mama. She will be so upset that she missed the birthing but I did NOT want her here. She would have prattled on and complained of her flutterings, calling for the smelling salt, and the actual patient would have been completely neglected!" She laughed. She sat at the desk and wrote a quick note and had the footman see to it.

"The midwife is calling for the wet nurse but I had to show Jane what to do for this night. Having one babe is so easy! I do not know what she was complaining about!" She giggled. "Shall we retire? And practice making babies?"

Darcy laughed. "I love you, Mrs. Darcy. I am glad you were here for your sister. I hope she was not too disappointed that her anniversary dinner was completely ruined. We men certainly enjoyed it. I had asked for some repast to be brought up for you after the baby arrived and after you wash, you can eat and I will massage you. Job well done, my love!"

"Oh, Fitzwilliam. You are the best of men! Thank you, my love." Elizabeth beamed in appreciation of her thoughtful husband.

~*~

The next day was as chaotic as Richard had predicted. The Bennet clan, as well as Mary and Aunt Philips, all descended to Netherfield, and Mrs. Bennet's ravings were heard throughout the house. She had been so disappointed that she was not called immediately after Jane went into labour but Mr. Bennet hinted that she would have been of no use and she finally conceded.

When she began to bemoan the fact that Jane had delivered a daughter when it was her duty to provide a son first and that she had not done as Lizzy had done to provide an heir, Mr. Bennet stood up, pulled her off her chair, and bid everyone good day, then pushed his wife out of doors to return home.

Jane was serene and cooed at her daughter. "Son or daughter, they are precious and I love my Betty Bingley best right now."

The Bingleys had decided to name their daughter after Charles' mother, Agatha: Agatha Elizabeth Bingley, nicknamed Betty. Elizabeth was pleased for them and after the rest of the visitors left, went to the nursery to check on her own sons.

She laughed when she entered the room. Fitzwilliam and Richard were on the floor, on their stomachs with coats off and playing with spin tops while the babies sat next to them laughing and clapping.

Oh, how I love all of my men in my life! Elizabeth gleamed.

~*~

"Richard! Are you well?" Elizabeth asked.

It had been two weeks since Betty was born and things were finally settling down. Elizabeth had been extremely busy assisting her sister on how to care for the baby, run the household for her during her convalescence, as well as manage the visitors, family, and neighbours alike. Her mother had been useless, as she had expected, but she had begun to teach Kitty and Lydia on how to be mistress of a home.

Kitty was being courted by Mr. Goulding Jr., who had been in love with her for the past six years, after working hard with Mr. Gardiner and successful in his ventures, was able to finally afford a wife. Lydia, though, only cared for parties and dresses still, and as she would be travelling to London for the season and staying with the Darcys, her head was filled with thoughts of meeting her perfect prince and dancing.

Elizabeth had finally some time to rest as Mary joined to assist Kitty and Lydia with several errands; the house was actually quiet and peaceful. Bingley had several questions for Darcy on a tenant issue so the two had ridden out while Richard stayed to answer to several correspondences.

Elizabeth checked the time on her pin-watch and walked towards the drawing room after seeking some light reading materials at the library. She spotted him pacing in the drawing room. *Ah! He is finally alone.* She thought.

"I am well. Everything is good, Elizabeth. May I carry those books for you?" Richard took the three volumes from her hands and offered her his arm.

"Thank you, Richard, but I saw you pacing. Is something troubling you? I feel as if I have neglected you these two weeks. I have been so busy! I know Netherfield is not large but it is not the same as running your own homes. Pemberley and Rosings were better organised, I believe." Elizabeth commented.

Richard was immensely happy to hear of her speaking of Rosings as her home. It was their home together and everything he had, it was hers.

As they reached her rooms, Richard looked around and seeing no one about, asked, "May I come in?"

Elizabeth smiled and quickly opened the door as he had missed him. In all their own homes, there had been so much space and time, and their joined sitting rooms had provided privacy so they could talk and be affectionate without prying eyes.

As soon as the door closed, Elizabeth was in Richard's arms and he was kissing her frantically on her lips, cheeks, neck, and back to her lips and he opened her mouth with his tongue to taste her deeply. Eventually, they broke for air. Still holding onto each other tightly, they huffed for air and Richard buried his face in her hair.

"I have missed you so much, Elizabeth. I have been dying to kiss you." Richard confessed as he sighed.

"Oh, Richard, I have missed you very much as well. I have been very busy; truly I did not mean to neglect you. Even poor Fitzwilliam was pouty and complained that it had been a whole week since we had been intimate. I have been exhausted but things seem to be finally better today." She smiled. "I hope to be able to spend the next week giving more attention to my dear," kiss, "poor," kiss, "husbands." She kissed with each word.

"Elizabeth, I need to speak with you. I received word that the Crofts, Wentworth's sister and her husband, would like to lease Rosings but because of Anne's recent death, the estate has some documents that need to be signed over and I must travel to London and then Rosings. I will most likely be gone for a whole week, and since we had planned to return to Darcy House in nine days, it would not make sense for me to return here, only to remove to London again. I will need to leave tomorrow and will not see you until you arrive at Darcy House. I wish I could take you with me, but you are needed here." Richard embraced her again. "I have not parted from you for so long and I despair of missing you already."

"Oh, my love. I understand you must go and all will be well. It will not be one hundred thirty-two days, Richard. I will miss you terribly but perhaps I can farewell you with a new memory that can sustain you until you return to me?" She arched her brow.

Richard gulped, as he did not know what to expect from this incredible woman. He watched her as she locked her main door, strode over to lock the servants' door, and lastly, locked the connecting door to Darcy's room. Elizabeth returned and led him to the chair near the fireplace. She pushed him down to sit and she sat on his lap after lifting her skirts, with her knees next to his hips and began grinding against him, with her arms wrapped around his neck.

Richard had never been so seduced. She was in control and she was making him insane. She began to kiss his neck and ear, making love to him and beguiling him far beyond when she had been intoxicated several months ago. She began to nibble at his lips and he attacked her mouth fiercely, losing all abandon. His arousal was massive and he had thought he would explode while kissing her but suddenly, she whispered in his ear, "Do not release yet."

He froze, not knowing what she was going to do. She put her hand in his waistcoat to pull out her newest handkerchief that she had given him and then she softened her kisses and trailed her hand down to his trousers where she grazed his manhood.

"Ahhhhh..." Richard moaned. She had never touched him like this before. He thought he was going to burst from feeling her hand on his erection. He was undone when she unbuttoned his fall and caressed his hard cock with her soft hand, exposing him completely in the air. "My god, Elizabeth, what are you... that feels so..." He could not think. All he could feel was her hand fondling him gently as she sat on his thighs. Richard moaned softly. "Elizabeth, I want to come. I need to..."

"Richard, kiss me."

And he obeyed immediately. His tongue was in her mouth and wrapping around her tongue with his hands on her hips to help her gyrate against him. She continued to rub herself on him as she held his hard cock with both hands, covering the tip with his handkerchief with one hand while pumping him up and down with the other. His mouth freed hers as he moaned loudly as he climaxed. He panted for breath as she continued to stroke and expel every last drop of his seed.

I have never lost control as I do with Elizabeth. I know it has been a month but how is it that she barely touches me and I explode like a pimple-faced boy? She is incredible! Richard wondered in amazement as he was catching his breath.

She wiped him off completely and pocketed the handkerchief. She buttoned up his fall for him and sat next to him, swinging her legs over both of his thighs. She leaned and rested her head on his chest, listening to his pounding heartbeats. "I hope I made up a little for the weeks of neglect and that you have a new memory of our time together. I will miss you very much, Richard." She sighed as she hugged him tighter.

"Elizabeth, you did not have to, but that was perhaps the single most important memory of my life. I love you. I cannot control myself when you touch me and it felt so good. Thank you for doing that for me." Richard was so grateful.

Elizabeth giggled. "You and Fitzwilliam are more similar than you would ever know. Being wife to both of you, I can assuredly tell you that you and he are about the same size, so very large and strong. Who would have known?"

"Minx! Do you not know a man wants to be the biggest?" They laughed. "You will tell Darcy?" Richard nervously asked. He did not want to keep anything a secret but he was not sure if Darcy would want to know such intimate details.

"He actually asked me to spend some time with you today. He knows that you have not initiated anything for a month and knew you would be desperate. Now that you need to travel alone, he must have wanted to make sure I give you some affection. You enjoyed it?" She innocently asked.

Richard kissed her, deeply and passionately. "Oh, yes, my love. That was by far the best feeling I have ever felt. I cannot wait to do it again someday." He kissed her again. "I care for you so much, more than for my physical needs, you must know. I cherish every moment with you and I am grateful for the love you share with me. I love you, Elizabeth. Thank you for your love, my dearest wife."

~*~

"Richard! Did you get some time with Elizabeth?" Darcy whispered when he saw his cousin. Richard had told him that he had to travel and had been devastated that he would be far from Elizabeth for nine full days.

Richard embraced him and tapped his back. "Yes, brother, thank you for allowing us some time together. It was kind of you to get Bingley away for a while. I cannot wait to be home soon, with our private sitting room and our own servants. I cannot thank you enough since I desperately needed her affections. She eagerly awaits you, kind sir. I will see you at dinner."

He quickly returned to his rooms to relieve another arousal after leaving Darcy at Elizabeth's door.

Darcy had returned with Bingley just a little while ago and finding both her bedroom and the adjoining door locked, he had guessed that Richard was finally getting some time with their beloved wife.

He smiled as he entered Elizabeth's room and locked the door to her room.

"I just met your lover as he was leaving. Having one man after another, what a wanton creature you are." He teased. "What beautiful, seductive, sensuous, lovely, sexual being you are." He lifted her skirts. "Did he make you wet? Did you enjoy his release?" He buried his head between her legs. "Mmm. You are so wet for me." He fingered and licked her. "Do you want my hard cock inside of you? Do you desire to be filled?" She was screaming out her orgasm as he thrust his fingers in and out of her.

"Oh, Fitzwilliam! Take me, please! I need you inside me!" She screamed.

"Do you wish for my cock to fill you or his?" Darcy asked as he began to slide his manhood inside her.

"Yours. Always yours, Fitzwilliam." She moaned. "You feel so good, my love! I am coming again!" She screamed as he pumped her.

Damn! She is so aroused. Such a passionate woman! Darcy thought. "Oh, Elizabeth, I love you so much. Please, please say that you will always save yourself for me. I want to fill you with my future children and I want to taste you and pleasure you always. Be mine, love, be mine." And he climaxed deep inside her.

After they finally calmed, Elizabeth whispered, "I love you. I love you till death parts us, Mr. Darcy. My body is yours. As much as I enjoy helping Richard, I do think of you and our love always. Truly I only need you to pleasure me. You are my world." She kissed him desperately. "I need you to fill me and I want your babies. I desire you so much that everything else pales in comparison to my love for you. I love Richard but he is not my true husband. As much as I consider him my surrogate husband, my heart is truly yours, my love. I am all yours. I made a vow to you and I will be true to you. What you have allowed, the love that I am able to receive from both of you, is something that is wondrous and astounding but I would give up Richard if you asked it of me. I belong to you, my husband. I do wish to be able to love you both but even as he kissed me, even as I stroked him so he could release, I thought of you and how I would like to unite with you."

"Thank you, my love. I know that you love him and you care for him very much but to hear your love for me comforts me. I am possessive and wish I could be more generous, but I love you and I honour you too much to allow you to break our vows. There is a fine line in our relationship, the three of us. The act of adultery is something that we cannot cross. The kissing and fondling, it might not be appropriate but not immoral, I believe. Our love for each other is so strong that we must have an outlet, but we also must be honourable as well. When I release inside your womb, it is an act of love, a vow to worship your body, and possibly to grow our child together. Elizabeth, please, lay only with me and save that part for me and only me. I would be heartbroken should your generous heart allow him in there. I would never stop loving you but I wish for one part of you, the most important part between man and wife, to belong to only to me. Only to us. I will never break my vows to you. I love you so much."

He buried his head in her wild and unruly hair.

"I will be faithful to you." She hugged him tightly. "I am all yours." She giggled. "When I was caressing his manhood, I was thinking of you. I told this to Richard that you two are very alike. Not just in your height and appearances, but your manhood as well! I would say yours is a little thicker but it would be hard to tell them apart at a glance!" She giggled.

"A man likes to be the biggest, my dear!" Darcy reprimanded but unable to hide his smile.

"That is what he said!" She burst out laughing.

"I am so glad I can talk to you about everything. What happens between the three of us is truly only for us and I am honoured by your love." Darcy held her tightly.

Chapter 7

"Stop pacing, Georgiana!" Richard commanded. He was getting dizzy from watching her pace, run to the window at every sound, sit on the chair, only to run back to the window and resume her pacing.

"What is taking them so long? They should have been here by now!" Georgiana whined.

Richard now stood and paced. "They were probably delayed leaving because of Mrs. Bingley or Mrs. Bennet." Elizabeth had managed Netherfield so well, too well, that they had continuously demanded her attentions.

Richard shook his head. *My Elizabeth is such a wonderful mistress. Jane Bingley may have had her baby only recently but she is nothing to my wife. Elizabeth was already ruling her domain by the third day.* He smiled. *I miss her so much. I am desperate to see her. Nine days without her is a lifetime.*

Attempting to distract his excitable cousin, he asked, "So, what do you have planned with Lydia? Have you heard anything more from Kitty? Anything that sounds interesting with her suitor?"

Georgiana smiled. "Oh! I am so excited to have Lydia with us! Aunt Susan will be taking her around and we have ever so many shopping trips planned. You most likely will not see us for days on end!"

Thank goodness, Richard thought.

Georgiana continued, "And Kitty just accepted Mr. Goulding's proposal! It is so exciting. She hopes to be married in June, right before you plan to return to Pemberley. Lizzy wants to stop back for a few days then head home while I remain with uncle and aunt. Perhaps *I* will get a suitor for myself!"

"God forbid! You are still too young, missy!" Richard smiled.

Georgiana gleamed, but then turned serious. "Why is it that you call all the Bennet daughters by their names except Jane? Oh, and we all call Lizzy 'Lizzy' but you call her 'Elizabeth'. Why is that, Richard?"

Because I love her with every breath in my body! How do I explain this to Georgie? He took a quick moment. "Well, I call all the girls by their names because they are young. I, I call Mrs. Bingley by her title because I want to be respectful to Bingley, and Elizabeth has been... it is what Darcy always calls her and I got used to hearing it so much that I say it now, I suppose."

He stood to look out the window. *Oh, my love. Where are you? I need to see you desperately.* His heart ached to be with his beloved once again.

"That makes sense. I hope Lydia will be up for going shopping today. I am so excited to show her all the wonderful shops. Oh! I need to send a note to Aunt Susan and see when she will be available. Please excuse me." Georgiana prattled and then left.

Richard's heart was still throbbing from talking about Elizabeth and aching to see her, then he saw Darcy's carriage on the street and immediately smiled. *She is here!*

He called to Georgiana that the carriage was approaching and they were waiting at the door for them when it arrived.

The two exchanged an excited look as they saw Darcy exit, handing out Elizabeth, then Lydia. Discarding propriety, Georgiana rushed out to greet them and squealed with Lydia as they were hugging each other.

Richard remained at the front door with his eyes only on Elizabeth. *She is more beautiful than when I last saw her.* His heart beat wildly. He saw her eyes lift and saw her bright smile and sparkling eyes trained on him. *I am certain I love her more. How is this possible?*

Richard remained very formal as the group entered the foyer. "Darcy, welcome back. Lydia, nice to see you again. Mrs. Darcy," he paused. He took her hand and kissed it briefly and released, barely meeting her eyes. He knew his hands were shaking. He could not say more without betraying his feelings in front of the others.

"Richard, how was your business at Rosings? All went well?" Darcy asked, seeing that his cousin was barely able to keep his passions in check. *Poor man. I know he must have missed her so. I knew he would be bad but not this bad!* He laughed internally.

"Good, good; everything went well. I will fill you in later." Turning to Georgiana, "Georgie, did you have something to ask your brother?" Richard smiled.

"Oh, Fitzwilliam, Lydia agrees with me and I was just about to send out a note to Aunt Susan. May I take her shopping today? After she changes out of her travelling clothes, I would like to show her the best shops today!" Georgiana asked.

"Already planning on spending a fortune?" He laughed. "Of course, Georgiana. As long as Aunt Susan agrees, you may do as you wish but Elizabeth will need to rest. We old folks have a limited energy and want to settle the babies in to make sure they are well. They had a difficult time travelling today from teething." Darcy answered.

"Thank you, brother! Rest well, Lizzy!" Georgiana grabbed Lydia's hand and scurried off to Lydia's bedroom.

After seeing to the babies settling into the nursery, Darcy led Elizabeth towards their shared sitting room. "My love, I know you will wish to wash up and rest but could we quickly adjourn to the sitting room for a while?" She nodded. "Richard, join us."

They walked to the room and entered. As soon as Elizabeth and Richard stepped in, Darcy stated, "I will see you in our rooms soon, Elizabeth?" She nodded and he closed the door, giving them privacy.

"Richard, are you well? You have been so quiet. I have missed you terribly." Elizabeth wrapped her arms around his waist and put her ear next to his heart. She had thought he would be more excited to see her. He had written to her once through her husband to explain how his business was going and although it was not explicit, he had referred to how he wished he had been back at Netherfield with the party and that he was looking forward to their return to Darcy House.

She feared something might have happened when she did not feel his arms around her as she held him. He had avoided meeting her eyes so far and she was briefly afraid that his passion might have died out during the separation. She looked up to see his face and saw him penetratingly looking at her. His stare was so fierce, she felt he was looking for faults as he pierced her soul.

She did not know what to think but continued to watch him when she felt his arms slowly wrap around her, with one hand behind her back and one on her cheek. She could feel his hand trembling on her cheek and realised that he was holding himself back. He leaned down very slowly to meet her lips gently, touching her lips several times with the lightest of kisses.

"Did you miss me, my love?" Elizabeth whispered.

Then, Richard pressed his lips hard and opened her mouth with his tongue, exploring her mouth and suckling on her tongue. He kissed her as if he had been a starved man. He wrapped his arms around her waist tighter and pressed her against him as he continued to kiss her fervently. His hand was stroking her hair and he was touching and caressing every part of her body that he had been allowed to stroke, his tongue frantically reaching for her soul.

Elizabeth was feeling faint as she could not catch enough air but his kiss was so ardent and loving, she continued to receive it and returned it.

He finally released her mouth but held onto her. As they struggled to fill their lungs with air again, Richard kissed her hair and temple and forehead, whispering, "I love you" again and again.

Richard finally lowered her feet to the floor then lifted her up to carry her to the couch where he resumed his habit of seating her on his lap. "I missed you..." He was still too emotional to continue.

Elizabeth cuddled into his embrace. "I was afraid that your love might have died out during our separation. I was afraid of losing you for a moment; you were so quiet and distant."

Richard quickly held both of her cheeks and looked directly into her eyes, appearing almost angry. "Never! I love you! Never, ever doubt my love for you. I have never felt so much love for a person in my life and even if I were to be away from you for weeks or months or years, my love will never die out. Do you understand me? I love you with an all-consuming fire and will love you until my last breath." He kissed her again most ardently until they both desperately needed air.

"Elizabeth, I wish to never be parted from you from this day forth. I felt as if my heart was left where you were and I was barely living. I know it was not four months but having tasted you, having held you in my arms, every day away from you felt like years. I missed you so much and I could not speak to you when I first saw you. Oh, my love. You are more beautiful than when I last laid my eyes on you. How is it possible that I love you more than before? I know it unlikely, but I wish to never leave you again. The past nine days have been the most miserable days of my life." He kissed her lips desperately again for several more minutes.

"I have missed you so much as well. Things were just not the same without you and even Fitzwilliam was most irritable without you by our side. We are a pathetic lot, are we not? Cannot live without each other." She smiled.

"As long as I am with you, I care not if I am pathetic. I am so in love with you, Elizabeth. More today than yesterday." Richard held her tightly and resumed kissing her neck and ear.

"And did the memory of our last kiss sustain you?" Elizabeth teased. She knew she was sitting on his massive arousal and it pleased her to be the cause of it.

"Minx! Yes, it kept me going and looking forward to the next time. You brought me so much pleasure. I think of it constantly." Richard buried his face in her hair and inhaled. He had been reliving that memory several times daily, unable to restrain himself and needing to find his release nightly as well as this morning in anticipation of their reunion.

Elizabeth felt his cock twitch beneath her and knew that if she kept pressing him, he would spend, so she changed the subject. "How was the business at Rosings? When will the lease start?"

Richard took a deep breath to calm himself. He was ready to explode as he remembered her hand stroking him once again. "They will take residence on the first of May. The Crofts are kind people; the admiral and his wife are an intelligent and respectable couple. The paperwork was all completed and the new will was reviewed without any problems. It is official that Richie will inherit Rosings."

"You are so generous." Elizabeth kissed him.

Richard relaxed after receiving her kiss. "It is my honour, my love." He continued after a soft moan. "I saw Abigail again." He felt her stiffen at the mention of his former mistress. He lifted his eyes to her to meet hers and caressed her cheek. "I do not mean 'saw', my love. I apologise for startling you. I saw her at Bromwell with a gentleman and we barely acknowledged each other. Word is that she is being courted by a widower with 1,000 a year. I am happy for her. She can move on and leave her past."

"And how did Abigail react when she saw you?" She tested out her name to see his reaction.

Richard answered, "She was surprised. I think she might have thought I had returned for her but I gave no indication of knowing her and I never sought her out. She was most likely relieved if she is interested in marrying the man. My love, I feel I can speak her name now, as you know I will never visit her again and will never look to another for as long as I live. Even if I never find another release, whether by your touch or my own, I will never seek elsewhere. I will be faithful to you always, heart and body. Please know that."

He began to kiss her again and she felt his arousal return in full force.

Oh, I have missed his kisses so. I am truly in love with two men and these two men truly love me. How blessed I am. Elizabeth thought.

As he continued his kisses, she shifted her legs so she could sit on his lap closer and gently caressed his erection over his trousers.

Richard moaned but broke his kiss. Holding his hand over hers, he gently rubbed himself using her hand and spoke. "My love, I wish to find my release with you again but I want to wait. Would you be... Could you ask Darcy if I may be allowed to love you before you retire with him tonight? I will not ask for more than what we have already experienced unless you allow it, but I wish you to be in my rooms and I wish to take a little more time with you. Could you allow it?" He asked.

"I will ask Fitzwilliam. He and I have discussed in detail what we wish from our unique relationship. Although I will not break my vows, he and I have outlined what we see as acceptable and what cannot ever happen. He is most understanding. I will ask." Elizabeth kissed his lips and rose. "I will see you at dinner. I will go and rest for now, Richard."

"I love you, Elizabeth, with all my heart." Richard smiled as he walked her to her door.

Elizabeth smiled brightly. "I love you, too, Richard."

~*~

Dinner was a joyous affair. Richard was once again laughing and joking with Darcy and Elizabeth, and Georgiana and Lydia described all the wonderful shopping that they had done as well as planned on doing tomorrow. Lady Matlock had desired to have more company so she invited Georgiana and Lydia to remove to Matlock House tonight for a week for an intensive course on housekeeping and etiquette. Lady Iris was to help prepare them and wanted to share all the details of her engagement to the third son of an earl.

Richard was relieved that they would have the house to themselves, even though Darcy House had been converted like Pemberley and Rosings, where the Mistress' room was now a sitting room, and a door was made from Richard's room to that sitting room.

The Rosings' tenants had asked why the Master and Mistress' rooms were so far apart, with the large sitting room in between, and Richard had joked that should the husband and wife have an argument, it would give them a wide berth. He also explained that because he was not planning to marry, he had wanted to give the best room to his cousin and his wife without foregoing the option of separate bedrooms if one should desire.

Although the sitting room would provide much needed privacy, he wanted to kiss and hold Elizabeth in his own rooms. Most of their affections were either from a sitting or standing position and he desired to lay down with her, not for intercourse, but to fully relax and not be rushed.

After dinner, the girls rushed to complete their packing to leave for Matlock House and Elizabeth went with them to assist.

Darcy poured Richard a glass of brandy. "So, you want to bed my wife tonight." He declared.

Richard gulped. It had sounded so much better in his head when he had made the request.

"Um, Darcy, it would not be... I would not be breaking your trust. I... Darce, I missed her so much, I wish to hold her and take longer to... spend time with her tonight." He coloured. *I do not think he will agree. I do not blame him. He cannot be THAT generous.*

Darcy chuckled. "Do not worry, brother. You will have your time with her. I saw the look on your face and knew how much you missed her. Elizabeth asked me what she should do with you." He sighed. "I wish the moral and legal limitations did not apply to us but we must respect the guidelines that have been established before us. Richard, I cannot, I will not allow you to bed my wife," he paused, seeing the disappointment in Richard's face, "to the point of Elizabeth breaking her vows. You must not, you must never violate that trust, Richard. But, I understand your love for her, cousin. If it were not illegal, if it would not be considered immoral, if it were possible for us to both be married to her, we would both take her to bed. But her vows are to me and she will be faithful, but in her innocence, she may give you more than intended. You know what you are about and you must not allow it. Do you understand?"

Richard acknowledged it. "I will not break your trust in me, Darcy."

"Richard, she will join you in your room after I join with her first. She will be my wife before she is anything else. She loves you and wishes to bring you pleasure but I will love her first. She will always choose me first. Be kind to her. Love her and care for her, Richard." Darcy concluded.

They shook hands and parted.

Chapter 8

"Are you well, my love?" Darcy asked.

He had spent an inordinate amount of time to pleasure and love her. He had poured all of his skills in satisfying her and reaching their climax together. Darcy had known that Richard was an experienced lover and wanted to make sure that Elizabeth would not regret marrying an amateur. Even though Richard was not to penetrate her, he was insecure that his cousin would exceed his skills, however illogical as it were.

"I am in bliss, Fitzwilliam, and I cannot imagine being happier than I am now. I have never seen you so dedicated. I feel limp and relaxed in ways I have never been. Are you well? Are you anxious?" Elizabeth caressed his face.

"I love you so much, Elizabeth. I wish I could keep you all for myself but I know that Richard loves you deeply and cannot live without you. I am confident in your love for me, my love, but I am also insecure that he can provide for you something that I cannot." He buried his face on her neck. "I wonder if he is a better lover than me. I wonder if he will satisfy you more than me. I wonder if you will prefer his attentions more than mine." He whispered apprehensively.

Elizabeth stroked his hair as she heard his trepidation and smiled. After all his professed claims of his willingness to share her with his cousin, he was nervous that he was not enough. All of his wealth and holdings and power that he exuded, he was gentle and vulnerable with his wife.

"Fitzwilliam, will you look at me please?" She waited until her eyes beheld hers. "My love, my dearest husband, I have no point of reference on your skills as a lover as you are my first and last husband. True husband. As much as we talk of Richard being my 'other husband', you are truly my one and only. I love you with all my heart and I know that I have all of your love. I do not know if Richard is a great lover. He is certainly more experienced than you, but that does not make it better. It matters not, because I will not take him in. My womanhood is only for you and you have pleasured me tonight above anything I have ever thought possible. I do not have to go to him, my love. I can stay in your arms and we can make love all night and you can keep me in your bed always. You do not have to share me. Richard desires an intimacy with me that satisfies his carnal need without the act of intercourse and I have given and received several times now that satiates my love for him. But my thoughts are always with you and he knows this. He will not take and I will not give more than what we are allowed. You own my body and you have control." Elizabeth paused. She kissed him several times and continued.

"I love him, Fitzwilliam. I do not know how it is possible but I have fallen in love with him and I do see myself as a wife of some sorts with him, but I do not crave him as I do you. He held on to me so steadfastly when we arrived and although I returned his kisses because I missed him and enjoyed his touches, you are always on the forefront of my thoughts. I wish to help him as we three awkwardly love each other but I am yours. Always yours." She considered the opposite situation and asked Darcy in honesty.

"My love, if I had come to you with a previous experience, let us say I was a widow with a prior husband, in a legal marriage, everything appropriate but he had died, and let us say that you loved me and you married me, would you still be wary of your talents as a lover?" She asked.

"I had not considered it. Yes, I would want to know if he was better, bigger, longer." He laughed. "A man wants to be the best."

She laughed as well. "Well, Richard has been with possibly two hundred women, Fitzwilliam. Not two, not two dozen, but two HUNDRED. That is an incredible number and I could never believe that my assistance in helping him would be above it. I cannot imagine that he is being truthful that he says I am better, but he, as well as you, has confirmed that being in love is what makes that difference and I love you so much that that is where the difference lies as well. Our love, our union, is something that he will not experience and will not ask for. He knows that we are constantly loving each other and he does not get jealous because he is content with what he has. I do not know if I could lie with someone who has had hundreds of lovers before me. Even while being in love, I do not know if I have the capability to accept such a past. Knowing that you waited for me is the most incredible gift that is impossible for anyone else to beat. I love that you saved yourself for me and I saved myself for you. I love you so much, husband." She kissed him tenderly.

"Thank you, my love. I love you with all my heart. I know Richard loves you with all his heart and that is the only reason that I am capable of sharing you. I also know you love him. You would not have allowed it if you did not, and I know his cares comfort you. It comforts me as well. I was miserable without him with us since I had not realised how symbiotic we have become. He does not know yet, but I am including him in my will, Elizabeth. He is not only a legal co-guardian to Georgiana but will be yours as well. Should I surpass you, he would be responsible for you as well as Bennet and Richie and will be your protector and advisor until Bennet is of age. I wish to live a very long life with you, but should something happen, he will be able to guard you and love you.

"He is now worth over £10,000, Elizabeth, and he is sharing everything with us. Should something happen to him, Richie is to inherit everything he owns. He has given me the settlement from Miss Bingley's trial to add onto our future daughters' dowry and he also told me that he has over £50,000 that he had saved from my father's will and his income, as well as the 30,000 from Cousin Anne's dowry that he inherited. Typically, he would have been very generous to settle £10- to 20,000 to his wife based on his wealth, but he wanted to give you all of it. He is gifting everything to you as due as his dearest wife. He has placed £80,000 in a trust in your name. With the 50,000 that I settled on you and your 5,000 dowry that I put back into your settlement, you have over £135,000 and are now worth nearly 7,000 a year independently. Our daughters, should we have any, will all be very well-provided for. Part of his businesses in London was to see to your trust. I never thought anyone could be so generous but he is giving you everything he has." He kissed her forehead and continued.

"It is not that he is purchasing your love, but his love is fierce and eternal. After your row in Bath, he had confessed to me that he had been holding something back, that he had kept an escape route open, should our lifestyle become uncomfortable or if we should change our mind and reject him from our lives. But after your argument, he told me that he wished to fully invest in his love for us and our love for him, and he had determined to give all of himself to you and to me. He has been working diligently to help Rosings prosper as well as Pemberley and our investments, my love, and our income is now nearly 50,000 a year. With Rosings and Richard's investments, we are at over 60,000 a year. He truly loves us and that is why I wish to ensure that he know how much we love him and value him. He is a good man, Elizabeth. Even with his two hundred concubines in his past, he has given you everything because he loves you with all of his heart. He told me that making you cry tore at his heart more than all of the battles he experienced and he wishes to never hurt you again. He would give up everything he has to please you. Accept his love and share your love with him, my love." Darcy spoke quietly.

Elizabeth was in shock. It mattered not the amount of her wealth, but the decisions that Richard had made, what he truly gave to them, all of himself and wealth and possessions, touched her heart deeply. She knew that he had not brought up once of any sacrifice on his part and he worked diligently with Fitzwilliam. She felt the love and protection of the two most worthy men and rejoiced.

Darcy spoke, "I believe he has been waiting for you for a long time. He is probably thinking that you will not show, since I have kept you for so long. I hope you will return to me tonight and I will love you again. If you wish to stay the night with him, I understand as well. After our lovemaking tonight, I believe I can part with you for a few hours." He teased.

"I love you. I will return to you. If you are still sleeping, if it is in the morning, I still plan to ravish you with my attentions again. I will remember tonight with the greatest pleasures." Elizabeth rose after giving Darcy a tender kiss.

~*~

Elizabeth washed herself and changed into a more modest nightgown. Donning her robe, she kissed her husband good night again and walked to the sitting room.

She was surprised to find Richard sleeping on the couch. He apparently had been waiting for her and fallen asleep. She smiled. Fitzwilliam had been so intent in loving her that they had made love for over two hours. *I wonder if he was able to hear anything. I hope he did not mind waiting so long.*

Elizabeth leaned down and gently kissed Richard's lips but he did not stir. She sat on the edge of the couch and touched his chest and kissed him again. She heard him whisper, "Elizabeth", but he was still asleep. *He dreams of me. Such a sweet man.* She began to untuck his lawnshirt slowly and began to caress his bare skin with her soft, warm hands. She touched his strong muscular chest and rubbed his nipple. She felt him jerk as he jolted awake.

"My love, you are here. I thought I was dreaming." Richard smiled.

"I am here. Shall we retire to your bed?" Elizabeth seductively asked.

Richard gulped. "Yes. Yes, you are ready? Darcy is well?"

Elizabeth replied honestly, "He was insecure and we had to have a long conversation. He knows that you are an experienced lover and he was afraid that I might be pleasured by you too much, but he knows that you will not fill me as he had done and I would not be able to achieve that pleasure with you so he is comforted. I love you, Richard, but we cannot ever unite in such a way. My body will always belong to my first love, my legal husband, my Fitzwilliam."

They began to walk to his rooms. "I know what you have done. He told me about the trust you set up for me, and I have no words to say how much it means to me. You and Fitzwilliam have taken such care of me that I will become vain again." She laughed. "But it matters not about your wealth. You are a good man and I love you. Please let me know how I can pleasure you, husband." And she slid off her robe to expose her nightgown that was still low cut to emphasise her large bosom. She had not been breastfeeding for almost three months now and her breasts were smaller now, but they were still quite voluptuous.

Richard stepped closer to her and held her cheek and waist. "I meant everything I said to you in Bath. I will no longer be an imposter. I give myself to you fully and freely, Elizabeth. You are my world and everything I have is yours. I cannot live without you and I am grateful for what you freely give and I will not ask for all of you but will treasure what you gift. You are so beautiful. I did not realise your hair was so long." He caressed it gently as he took in her form. "You are by far the handsomest woman of my acquaintance. Will you lie with me in bed? May I get undressed?" She nodded.

Elizabeth climbed into Richard's bed and lay down. She watched as Richard undressed. She had seen his neck and touched his manhood but his body had always been covered. He first took off his shirt then his breeches and stood next to the bed completely nude. He had a gorgeous masculine body. His dark hair and blue eyes were piercing; his facial hair had grown and gave him a rough masculine look. His chest was robust like Fitzwilliam's, with a little more chest hair, and it was obvious that he was not an indulgent man who sat and grew fat. He was muscular, with thick arms, and his thighs were strong from riding his horse and had several scars on his torso and arms. Elizabeth flushed at seeing his magnificent body with his massive erection pointing straight at her. She imagined that he must have satisfied all those women quite vigorously. She recalled her incredibly handsome husband taking her so hard and so long that she became wet with desire.

Richard climbed next to her. He had been nude with so many women before and he had never been shy, but he felt insecure with Elizabeth. *Does she find my body attractive? Am I too large? She is so precious to me; I only wish to please her.* He knew Darcy cut a dashing figure and he had seen his cousin's torso often while fencing. They were built very similarly so he hoped his naked body should not shock Elizabeth.

"I love having you in my bed, Elizabeth. I have never brought anyone into my bed before. Even with other women, it was never in my bed, in my home. This means the world to me, my love. I hope you are not displeased with what you see." Richard whispered shyly as he caressed her arm lying next to her.

"I am glad to be here with you. Your body is magnificent, Richard. I am certain all your ladies before were quite impressed as I am now. You have scars that I did not know you had. From the war?" Elizabeth asked, gently touching several on his chest.

"Yes, some from training, some from the enemy. This one was from the continent," pointing to the large scar on his left side, "it almost killed me but I was able to recover after two months." Richard smiled.

"I will kiss all your scars and replace the unpleasant memories." She proceeded to kiss every one of his scars on his body, from his face to his legs, while he moaned watching her lips on his body. She grazed his manhood gently as she kissed his scar on his hip and his phallus jerked in anticipation of his pleasures.

As Elizabeth kissed his scars and swirled her tongue on the larger ones, Richard thought he would explode. *She is such a seductress! I have never felt so out of control in my life! I wish had more scars...*

280

"What else shall I do? What do you intend to do with me, sir?" She teased.

"I wish to love you and kiss you. I wish for you to stay with me awhile." Looking at her breasts, he asked, "May I kiss you? May I touch you?" She nodded.

Richard stroked her cheek and kissed her lips. Starting gentle, the pressure grew until his mouth opened and she opened hers then licked her gently and sucked on her tongue. His shaking hands drew down to her neck and to her décolletage until he cupped her breast over her nightgown. She moaned as he whispered, 'perfect', and rolled her nipple with his fingers.

He rolled her onto her back and lay over her, keeping his weight on his knees on either side of her thighs and his elbows and kissed her deeply, causing Elizabeth to moan loudly.

Richard dipped his lips behind her ear and neck, continuing to caress her breasts as he lifted himself from her and exposed her breasts from her nightgown. He whispered, 'exquisite', before lowering his mouth to gently kiss her breasts one at a time and suckled her nipples. He returned to her neck and whispered, "I love you so much; you are more beautiful than I ever imagined. I love you, my Elizabeth, my wife."

He lay on top of her and Elizabeth could feel his gorging erection. It lay straight at the juncture of her legs with the tip near her navel, and he began to move his hips against hers and he returned his attention to her breasts. She rubbed on the smooth skin of his back, while he made love to her. As he groped her, he continued his thrusting motion against her belly and kissed her deeply again, his moans growing louder until he lifted his face from her and yelled, "Elizabeth!" He released his seed onto her nightgown and panted.

After shivering, he kissed her neck and lips frantically. "Oh, my Elizabeth, are you well? I hope you are well. My god, that was... you... incredible... so beautiful... lovely. That... I could not... imagined..." He could not think straight. To hold her and love her in his bed was the greatest privilege and pleasure he had ever received.

"Oh, Richard, that was lovely. I am delighted that you enjoyed loving me. Your kisses overwhelmed me. Do you truly find my body so pleasurable?" Elizabeth shyly asked. She could not believe that only touching her body like so could bring him pleasures when he had such extensive experience with so many women. If his mistress was an indication of the types of women that he found attractive, Elizabeth guessed his past lovers must have been extremely beautiful. She had seen the types of women that chased him and although she thought herself plainer in comparison, he had dismissed them as unattractive.

He was an incredible lover. She was not only damp where he had released on her but she was wet between her legs. She had enjoyed his kisses and his caresses, and his mouth on her breasts was so sensual, she was craving Fitzwilliam's hard manhood inside her again. *Richard is truly a fantastic lover! What a wanton creature I am. After spending two hours with Fitzwilliam and another half hour with Richard, I am craving to be filled again!*

Richard slowly lifted himself off and lay next to her. He gathered her in his arms and kissed her temple. "My wife, I love you so much. I have never had such pleasure before. I know you may not believe me, but my time with you, every kiss, every touch, has exceeded any other experience that I have had. I love you deeply with all my heart and our lovemaking satisfies my soul. I apologise for the mess," he looked below. He attempted to wipe his semen with the sheet, only for Elizabeth to giggle.

"That tickles, Richard." She laughed.

He smiled. *I love her more than before.* He kissed her again on the lips. "I wish I could pleasure you somehow but I will leave it for Darcy. I know he pleasured you many times and I am glad. Will you stay with me for a while?" He quickly added, "Not through the night; you should return to Darcy soon, but a little longer." He pleaded with his eyes. He wanted to hold her close.

"Of course, my love. I love laying here with you. You comfort me so much." Elizabeth answered.

His heart was elated as kissed her. As his tongue licked her lips, she opened her mouth to touch his tongue again and suckled it. He was burning with desire for her again and he delved his tongue into her again and kissed her passionately. He realised that within minutes releasing, he was hard again. *I just came! How is this possible? With other women, they had to suck me into an erection.*

His erection rubbed against Elizabeth's hip and she knew that he was aroused again. She smiled after he released her mouth. "Again?" She asked with mirth in her eyes.

"Oh, my love, I cannot seem to get enough of you. It will pass. You do not... Aahhh!!" He began to reply but moaned as he felt her hand stroke his rock-hard manhood.

Elizabeth turned her body to face him lying on her side and stroked him as she kissed him. She moved her hands up and down his full shaft with her right hand and caressed his hair with her left, bringing his mouth closer to hers. His hand was on her breast again and she sighed happily. Richard bent down to lick her nipples and Elizabeth let out a loud moan. Seconds later, Richard grunted forcefully and released in her hand.

Richard grabbed his beloved and panted in her ear. "My god, I love you, I love you. I worship your body and I am eternally grateful for your love and generosity. Thank you, my love. I will buy you a hundred new nightgowns. I love you."

Elizabeth giggled. "I have plenty, Richard. I love you, too. I am happy to love you. Now rest. I will wait until you are asleep if I can. Good night."

Richard held her close and smelled her scent. *Bliss!* He soon fell asleep and began to snore lightly.

Elizabeth caressed his face, kissed his cheek, and left his room after grabbing her robe.

~*~

When she returned to her room, she saw that Darcy was sleeping. *He had done so much work to pleasure me that he must have been exhausted*, she thought. *My sweet, sweet Fitzwilliam.*

She went to her dressing room and pulled out a third nightgown. *Hannah is going to wonder how many times he climaxed! There must be at least six stains.* She laughed. *Well, my two husbands are quite demanding!*

After donning a fresh gown, she crawled into bed and held Darcy's hand. He was sleeping soundly and she smiled. She was still wide-awake from being so aroused. Richard was truly a fantastic lover and even though he had not penetrated her and never touched her below, she was exceedingly wet from his kisses and caresses that she was beyond aroused. She found her husband most attractive and desired him. She began to touch herself as Darcy had done for her so many times and began to become desperate to be filled.

She knew she should let her poor husband rest, but when he turned onto his back, he was still naked below the sheets. She ducked under the cover and began to stroke his manhood as he slept. Although still lightly snoring, his penis became harder and she put him inside her mouth. She wanted some part of her to be filled and began sucking on his phallus that continued to grow. She heard him whisper, "Elizabeth", as she moved her head up and down, stroking his shaft. As it had grown very large, she lifted herself up and impaled herself onto his erection.

Darcy had been worried. He knew that Richard would be kind to her but hoped that she would return soon. He had wanted to remain awake but as soon as the candle was out, he had quickly fallen asleep. He dreamt of his beautiful wife, that she was mouthing him and he called out her name.

Suddenly, he was fully awake when he felt his cock being wrapped in her flesh and flashed his eyes open to see his wife riding him. The bed curtains were open so he could see her moving herself up and down, her luscious breasts bouncing as she moaned loudly. He thrust up to her and met her movements and when she cried out loudly as she reached her orgasm, he came again as he was incredibly aroused to wake up to his wife desperately riding him. She leaned forward and collapsed on top of him and he kissed her hair and held her tightly as she finished shivering her climax.

Richard must have gotten her quite rankled. Wow! I cannot believe I released again. As long as she wants me and she returns to my cock, I am satisfied with this arrangement. Darcy thought.

"Oh, my love, that felt so incredible! Were you mouthing me? You are well? Richard was kind to you?" Darcy asked, thinking, *He probably exploded on sight! Elizabeth is so delicious.*

Elizabeth panted for several more breaths and answered, "I am well. I was so desperate for you. I needed you to fill me and put you in my mouth until I could ride you. I love you so much, Fitzwilliam." She wanted to reassure her husband. "Richard was gentle. He took his pleasures twice and he was so grateful and I wanted you desperately after his teases. Oh, my love, there is nothing like our lovemaking. Tonight has been so special, Fitzwilliam. Thank you, my love."

"I love you. Thank you for returning to me." Darcy considered before continuing, "I do not know how often we should allow it but if this is the result after Richard spends some time with you, perhaps we should consider it a regular thing. I know I go insane without you for more than a week. We will need to talk with Richard on his thoughts on how we should arrange this but we will need to be careful and we cannot risk it when we have guests residing with us, but I am certainly willing to give you your heart's desires. Not every night, though, even if Richard wishes that! I need to fall asleep with you in MY arms, wife." He laughed.

"I love you. We will talk about it later. I have ruined three nightgowns tonight and I do not think Hannah can handle washing so many stains!" She giggled.

"I will buy you a hundred new gowns." Darcy answered.

"That is what he said!" Elizabeth laughed.

They fell peacefully asleep and woke quite late the next morning and all three were late to breakfast by quarter of an hour.

Chapter 9

Georgiana giggled as she lined up for her dance. She was standing with her brother for the first dance at her Coming Out Ball and she was excited to finally have her day.

Darcy smiled and pondered how quickly she had grown. He was genuinely proud of his baby sister and knew that he had so much to be thankful for. He looked lovingly at his wife and winked at her, who returned his smile, and proceeded to dance.

Elizabeth was dancing with Richard for the first set, one of the rare opportunities where Darcy was unavailable, as he was dancing with Georgiana. She saw her dearest husband contentedly smiling down like a proud father and knew that he was immensely pleased.

Looking at Richard, he smiled softly at her with his eyes passionate for her as always. It had been two weeks since they had shared the intimate experience and Elizabeth knew he was still revelling from it.

"Thank you again for your generous gift, Richard. I am in awe of it. It is such a beautiful necklace." Elizabeth expressed her appreciation.

"It is my pleasure. I was glad it was finally ready today after I had commissioned it three weeks ago." Richard answered as they continued their dance steps.

He had presented her a beautiful necklace that had an incredibly large emerald surrounded by diamonds, encased in gold with a long chain that she could wear over her dress or accompany it with another necklace. On the back, it had a simple inscription, *All my love.*

Elizabeth had been touched that he had purchased this incredible jewellery for her even before their night together. Ever since Bath, he was so generous and he had shown her daily how much he treasured her with his words and actions. The day after their lovemaking, he had a dozen red roses delivered to her as well as a bottle of the finest whiskey for Darcy. He continued to gift her with flowers and trinkets, from jewellery boxes to books to ribbons. Anything that she might desire, he thought of her and purchased them for her.

"I never courted you properly. I do not know how in the world I won your heart but it is my privilege to give you everything I have. I do not have family jewels to give you but I do wish you to be showered with anything I can offer you. I am thankful that Darcy is allowing it. He has so much more to give you but he wishes you to be happy. I am truly honoured that you have accepted the necklace, Elizabeth. You are my world." He whispered when they were close next time. In a louder voice, "So, is your dance card completely full, Mrs. Darcy? Even after being off the market for a year and a half, I see that you still have men flocking all about you." He teased as he winked.

He knew he himself was the most avid suitor of them all. He had seen several men, some married and some single, circling around her, most likely to attempt to seduce her or to arrange a liaison, as many wives of the *ton* did. He and Darcy had protected her as much as possible from the scavengers but it had been impossible to protect her from having some of them on her dance card tonight. He would kill any and all of them with his bare hands if they attempted anything.

Her melodious laughter filled the air. "That is ridiculous! You make it sound as if I am a meal and the hungry predators are all standing around so they can feast on me.

Surely Georgiana is the true centre of attention and I am only here to enjoy the party. Aunt Susan was instrumental in making her ball a success." Elizabeth changed the subject.

You still have no idea how beautiful you are. These men would risk life and limb to receive a piece of what I have been given if they thought they had a slim chance. Richard thought. "Well, I hope you will enjoy yourself because I know it is you, who are responsible for the planning and the details of making this ball so wonderful. Mother has commented that you are a true gem and she only wished I could find a wife like you. Little does she know." He smirked.

The set ended and Richard led Elizabeth to the punch table, continuing their banter while awaiting Darcy and Georgiana to finish conversing with guests who were congratulating his young cousin. Richard was to dance the next with Georgiana and Darcy was to dance with Elizabeth.

As he stood to wait, his mother approached and kissed his cheek and Elizabeth's.

"My dear Lizzy, this is, by far, the most splendid ball yet! Congratulations on all your hard work, my dear. You have made Uncle Henry and me so proud!" She gleamed.

"Thank you, Aunt Susan. I could not have done much without you, though. I truly appreciate all your help." Elizabeth humbly replied.

Then, Mr. Bennet approached. "My dear, I believe Lydia is quite upset with me for stepping on her toes twice. She says her shoe needs quick attention. Would you be able to assist before the next set begins?" He asked bashfully. The Bennets had arrived in London last week and the Darcys were hosting them for three weeks. The Bingleys remained in Hertfordshire due to the recent birth.

The plan was to stay in London for two months then remove to Netherfield for Kitty's wedding with Mr. Goulding, and afterwards, Darcy, Elizabeth, and Richard would finally return to Pemberley for the summer. The trio desperately desired time and privacy in their little paradise.

Elizabeth dipped a curtsey to Lady Matlock and rushed to assist Lydia and Mr. Bennet returned to his wife's side to ensure she remained proper in this company. She had improved much but still needed to be supervised.

Lady Matlock grabbed Richard's arm, not seeing that his eyes were following Elizabeth's delectable figure and began. "Richard, Lizzy is truly delightful and she makes such a good wife. I am glad to see you smiling and congenial today. I know you have been taciturn and unapproachable for over a year and it is about time you find yourself a wife. If Lizzy only had a twin!" She sighed. "But I must demand that you ask Lady Isabelle to dance. Not only is she a dear friend of Georgiana's but the daughter to our dear friends, the Duke and Duchess of Derbyshire. If you do not ask, you will offend their Graces. Come now. Let us go." She began to drag his arm.

Not wanting to cause a scene and unsure of how to get out of it, he resignedly walked to the young miss, who was speaking with Darcy and Georgiana. He bowed. His mother elbowed him. Rolling his eyes discreetly, he asked, "Lady Isabelle, how good to see you again. If you are available, may I have the pleasure of dancing a set with you?"

"Yes, Mr. Fitzwilliam," she shyly answered. "I am available for the supper set, sir."

He sighed, "Thank you." He bowed over her hand and left with Darcy to get another drink. *A stiff one! My mother and her matchmaking; when will she understand that I will never marry? I am already a husband to the most wonderful woman of my acquaintance and no one will ever match nor exceed her.*

"Oh, Aunt Susan is on fire tonight, Richard! She has arranged all of Georgiana and Lady Isabelle's cards as well as Lydia's. She wants to make sure that all of the most eligible bachelors see them paraded around." Darcy chuckled.

"Argh, I only wish to eat and dance with Elizabeth again and go to bed. Is that too much to ask?" Richard whined.

Darcy burst out laughing again. "If *I* have to be here, *you* have to be here, brother; although I am infinitely pleased to be married and not forced to dance with these young debutantes. Tongues will be wagging when you are seen with Lady Isabelle. You have not danced with a single lady except with Caroline Bingley in over a year."

Shit! I hope no one gets the wrong idea. Where is Elizabeth? I must let her know. Richard panicked.

"Do not worry, I will let her know how it came about, Richard. She will understand." Darcy winked, seeing Richard's pale face. Richard let out a sigh of relief.

~*~

The dances progressed and everyone was having a merry time, with Elizabeth dancing a set with Captain Wentworth and Darcy and Richard a set each with Mrs. Wentworth. Elizabeth was very pleased to see her dear friend and they chatted as much as possible between sets. She knew that Captain Wentworth was beaming with pride at his beautiful wife and guessed that they were quite enjoying the marriage bed again.

When the supper set arrived, Richard sought out Lady Isabelle to claim her for their dance. He had only danced with Elizabeth, Georgiana, his sister, and Mrs. Wentworth so far. He only had this set and then with Elizabeth again before having completed his duty for the dances.

Lady Isabelle was seventeen and very beautiful. She was tall with light brunette hair and large blue eyes. She had been a childhood friend of the Fitzwilliams and the Darcys as she was the same age as Georgiana, and he was not blind to the fact that she had a light figure and had grown into a very accomplished woman. But with the fourteen-year age difference and his heart being completely captured, he had not looked at her twice.

He was startled when Lady Isabelle had asked him a question. He had been reminiscing on the beautiful kiss he had received from Elizabeth after he had given her the necklace this afternoon and did not hear what she had asked him.

"My sincere apologies, Lady Isabelle, my mind was elsewhere for a moment. Could you please repeat your question?" Richard requested with embarrassment.

Lady Isabelle laughed softly. "I was asking if you were always so reticent while you danced. I saw that you were quite at ease for the other dances and suddenly you are so quiet. Shall we talk of books or philosophy?"

Richard smiled broadly, recollecting his conversation with Elizabeth when they had danced at Matlock House after the wedding. Lady Isabelle gasped softly, realising that he was the most handsome she had ever seen him with the smile, and flashed her own. Not realising the picture he presented, he spoke and conversed more freely, all the while thinking only of his beloved and glancing at her direction as discreetly as possible.

~*~

After the pair sat with Darcy and Elizabeth for supper, the four chatted comfortably. Georgiana was sitting with Lord and Lady Matlock, and Lydia was sitting with the Gardiners and Bennets. The Wentworths were sitting with several of Richard's military friends and all were a merry party.

Elizabeth looked at Lady Isabelle and saw a more confident version of Georgiana. Her hair was darker but she was friendly and very beautiful. Elizabeth guided their conversations to talk of general categories as well as the splendour of Chatsworth where she had visited and she smiled when she recalled that that was where she had fainted and Darcy had been informed of her first pregnancy. She had been ill for the past two mornings and she had guessed that she might be with child again. It thrilled her that she might be carrying Fitzwilliam's next child and knew he would be joyous.

She was watching Lady Isabelle and Richard in conversation and noticed that Lady Isabelle's eyes were drawn to Richard more often than not, and that she gazed at him in admiration when Richard was talking with herself or Darcy.

Oh my, I think Richard has captured her heart already! But of course! She grew up seeing him with her older brothers and most likely fancied him as a young girl. Elizabeth thought. *I must ask Georgiana if she is aware of Lady Isabelle's feelings. How disappointed she will be. Richard is so handsome; nearly as much as my Fitzwilliam and is certainly the most eligible bachelor here!*

Elizabeth no longer had any insecurities of Richard's love for her. She looked down at her gift and smiled. She was wearing two necklaces, with the longer chain under a set of the most incredible Darcy jewels.

She had been shocked when Fitzwilliam had finally been able to take her to the vault and showed her the massive collection of the largest and rarest jewels, only second or third to the Queen's. It was no wonder Darcy had been so coveted for a husband.

To see the combination of the Darcy emeralds and Richard's beautiful necklace perfectly coordinated with her dress had made her proud. How she loved her men.

~*~

As Elizabeth danced with Richard for the next set, she asked, "So, it seemed you enjoyed your dance and supper with Lady Isabelle. How did you find her?"

"She was pleasant but you know my eyes were only for you, my love." Richard whispered in her ear at the next pass.

Elizabeth's eyes shone in merriment. She knew full well that he paid her little attention. "Well, I hope she will not be too disappointed, Mr. Fitzwilliam. I understand she has been a long-time admirer of yours." Georgiana had confirmed that Isabelle had been in love with Richard since she was eight years old.

Richard coloured. "I know nothing about it. I always saw her as a little sister or even like a daughter. How could I look at her any other way when I am fourteen years older than she?"

"Well, she is no longer a child and very beautiful. You are nearly ten years older than me, Richard!" She teased.

"Yes, you are an old married woman who wants to wear a cap. Old woman, my arse!" He flirted back. How he loved her.

Elizabeth giggled. "Well, I wonder if you should ask another single lady to dance with you tonight. Rumours will be rampant that you only asked for one dance with one single woman."

"I could kiss you! That is the perfect solution to my dilemma. I was trying to figure out what to do, as Mother insisted that I dance with her and I did not want any ideas of my attachment to her. General Darcy, I shall follow your strategy." He glowed. "And you *will* get that kiss from me later, wife!" He quietly whispered. *So intelligent, my Elizabeth, my wife.*

"Well, I will recommend Miss Fairfax. She is brunette and genteel and quite single, but I am aware of her attachment to another gentleman who will soon make his intentions known. You will not injure her and perhaps help her suitor decide on her faster. Shall you always call me General, Richard? I find myself quite liking it." She winked.

Richard wanted to drag her to the study and make love to her right then. He would definitely need to find a few precious minutes with her soon. "Minx!" He laughed.

Darcy approached them after they completed the set. "So, I have heard rumours from several matrons as I passed that you are desperately in love with a lady known to you for years and that you have not sought out a wife for two years because you have been waiting for her to come out. I seriously hope you do not have any intentions towards my sister! It will be pistols at dawn for you should you desire to court that young lady!" He sternly commented, as they moved to a corner for some privacy. He then smiled and whispered, "As I know for a fact that you are already husband to the most wonderful woman in the lands, I will overlook the rumours... this time!" He teased. They laughed heartily together.

Richard answered, "Well, General Darcy here had a brilliant idea and I must carry out her orders. Sir," he dramatically saluted. "General." He bowed to Elizabeth with a smile and separated to ask Miss Fairfax to dance.

"You are brilliant, my love. Aunt Susan will not know what to do with having two ladies to try to attach to Richard." Turning to her and kissing her hand, he asked, "Are you well, Elizabeth? I saw you pale at dinner for a moment. You seem to recover quickly but I did notice it."

"Oh, you dear man. I cannot get away with anything from you, I suppose. I have been ill for the past two mornings and it is definitely too early but I may be with child. I have not had regular courses after I stopped breastfeeding and I am not certain how far along I might be, if I am indeed with child, but my best guess would be two months. Still too early, my love." Elizabeth whispered.

Darcy had the largest grin and he kissed her hands several times. "I wish I could take you to my bed and look at your body. Oh, my love. I wish for you to take good care. I know that your body had gone through so much with the twins and I am afraid that it might be too early. If you are two months, then when..."

"Early January." Elizabeth answered.

"Oh, my wife. I love you. Please promise me you will take care. May I get you a drink, some water? You should be sitting. Let us find you a comfortable chair." Darcy began to flutter.

"Fitzwilliam, Fitzwilliam! I am quite well. It is too early and we will have to wait, my love. I am well." She comforted him with a large smile. "I do not know what happened to my next dancing partner, though. Mr. Thorpe was to dance with me next but he appears to be missing."

Darcy smirked mischievously. "Well, I was told that he was on your dance card but Richard and I approached him to reconsider and he sends his regrets. While you were dancing the other sets, Richard and I ensured that he would never be without a glass of the best brandy in his hand and by the fourth set, he could not stand on his own two feet. Richard put him into his coach during the fifth set and you will be free this set to rest."

Elizabeth tapped Darcy's arm in jest. "Sir! How could you deny your wife a dance with a most eligible bachelor at this ball? I was looking forward to all his flattery and leering of my bosoms, not to mention the stench of the alcohol that was seeping through his skin by the end of the second set!"

Darcy burst out laughing, loud enough for heads to turn. "I dare refuse to allow that man to touch my wife and I know Richard was itching to give him a solid jab on his nose. John Thorpe is a vain, self-absorbed arse and he will be refused entry to our homes, even if he dare arrives with the Prince Regent. I was unhappy that he swindled his way in tonight and I was ready to disgrace him in public for requesting a dance with you, but Richard advised me to keep you and Georgiana happy and get the drunken scoundrel out of our home quietly. We will protect you always, my love."

Elizabeth beamed proudly. "I love you." They smiled at each other.

They watched the gossips fan themselves and whisper loudly as they saw Richard dancing with Miss Fairfax. They giggled when Lady Matlock's eyes bulged in shock and she hurried to her friends to obtain more information about the second unattached lady that her favourite son had danced with tonight. Elizabeth noted that Lady Isabelle appeared disappointed but was distracted by another gentleman who was talking animatedly with her during their dance.

Richard only had eyes for his beloved. He paid no mind to the half dozen married women or widows who attempted to capture his attentions to lure him into their beds again, nor did he even look at the directions of the single ladies that he had danced with last year. Unless he was with his cousins, his face was kept stoic and serious, keeping his eye out on his sister's or Georgiana's dance partners. He had no time or care for anyone else than his family's happiness and most importantly, Elizabeth's. He watched Elizabeth smile and enjoy herself and frowned at anyone who leered at her, ready to kick them off the property at a moment's notice should they misbehave.

The party ended and all toasted the belle of the ball as well as the hosts. After the guests dissolved, Darcy and Elizabeth retired to their rooms to celebrate, but not before Richard was able to find several precious minutes to make love to Elizabeth most passionately in their shared sitting room.

Chapter 10

The next weeks flew by. Georgiana had a string of callers every day and there were four gentlemen whom she was quite interested in getting to know better. Darcy and Elizabeth sat with her and sometimes Richard joined as well, to watch and interview those men to ensure they were suitable. There had been more than twenty callers, as Georgiana was quite eligible with her wealth and connections, but after each meeting with her fierce guardians, only four remained.

Darcy and Richard promised Georgiana that they would not be so stern with the remaining suitors and that she would need to determine which man was worthy of her notice. Lady Matlock sometimes chaperoned them when Elizabeth was not able.

The Bennets, with Lydia, who was only desperate to see the soldiers in Meryton again, returned to Longbourn to prepare for Kitty's wedding and Elizabeth had been very busy setting up her charity foundation. With her current wealth, she desired to help the poor and those in need and had fervently championed several charities already but also established the Darcy Fitzwilliam Foundation, in honour of both of her favourite men, supporting the arts and sciences as well as providing jobs for the poor and shelters for abused women.

It also appeared that she might indeed be with child. She had the symptoms of nausea in the mornings consistently and unable to tolerate some of her favourite food now. She had a nagging ache in her lower abdomen, though, and she attempted to rest as often as she could.

Darcy was ensconced in the study with Lord Matlock as they discussed Georgiana. He would be leaving with Elizabeth and Richard to Netherfield for Kitty's wedding and did not know if he should return to London after or head up to Pemberley as originally planned. He had not thought Georgiana would be so interested in marriage during her first season and had planned to allow her to stay with the Matlocks to attend the parties, but her suitors, especially one of them, appeared to be quite interested.

Lady Isabelle was disappointed when Richard Fitzwilliam did not call on her when she had enjoyed their dance so much. She hoped that he was attracted to her, as he smiled and made pleasant conversations during their dance and they both had enjoyed supper very much. She attempted to not dwell on their brief time together but she believed him to be the handsomest man of her acquaintance.

Her older brother by six years, who was much younger than Richard and Darcy, had become interested in his sister's friend and had begun to call on Georgiana. Although the third son of a Duke, he still had an income of 8,000 a year and a comfortable estate in Derbyshire and would be a fine match for Georgiana Darcy.

Elizabeth had just returned from her meeting with the ladies regarding her foundation and feeling queasy, desired to rest. She became dizzy and after sitting in the drawing room for a few moments, she slowly stood up, deciding that she needed to lie down in her bed.

As she began to rise, Richard entered and greeted her. He had just returned from his club and had been eager to see Elizabeth as his custom whenever he had not seen her for a few hours. "Elizabeth! I am so happy to see you!" He quickly noticed that she was pale. "My god! What is wrong?" He quickly rushed over to her side as she began to double over in pain. He caught her as she fell into his arms and fainted.

He lifted her up and saw that there was blood where she had been sitting and the back of her dress was damp with blood. He lifted her up immediately and boomed at the footman to fetch a doctor. He carried her to her bedroom and laid her down, calling for her maid and yelling for Wilkins to notify Darcy immediately. He cradled her cheeks and kissed her lips several times. "Oh, Elizabeth... I thought you might be with child. Oh, my love." He cried for the despair that she would feel.

Darcy entered his room and saw Richard kneeling next to the bed kissing his wife's forehead. He saw the tears fall from his face and knew the babe was lost. Richard stood as soon as he heard Darcy rushing to his wife and whispered, "I am sorry, Darcy." He shook his head and departed, seeing that Hannah and other maids were quickly rushing in to change her clothes.

Darcy sat with Elizabeth in bed and held her tightly. She began to stir but remained pale. As soon as she saw his face, she knew that she had lost the baby. "Oh, Fitzwilliam! I am so sorry. Our baby..." she sobbed.

He rubbed her back and comforted her. "It was not to be, my love. You did nothing wrong. He was not to stay but he was loved for the short time that he was inside you. When you are ready, we will try again. I love you, Elizabeth. Do not blame yourself. Remember that you are loved so dearly."

The doctor arrived and confirmed that she had suffered a miscarriage but having had twins prior and being young, that she should make a full recovery. Rest for two weeks with light activity was prescribed and Darcy stayed with her until she cried out her tears and fell asleep.

~*~

Darcy found Richard pacing in their shared sitting room as he wanted to make sure Richard was aware of the latest. His cousin was exactly as he had suspected; pacing frantically, eyes red-rimmed with recent tears, and dark circles under his eyes. *Poor, Richard. He truly loves her as much as I. I am glad I am no longer jealous of his attentions to Elizabeth. We both need him in our lives.*

"Richard."

Richard jumped and ran towards the door to stand in front of him. "Is she well? The baby?" He was desperate for news.

"She is well. The babe is lost. She is sad but physically, she will recover fully. The doctor prescribed two weeks of rest." Darcy took his usual seat and sighed. "She will need a lot of love, Richard. She blames herself."

Richard spluttered, "But... but that is not possible! Babes are lost all the time and she has been resting more than ever. I... she did not tell me yet but when I saw that certain food were starting to bother her and her bosoms were more tender, I had guessed it. She must not blame herself!"

"I know, Richard. But she takes too much upon herself. She confessed that she had felt more cramps and pain but did not seek help. There would have been no way to prevent it. I am going to write a letter for Aunt Gardiner to visit but I do not wish for her mother to know. She would only make things worse. I need your help, Richard." Darcy paused.

"Anything, Darce." Richard quickly replied.

"I need one of us to stay with her at all times. I am wrapping up business here and have several more appointments to go and I wish to take her to Pemberley as soon as Kitty's wedding is completed. We will have two more weeks here, spend two nights at Netherfield, then will leave for home. I do not wish her to be distressed at all and you and I can ensure it. Like we did before, Richard, can we do that?" Darcy asked.

"That is exactly what I wished to do. Anything for our Elizabeth. May I go see her? I need to see her." Richard agreed.

"Yes, I will write to Aunt Gardiner to arrive this evening. Do not be seen in our room but I will leave our bedroom door open later tonight. I give you leave to enter our rooms, stay as you had done after our attack like before, for as long as you wish. I know she will be comforted by your presence."

"Thank you, Darcy." Richard tapped his cousin's arm and ran to the door.

After he opened the door, he entered hesitantly to not awaken her. He sat on the chair next to her bed and gently caressed her tear-stained cheeks. *Oh, my love. You must not carry the burden. I love you so much.*

After a quarter hour, she began to stir. She opened her eyes slightly and saw Richard. She smiled gently. "Richard."

"Elizabeth, I am here. I will always be here, my love." He kissed her hands.

"Did you have to carry me all the way to my bed again? Why do I keep fainting in front of you?" She teased.

Richard smiled. *She is teasing me. After all this, she still makes me smile.* "I love you. It is my honour to carry you whenever you wish and you will have your house filled with many babies. It was too early after our sons. Your body needed rest." He kissed her hands again. "I will stay with you, my love. Sleep."

She softly smiled again and her eyes fluttered and she quickly fell asleep.

He leaned and kissed her on the lips and sat back, opening the book that she had been reading and staying next to her side until her aunt arrived.

~*~

Elizabeth was distraught at the loss of her baby but knew that it was common. She carried the guilt of not seeking help earlier, though. When Aunt Madeline arrived, she cried her heart out and despaired her loss but her aunt had reiterated again and again that she was not at fault and that she herself had suffered two miscarriages.

After being comforted, Mrs. Gardiner kissed her forehead and promised to return the next day. As soon as the door closed, she heard the sitting room door open. She smiled when she saw Richard enter.

Oh, the poor man. He must have been lying in wait by the door to return to me. Elizabeth thought.

"Elizabeth, how are you feeling?" Richard tentatively asked.

Elizabeth stretched her arm to hold his hand. He rushed over and kissed it and sat next to her on the bed.

"I am better. I will be better. Thank you for caring for me. Thank you for always being here, taking care of me and scooping me up to save me or protect me. I cannot imagine my life without having Fitzwilliam and you in it." Elizabeth cried as she smiled.

Richard was gladdened to hear that she was feeling better and that she was pleased with his love. "I will always be here and Darcy will be returning shortly. One of us will always be with you, my love. Your only duty is to rest and be well. We are at your beck and call, milady." He teased, as he caressed her face and kissed her tenderly.

"You are my world, Elizabeth. Everything will be well and I will take care of you."

Then, the door opened and Darcy entered with his two squirming and giggling sons in tow. "Look who wants to see their mama!" He laughed. He placed the boys on the bed and they quickly crawled over to Elizabeth and began to climb on her, calling out, "Mamamam". Darcy and Richard grabbed one of the boys each and placed them at her sides so she could cuddle with them. They both smiled at each other as they saw that their beloved was teary-eyed but happy to be with the most important men in her life.

The boys began to drool quite copiously and Richard laughed as he pulled out his handkerchief and wiped their mouths. Elizabeth thanked him and turned to her husband, "Fitzwilliam, could you grab that box on my dresser for me? I had wanted to wait but I believe I will give it to Richard now."

Darcy smiled and returned quickly with a small box about the size of a book. He gave it to Elizabeth.

Elizabeth handed it to Richard and spoke, "I know it is a little early for your birthday gift but since we are all here, I would like to give this to you. It is not much but I hope you will like it."

Richard received the box from the woman he loved and was curious what she had given him. It was light and he did not know what could be in it. He slowly unwrapped the beautiful ribbon and pocketed it then he opened the box and saw a stack of handkerchiefs that had his initials embroidered in one corner. His eyes teared up as he saw sprigs of lavender flowers beneath the initials.

Oh, my love. This is a treasure. No one had ever done this for him before; it was something that a wife would do for her husband and he knew that he was truly her husband now. To have been accepted by them both touched his heart. He gently touched over the stitches that her hands had made to embroider his initials. The time and the love that she poured into making these were precious to him.

"Thank you, Elizabeth. I shall always carry one with me. This is truly the best gift I could have received. Everything from you is precious, my love." Richard wiped his eyes. He cleared his throat. "Ahem. Darcy, thank you for allowing this. I am touched."

Darcy beamed. "Elizabeth has been embroidering for me for so long that I had almost forgotten how my first set affected me. Our Elizabeth is a treasure, is she not?"

"That she is." Richard laughed.

Suddenly, the boys were restless again and began to crawl. Then, Bennet, who was closer to Richard, reached out his arms to Richard to be lifted up. Richard easily took him in his arms and rocked him. Bennet blurted out, "Papapapa" and Richie also began to yell "Papapap", crawling to Darcy. The men were shocked. The boys had only spoken 'mama' for Elizabeth.

Darcy and Richard looked at each other and traded babies. The boys continued their babbling and Bennet put his head on Darcy's shoulder and sighed, "Papapa," and continued his chattering.

Richard held Richie and hugged him. He squirmed and screamed out, "Papapapa!!!"

Elizabeth laughed softly, "Our boys have publicly announced you both as their papas, gentlemen. Congratulations on becoming their fathers!"

The group laughed and continued to play with the babies. They knew everything would be well.

Chapter 11

By the time the group arrived at Netherfield, Elizabeth had fully recovered and was happy again. She had gone through periods of sadness and tears but Darcy and Richard continually assured her of their love and she was able to rally on.

Elizabeth sat with Jane in the mistress' private sitting room to discuss the event and to catch her up on the latest gossips.

"I was very sad but I am better now. I am glad that I already had the boys; to have suffered a miscarriage without having children already would have been devastating. They are so happy to be in the country. I cannot wait to go home." Elizabeth shared.

The ladies could see Darcy, Richard, and Bingley outside with the babies. Darcy and Richard were holding each boys' arms and having them walk to exercise their little legs, while Bingley grinned and carried his daughter in his arms. Laughter could be heard as Bennet or Richie would try to stand alone and fall again and again.

Jane smiled, "They are wonderful, are they not? Charles has been a good father these past four months and he has been so happy with the baby. You are fortunate that you have Mr. Fitzwilliam with Darcy. It would have been difficult for Darcy to have to look after two boys alone since they are so energetic! I cannot tell the difference between Darcy and Mr. Fitzwilliam on how they treat your boys. He truly treats your boys as if they are his own. He is very generous..." Jane drifted into her thoughts.

Is she still fancying Richard? Elizabeth thought. *I know he continues to keep his distance from her but it seems as if she desires his attentions again. He is very handsome, nearly equal to Fitzwilliam, but she should not be looking to him again. I cannot wait until we are back at Pemberley!*

Elizabeth replied, "Of course he loves them very much. Richard is godfather to them both and the boys even call him 'Papa' just like they do Fitzwilliam because he is constantly in their lives. He is very happy to be a part of our family and we are happy to receive his love."

"But why is he not marrying? Charles had said something about his being in love with a woman who might be deceased possibly, but he must want his own situation. I have never seen a more eligible bachelor." Jane blushed as she spoke the words. "Oh, Lizzy, do not get me wrong. Charles is a kind husband and wonderful father, but I am not blind to the fact that Mr. Fitzwilliam is so incredibly handsome. You spend all your time with Darcy, who is possibly the handsomest man in the world, as well as Mr. Fitzwilliam, who is a very close second, so you probably have not even noticed it. Those two men are quite likely the finest specimen of their sex." She flushed red as she responded.

Elizabeth laughed. "Oh, Jane! It sounds like you have quite a crush on my husband and cousin. I do agree with you that they are handsome and I am fully aware since I still have to fend off ladies who are throwing themselves at Fitzwilliam. So many have slipped their handkerchiefs with their cards asking him to call on them for a 'mutually satisfactory visit' and how I wanted to slap them and scratch their eyes out. Richard, too, have received the same, if not more, due to his being single, and some from the same women, might I say, but he has not turned his eye to them once. His heart is quite set, I am afraid."

"But who is she, Lizzy? I cannot imagine he will spend the rest of his life alone! He has a mistress, does he not? I cannot imagine him not... Charles was desperate after six weeks. We did not make love often but not so far apart. We had hoped that after the baptism, we will be able to return to sleeping together but I was so uncomfortable that we did not lay together for another two months. I... I find that I cannot become aroused enough to enjoy it. It is not that I cannot become aroused, I do not think, but Charles has been so eager that it is painful and I cannot tolerate his attentions. I told him he should seek a mistress so he can find his pleasures." Jane sadly spoke.

So that is the problem. So, she would feel justified to having her own pleasures outside the marriage if Charles had a mistress? And, she looks to Richard? Although I am certain Richard can get any woman to burst with desire with just one look, he will never go near her. Elizabeth thought.

"Jane, you said that it is not that you cannot become aroused. Does Richard arouse you?" Elizabeth asked candidly. She loved her dearest sister and wished her happiness but Jane needed to figure out for herself that another man or a mistress outside of the marriage was not acceptable.

She blushed again but answered, "Well, you know that I find him very attractive. I am constantly asking myself if he had flirted with me more and I returned his attentions when we first met, if he would have offered for me. With his 6,000 a year and his connections, I know him to be even more eligible than Charles. Yesterday when you all arrived, I could not turn my eyes from him. It seems he looks happier and handsomer every time I see him. Oh, Lizzy, am I wanton for desiring him? I do wish it," she cried, "I do wish Mr. Fitzwilliam would rapture me with his attentions and I would certainly go to his bed most willingly. He is so amiable and handsome and his body is incredible. I would do anything for him to flirt with me again!" She wailed.

"Oh, Jane." Elizabeth patted her sister's back as she cried. *But Richard might have remained a colonel with his 1,000 a year and you would have never considered him, and he would have never pursued you! He is not the same person as he was back then!*

After Jane settled, Elizabeth continued. "Richard does not have a mistress and he does not want one. He is also determined to be a bachelor for the rest of his life and has given away all of his wealth to the Darcy family. Little Richie is heir to Rosings and Richard is content to spend his days assisting my husband to continue to improve our estates together and Fitzwilliam is truly grateful. You know he saved our lives, right? After that awful event with Wickham, Richard has completely dedicated his life to being of service to us, similar to how he would have given up his life for King and Country. He will not be turned by you, Jane, no matter what. So you must get him out of your head and get Charles back in. With your permission, I will speak to my husband," *both of them!* "to guide your husband. Jane, I am slightly embarrassed to talk about marital relations but I believe it must be said. After my boys' baptism and after my miscarriage, I was also nervous and hesitant. But my husband, who has no practical experience before me, knows that it is always better when I am aroused and attends to my pleasures thoroughly and extensively before he enters me. Do you know what that means?" Jane shook her head in the negative. "Oh, Jane, how much you are missing. There is more than the act being filled to bring you pleasure. I must talk to my husband to talk to Charles. I will not go into more details but I do hope Charles will listen. Now, Kitty's wedding is tomorrow and Mr. Goulding will be joining our merry men to celebrate tonight. Shall we leave for Longbourn in an hour to give our dear sister all the wisdoms of becoming a wife in body? We certainly cannot let Mama talk her nonsense. She did well with me but only because of Aunt Madeline insisted on broaching the topic with her in London. Mama was horrible with you!" She laughed.

"Thank you, Lizzy. I hope you will talk to your husband soon. I know I must stop thinking of Mr. Fitzwilliam but it is so difficult. He is truly SO handsome." Jane blushed once more.

~*~

Elizabeth departed Jane's room, concerned that Jane was on the verge of committing an affair. If Richard had no scruples, if he were not already husband to herself, it would take no more than a look for Jane to jump into his bed. She knew that it was due to lack of satisfaction from her current situation as well due to his handsomeness and her desire for a sexual connection. If her husband was fulfilling her desires, perhaps she might not be so tempted by Richard.

She shook her head and sighed that so many women were willing to break their vows for that sexual release. *Fitzwilliam is so good to me. But then again, I also have Richard who constantly pours out his love on me so much that I do not need to look elsewhere. They are both such fine specimen of their sex!* She smiled to herself.

Elizabeth saw Richard hopping over towards his rooms as she neared her own door.

"Elizabeth! How are you? We were outside playing and Bennet decided to gift me with his lunch on my coat." He laughed. "Darcy remains outside with Bingley and I am quickly changing my coat."

Looking around and seeing no one, he quickly grabbed her hand and rushed her into his room. He quickly closed the door and kissed her frantically. He urgently touched her neck and her breasts then pressed his erection against her and rubbed, as he continued to wrestle her tongue and she pulled his lawn shirt to caress his bare chest.

"Oh, Elizabeth, perhaps a full change of clothing is warranted. Come, my love." He lifted up her body and carried her to his bed. He took off his coat quickly and climbed on her body. He lay over her and kissed her fiercely again, and dipped his head down to lick her breasts while he freed his raging cock from his trousers and pumped himself. He kissed her again and after Elizabeth moaned loudly as her breasts were being roughly fondled, she pushed him onto his back, grabbed his erection and stroked it with both of her hands while sitting on his legs. Richard lifted up his shirt to bare his chest and grunted loudly as his semen flew onto his stomach. He lay back several more moments while panting.

"Oh, my love, you are so generous. It has been an eternity since last night!" he jested. "Thank you for loving me two days in a row! I cannot get enough of you. I love you so much, Elizabeth." He kissed her long and deep again as she laid next to him above his face with her breasts exposed. "I hope I was not too rough. Are you well?" He asked as she fingered the liquid on his stomach together. He watched her in fascination as she dipped her index finger in the pool and brought it to her tongue to taste his seed.

Good lord! Does she have any idea what she does to me? Richard gasped. She was the most seductive woman alive and his manhood immediately twitched for another erection.

"Minx! You are getting me hard again, Elizabeth. I wish I had time to love you properly." Richard groaned as he licked her nipple. "I wish I could make love to you all night long, my love." He kissed her mouth then took a deep breath as he rose. He began to take his clothes off in front of her, unashamed for her to see him completely naked.

"Oh, Richard! You get me so flushed and excited." She exhaled loudly, fanning her face with her hands. "Jane was quite right that she found you so handsome!"

"Jane? What does Jane have to do with us?" Richard asked, as he continued to disrobe to change into a new set of clothing.

Elizabeth watched him as he lifted his shirt off and pulled down his trousers. He stood completely nude in front of her, wiping his still-erect penis and stomach with a washcloth, then putting on a new shirt and getting dressed.

"Jane mentioned that she still finds you handsome and sees you as a good catch. We watched you all play with the children and I think she was quite aroused by you. She said that Charles has not been able to arouse her enough during intercourse and she is looking to you for your attentions." Seeing his eyes widen and he began to splutter, she continued, "Do not blame her. She is just pent up and I can understand her. If you kept doing this to me and I did not have my dear Fitzwilliam to finish me, I would become desperate and lose my mind. You are quite a magnificent lover, you know."

She stood up and kissed him. She helped him with his cravat while he rubbed his hands on her waist and back. "There, now you are presentable."

He leaned down and kissed her. "Thank you, wife. I cannot wait for Garrison to return from his visit with his family." Smirking, he asked, "Do you want me to seduce your sister? Shall I give her a little taste of what you received? Do you think she would burst with lust if she saw me naked? What is your wish, milady?" He asked seductively while kissing her neck and massaging her breast. "I am hard for you again. Shall I let her see me in this state?"

"Do not jest, Richard!" She slapped him on his arm. "She would open her legs for you with just one look since you are far too attractive. She is desperate for affection and is not thinking straight," she kissed him on the lips again, "although I fully comprehend the temptation before me." She licked his lips. "Will you talk to Charles? I think Charles is rather thick on pleasuring his wife and needs a lesson or two from you. I must confess, I am quite proud to have such dedicated lovers at my disposal."

She kissed him fully on the mouth, delving her tongue inside him to tease him. "We must return. I need to change to visit Longbourn. Could you send Fitzwilliam my way?"

They walked towards the door and stopped. "Of course, wife. I would do anything for you, Elizabeth. Thank you for the quick love. I desperately needed it being at Netherfield again." Richard kissed her hand.

"I love you, Richard. We will be home in a few days and we will have more time there." Elizabeth smiled.

Richard laughed, "I cannot wait to be home to have you in my bed in Pemberley and take my time with you as well! I love you."

Opening the door and ensuring no one was about, Elizabeth returned to her room and Richard dashed to Darcy's side.

Chapter 12

"You have changed your clothes." Darcy commented. "I thought you were going to change out just your coat."

"I thought I might as well change for our dinner with Goulding now. The boys look tired. Let us return them to the nursery so they can nap. They will be out for hours!" Richard laughed.

Bingley took Betty to the nursery himself while the twin's nannies took the boys.

Richard whispered to Darcy. "Darcy, I ran into Elizabeth when I went upstairs. I sought a quick affection and had to change my clothes." Seeing Darcy smirk, he laughed, "I could not resist and it took me all of five minutes. She is waiting for you. She said she needs you *desperately*."

Richard's loud laughter roared behind as Darcy flew from his side to his wife's rooms.

Darcy flung the door open and immediately locked it. "WIFE! Where are you?" He boomed.

Elizabeth came out of her dressing room completely nude. "Here I am, husband. Is there something I can do for you?" She seductively asked.

"Well, I believe it is what I can do for you, milady. Come and sit on my face." He lay down on her bed after pulling off his jacket and shirt. As she knelt above his face, he pulled her womanhood down and began to lick and thrust his tongue into her folds. He took off his trousers and his massive erection sprung out. "Turn yourself around, Elizabeth. Taste me as I taste you."

Elizabeth shifted her body so she could mouth his arousal while he continued to kiss her nether regions.

Elizabeth cried out her pleasures as she climaxed and Darcy placed her on her back and slid slowly into her.

"Did you enjoy your time with Richard?" he asked as he began to pump her. "Did he arouse you and make you wet for me? Were you desperate for my hard cock to fill you?" She nodded as she moaned. "And my cock, do you love it? Do you like sucking on it and taking it deep inside you?" She moaned louder and nodded again. "I love that you are so wet. I love seeing you aroused and desperate for me. I love taking you hard," he pumped furiously then slowed down, "and slowly and carefully. I want to release inside you, my love. I want to try again to get you with child. I want to make you happy."

"Oh yes, my love. I want you inside me. I want all of you and I want your babies. I love you so much, Fitzwilliam. Love me until you release, husband." Elizabeth begged.

Darcy's cock twitched with her passionate demands. He thrust into her hard and grunted loudly as he came deep inside her.

He sighed as he relaxed. It had felt good to release inside her again. They had resumed relations two days ago and he had released his fifth time this morning, but they were not sure if she would want to become pregnant again so he had been letting go on the sheets.

I do not know how Richard does it. I would die to not be inside her and I was miserable that I could not release inside her. But he is content and it satisfies all of us. Oh, I love it when she is so amorous after a little time with him. Darcy thought.

"Thank you, Elizabeth. I love being inside you and releasing. I do hope we will have another child soon when it is time and we will take any blessings we receive." He kissed her lips. "I love you. Thank you for being my wife and desiring me so much. I am so glad you allowed me to come inside you. It was a mess this morning after the night we had." He laughed.

Elizabeth answered, "I love you. I know we will be well. I shock myself with how wanton I become sometimes and I cannot wait to be back at Pemberley as I plan on ravaging you more often there. I cannot get enough of you!" She paused. "Poor Jane. I told Richard this as well but it appears that Jane is desiring Richard's attentions again. She finds you and he to be the handsomest men and has told me that Charles is lacking in his skills. She has had discomfort in bed and he cannot stimulate her enough for her to achieve satisfaction. I know that she would never try anything with you, but she might become desperate enough to try something again with Richard. He would probably make her climax with just a look but you must help her, Fitzwilliam. You and Richard need to speak with Charles on how to pleasure a woman. I know that he is very experienced but I think he took pleasures without ever considering how to give. Will you talk with him? Will you try to help him love his wife better?"

Seeing a disgusted look on his face, she continued, "I know it is not a topic that you want to think about, but if you do not help Charles, Jane will either disgrace herself with Richard or any other man that shows her a little bit of attention and her life and reputation might be ruined. She also has offered that Charles take a mistress. I am certain, should he sleep with another woman, she will feel it justified to sleep with other men. It is in all ways horrible. I know intercourse is an important part of marriage and they must keep that part of the relationship healthy. Will you please help her? It would be helping Charles and Jane and even Richard. Please, please??" She begged.

Darcy laughed. "As you wish, my love, I would do anything for you. I have no idea how to approach Charles on coaching him how to pleasure his wife but Richard and I will figure something out. I might vomit but perhaps Richard can help." He paused for several moments. "My love, do you ever wish Richard can satisfy you while you satisfy him?"

"Well, I had not considered it. I always think of you and cannot wait for you to fill me but I would not take him in, my love, so it is not something to worry over. I will not break my vows to you." Elizabeth confirmed.

"Oh, my love, I know that. And I know that he will not enter you and I trust you both with my life. I only ask if you would like to be aroused and reach a climax with him. He can use his mouth and fingers as you are implying Charles do with Jane, and it will bring more satisfaction to you both without actual I intercourse. I would wish you to still burn for me to fill you. I want your passions for me alone, but I wish for your enjoyment with Richard as well. If Richard pleasures you, if he helps you climax when he is in bed with you, will you still return to me with your womanhood on fire for me to take you?" Darcy was hard again. He climbed over her again and fingered her.

"If he touched you like this," he thrust his long fingers inside her and rubbed her clitoris with his thumb, "and tongued your womanhood and made you scream in pleasure, would you still want," he thrust his erection into her powerfully, "me inside you? Would you demand for me to take you," he thrust in again forcefully, "and to fuck you hard, again and again?" He hammered his long cock into her repeatedly. "Do you want me?"

She screamed her climax. "Yes! Only you, my love!"

Darcy drilled hard into her and released again.

They both lay panting on their backs for several minutes. They could not get enough of each other.

Once they calmed, Elizabeth began. "Fitzwilliam, do you truly wish me to be satiated while Richard is seeking relief? I must confess that it is very one-sided when I lay with him. He touches my breasts and kisses me and I am desirous for more but I do not know how I would respond to his ministrations. I love joining with you and you arouse me so much and climaxing while you finger me and use your tongue is an amazing sensation but it is not the same as actual intercourse. I know that I would burn for you to fill me completely but I am afraid that once we cross that line of pleasure, do you not worry that Richard and I might actually have relations? What if he cannot control himself and inserts it inside me? What if I accept it? I dare not break my vows to you and I feel as if we are playing with fire."

"I love you so much and I am honoured by your commitment. I do wish for your completion and your constant attentions but I do wish for your happiness when he makes love to you. We should talk with Richard on it but if you wish it, I wish it for you. Richard has an iron will, as I have said before. If he does not believe he can restrain himself from the temptation, he will not attempt it. I do not know how it is for him, but for me, being inside your mouth is quite similar to being inside your folds. Having your tongue and the wall of your mouth wrap around me is the closest thing to intercourse and it is an incredible feeling. That would be one way for you to pleasure your other husband without breaking our vows." Darcy smiled. "You have two husbands, my love. When our sons called him 'papa', I resolved then that I would ensure his happiness as well as ours, and you make him happy. He is my best friend, my brother, and now my full business partner. I share everything with him, my home, even my children, and a large part of my wife. He cannot have you fully but I wish for both of your satisfaction. And I understand that you might fall asleep after your completion since I know you rest better after your release. Although I wish for you to return to me, do not be distressed should you fall asleep in his bed. I might come and abduct you from his bed in the middle of the night, but will you return to me if you can?" Darcy asked.

"Yes, my love. I will always return to you, even if it is late into the night. I do not know how Richard will respond since I am certain he will desire all he could receive but I do not want him to be tempted beyond his power. I do not know the workings of his iron will but I hope you are right, Fitzwilliam. Thank you for thinking of my pleasures and considering Richard's love. I love you and will always want you. I will always be desperate for you."

Elizabeth kissed her husband tenderly. He was truly the best of men.

Chapter 13

Richard awaited Darcy's return in the library. He thought of his liaison with Elizabeth and smiled to himself. She was so passionate and had no idea how alluring she was. He could not get enough of her and every moment with her was indeed an adventure. He only wished that he could satisfy her somehow while he took his pleasures and felt his arousal return so he quickly attempted to suppress it and looked around for a book. He walked by the bare shelves and found a copy of 'Much Ado About Nothing' and began to read it while sitting near the window and looked often at his beautiful pocket watch to check the time, to gaze at the engraving and inscription, then return to the book. He sat for over half an hour when the door to the library opened.

He smiled, expecting Darcy, as they were to receive Mr. Goulding soon, wondering how Elizabeth enjoyed his attentions, but was startled when he saw Jane Bingley enter. He immediately went into defensive mode and stood. With full intent to be a proper gentleman, he bowed and greeted her. "Mrs. Bingley."

Instead of leaving, seeing that he was alone, Jane closed the door, entered the room, then stood by the fireplace. She paced a little and seeing that Mr. Fitzwilliam was walking briskly to leave the room, she nervously asked, "Who is she? The woman you love?"

Richard stopped. *What do I say?* He resumed walking towards the door and opened it to maintain propriety since he did not want to be caught alone with her ever again. He took a deep breath and turned around.

"She is the love of my life. She is breath to my lungs and my heart beats only for her and I have never known anyone of her equal. She is perfection to my own heart and I will love her until my dying day. I think of her when I am awake, I dream of her when I sleep, and I will never look to another. She inspires me to be a better man and it matters naught that I cannot marry her and I will be steadfast and never deter from my course of loving her and only her. My life with the Darcys satisfies my soul and having my godsons to love is the greatest honour bestowed onto me. Everything I do, I do for her." He could not go on. He was afraid he would blurt out his beloved's name. "Good day, madam," and he walked out.

He was surprised to find Darcy and Elizabeth standing near the door. Darcy beamed and Elizabeth was in tears and smiling.

Richard pulled out his precious handkerchief that Elizabeth had embroidered and dabbed her eyes for her. He kissed her hand and whispered, "I love you." Darcy patted his shoulder and the two men walked to Bingley's study.

~*~

Elizabeth blew out her breath. She was an emotional wreck from hearing Richard's speech to Jane. She had known of his admiration for her; he had professed it to her many times and all of his looks and his actions were proof of his affections, but for her to hear those words of love spoken out loud to another person made it so real and there was no contesting that his love was true and deep. She fanned her face to dry her tears then entered the library. Jane was sitting by the fire and looking into it aimlessly.

"Jane, shall we depart? I believe the carriage is ready." Elizabeth asked, not knowing if she should let her sister know that she had heard everything.

Jane quickly wiped her eyes. "Oh, yes. It is time. Let us go." She was silent and still quite sullen after they entered the carriage.

"Is something wrong, Jane?" Elizabeth asked. She wanted to make sure her dear sister would be well.

Jane sighed and answered, "No, nothing is wrong. I have a confession to make, Lizzy. I entered the library knowing full well that Mr. Fitzwilliam was there alone. I was hoping that I would be able to show him that his advances would be welcome should he desire me and I asked him about the woman he loved. I... I have never heard such... ardent love, such dedication and resolution to love her. To love this woman that he could not marry... I am ashamed of myself for desiring to have an affair because I want him in my bed. To hear of his determination to spend the rest of his life loving her and only her, I was astonished at such a love. I do not know if Charles feels a fraction of that love for me and I am in awe. And I find myself jealous that he loves her. I wish it were I. I could not imagine receiving such a love and not returning it. I wish, I wish for attention and flattery. I wish I were loved so; to be dancing in a grand ballroom in his arms and under him in his bed. To be in his heart and receive such a love would be a dream..." Jane admitted to her dear sister.

Elizabeth smiled and looked out the window. *Fitzwilliam loves me so, and he had done so since the first moment of our meeting. And I agree, to receive Richard's ardent love, as he loves me, I was bound to love him back. I do love him very much. I dearly love my husbands and I am the most fortunate soul to have their love.*

"Jane, I believe, I know, that such a love is an honourable one and I agree that you cannot but love in return when someone loves you with such ardour. My dearest Fitzwilliam loved me just as fiercely, and that was the reason why I agreed to marry him only two days after meeting him. Perhaps it is a Fitzwilliam thing, but I have never seen two cousins so similar in temperament and character as my husband and Richard. They even look alike in their appearances, but I know that it is also a rarity. I do not believe everyone can have that equal of passion for love, as it also has to do with character. Fitzwilliam and Richard are both very dedicated and hard-working men. Richard might have been a bit of a rake before, but he has always taken his duties seriously and has seen the casualties of war. He has seen detriment and horrors that he will not speak of to anyone, but he has never been indolent. But I know that he had gone through a lot of learning to become the man he appears now, and it was partly because of that woman who captured his heart that he was able to change several things, see the errors of his ways, and be motivated to become a better person. That woman had helped him and he will love her and only her because of it."

She looked into her sister's face. "The problem is, Jane, you are in a marriage where enough time has passed, you have gone through some difficulty, and were able to work through it, and now you find yourself without focus and you want another challenge. Charles is exactly as he always was: Friendly, wealthy, with a happy demeanour. It is you who have changed. You were always told that you were the most beautiful so you should have the best; that because of outward beauty, you deserved the most. Now you find yourself a wife and a mother and the excitement of decorating your house has gone. You miss the balls and parties and being sought out as the prettiest girl in the room. You miss being the centre of attention and you see my Fitzwilliam and Richard, who are significantly above your husband's status, and you crave to be in their circle, to receive attention from a worthy man once again, to satisfy your need to have it all. If you only knew, Jane, if Fitzwilliam and Richard never have to step into another ballroom again, they would be happy. All they wish for is the peace and comfort of Pemberley."

Elizabeth paused to calm herself. She was becoming angry that Jane wanted what was hers. She knew that she was blessed with so much, but for Jane, who had been so highly praised all her life, now cared only for her own desires and comforts, upset her. Elizabeth had been called a hoyden, the least favourite child of her mother, and was constantly belittled as having no beauty compared to the beautiful Jane and the lively Lydia, but now that she was happily married with children and had two wonderful men who loved her, Jane had become bitter and was seeking an extramarital affair.

I must be generous. I have all of my heart's desire and I cannot fault another for wanting more. "Jane, you can be that woman for Charles. You can inspire him and motivate him; give him a challenge to become more and to love you so fiercely that you cannot but love him in return. I do not wish to compare but I argue with Fitzwilliam often. I nag and cry and drive him insane at times, but our relationship has grown and it continues to grow. I know his heart and he knows mine. We wish for each other's happiness above our own, and," she sighed, "to let go of our possessive nature instead of holding it too tight and killing our love when it is necessary. I would never be content with Charles because he was not meant for me, just like you would never be content with Fitzwilliam or Richard, because they are not meant for you. You were once content and you will be again, but it is up to you on what kind of wife you wish to be. Things were good for awhile, right, Jane? YOU must help him along. Sometimes men are clueless and have no idea how to get the job done. YOU must help him to become one, if you wish for a better husband. Do not seek out another relationship without fixing the one you have first, Jane." Elizabeth concluded.

They were close to Longbourn and Jane wiped her eyes. "Oh, Lizzy, I wish you could stay longer. Your advice is so good and you have helped with Netherfield so much."

"Jane, I am glad to be of service to you but you must take the reins of your own life and your own domain. Your husband, your home, are your responsibilities and I cannot fix everything for you. I want to go home. I wish nothing but to be home with my family. I am so happy for Kitty, but after the wedding, we will be leaving for Pemberley. I hope you will write to me often and let me know how things are and I pray that you will find happiness. Now, shall we go and scare Kitty about the fearsome creature known as 'husband' who will overpower her and brutally take her tomorrow night?" Elizabeth joked.

Jane laughed. "Gerald Goulding is the meekest person I have ever met! I do not believe they have even kissed yet!"

They arrived at Longbourn and continued their laughter, sharing with their sisters on the joys of the marriage bed.

~*~

The men gathered, playing their game of billiards and toasting Gerald Goulding several times. Darcy really liked this young man. He was very similar to Bingley, easy-going and friendly, but shyer and definitely inexperienced. Reverend Bertram was also in attendance but he had cried off after dinner that due to his profession, the men would enjoy the evening better without him and that he was needed by Mary's side in any case. Mary was with child and was due in September.

As they relaxed with their coats off and sharing stories of their courting days, Bingley bragged that he had the longest courtship while teasing Darcy that he had the shortest. Goulding did not know the full story and he laughed that Darcy had a one-day courtship and that he had proposed the very next day. He was shocked even further that Darcy had begun courting his wife the morning after first meeting her at the assembly. Goulding successfully won the title of being in love the longest, as he had waited over six years for Kitty.

Bingley, having taken a few more drinks than his norm, blurted out, "Make sure you take it nice and slow and do not stick your cock in her too fast." Not noticing that Goulding was bright red from mention of the marriage bed, he continued, "I took my Jane too fast and she did not enjoy it but she loosened up eventually. If I can only get back inside her now. It has been too long since I had a good fuc..."

Darcy quickly grabbed his glass away from him and splashed the cup of brandy onto his face. Richard ordered some coffee and grabbed Goulding away from the intoxicated and belligerent Bingley.

"Goulding, have I told you about my military experience at..." Richard wrapped his arm around the young man and walked him to the library.

Darcy yelled at Bingley, "What the hell is wrong with you, Bingley? Do not dare speak of your wife so! Blast it, Charles! Your lack of skills should not scare off Kitty's betrothed." Darcy huffed but realised that Bingley was quietly crying and he felt awful.

"Charles, I know about your difficulties in your marriage. Jane shared and Elizabeth told me." Darcy quietly spoke.

"Jane complained about me to Lizzy? Damn it to hell, Darcy! She hates me. She refuses to let me touch her and she avoids me. She says she is uncomfortable but she does not even want to spend time with me and... and she told me to find myself a mistress. I am seriously considering it. I never thought I could marry for love and end up so miserable. All that time to take things slow to court her properly, she wants to push me over now. I had a good whore in London when I prepared the settlement papers and I wanted to return to see her but thought I finally found love. I have been faithful since I made my vows, Darcy, but I am certain she wants to take on a lover. I have seen how she has been eyeing Fitzwilliam. I know, I know, he does not care for her at all; he does not even look at her direction, but she wants another man. She wants Fitzwilliam or anyone else to fuck her but not me."

He stood and huffed while he paced. "Well, fine! If she wants another man, I *will* get a mistress. Maybe even fuck in our own bed and make her watch. Damn it! What am I supposed to do?" He sat down and pulled his hair.

Darcy was concerned for his friend. Even knowing that he was still intoxicated, he was spewing more curses than he had ever heard from him. He saw the suffering and knew that if Elizabeth had ever denied him, he would be devastated. He was confident of her love for him and although he knew she loved Richard, she loved him first and foremost and was always in her thoughts.

He sighed as he gathered his thoughts. *How does Richard do it? To not be able to take Elizabeth fully but love her so dearly and desperately, and he has never once shown jealousy of my being her husband. He is such a good man. He loves Elizabeth with his whole heart and we are blessed to have him in our lives.*

"Bingley, your coffee will arrive soon and Richard will keep Goulding entertained for a while. Elizabeth told me that Jane's complaint was that you had not stimulated her enough and she was indeed having discomfort when you entered her. You never did read that book that I gave you, did you? She was not aroused enough to take you and the changes to her body most likely caused her to be too dry. And you, like a brute, still took her and did not care for her pleasures." He saw Bingley's eyes widen. "Yes, you imposed on your wife without seeking to pleasure her first."

He stood and paced. "Charles, I know you have known many women; prostitutes and Mrs. Wickham in the past, but I have known only one. I will never know another but I do know that when my wife is happy, our union is even better." He coughed. "I do not know how to say it so I will blurt it out. When I pleasure my wife, using all of the tools available to me," he waved his fingers and pointed to his tongue, "she is very eager for me. She gets aroused to the point that she climaxes quickly and repeatedly. It is wonderful to bring her pleasure and it pleases me to serve her first. Bingley, have you been a gentleman to service your wife first or have you always been only taking? Is it possible that Jane is dissatisfied because she is missing something in the marriage bed?"

"I do not... that is... I always thought I just... Damn it, Darcy. I have been a brute. I just stick it inside her; if she is too dry, I spit on myself and take her like I did with whores. Sometimes she climaxes but I do not know how often. I just come inside her and I might go at it again if I am horny enough. We used to do it more often, you know, in the beginning. Then she was pregnant and wanted me persistently for a while but then it settled down. Her mother would be constantly over and she would claim fatigue or headaches. I had her maybe two, three times a week near the end of the pregnancy and then nothing. After the baptism, I had her twice. TWICE. It has been a very long four months..." Bingley rubbed his face with his hands. "How often do you and Lizzy...?" He asked.

Darcy straightened. "Bingley, that is none of your..."

"Oh, come on! I used two or three prostitutes a week before marriage. How often? Once a week? Twice a week?" Bingley kept probing.

Darcy turned his back on him and smirked. *Idiot! My Elizabeth is nothing like Jane. Twice a day, my friend, sometimes more.* He turned back around and replied, "Bingley, I will not discuss my love life with you. My wife keeps me content and it is none of your business. The truth is, she does not turn me away because I think of her pleasures first. I make sure that she desires me as much as I desire her."

Bingley responded, "I thought women just lay there. When she wanted me often during the pregnancy, she did moan more but I suppose she was already aroused. She was most excitable when..." Bingley paused, "...when Mrs. Bennet was giving birth. After Samuel was born, she begged me to take her home so I could ravage her. That was when you and Fitzwilliam were here. It makes sense now, even then, she still wanted your cousin." He stood to puff again. "Damn it, Darcy! Why does your cousin have to be so attractive? Perhaps I will never invite him back!"

Darcy laughed. He was acting like a child. "Well, Bingley, if Richard is not invited, you might as well take me off your invitation, too. I would have to cut off our friendship and Elizabeth would never forgive you. If you anger Elizabeth, either Richard or I would call you out and Jane would be a widow. So, there you have it. Take the blame onto yourself and fix the damn mess you made with your wife or blame everyone else. It is your choice. I am going to join Goulding. I refuse to wreck that nice young man's last evening of bachelorhood."

Darcy left and joined Richard in the library.

The two experienced men spoke of how poor Mr. Goulding could be kind to his wife and subtly gave hints on how to pleasure her first.

Chapter 14

Elizabeth sat at the church pews, surveying the scenes and laughing. Richard sat to her left while Darcy sat to her right and her men were pleasantly conversing. Charles was standing up with Gerald Goulding but she could see the glares pointed at Richard and she scoffed as inconspicuously as possible. *So childish! Instead of fixing his own problems, he blames Richard because he is handsome. Ridiculous!*

Hearing her muffled laughter, both Darcy and Richard looked at her and knew exactly what she was thinking. Each took her hand and squeezed it lightly. Richard sighed and let go while Darcy held on.

Jane sat with her mother while Lydia stood up with Kitty. She quietly groaned and knew that her marriage was in trouble but she knew not what to do. She dared not look at Mr. Fitzwilliam again. He was dashing today in his dark green striped waistcoat, and it appeared that he could have coordinated his outfit with the Darcys. Elizabeth wore a dark green dress while Darcy wore a dark green coat. She sighed again, seeing that Mr. Darcy was too handsome as well. She looked at her husband who was eyeing Mr. Fitzwilliam once again and she sat in embarrassment that he was acting so foolish in public and paying her no attention.

The ceremony soon ended and the wedding breakfast was another achievement to Mrs. Bennet's credit. She fussed and bragged that she now had four daughters married off and only one more to go. She loudly complained that Lydia was not doing her duty to attract more worthy suitors, even after her dear Lizzy had thrown her in the paths of rich men. Mr. Bennet quickly pinched her arm and she immediately quieted and spoke of more genial things.

After returning to Netherfield, the Darcys gathered their last items while the servants were hurrying to load their trunks on the carriages and Elizabeth and Darcy went to the nursery to farewell little Betty.

When they returned, they were surprised to find Bingley hugging Richard and laughing. Jane soon appeared and they departed after another hearty embrace from Bingley to Richard.

Richard awkwardly received the hug, bowed to Jane, then entered the carriage. Darcy embraced Bingley and kissed Jane's cheek and waited for Elizabeth.

Elizabeth kissed Bingley's cheek and spoke, "Take care of my sister and my niece. I hope to see you soon after our travels are completed." Turning to embrace Jane, she said, "Love your husband. Write to me often and let me know how things are." She whispered.

Once they entered the carriage, Elizabeth asked Richard, "Whatever did you say to Charles, Richard?"

He smirked. "Only the secret of pleasuring a woman."

Elizabeth flushed bright red. She looked at Darcy who was grinning like a fool. "And do you know this secret, sir?" She demanded to know.

Darcy laughed. "Who do you think taught me?" He laughed louder as she blushed even more.

In concession, she shook her head and laughed as well. "Well, husbands, let us not make this 'Embarrass Elizabeth' day. Shall we play a round of chess?" She changed the subject and smiled.

~*~

Pemberley was beautiful. The trio took a deep sigh of relief when they saw the familiar vista of the home they loved. They were to stay for three months with no visitors and no disruptions, then travel to Scotland for two months. They would spend the next five months with no one but each other.

As soon as they arrived, the servants were busy unloading the carriages and the nannies rushed their charges to the nursery. The twins were excited to be back again where more toys were found. Baths were called for and dinner would be in their private sitting room just for the three of them.

Darcy held Elizabeth's breasts and rubbed them in circles. Elizabeth moaned as he pinched her nipples to harden and could feel his arousal behind her. "I believe you have cleaned them well enough, Mr. Darcy." Elizabeth stated, as she relaxed, sitting in front of him in their very large bathtub.

"Oh, one can never be too sure. We must practice constantly, you know." Darcy whispered in her ear. He trailed his hand and began to finger her womanhood. "This too, we must make sure that you are very clean. I am certain it is still full of my seed from this morning's activity at the inn." He lifted her body onto his groin and rubbed her clitoris. "As a matter of fact, I believe I will need to make one more deposit before we thoroughly clean you." He inserted his penis inside her core and pumped up.

Elizabeth turned her head to meet his mouth and they kissed as she rode him from above. Darcy had one hand on her breast and the other continuing to rub her nub. "Oh, Fitzwilliam! That feels so good! Oh my god, you are making me come again." She screamed several times and he thrust deep inside her and released again.

The bath water had sloshed around and water overflowed from the bathtub but they did not care. The servants had known that the couple enjoyed uniting in the bathtub many times before and always had piles of towels around the tub.

They climbed out after they reached their satisfaction and Darcy wrapped his wife with the soft towels and helped her with her robe, then he dried himself off and donned his robe.

Instead of dressing for dinner, they walked straight into the sitting room where Richard had been waiting for them for dinner. Richard stood from the couch, which was facing away from the Darcys' bedroom door, and his jaw dropped when he saw them both in their bathrobes.

"Well, when you said 'private', I did not realise you meant this private. Shall I leave you two alone or shall I go and don my robe, too?" He finally jested, still unable to keep his eyes off of Elizabeth's figure.

Darcy laughed. "We took longer than planned and did not wish for you to wait to dine. You may do as you wish. You can take off your coat should you like to relax a bit but I am famished. No time for you to undress." He winked.

They ate and laughed and made plans for the next few weeks. They knew that although peaceful, there were many duties that needed to be seen to, and as Spring Planting had been completed by correspondence for both Pemberley and Rosings, both masters would be quite busy catching up.

Elizabeth also had piles of duties to oversee. Her school for girls and several dinner parties, as well as her Foundation businesses all needed her attention.

After the meal was completed, Darcy kissed Elizabeth fully and fervently in front of Richard, caressing her buttocks firmly. "I will see you later, my love. Richard, be generous." He winked at him and retired to his room, closing his bedroom door.

Richard gasped. "Elizabeth, are you... now... are we..." He was shocked that she was to join him on the first night of their return to Pemberley. He had thought it would be at least a week, if not a month, until they would be able to find time. *Darcy is so generous.* He immediately stepped towards her and kissed her. "Has Darcy already had you? I thought he would keep you all night tonight. Did you two... in the bathtub?" He smiled as she blushed. *I should have guessed. Of course, they bathe together and of course he would not be able to stop himself. I certainly could not!*

"Let us go to your room, Richard. I need to get out of this robe." Elizabeth winked.

He gulped as he felt his cock twitch. *Seductress!*

He opened the door and led her to his room then watched as Elizabeth slowly unwrapped her robe and hung it at the foot of the bed. She stood next to his bed completely naked and he could not stop staring at her womanhood. Her dark tight curls were covering between her legs and although he had seen her leg up to her thigh when he was tending to her wound when Wickham cut her, he had been so desperate to stop the bleeding that he had not noticed anything else. Her long slender legs and her tiny waist with her large bosoms made his arousal so strong that he thought he would burst. Seeing her finally fully nude was an incredible sight, as her body was magnificent and she was the most erotic woman he had ever seen.

Then, she turned around and his heart thumped harder as he watched her taut buttocks facing him as she lifted herself onto her knees to climb into his bed. He saw the slit of her womanhood and thought he was going to die from his eyes being pleasured so much.

He knew he would not do more than what he had done before but he was desperate to see all of her again and quickly divested his clothes. Completely naked and his erection stronger than ever, he jumped into bed next to her.

Elizabeth quickly stopped him from climbing onto her with her hand. "Richard, husband, we have some rules to discuss."

Richard calmed himself and took several breaths and answered, "Of course, Elizabeth, wife, I will listen to whatever you wish for me to hear." His heart continued to beat rapidly.

"Richard, Fitzwilliam said that you have an iron will. Do you believe it to be true?" Elizabeth asked.

Richard contemplated, not certain which direction her question was going. "I believe so; once I am resolute, I tend to not sway from it. Why do you ask, my love? What do you wish from me?" He kissed her hand and held it, unable to remain disconnected from her.

Elizabeth continued, "I wish to be pleasured tonight. Fitzwilliam has given us permission for me to enjoy myself with you. I wish to pleasure you and in return, I wish to experience a little of your masterful art of loving, but we cannot, we must not engage in intercourse. I have no intention of breaking my vows and I cannot dishonour Fitzwilliam. If we are pleasuring each other and enjoying our bodies together, would you be able to swear that you will not enter my womanhood? I am afraid that in my ecstasy, I will forget that you are not my legal husband and if you enter me, I might accept it, irreparably damaging our trust with Fitzwilliam. He told me to talk to you about it and he trusts you. He said that you would be able to control yourself but if you could not, you must not do more than what we have done so far."

"I will be honest with you, Elizabeth, it is my greatest desire to have all of you. If you begged me to take you right now, I would; I have never been this aroused before. I know that I had told you before that if you were naked and begging for me, I would save you from yourself, but my love and desire for you have grown so much that I am barely able to contain myself right now. If you opened your legs and cried out for me to fill you, I would without a second thought, even knowing that I would regret it and would have to move to the Americas as a penniless servant. I could deny you nothing and I would do it, but if you do *not* ask of me, I will never. If it was both our wish to never join, I am more than satisfied having you in my arms, kissing you, enjoying your body, loving you as I have done before. I would never overpower you or injure you, Elizabeth. I would not take what does not belong to me if you do not offer it, because I love you too much to ever hurt you.

"I can solemnly swear to you that I will not enter you if you do not ask it of me. I wish to taste you and pleasure you but you will not be filled by me. That is for Darcy alone and I made a vow to him as well that I would not cross that line. If you will not ask of me, I will never break my vows to you and to my cousin. Your vow to Darcy is that you will be filled only by him. My vow to you is that I will not fill you there. Is that what you wish?" Richard asked.

"That is exactly what I wish, my love. I love that you know us and that you protect my vows as fiercely as I protect it. I must admit that I am curious to know what a man with such extensive education can do for me. Do you find being in bed with me more pleasurable when I am not wearing anything?" She asked, suddenly feeling less bold as Richard gazed at her intently.

"Oh, my love, let me show you." Richard began to kiss her passionately. He caressed her breasts and brought his naked body closer to her, revelling in the sensation of having his beloved's skin in full contact with his own. He ran his hand from her breast to her waist to her hips and down her thighs. He touched her left thigh and felt the scars that had healed well. He kissed her from head to toe, from behind her ears to her shoulders and fingers, to her bosoms and navel and hips, trailing his kisses on her thighs to knees to feet. He touched her everywhere he could see, then he gently grazed her pubic hair. He returned to attend to her breasts gently one by one as his fingers ran across her folds below. She opened her legs for him and he trailed his kisses to her stomach and finally to her womanhood, and he inhaled her womanly scent and he knew he was drunk on love. She smelled so good and he was desperate to taste her.

He opened her legs wider to expose all of her to him and moaned loudly. He was ready to burst but he gently inserted two of his long fingers to pump her and began to lick her. Slowly then fast and repeating his motions again and again, he felt her muscles grip his fingers and delighted in giving her everything he could, using all of his extensive knowledge to pleasure the only woman that he had ever loved. He plunged his tongue inside her womanhood and revelled at being so intimate with her. He had never been so dedicated to bring ecstasy to a woman before but this woman in his bed was the only one that ever mattered.

He wanted to give her every moan, every peak, every pleasurable sensation that he could deliver with his body without entering her. It was about *her* pleasure and he, for the first time in his life, did not care for his own. He made love to her as he had never done before until she cried out her climax twice, and he lay over her and rubbed his erection against her pubis while kissing her deep inside her mouth.

Finally having his Elizabeth in his bed, naked under him and crying out her bliss, he could no longer hold back and yelled out his release onto Elizabeth's flat abdomen. He was dizzy with such a powerful release and plopped down next to her to pant for air, then he fingered the liquid on her belly.

Elizabeth's breaths were shallow as well. Her husband was an excellent lover and she could not imagine that another man could exceed his skills, but Richard was truly masterful. There was something about his method that brought her ecstasy quicker and stronger than ever before, and although she missed Fitzwilliam's enormous phallus inside her, she had been pleasured beyond her expectations.

Richard watched her stomach rise and fall quickly and he pushed his semen around in circles to gather them into one mound. He rose to the side table and grabbed a washcloth and wet it with lukewarm water at his bedside. He wiped her between the legs, absorbing her juices and his saliva, then cleaned her abdomen, caressing her skin gently and enjoying her body.

Elizabeth smiled. "You know, the first time Fitzwilliam and I joined, he washed me as well. You and he are so similar."

Richard kissed her breast and neck and held her in his arms. "It is because we both desperately love you. I have never washed anyone before. You are so lovely. So, so lovely." He kissed her lips. He continued to caress her skin, basking in the softness. "I love you so much, my Elizabeth, my wife. I swear to you, you are the best thing in my life. Every time with you is a treasure that I will remember all of my life." He began to kiss her deeply again.

Elizabeth sighed in happiness. "I do believe it is said that 'it is better to give than receive' but I really did enjoy receiving. I felt that before, you made love to me and took your pleasures while I assisted in bringing it about, but now, I feel closer to you, having made love together. You are definitely a masterful lover and it was marvellous. I enjoyed your attentions very much, my love."

"Oh, my love. I cannot get enough of you." He trailed his tongue on her neck and caressed her breasts as his erection had already returned. He ground his penis at her hip and as soon as she grabbed him with her hand, he fingered her clitoris again. They touched each other while kissing until they reached another climax together, Richard releasing on her stomach again.

"That... was... bloody... fantastic..." Richard panted. He loved being able to touch her and hear her cry out while he released. He grabbed the cloth again and cleaned her once more. "I have never made love like this before."

Elizabeth giggled as he tickled her while wiping her. "You are so kind. Are you certain you have not had other women like this? How does one become so masterful without constant practice? Your mouth is skilled beyond expectations, Richard." She teased but appeared a bit sad.

"Oh, my love. I had never cared for anything other than my own completion before. Although I had 'practiced' it a few times, there was always something repulsive about kissing a loose woman down when I did not know how many were there before me. I swear I never have done that to a prostitute, either. You are my first and only to have my complete dedication, Elizabeth, and my last. You mean everything to me, Elizabeth." Richard kissed her gently to soothe her worries. He knew that she hated that he was so experienced even if she had enjoyed his talents. "I might have some experience but my heart was never touched before I met you. The other women, I never allowed any of them to call me by name, no matter how many times I used them. You are the only one to have my heart, Elizabeth."

"Thank you, my love. I appreciate your love and your devotion and I am grateful for all of the care you pour on me." Elizabeth smiled softly. She knew how much he had given to pleasure her. "Will you tell me why no one calls you by your given name? I realised that even Albert's wife calls you 'Colonel' still and I wondered why everyone else calls you 'Fitzwilliam'. You wanted me to call you 'Richard' from the first day we met."

Richard smiled. "I fell desperately in love with you from the moment I laid my eyes on you and I could not fathom any other name from your lovely lips. Like my heart has called you 'Elizabeth' from the beginning, I only ever wanted to hear you call me by my name, as would someone so dear to me." He shifted his position and held her in his arms to continue his story.

"When I was four or five, I had a difficult time with my 'R's and I could not pronounce my name. I kept saying 'Wichad' and up until about eight or nine, I still could not pronounce my name properly so I hated repeating it. I told my friends to call me 'Fitz' and I liked it and preferred it. I had only allowed my parents, my brother, and Darcy, and eventually Iris and Georgiana, to call me 'Richard', since they were family and I knew they loved me no matter what. I related using my given name with those closest to me and never allowed anyone else to assume such intimacy with me. I vowed to myself that only the woman I loved would have that privilege." He kissed her hair affectionately.

He paused and laughed for a moment, recollecting a memory. "When I was thirteen, I was at Pemberley and was thrown off my first stallion that my father had given me for my birthday and became afraid to ride it for several days, and George Wickham, knowing that I was afraid of my own horse and knowing that did not like being called 'Richard', teased me mercilessly, calling me 'Wichad the Chicken-heart' until I completely lost my temper and began to beat him to a pulp. Darcy, thankfully, was with me and pulled me off the idiot before I killed him." He snickered then. "He was bruised and had two blackened eyes for over a week. My father punished me by making me feed my horse for a month by myself, which had been a blessing, since I had quickly overcome my fear of the horse after I spent more time with him, and I knew that I could conquer any fear."

He lifted Elizabeth's chin to look into her eyes. "That is, until I met you. I had never been afraid of anything until you suddenly appeared in my life and I feared for your distance, your rejection, your safety, and your happiness. I have never experienced so much love and fear at the same time, Elizabeth. I love you so much and yet I am always afraid of losing you or not being with you. I cannot imagine life without you and there is no happiness if you are not with me. I will be devoted to you for the rest of my life." He kissed her affectionately for several minutes, as they relaxed in each other's arms.

"I love you with all my heart, my dearest wife. Stay with me for a while?" He asked, as he yawned.

Elizabeth replied, "Yes, husband. I will be with you always, if not in body, then in your heart." She kissed him lovingly and he quickly fell asleep. She soon gathered her robe and left Richard's room.

Darcy was still awake and reading. "Back already? He must have been quite desperate." He chuckled.

Elizabeth smiled. "He was very tired after doing so much work. Fitzwilliam, may I ask you something?"

Darcy put his book down. "Of course, anything."

"Do you know if your uncle or Albert is as passionate as you and Richard? I am curious if it is a family trait. Richard pleasured me very well and spent on my stomach twice and he washed me after each time as you washed me on our wedding night. The attentions that you both show are so astonishingly similar and I must believe it is a family trait, although Albert certainly looks nothing like Richard." Elizabeth pondered.

Darcy laughed. "Oh, my love. I do not believe that Albert cares for more than his own release. He likes his wife very much but he has a mistress, Elizabeth. I believe the current one is his fifth or sixth, Richard would know for certain. Poor Albert; he got his mother's father's looks while Richard and I have been told we look more like our grandfather, the earl. And my uncle, he used to have a string of mistresses. He and my aunt began to like each other more about eighteen years ago, and he became more kind to Aunt Susan. That is when Iris was conceived. It is the norm, my dear, and I am once again the rarity." Seeing her surprised face, he continued. "I am afraid I have cast a shadow on my family. Remember, even Richard has had a mistress."

Elizabeth was still in shock. "I never knew about Uncle Henry and Albert!"

Darcy chuckled again. "My love, you happened to have two men, cousins, might I add, who are desperately and whole-heartedly in love with you. I am certain Richard has never washed another woman in his life."

Elizabeth interrupted. "That is what he said!"

"And he will never do so with another woman. He loves you as dearly as I love you. Was he good to you? Did you enjoy his attentions?" Darcy asked, taking her robe off of her as well as his own.

"Oh, yes, he is a masterful lover. I enjoyed being pleasured very much, Fitzwilliam. He told me the story of why no one calls him by his given name and what he did to Wickham when he teased him after Richard became afraid of his horse. He does love me so much and I appreciate that you allow our relationship to grow. He told me that he was afraid of nothing until he met me."

She saw her husband smile and nod. "I should have known that he loved you when he asked you to call him by his given name. He had confided in me that he only wanted those closest to him to call him 'Richard' and even Lady Celia does not call him by name. I honestly thought he was doing so due to our friendship but I should have known better. Did you know Celia chased Richard before meeting Albert?"

Elizabeth was surprised. "No! I did not know. She is so wealthy and beautiful. I heard she had £50,000! Why did he not pursue her? She would have made him a good wife."

Darcy smiled. "He never looked at her twice. Richard told me that Celia was vain and obnoxious and..." he laughed, "he wanted larger bosoms from a woman." They both laughed. "Albert found her attractive enough and they married a few months later. She liked the title, even if Albert was not handsome, and she is aware of his mistresses and is content with her lot in life. Richard and I both liked to see a lot more in front of a woman." They laughed harder. "We were both waiting for you. No one kept my interest for longer than a few minutes and Richard would have had a string of mistresses if he married for connections or wealth. We were waiting for our perfect soul mate and until the day you showed up in our lives, no one sparked our hearts like you had done."

"I love you so much and I am so content with my two husbands." Elizabeth sighed and cuddled with him.

She kissed him again and rubbed his masculine chest. "Oh, my love, I do wish to still be filled by you. Although I climaxed strongly several times, it was not the same as being completely filled by you. Will you love me again?" Elizabeth nibbled on his ear.

"Oh, yes, my love. A thousand times, yes." Darcy kissed her passionately.

They lay in their arms and slept together after achieving their satisfaction on both parties.

Chapter 15

The months at Pemberley flew by. They often worked together in the study, picnicked together in the parks, and played with the twins, ensuring many laughter throughout the house. Elizabeth would sometimes overtake Richard's study, citing that she was saving him from the swarm of ladies while she needed to meet with her neighbours to plan for the school and work on fixing up the orphanage.

Many single ladies flocked to flirt with Richard, whether at Pemberley or at dinner parties, but now, he remained cordial but distant, no longer smiling and returning their flirtations. He only had eyes for one woman and it was evident to all that his demeanour was completely changed. He was certainly pleasant but made it obvious that he was assuredly not in the marriage market.

Darcy was buried in work in his study and was once again thankful for his cousin's partnership in managing Pemberley, Rosings, and their many other properties. He had become an excellent master and they had divided several tasks to ensure all of their investments were thoroughly reviewed.

Richard was in shock when Darcy had told him that except for Pemberley, all of the other properties and investments now listed him as a co-owner. Darcy had completed updating his will for Richard to be appointed as legal guardian to Elizabeth and his current and future children, and that Pemberley would be willed to Bennet but all the other properties, Richard would have equal share in the decisions.

"Darcy, I do not know what to say." Richard was touched. He was teary-eyed from the love and respect that his cousin had given him. "I thank you from the bottom of my heart. I truly appreciate that you provide for all in your lot and although sharing your properties is a great gift, being Elizabeth's legal guardian is truly an honour. I know we will spend many years together but seeing that you protect her even further pleases me." He rose from his seat and stood by the window to look out. "Darcy, I know how much you have given. Having Elizabeth with me in my bed once a week is something that I never thought possible. I... I thought I would suffer miserably and die alone when I first fell in love with her and for you to allow... for us to be where we are now, it is a dream. The trust and the gift that you have given me... I am touched and eternally grateful, brother."

Darcy knew Richard was not usually an emotional man and smiled as his cousin wiped away a tear. They had learned more from each other in the past year than all the previous years combined and he was very proud of his cousin. "Richard, our wife is the tenderest and most generous of souls, and that she loves us both so fiercely is a gift. I know that should I have never met her and married her, I would have been an arrogant arse who looked down on everyone and most likely remained single. If I were married, it might have been to an obnoxious, mercenary shrew, who would only have cared about how she could spend my money. You would have still been a colonel, possibly on the continent, still sleeping around with your harem of women. Who knows, you might have become infected and died from the French disease by now. The fact that she accepted me so quickly and grew to love you is a testament to our fortune."

He paused to stand next to him by the window. "I know that it is too early but she has missed her courses last month and she might be with child. By my calculation, if she is able to keep this babe, it would be April or May. I worry for her, Richard. Her last miscarriage was devastating and it broke my heart to see her cry."

Darcy tapped Richard on the shoulder and continued, "I need you more than you know, brother. I do not share Elizabeth with you only out of the generosity of my heart, Richard. I am a selfish being and I wish I had all of her. But your endless love for her guides my heart that we are stronger, us three, when we share our love, and she loves you so intensely that I cannot take that away from her. She is such a woman, that she deserves *two* husbands to love her as thoroughly as you and I love her. She deserves every happiness and she is so happy with us both. I do not know how you do it." He shook his head. "I told Elizabeth that you had an iron will and it truly appears that you do. To have lain with women and to give that up completely, I do not know if I could ever stop loving Elizabeth so. Thank you for keeping your word." He smiled.

"To hold her and love her is enough; I need nothing else. I will not break your trust, Darcy. Iron will or not, it is my love for her and my vow to protect her vow to you that will not allow me to take more than what I have been gifted. I have been given beyond all expectations and I am grateful for every kiss, every affection." Richard spoke emotionally.

Just then, there was a knock at the door. Darcy bid enter and grinned broadly when Elizabeth opened the door and the twins waddled in with giggles.

"Papa!" Both boys screeched. Bennet ran to Darcy, falling down a couple of times but lifting himself up, while Richie wobbled slower to Richard, raising his arms to be lifted. Richard had taken Richie, his namesake, to his heart and had spent a little more time with him, while Darcy had done the same with his heir, so the boys each had his own 'papa' that they preferred.

Elizabeth smiled proudly at her men and boys. Bennet was grasping Darcy's neck tightly and bouncing up and down in laughter while Richie lay his head on Richard's shoulder and was babbling, telling his godfather all about his fingers. Her eyes teared up to see such a familiar sight and she thanked the heavens for her husbands.

"Well, husbands," she began as she walked over to kiss each man's cheek, "I hope you are getting all your work done. I expected you to be buried in paperwork but to see you sightseeing by the window, I am glad to disrupt your playtime with our boys." She teased. "I thought we would have a last picnic before we depart tomorrow. I cannot believe how quickly the last three months have passed!"

They all agreed and the men carried the boys and headed outside where Elizabeth had prepared a light luncheon. They laughed watching the boys fight over a ball and trying to eat the grass, and Elizabeth asked the men about what types of games they played as children.

The small family of five relaxed in the sun and could not imagine a more blissful life together.

~*~

Scotland was beautiful. The greenery that surrounded the beautiful manor was beyond what Elizabeth had expected. She had seen paintings of all of the Darcy properties at Pemberley but seeing it in live colours took her breath away.

Darcy Manor was one of two properties in Scotland and they would spend six weeks here, another six weeks at Kieran Hall, located fifty miles east. This property was being leased but Darcy had scheduled it so the tenants would be traveling during their tours.

Elizabeth walked around the rooms and saw what might need updating and although very comfortable and pleasant, she saw that several furnishings would need to be replaced. She met with the housekeeper and the rest of the staff and listened to their needs and very quickly earned the respect and loyalty of the entire household.

~*~

A week after they arrived, Darcy and Richard were ensconced in the study when Elizabeth had visitors. They were two ladies, sisters, who were from a nearby estate and had been close family friends for decades.

Mrs. O'Shea and Miss Mulligan were both fiery redheads with beautiful pale skin and slim figures. They were very attractive and very eligible. Elizabeth found them pleasant and friendly and excellent conversationalists, and she was pleased to find two women whom she could know better here and invited them to dinner the next day.

After her guests departed, she strode into the office where her men were working hard. The property laws were a little different and Darcy was showing Richard the variances.

"I just had the most wonderful visit, husbands. The ladies told me that they were childhood friends to you both, from here in Scotland as well as in England. Do you recall Mrs. Emily O'Shea and her sister Miss Emma Mulligan?" Elizabeth asked as she sat on her favourite chair.

Darcy replied, "Oh, yes! Very pleasant ladies. I believe they are about seven and twenty and five and twenty now? I saw them often here and I believe Mrs. O'Shea lived in London for several years until her husband died, perhaps four years ago? I cannot recall when exactly. Do you recall, Richard?" Darcy asked, turning his eyes to his cousin who was suddenly standing by the window looking outside.

Shit! I forgot her family lived near here. I thought she would be in London still. Richard thought.

Turning to Darcy slowly, he answered, "Yes, four years ago. Died when his horse threw him off and he was too drunk to hold on tight." He could not meet Elizabeth's eyes. *Damn it! Will Elizabeth forgive me?*

"That is right. I recall that he was a little obtuse and liked his liquor. Reminded me of Hurst. Miss Mulligan is one of those young girls who tried to kiss me when I was, I think eleven or twelve, Elizabeth." He laughed. "I ran away from her screaming and I still remember my mother laughing as I hid my face behind her, yelling that she was *icky.*"

Elizabeth laughed heartily at this. She looked toward Richard and saw that he was not laughing but his brows were furrowed and was in deep thought.

"Something you would like to share with us, Richard?" Elizabeth asked. *I wonder what is the matter. I am certain he has a lot on his mind but he is usually not so serious.*

Richard startled when Elizabeth addressed him. *What am I to do? I cannot lie to her. Oh, Elizabeth, my love, please forgive me.* He coughed and answered, "Ahem, I... I knew Mrs. O'Shea well. In fact, I had seen her in London after her husband died." He sat down and covered his face in shame. "I knew her... intimately."

Elizabeth sat with her mouth agape. *He... he slept with her?* She was shocked. Other than seeing Abigail Harrington, whom she saw only for a few minutes, she had not yet met anyone who had been intimately involved in Richard's past. She had enjoyed speaking with her and liked Mrs. O'Shea's company.

Darcy saw the shock in Elizabeth's face and was worried for her. He knew she would feel strongly about a woman from Richard's past and did not envy his cousin of the guilt that he must be feeling. *Thank God I waited for Elizabeth. I would rather die than have my wife meet an old lover. Poor Richard. Oh, these two. Sometimes I feel like I am the only adult around here. Well, she will need some time to vent her spleen.*

"That is my cue; I will leave you to talk. Will you be well?" Darcy stood up. She nodded in a rush. She needed to think. He kissed Elizabeth's cheek and whispered, "Be kind, Love."

He walked over to Richard and tapped him on the shoulder in sympathy. "I do not envy your place right now but I know it was before you fell in love. She will forgive you... eventually." He left to give them privacy.

Elizabeth stood and paced. She knew Richard had a long list of lovers, scores and perhaps hundreds, in fact, but never considered that she would befriend one. Not that she would have demanded he name every one of his women; he probably did not even recall some of them, but to be shocked so did not sit with her at all. She wondered who else she knew that he had relations with. She was mortified that she could be friends with women who spread their legs for him and enjoyed his favours.

I know it is in the past but I am jealous and angry. I know it was before he ever met me but now, I imagine him over her and making love to her, doing what he cannot do with me. What I cannot do with him. She cried, she did not know why, but the tears kept coming. It was illogical but she felt betrayed. She pictured his gorgeous body laying over that beautiful woman and his rock-hard manhood vigorously plunging into her, taking her long and hard, doing the things that he could not do with herself. She could imagine him kissing her and passionately making love and his face in ecstasy as he released with that other woman and she wanted to scream. There was nothing to be done but she hated that he had been with other women. She needed air. She could not breathe.

"Richard, I... I cannot... I need air." She swallowed a sob and began to hyperventilate.

Seeing her in distress, Richard immediately stood and ran to her. "Elizabeth, you are pale. I am so sorry. You must breathe slowly." He fanned her with his hand. "My love, breathe." He led her to the couch and sat her down and continued his fanning and wiping her tears.

She finally settled down and was able to breathe steadily. She took Richard's handkerchief and wiped her face then sat, staring into empty space while Richard wrapped his arm around her shoulders and whispered into her hair 'I am so sorry' over and over.

She looked down and saw the handkerchief in her hand. Richard was true to his word. He had always kept one of her handkerchiefs on his person and she caught him several times looking at her embroidery and beaming. He had loved her gifts and she also knew he was constantly rubbing the pocket watch out of habit when he was thinking. He carried the first gift that she had given him with him before their deeper relationship began; he was never without his book of poetry and would often read to her from it, sharing his favourite verses and reciting love poems to her when he made love to her. He had not broken one promise to her, that he would love her and never ask for more than what she had given. He was a good husband to her, albeit unofficially, and had been a wonderful godfather to her sons. He had truly given everything of his life, fully and wholeheartedly, without asking for anything else in return.

She looked down to her hands. She was never without her rings; her wedding band to keep her vows to Fitzwilliam, and Richard's ring, which had always comforted her.

Once again, she remembered the love that Richard had resolved to show her and the promises he had kept. He had proven his love for her time and time again. Every day with his actions and words, every week in his bed, he loved her with his entire being. He would love only her for the rest of his life. She smiled softly and knew all would be well.

Richard was distraught with her tears. *I am such an arse! If only I had never been such a rake. Oh, Elizabeth, you have changed me so much but I cannot change the past. Please, please forgive me.*

When she stood suddenly, he was startled and was afraid that she wanted to walk away from him. He hated it when she turned from him. He wanted to touch her, wanted to be connected with her somehow, and desperately hoped she would stay with him. He knew she would forgive him eventually; she was intelligent and generous, but he knew he had wounded her deeply and did not know how much grovelling would be needed for her grace. He attempted to stand with her but she put her hand on his shoulder to still him.

His heart tore that she would leave his presence but when she turned around and lifted up her skirts to sit astride him, he was in shock. She placed her legs on either side of his hips and placed her hot core above his groin. She wrapped her arms around his neck and kissed him softly. His arms were immediately around her waist and he returned her kiss furiously. He delved his tongue inside her mouth passionately to prove to her that he loved her and only her. His arousal had sprung as soon as she had sat on him and he was desperate to love her. It had been over a week and being in this estate, they had not yet found the privacy and had not known enough about the servants to keep confidences.

There was only one other person who knew of the close relationship between the trio: Garrison, Richard's valet. He did not witness any intimate acts but was aware that Mrs. Darcy spent time in Mr. Fitzwilliam's bed once a week at Pemberley and that Mr. Darcy was fully aware. Richard had saved his life twice and trusted his valet with his life, as he was his batman throughout his military service.

Elizabeth unbuttoned his fall and began to rub her wet folds on his long shaft, gliding her damp womanhood against him as she had done weekly at Pemberley. They had found that this was as close to sexual intercourse they could experience together and Elizabeth was able to reach a powerful climax, as his hard cock rubbed against her nub, and her hand rubbing his tip had provided his. Without his phallus entering her, she ground herself against him and used her hand to stimulate his erection. Richard bared her breasts and licked and suckled on her nipples, attempting to hold off releasing until his beloved climaxed but he was too aroused and was about to explode. He felt completely wrapped in her love. He lifted his mouth from hers and whispered, "I need to come."

Elizabeth placed her handkerchief on the tip of his manhood and returned to her grinding. She kissed him again, taking control of the affections, and whispered, "I am so in love with you, Richard."

Richard immediately released with a loud grunt, holding on to his beloved tightly. He held her and did not let go while he waited for his brain to gather more air. He kissed her hair and temple and whispered his words of love to her. She lifted her head to look into his eyes and he saw her love for him as she smiled.

"I am completely and wholeheartedly in love with you, Elizabeth. There is no one for me but you. Thank you for forgiving me. I... I am devastated that my past has caught up with me and I am ashamed of who I used to be, who I was before I met you, but that is no longer me. You have changed me and that is not who I am now. I am all yours. I cannot recall if I shared with you but that day when I first met you, I fell in love with you at first sight. You made Georgiana laugh and your eyes were shining and your smile melted my heart. Realising how much I wanted you but could not have you, I became desperate and used a prostitute who ended up being Abigail and I kissed her daydreaming that I had you in my arms, but I could not go on to even look at another woman ever again. My lips have never touched anyone else since and will always be for your lips alone. I am so different now and it is all because of you. I love and respect you beyond anything that I thought possible. I have not even thought of other women in my past and I only regret that I *have* a past. I wish I had self-control back then; I regret not waiting for you, my love, my wife. I love you so much; I love you with every fibre of my being, Elizabeth." Richard held her tighter and kissed her repeatedly.

"Well, my husband," she kissed him lovingly, "I will take advantage of your lovely lips often." She kissed him ardently again. "I believe you should think only of the past as its remembrance gives you pleasure." She lifted herself off his lap and sat next to him, helping him button his fall and embracing him tightly. "I was wounded; I felt helpless when I imagined you laying with her, Richard, but knowing that I have your love completely now, seeing my ring on my finger," she lifted her right hand and looked at her ring again, "and that we cannot change the past but only look to the future, I know you are mine and will forever be mine, husband. I love you too much to waste my time being jealous." She kissed him. "Will you tell me how long you and she... How did it come about? I promise to not dwell on it too long but I only wish to have the facts. She is very beautiful." Elizabeth asked.

Richard kissed her hand and ring. "*You* are the most beautiful woman I have ever laid my eyes on, my love. No one compares to your beauty, inside and out. You amaze me, Elizabeth. I cannot imagine... you truly astonish me with your generosity." He kissed her lips again several times. "I became reacquainted with her in London after meeting her and her husband at a dinner party. Her husband's brother was one of my lieutenants and we dined often. After her husband died, I visited her for consolation and being childhood friends, she naturally leaned on me for comfort and I took advantage of it. She was not my usual... preference... but I only cared for my immediate gratification. I do not recall how often but I saw her a few times for a couple of months and I moved on. I honestly had not given her one thought afterwards."

Elizabeth hesitantly asked, "Was she... did she please you?"

Richard laughed. "You ask after what you just did for me? I barely recall what she looks like and have absolutely no idea if she was good or better than others. I just poked myself in, let myself go, dressed, and then left. That was always the case. I had never cared for anyone else's pleasures until I met you, my love." He held her face between his hands and caressed her soft cheeks. After kissing her tenderly, he continued.

"I will be honest with you, Elizabeth. Immediately after I met you, to try to purge my desires for you, as well as after abstaining for eight months then taking up a mistress to try to use her for my carnal needs, I could not be aroused unless I dreamt of you. Only the thought of loving you and holding you would allow my body to be inspired because my heart was with you always. My body would not cooperate if I tried to think of anything else and it would always turn to you.

"I cannot recall a single event that was more pleasurable than kissing you and loving you." He kissed her fondly. "Do you recall that first time I kissed you on Xerxes?" She nodded. "I had you in my arms and you were unconscious and I could not stop myself.

Touching your lips and tasting your mouth was the sweetest memory of my life. I remember every one of our kisses. In the breakfast room and library at Pemberley; in the study at Darcy House; in our sitting room at Rosings; on the couch at Ramsgate; on your bed at Netherfield. I remember every one of our embraces and our intimate times together. My head, my heart is filled with so many memories of you and love for you, that my past has no place in them."

Elizabeth leaned against him. "Oh, you sweet man. I do not know if it is my possible pregnancy that is causing me to be so emotional and I am terrified that I will be so illogical and horrible like the last time, but I am glad you and Fitzwilliam will be with me always." She suddenly startled. "Oh, my love! I invited her and her sister for dinner tomorrow. Shall I cancel? Do you think it will be a repeat of the luncheon with Lord Devon?" She giggled.

"No, no, no. I cannot imagine having another meal as bad as that." He laughed. "I will do as you wish. You do not have to cancel. I can be unavailable and you can meet her and interrogate her for more information or I can attend with you and prove to you that there is nothing between her and me whatsoever. I do know you wish for female companionship up here. I will do whatever you wish." Richard kissed her cheeks. "I must go and clean myself up. I cannot believe how much I released." He rubbed his groin. "Thank you for the handkerchief. Now I will have another memory whenever I look at it." He winked. "I love you with all my heart, Elizabeth."

"I love you, too, Richard." Elizabeth responded. He kissed her lips and departed.

On the way to his room, he stopped at the library where he knew Darcy would be. "Darce, thank you for marrying the woman of my dreams. She is a treasure. She awaits you." He winked and left.

~*~

Darcy returned to the study to find Elizabeth biting her nails and looking out the window from the couch.

"You forgive too easily, my love." Darcy sat next to her and kissed her temple. "I would have made him suffer a little longer."

She laughed, "Well, my love, that goes to show you that you have a cruel streak in you, whereas I am so kind and generous." She kissed his lips. "I could not hold his past against him. Not everyone is as saintly as you, Fitzwilliam." She climbed onto his lap as she had done with Richard. "I forgave him because his suffering is my suffering. When I suffer, you suffer, when we all suffer, we get nothing done. I invited the ladies for dinner tomorrow night and I do not know what to do."

She spoke while grinding her husband's arousal and kissing his neck. "I liked her. I really enjoyed her company and wished to know her better," she continued as she unbuttoned Darcy's fall and Darcy was licking her exposed nipples, "but I dread what pictures will be in my mind as I speak with her. I thought her so beautiful."

She inserted his arousal inside her and moaned loudly. "I was so jealous that he was doing this, what we are doing right now, with *her*. I pictured what I could not do with him, the love that we make together, but I know he loves me." She climaxed as she rode him wildly. "Oh, that feels so good. I love you so much." She rode him gently now. "What should I do? Do I cancel? Should Richard attend?"

She moaned louder as Darcy thumbed her clitoris. "What if Miss Mulligan wants to kiss you? Shall you run and hide behind my skirts?" She laughed between moans. "Will you tell me if you think they are beautiful? Would your head be turned?"

"Oh, Elizabeth, I cannot think when you are riding me. My love, keep riding me. It feels so good. I am close, Elizabeth. I love having your juices all around my cock. Oh, yes!!" Darcy released as soon as Elizabeth cried out another climax. He held her tightly on his chest as she gasped for air.

Elizabeth spoke when she finally caught her breath. "I was thinking of changing out this couch but I think I will keep it. It has serviced me well today." She giggled.

Darcy pulled out his handkerchief and wiped her then himself. As he helped her rise and he buttoned his trousers, he said, "I think you should hold the dinner and have Richard attend. It will satisfy your curiosity into his past relationship and Mrs. O'Shea will have confirmation that he is not the same person he used to be. You probably met quite a number of women that he has bedded in the past, Elizabeth. You were not acquainted with them and he never mentioned it, but at Aunt Susan's Ball and other parties we attended in London, I knew at least a half dozen that he had slept with."

Elizabeth gasped, "Who?! Am I friends with them now?"

Darcy smiled. "Those unmarried women who would bed men without an understanding are no ladies and no, you are not close friends with any of them. You know Miss Smythe; and Miss Grantley and her sister Mrs. Barnett who is married. And also, Dowager Lady Jersey's daughters, yes, all four of them, Richard had known them all. He has definitely been around the block, my love, but he does not even remember them and never looked at any of them once when you were near. He is not the same man before he fell head over heels in love with you; the most beautiful, intelligent, and generous woman in all of our acquaintance." He kissed her with each compliment.

Elizabeth hugged him tightly and spoke. "My goodness! They are some of the most beautiful and wealthy women I have met yet!" *I do not compare to those women and yet my husbands chose me.*

Darcy smiled and kissed her head. "But you have our hearts completely and he and I both fell in love with you at first sight. Never forget how much you are loved. You should hold the dinner, Elizabeth. We will be here for several more weeks and I know you desire female companionship. He will do as you wish."

Elizabeth giggled, "That is what he said!"

Darcy laughed loudly. "Your husbands are very wise!"

Chapter 16

Dinner began awkwardly but conversation began to flow as Miss Mulligan laughed and joked about Darcy as a youth.

"Mr. Darcy, I remember your running away from me to hide behind your mother. I was livid that you had spurned me but you must know that I was all of seven years old!" She laughed and the party joined as well. They spoke of the properties around and what types of families resided and if there were any good shopping nearby.

Miss Mulligan chatted of the neighbouring town about three miles away that had some shops of note but also said, "I do miss London. It has been years since I have been there. Last time was prior to Mr. O'Shea's passing. Emily, what was that shop that you liked? The one with all the ribbons?"

Mrs. O'Shea blushed, recalling her time in London with Mr. Fitzwilliam and replied, "I think West End Emporium, Emma." She raised her eyes to look at her former lover. *He is even more handsome now and he is dressed so fine. I have missed his gorgeous naked body on mine. He was, by far, the best lover I ever had, even if it was four years ago. I never climaxed before he used his mouth on me and it was better than I ever thought possible and he is still single. I must get him back in my bed!* She thought. Mrs. O'Shea had known several other men after her husband died but Mr. Fitzwilliam had impressed her most with his physique and skills in bed.

Elizabeth noted the exchange and hid her smile behind her teacup. Richard had barely acknowledged Mrs. O'Shea when she entered, bowing his usual greeting from a distance and turning to Darcy more often for conversation. She had been a bit guarded when Mrs. O'Shea first entered and saw that her eyes were immediately drawn to Richard, but seeing him roll his eyes discreetly and wink at herself and his refusing to touch Mrs. O'Shea, even with the civil greeting, had appeased her senses. She wore the necklace that Richard had given her in London and once again felt secure in his love.

Darcy had been also very kind, rubbing her back and whispering to her, "You are much prettier, Elizabeth. There is a reason why Richard and I both fell in love with you at first sight."

Elizabeth had placed Richard on her left with the two sisters on her right, Mrs. O'Shea further away from Richard and next to Fitzwilliam's left. She saw that Miss Mulligan was eyeing Richard several times but she was too distracted, as Richard kept rubbing his foot against her ankle between bites. She decided to get revenge by placing her left hand on his knee while the ladies were answering her husband's question. Richard choked on his food for a few seconds but she saw him smile while he drank some water.

When the women separated and moved to the drawing room, the ladies chatted and Elizabeth wondered if both ladies did not have feelings for Richard. Miss Mulligan was single and likely unattached, as gentlemen were few up in the north.

Elizabeth asked Miss Mulligan, "May I ask, is anyone calling on you? Are you being courted by someone?"

Miss Mulligan blushed. "There are not enough single gentlemen of notice up here. Most are in London or Glasgow at this time of the year and I stay with my sister and my parents for now. I was engaged to a naval captain but he died at sea two years ago and I have not been tempted by anyone since."

Elizabeth thought, *Until today!*

Miss Mulligan continued, "I do find Mr. Fitzwilliam very pleasing now since I had not seen him since he was a young man of three and twenty or so. Could you tell me a little about him? My sister will not say a word, although I know she is acquainted with him more recently from London. Emily only said that his situation must have changed much to be no longer be wearing a red coat and I imagine him very dashing in his uniform." She blushed.

Elizabeth noted the blush on Mrs. O'Shea as well. *Oh, my. Both sisters are after my Richard.* "Well, he has, as you know, retired from his service over a year and a half ago when his cousin, Miss Anne de Bourgh, charged him to take care of her estate due to her illness. She willed Rosings to him and he is master there now." She saw the ladies gasp in shock. "Do you know Rosings Park?" Elizabeth asked.

Mrs. O'Shea nodded. "Yes, it was Lady Catherine's property. We used to make fun of her and called her 'Dragon Lady' because she always scared us. I believe it is an estate of at least 5,000 a year and is quite grand."

Elizabeth smiled. She had fond memories of Rosings. "Yes, it is a beautiful estate and its gardens are one of my favourites. Mr. Fitzwilliam has worked hard and it is a very prosperous place and it is currently being leased but he continues to work diligently with the steward there and also has other investments. Rosings brought in £7,000 last year, from what I have heard." *I will not even mention the other three thousand!*

"So much! But he is still single. How has he not found a wife yet? He must be the most eligible bachelor in all of England!" Miss Mulligan quickly covered her mouth. "I apologise. I should not be so rude to ask. It was quite surprising to see Mr. Darcy and Mr. Fitzwilliam again after so many years and they have both turned out to be very handsome gentlemen. I only wish I was successful in getting that kiss from Mr. Darcy all those years ago!" She laughed.

Elizabeth heartily laughed. She knew she was keeping both handsome men all to herself and knew she was blessed.

The gentlemen returned from their quick separation and sat with the ladies. Darcy sat next to Elizabeth and Richard sat on a single chair, furthest away from Mrs. O'Shea. As they began to converse on other topics, one of the boys' nannies knocked and entered. "Mrs. Darcy, Masters Bennet and Richie have a slight fever and I wanted to report it to you right away, ma'am."

Concerned for her sons, she curtsied and immediately left.

Darcy was concerned as well and asked Richard without words if he could leave as well. Richard nodded and Darcy excused himself. Richard truly did not wish to be in the room with these two ladies but wanted to be a good host so he began to ask about their parents and how things were at their estate. The ladies relaxed and began to fill him in on the topic.

Mrs. O'Shea took the opportunity to move her seat closest to Richard and asked, "And how have you been, sir? I have not seen you these past four years. I have heard from Mrs. Darcy that you have had a career change and are now the Master of Rosings."

Richard sighed. *What did I ever see in her? I better get this over with.* "Yes, I took over management of Rosings two years ago and have been learning from my cousin Darcy on how to improve and look for other investments as well. Our stay here at Darcy Manor is to teach me about Scotland laws and we are leaving for Kieran Hall in a month. I am only here to focus on the task at hand and not sure how much socialising I will be doing, since even while Mr. and Mrs. Darcy attend some functions, I intend to remain here so I can continue to work." *There! That should make it simple enough to understand that I am not here to flatter them and dance with them both.* He changed the topic and addressed Miss Mulligan. "I recall hearing that you were engaged to a sea captain but he was lost at sea. I am sorry for your loss and I wish you happiness for your future. Ladies, my apologies; I would like to also check on my godsons and will need to end our evening short. I will call for your carriage." *Enough of this pretence. Get me to my sons!*

After waiting several minutes for the carriage, he farewelled the ladies and ran to the nursery.

Elizabeth was holding Bennet and wiping his brow while Darcy held Richie who was sleeping peacefully. Elizabeth smiled when she saw Richard. "Have the ladies gone? I am so sorry to leave you alone with them. The boys are doing better now. Sit with me. I think they are both teething the back tooth and were uncomfortable but Richie seems to be well now. They are slightly feverish but not bad." She smiled as Richard bent to kiss Bennet's forehead.

"Our poor sons... Shall I hold him for you, Elizabeth?" He asked in concern.

"That would be nice." She handed the baby over. "We might have a long night ahead of us if they continue to take turns crying. I have instructed the nurses to wake me should they need help. The boys kept crying out for their Mama and they had to get me tonight. I do not mind. My sons are precious to me."

"And that is why they cry for you. They love you because you are a wonderful mother." Darcy beamed. "My love, why do you not go to bed? Richard and I will watch them for a while. They seem to enjoy their papas holding them for now."

"I will. Thank you, my love." She kissed both men on the cheeks and departed.

It was indeed a long night for Elizabeth, as the nurses had to wake her three times during the night. Elizabeth was exhausted and napped several times the next day while the men worried for her.

~*~

Elizabeth was elated when she received an invitation to the Fall Ball that would take place next week. She had met several more neighbours in the past weeks and looked forward to wearing her party dresses again. She missed dancing with her favourite gentlemen and was saddened to hear that Richard was not interested in attending.

"But do you not wish to dance with me, Richard? It is certainly the food of love, is it not?" Elizabeth flirted.

"Minx! I will dance with you right here if you wish." He leaned closer and whispered, "Or in my rooms, completely naked."

Elizabeth blushed. It had been weeks since they had been intimate. Finding neither the time nor the privacy, the last time they had made love was that day on the couch.

"Well, I shall make sure to dance all of my dances with handsome gentlemen at the party and you shall hear all about how they flattered me and looked down my dress and Fitzwilliam valiantly fought them off, losing his teeth to protect my honour and you were not there to help us. Hmph! How could you, Richard?" She crossed her arms, suddenly angry at the imaginary scenario.

"Oh, you are certainly with child. You have not been this emotional since you were last pregnant." He laughed. He held her in his arms. "My love, I meant what I said to you before. Wherever you wish me to be, I will go with you. I will always be with you. If you wish me to be at the ball, where all the unattached ladies will be throwing themselves at the Master of Rosings and his 10,000 a year, and might even jump into my arms to rip their dress open so they can expose themselves to me in order to capture me, and I fall desperately in love with one just by the size of their bosoms and fluttering of their eyelashes, then we can certainly have it your way. Although, I must say, I have a pair right in front me that makes me drool every time I see them bouncing my way." He dipped his mouth onto her cleavage and licked her. "Damn it, Elizabeth, men *will* be looking down your dress. Now I will *have* to go with you." He leered and caressed her breasts.

"Language!" She giggled. "Has it been that long? I am sorry. We have two more weeks to go and we move to Kieran Hall. How will you make it until we return to Pemberley?" Elizabeth asked.

They had decided not to risk being caught having Elizabeth in Richard's bed at Darcy Manor. The footmen were about at different stations and there was no connecting door between the rooms. The few times that they had privacy had interruptions and it had been nearly a month since Richard had his release with her.

"It matters not, my love. Being able to kiss you and be in your presence sustains me." Trying to distract himself from his ardour, Richard commented, "I have heard from Wentworth. He was flowing with praises for his wife for giving him a son and as a personal thanks for my helping him through his difficulties, they named him Richard!" He laughed. "Richard Wentworth. I must say, I am quite accomplished to have two boys named after me now. Richard Darcy and Richard Wentworth. Perhaps they will become great friends in the future."

Elizabeth laughed. "I, too, have heard from Anne. She is so proud of her son and is ever grateful for my educating her through her pregnancy. She has such a kind soul. She does not have anyone to talk to about marriage, as Mrs. Russell, her confidante, has been widowed for so long and her younger sister is useless. She appreciates our friendship and I have you to thank for it." She kissed Richard's cheek. "You have very loyal friends. You must have done something right before you met me." She gently stroked his cheek.

"Minx! I might have done all right before meeting you but you made me infinitely better. Mmm... You are so sweet." Richard replied, as he began to caress her again and his mouth trailed her neck. "So tempting..."

Elizabeth moaned. "Oh, I wish we were in your bed right now."

Richard straightened quickly as he was about to explode. He kissed her lips and stepped back to take several deep breaths. "I need to calm myself before I burst. I love you more than for your body or my release, Elizabeth. I do wish you would rest more. I know you have been ill in the mornings." Richard kissed her hands, as he attempted to settle down his raging erection.

"You sweet man. I love you. Cook has been making sure I have toast available to me at all times and the tea here is fantastic. Thank you for finding it for me. The blend is delicious and I hope to take some with us back to England." Elizabeth beamed.

"I will personally see to it that you are never without it, my love." He kissed her lips this time. "Now, tell me before Darcy returns, which of these two books do you think he will like?" Richard had found two volumes of very rare first editions and asked Elizabeth to choose one.

"Hmm... I know I prefer *Utopia* but I believe Fitzwilliam will prefer *Paradise Lost*. I selfishly want to choose Thomas More but I know his taste. Oh, I cannot choose! These are both marvellous and must have cost a fortune!" Elizabeth cried.

Richard laughed. *She has 7,000 a year and is still frugal as ever. I love her to death.* "Well, since you are having so much difficulty choosing, you must let a *man* choose for you. Your feeble womanly mind must comply to a man's *superior* decision."

"Richard!" she hissed. She pinched him on the arm and he yelped.

Just then, Darcy entered the study and boomed, "Children! Cease your bickering!"

Then he laughed.

Richard burst out laughing as well while Elizabeth giggled. She ran into Darcy's arm. "Happy birthday, my love! We have a gift for you. Well, it is Richard's gift but I helped choose it. Well, I was helping him choose it but I am not sure which one we decided on. Good lord, what is wrong with me? I got distracted and do not know which one. Richard?" She looked to him for help.

Richard laughed loudly again. "Darcy, she was too busy pinching me that she did not decide. But I have told her that I would decide for her because I am a man and thus superior." He laughed again as he saw Elizabeth glare at him. "Here is your gift, from the both of us." He handed Darcy the copy of Milton's book.

Darcy was in awe of the rare volume. "How did you find this? I have been looking to add this to my collection for ages! Thank you, brother!" He hugged Richard. He kissed Elizabeth tenderly, "Thank you for trying to choose, my love." He took the volume and sat down to look at it.

Richard turned to Elizabeth, "Milady, I must apologise for my rude comments. You are in no way inferior to us weak men who will literally fall at your feet and grovel for mercy should you be offended by our stupidity. My gift to you, milady." He handed her *Utopia*.

Tears immediately sprung to her eyes, "But it was... I was to choose one! It is too much!"

Richard kissed her hand. "I always meant it for you, Elizabeth. I know you wanted it."

Without breaking eye contact, Elizabeth yelled, "Fitzwilliam?"

"Hmm?" Darcy barely replied, so focused on his book.

"I am going to kiss Richard now. I hope you will not mind." Elizabeth continued to watch Richard.

"Sure, my love." Darcy agreed without a second thought.

Elizabeth inched closer and closer until her body was flushed against Richard's and dipped his head down with her hands. She pressed her lips against his and opened her mouth to taste his lips and suckle on them.

Richard gulped, as he had never kissed Elizabeth like this before in Darcy's presence. He knew he was rock hard and would be embarrassing himself should he release in his trousers now.

But she began to attack his mouth and he lost all thoughts as he returned the kiss fervently, his hands caressing her back and hips as he was tonguing her deeply. He froze when he heard a cough. *Damn it! He is watching us.* He quickly broke the kiss and parted, sitting back down on the desk to hide his arousal.

"She started it!" He accused like a child.

Darcy burst out laughing. "I know, Richard, I know." He smiled and returned to his book.

Elizabeth arched her brow and took her book to sit next to Darcy, eager to browse through her gift.

Richard smiled as he shook his head and went back to work. *I love my life!*

Chapter 17

The Fall Ball was held at Stirling Castle and it was magnificent. It belonged to a duke, and he and his wife were elated to see Darcy and Richard again. Their Graces spent some time in London but it had been three years or so when their visits had aligned. They had been long-time family friends and were delighted with Elizabeth and commented that Darcy's personality had changed so much since his marriage that he was nearly unrecognizable.

Unfortunately for Richard, Her Grace wanted to personally introduce him to every eligible lady in attendance and there was no polite way for him to decline. Prior to arriving, Richard had begged and pleaded for Darcy to switch their supper set, as he did not want to be forced to dance with some insipid creature and have to sit with her for the meal. Darcy finally agreed, in exchange for Richard accompanying Elizabeth for the next shopping trip and carrying all of her purchases.

Darcy danced with some of the matrons with whom he was familiar but mainly stayed with Richard and Elizabeth. Elizabeth was once again very popular, as many had known Darcy to be a stoic fellow and was pleased to see his wife liven him up.

Richard was pressed to dance almost every set and was exhausted by the supper set.

"You have danced with so many eligible ladies, Cousin Richard, have you found anyone worthy of a second dance?" Elizabeth spoke a bit loudly to spur on gossip.

"Minx!" Richard whispered as he attempted to maintain his stoic face. He was trying to emulate Darcy's old habit of keeping distance from all the ladies but was failing miserably with Elizabeth. He said louder, "No, Cousin Elizabeth, I find that all the ballrooms are the same. This castle is quite beautiful but I am only enjoying my dance with my dear cousin and I only wish to for the night to end. You know I have no plans to marry, Mrs. Darcy. I am fully enjoying my bachelorhood and0 intend to keep it that way. I am perfectly content with my life as is, thank you." He concluded.

Elizabeth could hear the disappointed sighs around her. *Success! That should keep the gossip to a minimum.*

Richard whispered at the next close movement, "You are a master manipulator, wife, and the mistress of my heart. I wish I could dance with you again."

Elizabeth laughed merrily. "These ladies really do want you, Richard. They only wish they could get their claws on you but you belong with me and I am glad you are here with us. We will dance again soon, I promise."

Richard thanked her for the dance with a full smile and they walked to supper with Elizabeth on Darcy's arm.

~*~

Richard's last dance, though, was with Mrs. O'Shea. Somehow, the Duchess had arranged his set and he was forced to dance with the lady. Giving a silent apology to Elizabeth, he led his former lover to the line and stood next to Darcy who was dancing the quadrille with Elizabeth. *I wish I were dancing with Elizabeth again instead.*

They had met only a few times during other dinner parties in the neighbourhood and he had avoided speaking with her as much as possible, but Elizabeth had warned

Richard that she felt Mrs. O'Shea was still seeking his attentions. After reassuring Elizabeth several times that he found nothing pleasing about Mrs. O'Shea and that he infinitely preferred the beauty and grace of his beloved wife, he knew that Elizabeth was finally comfortable being in that woman's presence.

As the dance started, Mrs. O'Shea asked quietly, "How have you been, Mr. Fitzwilliam? I have missed our times together."

Richard briskly answered, "I am well." He did not know how much more to say.

Mrs. O'Shea began her flirtations. "I see that you are. Quite well. You look dashing tonight, my dear Richard. May I call you 'Richard'? I do miss seeing a lot more of your magnificent body in private, Richard. We were so close before, can we not be so again, my dear?"

"Please stop addressing me so informally, Mrs. O'Shea." He hissed. *She is crass and rude! I cannot stand to hear my name from her. How dare she address me so intimately?!*

"I remember our times together well, Richard. Do you recall how well I pleasured you with my mouth? You were the biggest I had ever had, dearest. I understand you are unattached and also know that you intend to remain a bachelor but perhaps we can be of use to each other once again. I am looking for a situation to return to England and heard Rosings has several cottages you can use for your 'personal needs'." Mrs. O'Shea blatantly continued to flirt during the dance.

Richard was fuming. For her to speak of such things in a ballroom where it could be overheard was inappropriate and the act of a desperate woman. He could see that Elizabeth had heard some of her words by her gasps, and his shame of having used so many women in the past returned in full force. He was kicking himself that his bad behaviour in his past gave way for women to talk to him so. He saw that Elizabeth, who was dancing with Darcy, appeared worried for him but noted her soft smile. He felt his heart lift when he saw his beloved. *My Elizabeth is so wonderful. I will be resolute but a gentleman.*

He stopped in the middle of the dance and spoke clearly but quietly to Mrs. O'Shea. "Madam, I have kept myself quite busy and made many great changes in my life. That man that you knew is no longer who I am now. I will never return to that old self and am very happy in my lot. Please do not approach me again. Good evening." He bowed and left in the middle of the dance.

There were loud gasps and conjectures as he walked out, with people wondering if he had just cut Mrs. O'Shea or if he was simply not feeling well. He did bow so it appeared that he was not cutting her in public.

Richard removed himself to the balcony where several guests were getting some fresh air. He was still fuming but attempting to control his anger towards the tactless woman as well as himself, when he felt Elizabeth's hand wrap around his left arm and Darcy standing to his right.

Elizabeth softly spoke, "I do not know exactly what was said, but I can make an educated guess by your expression. You did well. You did not humiliate her but you spoke what needed to be said. I am proud of you, Richard."

Darcy tapped his hand on Richard's back and held his shoulder. "You did well, brother. I do not know if I could have handled her as well as you did. Let us take our leave and return home. Elizabeth is feeling poorly."

Richard was immediately concerned for her. "What is the matter, my dear? What can I do for you?" He turned and rubbed her hand on his arm.

"Oh, you dear man. I am only exhausted. Supper was too heavy and I need some toast. I will be well once I get some rest." Elizabeth gleamed.

"Let us go now." Richard hurried.

~*~

After thanking their Graces, they loaded into the carriage and departed for the one-hour trip back to Darcy Manor.

Elizabeth leaned on Darcy and asked sleepily, as her eyes were closing, "Richard, what did she mean when she said you were the biggest she ever had? What was so big? Bigger than what?"

Richard's eyes bulged while he looked straight at Darcy. Darcy was muffling his laughter and turning red, attempting to keep quiet.

Richard spluttered, "Well... she was... my dear, she was speaking of the... size of my..." He turned his eyes to Elizabeth and ceased speaking. He huffed out his breath in relief.

Elizabeth had promptly fallen asleep, resting on Darcy's chest, and Richard watched her carefully as she snored lightly.

Darcy, trying not to shake, let out a snort. "You know she is not going to forget! You will have to answer that one." He laughed as quietly as possible. "Oh, my dear brother, how you get yourself into these situations..."

Richard smiled shyly and scratched his head. "I know she is so innocent and I love her so much for it. She does not forget a thing and it is embarrassing but she makes me happy and I am willing to bear anything for her. Do you remember my telling you about my cock fight with Albert?"

Darcy laughed again, this time quite loudly. He froze when Elizabeth stirred for a moment then settled and began to snore again. Relaxing, he replied, "I think I was eleven or twelve. You were so proud that you beat your older brother of two years and that your 'sword' was twice his size to everyone. Did your father not give you a whipping for that? I remember my father laughing for days."

Richard grinned. "The ten paddles I received were well worth it. Father told me to never speak of it again, as gentlemen did not discuss those things, but I was so proud to have the bigger cock and teased Albert mercilessly for years that he had a tiny weenie." He laughed. "I bedded one of his courtesans a few years ago. Apparently, he still has a tiny weenie." They both burst out laughing again.

Elizabeth turned and repositioned herself while the men sat silently once more, suppressing their chuckles.

Richard quietly spoke after Elizabeth settled. "I would give anything to have waited for her. I fucked my way through whores in my youth, believing that as a second son, I could do whatever I wished with no repercussions, and I honestly never believed I would find someone. I knew you were waiting for your perfect woman and thought you were a fool. Who would have ever guessed that your perfect woman is my perfect woman... All those women I bedded were all the same; whether they were prostitutes or distinguished ladies, they opened their legs for immediate pleasures without any thoughts of regret. Elizabeth is the love of my life and I regret that I cause her so much heartache with my past bad behaviours."

"She loves you, Richard. I am so thankful that she loves us both. She is the most generous and forgiving person I have ever known and I will never take her love for granted." Darcy affirmed his cousin.

"Neither will I." Richard's eyebrows furrowed while he stared at his beloved. "She is so exhausted."

Darcy saw his concern and spoke. "She will be well. She has been very tired but had been enjoying herself so much that I allowed it. I hope she will stay in bed the full day tomorrow. She will be well, Richard. If we started worrying now, we will be miserable for the next seven months and our misery will lead to her becoming angry with us." He smiled. "She says she is too much trouble but she is worth it."

"She certainly is, Darcy. She is most precious." Richard agreed.

As soon as they arrived home, Darcy carried his beloved into the house. As they parted towards each rooms, Elizabeth opened her eyes and whispered, "Good night, Richard. I love you."

Richard smiled and fell asleep holding his favourite handkerchief in his hand.

~*~

Two days after the ball, Miss Mulligan visited Elizabeth alone. She had tears in her eyes and asked for forgiveness. "Mrs. Darcy, I am sorry to intrude on you. I see that you are packing to leave in a few days but I had to come to apologise about my sister. I needed to find out what happened during her dance with Mr. Fitzwilliam and she finally confessed it all this morning, that she was propositioning herself as a mistress and that she had hidden her previous relationship with him but was using that information to offer herself; it was disgraceful and dishonourable.

"It is obvious that Mr. Fitzwilliam is now such a respectful gentleman and we, both my sister and I, did not consider it when we flung ourselves at him. I was hopeful that he might be interested in getting to know me better but I could tell right away that he had no such thoughts. I saw that he was distant to Emily as well but until the ball, I did not think anything of it. When my sister told me that she had a relationship with him for two months immediately after her husband's death, I was initially angry with Mr. Fitzwilliam, thinking that he took advantage of her grief, but when she confessed to me that she had seduced him then and now wanted him back in her bed desperately, and with his wealth, how she wanted to become his mistress, I was mortified. He is so different than how he used to be, even just a few years ago and all the rumours from the past is nothing like how he is now. He is such a respectable gentleman and for my sister to have... disgraced herself, I am so ashamed. I am only grateful that he did not cut her in public for being a loose woman and he saved my reputation as well. If possible, would you be agreeable to have him join us so I can apologise for myself and on behalf of my sister?" She cried.

Elizabeth really liked this younger sister. She was intelligent and open and she had no guile and spoke freely. She was similar at laughing at the follies of humans like herself and Elizabeth wished her the best.

She gave a quick word to the footman for Richard and within minutes, he appeared in the drawing room. "Miss Mulligan." He bowed and took his seat next to Elizabeth.

Miss Mulligan explained the situation and begged for his forgiveness and thanked him for avoiding a public cut.

He accepted her apology and wished her well. Elizabeth also thanked her for her openness and hoped to continue correspondence with her. She truly liked this young lady and could not fault her for having a loose woman for a sister. *Like Jane! So many pretty ladies after my Richard.*

After Miss Mulligan took her leave, Elizabeth walked back with him to the drawing room and asked Richard, "Miss Mulligan told me that Mrs. O'Shea seduced you after her husband died. I was under the impression that you had... initiated the relationship. Will you tell me about it a little more?" She was curious how the affair had come about.

Richard coloured. "I do not like to talk about my past, Elizabeth, but you know I will never keep anything from you." He took a deep breath.

"I visited Mrs. O'Shea to offer my condolences the day after her husband died and did not think twice about being alone in her company, being as irresponsible as I was back then, and when she cried of her misery of being a widow, I offered her my handkerchief. When I drew closer to her, she wrapped her arms around me and proceeded to... kiss me and... sat on my lap... and things followed from there. I really was not attracted to her but still allowed it to happen. I am ashamed that I fell so easily into such seductions but it was not... uncommon for women to throw themselves at me. I had known it was not appropriate to lay with her when her husband's body was not yet cold in the ground but I had not cared for more than for my immediate gratifications and took my pleasures whenever I had the chance.

"As much as she took advantage of my weakness, I should have known better and comported myself more gentlemanly. Because of my failure to keep myself in check, you have suffered for it and I am still very sorry." Richard kissed her hand several times. "I love you so much, Elizabeth. Having your love returned and your affections are the best thing in life and I only wish I had waited for you. You are my soulmate, my wife."

Elizabeth smiled. "Oh, Richard. I am sorry to dredge up an old memory. I know you had many women chasing you as you are SO handsome. I was only curious how a woman might seduce you to the point of your losing control." She winked. "I could use some pointers." She lowered her sleeve on her left shoulder to expose her skin.

Richard pounced on her when he saw her smooth skin, his kisses trailing from her lips to neck to her exposed shoulder. "Minx! You know you have seduced me to the point of losing *all* my self-control. I will never get enough of you, my love." He kissed her mouth again while he rubbed his arousal against her as she lay under him on the couch. "Mmm... It is not that I had no control but I did not exercise any with those other women. But you tempt me beyond every control I have because I have never been at anyone's whim as I am with you. I am at your mercy, milady."

He lifted himself off of her and he caressed her cheek. "I wish nothing more than to take you right here, right now, but I will be a gentleman. I love you too much to overpower you or to injure your reputation with my bad behaviour." He knew the servants were about and could not risk being caught.

"I love you, Richard. We will certainly talk more about her mouth being on you when we have some privacy. I feel so ignorant for not realising what she was talking about you being the biggest." Elizabeth arched her brow in mirth. "Having Fitzwilliam and you as the standard, I did not realise there were such drastic differences in the size of a man's... equipment." They both laughed. "I must admit I am very proud to have two such *large* tools available to me for my pleasures. A man wants to *be* the biggest, a woman wants to *have* the biggest." She winked.

Richard gulped as his cock twitched. "Damn it, woman. I will now have to go find some time alone." He whispered. "It is never going to go down if you keep tempting me. You will have to hide me behind your skirts up the stairs."

Elizabeth giggled and nodded.

Richard helped her rise, kissed her hand, and walked her to her door to rest. She was still nauseated all the time, especially in the mornings, and needed to rest throughout the day.

He kissed her cheek at the door and whispered, "Rest well, Elizabeth. I will let Darcy know to comfort you. Thank you for your love. I love you. Only you."

Chapter 18

Kieran Hall was about twice the size of Longbourn. It was Darcy's smallest estate and it had sat vacant for about a year. Darcy had planned to visit last year so he could make some updates but due to Elizabeth's pregnancy with the twins, that plan had been postponed until now.

Elizabeth quickly took a tour with the men. It was an older house, but structurally sound, carefully maintained, and in a peaceful setting that was very calm and restorative. It also contained fewer servants, as only the minimum was needed.

Elizabeth was exceedingly happy to see Agnes, the woman that she helped escape her abusive husband at Pemberley, looking so well, and the housekeeper, Mrs. Cleveland, complimented the young lady for being an excellent worker and that Mr. Smithson, Agnes' husband, was on hand to help with any task needed on the estate. Agnes had praised Mrs. Darcy to the skies and all of the servants quickly took a liking to the new mistress. The cook, the butler, and the caretaker were the only other servants present due to its vacancy and they all had been in the Darcys' service for decades.

For this visit, four maids were hired to help with the addition of the Darcys, Richard, two babies, two valets, one lady's maid, and two nurses, not including all of the footmen and grooms.

As Elizabeth surveyed the rooms, she noted that the bedrooms were quite out of date but she liked the cosiness of the small manor and actually preferred it over Darcy Manor. This home had a warmth and intimacy that she would enjoy for small family holidays.

She spoke with the housekeeper and planned out the menu for the week and returned to the gentlemen who were busy working with the steward, who did not reside in the servants' quarters. Elizabeth waited and listened to the discussions, as she often did, as her husbands insisted that she be aware of estate matters and made the proclamation after the steward departed.

"Fitzwilliam, Richard, I have an important matter to discuss with you. As you know, this home is quite outdated and all the guestrooms' wall coverings and furniture will need updating. Unfortunately, there are too many of us here and not enough space so we will need to squash up in order to get the renovations completed in time. If you are agreeable, I recommend that the twins take up the current nursery with the bedroom attached for their nurses, the other eight guest rooms be updated immediately, and unfortunately, Mr. Darcy, you and I will need to share the Master's room, while our dear cousin Richard take the Mistress' rooms. I have explained this to Mrs. Cleveland and she is absolutely adamant that although it will be quite uncomfortable for us, it is the only solution. What say you, gentlemen? Are you willing to suffer such discomfort for the next six weeks while we remain here?" She smirked.

Richard brilliantly smiled. *We will finally have some privacy!*

~*~

Richard lay back and panted. He was dripping sweat and his heart was beating frantically and he had the biggest smile on his face.

He had been desperate for Elizabeth to be in his bed as it had been over six weeks since he last made love to her in his bed. She helped him release five weeks ago but it had been truly too long.

The walls were definitely thinner in this house and he could hear Darcy laughing and taking his pleasures with his wife for a full hour. He could hear the moans and the bed thumping against the wall and thought surely after the second time Darcy grunted, he would be done! But no, this was the third time and he could no longer stand it. *Damn you, Darcy! Taking dear Elizabeth so many times! I can only imagine how fantastic she must be. I have never taken a woman three times in a row! I do not think I ever released three times in one night in my life! God, I wish we could have sex!*

He reached for his manhood and stroked it, dreaming of Elizabeth receiving Darcy's attentions and hopefully soon, his own, and came into the cloth that he had prepared. He shuddered as he released and hoped he would not disappoint Elizabeth too much when she finally came to his bed.

Richard heard some noises and talking and then silence for about ten minutes. He thought perhaps she fell asleep and was disheartened that she might not visit tonight, but his heart began to beat faster as he heard the door open to his room. This room was quite feminine but he did not mind one bit since he would be able to lay with his beloved and he had no thoughts for anything else.

"Have you been waiting long for me, Richard?" Elizabeth asked as she climbed into bed.

"All my life, my love. I am glad you are finally here. Did Darcy truly take you three times just now?" Richard asked with a smirk.

"How? You could hear us?" Elizabeth was flushing red.

"Yes," Richard kissed her cheek. "I could hear almost everything and I had to release myself hearing your pleasures. I love hearing you climax." He kissed her lips gently. "But we will have to be quiet, unless you do not mind Darcy hearing us. He might burst through the door and take you away from me." He cradled her breast and exposed her nipple from her nightgown. "Please let me love you; I am desperate for you. I missed you so much, my wife." Richard began to suckle on her nipple and took turns while kneeling between her legs. He was surprised how quickly his erection had returned. He lifted up her silk gown to feast on her womanhood with his hand and mouth.

She began to moan softly. "I do not know how it is possible to be pleasured so much. I am so wanton for having two men love me for hours and I cannot get enough, Richard. Oh, that feels so good." She began to moan louder as he fingered her and licked her nub.

She thrust her hips upwards to get the full length of his fingers inside her and climaxed, unable to keep quiet, cried out her pleasures.

Richard smiled at her passion and climbed on her to lay his huge arousal on to her abdomen as was his wont, but Elizabeth asked him, "Richard, I wish to pleasure you. Will you lay back on your pillow?"

He smiled and complied. He was hoping she would sit on him to rub herself against him and he was glad that he had released before she arrived since they would be able to take their time and enjoy the lovemaking for as long as possible. He placed his arms behind his neck and watched her, as she opened his legs and sat on her legs between them. She rubbed his erection with both of her hands and he gasped loudly as she bent forward to take him into her mouth.

"Elizabeth... Oh... Ah... my god... that feels.... so good...." Richard could not control himself. He moaned louder than he had ever done in his life. He had many prostitutes do this to him but for Elizabeth to take him into her soft, beautiful mouth, for his flesh to be enveloped within her oral muscles, she felt better than any womanhood he had ever entered. He could not blink, unbelieving that this was truly happening, and was afraid it was all a dream. He watched her intently as his cock throbbed being inside her orifice.

Elizabeth licked the shaft from the tip all the way down to his testicles and wrapped her mouth around his jewels. She spoke with her tongue gliding around his erection, "I recall hearing that you liked to take your pleasures in a woman's mouth." She licked the tip again and seductively looked up. "Do you like it? Do you like your *biggest* manhood in my mouth?" She bent and covered her mouth on his cock and bobbed up and down to plunge him as deep inside her mouth as possible repeatedly and vigorously.

He began to thrust into her mouth and she met him, thrust for thrust, with her tongue rubbing against his shaft and sucking him so strongly that he thought he would faint. "YES! I... God! I am going to come!" He did not know if she would take his seed in her mouth but she would not let go and suckled even harder. "ELIZABETH!" He screamed out, as he had the biggest release of his life.

Richard panted and gasped and held on to the headboard as he shuddered. He was dripping sweat and his heart was beating frantically. He thought he would fall off the bed from the ecstasy he just experienced and when his eyes could finally focus, he saw Elizabeth wiping her mouth with the sheets and smiling.

"Was that worth the wait, my love?" She seductively asked.

"Oh, my love, my wife, I... I cannot... believe..." He could not speak clearly. "That was the best feeling that I have ever felt... That was better than every pleasure I have ever experienced." He kissed her frantically all over her face, mouth, and neck.

"Fitzwilliam said that it was most similar to being inside a woman but the texture of the mouth and of course the wantonness of it all makes it most pleasurable. Is it the same for you?" Elizabeth asked.

"Yes, a thousand times, yes. I care not that I will never enter your womanhood if we could repeat that. That was amazing, Elizabeth. Just amazing." He was gasping for breath still. "No one, I swear, no one has ever made me release like that, my love. Your mouth is astounding. You are incredible." He kissed her mouth and neck again and caressed her breasts.

Elizabeth moaned as he masterfully made love to her with his kisses and caresses. She knew he was well-experienced and to be intimate with Richard was heavenly but she missed having Fitzwilliam fill her and unconsciously began to rub herself while Richard lay next to her, licking her nipples.

Damn! She is aroused and is touching herself! Richard watched in astonishment as Elizabeth's finger circled her clitoris and her moans became louder. *Good lord, I am hard again. How is this possible? I want to give her everything I have; all of myself.*

Richard climbed on top of Elizabeth and kissed her, tonguing her mouth as deeply as possible and held her hands above her head, rubbing his erection against her curly hairs between her legs.

"Do you trust me?" Richard asked, as he kissed her neck.

Elizabeth moaned, "Of course, Richard." She was extremely aroused with Richard's talented skills and having him completely cover her naked body with his long muscular figure. She wanted to reach another climax and squirmed under him to rub herself against his body.

Richard kept her wrists pressed so that she could not move. He held her in his power and his cock twitched, knowing that he could take anything he wanted at this moment. *I wish we could make love all the way. I wish for all of her more than anything in my life but I will honour her. She has given me so much more than I ever thought possible.*

"Mmm... I love you with all my heart and body, Elizabeth. I want to love you as intimately as possible. I will not break our vows but you must promise me that you will keep your legs closed and straight. Can you do that?" He asked.

Elizabeth nodded. "I will do whatever you wish." She straightened her legs.

Richard kissed her again. "I love you so much. I am going to make love to you but I will not enter you. Keep your legs straight when I tell you to." He lifted himself off her body and fingered her core and gathered her moisture and rubbed it against his erection. He lay back over her, closing her legs together with his legs, and moaned loudly as he plunged his hard cock between the apex of her legs, rubbing her clitoris with his long shaft as he stroked up and down. He had done this to prevent intercourse a few times but he could not resist the temptation and ended up plunging inside those women and gave up trying. He had wanted his own satisfaction above anything else and had not cared if they were married women or if he got them with child.

Elizabeth writhed as she felt her bundle of nerves being rubbed as hard as when Fitzwilliam was thrusting into her and began to moan louder and louder.

"Oh my god, Elizabeth! This feels so good!" Richard cried out as he was bouncing on her petite body. He took care to keep his weight off her baby bump but revelled in the incredible sensation of plunging into his beloved. It felt nearly as equal to intercourse but of course having Elizabeth under him made a world of difference. He wanted to pleasure her but was determined to keep his vow even if she might open her womanhood to him.

Until now, they had rubbed on each other and Elizabeth had sat on his erection, or Richard had used the folds of her buttocks to stimulate himself but it had never been this close to intercourse, this intimate.

Elizabeth screamed out her climax as it was nearly as strong as being filled. "Oh my god! It feels so good, my love! I am coming, Richard!"

Richard grunted noisily as he thrust himself between her folds and released immediately as soon as he heard Elizabeth climax. "I LOVE YOU!" He screamed out.

They both lay panting for breaths as they reached their pinnacles together so strongly for the first time. Richard had kept most of his weight on his arms and knees and after regaining his senses, he lifted himself off of his beloved. He grabbed a towel and wiped his semen off her womanhood and cleaned himself afterwards. *I have never... Three times?! My dearest Elizabeth is a wonder.*

He held her tightly in his arms. "That was... you are... most incredible. Will you stay with me for a while?" She nodded. "I love you, wife."

"I love you, too, husband." They wrapped their arms around each other and fell asleep in exhaustion.

~*~

Darcy realised that the walls in this house were very thin. As soon as Elizabeth left him, he had intended to stay up for a short while to read then go to sleep. But he could hear the muffled sounds of conversation and soon, silence. Then he heard his wife's moans as they grew louder and louder. *Oh, my Elizabeth is enjoying herself. Even after climaxing six times, she still has more to give.* He smiled.

He continued to hear the moans and heard her cry out her climax. He felt his cock twitch at the sound and looked down. *Again? I just came three times and it is getting hard again. Oh, my lovely wife.* Then he heard Richard's moans. *Wow, she must be pleasuring him well.* Richard's moans grew louder and louder and after several minutes more, he heard him cry out, 'ELIZABETH!'. *Ah, there it is. He got his release. Good job, man. I wonder if he will go for another or if Elizabeth will return to me shortly.*

Darcy smiled widely when he heard Elizabeth's moans grow louder again. *Damn! She is enjoying herself yet again. How many times can she climax?* Soon enough, he heard Richard grunt "I LOVE YOU!" and knew his cousin had taken his pleasures again. *I hope she comes back soon. I cannot believe I want her again. Thank goodness she is such a passionate woman.*

Curious, he waited several minutes but there was only silence. He closed his eyes and drifted off to sleep, only to awaken about an hour later. Seeing that Elizabeth had still not returned, he got up to see if she was ready to return. *Probably fell asleep there. I will carry her back; I want to have her again right now.* He was used to her returning to him; even if it was hours later, she had always returned before daylight.

He quietly entered Richard's room and the fireplace was still burning that lit up the room softly. He saw that she was indeed asleep. She had her nightgown on but Richard was nude and had his hand on Elizabeth's breast as he slept.

He walked towards Elizabeth's side and she was sleeping so peacefully in the middle of the bed that he decided to lie next to her there. As he held her hand and heard her soft snores, he also fell asleep.

Darcy awoke when Richard cried loudly in his sleep during what appeared to be a bad dream. He alerted himself to where he was sleeping, seeing the faint daybreak, and realised that Elizabeth was lying next to him and also dreaming. He heard her whisper, 'Fitzwilliam' and loved her more right then. *She is so beautiful! Even after loving her other husband, she is still dreaming of me!* He knew Richard was a good lover and Elizabeth had openly shared all of her experiences. Knowing how dedicated Richard was in bringing Elizabeth's happiness, he wanted to love her deeply as well and give her every part of himself all over again.

He was aroused to have her in this bed with another man next to her on the other side. He knew he should carry her back to his room to make love to her but he was desperate to be inside her. Caressing her breasts and coaxing her legs to open, he fingered her and found her wet. He rubbed her clitoris and she began to moan in her sleep. He suckled on her nipples and climbed over her and massaged his manhood at her entrance.

As he had done many mornings, he slowly slid his erection inside her, lubricating his tip slowly to fill her. He was half way in when she jolted awake and yelled, "Richard, NO!"

She began to push him off and cried, "NO! You must not!" while Richard jumped up and yelled, "Darcy!"

Darcy whispered again and again in her ear, "It is I, it is not Richard; it is I," until she calmed and saw his face.

The relief on her face was so evident and Darcy felt awful that she thought Richard was penetrating her. "I am so sorry, my love. So sorry. I slept here all night when you did not return to me and you looked so lovely, I was a brute. I am so sorry." Darcy kissed her all over her face, still aroused and inside her but feeling terrible for causing her to panic.

"Damn it, Darcy! You could not wait to take her in your own bed? Argh!" Richard grunted, throwing his pillow over his face to calm his heart after waking so shockingly when Elizabeth yelled out his name.

Darcy knew he should stop but he could not. He continued to rock his erection inside her and kissed her. He kissed her deeply. He loved her so much that even with all the love that Richard poured onto her, that she had still dreamt of her true husband; she had called out his name; she had tried to protect her vow to save herself only for him. "I love you, my wife. I love you so much. Please let me love you." He continued his thrusts.

Richard knew what Darcy was doing and grunted as his cousin was penetrating the love of his life right next to him while he was but a foot away. He heard Elizabeth's soft moans and knew his cock could not take it much longer. He pulled the pillow off his face and watched as Darcy feverishly pummelled his phallus into his wife and Elizabeth's moans grew louder. Elizabeth lifted up her legs and wrapped it around his waist to take him deeper inside her and Richard could see Darcy's cock pumping into her. He watched her face while she was being pleasured in a way that he could not but he jumped when her eyes opened and met his own. He had been stroking himself watching them in the act and was embarrassed that he was so aroused by it.

Elizabeth smiled softly at Richard. "Fitzwilliam, my love, may I pleasure my other husband while we make love?"

Darcy laughed. "Yes, we are in his bed. And I owe him for interrupting his night with you. I am sorry, Richard." He lifted himself off and waited for Elizabeth to position herself.

Elizabeth turned around and pointed her bottom towards Darcy on her hands and knees, lifting her nightgown up to expose herself to her husband. She leaned forward and kissed Richard on the lips and licked them, then bent down to mouth his bulging erection.

Darcy entered her from behind and began to pump slowly as he watched his wife mouth Richard's long, hard cock. *Fuck! This is the most erotic thing I have ever experienced!* He continued slowly as he knew he would explode any moment now.

Richard watched Elizabeth's mouth and hand on him again and he dared not blink. He watched her head bob up and down as she took him deep into her throat and moaned loudly as Darcy was thrusting into her in slow successions. *Fuck! This is the most erotic thing I have ever experienced!* Richard thought.

Soon, Elizabeth's moans grew louder as she began to climax and Darcy pumped fast and furiously until she released Richard's manhood from her mouth and cried out her orgasm. Darcy yelled out his release loudly as well and while he was still coming, Elizabeth's mouth returned and she sucked Richard harder with her mouth and stroked faster with her hand. Richard grunted, "Oh, god!" and he came inside her mouth again.

The three laid side-by-side, panting for air and realising the significance of what had just happened.

Elizabeth was the first to recover. "Husbands, can we do this again sometime? I know this would be quite frowned upon by others, but I must tell you that it was the most wonderful feeling I have ever felt. I know Richard has told me that you both are larger than most men and it is an incredible sensation to have both of you inside me." She panted as she was catching her breath.

Darcy spoke next. "I... I had never been so pleasured before, my love. If you wish, I certainly would deny you nothing. You were incredible."

Richard immediately agreed. "I think it only natural that you want to take both of your husbands at once, my love. It was the most erotic thing I have ever experienced. I think we are too loud for it, though. We were making such noises and I am certain the whole house overheard. Perhaps when we return to Pemberley?"

"Oh, I agree. Fitzwilliam, Richard could hear everything we did in our room last night. Did you hear us?" Elizabeth asked.

Darcy grinned. "Yes, I was so aroused by it, that is one of the reasons that I came into the room. I had originally planned to carry you back to our bed but you looked so lovely, I laid down next to you and fell asleep. I am so sorry for scaring you. It pleased me to no end that you were still keeping your vows even when half asleep."

"Oh, Fitzwilliam, please do wake me up first next time. I did not want Richard to break his vow or else our relationship would have been irreparably damaged. I love you both too much to lose either of you in my life. I know our relationship is unconventional and possibly immoral in the eyes of others, but I love you both so deeply, husbands, that having both of you in my life brings me the greatest of pleasures." She smiled broadly. "I am so thrilled to have two of the biggest and the best men at my disposal." She winked. "Well, I need to go wash and dress. I am certain my morning sickness will return soon so I need a piece of toast. Please excuse me, husbands." She grinned again and walked towards her room.

"I am sorry, Richard," Darcy spoke. "I invaded your privacy and nearly gave you a heart attack. I hope you do not mind how things turned out."

Richard beamed. "Not at all. Elizabeth favoured me with her mouth twice now and I was able to love her most intimately last night. Having her in my bed all night long, Darcy, I feel as if she is truly my wife now. Not just a borrowed one for a few hours in the night but truly, I have her body and love without breaking my vows to keep her marriage to you safe. I have lain with a few women until the morning but I was usually sneaking out quietly to avoid detection. It is unimaginably gratifying to lay with our wife and to love her so many times. Is it wrong for two men to enjoy one woman so much? I finally understand when she said we are similar. I think my arms are a bit thicker than yours but we do have very similar physiques." He laughed. "Even our cock sizes are similar, just like Elizabeth said."

Darcy laughed loudly. "Thank goodness I am not as small as Albert!" They both burst out laughing. "No wonder she wants us both. Imagine having two Elizabeths in your bed!"

Richard froze, "No, I would die too early from exploding or a heart attack. I believe one Elizabeth between the two of us is more than sufficient! She is already too much for both of us!"

They laughed loudly but shut their mouths quickly when they heard through the wall, "I CAN HEAR YOU!"

They burst out laughing again and both yelled, "WE LOVE YOU!" at the same time.

The men shook hands in silent agreement that they would love their wife again together and pleasure her every way possible.

Chapter 19

The six weeks at Kieran Hall flew by quickly.

Not only did the men have a lot of work to oversee at this property, Elizabeth was constantly looking at wall patterns, furniture catalogues, and discussing household improvements with the housekeeper even while the rooms were being updated.

They had decided that once their six weeks were up, the master and mistress rooms would also need additional soundproofing. All three of them had treasured the memory of their lovemaking in this house and they wanted to use this as their main holiday to Scotland in the future instead of Darcy Manor.

Elizabeth was feeling energetic, unlike the last pregnancy, and she was not growing too fast. The nausea dissipated quickly and she had been in the drawing room when she jumped and cried out, making both Richard and Darcy drop their teacups in surprise.

"I felt the quickening, my dears! Oh, it is true, you will be a papa again." She cried. Richard shook Darcy's hand in congratulations and smiled broadly.

Suddenly comprehending that plans needed to be made by the time they arrived back at Pemberley at the end of November, Darcy frantically rushed to his study and returned with the calendar.

"When we return to Pemberley next week, we will soon have Christmas upon us. We have no plans made and will need to decide what to do. I received a letter that

Georgiana's courtship is going well and Aunt Susan believes she will most likely become engaged. Elizabeth, you are now at four months and if I had to guess, you are carrying a singleton, as you are nowhere as large as you were with the boys. Would you be well enough to travel to London? I am certain you will wish to get some shopping done." Darcy winked. "If this young man is in earnest to get himself married to my baby sister, he will have to go through her legal guardians and I would like to spend some time with him. Shall we head to London after a quick fortnight respite at Pemberley?"

"That sounds wonderful, Fitzwilliam. I would like to be home longer but it makes sense to enjoy Christmas with Georgiana. I miss her dreadfully but she is very pleased with the courtship and he makes her happy and she loves him, Fitzwilliam. But I also reckon that Lady Isabelle will often be in company since she and Georgiana have been spending most of their time together. Will you be all right with that, Richard?" Elizabeth winked at him.

Resigned, Richard agreed, "I will do whatever you wish, my love. I would not mind seeing some of my former officers and friends and I do have a debt to pay. I still owe my lady some shopping." He grinned.

"Oh, and I found someone who is interested in leasing Kieran Hall. After our departure, all the renovations should be completed by the New Year and they could move in by February. What do you think?" Darcy asked.

"That is wonderful, Fitzwilliam! I do hope to return here. I have *very* fond memories of this place." Elizabeth arched her brow.

Both men gulped. They had not been intimate in a similar fashion since the first night of arrival five weeks ago, and every time they had thought of it, they were both immediately aroused.

Richard stood by the window while Darcy grinned widely and sat next to his wife, with a very obvious protrusion.

"Well, I hope to have a chance to make more memories at every one of our homes eventually. We just need to have you be well, my love. I know that you have been exhausted. You must rest often."

There was a knock on the door. The butler entered and advised Darcy that the prospective tenants had arrived for their meeting and tour. Darcy kissed Elizabeth and left for his study.

"Are you well, Richard?" Elizabeth asked. *He must have deflated by now!* She walked over to the window to stand next to him.

"Yes, my love. I am well. I just worry for you. I know you have not been well and it has been a long fortnight that Darcy nor I have been able to make love to you. I appreciated your sleeping with me last night. It did comfort me to have you in my arms all night." Richard replied.

He was pent up and he knew Darcy was equally frustrated. After experiencing her love so deeply, he realised that he had never before released four times in one night as he had done with his beloved and he was dying to love her again.

For the first two weeks, the men had taken their turns with her nightly in their own beds due to her high demands, but they had not congressed as a threesome again. But then Elizabeth had some spotting and although the doctor confirmed that it was common and no cause for major concern, he had placed a restriction to avoid intercourse for a month.

Two more weeks to go! Richard thought.

"I keep offering my other services but you and Fitzwilliam keep turning me down. The offer still stands, Richard. I miss having you in my mouth." Elizabeth whispered.

"Minx! The visitors will be here any moment and look at this!" He pointed to the protrusion in his trousers. "No, my love. We do not wish for you to overwork yourself. I am still able to take care of myself and I did while you slept. So beautiful," he kissed her lips gently and rubbed her round bump, "my love, my wife."

Clearing his throat, "Now, Seductress, have a seat and rest. I will order some tea with your favourite blend." He smiled.

~*~

The prospective tenants were very pleased with the property. They were impressed with the rooms that had completed the renovations already and looked forward to moving in. Papers were signed and Darcy and Richard agreed that it was a great trip to see to this property.

The next week, the small family of five boarded their carriages and looked upon this small piece of heaven with fond memories.

~*~

Their two-week stay at Pemberley was short but sweet. Elizabeth had no more spotting and was able to resume relations with each husband but continued to be tired. During the first week, she would fall asleep in Richard's bed after making love, and Richard, to appease Darcy for his generosity, would carry her back to Darcy's bed, or allow Darcy to enter his rooms to sleep next to Elizabeth and the three would awaken together.

By the second week, they gave up and slept together, not taking her together, due to her exhaustion, but each taking his turn while the other watched and gratified himself.

Elizabeth knew that it was of utmost importance to take care of the babe and she was grateful that Darcy and Richard could handle the rambunctious boys who were terrorising the gardeners by trying to pull out all the flowers.

It took four days, again, to travel to London, to give plenty of chances for the twins to run around and play, and for Elizabeth to rest.

Once they arrived at Darcy House, though, chaos ensued.

Chapter 20

Richard went to his study to work on his correspondences and saw a letter from a solicitor who was unknown to him. He opened the letter and read it and immediately paled.

Darcy and Elizabeth were laughing when they entered Richard's study. They were to meet with Richard to make dinner plans for the next two weeks before attending the Christmas Ball, as the Darcys had a high stack of invitations which Elizabeth had sorted through already.

"Good god! Whatever is the matter?" Darcy exclaimed when he saw Richard pacing frantically and pulling at his hair. He did not seem to had heard and was still mumbling and rubbing his face with both hands.

Elizabeth approached him and gently tugged at his arm. As soon as he saw her, tears rolled out and he hugged her tightly but would not speak.

Elizabeth did not know what to do. She asked, "What has happened? What is wrong, my love?" *Why is he so distressed?*

Darcy asked again, "Richard, what is the matter?" He watched as Richard continued to hold onto Elizabeth as if for his dear life.

Richard pointed to the letter sitting on the desk and Darcy walked over to read it. "MY GOD!" He exclaimed.

Elizabeth was frustrated. She was being gripped by Richard and Darcy had not said anything that would reveal what was happening. "What is going on, Richard?! Fitzwilliam?!" She demanded.

Richard whispered in her ear, "Please forgive me. Do not leave me. Please." And he continued to hold her, repeating the words.

Darcy finally spoke. "It seems that Richard received a lawsuit to recompense for his natural child, who is nearly two years old, by a Mrs. Maria Rushworth. The claim states that he fathered a child with her and she is demanding £5,000 for the upkeep of the babe as well as her lifestyle that was promised to her during their three months of relationship. He has until December Thirty-first to pay the amount or the case will go to public court and the amount will be doubled to £10,000. It looks like copies were sent to Pemberley and Scotland and he received this one first. I believe they are hoping to rush him to make restitution to give him a chance to keep it quiet, knowing of his status and connections."

Elizabeth closed her eyes. *It seems as Richard is in Charles Bingley's shoes, although not with a maiden and it is more than the £3,000 that was given to that woman. How dare she even demand such an amount!* Richard had confessed that he was tempted beyond his moral code and would have taken Elizabeth as a virgin if he ever had the opportunity but vowed that he had never taken a maiden before, even with his expansive previous experiences.

Elizabeth was red with anger and began to pace.

Richard had let her go while Darcy was speaking, mortified that his mistake from his past was once again catching up to him, this time possibly irreparably. He watched Elizabeth as her eyes were squinted and her nostrils were flared and her fists were tight in her hands. *She is readying her tongue-lashing and I fully deserve it but I could not bear it if she leaves me. I am nothing without her. I cannot believe that I was so careless and dishonourable. Blasted!*

Darcy saw her rage and walked to her. He held her tightly and whispered to her. "Elizabeth, I know you are very angry but it is not good for the babe. Please breathe. We will work through this. We will make it work. Please be calm, my love." He rubbed her back and watched her as she began to relax.

"Thank you, my love. I do not know if I have been this angry before but I must think of the baby. Thank you." Elizabeth replied, holding Darcy closely. She kissed him and released him. Turning around she called, "Richard."

Richard was devastated to see her reaction. *What must she think of me? A rake and a cad, a father to a bastard, and utterly dishonourable. Who knows if this is the only one? There could be dozens out there. Why, why could I not have been more like Darcy?* He tormented himself. Upon hearing her voice, he could not face her. He remained staring into the fire wondering, not for the first time, if he should jump in and burn.

Darcy shook his head as he watched his dear cousin in pure misery. *Why this has to happen to poor Richard again is such a shame. He has been such a good man and he loves Elizabeth dearly. He must be wretched that another past lover has sprouted. She will forgive him. I do not even think she is upset with HIM. This woman is a menace and she sounds mercenary.* He turned and asked Elizabeth, "Would you like for me to stay or go?" He recalled the resolution to Mrs. O'Shea was brief but Elizabeth had been very affected by it.

Elizabeth answered, "Would you return in a half hour? Thank you, my love." She kissed him and took a seat and waited. Darcy left after tapping Richard on the shoulder.

Richard was still silent and would not look at her direction.

"Richard?" She called again.

Resigned, he turned and faced her to receive whatever punishment she saw fit. "Yes, Elizabeth." He could not meet her eyes, though.

"Did you love her? This Mrs. Rushworth?" Elizabeth asked quietly.

Richard swiftly rushed over. He might have been a rake and a reprobate in the past, but there was no way on earth he was going to allow Elizabeth to believe that he ever loved anyone else. "NO, Elizabeth! I swear to you, I never loved her. I have so many regrets but I will have you know that I love you and have never loved anyone else. You are my first love and the last. I am not the man I was and I am so sorry that I have to have you suffer through this again. I cannot... I did not know and I am certain it is my wealth that she is seeking. I do not know why else she would have waited so long if not for mercenary reasons. I am so sorry..."

Elizabeth leaned into his embrace and listened to his heart beating. *He is such a good man. His past is in the past but he continues to suffer so because of his wealth. If only they knew that he has given me everything. If he were married, he might have been safer, but he must endure these kinds of mercenary women because of me.*

"We must speak about this, Richard. We must decide what to do." Elizabeth started.

Richard replied, "I know, my love. I know you are angry with me..."

Elizabeth cut him off. "Angry with you? Why would I be angry with you, my love?"

Richard sat straight up. "You were furious, you were red and I thought you would break a window. I had never seen you so angry."

"Do not be ridiculous, Richard! Why would I be angry with *you*? I wanted to kill that woman who is using a poor child to get funds off of you so *she* could live comfortably. Fitzwilliam read, 'to upkeep her lifestyle' and that tells me that she is a mercenary shrew who deserv..."

Her speech was cut off as Richard frantically kissed her. His lips and tongue, his hands and legs were completely wrapped around her and she found herself pinned under him as he continued to kiss her neck and caress her breasts. She released a soft moan, as it had felt so good to be kissed. *It has been too long. I hope I have the energy tonight for both of them.* She thought.

Eventually, Richard lifted his body and helped her sit up. He still held her in his arms and kissed her hair and temple. "Oh, my love. You are the most wonderful, the most generous, the most beautiful woman in the world. I love you, I love you." He kept kissing her. "You are not angry with me? Even though I..." He asked.

"Richard, we cannot change your past. I love you, blemish and all, and we will fight this shrew together. Do not give a penny to this harlot. I would rather take this child from her and bring the baby here and raise it as our own. If she is so incapable of raising a child that she needs £5,000 from you when she was the one that opened her legs without a marriage vow, she has no business raising any child of yours." Elizabeth emphatically stated. She grabbed him by both cheeks and looked into his eyes. "I love you, Richard Michael Fitzwilliam. I know that our relationship is our secret and although I am not ashamed of it, it is something that people will not understand. But I want you to know that I love you and you have my heart. There is nothing that you can do that you have to fear I will leave you. I never want you to beg me to not leave you again; do you understand me? We will be together always. You are my husband and I am your wife. I will be with you and you will be with me and Fitzwilliam."

"Elizabeth?" Richard quietly called after kissing her again tenderly. Meeting her eyes, he continued, "I believe I love you more than ever right now. I do not know how it is possible, but I love you until my heart wants to explode. I wish to buy you trunks of jewels and fill the bathtub with them so you can soak in all of my money but I know you do not care for such a thing. I wish for life with you, spending all of my days by your side, your children are my children, everything I have, everything I possess, it is all yours. Today, you have shown me what it is to be fully loved in return and I cannot thank you enough. For you to love me, for you to trust me, I have never known such love." He wiped an unshed tear. "There is nothing that I have that does not belong to you: my heart, my wealth, my body, they all belong to you. If I could only give you my name. You truly have all of me, Elizabeth." He finished.

Elizabeth grinned broadly, "Well, I do wear my ring here, where you have made your vows to me, husband. Great coincidence, it is, that my name is Mrs. Fitzwilliam... Darcy... It could be noted that I am both Mrs. Darcy and Mrs. Fitzwilliam." She arched her brow.

"Mrs. Fitzwilliam..." Richard whispered. "I love you, my wife. Always you. Only you." He kissed her gently.

Elizabeth smiled brightly at his affectionate words. "So, what are we going to do about this strumpet?" She winked.

~*~

Darcy rolled his eyes as he entered the study without knocking. He heard Richard laugh and knew all was well. "When will you ever be properly angry with this rogue? You forgive too easily, my love." They laughed. "Since I am certain Richard has done nothing but kiss you the last half hour, I believe it is my turn."

He lifted Elizabeth who was sitting next to Richard, as she squealed in joy and placed her on his lap. He kissed her deeply while rubbing his hand on her breast over her dress.

"So, what is the plan?" Darcy grinned at Richard, who was watching with a smile on his face.

Elizabeth attempted to sit back on the couch and Darcy held her in place. "No, woman. I need you right here for a while."

She giggled, as she knew his erection was massive. "Fine. You can be my chair for now. We were contemplating what to do with this woman, this hussy, Fitzwilliam. She sounds mercenary and cruel to use her child to practically blackmail Richard. What are our options?"

Darcy was quiet for a few moments. "We need more information on this woman and you can write to Mr. O'Connor to use his services again." He thought for a few moments longer. "Richard, do you recall when you last met with her?"

Richard thought for a minute. "I know that it was a little before I met Elizabeth. As you know, I was at training camp and had returned that same day when I met you here, my love. I was gone for a month of training at Dover, so I was not in London in September to the beginning of October." Reluctantly, he shared, "I hate to be an open book but I guess I have no choice. I visited her a few times in August? It is a blur. I do not think I saw her for more than a month; I am certain I did not visit her for three months. I was... I was always rather fond of larger breasted women, ahem."

He cleared his throat, "Large bosoms, petite, and brunette," he looked at Elizabeth and smiled softly, "with sparkling eyes." Elizabeth giggled. He continued, "And she is quite small up top, from what I remember. Ahem." He cleared his throat in embarrassment again. "Oh! Wentworth! I just remembered that Wentworth slept with her, too. I shall need to write to him and tell him of what she is accusing me. If she had relations with several men, how is it possible that I am designated as the father? Although... Although it is possible that he or the other men did not take their release inside her. I was so thoughtless! I did not care for anything but my immediate pleasures and I was not thinking straight, especially that summer."

He walked over to the window and stood for a moment then turned. "I was recovering from my injury in June, you know, with the musket ball, Darcy, and I did not have the... energy... to make any visits during that month. I used a few ladies in July and sought the energetic ones... ones who would do the work, but it was only a couple of times, as I was still recovering. I was quite busy in August, preparing for the Dover assignment and had time for only a few... appointments... and made the visits, knowing that Wentworth and a few others were seeing her on other days. I thought her a bit too old but it was an opportunity and thought I could go right back to my regular routine and was trying her out." He rubbed his face as he continued his confession. "I am ashamed to say that in September in Dover, I... had more time and... I was... determined... and used three or four younger whor... women... a week. The last one was two days before I met you, my love, then you know about Abigail that same day..." He coloured in embarrassment as he looked at Elizabeth. Thankfully she did not appear angry. "I am so glad I will never return to being a rake again. I love my life with you so much, Elizabeth."

Richard smiled fondly at Elizabeth and continued. "Mrs. Rushworth is the disgraced ex-wife of Mr. Rushworth, who is an idiot, by the way, who was not enough for Maria Rushworth née Bertram. Your sister Mary is actually related by her husband to her. Sir Bertram is brother to Mary's husband's father. I noted the connection and Parson Bertram and I talked about it in general terms several times. Well, Maria Rushworth ran off with a Mr. Crawford a little after six months of marriage and there was a big scandal. She was living with her shrew of an aunt but often invited men to visit with her and I was one of those fools. I do not know much else, Darcy."

Darcy was in deep contemplation and had finally released his wife to straighten their clothing. Elizabeth wondered if she had missed something and had the letter in her hand and was reading it for the third time. Elizabeth soon announced, "I think you have missed a vital point, Richard. The letter here is vague and I believe it is intentionally ambiguous. When I refer to our boys, it has always been by their months of age at this point. Until they reach the age of two, it is more common to refer toddlers as how many months they are. Our boys are 15-months old, for example. I would not round down or round up during their youngest years. The letter says nearly two years old. Why not eighteen months or twenty months? I may be mistaken but it seems something nefarious is at stake here. It is possible that the child is nineteen months old and may fit the timeline according to your visits with her, Richard, or that she is lying about the paternity and they are trying to make you more desperate to just pay her off."

"Your brain is first-rate, Elizabeth. I knew there was a reason I married you." Darcy beamed. "You can write to Reitling as well, Richard. If O'Connor finds evidence to the contrary, we will have Reitling file a countersuit for slander and blackmail."

A moment later, he continued, "Richard, why do you not write to O'Connor and I will write to Reitling. We are fully behind you, Richard. No one dare messes with our family." Darcy smiled.

"Well, I will rest for a while and will see you gentlemen for dinner. I love you, husbands." Elizabeth smiled and kissed their cheeks.

"We love you, wife." Darcy and Richard chimed together as they grinned at each other, loving their wife fully with their hearts.

Chapter 21

Mr. O'Connor arrived four days later.

"Good to see you again, Mr. O'Connor." Darcy shook his hand. Richard also shook it.

"Gentlemen, it is a pleasure to see you again even though not under these circumstances. I apologise for taking a day longer than expected. As my note indicated yesterday, we have been waiting for a rider to return so I have a full report for you today. I shall begin.

"Mrs. Maria Rushworth née Bertram is twenty-six years old, daughter to Sir Thomas Bertram; she was married to Mr. James Rushworth but after seven months of marriage, was caught having an affair with a Mr. Henry Crawford and fled together. They remained in a carnal relationship lasting three months living in Bath but after she became pregnant, Mr. Crawford abandoned her to pursue an heiress. She ended up with a miscarriage the next month and was relocated to live with her aunt, a Mrs. Norris, and she began to seek male attentions, mostly from the militia where several men were seeking companionship. It is noted that during that summer in question, Colonel Fitzwilliam," he pointed at Richard, "was witnessed entering her home during the month of August. This was specifically noted, as several other gentlemen visitors wore Navy blue coats while Colonel Fitzwilliam wore red. One particular milkmaid was able to capture the exact number of visits, as she had told us that she eagerly waited to see the handsome soldier in a red coat every week. She reported seeing the red coat once a week, three times in August and then no more.

"There are also reports that Mr. Crawford had returned after failing to capture the heiress and was seen making his visits once again. It is reported that he began his visits in October and continued until December of said year. He promptly grew tired of her once again and is currently married to the former Miss Kingston who had a dowry of £10,000.

"Now, the most important part; the child is a daughter named Jane and her solicitors are desperately attempting to remove her middle name in the registry and it would have been done next week if you had delayed seeking the services of Mr. Reitling. The daughter is registered as Jane *Crawford* Bertram. Due to the lawsuit, Mr. Reitling was able to stop the name change as noted in the original registry.

"It will relieve you, Mr. Fitzwilliam, that it is impossible for you to be the father of the child, as she was born on the twenty-third of July and would have been conceived at earliest, mid-October, and there has been no witnesses attesting to your visits in October. From your word, you were in London continuously. You were seen with the Darcy family throughout the month and it was confirmed that you were either at your office with the military or here at Darcy House. Due to your status as Lord Matlock's son, Mr. Fitzwilliam, society pages also noted your presence with the Darcy party at nearly every outing. Between your work schedules and public outings, there does not appear to be any time apparent for you to travel the one-hour distance to visit Mrs. Rushworth and return in time."

Richard smiled softly at this. *I was drooling over Elizabeth who had not looked at me once. I was following her everywhere she was like a lost puppy.*

Darcy asked, "So, it is impossible that Mr. Fitzwilliam is the father of the baby, O'Connor? Do we have sufficient proof to take to court?"

Mr. O'Connor replied, "Yes, I have been working with Mr. Reitling, who is an excellent barrister, by the way, to gather evidence and signed statements. I believe he will update you tomorrow on his plans but I do not believe you have anything to worry over. It is obvious that she is mercenary and falsely accusing Mr. Fitzwilliam. It is impossible for a woman to confuse the three liaisons from August and to accuse the one man while at the same time sleeping with several others, and it is clear that she became pregnant in October. It is also noted that the child does look more like Mr. Crawford as well, with light blonde hair while Mr. Fitzwilliam as well as Mrs. Rushworth both have dark hair. Even if she became with child in August, we could argue that the paternity might belong to one of," he looked at his notes, "four other men who visited her during the summer. The Navy had several summer holidays and apparently these naval officers had a lot of time." He suppressed a chuckle. "Do you have any questions, gentlemen?" Mr. O'Connor asked.

Darcy answered. "No, not from me. Richard?" His cousin shook his head. "Thank you once again. You have been most thorough and I am again impressed with your work. Good Day."

Mr. O'Connor bowed and left.

Richard blew out loudly. "My god, Darcy! This woman just wants my money. Thank goodness; I was terrified that I fathered a child. After all this time, I thought I left that life behind and it was a horror to wait to see how it would turn out and I am relieved beyond belief. I did not realise she was such a harlot. Wentworth wrote me and told me that he was horrified that I could be in this situation and was also thankful that she did not chase after his money first since he is so happily married now. He told me that he used her and released inside her for two full months, visiting her two or three times a week during all of July and August and was terrified that it might actually be his issue and that she might come after him next. He will be relieved that he did not father a bastard, either. He had so many regrets about not waiting for his Anne after hearing of your chastity and it would have killed him to father a child out of wedlock. I am tremendously relieved, Darce. I am certain she picked me because I am wealthy and unmarried. With my money and connection to you and my father, she must have thought she could weasel the most money out of my purse." He paused and smiled. "But our dear Elizabeth, she told me that she would have taken that child in and raised it as her own. She is so generous. I never thought... I never expected such love."

Darcy returned the smile. "She is amazing and her love for us and our boys is ever generous. We are the most fortunate of men, Richard." He stood. "I am glad we will be able to get this harridan in court and expose her for the whore that she is. It will be difficult for you but she must not make any false accusations again. We will ensure that your friends are safe and no one will ever believe a word from her mouth again." He paused then spoke, "Richard, Elizabeth is going through her insatiable phase again. I think all of the travels had exhausted her but now she is well and back to normal. She has demanded my attentions three times already today and I am certain as soon as you are done closeting yourself in your study today, she will seek you out. She has left you alone only because she knows you had a lot on your mind." He walked over to the door to his study and before he opened the door, he said, "And, she wants us *both* tonight." He winked and left.

~*~

Richard stood frozen. He had an immediate erection, as the images of Elizabeth taking Darcy and him at the same time flooded his mind. He felt guilty that even though he knew she loved him so much, he had avoided her these past four days and had slept in his own bed after working late. Now that he had confirmation that he had not fathered the child, he was elated and that burden had been lifted.

He looked at his pocket watch and tried to determine where she would be. It was still visiting hours but even if she might have guests, he was desperate to see her. After he wrote a quick note to Captain Wentworth, he left his study to search for his heart's desire.

Richard heard her voice in the drawing room and his feet immediately followed. He smiled to himself to hear her laughter, as it brought much joy to his heart.

He entered the drawing room without any other thought than seeing his beloved but was stopped short when he saw that Elizabeth's guests were Lady Isabelle Chatsworth and Miss Jane Fairfax.

Georgiana was also in attendance and was the first one to notice him awkwardly standing in the doorway. "Richard! How good of you to come see us! Brother just left. Come, come. You remember my guests, Miss Fairfax from my ball and of course, Lady Isabelle." She grinned widely.

Richard internally groaned. *But of course the two and only two women that I danced last spring are the ones that are here.* He bowed to them and greeted all the ladies like a gentleman. He took the seat next to Elizabeth where Darcy had most likely sat. *Traitor! He should have told me they were here.* He smiled at Elizabeth. *Oh, my love. I missed you.*

"How have you been, ladies?" Richard started courteously.

"Very well, thank you." Both ladies confirmed.

Georgiana excitedly shared, "Miss Fairfax is engaged! She is going to become Mrs. Frank Churchill next month. Finally!!"

"Congratulations, Miss Fairfax. I know Churchill! I had heard that he was in love with a lady for two years. I understand he will complete his mourning next month?" Richard spoke friendly to her with a full smile, now that she was an engaged woman.

"Yes, it has been a long time. I am quite anxious for next month to arrive." Miss Fairfax softly answered.

Georgiana chimed in. "Mr. Churchill proposed two days after my ball. Jane says it was good luck." She innocently added.

Richard smiled. *Elizabeth was correct! But of course she was. No wonder Churchill appeared upset with me that day after. I did not make the connection. Haha!* He looked at Elizabeth who was smirking at her success. *Minx! I would love to wipe that grin off her face.*

He turned to Lady Isabelle and asked, keeping his face more stoic since he did not want to give her any encouragement, "And how was the rest of your season? Georgiana has been going on and on about her fiancé but not much else." He winked at Georgiana. Lord Andrew Chatsworth had finally worked up the courage to propose and asked for consent from both of her legal guardians yesterday.

"I have been well. I am looking forward to the Christmas Ball and seeing many of my friends again." She blushed. She found Mr. Fitzwilliam most handsome.

Richard looked her briefly and thought deeper while the ladies spoke about his mother's Christmas Ball next week. He had quickly surmised that Lady Isabelle had not accepted anyone's suit this season because she was still hoping for his attentions. Georgiana had talked about her in her letters briefly that her dear friend could not find anyone worthy of her notice and that she was waiting for the right one, and Elizabeth had mentioned that Lady Isabelle had been in love with him since eight years old. She was beautiful. Tall and brunette and had a £50,000 dowry. Being the daughter of a duke and a family friend for decades, she would have made the perfect society wife. She was young, now eighteen, and her figure was pleasing, even if her bosoms were smaller than his wont. His own mother would have pressed and most likely, he would have conceded in marrying her if he were single. She would have fit every criterion to be a good Mrs. Fitzwilliam.

He turned to Elizabeth. *My wife. The love of my life. The absolutely most gorgeous woman of my acquaintance. The only one that could make my heart beat like so.* She was subconsciously rubbing her baby bump while she spoke with the ladies. Her eyes glistened and his heart jumped at the sound of her laughter. Lady Isabelle could not hold a candle to this beautiful woman sitting next to him and he cared naught for wealth or status. He never knew such happiness until Elizabeth entered his life and even when he was miserable because she was not in his reach, even before their first kiss, he would have rather suffered the thought of loving her from afar than to marry anyone else. He let out a sigh of contentment.

Elizabeth heard him. She turned and saw that he was looking at her with passion in his eyes and her heart fluttered. "Are you well, Mr. Fitzwilliam?"

Richard smiled. "I am well; very well, Mrs. Darcy. I noticed you were rubbing your stomach and wondered if you needed anything. Something to tantalise your taste buds? Perhaps these plump grapes that will burst in your mouth?" He took one and popped it into his mouth. "Or would you like something more savoury or meaty?" He asked, keeping his eyes on hers.

Good lord, he is such a flirt. I need him now. "No, but I am feeling rather tired at this moment and I believe a quick rest is warranted. Georgiana, I will leave you with your guests. Mr. Fitzwilliam, would you kindly assist me? Good day, ladies."

"Of course, Lizzy! Take good care of the baby!" Georgiana responded.

~*~

Richard held her hand, which was resting on his arm. "Are you feeling ill? You must rest for your health, my love. I was teasing you but I did not know you were feeling poorly." Richard asked in concern.

Elizabeth continued to walk with him to the sitting room between their bedrooms. "I am well, Richard. I just have one thing that I need right now." They entered the room and Elizabeth pulled him to the couch. She pushed him to sit and climbed onto his lap. "You were so naughty, talking about putting something in my mouth. You will get your turn later but I need a release now, husband."

She began to rub herself on his erection and kissed him fiercely and Richard began to fondle and lick her growing breasts. He lifted her skirts to expose her womanly flesh and moaned. He rubbed her clitoris and began to finger her and she began to get more wet and moaned louder. He continued suckling on her breasts and increased his fingering as she climaxed loudly and he grunted and released all over her womanhood.

"Good lord, Elizabeth, I love you so much. I love that you want me." Richard panted.

Elizabeth continued sitting on his groin. She knew she was dripping all of her wetness onto his groin and she could feel his semen all over her clitoris, which aroused her again. She continued to attack his neck and spoke to him. "I missed you. I have barely seen you these past four days."

Richard continued to hold her buttocks and helped her rub herself against him. "I know; I apologise, dear wife. I was torn with the possibility of fathering a child and I felt unworthy of your attentions. It will never happen again. I love you so much."

He moved his hand between her legs from her behind, inserting his fingers deep inside her and kissed her breasts again. Her nipples were bouncing in front of him and he tongued one at a time. *Damn! I am hard again. How does she do it?*

He continued to rub himself against her and with her folds already damp with his semen and Elizabeth's juices, he could feel her heat greater than ever. "My god, Elizabeth, you are so hot for me. I love you so much." She began to release her climax. "Yes, come for me, my love, that is it. Let it go." And he grunted another release soon after she cried out.

It took several minutes longer than usual to catch their breaths. Richard rubbed Elizabeth's back as she collapsed onto his chest and was holding him tightly. They were a sticky mess together but did not want to part.

Elizabeth kissed Richard's neck and asked softly, "Do you think you would have married her?"

Richard laughed and kissed her hair. "I kind of like it when you get jealous, Elizabeth. And I already have a wife, thank you."

"Oh, my love. But she would have been perfect for you; young and beautiful and rich with a £50,000 dowry and daughter of a duke. She even has bigger bosoms than

Celia; I heard she chased you before Albert. You could not handpick a better wife than Isabelle and she is in love with you, I can tell. She blushes and smiles and desperately wishes for your eyes on her. I hope you will not regret me when I am old and grey and a new debutante is throwing herself at you. You are *so* handsome, Richard." She nibbled on his ear.

Richard chuckled. "I will never regret you, my dearest Elizabeth. I confess I did watch her most carefully today. With the fourteen-year age difference, I would have not considered her but if I had never met you and my situation had remained the same as it were, she would have made the perfect society wife. She would have been attractive enough for me to bed and to have children with, but I would have tired of her quickly and I am certain I would have obtained a mistress or continued to visit with whores. I would not have changed my ways because my heart was waiting for you.

"She is not you, Elizabeth. That one fateful day when my dear cousin brought you into this house and I heard your laughter, my heart was irrevocably lost. You are the only one to have touched my heart. I had given up all hopes of falling in love and even though I tried to deny it, my heart was yours the first moment you smiled at me." He kissed her lips tenderly. "I will never regret us. I have a wife, I have a home, I have our boys, and another babe on the way. I have never known such love and happiness, Elizabeth. After I looked at her and I turned my eyes to you, she could not hold a candle to your beauty, your intelligence, your wisdom, and your infinite kindness. You are my dream wife and I have you in my arms. I cannot imagine greater contentment."

"Oh, you dear man. I love you and your love for me brings me much joy and I cannot let you go. I wish for us to stay together always and I will show you tonight exactly what I want to taste." She kissed him again. "I must go and change. I cannot believe how much of a mess we just made. You are wonderful, my love."

Richard helped her rise and watched her enter her bedroom. He beamed, *I am most fortunate. I hope Darcy appreciates that I am helping him through her insatiable period!*

Chapter 22

"Elizabeth, I ran into some buddies at my club and I would like to throw a dinner party in a few days. Would that be acceptable? I know it is short notice but would you be willing to be hostess? Darcy agreed with me; he knows several of them and a few of them are married and will be bringing their wives." Richard asked Elizabeth.

"But of course, Richard! You are welcome to invite anyone you wish. This is your home as well and I would be happy to be your hostess any time, my love." Elizabeth smiled. "Would Friday work? How many guests do we expect? These are your friends from university or from the military? Will the Wentworths be joining us?" Elizabeth cheerfully asked, as she leaned and looked at her diary on her writing table.

Richard stood behind her and caressed her back and buttocks. "These are actually my old friends from the military base. Some are naval officers and some are from the army. It will be about twenty including their wives. I will get you their names today. The Wentworths are in Bath visiting Sir Walter and Miss Elliot with the baby. The captain took his wife a few days ago as a part of his atonement for his past mistakes after confessing to her about the women he used. She was very understanding but he feels awful just as much." He laughed. "I am told Miss Elizabeth Elliot is green with envy and is distraught that her suitor has slipped through her fingers. She had hoped to catch Mr. Elliot again but apparently her *dearest* friend, Mrs. Clay, is carrying his bastard and he abandoned both of them again for some wealthy heiress in town."

Elizabeth was shocked hearing of Mr. Elliot's dishonourable transgressions. "I am so glad you are an honourable gentleman. I am grateful for your love, Richard. I am at your disposal, sir."

He hugged her tightly from behind. "Thank you, my love. I truly appreciate having a hostess for my own use." He began to kiss her neck as he rubbed her growing belly with his hands from behind her. "You are so tempting, Elizabeth. I cannot get enough of you."

Elizabeth laughed. "I should hope I have been keeping you satisfied. After twice today already, I do not know how much more you have left to give!" She jested.

Richard rubbed his arousal on her buttocks, "And yet, I am aroused for you again, love. Do you have time for a quick love? I have never been so happy in my life, Elizabeth. You are my world." He caressed her breasts and began to tongue her mouth.

"Mmm... We have to wait. I am expecting company very soon, Richard, and you will have to make yourself scarce. Miss Mulligan is in town to visit her aunt and she will wish to jump onto your lap to compromise you if she sees you. She still fancies you, you know. I see the lust in her eyes, although I think she thinks Fitzwilliam also quite handsome, she finds you an eligible bachelor and wishes you would court her." Elizabeth moaned as her neck was being attacked.

Richard took several breaths to calm his arousal. *Damn! I am so hard right now. No time. Calm down, man!* "I desire you desperately but I will behave until tonight." He turned her around and looked deeply into her eyes. "I truly have not looked at her twice. She is nothing to you, no matter how pretty you think she is. I like my woman married and pregnant." He laughed, as Elizabeth pinched his arm. "I love you, Elizabeth. Have a good visit. I need to get back to working with Darcy and he is going to be so jealous when I tell him I got to fondle you for a while." He winked and kissed her lips and departed.

Elizabeth fanned her face with her hand. *That man! My husbands are so good to me.*

Soon, there was a knock and Miss Mulligan entered. They were able to chat comfortably for half an hour and Miss Mulligan departed with the promise to see each other again next week.

~*~

The dinner party was rowdy and loud. The military men were fascinating and memories were shared and future prospects were discussed. The wives were genteel but obviously used to the roughness of the military men and Elizabeth found the group a fascinating character study. She saw a side of Richard that she had not seen before as he relaxed and spoke about some of his war experiences that he had seldom shared. She noticed immediately that as Richard conversed with this party, he took on a different posture and was a commanding figure in his speech and motions. He was heralded by these men as a true hero who had saved numerous lives and had been a great leader to them all. It was obvious that they had the highest respect for the former colonel.

She flushed with desire seeing this side of Richard. *I understand why so many women want him! And he is mine!* She looked at Darcy who was beaming with pride at his dear cousin and smiling broadly. Their eyes met and she grinned as her dear husband winked at her. *I love my husbands so much; they are both so incredibly handsome and so dear to me!* She reached under the table and tenderly caressed Darcy's hand.

The men spoke of the lingering trauma of seeing such devastations and how the recovery was long. She had known that Richard had nightmares about the war occasionally but he had assured her that having her in his arms alleviated his anxieties, and she had seen that since they began to sleep together regularly, he had slumbered much better throughout the night.

The only uncomfortable company was one of the men who had not been invited but had strung along with another lieutenant and they had to set his dinner place at the last minute. Elizabeth was slightly wary of Lieutenant Anderson whom she noticed was drinking more wine than the others and his eyes kept turning to herself. She tried to discern if they had met before or if he knew her from some other place and kept her distance and avoided him.

Richard was immensely proud of his Elizabeth. The food was sumptuous and Elizabeth took well to the ladies present and conversation flowed freely. *She is the perfect Mrs. Darcy but she would have been a perfect colonel's wife. So intelligent and kind. My perfect Mrs. Fitzwilliam.* He did notice Anderson's odd looks at Elizabeth and wondered what was going on with that man. He had never liked him much but he had weaselled his way in through another officer and it would have been rude to kick him off the property without cause.

While the sexes separated, Richard observed Anderson gawking at Elizabeth's form. Richard eyed Darcy and whispered to his cousin, "Anderson has been ogling Elizabeth and I do not trust him. He is one of the... men that I was... behaving badly with when I was in the army. I did not associate with him often but he and I shared several... whor... women together and he is still stuck in that place from ten years ago while I have moved on. I do not like the way he looks at Elizabeth, Darce. He will never set foot in here again but for tonight, we must be vigilant."

Darcy agreed immediately. "I had noticed it as well. The other guests are all welcome but I do not like him. Let us make sure he is not near our wife."

The men conversed and also caught up on some of the more masculine stories unfit for ladies' ears and laughed loudly as they shared their after-dinner drinks.

Anderson belched loudly and asked, "Colonel! How is it that you are still not married? I suppose with all your wealth now, you do not need to be tied down to one woman. You must have a dozen mistresses!" He laughed loudly, not realising that no one else was laughing.

Richard gruffly replied, "Anderson, whether I have a mistress or not is none of your business and I hope you are able to behave yourself when we join the ladies again. I will not tolerate any disrespect in my cousin's home."

Anderson snorted, "My apologies, your highness. If I had your wealth, I would be bedding a new woman every night. So, tell us more about Rosings. It sounds like a lot of work."

Richard was fuming but he maintained his composure and spoke to the men about the estate and of Wentworth's sister residing there now with the Admiral.

Soon, it was time to join the ladies and Darcy and Richard both breathed a sigh of relief when they saw Elizabeth conversing pleasantly with the other wives. She was laughing and happy and beautiful.

352

~*~

Darcy spoke pleasantly to several officers and their wives. Some men he knew already, either from Richard's acquaintance or they were second or third sons of gentlemen or nobles. He had felt more comfortable in company with Elizabeth by his side and turned his eyes often to ensure she was content.

After she sang and played a beautiful song on the new pianoforte that Richard had gifted, Elizabeth asked some of the other ladies to entertain. She had to use the water closet often due to her pregnancy, and quietly excused herself, letting her husband know she would return soon. He offered to attend her but she insisted that he remain to host and that she would return shortly.

Shortly after, the butler entered to alert his master of a small accident with one of the stable-hands. Darcy whispered to Richard that he would see to it and left.

Richard looked around and seeing that Elizabeth was not there, his heart suddenly dropped. He had been conversing with one of the officers and had not seen her leave. He guessed that she was visiting the water closet, as her girth had been increasing, but knowing that Anderson had excused himself to the dining room to sober up ten minutes ago, he felt a sense of dread, similar to when he was stabbed in battle and had nearly lost his life.

He calmly rose while a new pianist was performing and headed towards the water closet when he heard voices coming from the dining room.

"Please, Lieutenant Anderson, we must return to the drawing room." He heard Elizabeth's voice beg.

Richard heard, "Oh, Mrs. Darcy, you are just the type of woman Fitzwilliam and I used to share. We both loved fucking brunettes and I am sure he would love taking you but he is too high and mighty to betray his cousin. I just want a little taste. Your teats are truly magnificent!" He flung the doors open to see Elizabeth cornered against the wall, nearly within Anderson's reach, who was ready to grab her and assault her.

"ANDERSON!" Richard boomed. He was beyond furious that this scoundrel would trap in his beloved and attempt an attack.

He ran to the disgusting man and pushed him as far away from Elizabeth as possible. Anderson spun around and threw a punch but Richard was too quick and was able to dodge the strike. Richard hit him in return and landed a hard punch on the villain's jaw.

Anderson fell back but laughed as he rose quickly and wiped the blood from his lip. "You were always a righteous prick, Colonel. Even when you used those whores with me, you still thought yourself so damn above everyone else. Mrs. Darcy is bloody gorgeous and I bet you want to get your cock in her just like I do. Come, come, let us take her together. You take her cunt and I will take her arse. You used to take two or three whores at a time and there is no way in hell you are keeping your famous cock to yourself now, living like an insipid gentleman. I would rather die than be as dull as you!" He stepped forward to attack again but he was no match for the former colonel.

Richard bent and avoided Anderson's fist again and landed two strong punches in his former friend's abdomen. He grabbed Anderson, who was winded and moaning from the pain, by his collars and pushed him against the wall and held him up by the neck with his hands. He was ready to murder this rogue. "You disgust me. How dare you assault my wi... my cousin's wife in her own home?"

Richard realised he almost slipped but since he was not legally married, no one would notice the gaffe. He grew angrier as he thought of his precious wife and began to choke him harder. He cared not for his own insults but only for Elizabeth, who was shaking in the corner, watching the scene. Anderson's feet were dangling and his face was turning bright red.

Richard called out to Elizabeth, "Are you well, Elizabeth? Did he touch you? Did he dare put his filthy hand on your person?"

Elizabeth was in awe of Richard's strength. Anderson was not a small man and for Richard to be able to lift him up and begin to squeeze the life out of this man was an astounding sight. She knew he would protect her at all cost and now felt safe but also knew that she needed to stop him from murdering the lieutenant, so she bravely walked behind him and gently rubbed his back to speak softly, "He touched my arm to lead me into this room but he did not touch me anywhere else. He is obviously drunk and does not know what he is doing, Richard. You must put him down for air, he is turning blue, Richard. Please."

Richard had finally calmed as he felt her touch and she spoke composedly to him. He noticed that the guests had heard the commotion and ran in to assist. He dropped Anderson like a sack of flour and the scoundrel fell, sitting on the floor with his back against the wall while gasping desperately for air.

The former colonel turned and looked at Elizabeth to ensure that she was well. When she smiled softly, he returned it with all the love in his heart, knowing that he had done his part in protecting her from further harm and called out to his friends. "Captain Saunders, Lieutenant O'Shea, I will be pressing charges against him for Conduct Unbecoming an Officer and I apologise that we have to end our dinner party this way. Throw him in the brig and have him locked up. I will be making a personal visit to have him court-martialled tomorrow and will speak with General Wentington himself." He saw Anderson pale. "I know you are not as drunk as you act; I know you well, Anderson. You should know that I am most vigilant to protect my family and your offences against them will not be taken lightly. I ensured that Wickham was hung for harming Mr. and Mrs. Darcy, and you are fortunate that you did not get a chance to do anything else. I would have killed you and it would have been justified."

Richard noted that Darcy had returned and was holding Elizabeth in his arms. He saw his cousin's furore and spoke again to Anderson. "If Darcy were here earlier, your limbs would have been shredded from your body." *How dare he touch our wife?!* He grabbed his right hand with both hands, appearing as if he was going to shake hands with the villain, and saw Anderson slightly relax. Then he squeezed his hand so hard that his guests could hear bones crack. "That is for touching her arm. No one dare touches her without her permission."

He turned to Saunders and O'Shea. "Please get this rubbish out of my home. I will see you tomorrow." Turning to the other guests, "I apologise for the abrupt end of our evening. It was a very pleasant evening otherwise and it was nice seeing all of you. Gentlemen, I will see you at the base or at the club. Good night."

~*~

Richard watched Darcy take Elizabeth upstairs and he continued to farewell his guests as they gathered their cloaks and carriages were called. He observed Saunders and O'Shea roughly push Anderson into their carriage, while the belligerent Anderson cried out while guarding his broken hand and cursing out that he had not been successful in seducing Mrs. Darcy so he could not press charges, and that Richard Fitzwilliam was no longer in the army so his buddies should have protected himself instead.

Idiot! I nearly killed him and I would have, if Elizabeth did not stop me. I hope she is well. I should have kicked out Anderson when he first stepped foot in the house. Richard begrudged himself for allowing him to stay at Darcy House for as long as he had.

After the last guests left, he rushed upstairs to their sitting room. Darcy was holding Elizabeth in his arms and they were talking softly. Richard rushed over and began his apologies.

"I am so sorry that I let that rogue near you. I should have never allowed him to enter our home, knowing what he was. He was never a good man and he is not my friend. I am so sorry." Richard kissed her hand multiple times.

"Oh, my love. You have done nothing wrong. I was telling Fitzwilliam what had happened before he arrived. You were magnificent, Richard! I knew you were strong but to see you in action, I felt hot all over and it was an incredible sight. You saved me again and I appreciate you more than you know." Elizabeth kissed his lips. "So, from what he said, I am your type; is that right?" She teased.

Richard coloured, "Darcy knew this already. You are *exactly* my type; all of my desires and preferences before meeting you was my soul waiting for my perfect mate. Everything I wanted, my heart was waiting for you, my love. There is none other and will never be any other type for me, Elizabeth." He smiled.

Darcy chuckled, "So true. I knew right away that you loved her when I discovered that your heart was taken. Elizabeth is our perfect wife. I cannot believe you broke his hand like that! There will be no doubt in anyone's mind that you are our most fearless protector now. Wow, brother, he is also going to have a deep bruise around his neck for a week! You were quite fearsome and I am glad you protected our Elizabeth while I was seeing to the stables. Thank you, Richard." He tapped his cousin's shoulders.

Richard smiled brightly. "It is an honour. I will protect you with my life, Elizabeth. No one touches you and gets away with it. I love you." He kissed her hand again and caressed her cheek. "It is my privilege to love you and guard you." Turning to Darcy, "Was the situation with the stable-hand all well? What happened there?"

Darcy replied, "The new boy, James, got kicked by one of the horses, which ended up being Anderson's horse, by the way, after trying to feed him some hay. That horse was severely abused and now knowing the master, I am not surprised by it. The lad will be well; he was just knocked out for a few seconds but I ordered him to rest for a full week and he will recover. Perhaps you can use that information when you meet with Anderson's superiors tomorrow?"

Richard agreed. "That is a good suggestion. I will not let that bastard get away with anything at all. He was a terrible human being before and part of his... influence resulted in my behaving badly a few times but that was more than ten years ago. I will make sure he gets the full extent of his punishment."

Elizabeth held Richard's hand and asked innocently, "Richard, can you tell me what he meant by your having two or three women at a time? How does that work?" *I wonder if he desires it now. Not only is he sharing me with Fitzwilliam, he does not go inside me.*

Richard positively flushed from embarrassment now. "Damn it, Elizabeth! Why is your hearing so good?" Seeing that she was not angry but simply curious, and that Darcy was quite amused with his humiliation, Richard was resigned and took her hand and kissed it. "I am sorry for cursing, Elizabeth. Darcy already knows of my many 'conquests' and he is laughing at me even right now." He also laughed at Darcy's wide smirk. "I used a lot of women back in my youth and it did not matter who was in my bed or how many. I just... I did whatever I felt was pleasurable."

Elizabeth smiled at his honesty. "And how was it to have so many women at one time? Do you miss it? You have not... been inside a woman for some time now. Do you miss the adventures?"

Richard saw the love in her eyes and knew that it was not jealousy or anger with his past behaviour but rather a curiosity and amusement. He kissed her hand seductively and twirled his tongue on her inner wrist. "I have all the adventures I ever want here, Elizabeth. I have never felt so satisfied and fulfilled in my life. Having you in my arms is the best thing in my life and I enjoy sharing you with Darcy. As I have said before, the love that I make with you is better than all the women I ever had and I will never regret you. My past misbehaviours have taught me that having the woman of my heart is the best love in the world. Whether two or two hundred, there was always something missing and now I am dedicated to your happiness."

Elizabeth smiled fully but then furrowed her eyebrows in contemplation.

Richard asked, "What is the matter? What has you in deep thought, my love?" Darcy sat up in concern as well.

Elizabeth blushed and spoke shyly, "I just recalled Lieutenant's other comment as well and I... I am confused but I am hesitant to repeat it..."

Richard paled. "Blast it, I know what you are thinking. Damn Anderson!" He shouted.

"Of what are you speaking, Richard? Elizabeth?" Darcy asked in confusion.

Richard was standing and huffing in anger and Elizabeth timidly answered her husband. "Well, Fitzwilliam, while the Lieutenant was mocking Richard, he mentioned... having me... together with Richard. I do not know how it is possible but he said... he said he would take my... my..." she could not speak the words out loud.

Richard grunted. "Blasted! His language was not meant for your innocent ears, Elizabeth. I am so sorry that you were exposed to that son of a..." He took two deep breaths. "Darcy, he intimated that I take Elizabeth's womanhood while he... while he buggered her. Damn him! I am going to knock his teeth out next time I see him! He used fouler language, of course, and he corrupted our dear Elizabeth's mind."

Darcy sat in shock. To suggest buggery was deviant in itself but for two men to share a woman at the same time was not something that he had heard of. He could not imagine a woman agreeing to such an act, nonetheless enjoying it.

"Have you, Richard... had you done this with Anderson before?" Darcy finally asked several moments later. He knew his cousin was experienced beyond the norm of society's expectations but this was too much. He had read enough to know that sodomy without precautions could cause tremendous pain, but for two men to overpower a woman like that would be unforgivable.

"NO! Never! I... I am sorry, Elizabeth. I will always be truthful with you; I promise you I never did that with anyone." Richard sighed and sat. "I used a prostitute in France and was in the same room with Anderson and another soldier. While I was... busy with my... woman, the two men had another prostitute together and I... I watched them perform the act. It was... It was not unpleasant, I believe. That woman seemed to... enjoy herself very much and although I was asked to participate, I refrained and kept to my own... party."

Elizabeth asked in shock, "The manhood goes up the other... in the...? I cannot imagine that being comfortable! And at the same time as one in the womanhood? I cannot imagine such a thing!"

Darcy caressed her cheek. "Dear Elizabeth, I am sorry that you have been exposed to such vices. Although buggery is illegal, especially between two men, it is more common than generally known. My acquaintances at University spoke of enjoying overtaking women like so, and I know of several men who secretly met for their own liaisons, and two men were foolish enough to practice it where I witnessed them in the throes of passion. Those men had divulged to me that with proper preparations, it was incredibly enjoyable and that they indulged in it as often as would using a woman and begged me for secrecy. Before I met you, I was actually propositioned by a few men who thought I did not care for women because I had remained chaste for so long." Darcy smiled, seeing Elizabeth and Richard's shocked faces. "Yes, some of these men thought I wished for male companionship and could not fathom that I was awaiting my perfect soul mate. I did not think it was something that women would enjoy but I am certain Richard's observations are accurate, and even if it could be pleasurable, it is something that we will not practice." His eyes met Richard. "Richard honours our vows to each other and we will not impose on you in any shape or form."

Elizabeth giggled. "I am getting an extensive education today, husbands. I cannot believe there are so many ways to have relations and I have heard of homosexual men but never knew that was how they had intimacy. Lieutenant Anderson's actions today certainly added to my edification on intercourse."

Both Darcy and Richard relaxed and laughed. She had such a light and innocent heart and they both loved how quickly she was able to rebound from her worries. Richard bent and kissed her neck. "You know too much about relations already, milady. You serve both of your husbands very well as is, and we cannot get enough of you." He kissed her lips gently. "I would never cause you harm. I will never hurt you if I can help it and you own my heart and my body completely. You make me happier and more satisfied than every experience I have combined, and my biggest regret in life is not waiting for you. I will do everything in my power to love you and keep you happy, my love. I know Darcy is even more committed to your happiness, otherwise he would have kicked me out of your life long ago. I love you, Elizabeth Darcy, with all of my heart."

Elizabeth melted at the words and knew that Richard's heart was completely hers. She felt Darcy behind her as he kissed her neck and began to caress her breasts, and knew that she had the love of her husbands wholeheartedly. She smiled broadly at both men and arose.

"Well now, I am ready for bed. I think I need both of you to 'soothe my nerves' for an hour or so. I will need a lot of attention to erase the distasteful events today." Elizabeth arched her brow as she rose and headed to the bedroom, slowly pushing down her dress off her shoulders, one at a time.

Darcy and Richard looked at each other and smiled brightly. "Our Elizabeth is the best," Darcy commented as the men arose to obey her command.

Richard agreed, "That she is. She is the most amazing woman in the world."

~*~

Richard spent the next three days riding to his old military base and speaking with

Anderson's supervisors as well as General Wentington who was wrapping up businesses for the holiday. The General was particularly upset that this ruffian attempted to attack a gentlewoman, Mrs. Darcy, of all people, whose Darcy Fitzwilliam Foundation had helped hundreds of soldiers who were wounded and were looking for employment after leaving the military. Due to the General's pressure, as well as the commendable former colonel's input, the court-martial took place on the third day and Lieutenant Anderson was quickly found guilty and received 100 lashes for attempting to force himself on a lady. Oddly enough, the abuse of his horse got him a two-year sentence at Newgate Prison.

Darcy shook his head at the irony that abusing a horse carried a steeper sentence and how society still viewed women as inferior possessions.

"I am glad we had the horse as proof of his crimes, then, but Mrs. Darcy, your worth is above all the rubies in the lands. We love you more than our stallions, although sometimes I wonder how much Richard truly loves Cyrus." Darcy joked.

Richard laughed loudly. "I do love my horse but it is nothing to how much I love you, Elizabeth. You might be happy to know, he will most likely never be able to gain full function of his right hand. The doctors botched setting his bones and he will most likely never be able to grab onto a horse's reins or anything else with that hand. It will remind him to never touch a woman without permission."

Elizabeth smiled. "I am still awed at your strength. I had discovered Fitzwilliam's power after Wickham but I forget that you both are exceptionally strong, especially when angered. Thank you, both, for being so kind and gentle with me always. I hope to never incur such a wrath from either of you!"

"Never. We love you and you already know we would kill each other if one of us hurt you. We are completely at your submission, milady!" Richard laughed.

Darcy kissed her. "We love you and are fiercely protective of you, even from our own selves. We will never let any harm come to you if we can prevent it."

Elizabeth's eyes teared with so much affection from her husbands. "You two are truly the best of men. Thank you for your love, husbands." She cleared her throat, "By the by, Miss Mulligan enjoyed meeting Captain Saunders. He and Lieutenant O'Shea and his wife seemed to enjoy dinner last night and Miss Mulligan seemed to find the captain quite dashing. She only looked at you both the other half of the time but I think she likes her men in uniform." Elizabeth teased. "If they begin to court, my record will be two for two!" She laughed heartily.

Richard kissed her neck as he sat next to her on the couch. "Darcy, our wife is too tempting. Perhaps we should retire to our bed? I am quite desperate for an afternoon rest. What say you?"

"Oh, I agree. I think we should all rest with her. It has been," Darcy looked at his beautiful pocket watch, "six and a half hours since we 'rested' together. With your permission, Elizabeth?" Seeing her nod, he lifted her up and carried her to the bed from their sitting room, where both men began to strip their clothing and made love to her for the next hour.

~*~

"How is it possible for a woman to be so demanding? I have never heard such a thing!" Darcy exclaimed.

Richard laughed heartily. "And with both of us! I think it is more frequent than the first pregnancy!"

"Infinitely more. To think that carrying twins, she was actually holding herself back." He sighed deeply. "I am so glad you are here to do your share. My cock is sore from enjoying itself so much." Darcy laughed. "I never thought I would complain of having too much sex in my life!"

"Mine is sore and raw from the friction from her mouth and her riding me. I have never released six times from morning to night before. Good lord, she is amazing." Richard chuckled.

Darcy laughed loudly again, "Yes, she is worth every pain. Not that it is really a pain. A good pain. I think she is finally resting and will sleep throughout the night."

The gentlemen were sharing some brandy after they left Elizabeth fully satiated in Darcy's bed. They had planned on their ménage a trois once a month or so to avoid indulging too often, but due to Elizabeth's demands, they had congressed for the twelfth time in the past eight days.

"So tomorrow's ball, do you have any plans to dance with single ladies? Your mother will be relentless and I know you have been avoiding her repeated demands to court Isabelle. She has been pressuring me to convince you of it, brother. Isabelle is a lovely young lady but a child. Elizabeth, oh, she is a woman." Darcy smiled as he recalled his wife's soft skin. "How are you going to kill the rumours? Word is that you were too busy to court her last spring due to your travels and that she had been waiting for your return. Miss Fairfax is engaged so your dancing with her will not squelch it this time. Elizabeth still turns a little green whenever I mention her, you know. She thinks Isabelle would have been your perfect wife." Darcy commented.

Richard rubbed his face. "Can you see yourself marrying Isabelle after loving Elizabeth?" Darcy laughed and shook his head. "My god, if she could understand how tempting she is. If I had married Isabelle and then I met your wife, you would have murdered me because I would have done everything in my power to seduce her to my bed. With any other wife, I would have taken on a mistress after the first few months of trying to behave myself. With Elizabeth, she is enough woman to take on both of us on and we bend to her every whim. I will never get enough of her and cannot imagine a better life, brother." He stood. "I will not dance with anyone tomorrow except with Elizabeth and Georgiana. Now, I shall retire. Return to our beloved; she might want you again soon. Wrap your cock on some cool cloth. I plan to do the same." He winked and left to his own rooms.

Darcy slid into bed and wrapped his arms around his wife who was sleeping soundly. *I love my life!*

Chapter 23

The Christmas Ball was splendid. It exceeded everyone's expectations, as Matlock House gleamed with soft candlelight and excellent wine.

Richard rolled his eyes as his mother was pressing him to ask Lady Isabelle for the first dance yet again.

"You must ask her as soon as she arrives before someone else does, Richard. Thank goodness you arrived early with Darcy and Lizzy and Georgiana will be so happy to be married soon and you must snatch up Isabelle quickly. You must make your intentions clear and dance two sets with her. The first and the supper or the last should suffice. I

---

know you always dance two with Lizzy and I know you love her," Richard's heart jumped, "like a sister, and everyone knows that you saved her and Darcy's lives and is no longer surprised by it, but if you dance two with Isabelle, everyone will know of your claim to her."

Richard quietly let out his breath in relief. He did not want rumours of any illicit activities with Elizabeth to be spread. He was glad once again that it was common knowledge of his fierce loyalty to the Darcys, and their public outings with Elizabeth, even without Darcy, no one batted an eye.

"Mother, you know I have no intentions towards Lady Isabelle. She is a child and I will not marry anyone. Since when did you start believing in gossips? Mother," he held her hand and kissed it. "I am happy as I am now. I could not be more content. Please, accept my choice and encourage her to seek elsewhere as I will never offer for her. I do not wish for anyone to have any hope because they will only be disappointed. I do not wish to dally or cause false hopes and I certainly do not wish to offend their Graces. Will you help me, please?" He gave her the most pathetic look he could express.

"Oh, Richard, my dear child. I understand. I am sorry for pushing you. I know that you are your own man and am so proud of who you have become. You are honourable and have become more like Darcy than ever and it is hard to tell you apart sometimes, so alike your character and honour. I wish for your happiness and if you are happy, I will not press. I only want for more grandchildren." Lady Matlock patted her favourite child's cheek.

"You will have to love the ones you have and hopefully will gain more. I know Albert had his heir but perhaps he will desire more and Darcy has two, whom you consider as grandsons and another on the way. I am truly happy, mother. Thank you." He kissed her cheek and walked her to the receiving line.

Tonight, for the first time in his two and thirty years, he would stand in the line with his family.

~*~

"Mr. Fitzwilliam, it is a pleasure to see you again, sir." Lady Isabelle curtsied.

Richard bowed over her hand. "It is good to see you as well, Lady Isabelle. I wish you a pleasant evening." *Truly, she is nothing to my Elizabeth.*

Lady Isabelle blushed as he held her hand and her heart beat frantically. *He is so handsome.* But she was disappointed when he did not ask her to dance. *Perhaps before the ball begins, he will ask me for a set.*

Richard turned to Georgiana's fiancé, "Andrew, I wish you a wonderful evening," he said more cheerfully. "Make sure my cousin is happy, or else!" He gave a fearsome glare. Seeing the young man gulp, he laughed and patted him on the shoulder. "Do not fear me, future cousin, I swear I am the easier of the two guardians. Darcy is MUCH scarier." He laughed jovially.

The wedding date had been set to the first of February. Due to Elizabeth's confinement, they did not want to risk waiting longer and Elizabeth had been determined to birth the babe in Pemberley. The trio would travel north after the wedding and were to remain there throughout the summer. They were looking forward to the peace and comfort of their country home once again.

As the first notes of the music began, the gossips watched carefully as Lord and Lady Matlock, Viscount and Viscountess Fitzwilliam, Mr. and Mrs. Darcy, and Miss Darcy and Lord Andrew lined up to dance. Richard Fitzwilliam was standing on the side watching the dancers and talking merrily with his friends, while his so-called love of his life was dancing shyly with the son of an earl. Lady Matlock had been effective in arranging this young woman's dance card tonight and respecting her son's wishes, had filled it with everyone but Richard.

Richard had eyes for no one but his Elizabeth. He hoped the guests would not notice but he had almost drooled when he first saw his beloved and could not stop staring at her all night. He kept thinking about their liaison only hours ago when they made love most passionately in the sitting room.

Elizabeth was gorgeous in her beige dress with shimmering golden trims and she looked like an angel. Her figure was most pleasing and her pregnancy had once again made her perfect bosom even more voluptuous. *Damn, I am getting hard again. Must think of something else.* Richard smirked.

Darcy and Elizabeth ended their dance and walked towards Richard during the short break between sets. Just then, Lord Harold greeted Richard.

"How have you been, Fitz? It has been a while." Lord Harold smiled. "I heard all the gossip about how you took down that villain at Darcy's home a week ago. Fine job, fine job." Word quickly spread that Richard Fitzwilliam had defended Mrs. Darcy's honour after a soldier attempted to seek her attentions while Mr. Darcy was unavailable. Ladies nearly swooned at his gallantry while men who knew him expected nothing less from the ever-honourable former colonel.

Lord Harold's disgrace had been forgiven, only due to Darcy writing to his father, the Duke, to explain how instrumental his son was in the criminal trial against Caroline Bingley, and after Haversham's heartfelt apology, Lord and Lady Matlock agreed to invite him to their ball once again.

Lord Harold had brought his wife to the ball this time and was behaving himself while Lady Haversham was conversing with her friends. He greeted Mr. and Mrs. Darcy while they stood with Richard. "Mr. Darcy, Mrs. Darcy," he kissed her hand and leered at her magnificent décolletage but snapped to attention when Darcy coughed.

"Haversham." Darcy coldly replied.

Elizabeth suppressed a giggle and briefly curtsied.

"I am glad to see you here with your *wife* this time, Haversham. No need to look at another's, am I correct?" Darcy subtly threatened.

"Yes, yes. Of course." Haversham quickly averted his eyes from Mrs. Darcy. *Damn fine. She looks more beautiful but I know both Darcy and Fitzwilliam would kill me if I misbehave.* Turning to Richard, "Say, how is Abby? Do you see her often?" He spoke quietly but Elizabeth had heard.

Richard flushed but remained calm. *Elizabeth already knows so I have nothing to worry about. Be calm.* "I would not know, Haversham. I know nothing about her. Shall we go to your wife and ask her if *she* knows?" He glared at his friend. He leaned closer and whispered, "Do not mention her ever again. I might have seen her a few times but she has been retired for a year and is not worth thinking about, do you understand me? Your invitation here can be revoked at any time if you continue to speak of your old mistress."

Turning to Elizabeth, "Mrs. Darcy, I believe it is time for our dance. Shall we?" And they left Haversham standing alone.

~*~

"I know you heard her name. I am sorry, Elizabeth." Richard apologised. He still felt awful that he had hired a woman for his needs and still felt the betrayal committed against his beloved.

"I have not put a second thought about it, Richard. Do not dwell on it. It is all forgotten." Elizabeth smiled. "Now, I do have a bigger problem. Apparently two of my former suitors have decided to join the party this year; I see that Lord and Lady Devon are in attendance. I certainly hope they will not annoy us."

Richard laughed. "You have had too many for my taste, Elizabeth." Standing closer during a dance step, he whispered, "Perhaps we should retire early so we can engage in a similar activity as last night."

Elizabeth blushed profusely. She had been unstoppable last night, taking them both at once and then taking turns with each of them throughout the night. Each of her men had completed three times before the morning arrived and she had begged for twice more today.

"Richard, do not speak about it!" She snipped. "I am hoping to control myself but it could not be helped. I do not know what is wrong with me." Then suddenly, she started tearing up, "There must be something wrong with me, Richard. Perhaps I need to deny myself and cut off all of the activities."

Richard felt terrible to see her unshed tears but knew she was going through her emotions once again. *This pregnancy is going to be the death of me! From too much pleasure! She is so adorable when she cries.* He smiled. "I am sorry for teasing you. You are wonderful and nothing is wrong with you. You must not worry and Darcy and I will make sure you are well. We will talk about this later. I will not be fit to finish the dance if we dwell on it." *I am getting hard. Think of something else.* "Elizabeth, do you see Lady Devon circling around your husband like a vulture?" She nodded. "What do you think of it? Shall we have a plan of attack, general?"

She smiled brightly at this. "I like it when you call me general." She laughed merrily.

There is my girl. I love to hear her laugh. Richard smiled tenderly at the woman he loved.

~*~

Darcy stood against the wall during the second set. Georgiana was dancing with Uncle Henry and he had no wish to dance with anyone else so he conversed with a few of his friends and mostly watched his beautiful wife. He saw that she was smiling and then a bit teary, then smiling again. *Richard, that rogue! Probably took a joke a little too far. My Elizabeth is too emotional right now. God, I love her when she is with child. It certainly makes everything quite exciting.* He smiled brightly, not realising the picture he presented.

Lady Devon had been observing him closely. She had found him most handsome and much better than her husband, since although Lord Devon had been quite enthusiastic in bed before they married, she knew he had been sleeping with Mrs. White behind her back. *Thank goodness Mrs. White left my house after my sister got married off to that dull lieutenant in the summer. And I was so sick of Grace complaining about*

Richard Fitzwilliam. He is dashing but Mr. Darcy is certainly more handsome and so very fit. I have not seen Mr. Fitzwilliam with anyone else than Mr. Darcy and that hoyden Mrs. Darcy. She looks a little plump and thick in the waist. She must be with child.

She then had a brilliant idea. It was common knowledge that most wives promptly kicked their husbands out of the marriage bed after getting with child and men often looked for options outside. Mr. Darcy would be the crowning achievement of her seduction as she found him more handsome than any other men of her acquaintance. He was tall and strong and when he smiled, her heart fluttered. Even though she had a few liaisons with some of her friends' husbands for her enjoyment, they were nothing compared to the most attractive Mr. Darcy. She circled around a bit to find a way to attach herself to him.

Mr. Darcy was still revelling in his wife's beauty and when she laughed at something Richard said, he felt his desires rise, as he recalled her laughing after a spectacular climax last night. Knowing that he would disgrace himself with the quickly rising protrusion in his breeches, he scurried off to find a private moment to calm himself. He stepped out of the ballroom and walked to the library.

He sat on a chair and attempted to deflate his raging erection but he could not stop thinking of his beautiful wife. *Maybe I can get her in here and take advantage of some private time. It would take me thirty seconds.*

Just then, he heard the library door open. He smiled. "Elizabeth, have you followed me here seeing my distress?" He stood and turned around to greet his wife but suddenly paled, seeing that it was Lady Devon standing in front of him.

"I am not Elizabeth but I can certainly help you with any distress, Mr. Darcy." She walked towards him slowly, lowering her sleeves to expose her pert breasts to him. "I would be willing to do *anything* you like to bring pleasure to you. I know you enjoyed my company last time we dined and I find you to be *most* attractive." She continued to walk towards him as he began to back away looking for an exit, keeping his eyes away from her.

Damn it! I should have been more careful. How did I get myself into this? Elizabeth is going to kill me! Darcy thought.

He was backing slowly towards the library door, taking the long way around the furniture, when the door suddenly opened and Richard and Elizabeth both barged in.

Richard and Elizabeth had been watching Lady Devon during their dance, realising that she was seeking her prey and Darcy had not noticed. When Darcy left the ballroom and Lady Devon slowly followed after, Elizabeth feigned illness and asked Richard to lead her out for some air. They guessed Darcy would be in the library, his favourite room at Matlock House, and entered to see Darcy ten feet away and backing out while Lady Devon's bosoms were exposed with her nipples hard against the cold air.

Darcy breathed a sigh of relief. "Oh, thank god!" He spoke loudly.

Lady Devon spluttered and quickly covered herself. "Mrs. Darcy! I... I hope you understand, your husband was in desperate need of relief," she had seen his arousal when she entered the room, "and I came to offer my services. You see, I can provide a service to our mutual benefit during your pregnancy and I am certain we can help each other out. I know Mr. Darcy desires me, as he was clearly aroused when I was standing near him."

Elizabeth laughed out loudly at this. *If she only knew how often he is relieved.* Then she was angry. She was tired of these loose women attempting to throw themselves at her husbands. It was one thing to suggest in words or give calling cards offering pleasures, but for this harlot to seek her husband out alone and bare her chest to him was entirely another story and it was unforgivable!

She walked over to Lady Devon and slapped her across the cheek as hard as she could. Lady Devon was shocked at the attack and as soon as she recovered, she raised her hand to strike back but her wrist was quickly captured by Richard.

"If you dare to lay one finger on her, I will *kill* you with my bare hands." Richard growled in anger.

Lady Devon became very afraid with his threat. She had heard about the fierce loyalty that Richard Fitzwilliam held for his cousins after returning to town from Bath. After saving their lives two Springs ago, it was widely circulated that he had become their guardian and protector and why he was seen with them everywhere, even dancing twice with Mrs. Darcy at every function when it was typically reserved for married couples to do so. Her husband had confessed that Mr. Fitzwilliam was quite 'severe' in their attempts to connect her sister with him in Bath and that threats were made due to the Darcys being unhappy with the Earl. Only last week, that gentleman had been successful in having a soldier court-martialled and broke his hand just for touching Mrs. Darcy's arm. Her own father had bragged about Mr. Fitzwilliam's valour during his service and his magnificent skills with a pistol as well as a sword, and she knew he was fully capable of easily squeezing the life out of her.

"My apologies. I... I only wanted to comfort Mr. Darcy... I am certain he wanted me to..." She looked over and saw him in a tender embrace with his wife, his hands were around her while kissing her deeply.

"I will escort you to Devon myself. Darcy, I shall return in several minutes and knock. Make sure to lock the door." Richard commanded. Dragging Lady Devon by the arm, he closed the door behind him.

Elizabeth spoke to her husband when their kiss ended. "You poor man. Are you well?"

"Oh, Elizabeth, I was afraid you would be angry with me. I did NOT invite that woman in here. You know I only have eyes for you." Darcy replied.

Elizabeth laughed. "I know, my love. Richard and I were watching you and then we noticed her circling about. Why did you leave the ballroom, though?"

Darcy rubbed his erection against her. "I desired you so much I started becoming too aroused to stand there. Oh, my love, how you took us in last night, I cannot help but be aroused all the time now. Will you turn around for me? Lean against the couch arm?"

Elizabeth smiled and turned herself around, bending over the arm and lifting her dress. She felt his fingers rub her folds and felt his stiff manhood enter her. She moaned loudly. "Oh, you feel so good. It has been three hours since I had you last, Mr. Darcy. Far too long." She continued moaning and a few minutes after he entered her, Darcy released.

"Oh, my love. I cannot get enough of you." Darcy panted.

While straightening their clothes, there was a knock at the door.

Darcy opened it carefully to see Richard. He allowed entrance and locked the door again. "Thank god Lady Devon was stupid enough to leave the door unlocked. If I was stuck in here with her and you did not get to me in time, I might have been unable to escape without striking her." Darcy laughed. "Thank you for guarding us, Richard. What was Devon's reaction?"

"He was finishing his set with his sister Lady Christina. I left her with Devon's brother, David. Shall we go and tell him the good news ourselves?" Richard winked.

He turned to Elizabeth and asked, "Are you well, my love?" Richard held her hand and examined it. "I loved hearing the slap against that woman's face." He laughed. He looked over her palm and seeing no damage, kissed the palm and the back of the hand.

"Let us go and put this harlot in her rightful place!" Elizabeth commanded.

"Yes, ma'am, General, ma'am!" Richard saluted with a full grin.

~*~

When they returned, the set was just ending. They spotted David Carlisle with a furrowed brow, hissing at his sister-in-law to remain where she was. She was attempting to flee before her husband returned to her side.

Richard could hear David whisper, "...or else I will publicly humiliate you right now for being a harlot and your father will hear from one of these guests!"

Richard liked this young man. He was definitely more respectful and more like the young Devon who had been friendly and honourable before he inherited his title.

"David! Thank you for keeping her here. I need to talk to your brother and make sure he understands what has happened. Ah, here he comes."

Richard waited for the earl to approach after he released his sister to her next dancing partner.

"Fitzwilliam, what is happening here? What have you done to my wife that she is so agitated?" Devon demanded loudly.

Richard lowered his voice and hissed. "Do you wish for privacy or do you want it all aired in public? There are eyes trained on us right now and it is your choice. I assure you, the fault lies with your stupid wife completely." *Do not dare think I am at fault, you arse!*

With a shocked look on his face, Devon quickly spluttered, "Let us find some privacy." He grabbed his wife by the arm and led her out.

Richard turned to David, "Let us have lunch tomorrow at the club, David; you did well." They shook hands. Richard had only told David that his sister-in-law was behaving like a harlot and not much else was told to him.

The Darcys followed the group, knowing full well that several guests were watching and whispering amongst themselves. Darcy smiled and kissed Elizabeth's hand and Elizabeth returned the smile and leaned against his arm, and it was obvious that whatever might have happened appeared to be Lady Devon's fault and more than one gossip wondered whose handprint was on her left cheek.

As soon as they entered the library, Devon boomed, "What the hell did you do, Alicia?!"

"Me? Why do you immediately suppose it was my fault? What if I am the offended one? That whore slapped me and you dare not protect my honour?" She screeched.

As soon as her words left her mouth, Darcy stepped in front of her with a severe frown, appearing ready to thunder down his terror. "Say one more word against my wife and I will ensure that everyone is aware of your attempt to throw yourself at me. I find nothing about your person or character pleasing and I am certain Mr. Fitzwilliam," Darcy met his eyes, "will ensure that your father knows all about your loose morals." He stepped back and wrapped his arm around Elizabeth. "Devon, get your wife under control or it will be pistols at dawn with Richard as my second. I will not hesitate to shoot you in the heart after what you tried with Mrs. Darcy in Bath. I have not forgotten nor have I forgiven you for that infraction." He sternly warned the earl.

Lord Devon paled at the thought. Fitzwilliam was the best shot he knew and Darcy had been reputed to be a close second with the pistol, and his skills with the sword exceeded even that of the former colonel.

Darcy continued, "Richard, if you do not mind, I will take Elizabeth back to the ball to enjoy our time while you take care of this situation. Please describe in detail of his wife's flat bosoms and the colour of her areolae which made me ill." The Darcys promptly left as Devon stood with his mouth agape in horror.

"You bared your breasts to him?" Looking at Richard, "To him, too?" The earl was red with rage.

"She offered herself to him most avidly and was caught with her bosoms bared. And for her to call Mrs. Darcy a whore? Who is the true whore? I am no longer surprised you took her to bed before your vows were made. Are you sure she was a maiden when you took her? You know I have spies everywhere. Why do you not ask her about her activities last week? Rumour is, she was entertaining two men at the same time, Devon. I leave this to you, Devon. Leave my parents' home immediately and take care of your household affairs and your wife will no longer be welcome in any of the Matlock and Darcy properties. Good night." Richard coldly stated and left the room.

As he was about to close the door, he could hear another slap and crying. *No woman should be struck by her husband but I dare not interfere. I am afraid I will hit her myself. How dare she call my Elizabeth a whore?* He burned with rage but calmed himself, as Elizabeth not only protected what was hers by slapping that harlot, but Darcy and he had guarded her. *I would give up my life for my beloved.*

He returned to the ballroom and asked for another set with Elizabeth as their second set was so rudely interrupted.

Chapter 24

This January day began with a gentle fall of snow. Elizabeth slowly opened her eyes and saw Richard's face in front of her, lightly snoring and appearing very peaceful. The drapes were closed but enough light was coming through that she could see his bare chest rising and falling. He had never stopped his daily exercise, whether riding or fencing, and even resuming his pugilist training recently, stating that he needed to fight off the women that Elizabeth might fight in the future. She saw his right hand where he wore her ring. She had given him a masculine gold ring for Christmas with 'E' engraved on the inside and he had never taken it off since.

She thought how similar indeed his gorgeous body was to Fitzwilliam's. But of course, they exercised together and they were partners in everything; even sharing the woman they loved together. They were truly content with spending much of their time together, from dining to going to clubs, and working on businesses to sleeping in the same bed. The two men she loved had become closer than brothers and it was all due to their love for one woman.

Her husband had explained to her that while he was growing up, his favourite memories were when he was with Richard and that ever since they resided together permanently, he had his best friend and brother whom he trusted and loved. Darcy loved having a constant companion, other than Elizabeth, of course, with whom he could share all of his joys as well as burdens. He was also ecstatic that having a competition for Elizabeth brought an excitement to court his wife continuously and invigorated a challenge that they both enjoyed. They both showered her with flowers and gifts constantly, and she laughed at their attempts to out-spend each other this Christmas, as she had received fur-lined cape, boots, and gloves from Darcy, while Richard gifted her with three adorable puppies to protect her if her husbands were not with her.

She felt her husband stir behind her. His arm was wrapped around her growing abdomen and she felt his manhood twitch against her buttocks. She kissed his hand around her chest where he also wore a wedding band on his left, which she had engraved *'F&E forever'* inside for Christmas and he had loved it and wore it all the time as well.

"Mmm, good morning, my love," Darcy whispered. He lifted up her nightgown and rubbed his arousal against her bottom. "Did you sleep well?" He caressed her breast gently as it had become more tender recently.

"Oh, yes. My wonderful husbands wore me out and I slept ever so peacefully." Elizabeth replied.

Darcy kissed her ear and neck and slowly slid his erection inside her folds and she released a soft moan. He began to rock her gently, moving himself in and out of her slowly. Her moans grew louder as she turned her head to receive Darcy's tongue into her mouth.

"Mmm, I love having you in the morning. I see that Richard is awake. Shall you have him for breakfast?" Darcy teased.

"Ugghhh... All I wanted to do was to sleep in a little this morning but no, *someone* is hungry for morning sex again..." Richard groaned in jest. His cock was hard as he awoke to the sounds of lovemaking and it had tented the sheets for the copulating couple to see.

"Good morning, Richard," Elizabeth called. "I think I need something meaty in my mouth for breakfast. Will you comply with my wishes, sir?"

"At your service, madam!" Richard immediately rose and kissed her mouth deeply as Darcy continued his gentle thrusts. He sat up so Elizabeth could mouth his long erection and suckle on it. He reached down and rubbed her nipples gently and stroked her hair as he gazed adoringly at her while she mouthed him.

Darcy began to thrust harder and Elizabeth's groans became louder. She released Richard's phallus from her mouth and he rolled down to lay beside her and kissed her mouth as she was crying out.

Elizabeth stroked his erection as he tongued her mouth as she climaxed, and after Darcy grunted and released his seed deep into her, Richard rubbed himself against her clitoris and sprayed his seed near her womanhood.

Richard lay back on the bed with a smile on his face. *She is amazing!* "Thank you, Elizabeth. You are ever so generous!"

Darcy lay on his back with his arms behind his head. *She is amazing!* "Oh, my love, I will never tire of loving you!"

Elizabeth sat on her knees between the men and looked at them both. They had the exact same expression on their faces, glowing with post-coital happiness. "I love you, husbands. Thank you for pleasuring me so thoroughly. I am going to take a bath now." She smiled. She kissed them each and left with Darcy assisting her off the bed.

Darcy returned to bed after promising to join her shortly. Plopping back onto the bed, he asked Richard, "I love my life. I cannot wait for the babe to arrive, though. She hopes for a girl and she is thinking Amelia Anne, after your grandmother and my mother, or Madeline Anne, after Aunt Gardiner. If it is a boy, she wants to name him Michael William after your middle name and our names shortened. What do you think?"

Richard was surprised at the honour. "To name her Amelia or him Michael would be an honour. I am so touched by it, Darce. I do not know what to say. She truly loves us."

"That she does, Richard. I cannot imagine a happier marriage. And you? Is our situation satisfactory to you? You do not wish for your own situation?" Darcy asked.

"Never. I could not imagine a better life. I have the love of the most important people in my life and I have never been so sexually satiated. I am so thankful that you enjoy pleasuring her together. It is not something that society would understand but making love to our wife is the most incredible experience of my life and I would not give it up for anything. I know it will not be long before she becomes too exhausted for our lovemaking but I want to enjoy it every moment possible. Best month of my life, sharing the bed with you two." He grinned.

Darcy contemplated, "Richard, I have been thinking that perhaps we can come up with a way to see if Elizabeth can carry your child next without breaking her vows to me. To introduce your seed inside her without your entering her might result in conceiving your own flesh and blood. We will consider it after she is fully recovered after this child she carries. Whether yours or mine, all our children will be raised with all the love in the world."

Richard beamed at the thought of his own child with Elizabeth. "I will gladly receive any gift you and Elizabeth will give. To have my own issue would be an unfathomable joy. It matters naught, though. All of you and Elizabeth's children are my children. I treasure every moment with her." He sighed. "We will have to face that nasty business in court today. I hope it is over quickly. Go and join your wife in the bath. I will need one, too. Thank you, brother." Richard left for his own rooms, walking away completely naked and not caring one bit.

Darcy rose and joined his wife in the bathtub, ensuring that every inch of her was squeaky clean.

~*~

"So, you are not denying your history of a sexual relationship, Mr. Fitzwilliam?" The barrister demanded.

Richard was disgusted. *If I never see her face again, it will be too soon!* "No, I do not deny it." Gasps were heard. He cared not that his reputation was being dragged through the mud right now. He would have his vengeance soon. "I did have a sexual relationship with her but I am denying that I fathered her child and I am denying that the relationship was as long as she claims it." Richard firmly answered.

"Just 'Yes' or 'No', please. Did you use a sheath? Did you spend outside of her?" The barrister asked.

"No." Richard answered. Gasps were heard from the audience again.

"Then I wonder, sir, how you can be so confident that you did not father a child with her. For all your professing of being a respectable gentleman, how dare you shirk your responsibilities? We claim that you had promised her a life of comfort and after you thoroughly took what you wanted, you abandoned her to pursue other women! She deserves justice, sir!"

Mr. Reitling stood, as he knew it was his turn. "Your Honour, may I ask questions to the defendant in accusations of these claims?"

Judge replied, "Proceed."

Mr. Reitling slowly gathered his papers and walked to Richard and asked clearly, "What was your income as a colonel when these events took place?"

Richard answered, "1,000 a year."

Mr. Reitling asked, "And what kind of a life of comfort would be available to be a mistress of a man with 1,000 a year?"

Richard smiled, "Perhaps a small leased cottage, no servants, might be enough to eat. I could probably afford to give her £50 a year, if that. Enough for shelter and food."

Reitling looked at the jurors, "And Mrs. Rushworth is demanding £10,000 in restitution. It would be an impossible sum for a colonel, no?"

Richard answered, "It would take ten years with every penny being saved to raise such funds." The crowd gasped again.

Reitling spoke to the jurors, "Please make note that her demands did not arrive until the child was sixteen months old, AFTER Mr. Fitzwilliam inherited Rosings. Mr. Fitzwilliam, how much is your current income?"

"Ten thousand pounds annually." The crowd's voices grew louder. Richard knew most thought his income to be around 6 to £7,000 a year so it would be shocking that he was as wealthy as Darcy's rumoured 10,000 a year.

Reitling continued, "And can you give us your history of your relationship with Mrs. Rushworth?"

"Yes, I met her during the summer last year in August, at a party given by a colleague of mine. He was a naval officer and due to my inter-military office duties, I had training responsibilities and worked with the Navy. He invited me and I met Mrs. Rushworth and was promptly invited to a private party. I understand my colleague, as well as several other navy men were also invited to their own private parties."

The crowd's murmurs grew louder.

"And how often did you attend this private party?" Reitling continued.

"Once a week. I only had time on Thursdays in August. I travelled in September to Dover." Richard answered.

"So, you had relations with her for only one month?" The lawyer asked.

"Yes, although I have a witness testimony that it was exactly three visits." Richard answered.

Reitling shared the documentation with the judge and sent it around the jurors.

"You are stating that the relationship lasting three months is false?" He asked.

"Indeed. I visited her three times in one month. I did not find her attractive enough to keep my interest." The crowd buzzed loudly at this statement.

"The court will note that the maid signed the document with absolute certainty that she noticed the red coat on Mr. Fitzwilliam and counted the exact number of visits. Also, there is a witness statement that several other naval officers were noted to visit on different days of the week throughout the month." The spectator's murmurs grew louder when it became significant that she had more than one gentleman caller.

Richard looked directly at Maria Rushworth, who had been sitting throughout the trial, her eyes teary and presenting herself as an abandoned woman who was scorned by her wealthy suitor. She was now flushed red, in anger or embarrassment, he could not tell. He looked at her with disgust. *What did I ever see in her? My womanising ways did not care one bit as long as I got between her legs. How shameful I was. I deserve every criticism here but I am no longer that man!*

Reitling continued, "And are you courting or have you courted anyone after you parted company with Mrs. Rushworth? Are you engaged or married?"

Richard confidently answered as he thumbed his right-hand ring, "No. I have not courted a woman for marriage nor do I have plans to ever marry; I have been working with my cousin to learn about estate management, as I do not wish to be an idle gentleman but I will never marry." Murmurs grew once again, as it was common knowledge that he sought no single ladies and he was deemed an outstanding and respectable man.

Reitling asked, "We also wish to note that it is certain that Mr. Fitzwilliam could not have fathered a child based on the dates of the visits. Your Honour, I have here records and witness statements from several prominent doctors on the dates of conception that as the child was born on the Twenty-fifth of July, the child must have been conceived from anywhere between the tenth of October to the fifteenth of November. There is absolute proof that Mr. Fitzwilliam is NOT the father of this child."

The courtroom burst with loud gasps and exclamations. The judge banged down his gavel, "Silence!"

Once silent, the judge asked Reitling, "Any more to add?"

Reitling answered, "Yes, Your Honour. Due to the defamation and slander against my client, he has had to face public scrutiny of opening his private activities in court. My client would like to file a counter-suit against Mrs. Maria Rushworth for the amount of

£10,000, the same as she had demanded."

Maria Rushworth fainted.

When she awoke in the small room next to the courtroom, her barrister told her that not only did she lose the case but that the judge granted the £10,000 restitution against her. He criticised her for withholding valuable information until too late and for lying to him that Mr. Crawford was not the baby's father, and that he would be sending her the £100 fee as well. He promptly left her sitting alone and sobbing.

~*~

Richard gathered his belongings and was stepping away from the courthouse with the Darcys when he heard his name being called. He turned around and found Maria Rushworth several feet away.

They had remained to sign the documents and for the court to obtain the settlement on his behalf and had delayed his departure to avoid the numerous spectators who quickly left to gossip and spread the word. They were sure all the details would be laid out for the world to see in the papers tomorrow.

Mrs. Rushworth grabbed his arm. "Colonel! Sir! Why have you been so cruel? You could have shared all of the information to me beforehand to avoid my public humiliation and to save yourself from exposure as well." She changed her approach and began to caress his arm flirtatiously. "Did I not serve you well during those intense times we spent in my bed?" She spoke softer but did not care if the Darcys could hear her. "Colonel, I know how much you enjoyed my body. I remember you above all others because you ravaged me for over an hour, making me climax so many times in a row. You were magnificent. You released inside me twice each time you made love to me and I know you loved hearing me scream my pleasures. Do you not wish for a mistress? I could be at your beck and call anytime you want to take your pleasures." She stood closer and pushed her chest forward to show her assets.

He shook her hand off of him in disgust. "You are revolting, madam. I have no wish to ever see you again. I wish I never met you!"

She screamed in anger. "I hate you! Just like a man to take his pleasures and leave! I only just received half of my dowry from my former husband after a thorough negotiation, and now I will have nothing left. All I wanted was more funds so I could start my life over somewhere in the north but you have ruined me! You are so wealthy; why could you not just pay me and prevent such publicity?" She yelled.

Richard gruffly replied, "You should have been more content with your lot, madam. No one dares attack me or my family and gets away with it. I care not for my public image; I am already honourable and well-regarded. Those who know me know that I am not the same man as I was then and they know me to be a powerful but generous master and I will not stand anyone trespassing upon my goodness. I am determined, if my exposure will prevent you or anyone else from falsely accusing another, so be it. Why do you not crawl to Crawford and see if he will give you a farthing for his daughter? Yes, I know he is the father. You should have just gone to him instead of hoping to catch the bigger fish."

Richard drew three guineas from his waistcoat. He grabbed her hand and placed the coins in her palm. "Here is payment for your services, madam. It is what I should have paid you for opening your legs to me back then like a whore and my payment would have been complete. It is more than you deserve, but then again, you are a *lady*." He scoffed. "Do not dare touch me or come near me ever again." Richard glared and turned, leaving Maria Rushworth despairing and alone.

~*~

As soon as they entered their carriage, Richard leaned forward and kissed Elizabeth's hands. "I am so sorry you had to witness that. It is over. Thank you for your support, Elizabeth. Watching your face was the only thing that kept me from jumping over the tables to choke her neck. Darcy, thank you, brother. Truly, I could not have gone through this without you both."

"She was very beautiful, Richard. I see why you were attracted to her." Elizabeth spoke softly. It had been difficult to hear the sordid details of Richard's relationship with her in court as well as just now. "She is one you used your... mouth..." She took a breath. "I have met three women from your past now, and I know some of the ones who chased you; they are all incredibly beautiful and I can never compare..." She felt herself inferior to the women of his past, as they all seemed to have had great beauty or remarkable skills in bed or huge dowries. She was absolutely amazed at how beautiful these women were and of how little consequence she herself was in comparison.

Richard closed the drapes on the carriage quickly and pulled her tightly onto his lap. He kissed her mouth fiercely to show her how much he loved her. He felt awful to see her denigrating herself. "Oh, my love, she is nothing. You must know that you are the handsomest woman of all my acquaintances and I find you infinitely more beautiful and charming than anyone else. I have told you her figure is lacking and she could not inspire a fraction of the desire I have for you. She could be announced as the most beautiful person by the Prince Regent himself and I would find her horrid. She is so ugly inside that anyone who looks closely will see it immediately, now more than ever. I love you, Elizabeth Darcy. You are so beautiful inside and out and no amount of beauty or wealth matters to me. They are not you. None compares to you; I swear it. I am so sorry for my past, my love. You are the only one that I love and have ever loved. I regret my behaviours before I met you and wish I could make them all go away. You are so beautiful and my heart is all yours. You have all of me, Elizabeth. I swear to be true to you until my dying breath. You are the only one for me."

"I agree, Elizabeth. You are most beautiful to both of us. You have a beauty that none can compare; your beauty shines from within your soul, with your tender heart and generosity and I cannot imagine another woman worthy of so much love. I love you; we both love you, because you are worthy to be loved." Darcy chimed in and kissed her temple as Richard released her and he lifted his wife onto his own lap.

Richard rubbed her hand and kissed her neck. "I will certainly ravage you later to show you how dedicated I am to your happiness, Elizabeth. Darcy and I will ensure that you never forget how desirous you are and how much we enjoy your body. You know we both cannot get enough of you."

She smiled in appreciation. They were both very kind to her. She caressed Darcy's cheek tenderly and kissed him. "Thank you for marrying me, my love. I know Richard would not have considered me if I was not already taken," she winked at Richard, "but your choosing me to be your wife has brought many blessings into my life and I love you so much for it."

She squeezed Richard's hand. "Thank you for loving me, Richard. I am blessed to have your love and am honoured by your commitment to us. Now, enough with the flattery! Stop it, both of you."

Elizabeth knew that there were plenty of extraordinarily beautiful women in the world who all seemed to want her husbands' attentions, but she was reconciled to the fact that both of her men found her beautiful and loved her dearly for the person she was.

"We have to prepare for Georgiana's wedding and I still have a lot of shopping to do! Whose turn is it to take me shopping?" Elizabeth arched her brow as she took her own seat once again.

Both men avoided eye contact and hesitated to answer. Richard was the first to reply, "Well, I believe I was the last so it is your turn, Darcy?"

Darcy spluttered for a second and replied, "Well, since it was your day of winning, I thought you could celebrate and get yourself something nice while you shop with Elizabeth. I do have quite a pile of correspondences..." Darcy deferred.

"HUSBANDS!" Elizabeth shouted. Then smiling, "I wish to go shopping for some nightgowns and wanted your opinions." She lifted up her skirt to expose her stockings, "I need to shop for some undergarments as well. How *ever* shall I choose them by myself?"

The men both gulped and responded at the same time, "I will go with you!"

She smiled broadly. "Thank you for volunteering, husbands. I am so glad you will both go with me."

Darcy and Richard looked at each other and began to laugh. Darcy recovered first. "I cannot believe we fell for that, but we are certainly at your beck and call, milady." They all laughed together once again.

Chapter 25

Georgiana married Lord Andrew Chatsworth on a bright but brisk day in February. Kitty and Lydia were in attendance as well as many of Georgiana's friends and acquaintances and it was a huge celebration with nobility attending for both sides. The Bingleys and other Bennets could not attend due to their infants being ill due to colds and due to Elizabeth's pregnancy, Lady Matlock offered to host the wedding breakfast and Elizabeth assisted as much as possible. The twins were dressed in cute, little outfits and were adored by everyone in attendance.

Rumours and news about the court case were still rampant and although somewhat embarrassing for such affairs to be publicised, Richard took it with a grain of salt and was soon heralded as a hero for exposing the shrew's deceit.

The only awkward time was when Richard had to stand up with Andrew because his best man became ill at the last moment. Lady Isabelle was standing up with Georgiana and he noticed the forlorn look on her face when she looked his way. He rolled his eyes throughout the ceremony.

As they exited the chapel, he bowed over her hand and softly spoke to her as she gazed adoringly at him, her eyes full of admiration. "Lady Isabelle, you have done a fine job for Georgiana today. As you have seen, Darcy is a father figure to Georgiana and with our vast age difference, I always considered Georgie like a daughter as well." *Get the hint, woman! I will never look at you like I do my Elizabeth. Elizabeth told me to be kind so I need to be gentle. Oh, that wife of mine...* "My E... My dear cousin Mrs. Darcy has asked me to introduce you to a good friend of mine. Will you allow the introduction?" Richard asked. She nodded shyly with a blush on her face. *Good lord, Elizabeth and her matchmaking!*

"David! This is Lady Isabelle Chatsworth, sister to my new cousin, the groom. This is David Carlisle, brother to the Earl of Devon, please do not discredit him due to his family connection; he is the better brother." Richard winked. He left the couple to chat and hustled over back to his beloved.

Darcy laughed. "Nicely done. Elizabeth is proud of you for helping her with the match. She thinks they will get along fabulously."

"My current record stands at two for two and I have been too busy to matchmake. I must see if I can get it up to three for three!" She giggled. Miss Mulligan had recently sent word that she was being courted by Captain Saunders.

Richard bent and whispered quietly, "You are a fine matchmaker, but no one will be as happy as us three." He smiled tenderly.

When it was time for departure, Georgiana hugged her guardians tightly as tears rolled down. "I love you, brother. Thank you for everything you have done for me."

She hugged Richard, "I love you, Richard. Thank you so much for being my guardian and protector."

"Lizzy! I am so glad you helped me. I do not know what I would have done. I feel so much better talking to you about marriage topics and I will write to you often. I love you!" Georgiana thanked Elizabeth.

There were tears in Darcy, Richard, and Elizabeth's eyes as the newlywed sped out in their white carriage that Darcy and Richard had gifted. They left arm in arm to walk the two blocks to Darcy House and spoke of the people they saw and the food they ate and could not wait to get back to Pemberley.

~*~

"Please, no, Elizabeth. I do not wish for a repeat of the last time!" Richard complained, twisting his ring on his finger.

"Oh, Richard, she has written me and promised that things are improved. She will not bother you now. Please, pleeeeaaaassseeee? I know that we had planned on going straight back to Pemberley but I dearly wish to see my father and my sisters and brother. I promise to stay with you as often as possible or you can escape with Fitzwilliam. Please?" Elizabeth begged.

She knew that after the baby was born, she would be in the north and it would not be until August until she could travel again. The plans were to visit York and Manchester this fall and return to Pemberley for Christmas. The whole family was invited and the reunion would be a very large one, but it seemed too far away to wait nearly a year to see her family.

Darcy had immediately agreed as he looked forward to seeing Bingley again. He had written that he was much happier and had used Richard's techniques in his favour and that there were several new tenants at Netherfield that he was very pleased with. He had completed the purchase four months ago and was thrilled to be a landed gentleman.

Richard was not so pleased. He knew that being at Netherfield was stressful and to avoid Jane Bingley and to keep Bingley from becoming upset with him had been a challenge. He and Bingley got along famously now, but he had received letters from Bingley which even Darcy did not know about and he did not know how to share the information.

He coughed and faced the window. It was a cold day and there was a thin layer of snow on the ground. Hopefully it would melt in two days when their travels would begin.

"Elizabeth, I... I have been keeping something from you. Nothing that affects us, no. But it has to do with Bingley." Richard paused. *How do I tell her?*

"Richard, you are scaring me. What is it? Will you tell me now?" Elizabeth immediately cried seeing his solemn countenance.

"Oh, my love. I am sorry to worry you so." Richard immediately saw the change in her demeanour and rushed to hold her. He kissed her forehead several times as they sat on the couch.

"You know that after my advice to him last June, he has been writing to me regularly, asking for one advice or another and how to pleasure a woman. Well, I have been sharing some of my... methods... of what was helpful and his letters had become more descriptive as time passed. Well, with all our travels and your pregnancy then the business of Christmastime, I did not know how to bring this up and I should have discussed it with Darcy, but Bingley swore me to secrecy from him. I hate to break confidences but as my wife, I believe you have the right to know. I am certain he did not share with Darcy because Bingley knew he would share with you, and me, technically being unmarried, he thought I would keep it to myself. I would have and have done so far, but if you wish to travel to Netherfield, I feel it is imperative that you know." Richard continued.

"Is he dying? Is somebody dying? What is it?" Elizabeth desperately asked.

"I believe you might murder him after I tell you this. Elizabeth, he has a mistress." Richard confessed.

"WHAT????!!!! That no good lying son of a..." Elizabeth's lips were shut by Richard's mouth.

"Elizabeth, my love, you must not get overexcited. Remember the baby." Richard gently reminded her.

Elizabeth wrapped her arms around his waist and leaned back on the couch. "Yes, my love." She was so angry that she began to cry, but she took several breaths and settled herself while Richard rubbed her back and kissed her hair.

"How long? Who?" Elizabeth softly asked.

Richard pulled out his handkerchief. This was a new set that Elizabeth gifted, with the ever-familiar emblem of a triangle with a heart inside.

He wiped her tears. "Four months. It is Mrs. White. Devon's sister-in-law's friend."

"WHAT! That good for nothing harl..." Richard was kissing her again. He held on to her lips with his until her breathing calmed. He released her after gently plucking her lips.

"My love, please." He begged. "I know you are angry but slowly, my love. There is more but I cannot tell you until you promise to be calm."

She huffed and folded her arms across her chest. After several moments, she looked at Richard who had not continued his explanations. "Why do you look at me so?" She asked.

Richard gulped. "I have difficulty concentrating on anything else but your breasts at this moment, my love. You are getting so large again. They are beautiful."

Elizabeth laughed and Richard smiled. *That is my girl. I love to hear her laugh. She will not be laughing long after I tell her the news, though. Poor Elizabeth.*

"Fine, Richard. Thank you, husband, for getting me out of my foul mood. I know I am so changeable but I have a right to be angry, but I will remain as calm as possible." She rubbed her belly with Richard's hand. "Our child is most important to us."

"You know the twins call me 'Papa' just as much as Darcy. What shall this little baby call me? What shall we have all our babies call me? Uncle Fitzy? Cousin Wichad?" Richard laughed as he began to kiss her neck and jaw.

"You will be a father to all my babies. I know Fitzwilliam spoke with you about your fathering our next. I hope it will be successful. I would be so happy to give you a child." She kissed him passionately.

"Mmm, perhaps you and Darcy shall name me godfather to all your children. I am legally their guardian so it would not be frowned upon, would it?" He smiled after their kiss. "I would love to be 'Papa' to all of them." He kissed her again ardently. "I love you so much. Perhaps we should go to bed instead of sitting here in the library."

Elizabeth giggled.

"Why am I not invited to this party?" Darcy boomed as he entered the library and saw them in an embrace.

He laughed as he gathered his wife into his arms and placed her on his lap, sitting next to Richard. He had stopped being jealous long ago, as he knew she loved him deeply and he enjoyed his wife being flushed with desire for himself after time with Richard.

After kissing her husband sweetly, Elizabeth spoke. "Oh, Fitzwilliam, Richard was giving me some bad news and I kept losing my head so he was comforting me. He succeeded so well that I nearly forgot what we had been speaking of. Prepare yourself for something dreadful, my love. Bingley has a mistress!" Seeing the shocked look on her husband's face, she continued, "And it is Mrs. White! That harlot who was chasing you around with Lady Devon and sent both of you notes to offer herself you!"

"Wha... How? Richard, Bingley has mentioned nothing to me. How do you know this?" Darcy asked, still in shock.

"Well, he has been writing to me about lady advice and he bragged to me that he took her on four months ago and that she lives in one of the tenant properties. He had the gall to tell me how good she is in bed and that she does things that Jane does not. He visits her daily, Darce. And..." Richard paused to look at Elizabeth, "he has arranged a lover for Jane. Jane is bedding another man for her pleasures. Bingley wrote that he forbids the other man to release inside her because he still wants an heir, but after four months of trying to repair their marriage, they both agreed that if each took on a lover, they could live harmoniously as well as pleasurably. It was a mutual decision."

Elizabeth was crying again; not in anger this time, but in sadness that her dear sister's marriage ended up like the common marriage of the *ton,* where such arrangements were the norm. She looked at her husband and Richard and thanked the heavens that she was so loved. She was absolutely adored by these two men, body and soul, and not to be discarded and put on the shelf like many wives were.

"Do you know who Jane is seeing, Richard?" Elizabeth finally asked.

"I do not know for certain. From the sound of it, it appears to be one of the servants, perhaps a footman. I heard rumours that Caroline Bingley had paid a footman named John to service her and I would not be surprised if it is the same man. He is known at Netherfield to... take care of the women there." He paused for a moment to soften the next blow.

"Bingley offered... his wife to me, he explicitly wrote of it, that if I wanted to... have her, he would not mind watching and that she would certainly welcome it. He actually wrote that talking about me taking her made her flush with desire and it had been a fantasy of hers for months and they... they wanted... to do what we three do now... to be in bed together but more... and take turns. I am afraid that my visiting Netherfield will not be a good idea." Richard looked at Elizabeth and held her hand. "I am so sorry to tell you this."

Elizabeth's eyebrows suddenly furrowed. "My sister is a harlot! She dreams of another man while her husband is making love to her and she is sleeping with a footman?! She wants two men to take turns in her... space and ignore her vows because she wishes to indulge in a fantasy without promises or love? And her husband has a mistress? What has this world become? What happened to the sanctity of marriage? What happened to honouring their vows?" She stood up and began to pace.

Darcy and Richard looked at each other to see if they should stop her or let the floodgates open. Darcy began to stand up to comfort her and she put her hand out to stop him.

"I am perfectly well, gentlemen. I may be angry but I am in control." She took deep breaths. "I have kept my vows and I know I have two husbands to love me and I cannot imagine being more fulfilled in my life, but our love is a deep commitment; vows and promises were made, AND KEPT! We three are not together to fornicate out of desperation to commit adultery; we are a *family* and we are raising our children together and you watch out for each other closer than brothers.

"Our love is not a passing fancy nor is it taken lightly. We are committed for the rest of our lives together and we will love each other until death parts us! I am most fortunate of souls and I can face God with a clear conscience that I have loved fully and have been loved in return, but for Bingley to take up a mistress and arrange for his wife to have assignations so he can shirk his duty, well, that is beyond wrong. And for Jane to... for my once-virtuous sister to fall into the trap of carnal desires so deeply that she enjoys and welcomes this arrangement, it breaks my heart.

"I know that I would like to visit Hertfordshire, as I do miss my father and would like to see my little brother. He and my boys would get along famously but we cannot stay at Longbourn and we certainly will not stay at Netherfield. I want to straighten out both Charles and Jane and give them a piece of my mind! I know I cannot fix everything for them but I will certainly not let them get away with this! I will not let Jane within ten feet of you, Richard. You are mine and she will not taint you. And I did not forget that Mrs. White was eyeing you, Fitzwilliam! That harlot will not come anywhere near your person, or you, Richard! You are both mine and I will protect what belongs to me!" Elizabeth exclaimed.

Darcy elbowed Richard and they both sniggered. They loved seeing this fiercely protective side of her.

"So, what do you suggest, General Elizabeth?" Richard asked with a wink.

Chapter 26

Being six months pregnant, Elizabeth had difficulty sitting at length and knew that to travel from London to Hertfordshire for four hours, visit with the family, then return to the carriage for another four to six hours till dusk would be too arduous.

They decided to stay at the inn for one night and Darcy immediately wrote to Meryton Inn to make arrangements for the entire inn to be made available to them to accommodate his family and servants.

Elizabeth also wrote to her father to alert him of their arrival in two nights and that due to unforeseen circumstances, they were required to stay at the nearby inn. She asked him for a large family dinner to be prepared the first evening and to invite all of his offspring to attend.

As the trio lay in bed the night before their departure, they knew that it would be several days until they could resume their lovemaking like this, so they began slowly and made love thoroughly before they departed for Meryton the next morning.

~*~

"How good it is to see you, my child! You are positively glowing, Lizzy!" Mr. Bennet hugged his favourite daughter. "Darcy, Fitzwilliam, Welcome." He shook his hands with his favourite son in law and his cousin. They were the best men he knew and was very happy to see them, as these two men were intelligent and generous and had been champions for his favourite daughter. He kissed his grandsons, each being held by one of the gentlemen, and grinned proudly. They were two months younger than his son and the three boys would get along well.

"Papa!" Little Richie hid his face on Richard's chest in fear of the stranger.

"It is your grandpapa, Richie, it is well. Say 'hello', Richie." Richard coaxed.

Richie turned and looked at Mr. Bennet and buried his face again.

Richard laughed. "Richie is definitely shyer than Bennet. Bennet, say 'hello' to grandpapa."

Bennet turned and said, "'ello." Then he reached out for Richard to hold him. "Papa." He called.

Darcy laughed. "Why do I not take them both, Richard? The twins like to console each other." He held both in his arms and bounced them up and down.

Both boys squealed in joy. "Papa! Up! Up!"

Elizabeth beamed at seeing the boys laugh. They walked inside to the drawing room and allowed the boys to walk around and stretch their little legs.

"The boys call Fitzwilliam 'papa'? That is unusual." Mr. Bennet commented.

"Well, they have a hard time saying 'godfather' so it is still 'papa' for now. Richard is so constant in their lives that I do not think they differentiate between the two."

Elizabeth smiled.

"And Darcy does not mind? I would think most men would not want their children to call another man 'papa'. Rumours might begin." Mr. Bennet joked.

"Oh, papa. He loves that the boys are loved. The boys will figure it out eventually." Elizabeth kissed her father's cheek.

"Your mother will be down shortly. Samuel just woke up from his nap so he is still irritable. Have a seat."

"Thank you for having us early. We wanted to talk to you about something before everyone arrived. It is actually good that Mama is not here. Have you heard or noticed anything going on with Jane and Charles? Any rumours?" Elizabeth asked.

"Well, to be truthful, there is talk of Bingley riding out more often than his usual but it is such a small matter that I did not think further upon it. I have not seen anything different between them. What are you thinking? Is there a concern?" Mr. Bennet asked with a furrowed brow.

Elizabeth sighed, *How much do I tell Papa? I cannot burden him with Jane's disgrace.* "No, Papa. I only wanted to ensure they were happy. I had hoped for another niece or nephew from that couple by now." She laughed, "Mary is already working on her second!"

Mr. Bennet appeared relieved and shared the laughter. "Yes, they are certainly practicing being fruitful and multiplying!" They all laughed. "And you shall have your second pregnancy complete in two months. Your third child. I could not be prouder, Lizzy. You and your young man here, and Fitzwilliam, as well, look very content. I am happy for your growing family, Lizzy." He kissed Elizabeth's forehead.

Then, Mrs. Bennet and Samuel entered the drawing room and the twins squealed, curiously looking at each other and the other young boy that did not look like themselves. Samuel inquisitively looked at them both and then proceeded to hand them a toy in his hand and they began to babble and look for more toys. The adults watched in delight and conversed of the local news and town gossips.

~*~

Jane and Bingley arrived next with Betty and they decided to take a walk in the gardens. Bingley, Richard, and Darcy were chatting away on one side of the gardens while Jane and Elizabeth conversed on the opposite side. Mr. and Mrs. Bennet desired to watch the young ones in the nursery where more toys were available so they took the children upstairs.

Jane spoke first, "It is so good to see you, Lizzy! You look wonderful! You are significantly smaller with this child. Do you hope for a girl or a boy?"

"I know I will be happy with either. I do wish for a girl but I have a feeling it will be a boy. Some of my symptoms are too similar to my last pregnancy to ignore it." Elizabeth smirked. *My cravings are even more than the last. Although, it could be because of my wonderful husbands.*

Jane whispered, "Are you speaking of your insatiable phase?" *I cannot believe she has relations so often! I know John has been able to take me three times in one day but that was the most ever.*

Elizabeth blushed remembering last night's activity, rather this morning's. *My husbands are so handsome and I cannot get enough of them! Oh, how I want their mouths and hands on me right now.* Shaking her thoughts, she whispered, "Yes, I cannot seem to get enough." *Perhaps this is a good time to begin my battle plan.* "And how about you? Are things well? Has Charles been satisfying you better since our last talk? Your letters seem to indicate you are quite pleased." She smiled, knowing exactly what was happening.

Jane blushed profusely. "I... Yes, I have been quite content. I am finding myself more fulfilled than ever and have been enjoying relations. Oh, Lizzy, I did not know that it could be so pleasurable. I understand how you can crave it so often." She revelled in her pleasures from this morning when John dedicated his time in reaching her climax twice and she made a grave error of speaking without thinking, "I enjoy his mouth on me more than I ever thought possible. John was so good this..." She slapped her mouth with her hands and paled.

Elizabeth knew she had her. She whispered quietly, "Who is John, Jane? And why is his mouth on you?" She knew this must be Jane's lover. *The same man that plunged into Caroline Bingley! How disgusting!* "Jane, are you a fallen woman? Have you finally succumbed to another man's attentions?"

"Lizzy, please do not speak of it. Charles knows. In fact, he is the one who arran..." Jane shut her mouth again. She was flushing red in embarrassment and could not believe she had slipped. She had been too excited to share with her dear sister of the most exhilarating event that had happened since the wedding and the baby.

Elizabeth fumed, "So your dear husband actually arranged for you to have a liaison with another man in order to shirk his duties? Or is he bedding someone else as well? That sounds like the plan that you had desired last June and you made it come true." *I will not become too angry. I must stick to the plan. I knew all of this already.* "Jane, are you happy? Is this arrangement truly what you want in your marriage?"

Jane cried, "I do not know. All I know is that John pays me the attention that I crave and although not handsome, he knows what he is about in bed. Charles still visits me weekly and he wants an heir, but John lays with me nearly every night, sometimes until the morning. Charles visits his mistress daily and he says that this arrangement is most satisfactory to him. I am willing to take what I can, Lizzy." She cried gently. "I do wish for Mr. Fitzwilliam's attention more than any other." She gazed at him with lust in her eyes. "He is most handsome. Your husband, too, Lizzy. I cannot believe you spend all of your time around two such handsome men and I am jealous that I cannot get a minute of their attention. I dream of having Mr. Fitzwilliam in my bed. I wish to bed anyone *but* my husband, Lizzy. How awful is that? He has improved but I wish for adoration and dedication. I wish to be courted and desired; to be aroused and filled by men who enjoy my beauty and body. I am so wanton and I hate myself for it but I no longer find enjoyment with my husband. He is too busy bedding his whore... but I realise that when he set up John to visit me, I have become one as well. Oh, Lizzy, I do not know what to do!" She burst out crying.

Darcy and Richard saw that Jane was crying in Elizabeth's arms. They had been chatting with Bingley of inconsequential things but knew that Elizabeth must have been addressing Jane's affair. Their instructions from 'General Elizabeth' was to keep Bingley distracted, so after confirming with Elizabeth by a silent nod, they took Bingley into the study for a glass of brandy.

Elizabeth continued with Jane, "Jane, I do not know what I would do if Fitzwilliam had a mistress and he set up someone to bed me. I do not believe I would take him up on that offer, as I would never even consider breaking my vows, but the choice to continue to sin is up to you. You do not love John, am I correct?" Jane shook her head in the negative. "Whether Charles is committing adultery or not, it is on your soul to make your choice. I do not condemn you. I know that you had been apathetic with your marriage and you looked for excitement outside of your marriage but it sounds like John is not enough. If he is staying with you throughout the night, can I assume that he is a servant?" Jane nodded. "Oh, Jane, to bed a servant... Your desires to be adored and courted would never satisfy you if you do not look to your husband. You must take hold of what is yours. Charles loves you. He loved you at one point and took his time to court you properly and there was a reason that he married you. You must find that source again. You must look to yourself to find out what has changed. Do you no longer love him? What has changed in *you* and what has changed in *him*?"

"I think I still love him, Lizzy. I know that he is a good man, but he has no drive, he has no desire to improve himself. He is not necessarily indolent, but he takes on other people's opinions and I do not know if he truly has his own. When I brought up the idea of a mistress a second time after our reconciliation last June, he was initially reluctant but a woman he met appeared to please him enough and he set up lodgings for her four months ago. Charles is just happy with his situation as it goes and does not strive to be more. After his purchase of Netherfield, our income is lower, from what I happened to hear, at about 2,000 a year now. The house itself is grand but the properties are the same size as Longbourn and he has not been managing it well with the steward. But he is content with his lot and has no motivation to do more or to improve himself. I found myself losing respect for him. I suppose what is why I continue to look towards Darcy and Mr. Fitzwilliam. They work hard and they are two of the most respectable men in society and of their properties. It is as if Charles gave up and does not care to provide more for his family." Jane ceased crying but was now looking into space, realising the truth of her station.

Elizabeth understood her sister better now. No matter how hard she tried, if her husband or husbands did not care for her and the boys, if the men in her life were not the outstanding gentlemen that they were, her efforts would be limited and possibly in vain. She thanked the heavens for her dearest husbands once again.

"Jane, you must not give up. I know Fitzwilliam and Richard can help him and I will ask them. Do not give up. But I have something to ask of you. You must not look towards my husband or Richard. You will keep your distance from them and you will never be alone with Richard, do you understand? We are staying at Meryton Inn because Richard vehemently refused to be in your company. You have pushed him too far and he, one of the most respectable and honourable men of all England, refuses to be in my sister's presence. It broke my heart to hear him speak so. You will not approach him and you will absolutely keep your distance. Is that understood? I would hate to have a break in our relationship, Jane. I love you dearly but I would choose him because he is in the right. Do you understand me?" Elizabeth sternly spoke.

"I understand, Lizzy. I am sorry for making your life complicated. I will behave and I promise to never be alone with him or approach him." Jane agreed.

"Let us return. It is getting cold and I have a feeling that change is coming your way." Elizabeth softly smiled.

~*~

"So, Bingley, how are things going with your mistress?" Richard tactfully asked while Darcy was observing his wife by the window.

Bingley immediately smirked. "She is fantastic, Fitzwilliam. I have never been so happy. I met her in London while I was completing the Netherfield purchase and she was attentive to me and flattered me exceedingly. I use her every day and my cock has never been so satisfied and she has huge breasts and allows me to do anything I want with her. I had her even this morning." He bragged.

Richard thought, *Hmm, I know all about having a whore without love. It is nothing to my satisfaction with my beautiful wife. Blast it! Do not think of this morning. I am going to get hard.* "Well, Bingley, is your wife happy with the arrangement? Is that servant of yours giving her what you cannot?" *Plant the seed.*

"Well, she says she is happy. I know John visits her often, but I do not know how often. It must be once a week? I lay with Jane once a week. But now that I think of it, I think he is there more often. I saw him yesterday and this morning... What do you mean giving her what I cannot?" Bingley suddenly looked confused.

Idiot! Your wife is probably fucking that servant of yours constantly! I am sure she enjoys that lowborn cock more than her own husband's! Just like all the vapid slut-wives in town. Richard thought to himself.

"Well, if you are not keeping her happy, even with the techniques that I shared with you, certainly she is getting her pleasures from that other man." *I heard John pleasures all the women at Netherfield. Now, even the Mistress. How can Bingley keep such a rake employed to penetrate his own wife?* "I may not be married, but I cannot imagine my wife in bed with a servant. I would be mortified. I would be humiliated that my wife wants a lowborn footman more than me. I would want my wife to desire me constantly and offer me satisfaction beyond what I could get from a harlot and I would want my wife to *beg* me to take her." *Like Elizabeth begged this morning. Damn it, I need to go stand next to Darcy.*

Bingley continued to sit to ponder what was just said to him while Richard walked and stood by the window with Darcy. He saw Elizabeth speaking animatedly with Jane Bingley and looked at Darcy who had a soft erection. He chuckled seeing his own. Their eyes met and knew instantly that they were thinking of this morning's liaison. They could not get enough of their Elizabeth and their wife could not get enough of them both.

~*~

As the ladies entered, the gentlemen moved to the drawing room. The other sisters would arrive in the next hour and they knew time was short.

As they sat and conversed of the Christmas Ball, Elizabeth loudly spoke. "The women in town are awful! Fitzwilliam gets offers from widows and married women often and I have to fight them off. I even slapped a countess across the cheek!" Bingley and Jane both gasped loudly to hear of Elizabeth becoming violent. "And what was that woman's name? The one that propositioned both you and Richard last summer? She had the nerve to slip in a note to you both the same day. She must have been so desperate. What was her name?" Elizabeth asked nonchalantly.

Darcy replied, "Mrs. White. Claire White. Friend of Lady Devon's sister who had the affair with Lord Devon. What a mess that was! I heard Lord and Lady Devon are shunned in public now, especially with all the extramarital affairs that besmudgeoned both of their names. Lady Devon's father cut her off and has threatened to chop off the earl's private parts and they are exiled to some remote town until the gossip dies down. I heard Mrs. White was quite on the hunt for a new benefactor and offered herself to at least a dozen men, giving her services in order to capture anyone that might fall into her trap. She certainly did not succeed with me. Not when I have the most wonderful wife in the world." He kissed Elizabeth's hand and smiled.

Richard also commented, "I found nothing pleasing about her. I never cared for fair-haired ladies." *Get the hint, Mrs. Bingley!* He watched her stiffen from the corner of his eye. *Ha!* "She was too aggressive and vulgar. Nothing like an intelligent, compassionate woman who would catch my eye." *Like my beautiful wife!*

Darcy and Richard noted that Bingley was frozen in shock. They changed the topic to speak with Jane to give time for Charles to recover.

Bingley was surprised beyond belief that Mrs. White was offering her services to several men and he had been the fool that was captured. *No wonder she was so good in bed. She is no better than a whore and I was the stupid fool that she caught! Well, I am going to give her a piece of my mind! What I complete dolt I am! Will I never be my own man? Sarah wanted Darcy, Claire wanted Darcy and Fitzwilliam, and even Jane wants Fitz. I am never going to be good enough. Blast it! I cannot believe I have been fucking Claire for four months and I thought she actually loved me. That wench!*

Seeing that Bingley was becoming redder by the moment, Darcy eyed Richard to take Bingley back to the study.

Richard nudged Bingley and they both walked out of the room quietly.

Moments later, Mr. and Mrs. Bennet returned with all the children in tow, who were happily fed and changed and excited to see their parents.

~*~

"Are you all right, Bingley?" Richard asked.

Bingley fumed. "That whore! I cannot believe I fell for her tricks. If what you and Darcy say is true, she laid her traps and I was the bloody idiot that fell for it. She told me that she fell in love with me the day we met and she went down on her knees on me that same day. I should have known better than to touch that wench! I have been releasing inside her for months so she could have my baby, Fitz! I thought I loved her and wanted to breed with her since Jane was not high in the belly again all this time. I gave her more than £2,000 worth of money and gifts already and she keeps demanding more. Damn it to hell! Why was I so blind to her greed?" He vented several more expletives and Richard just listened.

Richard was quite used to curses from his military men but was surprised to hear such foul language from the normally amiable Bingley. He shook his head, thinking about the money that Bingley threw away on the harlot and how Elizabeth would have cringed at the waste. Jane Bingley's lover was probably being paid a lump sum for secrecy as well. Richard was thankful that his former mistress was not so greedy and was grateful for whatever he had gifted her. *I would gift every farthing to my Elizabeth for her love but thank god she is not after my money. She is so frugal, even when she is wealthier than Bingley!*

After Bingley appeared to calm for a while, Richard commented, "You were too busy thinking with your manhood, Bingley. She never loved you; loved your money, I bet. You chose to be blind because you were too busy looking for your own pleasures. I wonder why you feel more betrayed at the woman who seduced you than at yourself for arranging to have a servant bed your wife. You failed your duty as a husband and supplied a substitute source of pleasure for your wife, seeking your own outside of your marriage, Bingley. You have a good-looking woman as your wife and you are throwing it away because you lost your focus." *Of course, **I** would find her completely insipid and I would never have married her!*

He continued, "I certainly do not appreciate that you allow, nay, *encourage* her to fantasise about me while you have relations with your wife. It disgusts me that you are using me to get what you wish from her and I am affronted that you would treat our friendship in such a way, Bingley. I know you have your preferences but I never found your wife even remotely tempting and would never accept nor condone such an offer to chase only after lust and temporary gratifications. I beg you to leave my name out of your bedroom or else I will terminate our friendship immediately.

"Is your love for her so limited that she is not worth more effort? If I could have married the woman I love but she began to lose interest in me, I would do everything in my power to win her back. I would work hard to never lose it in the first place. I would be grateful for every affection, every moment with her. You have a child together; you courted and fell in love with your wife to marry her. This was no arrangement with an excuse of lack of affection. You loved her once before and it is a shame that you have forgotten. The mistakes are on your head, Bingley. If something is wrong, fix it. Stop blaming your wife, Sarah Fleming, or Claire White, or even myself or Darcy. If you are not the man your wife wants, find out what she *does* want and fix it."

Richard had to calm himself. In his past life, he would have been the same way; if he had ever married, he would have kept a mistress himself and never bat an eye at another man for doing the same. But he was different now. He was faithful to his beloved and could not imagine looking for another outlet ever again. *I wish I were in bed with Elizabeth right now!*

"Charles, I sympathise with you and understand that you have needs, but I find that loving someone with all my heart changes a man. I know if I marry out of duty, I would have a mistress and care not for my wife's needs, but you married your wife because you loved her. I doubt that Darcy would ever allow Elizabeth to become tired of him, although Elizabeth would surely take her husband to task and fix it. It is your choice. Whether Mrs. White or another loose woman who wants to get in your purse and your breeches, the result will always be the same. You will never be truly happy with the distractions of the world if you are not faithful to your wife. Do not give up. Stand up for what is yours and be your own man, Bingley. I wish you the best. I truly do, but since you are married and have a family, you must own up and fix it." Richard finished. *Thank God for my Elizabeth!*

"Thank you, Fitz. I must contemplate and see what direction I want to take. I do love Jane. She is so beautiful and I know she is disappointed in me. She is so quiet and serene most of the time that I forget she has feelings, but I am sorry for violating your trust. I will not use or allow Jane to use your name to stimulate her again. I know she is attracted to you and I am thankful that you are honourable to not dally with my wife." Bingley scoffed and continued. "I am jealous of Darcy. At times I wish I pursued Lizzy first. Darcy thought she was barely tolerable and I might have been successful in getting her attentions if I had not been turned by Jane's hair colour. How shallow am I that I pursued a woman just for her colouring? Lizzy is very beautiful and has a fiery personality that would make any man burn for her." Bingley confessed.

I burn for her constantly and so does Darcy. Oh, Bingley, she is too much woman for you. She would have seen right through you and not given you the time of the day. She would have burned you alive and you would not have survived. Richard laughed. "I believe Darcy will call you out and challenge you to a duel for speaking of his wife so, but I do agree with you. She certainly is vivacious and you would not have survived. She is not the woman for you, Bingley." *But she has my whole heart!* "Forget about other women, Bingley. Care for what you have. The grass is not greener. You must cultivate it and enjoy the fruits of your labour. Love your wife; lose the mistress. Darcy has told me that he discouraged you from taking on a mistress when Sarah Fleming broke your heart. I stand by his advice and give you the same guidance. You must find out what you want from your life. Are you satisfied being a mediocre landowner with a daughter and a mistress and a wife who no longer loves you? Or do you wish for more? Do you wish to be a good master, a good husband, and a good father? The choice is yours." Richard concluded and left for Bingley to ponder.

When Richard returned to the drawing room, his eyes were immediately fixed on Elizabeth who was waiting for his return. He smiled softly and she beamed proudly with her sparkling eyes. His smile grew. *My Elizabeth, my wife. The things that I do for you, my love.*

He walked to the Darcys and sat near them. Darcy patted his back and smiled. They knew they did all they could to help the Bingleys and the next step was theirs to make.

~*~

The dinner was splendid. All five Bennet daughters and baby Samuel filled the house with laughter, and all of the grandchildren and the expected babes to arrive made Mr. and Mrs. Bennet's hearts full. They knew that reunions such as these would be fewer in between and enjoyed every moment they could. Mr. Bennet was especially pleased that his wife was able to control her speech better and did not offend too much this time around.

The merry group parted, promising to see each other for Christmas at Pemberley.

Chapter 27

The Pemberley Party departed the next morning with an eagerness to return home. They knew that their quick stay in Hertfordshire was significant and it brought them peace to have at least attempted to help the Bingleys in their relationship. They sighed in contentment as they entered the foyer of the grand mansion It was not a place of wealth and prestige; it was a warm home to them.

As soon as the boys were settled in, the men gathered their energy to love their wife and rested comfortably. The trio resumed their lovemaking as soon as Elizabeth recovered from their travels and they were blissfully happy to be home.

~*~

Darcy and Richard sat in the study about a week later, working on the latest spring planning for Pemberley and Rosings when Elizabeth excitedly entered the room.

"I just got a letter from Jane and it looks like there is one addressed to both of you from Charles. I hope things are well with them." Elizabeth handed Darcy the letter and sat down to read hers.

Richard was not particularly interested in Bingley's correspondence, as the last had been filled with details of bedding his mistress, but Darcy opened it to see what news it contained.

Suddenly, Elizabeth gasped and yelled. "What?! How?!"

Richard immediately ran over to her side and sat with her, concerned.

Darcy also yelled out, "Damnation!"

Richard asked, "What has happened?" Hoping one of them would answer.

Elizabeth shared her letter with him. "Jane says that Netherfield has suffered a fire to over two-thirds of the structure. The devastation is massive and Charles was injured but not severely. She says that her lover, John, died in the fire and she feels tremendous guilt, as he died in her bed. She says that after they had relations, they fell asleep and she awoke to Charles lifting her up to carry her out, covering her with a thick blanket but her lover never made it out. Charles suffered burns to his leg when his clothes caught on fire while carrying her but they were able to escape the fire and that he had saved her life. They will be moving to their London townhouse while the house is repaired but believes the cost of reconstruction will be colossal. The house might have to be reduced to perhaps less than half of the original size and she is distraught that many changes will need to occur to avoid retrenching. How awful, Richard!" Elizabeth cried.

Darcy also added, "I finished the letter from Bingley, Elizabeth, and he offers more information. He states that after we departed, he visited Mrs. White two days later and was unable to contain his anger. He wrote here that he actually struck the woman in rage and she became unhinged. She threatened to tell his wife and his in-laws of the affair and to ruin his name in society. She taunted him that he was not man enough to get her pregnant after their four months together and that his daughter was probably a bastard since his wife opened her legs for the lowborn cock so often. She actually had the gall to tell him that she had wished myself or Richard had taken up on her offer and that in getting Bingley, she was hopeful that she would cross paths with us to seduce one or both of us.

"Bingley lost it and struck the woman again, knocking her out cold, then left her. That night, it appears that she snuck into Netherfield to set his bed raging with fire but Bingley was able to escape by knocking her out with a vase but it was too late; the room was on fire and he grabbed his wife to run outside. Betty and the nurse were safe, as they were much further away and everyone else was safe but Mrs. White and John the footman both died in the fire. Due to the deaths, he had to let the magistrate, Mr. King, know that his mistress started the fire after he ended the relationship and everyone now knows that he kept a woman within a mile of Netherfield. He says that Jane explained to her parents that she had encouraged it due to having post-birth issues and your parents are satisfied with the explanation, even if very disappointed in him. Bingley has kept Jane's infidelity a secret as feels guilty that he had hired the man. He paid £200 to the footman's parents for restitution as he told them he was on duty and perished after a brave fight.

"The damage to Netherfield was extensive as it burned the entire east wing and half of the west wing, and even after reducing the rebuild to less than three-fourths of the original size, the repair costs are still estimated at over £10,000. He has yet to receive the £2,000 from his tenants and after the original purchase price of 88,000, which he paid much too high, I might add, he only has about £12,000 left, so using £10,000 will be depleting most of his savings. He will need to sell the London townhouse after Netherfield is repaired but he is doubtful he will ever increase his income back to £5,000 a year. He will need some investment opportunities but does not have the funds until the house is repaired and the townhouse sold. I am afraid it will be a long road to recovering the funds. He begs for help and as he knows Elizabeth is expecting, asks if Richard would be able to assist, to join him in London to oversee the reconstruction and search for investments, which might take three to four months at least." Darcy finished.

Elizabeth stood and paced. Even though it was more of a waddle, she did her best thinking when up and moving.

"Richard, you cannot go." She cried out. "I know you are so generous with your time and advice, but you cannot leave me!"

Darcy held her as he stood next to her. "He is not going anywhere, Elizabeth. I would not allow it." He nodded at Richard, who was standing and approaching them. "I depend on him too much and he loves you too much to be so far, remember?" He kissed her lips to ensure she was paying attention.

Elizabeth replied, "Oh, my love. I am sad for Jane's situation but also angry as well. This all could have been prevented if Charles had not sought out a mistress. His weakness brought calamity to all."

Richard rubbed her back and held her hand. "I was never intending to agree, Elizabeth. I thought I would die to be away from you after nine days. I would never leave you by choice. Darcy, may I?"

With a smile, Darcy released Elizabeth after kissing her temple. "Of course, brother."

Richard embraced her and kissed her forehead. "I love you. I never wish to be parted from you."

Feeling the love and comfort, Elizabeth finally relaxed. "I blame my pregnancy. I did not think straight and was so afraid that you would leave me. I desperately need both of my husbands with me." She wiped her tears. "Thank you, my dearest husbands." She straightened and took her seat again.

"Is there anything we can do to assist? Should we offer a loan? What can be done?" Elizabeth asked after several moments.

Darcy was the first to speak. "I do not believe we should, my love. This is a test that Bingley must face alone and we can advise him through letters but he must bear this and grow from it. It is unfortunate but it will give time for him to reflect and find that motivation to improve himself. To offer him an easy way out would not only stunt his growth, but he might depend on it in the future."

Richard agreed, "I think having him go through this challenge will be vital for growth as well. But what about Uncle Gardiner? Could he not help him? He is wise and knows many investment opportunities. I have been writing to him about the latest railroad ventures and he and I have been partnering with several other investors. Some of the investments, the initial growth may be slow but the return might be astronomical if it succeeds. But they are all a risk and Bingley does not have the initial funds right now. It might be too late for Bingley for current opportunities but there may be something else that Uncle is aware of coming up."

Elizabeth beamed. Her husbands were sitting on each of her sides. She turned to Darcy and kissed him tenderly on the lips. "Oh, you dear man, I love that you want Charles to grow. You are infinitely wise and I cannot imagine a better father for our children."

She turned to Richard, "I love that you refer to my uncle as your uncle. To hear you share your respect for him when I know how much he respects you, it warms my heart. Thank you, Richard." She kissed him on the lips as well.

Speaking to both, she continued, "I hope that some time in London will be helpful to Jane and perhaps she will be grateful to Charles for saving her life. It might teach her some humility to know that as beautiful as she is on the outside, she must be beautiful on the inside as well."

Darcy scoffed, "She is not that beautiful, my love. She smiles too much. I found her colourless when I first saw her and you outshine her by far with not only your looks but your accomplishments as well. She is not even half the woman you are, my dearest wife. You are still blinded by what your mother repeated and your mother is wrong. You are the most beautiful by far."

"I agree, Elizabeth; she is nothing to you. I have known enough women to know that her so-called beauty will fade quickly. Darcy and I have seen all types of women paraded around and no one had ignited the fires in our hearts until we met you. I saw nothing tempting about her and never looked at her twice and I have seen men react to you and it is quite obvious that you are the prettiest of them all, my love." Richard agreed with Darcy.

"Too much flattery! Well, perhaps having two husbands has its benefits. This certainly seems to be one of them. Another might be that I have a need for some comfort and I need one of you to take me to bed now. Whose turn is it?" Elizabeth raised her brow with her question.

Both men gulped. Both answered, "Mine!"

"Thank you for volunteering, husbands. I would be more than happy to rest with you both right now." She laughed heartily as she began to waddle towards her room.

Darcy and Richard looked at each other and grinned. Richard shouted, "First one to the bedroom door gets the first kiss!" and dashed out.

Darcy scrambled and ran after him shouting, "Not fair!"

As they both passed the unhurried Elizabeth, she shook her head and laughed. "Boys."

Chapter 28

Jane Bingley sat in Lady Matlock's drawing room after an exclusive dinner with several members of the *ton*. Her invitation had been due to her status as Mrs. Darcy's sister and Bingley took it as an opportunity to learn more about investment opportunities. Darcy and Fitzwilliam had written to him about seeking assistance from Uncle Gardiner and her uncle had been able to connect him with several prominent gentlemen at this dinner.

Jane looked around and saw that there were very many beautiful ladies. She wondered if her dress was nice enough at this dinner after seeing the bejewelled women. It had been too long since she had been in London for more than a fortnight at a time, and she felt uncomfortable, as she realised she did not know the gossips or the people who were being gossiped about.

She heard the word, 'Fitzwilliam' that sparked her interest, though, and she focused on the ladies who were conversing.

"Lady Matlock, how is Mr. Fitzwilliam? We have not seen him in ever so long. We dearly miss his charming addition to your dinner parties." One of the young ladies asked.

Lady Matlock responded, "He is doing very well. He is at Pemberley with the Darcys and is quite busy with the spring planting. You would think by seeing so many landowners around here that these gentlemen sit and play all day long, and yet Darcy and my son have chosen work over ballrooms. Mrs. Darcy is expecting in April and they will stay in Derbyshire this season."

Another younger lady chimed in, "Oh, he is certainly dedicated to the Darcys and I have heard of his valour and loyalty. It certainly makes him so much more worthy but I hope he will join you soon. I am certain you must miss him very much and want him near you." She subtly implied, everyone full knowing that *she* wanted his presence for her own selfish motives.

Lady Matlock scoffed at the mercenary woman but replied, "Richard has given so much for King and Country that he finds the peace at Pemberley to be most essential to his mind. He has been pursued relentlessly since he became master of Rosings but enjoys doing all he can to help his family instead. He has been supporting my son at Matlock and we are most pleased that he has been his happiest in years."

"Lady Isabelle, I recall there were rumours of your attachment to him. Something about his waiting for a young debutante for years, but nothing seemed to have happened. You are now being courted by Mr. Carlisle?" An older lady asked.

Lady Isabelle blushed, "Yes, I am in courtship now. Although I have known Mr. Fitzwilliam since I was a child, there was neither understanding nor expectations. Even though I certainly would have been honoured, Mr. Fitzwilliam was not interested. He is very gallant, though. He introduced me to Mr. Carlisle and I am very pleased."

"Yes, yes, my son is too busy to dwell on the pursuit of a wife. His military background has ruined it, I suppose. He loves being a proper gentleman now and has dedicated his life into being a quiet farmer and enjoying life with his godsons. He writes to me about the Darcy boys and I absolutely adore them. Grandchildren or grandnephews, in this case, bring so much joy; much more than your own children!" Lady Matlock laughed.

The conversation turned to children and grandchildren while Jane Bingley continued to dwell on Richard Fitzwilliam.

He has been pursued by a daughter of a duke and turned her down? And all these other women, they appear to have wanted him as well, either for herself or for her daughter. I am nothing compared to them!

She looked around and saw the daughter of duke, daughters of earls, an heiress with £50,000, and some of the most beautiful women whom she had ever met. She had been told that she was beautiful all her life and she knew she drew the eyes of some men but her dress was slightly out of fashion, she had only a £5,000 dowry, and was a daughter of an inconsequential gentleman with 2,000 a year. Being honest with herself, she knew even her natural beauty was not equal to the ladies here. They were extremely beautiful with alabaster skin and tall, slim figures. There was no way that she would outshine even one of the ladies here in attendance.

Jane suddenly felt like she was served a slice of humble pie as she realised that this was Lizzy's sphere. Her dear sister, who was called unruly and a hoyden, who had been her mother's least favourite child, belonged in this world with Darcy and Mr. Fitzwilliam by her sides. She had still heard of Darcy's eligibility as a bachelor before his sudden marriage to a poor wife who was lauded as the belle of the *ton* now, and the astonishing tasks that the new Mrs. Darcy infused into establishing and running multiple charities, most importantly the Darcy Fitzwilliam Foundation that garnered over £100,000 in donations and saw to the needs of hundreds of people in need, providing education for girls and workhouses for the poor. *My sister takes it upon herself, after being attacked by Wickham, after delivering twins, and now expecting another, and she has done all these things while keeping her husband deeply in love with her. No wonder Mr. Fitzwilliam is so fiercely protective of them. She is fearsome and she is my own sister. I am nothing like her and I am ashamed.*

As conversations continued, Jane realised that none of the men in attendance, who now joined the ladies, paid her any attention. They were all far above Charles' consequence but she was the least in rank as well and she could not blame Charles' station in life. She had no beauty, no conversation, no connections other than Lizzy, and no status compared to the ladies of the ton. She had not read much, she did not play the pianoforte, and she felt her inferiority most acutely. *My mother, my own mother was the only one to tell me that I was most beautiful and I let it go to my head. It is obvious that Elizabeth is highly regarded in society here because of her beauty AND accomplishments. She has had many men attempt to court her and I thought I was more worthy than Lizzy? I am so ashamed that I fooled myself all these years.*

Jane had hoped that she could find herself a new lover in town while Charles was busy with re-establishing his connections and looking to increase his income, but she comprehended once again that the one man that she was able to bed other than her husband was a servant whom her husband had paid off to service her, whom she knew had relations with other servants within Netherfield. He was not handsome at all but was known for his eagerness and when he was not in her bed, she had found out that he was bedding her own maid, the cook's daughters, as well as Betsy's nurse. She was not jealous and had not cared for more than her own pleasures, but she offered him more money, that the more he could satisfy her, the more coins she would give him. Soon, John was lifting up her skirts and pleasuring her at any given time throughout the day whenever privacy could be found, whether in the dining room or the drawing room, and several times through the night nearly every night. She had been quite content with this arrangement, having his sole attentions, two or three times daily, without care that she become impregnated by a servant.

She felt her shame grow again that she had jumped at the chance to commit infidelity because she felt justified that her husband had a mistress. She knew he had visited his mistress daily but she had been looking forward to being away from him so she could have her time with John. She had only thought of her own pleasures.

Jane had been content that she and her husband had an 'open' marriage, where they could plainly speak of their affairs with their paramours. Charles told her that he wanted a large family and was releasing inside Mrs. White, and he had even called out 'Claire' during his climax a few times, but she had not cared and dreamt of Richard Fitzwilliam filling her instead. She would imagine Darcy at times as well, knowing full well that as long as she was being filled and it was pleasurable, she did not care whose manhood was inside her. She shared her desires for Mr. Fitzwilliam and screamed out his name while Charles took his husbandly rights for an heir and Charles had encouraged it because she was more wet with desire.

She did keep it a secret from Charles that John was constantly filling her several times a day. She enjoyed being filled by a man who was more eager than her husband and wanted to have a child so Charles would cease his attentions. The original plan was to use John once a week but Charles was so busy with his mistress and never knew that she was having constant intercourse with the footman, who spent more time in her bed than his own.

She also guessed that she might no longer be fertile, as she had taken John's seed numerous times a week for months, as well as Charles' once weekly, and she had still not become pregnant. She knew John had at least a half dozen bastards and even her maid had divulged that she was carrying his child. She felt the guilt of not being a good wife, sleeping with a servant, constantly dreaming of other men pleasuring her, all the while not being able to bear an heir for her husband.

She looked at Charles who happened to catch her eye and he smiled brilliantly at her.

Her heart fluttered at his attention, appreciating that Charles was happy to see her there. He had been more stressed and anxious but continued to be more attentive to her and tried to reignite their marriage. He continued his visits weekly and had become quite eager to join with her, and she knew that he no longer desired to take on another mistress and was working hard for his family. She recalled the concern on his face when he lifted her out from the Netherfield fire and although she was lying nude with her lover, he cared only for her wellbeing and had carried her out through three sets of stairs, burning his leg during the narrow escape.

Jane stood with a sudden realization. She loved him! *How could I have forgotten how much I cared for him? All those months of courtship, I had known exactly what he was. Even with Mr. Fitzwilliam's flirting with me, my head was not turned then because I loved Charles. It is my fault that I let it go. Lizzy was right. I had to decide what I wanted in my marriage and it is my fault that I was not a better wife. I threw myself at the first man when I felt wounded and I was stuck with my arrogant attitude that I deserved someone better than Charles after finding out about his illegitimate daughter. I never truly forgave him of that deed because I felt as if I deserved more for his past mistakes. I never allowed myself to enjoy being loved by Charles and I pushed him away. Oh, what a wretched creature I am. I wanted something else because I thought I deserved it because I thought I was beautiful. But I am not. I am nowhere as beautiful as some of these ladies here and am much uglier on the inside. How do I make it up to Charles? How do I make our marriage work?*

She considered the advices that Lizzy offered and was determined to work harder for her marriage. *I am resolute; I will be a better wife. I will speak my mind to my husband and we will talk it out. We can make it work and if I am a better wife, he will be a better husband.*

Jane walked over to Bingley and stood next to him as he concluded his conversation. She felt assured that his hand was behind her back, rubbing small circles, and was comforted that he sought to touch her. After his conversation was done, she whispered in her husband's ear, "I am feeling quite amorous, husband. Whenever you are done here, I wish to retire in your bed. We have many things to discuss, my love."

Bingley's eyes widened at the suggestion. She had not initiated any lovemaking since the day Samuel Bennet was born. "Yes, of course, my dear Jane." As soon as possible, they quickly thanked the hosts and departed home to discuss their relationship.

~*~

The Bingleys lay panting and looking at the canopy above them for several minutes.

Bingley turned to see a flushed, sweaty, and unkempt wife next to him. He himself was dripping with sweat and was aroused once again as he reached over and fondled her breasts and she moaned.

"Jane, I love you. I am so sorry that I was such a terrible lover and husband. I should never have taken on a mistress and should have never arranged for you to take on another man. Forgive me for my lack of talents in bed and I promise I will try harder. Darcy gave me a book and I only began to read it after meeting Mrs. White, when I should have used that knowledge to keep my own wife happy. I am so sorry and I hope you will forgive me. Can we try again? I know I am no longer a wealthy suitor; the next several years will be difficult for the both of us, but I promise you, with you by my side, it will give me the courage to be a better man. To provide for you and our daughter. To be faithful to our marriage and find happiness in working hard. I love you so much, Jane. I always loved you. Can we try again?" He begged.

Jane cried tears of joy. "I love you, Charles. I had forgotten it because I was still holding on to my grudge since learning of your illegitimate daughter and I never let that resentment go. I hoped for another's attention, believing that I was better than you, that I deserved more, and I was so wrong. I am not the most beautiful and I have certainly become most-ugly on the inside. I wanted what was not mine or what could never be mine, and desired to be put on a pedestal once again to be worshiped and adored because I had forgotten how much I love you and how deeply I desired to be your wife and that you are a good man. My handsome and kind husband, I hope you will forgive me. I forgive you fully and wish to try again as well."

They kissed and were resolute that they would make their marriage work. Money and status no longer mattered. Their relationship, their family, their love together; these were the only things that they would never take for granted.

Chapter 29

It was now April and Elizabeth was constantly uncomfortable. She was restless at night and her husbands worried for her incessantly.

Due to her restlessness and irritability, the men had determined to take turns sleeping with her so one could get some rest. Darcy took to sleeping in Richard's bed and Wilkins and Garrison laughed that their masters were at the whim of the mistress.

Darcy and Richard had spoken to their valets of the unconventional relationship together and requested their absolute confidence. They explained to them that Mrs. Darcy's love and health was of utmost importance and that although it may appear that Richard and Elizabeth were in an adulterous affair, they emphasised that vows were being kept and that Mrs. Darcy was not tainted by Richard.

Elizabeth also spoke with Hannah and confided in her that she had been sleeping with Mr. Fitzwilliam but were not having intercourse. Hannah finally understood the number of stains that she had washed out on her mistress' nightgowns. She thought both men absolutely handsome and after Mr. Fitzwilliam had saved Mr. and Mrs. Darcy's lives, she understood the loyalty and dedication that he committed to them. Knowing that Mr. Darcy was fully knowledgeable and participating in the lovemaking, she agreed that this was a unique love and pledged her secrecy.

~*~

As Richard rubbed her sensitive spot, Elizabeth cried out her pleasures and gasped for air.

"Oh, my love. It has been a while, has it not?" Elizabeth panted. Richard was behind her, stroking his manhood between her buttocks. She turned her head to kiss him after catching her breath and he licked her lips and sucked on her tongue until he released onto her womanhood.

After huffing for several moments, Richard replied, "Yes, it has been two weeks, my love, but all is well. I love just laying with you and having you in my arms. I am glad you are feeling better today." He rubbed her very full belly as he tenderly kissed her neck and shoulder. "I think this child is ready to come out very soon. I am worried for you but excited to meet our baby as well. Please promise me you will take it easy today. You worked too hard yesterday." He kissed her fondly as he held her in his arms.

The door opened and Darcy entered with a smile. "Good morning! It looks like you already had your first course." He spoke as he saw Richard's deflated manhood.

"Good morning, husband! Have you had much rest? I was telling Richard that I was feeling better today and he was able to provide one release but I desire you as well." Elizabeth cheerfully responded.

"I think you are very near, my love. Promise me you will take it easy today. You worked too hard yesterday." Darcy was concerned. She was due any day now and appeared ready to pop.

Elizabeth smiled brightly. "That is what he said!" She pointed to Richard. She kissed Richard fully on the mouth.

"You have husbands who love you very much, Elizabeth." Richard gleamed. "Enjoy yourselves. I am going to get dressed. See you downstairs for breakfast." He kissed her lips again and departed.

Darcy took Richard's place and held his wife against his chest and kissed her deeply. "I missed you in bed but this arrangement has been working well. I slept well and am refreshed and ready to meet your demands, milady." Darcy inserted his long penis inside his wife and glided in and out of her gently. "Richard left quite a load down here, my love. He must have been quite pent up, just like I have been. I know he usually washes you but he forgot this morning," he said, as he looked down to see the globs of semen on her womanhood. He used his erection to gather the liquid and pushed it inside his wife's vagina. "There, I have filled your womanhood with your lover's seed. If you were not already with child, perhaps he might impregnate you this way." He kissed her neck gently. "Would you like that? Would you wish to make a baby with him? I can help guide his seed inside you. Oh my love, I cannot wait to meet our baby. Having another child of my flesh and blood is such an honour. I love you, Elizabeth." He began to pump harder. Her moans grew louder and she climaxed long and Darcy released deep inside her.

"Oh, Fitzwilliam! I love you so much. I love the thought of having Richard's seed inside me. It is so thrilling to be filled by both of my husbands without breaking our vows. I love you, Mr. Darcy. You are truly the best husband. You would not mind? That child would still have to be a Darcy but you would not love him as much." Elizabeth suddenly cried.

"Oh, my love, I do not know if I could keep myself from not releasing inside you for weeks on end. It would be a mix of our seeds inside you as I would fill you with his and my own and we would most likely not know whose issue. It would be both of ours. He and I are so similar with same hair and eye colour, there would be no way to tell if you begot his child or mine. But I know that it will bring Richard happiness with the possibility of his having a child with you and I would still be content, knowing that you have kept your vows and it would still be my child, our child together.

"Whatever the true paternity, you are married to me and he would be a Darcy. I am so grateful to have Richard in our lives. He has supported the both of us in ways that I never thought would be possible and I am as dependent on him as much as you are. We have a special love together and we are stronger and better because of it. I am still in awe that he is satisfied without ever entering you. He reminds me often that he thought he would spend the rest of his life in your shadow, watching you from afar, desperately needing to be in your presence the once or twice a year he would normally visit. But us being together, sharing our lives together, sharing our bed and intimacy as we have, he never imagined such bliss. He knows after the child is born, he will be resigned to his own bed once again and seemed saddened by it but understands. After the baptism, shall we have you resume your weekly schedule with him?" Darcy asked.

"Oh, I do not wish him so far away, Fitzwilliam. You make love to me whenever you wish now, whether he is participating or not, and he does the same whenever possible. If it is agreeable with you, I would like him to continue to share our bed as we do now. I do not mind being in the middle and it comforts me to have you on each side. I know I have made you both miserable these last few weeks with my constant shifting and restlessness and I am glad there is an option for the other bedroom. Perhaps I shall sleep in my own bed by myself and you might have to bear sleeping with Richard on your own!" She teased.

Darcy chuckled loudly. "No, my love. Having Richard in bed alone is NOT a choice. I would sleep on the couch instead. Imagine how shocked Wilkins and Garrison would be. They would quit their service immediately and they are too valuable!" They both laughed. "Now, shall we get you to our bath, milady?"

Darcy stood to help Elizabeth sit up and suddenly she yelped out in pain. There was a gush of fluid from between her legs and she groaned in pain.

Darcy opened the door to the sitting room and yelled for Richard.

Richard, who was dressed by now, ran in to see that her labour was starting. Darcy was still standing naked but he tossed Richard his wife's nightgown as he put on his robe, and Richard dressed her as she was panting for breath. "You will be well, my love," he comforted her. He carried her to his own bedroom where the bed had been just refreshed and placed her on it.

Hannah came rushing in to tend to her mistress and Darcy was already calling for the midwife and Mrs. Reynolds.

"Richard, stay with her while I dress. The midwife should be here shortly." Darcy ran off.

Richard cradled Elizabeth in his arms as she grunted through the labour pains. He wiped her brow and kissed her forehead. "You are doing wonderfully, my dear."

She screamed out, "HOW WOULD YOU KNOW, BEING A MAN?!" She panted several more breaths then grabbed his cravat and pulled with the next labour pain.

Richard was shocked at being yelled at and could not breathe, as she tugged his neck so tightly. He was tremendously relieved when Darcy entered, sans cravat, and helped him.

"Yes, dear. Oh my love, let go of Richard. Let him go..." Darcy gently coaxed. She released her hand and Richard fell back to gain colour back to his face.

"THIS IS ALL YOUR FAULT, FITZWILLIAM DARCY!" Elizabeth screamed out again.

"Yes, dear. I know, my love." Darcy stroked her hair. "I love you very much, Elizabeth. Remember; we are waiting for Michael or Amelia."

At this Elizabeth instantly melted. "Oh, Michael or Amelia. How I long to meet our child, Fitzwilliam. I love you so much. I want to have so many more babies. I love you."

Darcy laughed and Richard was finally able to smile. *So, this is what Darcy had to go through with the last delivery. Haha! I feel like a proper father now!* Richard thought.

~*~

394

Soon, Mrs. Meyers arrived. She was ever congenial and saw that Mrs. Darcy was further along than expected.

Darcy remained in the bedroom once again and Richard moved himself to the sitting room, where he could hear her every cry. He wished he could be with her but also knew that it was not his place. He trusted that Darcy would care for her and waited patiently, spending some time with the twins and working on his correspondences from the sitting room. He knew the next several days would be spent in catering to her every whim and he and Darcy would be quite busy.

After hearing several screams, Richard held his quill in the air as he heard a soft cry of a baby. His heart filled with love for this child already. *Oh, my love. I hope you are well. I am so proud of you!*

Darcy flew into the sitting room and ran towards Richard to embrace him tightly. "Elizabeth is well, Richard. She has given me another son. Michael William Darcy! Another Darcy boy to carry on the family name." He beamed. "He is beautiful and everything is well." They laughed and cheered.

Richard poured Darcy a small drink. "Congratulations, Darcy. I am immensely proud of you and Elizabeth. She promised you many more babies and I know I will love every one of them like my own." He wiped a tear. Although he knew Elizabeth was receiving the best care possible, he was always afraid for her well-being and was tremendously relieved that she was well. "I am so pleased to be part of your family, Darce. When can I see her? And meet Michael?"

"They are cleaning them up and it will be a quarter hour or so. He is a beautiful boy!" Darcy beamed. He paused for several moments and spoke to Richard in a quieter voice. "Richard, I know you have honoured Elizabeth's vows to me and I appreciate it more than you know. To love her as I love her and not be able to obtain that one last part of her, I do not know if I could survive not being her full husband but I am married to her and it is my privilege and right. The next six weeks will be difficult without her but she still wishes to have both of us in bed with her. She is comforted by your presence, Richard. And when the time is right, perhaps after Michael is a few months old, we would like to see about getting her with your issue. You would not enter her but I would guide your seed inside her on your behalf."

He rubbed his face. *Thank goodness I can talk to him about everything.* "This morning, you released at her entrance and when I entered her, I pushed your spending inside her." Seeing Richard's surprised look, Darcy continued, "It might not work and I could certainly not prevent myself from releasing inside her, but it would be our child. The possibility that the next child could be yours should appease the both of us, knowing that our love could result in Elizabeth's next child." He laughed. "She just gave me my third son and here we are, speaking of the next one. She wants to have our babies, Richard! She loves us so much. She is a wonder."

Richard laughed. "It would be an unfathomable joy to have a child with Elizabeth; my own flesh and blood. But Darcy, I already feel like your children are my own. I love them because I love their parents. Any gift from you and Elizabeth, I receive with honour and gratitude." *Oh, to have a daughter in her mother's image. I love you so much, Elizabeth!*

"I know, Richard. You are a good man. We will love our family together and continue to work hard for our family." Darcy finished.

The door opened and Mrs. Reynolds entered. "Mrs. Darcy is ready for you both, gentlemen." She smiled brightly. She loved both these young men, having known them all of their lives, and although Mrs. Reynolds did not know about their sleeping habits, she understood that Richard Fitzwilliam fiercely loved his cousins and how concerned he had been for Mrs. Darcy's health.

Richard entered and saw his beautiful wife with a single bundle this time. Without hesitation, he flew to her side and sat next to her in bed. He saw the beautiful baby boy in her arms and wrapped his arm around her. "Well done, my love. He is beautiful. I love you so much." He kissed her tenderly in appreciation for all of her hard work and for the safe delivery.

Elizabeth beamed. "Such proud fathers." She kissed both of her husbands and looked down to her new-born. She bared her breast and began to feed him while Darcy and Richard gawked at the scene. It was beautiful and sensual and completely appropriate.

Chapter 30

The next several weeks flew by. Elizabeth was out of bed the day after delivery and already writing correspondences and seeing her friend by the week's end.

Charlotte Tinsley was a daily visitor, being closest of all her family and friends, and they shared stories of the childbirth and pregnancy experiences. Charlotte had given birth to a daughter a year ago and was expecting again.

Charlotte blushed when Richard spoke with her. He had become more friendly after her marriage and although maintaining proper distance, he laughed jovially and teased Elizabeth often, especially when Charlotte told stories of their childhood together to Mr. Darcy and Mr. Fitzwilliam. She was grateful that she found Mr. Tinsley, who was a caring husband and provided well for the family, seeing that Mr. Fitzwilliam remained unattached and appeared perfectly happy in his bachelorhood, living here with the Darcys and their three children.

He would have never offered for me. He never looked at me twice. Charlotte thought. She had been kept apprised of all of the events in London and knew that Mr. Fitzwilliam was coveted for his looks and wealth. *He is SO handsome. And Mr. Darcy, too. I have never seen him prouder but Eliza did give him three sons to carry on the Darcy name. I am so pleased for my friend.*

After the gentlemen left for the ladies to chat, Charlotte spoke to Elizabeth holding her hand. "Eliza, thank you for marrying Mr. Darcy and for bringing me to Pemberley. I cannot imagine what my life would have been like if I did not marry my dear Mr. Tinsley. I owe my happiness to you, my friend."

"Oh, Charlotte, I am glad to have you near me. I did not wish for my mother to attend and Jane is not in a place to visit. My Aunt Gardiner wished to be here for the confinement but my uncle's business is incredibly busy right now and she could not leave. I am glad you are here. Thank you for being my friend." Elizabeth was teary but joyous.

"You are so very loved, Eliza. I am happy to be here for you." Charlotte embraced her dearest friend.

They continued to chat about the needs of the parish and what could be done to improve the School for Girls and continued their visit.

~*~

"Richard, can you explain to me Uncle Gardiner's letter? I think I missed this part of the communication and need your help." Darcy asked, holding the latest letter from the investment that he and Richard had been participating in.

"But of course. Ah, yes, this was last month's result. It seems that the railroad venture has been quite successful and is showing a great return on our share so far. Because we were the first and largest investor, we are seeing the biggest outcome and own forty percent of the holdings. Our initial investment of £40,000 has returned £160,000, and because of the rapid growth and partnership, I expect to see another £300,000 in the next ten years without adding another penny." Richard saw the shock on Darcy's face and smiled.

"I was glad my grandmother's cottage's sale was profitable and I was able to use that fund for this venture. And Darcy, I have a surprise for you. I had been keeping an eye out on Kellynch Hall ever since we met that pompous arse, Sir Walter Elliot. The solicitor wrote to me last month that the idiot was finally forced to sell his estate due to failure at retrenching and I purchased it using my half of the investment earnings. The paperwork finally went through and I received confirmation that we own it as of yesterday. Kellynch Hall currently brings 5,000 a year and it will be for your third son, Michael, as Bennet will have Pemberley and Richie will have Rosings. I will be leasing it to the Wentworths for several years until they are ready to purchase something of their own and it will be in good hands. My gift to you, brother." Richard concluded with a large smile.

He was not ready for the surprise when Darcy attacked his person with the biggest embrace that he had ever given. Richard smiled and patted his cousin's back as Darcy continued to hold on to him. He knew Darcy was touched.

"Richard, I did not know... I am overwhelmed and honoured by your love for our family. I know that you have been working hard with this investment and I had left it to you to handle the details. You should keep all of the returns. I am grateful that you thought of my third son before he was even born. I cannot imagine your arranging all this and I insist that you keep all of the proceedings, brother." Darcy wiped away his tears.

Richard laughed. "Darcy, everything I have, I share with you. You have given me the greatest treasure and £75,000 is pittance to the life you share with me. Even after setting up Elizabeth's trust, I still have Rosings and some of my old investments, and I have more money than I know what to do with even now. If we have daughters in the future, our daughters will have at least £50,000 each and possibly up to a £100,000 dowry each, should all our ventures succeed. We only need to ensure our dearest Elizabeth can handle having so many of our children. Should we have another son, we will ensure his future is secure as well. We will continue to work hard and everything I have, it is yours and Elizabeth's."

"Thank you, brother. Your dedication to us means the world." Darcy was truly grateful for Richard. "Now, perhaps we can get some time in to fence together. We are both out of shape and it would not do to let ourselves go now. We have to continue to please our wife!" He smiled broadly. *God has been so good to us. I am so thankful for Elizabeth!*

~*~

Elizabeth lay panting. Her eyes were closed as she felt hands all over her body and both of her husbands had licked her leaky breasts on each side. She had hands caressing her everywhere and felt kisses down to her stomach and core. Having a mouth on her womanhood and another on her breasts was more pleasurable than she remembered. *It has been too long.* She thought.

She opened her eyes and saw Darcy's face as he tongued her mouth and she grabbed onto Richard's hair as he continued to attack her womanhood with his tongue. She moaned loudly as she climaxed and she saw Darcy's election near her face. Looking up at him, she took him inside her mouth and suckled on him while Richard continued his tongue thrusts and she climaxed once again. She turned her head to the other side and saw Richard's massive phallus now. She mouthed his erection first then held both manhoods in her hands and stroked it.

"I love to see them so eager at attention," she continued to stroke both. "I love having you both, my husbands." She took turns licking each and then Darcy proceeded to enter her womanhood between her legs.

"Oh, my darling wife. I have missed you very much. Six weeks without being inside you has been difficult." Darcy pumped in hard thrusts several times. "Yes, my love, mouth Richard's cock. He is throbbing for you. We are going to start practicing getting you with our child again, my love. Oh, yes. He is close. You are such a seductress, Elizabeth." Darcy guided her.

Richard was ready to explode. Elizabeth had been generous and had pleasured each of them with her mouth several times, a fortnight after Michael was born. But to see her climaxing and enjoying their lovemaking had been most thrilling. He stood quickly and moved between her legs, where Darcy had just been pumping and he was ready to release. He knelt up and spread her legs wide open to shoot his release directed into her womb while he used his left hand to keep her womanhood gaping open. He collapsed next to Elizabeth and continued to kiss her as Darcy gathered the residual semen with his penis and inserted deeply into his wife. Richard watched Darcy pump his wife and saw that his seed was being pushed in and filling Elizabeth by proxy. He returned to kissing her deeply. "Oh, my wife. The mother of my future children." He whispered.

Darcy grunted loudly and released his seed inside her after several more strokes. He fell to the other side of his wife and panted for air.

"That was by far the best intercourse I have ever had. It gets better and better, my love." Darcy kissed his wife's cheek and neck.

"You do not find me flabby and unattractive?" Elizabeth teased. She knew perfectly well that her men were thrilled by her body, even if a little plumper and softer. She had quickly resumed her exercise and worked hard to maintain her figure.

"Minx!" Richard laughed. "You know full well that we cannot get enough of you. I love you. Thank you for taking us both tonight. I lost the bet but Darcy was kind enough to allow me to join you."

"What bet? Do not tell me that my husbands are now gamblers!" Elizabeth feigned shock.

Darcy laughed loudly, "Richard bet me that Reverend Tinsley was going to make Michael cry during the christening but who would have thought he would sleep through everything? Haha! Even when Bennet and Richie ended up crying because they wanted their 'GaPapa' to hold them through the ceremony because they wanted to stand with us! It was very nice of you to hold them, Richard, so that is why I agreed. And of course, Elizabeth would have been upset with me if I barred you." He laughed loudly again.

"I am glad you will be godfather to all of our children, Richard. You have given so much." Elizabeth's eyes immediately teared. She was told about Michael's future estate and could not imagine a more generous gift.

"I sacrifice nothing. I give because I wished and I wanted to be prepared for our future children, Elizabeth. I only receive, even when I give." Richard kissed her softly.

"Will you get on your hands and knees, Elizabeth? I am ready for another round." Darcy requested, as he stroked his manhood with his hand. He knelt between her legs and began to pump her again while Richard positioned himself at the head of the bed to sit in front of Elizabeth's head so she could lower her head and suck on him again.

"I love my life." Richard said, after he released in Elizabeth's mouth.

"I love my life." Darcy said, after he released deeply in Elizabeth's womb.

"Oh, husbands, I love my life and I love you for loving me so thoroughly." Elizabeth panted as she lay between her favourite men in the world.

Chapter 31

"Lydia is engaged!" Elizabeth shouted.

"Finally, it is about time." Darcy commented. "She has been stringing that poor fellow for ages. Georgiana already has had her son and Mary is working on her third. Kitty is finally with child and even Jane is pregnant again. When does she expect to marry?" Darcy asked.

"March. Still a two-month engagement but at least there is an end in sight. Lieutenant Denny must be squirming in his seat if she is as flirtatious as she has been." Elizabeth giggled.

Darcy laughed, "I have a feeling they have anticipated their vows, my love. They looked far too comfortable when we saw them at Chatsworth last. Poor Georgiana had to play chaperon but with her pregnancy, she could not be everywhere at once."

"Shocking! You think my sister so loose to anticipate her vows?" Elizabeth feigned her surprise. "Oh, Fitzwilliam, I have no doubt. I recognise intimacy when I see it. I still am shocked at how well you and Richard behave in public. Richard more than you, for certain, since you are allowed to touch me and hold my hand. I do not know how he does it. He truly has an iron will." Elizabeth sighed. "When do you think he will return?"

Darcy held her hand and kissed her temple. "He will be back soon, my love. Be patient. He does not know yet, does he?"

Elizabeth shook her head. "No, not yet. He is observant but with the latest business tasks, I do not think he noticed. I hope Richard will be happy."

"Happy about what?" Richard boomed as he entered. It was raining outside and it had taken him longer than expected but he rushed in as quickly as possible.

Elizabeth jumped and hugged Richard as he entered. "You have returned to us!" She began to cry.

Richard chuckled as he continued to hold her. "Darcy, why is our wife so emotional? I was only gone for several hours for dinner. She has not been this bad since... wait...

are you? Could you be?" Suddenly wondering if it could be true, he looked into her eyes and received confirmation as she nodded.

He embraced her as firmly as possible and swung her around in circles. Lowering her carefully, he continued, "You are with child? Are you certain?" She nodded.

"Darcy," Richard spoke without breaking eye contact with Elizabeth, "I am going to make love to our wife right now, right there." He kissed her deeply. "Shall you watch or join us?" He continued to kiss her excitedly and brought his head down to suckle on her breasts.

Darcy laughed. "I shall watch. I just released half an hour ago. You enjoy her and I will finish her off for you, brother." He stood to lock the door and found a place to observe Richard's talents. Both men had become more comfortable with having relations with Elizabeth all over the house as long as the door could be locked. While their wife was not pregnant, they had experimented with many positions to bring her ecstasy as well as their own at least twice daily, and even during her courses, she had allowed them to be pleasured.

Richard immediately took Elizabeth over to the couch and kissed her and fondled her. He kissed her abdomen where the babe lay and mumbled his words of love, then he rubbed his manhood against her thigh, lifting her dress to finger her. "I missed you, my dearest. Oh, yes, Elizabeth, let it go. Oh, my love, you are so beautiful." He continued his fingering as he tongued her mouth and licked her nipples. She moaned louder and began to cry out her pleasures and Richard used his other hand to unbutton his fall. As she finished her climax, Richard looked at Darcy and grinned. He lay over her with his erection between her legs and began to thrust up and down, his shaft rubbing against her clitoris while his phallus was surrounded by her flesh without penetrating her womanhood. He moaned with his tongue inside her mouth until he was ready to explode and after she screamed out again, he stood at her head and coaxed her mouth to open for his raging erection.

Darcy rolled his eyes. *How does he do it? The technique seems the same but he gets her so hot.* He laughed. *Damn it, I am hard again. My turn.* He walked around the couch and took Richard's previous position and slid his firm erection deeply inside his wife.

Elizabeth moaned with a mouth full of Richard's manhood. She loved taking them both. Richard soon released inside Elizabeth's mouth with a loud groan and she swallowed his semen fully as Darcy held himself inside her. She sat up and took Darcy into her mouth as well and swallowed, as he grunted his release.

"Thank you, Fitzwilliam, Richard. I love you both so much." Elizabeth kissed Darcy's cheek as he helped her stand and fix her appearance. "I love it when you pleasure me so well." Turning to Richard and embraced him on the couch, she said, "I missed you terribly. How was your dinner?"

"I feel like I need to go out to dinner more often if this is the welcome I would receive." Richard jested. Seeing her false frown, he laughed harder. "Perhaps Darcy needs another outing."

"Oh, no. The last time I left Elizabeth alone with you, you kept her in bed the entire time I was gone." Darcy retorted, as he fixed his appearance and offered both a small glass of wine.

"And what have you been doing while I was gone these last," he looked at his favourite possession, "four hours and twenty minutes?"

Darcy grinned. "Kept her in bed the whole time." They burst out laughing.

Richard knelt at Elizabeth's feet and rubbed her stomach. "When?"

Elizabeth held her hand over his as he caressed her. "July."

"Oh, my wife, I love you." Richard kissed her abdomen and her hands, then took a seat next to her.

"I hope for a girl this time. We have positively run out of names for boys!" Elizabeth giggled. "But whether we have a houseful of boys or girls, I will love all of my children the same. They are all so precious and I love filling the house with little Darcys. Oh, our time in Manchester was definitely fruitful. It was such a heavenly little cottage. I think I like Kieran Hall and Chester Cottage the best, other than Pemberley and Rosings, of course. I did not care for York at all. I know that is where your father met Charles' father, but it reminded me of Caroline Bingley too much. I am glad you decided to sell it, Fitzwilliam. I was quite surprised how well Mr. Hurst looked. They will be happy in that house. It was not for us." Elizabeth spoke her mind.

Darcy agreed. "The Hursts definitely worked hard to make their marriage work and I was pleased to see them happy with their two children. Mrs. Hurst was positively beaming and she adored our children. Richard and I agreed that we should not like to return to York and it was no loss. Hurst received a good deal and it was mutually beneficial."

"So, do we need to plan out our travel plans?" Richard asked. "I know you were disappointed you could not see Mrs. Bingley for Christmas, although I thought Pemberley was going to burst at the seams with all of our guests."

Elizabeth laughed. "Oh, Richard, we still had enough room to house thirty more guests. Our home is quite large, mind you."

"But it feels so small when I cannot kiss you and love you often. It was a long three weeks for me to sleep alone." Richard pouted.

"Well, I made sure to satisfy you before you had to drag yourself off to your lonely bed. I hope I made it up to you these past two weeks, my love." Elizabeth kissed him on the cheek in consolation. "I have a letter from Jane that she is due any day now and that Lydia is getting married in March. Can we please go, Fitzwilliam? I would dearly love to do a little shopping in London as well. I will need to alter my dresses again. I feel as if I am constantly pregnant!"

Darcy laughed. "Well, with two husbands continuously needing your attentions, I am unsurprised at your constantly being in the pregnant state. Shall we go for a dozen? We can be a traveling circus, The Dozen Darcys, and show off our talents of being taciturn and grumpy." They all laughed. "I cannot believe how much our twins have grown. Nearly two and a half and so loud! I cannot imagine having the twins and Michael and having to take care for them by myself. Most grateful for you, 'GA Papa'! Yes, my love, we can go to London. There are a few items that require our personal attention," he eyed Richard, "and it would be better done sooner than later."

"Thank you, my love! But Netherfield is still under construction and it barely houses the Bingleys now. Where will we stay for Lydia's wedding?" Elizabeth frowned. "We have such a large party, staying at Meryton Inn was not comfortable for our group and we have another baby now." She stood and began to pace. "Purvis Lodge was available for a while but it is being leased. I heard Westwood Manor was on the market but it was recently purchased by someone unknown. Oh, have I told you about

Westwood Manor? It is double the size of the old Netherfield mansion, about half of Rosings, and is the most beautiful estate in Hertfordshire. The owners prior were kind people but I believe there was an issue with the entailment and it was wrapped up in a lawsuit for years. I heard it finally ended and they were able to sell it off. My mother loved Netherfield because it was so close to Longbourn but Westwood is by far the most grand estate, even if it is five miles away from Meryton." She noticed Richard and Darcy giving each other looks. "What? Have I been rattling off again? This pregnancy is going to make me insane again, will it not?"

Darcy smiled and kissed her hand. "No, dearest. We have a surprise for you, although we wanted to share it with you for Christmas since the paperwork had not been finalised yet. You know that Richard purchased Kellynch Hall for Michael. Well, after much consideration, we knew that you would want to see your family again but Netherfield would no longer be an option, even when the reconstruction completed, so I worked with Richard to purchase Westwood Manor for you. It would be yet another household for you to manage but one in Hertfordshire that we can visit and stay whenever we travel to London."

"But how?! How can we afford so much? I cannot comprehend how much Westwood Manor must have cost! And Kellynch as well! Are we that wealthy, Fitzwilliam?" Elizabeth was shocked.

"My dear, with Richard's and my income together, your two husbands are possibly the top fifty wealthiest men of England. We have worked hard these past three years to increase our income as well as make sound investments. You have over £120,000, with interest growing since you refuse to spend any of your money except for your charities, which is performing amazingly, by the way, and our annual income is at £70,000. On top of that, we had £160,000 from our investments which we used 75,000 for Kellynch Hall, which now brings in 6,000 a year, and another 60,000 for Westwood Manor, which brings 5,000 a year. When we take all of our savings into account, the three of us put together have over £750,000 to our names." Seeing the shocked look on her face, Darcy drew her into her arms.

"My love, do you recall before I asked you to marry me that you were shocked about my 45,000 a year and I told you I would give up everything for you?" She nodded with tears in her eyes. "I meant it then and I mean it now. Richard has already done so to give you everything he owns to you and our family. If you do not desire it, if you would rather have a poor husband who will work the earth with his own hands, I would give all of this up in a heartbeat if it meant being with you. I know Richard feels the same. You do not care about our wealth or rank but you love me for the man that I am; you love Richard for the man that he has become. Our family, our love, is truly blessed and you, my dearest Elizabeth, are worthy of our love. Life with you has opened so many possibilities and because of my one good decision to ask you for your hand, we are where we are now. We have been given much and we have done much good with it. Truly, I thank God for you every day that you forgave my slight when I called you 'tolerable' at that assembly that fateful evening in Meryton." He kissed her tenderly and wiped her tears with his handkerchief.

"I love you, Fitzwilliam. I have been in love with you since the first day I met you. You captured my heart and I was yours from the first moment our eyes met. Thank you for loving me with all of yourself." Elizabeth smiled with tears in her eyes and softly kissed him again.

Richard smiled when she turned to him. "My life was forever changed when this rogue introduced me to the most beautiful and bright woman of my acquaintance. I know that I am not married to you and I am here as in interloper between you and Darcy's marriage," she opened her mouth to argue but he placed his thumb on her soft lips, "but that you have both accepted me as a full partner into your life, being your other husband, being a brother, a father to our children, and possibly my own," he touched her abdomen, "has brought me more joy and fulfilment than I had ever expected or hoped. You have given me a gift and I would be a fool to refuse it. We do have an unconventional relationship. We have a unique love that outsiders would not understand; but we have the deepest of friendships and respect with each other that others certainly recognise as something special and untouchable. I love you with all my soul and I promise to spend the rest of my life showing you every day how much you mean to me." He released her lips and kissed them.

"I love you, Richard. Your love for me overwhelmed me and I knew I had loved you, I thought as a brother or a cousin, but I was bound to fall in love with you. It would have been an impossible task to not return your love when you loved me so fiercely. That you are truly committed to me makes you my husband and my love for you makes me your wife. Thank you for giving your best to me always and thank you for honouring my vows to Fitzwilliam. I know life without you would not be the same and your love has brought us the utmost joy and contentment ever imaginable. We three are truly blessed and I am most pleased to have your children and live out the rest of my life with both of you at my sides." Elizabeth kissed Richard tenderly.

The men both wiped their eyes quickly and coughed. "Well, ahem, you will always have our love, dearest wife." Darcy spoke as he tenderly kissed her hand. "Oh, Richard, by the by, there was a letter that arrived while you were gone. I believe it was from Captain Saunders." Darcy pointed to the desk.

Richard thanked him and walked over to browse at the letter but gasped as he read the contents and plopped heavily on the chair to continue reading. He gasped again and let out, "Shit!"

Darcy and Elizabeth rushed over to his side in concern.

"I have disturbing news." Richard began. "Saunders wrote this three days ago and explains that Lieutenant Anderson escaped from Newgate Prison last week. Apparently, the idiot has not learned his lessons and the first thing he did after his escape was to visit Saunders and O'Shea to condemn them for their betrayal that led to his court-martial, and he has vowed to take his revenge on me for ruining his career and for breaking his hand. He quickly left and is in hiding."

He stood and paced while Darcy was overlooking the letter now. "I promise he will not near us. But, Elizabeth, he has also sworn to have you. Saunders says that Anderson believes that if you had agreed to lay with him, he would not have been jailed. I swear to you, I will not let him hurt you." He held her tightly.

Elizabeth was very afraid of the threat. Darcy had rushed over and held her as well, caressing her hand and kissing her temple to soothe her. She sat quietly, contemplating what could be done. Now that she was with child again, she knew she could not run fast or fight off a large man like Lieutenant Anderson. She knew her husbands would guard her with their lives but she did not want to sit quietly and await her fate.

She took a deep breath. "I know you will guard and protect me. What can we do to find out where he is? I wish to learn to defend myself as well. I am with child but I will not be left vulnerable. Will you teach me how to shoot? Will you teach me how to fight?"

Darcy spoke first. "I will send an express to both Mr. O'Connor and his brother to investigate. He has the best men to locate this villain and we will have him sent off to the colonies or hung, if he tries anything. He will not get close enough to do anything to you, Elizabeth. I swear my life on it. I will not risk any injury to you. We must find out if he is in London or if he is in Derbyshire but we will protect you at all times. I will hire more men to guard all of us."

Richard also chimed in. "I will have Saunders and O'Shea monitor him also. Saunders has spread the word to have anyone that Anderson approaches will keep him informed of his movements. He has few friends and he is poor. I doubt he will have the resources to last long." He caressed Elizabeth's cheek. "I will teach you how to shoot a rifle and a pistol. I will never leave you defenceless." He kissed her hand several times.

Darcy kissed her other hand. "And I will teach you how to fence. Whether a sword or a dagger, you will learn how to use it to be able to defend yourself. I never believed fine ladies should only sit defencelessly, and you already know how to use your knee. I taught Georgiana how to fence a little and I will certainly teach you. You must promise to not overwork, though, my love. We will care for you while you care for our babe."

Elizabeth smiled for the first time in the past quarter hour. "Thank you, my dear husbands. I will trust that we will do everything in our power to catch this mad man and I know we cannot live in fear. We will do what is within our control and hire the best to take care of the rest. Thank you for your willingness to teach me. Even if I never shoot or stab anything, I would feel more comforted, knowing that I have done what I could to protect myself."

She stood tall and proud. "Well, I believe we all have several tasks at hand. I will need to write some letters as well. I love you, Fitzwilliam. I love you, Richard."

She walked to her desk where she began to write several letters.

The men looked at each other and smiled. They were pleased with Elizabeth's courage, and although extremely concerned for her safety, they knew they would do all in their power to make sure this insane man would be brought to justice.

Chapter 32

"Oh, Jane, he is beautiful!" Elizabeth gleamed. "His hair is so red! Betty is fair just like you and he is the spitting image of his father!"

"Oh, Lizzy, I have not known such happiness. With Betty, I was so new to the married life and did not know what I was doing, but William is so precious to me. Mama says it is because he is the heir but I care not for that. He is precious because he is a reminder of the renewed love between Charles and me. We named him William in honour of both Darcy and Mr. Fitzwilliam, as they both have 'William' in their names, since they were so vital to knocking some sense into us. Bingley told me about the letters and talks between both your husband and cousin and we are eternally grateful that they were so kind to us even after all of the mess we made. Charles is working hard now and although our home will be completed soon, we are content with our smaller home and our station.

"Charles promised me plenty of parties and Balls to be had and I am satisfied, more than satisfied, but rather grateful for my lot in life to have a husband who dearly loves me, to whom I return his love with our two beautiful babies to raise. We are not poor and Charles is working to increase our income. Uncle Gardiner has been instrumental in finding new opportunities and I have never seen my husband so dedicated to support his family. He has been loving to me and although it will be a few more weeks until we can be intimate again, he has been kind and has not mentioned any frustrations. We talk about everything and I owe it to you, sister, to knock me off my pedestal as well." Jane wiped her tears.

She continued, "I was so wrong. I was vain and proud, growing up hearing from mama that I was the most beautiful and the most deserving, but to hear of other women's achievements and to come to realise that I could not hold a candle to them, but recognising that my husband loved me above all and chose me to marry me those years ago, it brought me back down to earth and I begged him for forgiveness. I beg your forgiveness as well, Lizzy. I always thought I was the better of the sisters and I was conceited to believe that whenever you showed up with Darcy and Mr. Fitzwilliam on your arms, I deserved what you had. But then when I was in London, I heard Lady Matlock's praise of you and every one of the ladies in attendance had nothing but praise for you. I do not know how you were able to have three children, now carrying your fourth, to manage the number of estates that you own and still work on your Foundation, at the same time to keep your husband contented. I am in awe of what you have done and what you were able to accomplish within a few years of your marriage. With Wickham's attack and Georgiana getting married and then having to support Mr. Fitzwilliam through two terrible court cases, I could not fill even a fraction of your shoes. You are truly a wonder, Lizzy, and I am so proud to be your sister!" She cried.

"Thank you, Jane. Your praise is not necessary but I appreciate your kind words." Elizabeth replied. "I am very happy to see you reconciled with Charles and it is obvious that he is once again deeply in love with you. You will be happy together as long as you remember it and never stop giving your best. I love you, dear sister. You must rest now. I see that William is hungry. I shall leave you to care for him and will see you for dinner at Westwood Manor tomorrow."

~*~

After farewelling, she returned downstairs to the library where the men were gathered. She stood by the door when she heard her name. Not meaning to eavesdrop, she was curious as to why she was the topic of conversation.

"Elizabeth would have burned you alive, Bingley!" Darcy laughed.

"That is what Fitzwilliam said! She was and still is completely out of my league. I cannot believe it! She turned down an earl and a son of a duke? Well, I am certainly happy with my Jane now. Though not always, she is perfect for me now. Thank you, gentlemen, for pushing me to be a better man. My son is the direct result of your help and I will continue to work hard for my family. I am amazed at how much you have been able to accomplish between the two of you but I am certain Lizzy gives you a good kick on your arse should you misbehave, Darcy, and you, too, Fitzwilliam. I cannot imagine your cousin allowing you to be a slacker and will probably kick your arse as well!" They all laughed loudly.

Richard replied, still chuckling. "So true, so true. Elizabeth will never tolerate indolence. She is such a lady."

"My wife is the best, as all wives should be to their husbands, Bingley. Elizabeth was not meant for you but I have a feeling she would have moulded anyone into her ideal eventually. I am the fortunate soul that married her and Richard, here, has to suffer along, being our guardian and godfather to our children, and I could not have asked for a better life." Darcy smiled. *I miss her. I hope she will be here soon.*

Then Elizabeth knocked and was bid to enter. "Gentlemen, have you been having a good time? Jane is resting and I believe we should return." She rubbed her tummy as she turned her face away from Bingley. "I need some rest as well. I am craving something meaty and savoury right now, and I have just the thing I want to taste." She subtly smirked then returned to her sister's husband. "It was nice to see you, Charles," she kissed his cheek, "Love your wife and be kind to her. See you tomorrow."

Richard and Darcy both gulped at her innuendo. She had been insatiable once again but this time surpassed the other two pregnancies. She had no morning sickness and while the men had pleasured her up to five or six times in one day before, with this pregnancy, there was no stopping her. Yesterday, she had reached nine times and was begging for more this morning.

Darcy hurriedly shook Bingley's hand while Richard called for the carriage and they said their goodbyes quickly.

~*~

The Darcys and Richard had determined to proceed with their life as usual, even with Anderson's threat of revenge, after discussing options. One option had been to remove to Scotland for a period of time but Elizabeth was resolute that the criminal would not put more fear or upheave their lives further and they had arrived in Hertfordshire last week.

Letters to both Mr. O'Connors were sent and no expense was too great to track down Anderson. Men were hired to find out everything about him and everyone connected to his past. It was found that he had a string of debts and Richard purchased all of them to use against him for debtor's prison if needed.

Elizabeth had taken well to learning how to shoot a rifle as well as a pistol from her excellent teacher, and although somewhat uncomfortable in the beginning, she had managed to learn how to use a small knife that Darcy commissioned for her. It was a small dagger with several precious jewels on the handle, and although her safety was of the utmost importance, he wanted her to have something beautiful that she would love. She found a way to carry it on her leg under her dress using a garter belt and she often joked that anyone looking to find a surprise under her skirts would surely find one.

They pledged to live their lives without fear and continued to make plans to visit family and friends, even if they were traveling with a larger entourage now.

~*~

"Is it possible to die from having too much sex?" Richard asked Darcy as they took their lately regular nightcaps and rubbed the cold glass against their groins.

"I think not. If it were the case, Elizabeth would have died after the tenth time. She climaxed over twenty times today, I believe. She is unstoppable and we are in trouble. It is only the first of April and she is not due until late July. I do not know what would have happened if you were not here, Richard." Darcy laughed. "It is a pleasure to pleasure her, though."

"I agree. I thought she was slowing down last weeks with Lydia's wedding preparations but she still demanded us to attend to her and today has been the most times ever. How she has the energy to take us both on for so long, I do not understand, but I cannot complain. I am so sore, though. I want to dip my cock in this brandy to numb it." Richard snorted in amusement.

406

"Well, she might slow down once we are in London next week. A month there and we will be home once again. Are you certain you wish to go to Rosings by yourself? Elizabeth will despise the separation. Last time you were away for nine days, we were both miserable and you were absolutely despondent when we reunited." Darcy asked.

"It would not be for nine days. The inn there is small and cannot accommodate all of us but it will only be two nights. I do wish you could come with me to look over the paperwork but I dare not leave her alone with Anderson still loose. Father understands that Elizabeth is with child and does not expect her to travel, but he does ask you to part with your wife for two days for the funeral." Richard answered.

Darcy rubbed his face with both hands. "I have never been away from Elizabeth since our marriage. I know it is a rarity but I cannot be away from her for even for that long, especially now. I know she will be safe here with her family and the bodyguards but we should ask Elizabeth. She will most likely want to come with us. Perhaps I can ask Georgiana to watch the boys. Georgiana will be thrilled to mind them for two nights with their nannies and perhaps you can ask the Crofts to house your parents as well as the three of us. What do you think? Should we tell them about Anderson?"

Richard smiled. "Yes. That is a great suggestion. The boys will be safe with the Chatsworths and she will be with us. Once the Crofts hear of our situation with Anderson, I am certain they will not mind, even if I had not wished to be an overbearing landowner to them. The Crofts are very kind and the Admiral might have ideas to help us as well. Rosings is much more comfortable than the inn and it is an excellent idea, Darcy."

Elizabeth was distraught to hear that Richard had to go away for two days then she paled at the thought of Darcy attending with Richard. Her eyes watered up and the men were afraid of sudden flooding but Richard quickly added that they could all stay at Rosings and Darcy suggested asking Georgiana to watch the children for the short duration. She finally smiled and agreed that it was the best option, and that since Georgiana had been begging for more time with the little ones, it was a great resolution all around. The gentlemen were relieved that a potential disaster had been avoided.

~*~

It was April and the Season was in full swing. Georgiana and her husband, Lord Andrew, were pleased to care for the baby and the toddlers, as they just had their own in December and had travelled to London for the Season to show off their offspring.

The Crofts were more than happy to host the Fitzwilliam family for two nights to intern Lady Catherine to her last resting place next to her daughter Anne de Bourgh.

As they gathered at the church, several neighbours attended the service and Richard and Darcy recognised many of them from the Winter Ball. They were very caring and the service was over soon and the ladies prepared to depart before the gentlemen continued with the burial.

Elizabeth stood with Darcy while Richard was finalising the arrangements with Reverend Brown for the next steps, and she saw a face that she had only seen once before. She softly gasped and Darcy heard it but before he could find out the reason, Mrs. Croft, who had been speaking with them, called out. "Mrs. Johnston! How nice to see you. Allow me to introduce you to Mr. and Mrs. Darcy; this is Mrs. Abigail Johnston. She has been instrumental in improving our orphanage in Kent and has worked hard to help educate them."

The women curtsied to each other, unable to speak a word.

Darcy bowed, "Pleasure to meet you, Mrs. Johnston. Are you from these parts? I recall a Mr. Johnston but he was widowered several years ago."

"Oh, yes; no, I am not from here but I have resided here for about three years. I met Mr. Johnston and we married two years ago." She responded, unable to meet Mrs. Darcy's eyes.

Just then, Mrs. Croft was called away and the three stood awkwardly for several seconds when Richard approached with fire in his eyes. His face was red and Elizabeth could tell that he was extremely angry.

Before he could say a word, she touched his arm and shook her head gently, capturing his eyes. Turning back to Richard's former mistress, she spoke, "Mrs. Johnston, it is nice to meet you. I am very pleased to hear of your work and appreciate anyone who looks out for the interest of those in need. I applaud you and encourage you to continue your efforts. If you should ever require additional support, here is my card. It has my information for the Darcy Fitzwilliam Foundation and the secretary there will be happy to arrange a time for you to meet our board for any assistance. It was a pleasure meeting you. Good day, Mrs. Johnston."

"Thank you, Mrs. Darcy." Abigail smiled in gratitude. *She is every bit fearsome as I expected. Magnificent! She has her husband's and Mr. Fitzwilliam's love completely and I fully understand why!* Curtseying at all three briefly, she took her leave and returned to her husband.

"Do not speak, Richard. We have a long day ahead of us still and I know you are angry but you do not need to be. I am not injured and I know you love me. Please, be calm, Richard. Mrs. Croft introduced us and we could not avoid it." Seeing that he was beginning to relax, she whispered, "I love you, blemish and all."

Richard's heart fluttered. *How is it possible that after all this time, all these years of loving her, my heart grows to love her even more?* He smiled softly and whispered, "You are my world, Elizabeth. I love you."

Darcy whispered, "THAT was Abigail? THE Abigail? Good Lord, Elizabeth, you handled yourself most nobly. I cannot believe that you actually gave her your card. What made you decide to do that?"

"She once comforted Richard and I cannot begrudge her for it. She is doing something good with her life now and we must encourage such goodness. She has changed her life around and is not who she used to be," turning to Richard she continued, "just like you are not who you used to be. Your past does not lessen your love for me and I am content." Elizabeth finished, as she gazed into Richard's eyes with a soft smile.

"Darcy, I would like your permission to purchase a new carriage for her, perhaps five dozen new dresses? I never thought it possible to love her more but my heart continues to grow for her." Richard spoke to Darcy without leaving Elizabeth's eyes.

Darcy laughed quietly. "I feel the same every day. Perhaps a small piece of jewellery? Your last carriage is still new. Our Elizabeth cares little for material objects."

Elizabeth giggled softly. "I have everything I need in my arms."

Both gentlemen gleamed as she held each of their arms.

"You are the best thing in my life, Elizabeth." Richard lovingly whispered. "Thank you for marrying her, Darcy."

~*~

Their time in London was short but sweet. Richard did present Elizabeth with a beautiful row of diamond bracelet and made love to her for a full hour.

Darcy did not want to be outdone so he presented a bracelet of emeralds that could be worn as a set and loved her for a full hour.

As Elizabeth was wrapped between the two men she loved, she looked at her rings and her bracelets and smiled. "I love you, husbands." She whispered, before falling asleep peacefully in their arms.

Chapter 33

"He has been spotted!" Richard exclaimed, after he read an express from Mr. O'Connor in London.

They were in Pemberley now and Elizabeth had become quite round. She had another two months to go but instead of just sitting and embroidering for the child's dresses, she continued to practice her shooting and sword skills. Darcy and Richard were both immensely proud of her but worried constantly that she might be pushing herself too much. All of their walks or rides were fiercely guarded and all they could do was to wish for the nightmare to be over.

Richard shared his letter with Darcy and Elizabeth. "Mr. O'Connor writes that one of his men finally tracked him down to Cheapside and he was seen leaving a pub after wenching. Apparently, he had enough funds to use a prostitute for an hour and buy several rounds of drinks for some customers. He was followed to a small lodging where he was using the name 'Richard Williams' and had enough money to pay for a full month. No wonder we were unable to locate him for so long!" He whistled. "Mr. O'Connor worked with Mr. Reitling again to trace out where his funds came from, and what is this?! He has been using Caroline Bingley's money! That harridan had set up funds to hire him to take her vengeance on us as well and she gave him £500 to seek his revenge. I do not know how she managed it, but *she* is responsible for keeping Anderson so well-hidden. I am going to KILL that blasted woman with my bare hands!" Richard yelled, as he threw down the letter in anger.

Darcy continued reading to Elizabeth. "O'Connor's man made more discreet inquiries and although he fled his last lodgings, he appears to be still in London. He is working with Uncle Edward to see if they can find him again and he is confident that he will be spotted again soon. You were right, Elizabeth," Darcy looked at his wife, "Uncle Edward has had his network out and I am glad you had him work with O'Connor. Uncle's people had spotted him and alerted O'Connor right away. It is only a matter of time until he is discovered again. He will become more desperate, now that he knows he is being tracked. Anderson might be able to hide for a while with the funds that Caroline Bingley provided, but we will get him, my love."

Richard was still fuming, though. "I am going to write to Bingley and let him know that I might murder his damn sister if I ever get my hands on her. We need him to close this account of hers so that Anderson does not receive another farthing. She still has at least £5,000 left from her dowry and I do not know how she got that far, but she must be stopped. I will get Reitling to find out how she was able to coordinate this from Australia. That vicious woman will be stopped. I am going to strangle her."

Elizabeth rose and walked to Richard where he was pacing in front of the fireplace. She laid her hand on his arm and waited until he looked into her eyes. "Thank you for being my vigilant protector. Remember, he has vowed to hurt you first. Please promise me that you will take care of yourself, Richard." She caressed his cheek.

He finally smiled, seeing the concern in her eyes. "Of course, my love. I wish to spend many more years with you and I promise not to do anything rash to get myself in prison, either." He winked. "I know Darcy would love having you all for himself but I certainly wish to see our children grow and to grow old with you." He kissed her tenderly.

Darcy laughed and approached them. "After all this time, Richard, if I am not tired of you by now, I think I can keep you around for a few more decades. You are vital to the Darcys and you are one of us. I could not have shared my Elizabeth with anyone less worthy."

Elizabeth embraced both men closely and kissed them both on the lips. "Make love to me right now, husbands. I need your comforts desperately."

Her husbands obeyed instantly and after locking the study door, the trio passionately loved each other.

~*~

July arrived quicker than expected. Elizabeth had arranged for the Gardiners, Mr. and Mrs. Bennet, and Jane and Bingley to attend her during her confinement and although initially hesitant, Richard could deny her nothing and agreed to be cordial with Jane Bingley but maintained his distance more than ever.

The group enjoyed a picnic on the lawns while watching Samuel, Bennet, Richie, and Betty run around and play with the Gardiner children, and Michael and William were sitting under a large tree, gurgling and laughing at their papas making funny faces.

Elizabeth sat next to Richard and they were watching the scene. They were on a bench with a large trunk behind them to lean on. Their hands were on the bench, fingers grazing each other discreetly as they relaxed in the warm breeze.

Elizabeth wore a large sapphire ring that Richard had given her after it was found that Lady Catherine had one redeeming quality and that was her choice in jewels. A large strongbox of heirloom jewellery was discovered after her death and Richard reset more of the gaudy pieces to Elizabeth's tastes and gifted her majority of the most expensive diamonds, emeralds, rubies, opals, amethysts, and pearls to her, including this sapphire set of 10-carat ring, the matching 40-carat necklace, and the 20-carat bracelet. Richard was immensely proud that he finally had family jewels that he could gift to her and insisted on her having the best sets. He gave the remaining few pieces to Georgiana, his mother, and his sister.

Richard whispered, "I love you, Elizabeth," without looking at her direction.

Elizabeth replied, "I love you, Richard."

They looked at each other and laughed. Suddenly there was a flood of water on the bench and Elizabeth groaned.

Richard caressed her cheek, "It is time, love." Turning to Darcy's direction, he yelled out, "Darcy! It is time!"

Darcy immediately jumped up and ran towards Elizabeth and smiled. "Today is a good day, my love," then he carried her inside. Knowing that she was due any time, they had remained close in the backyard. The rest of the adults smiled, as they knew a new Darcy would be born today.

Richard picked up Michael and carried him. He called out, "Bennet, Richie, time to go!"

Bennet and Richie dropped their toys and followed, calling out, "G-O, go! GaPapa, GaPapa!" and ran after him in laughter.

Jane Bingley watched in fascination as Richard Fitzwilliam cared for the three boys as if his own and helped the twins up the stairs one step at a time to lead them back to the nursery. *He would have been the most wonderful father.* She paused. *But he **is** their father. He is godfather to all of the Darcy children and is a part of their family. How blessed Lizzy is to have so much love around her.*

She was no longer jealous. She could not shake her attraction to Mr. Fitzwilliam but knew nothing would ever come of it and did not pursue any attention from him. She turned to Betty and William and joined Charles in playing with their precious children.

The rest of the family spent the rest of the luncheon knowing that it would take hours, slowly gathered their belongings to await news, with only Aunt Gardiner following after Elizabeth after giving instructions to Mr. Gardiner on what to do with their children.

~*~

Aunt Gardiner entered the drawing room where Mr. and Mrs. Bennet, Charles and Jane, whom Elizabeth had made her promise to keep their mother away from her during the birthing process, as well as Mr. Gardiner were awaiting word.

"Mother and baby are well. We have a new Darcy in our family: Amelia Anne Darcy. She is beautiful with dark curls and green eyes just like her mother. And Lizzy insisted that we enjoy our dinner and apologised that Darcy and Mr. Fitzwilliam will not be able to join us." Aunt Gardiner beamed.

Bingley asked, "Where is Fitz? I expected him to pace around here and be grumpy."

Aunt Gardiner smiled. "He remained upstairs near his rooms, I believe, and Darcy was giving him updates. He is fiercely protective of our Lizzy, as you know. Darcy laughed that even though he could not be in the birthing room, his cousin could not be further away than the shared sitting room." They laughed.

Aunt Gardiner suspected that Richard Fitzwilliam was desperately in love with Lizzy by the way he looked at her and smiled at her when speaking with her. He had no eyes for anyone but Lizzy. If her niece was not already married, she suspected that Mr. Fitzwilliam would have begged for her hand a thousand times until she accepted him.

But he and Darcy were very close and it was evident that Mr. Fitzwilliam had great honour and respect for his cousins. Even if his words and care were more like a husband than a cousin to Elizabeth, nothing that he did was ever improper and Darcy was always with them. *I believe he must have been in love with her all these years. Only Lizzy could garner the attentions of two such suitors. Darcy is so deeply in love with his wife and Mr. Fitzwilliam would die to protect them. How blessed she is.*

~*~

Richard had been literally sitting by the door, hearing every scream and complaint and words of love. Elizabeth would yell through the door asking if he was there several times and he would always reply, "I am here, Elizabeth."

When he heard the soft cries of a baby, he knew it sounded different. Within several seconds, Darcy popped his head out, "It is a girl, Richard. A daughter. She is beautiful. Elizabeth is well and is smiling right now." And he popped back in.

Richard buried his face in his hands and cried. He pulled out his handkerchief, this time embroidered with tiny baby's breath flowers, and wiped his face.

My daughter. She had our daughter.

He knew this was his child. Darcy had given three sons to her and after their efforts to impregnate Elizabeth with his seed, he just knew this was his own flesh and blood. It had been unfathomable at one time, that he would be living with Elizabeth and loving her every day, but to have his own child with her was a blessing that he would treasure forever. But it mattered not. He would love every child that came from the love of his life.

After the room was tidied and the midwife and Mrs. Gardiner left, Richard entered with tears in his eyes.

"Elizabeth," he whispered. This was the third time seeing her after her deliveries and he could swear she was more beautiful after each time. He crawled into bed with the Darcys and laid his eyes on the most beautiful baby girl, in the image of her beautiful mother and cried. "She is beautiful. Our Amelia Anne. Thank you, Elizabeth. Thank you, Darcy. She is ours, she is truly ours together and I love her so deeply. I love Bennet and Richie and Michael with all my heart, but our first girl, she is truly special."

"You are most welcome, brother," Darcy replied. "Thank you, too, Richard. We are truly a happy family."

Elizabeth kissed his cheek as he held Amelia in his arms. "I love you, Richard. I could not have imagined a happier family together."

Chapter 34

It was over. The nightmare was finally over.

Elizabeth's hand shook as she bent over and gently placed the pistol on the ground. Smoke was still coming out of the tip and she did not know if she would go to jail now or what her punishment would be, but she had just killed Mr. Anderson and she had no regrets.

It had been seven months since anyone had any news of Anderson and his whereabouts, when the Darcys and Richard had decided to spend Christmas and New Year with the Bennets and their extended family, as well as the Gardiners, the Matlocks, and Georgiana and Andrew Chatsworth. Elizabeth was hosting everyone at Westwood Manor and planned to have a grand celebration with all of the family members.

Elizabeth was still uncomfortable with having an entourage of bodyguards around her when she made her visits to her sisters' homes but she understood why Darcy and Richard were adamant that she be protected at all times. She had complained time and time again that she did not need all three guards to follow her everywhere but her husbands would not relent.

Richard was escorting her this time, as the gentlemen took turns to keep her company when she made her visits, and they had just finished seeing Lydia and her screaming child.

Richard commented to Elizabeth in the carriage, "I know you found the situation amusing but I do not know how in the world you were able to listen to that baby cry for so long. None of our children were like that, you know. Michael might have been a bit louder than the others but Amelia is certainly an angel compared to that demon child!"

Elizabeth laughed loudly at this. "Your daughter is nothing like baby Kitty. Lydia was told by my mother, MY MOTHER, of all people, that babies should not be spoiled by being carried so much. My mother does nothing but dote on Sammy and she gives such terrible advice to Lydia. I did not wish to overstep my authority by picking her up but I am glad you did. Kitty took to you right away and she was cooing and smiling at you. I think you have yet another admirer, Richard." She kissed his knuckles.

"Well, it was either picking up the baby to try to soothe her or throwing her out the window. That baby girl is innocent so I could not do that to her. I am glad I have not lost my touch. I know babies love me." Richard smirked.

"You are such a good father. I know Lydia watched you in wonder. I do not believe Lieutenant Denny ever carried that child before but you rocked her and calmed her and she fell asleep soon after." Elizabeth beamed.

"I did have a lot of practice. I love our babies, Elizabeth, and I will love any future ones. I am glad you are not with child right now, my love. Your body still needs to rest." Richard caressed his wife's hand.

Elizabeth laughed loudly. "I know I scared you when we awoke this morning with blood on the sheets. My courses have been so irregular for several months; I had not expected it so suddenly. I do apologise for the mess."

Richard laughed with her. "As long as you are not dying, I am fine with blood. You are usually better-padded when you are near your monthlies and I was just caught off-guard today. I still love having you in my bed, Elizabeth. I cherish every moment with you, whether we are making love or just sleeping. Darcy panics more than me so it was a good thing he was already out of bed. He gets so worried for your comfort. He had to attend to business with several tenants early since I won my bet, although considering this morning's event, I might have lost!" They both burst out laughing.

"And what have you been betting on, sir? I know men bet on ridiculous things and I am glad you only play with Fitzwilliam. I have heard of men losing a fortune by betting on horse-races to rainy days and it always amazes me how nonsensical this world can be." Elizabeth commented.

Richard grinned. "And that is why I love you; you have common sense and beauty. Our bets are only for fun, you know. I bet Darcy that Bingley gets to bed your sister twice a week and he said three. We confirmed it with Bingley and I was correct." He sneered.

"Oh, my! Do men really talk of those things? Do you and..." Elizabeth was shocked.

Richard chuckled loudly. "Yes, men talk of their 'conquests' all the time, but no, Darcy does not brag of his times with you, even if it is two or three times a day at times." He laughed loudly seeing her blush. "I did have to offer up to Bingley that I have a hand or two to help me out a few times a week. If only he knew how good your hands are at relieving me two, three times a day... You got me excited again, Elizabeth." Richard whispered as he grabbed her hand and began to rub his arousal with it.

Elizabeth leaned in and they began to kiss passionately when the coach suddenly stopped unexpectedly.

Opening the curtains and seeing that they were still only half way to Westwood Manor, Richard immediately reached for his pistol and walking stick.

Elizabeth had gifted both men with a special walking stick, Richard's, decorated with an exquisite lion's head on the handle, while Darcy's had a fearsome dragon. The stick was actually a hidden sword inside the sheath that was sharpened to penetrate human flesh with ease. Her husbands had loved it and admired the workmanship so much that they had commissioned a few more, for their own use as well as special gifts.

Richard took a deep breath and handed Elizabeth her small pistol. He did not like her carrying it on her person but had kept it with his pistol in the carriage.

"You have your dagger?" Richard whispered. She nodded. "I hope it is nothing but I will check. Please stay in here and keep quiet until I return." He commanded as he kissed her quickly on her lips.

Richard opened the door and asked the driver what was happening.

"The path is blocked, sir. There is a fallen trunk in the way and I have four of our men removing it right now. There is nothing else here so it must have been just an accident." Mr. Woods, the driver, answered.

Richard had a bad feeling. The roads were maintained well and there was no reason for the tree trunk to be in the middle of the road now, when it was not there before.

He stepped outside to assess the situation and gave a signal to one of the bodyguards, Mr. Wesson, to ride to Westwood Manor for more men. He knew something was not right.

The second of the bodyguards, Mr. Smith, was helping with the tree trunk while the last bodyguard, the older brother of Mr. Smith, patrolled the area, circling the carriage to see if anything was amiss, when four men suddenly jumped from behind the bushes and trees and struck all four of his men on the head with wooden bats, knocking them unconscious. The elder Mr. Smith was able to shoot one of them down and Richard shot down another. As they were reloading their pistols, the driver fired on one of two remaining attackers but received a bullet in the shoulder and the bodyguard was now on foot, fighting off the remaining offender who had fired on Mr. Woods.

Elizabeth heard the shots and was fearful but continued to wait quietly for several minutes. She opened the curtain to see that Richard was checking on the unconscious men, and Mr. Smith, the only bodyguard standing, was tying up a smaller man, who was unconscious after receiving a beating from the very large guard. She could not see anyone else and heard the driver above telling Richard that the bullet only grazed him.

She opened the door to be of assistance to Mr. Woods when Richard turned around and their eyes met. Richard smiled, believing that the situation was under control, when Anderson unexpectedly leaped out from a tree trunk behind him and grabbed him by the neck.

414

"Fitz! I finally have you where I want you, you arsehole! I am going to enjoy killing you slowly. Ah! Mrs. Darcy! Come join us. I have been waiting for you for nearly a year to get my revenge on you and I will finally have it today." Anderson taunted.

Elizabeth saw that Anderson was holding a knife at Richard's neck with his left hand. Richard was taller and Anderson could not quite get his right arm around Richard, but the knife was already puncturing the skin and she could see a small amount of blood soaking through his white cravat.

Richard still had his pistol in his hand but appeared fearful for Elizabeth. She saw the concern in his eyes for her safety and she wondered where Mr. Smith was.

She took a deep breath. She knew she needed to save Richard above anything else and tried to think of what Anderson wanted.

Anderson then commanded Richard to drop the pistol and Richard obeyed. "I cannot fire a pistol, you bastard. My hand is lame and I am going to make you suffer for it. I know how loyal you are to Mrs. Darcy and you can watch me fuck her and you will be helpless to do anything about it, you prick!" he taunted.

Elizabeth spoke smoothly. "Mr. Anderson, how nice to see you again. Although I wish it were under different circumstances, I am actually relieved that you have finally appeared before us. All of the months of waiting were driving me *absolutely* insane." She flashed a large smile while she hid her right hand behind her skirt. She was still holding on to her small pistol that Richard had custom-made for her feminine hand.

"Ah, you are a delight. I have been watching you and learning of your moves for several months and finally learned of your travel to Hertfordshire. Miss Caroline Bingley sends her greetings, by the by. She wished you dead as soon as possible but since she is not here to chastise me, I delayed it this long so I can get some good use out of you. I waited for you to have that child of yours so I can get my seed in you and make you my whore for a few days until I get sick of you and kill you for my reward. If you are really good to me, I might keep you alive if your husband pays double what Caro is supposed to pay. You are delicious when you are with child with your huge teats and I would love to get you with my babe inside you. You should have let me fill you that night, Mrs. Darcy. You would have enjoyed it and begged for more. All this could have been avoided if this son of a bitch had not interrupted me. I do love taking the pregnant ones but I enjoy filling them up with my bastards even more. You are so delectable, I cannot wait until I get my cock inside you and I love the ones that fight back. The more you resist, the more I am going to hurt you." Anderson continued to goad.

Richard was fuming and was ready to murder this man but he could not think of a way to get his knife away from his neck. He felt no pain due to his rage but he knew he was beginning to drip more blood from his neck where the tip of the knife was digging in. He also knew Elizabeth was still holding her pistol behind her skirts and he was able to see that Mr. Smith was hiding behind the carriage, waiting for the vantage shot. They were both waiting for him to move out of the way. He held his walking stick in his left hand still and Anderson was too busy chatting with Elizabeth to notice it.

Elizabeth knew Anderson's focus was on her and she was the only one who could divert his attention enough for Richard to get away. She knew what needed to be done when she saw a small boulder next to her on the ground.

"Mr. Anderson, I am certain you are quite anxious to have your way with me soon, but I do have a request." She stepped towards the rock slowly and placed her right foot on it. As she lifted her skirt slowly with her left hand, she spoke seductively, "Would you be willing to tell me what you think of this?" She continued to lift up her skirt slowly until it was up to her knee.

She could see that Anderson was definitely distracted and met Richard's eye. Richard had a small smirk and knew what she was doing. She continued to pull up her dress higher up to her thigh to show him her leg that held the shiny, bejewelled dagger.

Richard felt Anderson's grip loosen and the knife drop from his neck. He lifted his walking stick and pushed Anderson away with the tip as hard as possible as he dove down to the ground and yelled, "NOW!"

Two shots were heard. Richard turned himself and landed on his back and drew the sword from the walking stick, ready to fight, and saw the criminal fall. He stood up and watched Anderson gasping for air flat on his back, with blood beginning to pool on his shirt on his torso and right arm. From the angle, he knew Mr. Smith had shot Anderson on the arm. *Elizabeth saved me. She shot this arse in the stomach and it was a perfect shot. I owe her my life!*

Richard walked over to Elizabeth and embraced her tightly. She was beginning to shake and soon, cried softly.

"Smith! Check to see if that bastard is still alive. I will take Mrs. Darcy into the carriage." Richard commanded. "We will need to tend to Mr. Woods as well. I will return in a moment." He pocketed Elizabeth's pistol and lifted Elizabeth and carried her to the carriage. He closed the door quickly and kissed her deeply. He kissed her lips and neck repeatedly and whispered quietly, "It is over. You saved my life, Elizabeth. It is all over and I owe you my life. I love you so much. I love you, Elizabeth. Everything will be well."

Elizabeth hiccupped but calmed quickly with his affections. "I love you. I was so afraid for you, Richard, and I am so glad you are well. I love you." She repeated. "Oh, Richard! Your neck!" She pulled out her handkerchief and pressed it on his neck where the knife had cut him. Her tears were pouring down in concern but she kissed his jaw and ordered him to keep pressure. "Hold it down firmly. I do not believe it is bleeding fast but you must keep pressing it."

Richard beamed. "I will be fine, milady. I love you so much." *She is precious!* "You are everything to me, Elizabeth. We will speak of this more but I must check on the men. Will you be all right? I am certain Darcy is on his way. Will you stay in here?"

She nodded. "I will be strong. I will stay here. I love you, Richard."

Richard kissed her forehead and closed the door while Elizabeth sat with her eyes closed, pondering her fate for killing a man.

Chapter 35

Darcy yelled for his horse to be readied immediately and ran to the stables as quickly as possible. Mr. Wesson had arrived with the news that there was a roadblock from Mrs. Denny's home and that Mr. Fitzwilliam had sent for reinforcements in case trouble was ahead.

Gathering a dozen men, Darcy followed the bodyguard towards the direction where the carriage was blocked. Suddenly, there were two shots fired and then silence.

His heart dropped and he raced to the sound as quickly as possible on Xerxes. He saw his men beginning to rise from where the fallen tree trunk was located. He quickly noted three unknown men lying on their backs with blood pooling under their bodies and saw Mr. Smith over another body. He could not tell who it was but breathed a sigh of relief when he realised that it was a man and the boots did not belong to Richard.

He then saw Richard exiting the carriage and their eyes met. Richard smiled and Darcy was relieved beyond belief.

Darcy quickly jumped off Xerxes and embraced his cousin. "You are wounded. Where is Elizabeth? Are you both all right?"

Richard returned the hug and spoke. "I am well. She was amazing. She saved my life, Darce. She shot the bastard and it was the perfect shot. She is shaken up but she will be well. She is the most incredible woman and she is ours. Amazing, just amazing."

Darcy was finally able to smile. "I will see her while you take care of the mess out here. Send someone to Mr. King. He is the magistrate and we will need to make sure Elizabeth's name is clear of this. I care not that everyone knows the truth of her bravery but I know society will not appreciate a woman firing a pistol."

He left Richard and entered the carriage to see his wife.

Elizabeth immediately jumped into his arms and wept. "Oh, Fitzwilliam! I know I needed to do it but I still feel awful that I shot someone. I believe I killed him, my love. I have never killed anything before and I would do it again in a heartbeat to help Richard but I still feel awful." She continued to cry.

Darcy held her while she continued to cry. He rubbed her back and comforted her. Once she settled, he spoke. "You saved Richard's life. I know Richard will be able to comfort you about taking a life, but you saved yourself and you saved Richard. You are a heroine, Elizabeth. I know the thought of killing someone is not pleasant but you had to do what you did to defend yourself. I am proud of you. I am SO proud of you."

She raised her head and smiled. "Thank you, my love. I would have done anything for you and Richard and I am glad all of the lessons were effective. I had to lift my skirts up to my thigh, Fitzwilliam. I hope you do not think me a hoyden." She joked, even as tears were still falling.

She is teasing me after this event. She is a wonder. Darcy thought to himself. "I will forgive you of any trespasses, my love. You are an incredible woman and Richard will be at your feet to worship you for the rest of his life." They laughed. "Everything will be well. We will be well." Darcy kissed her lips tenderly.

There was a knock on the door and Darcy opened it. Richard stood outside. "Anderson is still alive. Elizabeth's bullet was small; I am certain it was the size of her small pistol, but it was not enough to kill him. I ordered a cart to be brought so we could transport him. He will be hanged, Elizabeth. You did not kill anyone." Richard beamed.

Elizabeth breathed a sigh of relief. "Oh, thank God!"

Richard continued, "Mr. Woods will be well. His wound is to his shoulder and the bullet only grazed him. The other men were hit on the head but they will be fine after some rest. Two of Anderson's men are dead, from Smith's and my pistols, and the third is wounded from Wood's and will most likely die in the next few hours, and Anderson and his fourth accomplice will be hanged. But I found this letter in his pocket, Darce. You need to read it."

Darcy took the letter from Richard and silently read it. He shook his head and handed it to Elizabeth.

Arnold,

I am quite disappointed that you have not been successful in killing Eliza Bennet yet. I have promised you £1,000 more when you dispose of that whore for good and another £1,000 when you have killed Richard Fitzwilliam for betraying me. I have spent much of my energy to escape the prison ship and I can taste my revenge. You will get your money after you have ridden both of them from this world.

I will meet you again for an update on the last day of this month at two o'clock at my townhouse in London. I know how much you enjoyed my favours during the years we have been intimate and I will make certain you get your heart's wish with my body as well as my money as soon as you succeed. I wish nothing more than to be Mrs. Caroline Darcy after you kill his temporary wife. I know I will be successful in my task once you complete yours.

Caroline

Elizabeth sat back on her seat. "That awful shrew. She is in town. I do not know how she escaped and kept from detection for the past two years but she is here and we must find her! She will try again once she finds out about Anderson."

Darcy scratched his head. "Tomorrow is the last day of the month but this letter does not tell us where she will be. If we can capture her at the location, she will be hanged, based on this letter alone."

Elizabeth began to cry softly. Darcy wrapped his arms around her and Richard rushed back into the carriage and closed the door.

Darcy was distraught for Elizabeth but when he looked up to Richard, he saw that Richard had a huge grin on his face and Darcy became angry that his cousin was not taking the threat seriously. He lightly punched Richard's shoulder and snarled, "What are you grinning at, you arse?"

"Language!" Richard laughed loudly. "I am grinning because I know where she is. I would never mock Elizabeth or your pain. She wants *me* killed, too, you know! But I know where she is and we will get this harridan."

Elizabeth looked up. "Where, Richard?" She grabbed his hand. "Tell us!"

Richard kissed her hand. "I know I have so many regrets of my past but if it will help us now, I thank God for it." He kissed her hand again apologetically. "Before I hired Abigail as my mistress, Haversham had given her a townhouse. When she decided to retire to Kent, she wished to have more funds for her retirement and to disconnect herself from Haversham entirely. She sold it back to Haversham and guess who he gave it to? Caroline Bingley! Even though she did not ask for money, Haversham did not want to travel too far and gave the townhouse to Caroline for their liaisons several times a week."

Darcy chuckled. "You are brilliant, brother. We will get her. We will trap her and have her arrested and will finally have peace!"

~*~

Darcy and Elizabeth returned to Westwood Manor while Richard stayed with Mr. Smith and Anderson. He spoke cautiously to Smith about keeping confidential about Mrs. Darcy's involvement. "Details can be kept as simple as possible, Smith. Mrs. Darcy saved my life but her actions will be frowned upon should society know. She should be heralded as a heroine but we will have to keep her bravery a secret."

Smith was in awe of the incredible courage that Mrs. Darcy showed. He was impressed by her shooting skills also and vowed to protect her from her enemies. If gossip were to be her enemy, he would protect her from it. She had earned his fierce loyalty and he could understand why a brave man like the formal colonel was so devoted to the Darcys.

"You have my word, sir. She is an incredible lady and she has my full loyalty. I would like to share with Wesson and my brother about her actions but will keep it a secret to all others." Smith humbly replied.

"That is fine. Thank you, Smith. I appreciate your discretion. Has Anderson been talking?" Richard asked.

Smith smiled. "He is an idiot, sir. He has been blabbering on and on about his revenge and how he should have taken Mrs. Darcy long ago and how you had interrupted his plans several times. There is nothing in his brain that did not spill out and the magistrate was there for the whole thing. We have a dozen witnesses now and he will certainly be hanged."

Richard laughed loudly. "He was never able to keep his mouth shut. Please work with Mr. King and ensure that he is tried and punished as soon as possible. I will need you and Wesson to go to London with me today. I will return to Westwood now."

"Of course, sir." Smith bowed and returned to the other men.

~*~

Richard hopped into the shared sitting room between the Master and Mistress' rooms and found the Darcys there, with the twins and Michael squealing on the floor while Darcy was tickling them and Elizabeth holding Amelia in her arms on the couch. *Such bliss. I love my family.*

After explaining what happened at the scene and Anderson being taken away, they discussed their next course of action.

Elizabeth was saddened that Richard would travel to London on his own, but agreed that she needed to stay in Hertfordshire for the New Year Ball that the Bingleys were throwing. Her sister's financial situation was stabilizing and they would have a large party to celebrate.

She looked at Darcy who was sitting on the floor with the boys. She met his eyes and spoke, "You wish to go, too; am I right?" She asked in resignation.

Darcy smiled softly and nodded.

Elizabeth rolled her eyes. "Boys," she smiled. "I love you, Fitzwilliam. I know that you have never been away from me but I wish for you to keep each other safe. I know Mr. Smith and Mr. Wesson will do a fine job and the younger Mr. Smith will keep me safe. Will you promise me to come back to me whole? Will you return in time to dance with me? If you miss the first set, you have to dance with my mother. And Richard, if you miss the second set, *you* will have to dance with my mother. And if you miss the supper set, you will dance with my father. Both of you! Can you promise me that?"

She smiled but there were tears in her eyes. Richard immediately grabbed her and kissed her fiercely. The twins saw and laughed loudly and stood to join them. "'Iss! 'Iss!" they both shouted while Michael wobbled to wrap his arms around her legs.

Darcy also arose and sat next to them, lifting the boys up to stand on the couch while they hugged Elizabeth and kissed her face. Richard took Amelia from her while she returned the boys' kisses and Darcy eventually kissed his wife.

"I suppose we should stop kissing in front of the boys." Richard laughed. "They might start talking."

Darcy laughed. He leaned forward and kissed Elizabeth tenderly. "Yes, I suppose we should. Just one more." Darcy kissed her deeply.

Richard laughed. "Yes, just one more." He leaned in and kissed Elizabeth again after Darcy was done.

They both loved their wife with all of their hearts.

Chapter 36

Caroline Bingley looked in the mirror and was pleased with what she saw.

She had been shipped off to the colonies after losing £10,000 of her money to Mr. Darcy and Mr. Fitzwilliam and sentenced to seven years transportation. She was to go to Australia but as soon as she got onboard, she weaselled her favours with the captain of the ship and invited herself into his cabin and promptly opened her legs for him.

After paying off the £10,000 penalty, she had a little over 5,000 in her bank account. She used some of her funds to hire a solicitor to sell off her main townhouse and all of the belongings, moving her favourite pieces to Haversham's townhouse as stealthily as possible. He had signed it off to her months prior and no one else had known about it.

Her money paid for her clothes to travel with her and some of her scanty negligee certainly paid off in seducing the captain as well as several of the other officers. She provided her services for a full fortnight, taking more than one man at a time and showing off her newly learned skills in sexual pleasures. She had gotten close enough to them to be able to access the laudanum cabinet and once they docked in Spain to transport containers of supplies to Australia, she drugged them to be able to sneak off the ship and paid off several others to get her belongings to an inn. She gave her name as Catherine Darby and presented herself as a wealthy heiress.

It took her nearly two years, after hiding out in Portugal, after spending over £3,000 to set up an account under her alias and to live luxuriously to capture wealthy men. She began to write to a few of her former lovers to see who could help her get her revenge. She was more than surprised that Arnold Anderson wrote from Newgate Prison that he was incarcerated after his attempt to assault Mrs. Darcy and that he had wanted to kill Richard Fitzwilliam for his interruptions. A plan formed in her mind to seek her revenge once Arnold escaped his imprisonment with the bribery that she set up and she quietly returned to England, disguising herself under the other identity.

Now, she knew it was close. She would have her revenge when her lover killed that Eliza Bennet and Richard Fitzwilliam, then have a liaison with Arnold, and afterwards, slip in enough laudanum for him to fall into unconsciousness, then she planned on smothering him with a pillow while he slept. She had promised him £2,000 in addition to the £500 that she had set up for him already, but only had about 1,500 left. She would be able to get her hands on another £1,000 once she was able to get in touch with her solicitor but knew she would have to pay off the solicitor to not turn her into custody when she used her real name. Her only redemption would be that when Mr. Darcy fell in love with her after her consolation of his wife's passing and that his money would pay for anything, even getting a full pardon for the charges of burglary at Darcy House. She was certain he would get the charges dropped and her criminal records expunged.

She stood waiting for Anderson in her nightgown. She looked at herself again and was a little disappointed that her stomach still appeared frumpy after having given birth to a son whom she promptly discarded at an orphanage in Portugal. She had no idea who the father of the baby was, since she had slept with at least three men during the time of conception. She rolled her eyes as she thought of the child. *I hope he is dead. What good would a child do for me?* She thought while she waited. *It has been a month since I had a man. Trying to keep a low profile is such hard work. I hope Arnold shows up soon. I need a man to pleasure me.*

Caroline smiled when she heard the door knock. *Finally! I hope he has good news for me as well.*

She opened the door herself in impatience and was shocked to see Wilkins standing there. She gasped and attempted to shut the door quickly but he pushed her in and widely opened the door. He grabbed her with his full body and pinned her against the wall, wrapping her arms behind her back to hold her in place.

"Let me go, you brute! How dare you attack me in my own home?" She screamed.

Wilkins shouted towards the door, "I have her, sirs! She does not have a weapon on her."

Caroline nearly fainted when she saw Darcy and Richard enter, along with two very large guards and another four men, who ended up being a constable, a magistrate, and two officers.

She began to wail and cry copiously. Wilkins let her go after the men entered and closed the door and then Caroline's maid was called to cover her with a blanket and to stand as a witness.

"So, Catherine Darby, this is not your home, if you are indeed Miss Darby, unless you are Caroline Bingley, fugitive and an attempted murderer. You have two choices: Confess to everything now and save your life, or you can face the judge and hang for your crimes. Anderson confessed and we have a letter in your own hand, hiring Anderson to murder two people." The magistrate began.

Caroline looked at Mr. Darcy who was sitting as far away from her as possible. He looked more handsome than before but his face showed full disgust. She looked at Mr. Fitzwilliam. He was looking even better than he had at the Christmas Ball and she hated that he wanted nothing to do with her. He had a smirk on his face watching her misery and she wanted to kill him.

When her maid came with the blanket, Caroline took a seat at her favourite chair where she had kept a knife hidden behind the cushions. She discreetly reached for it and gripped the handle. If she was going down, she would make sure to take Richard Fitzwilliam with her.

She pretended to cry once again and asked the constable for a glass of wine. He stepped back to allow the maid to do so, and as soon as her maid stood to fetch a glass, Caroline arose behind her and raised her dagger to run toward Richard, who had his back on her while talking with one of the large men.

Caroline Bingley never saw it coming. She was suddenly immobile as she felt an unimaginable pain in her abdomen. She looked down and saw a sword in her stomach and when she followed the shaft of the sword to the handle, she saw Mr. Darcy's furious eyes staring at her, as he held the steel that would kill her.

She dropped the dagger in her hand and wheezed, "I only ever wanted to be your wife. You have killed me. Why could you not love me?"

Darcy pulled out his sword swiftly and coldly responded, "Elizabeth is the only one worthy of my love. You tried to kill my wife and my cousin and I hope you go straight to hell."

Richard had turned around just in time to see Caroline's dagger raised to strike him and then Darcy had opened his walking stick to save him. He saw the harridan fall and after a few more moments of groaning, she died.

Richard plopped down on the nearest chair. "Darcy, I do not know what the count is but you owe me nothing. I nearly died twice in two days and I survived due to you and Elizabeth. Everything I have is yours. I will live the rest of my life to be at your beck and call."

The magistrate and constable as well as the other witnesses in the room smiled. They all knew or had heard of the former colonel's bravery and honour before and guessed that he would stand by the Darcys until his last breath.

Darcy tapped Richard's shoulder. "I think we are even, brother. You have saved Elizabeth and me more times than I can count and I am glad to have been at your service." He turned to the magistrate. "I know I will need to sign some paperwork and will have to finalise any evidence, but we have a promise to keep and will need to return to Hertfordshire." He handed him his card. "Contact me at Darcy House for anything you need and they will know where to find me and get any messages to me quickly. I leave the rest in your good hands for now, sir. Thank you." They shook hands and Darcy's group swiftly departed.

~*~

Elizabeth bit her nails and watched the clock. She was dressed for the ball and at Netherfield, attempting to make pleasant conversation with her family and several of her friends in the neighbourhood.

As the clock struck seven, she heard the strings preparing for the first set. She closed her eyes and took a deep breath. She did not care about the dance or the people or the food. She could not care less about her dress or the decorations of the Ball or what her mother was speaking of. She wanted to know where her husbands were: If they were safe and well, and if this nightmare was finally over.

Then she saw them. Darcy and Richard both entered the room, dressed as fine as ever and beaming. She could not move and she knew tears were falling but she stood stock-still as her husbands approached her. Both men took her hand each and kissed it tenderly.

Darcy put her hand on his arm and guided her to Bingley's study attentively while

422

Richard followed. As soon as he closed the door, Richard locked it and Darcy began to kiss Elizabeth wildly. Richard rubbed her back and kissed her neck and when Darcy released her for breath, Richard turned her around and began to kiss her mouth as well.

Elizabeth laughed while still crying as both men were on her neck and face and caressing her breasts. "I am so glad you have both returned to me. I have missed you so much. I worried and panicked and prayed for you. I am so glad you are returned to me."

Darcy spoke to her while still trailing his kisses on her neck. "It is over. Caroline Bingley is dead and will never bother us again."

Elizabeth gasped and Richard continued. "Darcy saved my life when she attacked me and he used his walking-stick sword. She is gone. All is well, Elizabeth. It is over."

She sighed a breath of relief. "I am sad that it had to happen but I am thankful that you are both well and I am very glad you looked out for each other. I cannot live without you both, husbands. I love you so much!"

Darcy and Richard began to rub against her from front and back and caressed her breasts. Elizabeth knew that she had to calm both men. Their protrusions were massive and she could hear the strings playing louder to start the first set. She knew she had to go back out soon.

She took a deep breath. "My loves, husbands, I wish I could take you both right now but my family will be looking for us. We must return. You must be relieved that you do not have to dance with my mother!" She laughed. "I promise to take good care of you tonight, husbands. I love you both with all my heart."

Both men took calming breaths as well. They knew their reunion tonight would last hours so they agreed that they would leave the ball as soon as appropriate.

~*~

Elizabeth enjoyed her three sets with Darcy and two with Richard. While her husbands danced with her sisters, she could hear whispers of how handsome both men were and how noble they appeared.

Word began to spread quickly about Anderson's murder attempt, as well as what had happened in London earlier that day with Caroline Bingley.

Anderson would be tried and hanged in a few days and it was known to everyone that Caroline Bingley was responsible for hiring him. No blame was placed on Charles and Jane Bingley, as everyone comprehended that Caroline was insane and all ties had been severed years ago.

Elizabeth revelled having her husbands back in her bed as she pleasured them all night long and through the morning. The men vowed to pleasure her next week when her courses were completed, and Richard promised his dedication to both Darcys once again in appreciation for their saving his life. Darcy and Elizabeth reaffirmed him that they would do everything to watch out for each other in their special love as husbands and wife.

Chapter 37

The Darcys returned to Kieran Hall in Scotland to celebrate their wedding anniversary, two and a half years after Amelia's birth after making arrangements with the current residents to take a holiday for two months. While relaxing after a wonderful meal, Darcy spoke candidly with Richard about their relationship. Darcy and Elizabeth had already agreed on their next course and hoped Richard would agree. They shared a bottle of orange wine, taking measures to ensure that Elizabeth did not over-imbibe and Darcy spoke.

"Richard, I know that Elizabeth and I have kept our vows to each other and after six years of marriage, we are most content with our relationship together. But I do realise that we three are permanently sleeping together and you and Elizabeth have done nearly everything that a man and wife do together. I truly appreciate that you have kept that last piece of becoming one with Elizabeth, Richard, and that you truly do have an iron will. Our love for each other is everlasting and I agree with Elizabeth's view that we have loved each other fully and have a clear conscience to face God, that we loved and have been loved." Darcy patted Richard's shoulder. "Elizabeth wears both of our rings and she has been our wife for many years and I cannot imagine our lives any better. We need each other and we honour and respect each other with every fibre of our being.

"While we are here, Richard, I would like for you to make your vows with me and Elizabeth, even if it is not legitimate, so that we three can live as husbands and wife. I know it is not legal and it would continue to be our secret but I would like for us to make our commitment to each other out loud. Richard, while she will never be your legally wedded wife, with your vows to us and our vows to you, we three would commit ourselves to each other for the rest of our lives. You have already been a good husband and dedicated partner in our lives and Elizabeth and I decided it is time for that last step. Would you be willing?" Darcy asked.

Richard's heart beat wildly. "I am committed to you both and would be willing to take any vow to pledge my commitment and my life to you both. I am content with our current situation, as I have been given more than I had ever expected, but are you certain? If I am hearing you correctly, you will allow for me to finally take the step to making Elizabeth my wife in body?" *I have been having relations with Elizabeth for five years but I have never had intercourse with her. I cannot imagine such generosity!*

Darcy smiled. "Yes, Richard. You would finally unite with our wife in body. You would love her fully as I love her and have that last piece. You would be my full partner in life; Elizabeth and I agreed that we needed to modify our vows to make room for you because we both love you and your love for Elizabeth validates it. We wish for you to be in our lives always."

"I will make my vows to you right now. I will sign anything in blood." He turned to his beloved and continued, "I would die for you, Elizabeth. I love you with all my heart." Richard kissed Elizabeth's hands. "I love you. Thank you, my wife."

Darcy laughed. "I am glad to hear it. Please repeat the words that I prepared and I would like for you to give your ring back to Elizabeth. You will place the rings back after our vows are made. Elizabeth, here is my wedding band. I will hold yours for now."

Elizabeth took Richard's grandmother's ring and handed it to him while Richard took off his band and gave it to her. She did the same with Darcy.

Richard repeated after Darcy's guidance, "I, Richard Fitzwilliam, commit myself to thee, Elizabeth Darcy, to be my soulmate and wife, and to Fitzwilliam Darcy, her husband, to have and to hold, from this day forward, for better, for worse, for richer, for poorer, in sickness and in health, to love and to cherish, till death do us part, forsaking all others and keep thee only in my heart and body."

Elizabeth shed a tear as she vowed, "I, Elizabeth Darcy, take thee, Fitzwilliam Darcy and Richard Fitzwilliam, to be my soulmates and husbands, to have and to hold, from this day forward, for better, for worse, for richer, for poorer, in sickness and in health, to love and to cherish, till death do us part, forsaking all others and keep thee both in my heart and body."

Darcy spoke next. "I, Fitzwilliam Darcy, take thee, Elizabeth Darcy, to be my soulmate and wife, and Richard Fitzwilliam, her husband, to have and to hold, from this day forward, for better, for worse, for richer, for poorer, in sickness and in health, to love and to cherish, till death do us part, forsaking all others and keep thee only in my heart and body."

Darcy placed Elizabeth's ring on her finger and she placed Darcy's ring on his. They whispered to each other, "I love you."

Richard placed his ring on Elizabeth's finger, "I love you, Mrs. Fitzwilliam. With all my heart and soul."

Elizabeth placed her ring on Richard's finger, "I love you, too. Thank you for your commitment to us. We are better for having you in our lives and I am truly honoured to be your wife."

Darcy chuckled. "I pronounce us husbands and wife. We may kiss the bride."

Richard gently kissed Elizabeth's lips. Somehow, it felt different. Saying the words, making the vows out loud, brought a significance that he had not thought possible. His heart fluttered as he embraced her. *I love her more. I do not know how it is possible but I truly do.*

Elizabeth turned to Darcy and kissed him tenderly as well. "I believe we need to celebrate our wedding night right away. May I have a half hour to refresh myself?"

Darcy smiled while Richard gulped. "But of course, wife. See you in our rooms. We, men, have some refreshing to do as well." Darcy replied.

Darcy wrapped his arm around Richard's shoulder while she headed towards her dressing room after handing Richard a small amount of brandy.

"You must fortify yourself, Richard. I imagine pleasure beyond your imagination awaits you tonight. I will give you an hour with her and then join you. Remember, your vows might be to Elizabeth first but her vows are to both of us and I fully intend to participate in our wedding night." He laughed. "It is an unusual and unorthodox relationship but I am willing to bear it. You are so vital to our lives, I can fully share my wife with you and feel good about our life choices."

Richard took a small sip of the brandy. He wanted to have a clear head to enjoy finally uniting with the love of his life. His manhood twitched at the thought of entering her. "Darcy, I am truly honoured. I know I am going to be an absolute fool and probably will last all of ten seconds with her. I will go and prepare myself. I think I need to release before seeing her."

Darcy laughed heartily. "It reminds me of my wedding night. Yes, I recommend that you do so. I nearly exploded seeing her at my door, I recall. Enjoy yourselves and I will join you after an hour."

Richard went to his dressing room to change out of his clothing. His hands were shaking, his anticipation was so great. *I have been loving her most intimately for five years and I am nervous now? I suppose it has been five years of foreplay. We have seen each other at our best and worst but the thought of having that last piece is going to make me a bumbling fool!*

He washed himself thoroughly and quickly masturbated so that he would not explode on sight. *God, I love her. I cannot imagine a better life.*

Richard awaited Elizabeth in their shared room. Richard had his own room, mostly for his belongings, but it was just a formality in all of their homes. The three had shared their bed for years now and almost always slept together.

"How is it possible that you become more beautiful each day?" Richard asked Elizabeth as she entered the bed with her hair flowing down and dressed in a seductive red nightgown.

Elizabeth merrily laughed. "You are blind, sir. I have become much older and wider after each babe and am certainly no young maiden."

"No, my love. You are my dream and the most beautiful woman in existence. Please, let me fully love you for the first time. Darcy will join us in an hour." Richard smiled with love in his eyes.

Richard lay with Elizabeth in bed and kissed her as his wont, fondling her and licking her for several minutes. She moaned with desire and as he rubbed his erection against her, he whispered, "I love you, Elizabeth, with all of my heart and now with all of my body."

She responded in return, "I love you, Richard. I wish to be your wife completely. I wish for you to have all of me. Make love to me and take all of me. I have desired it for so long." She moaned.

Unable to delay any longer, he placed the tip of his long erection onto her entrance and slowly pushed himself in. He kept his eyes open as he lay over her, watching her face as he loved her fully for the first time. He took an eternity to enter her core, as he revelled in the sensation that he had never expected to feel again. He had relations with so many women for years until he fell in love, but to finally hold Elizabeth, the love of his life, and to feel her womanhood wrapped against his hard phallus was intense and incredibly unique. She felt tighter than he had ever thought possible and after he filled her up to the hilt, he looked deeply into her eyes. A tear fell from his eye as he gazed adoringly at his beloved under him. He kissed her reverently on her lips while he kept himself deep inside her.

"I never thought this could happen, Elizabeth. I have loved you for so long and to have all of you is a dream come true from the first moment I laid my eyes on you." He began to move in and out of her. "You feel so incredible, Elizabeth. I have never known such bliss. This is the most wonderful feeling I have ever experienced." He groaned between pumps.

"I love you, Richard." Elizabeth moaned. "You have guarded me and protected me and honoured my vows to Fitzwilliam, and I am so glad that we could make a new vow together. Our love is so special, I cannot live without you."

He began to move slowly; he had wanted to be gentle in taking her, his precious wife, but he could not help himself as he began to pound harder and thrust himself into her quickly as he held her tightly in his arms. "Oh, god, Elizabeth! You feel so good!" He screamed, as he continued to love her.

He held himself back from releasing and lifted her up to sit her on his lap with her legs completely wrapped around him while she bounced on his groin. To have her in this position as he had often done, but to penetrate her and fill her up completely had been a dream come true. He kissed her deeply and could no longer hold himself back as he thrust up into her like a madman.

Elizabeth revelled in having Richard's erection deep inside her. He was truly masterful. She had been jealous of the women in his past whom he had filled and had wished that she could experience his love, but she had been faithful to her lawful husband and enjoyed the other experiences that Richard was able to provide. But finally having him inside her was immeasurably pleasurable. He was similar to Darcy and although Darcy was an excellent lover, Richard's talents always aroused her greatly. She continued to scream her pleasures as well. She loved him so much and finally joining his body fully felt as if their souls were finally connected, but she still missed her first husband. *My lord! Richard feels so good inside me. I cannot get enough of my husbands. I will now have both to fill me and satisfy me completely! I hope Fitzwilliam will join us soon. I want to take them both so much. My heart truly belongs with two men and I need both of my husbands!*

Richard grunted loudly as he exploded inside her. He could not hold back as Elizabeth moaned and kissed him. Being inside her and taking her fast and furiously had been his deepest wish for years and after loving her intensely for half an hour, he could not hold back and released his seed inside her as he shuddered.

"Oh, my love. That was... that was amazing... I never thought... You are so beautiful. I love you." Richard kissed her repeatedly.

"Richard, I love you and I love having you inside me. Your seed has entered me so many times before but having you deliver it was amazing."

~*~

Darcy joined as Richard was fingering Elizabeth's womanhood with her laying above him. "I hope I am not unwelcome."

"Oh, my love. We were waiting for you. Richard had me twice already and he was waiting for you to join us for another round. Come here, my love." Elizabeth begged and her husband eagerly complied.

Elizabeth lay on her back later that night in exhaustion. She had never had so much pleasure in her life. Being loved by two men was beyond all her imaginations and previous experiences, and she lay panting, amazed at how wanton she was for being such a wife to two men. She lay back contentedly and closed her eyes while she felt hands on her breasts and kisses all over her body. A warm towel was cleaning her bottom while a hand was massaging her breasts.

She fell asleep with each of her husbands holding her breast, only to awaken again and again all night long, with whispers of "I love you" from her husbands with her womanhood being filled until she climaxed repeatedly throughout the night.

When morning arrived, she awoke to find Darcy pumping her gently and Richard licking her breasts.

"Oh, my husbands. How many times have you taken your pleasures?" She smiled. "I felt like I had one of you inside me all night long. It felt amazing to climax so often." She moaned while her body was being rocked steadily.

Darcy grunted his release loudly. "Oh, you did, my love. Richard and I kept waking each other up to take our turn with you. It had become a sort of competition on who could love you more often. I think I won. Richard said he came three times before I joined you but I still managed to fill you five times just now while he only hit four." Darcy gloated.

Richard was now riding her gently and Elizabeth began to moan again as he rubbed her swollen clitoris.

"Well, I am going for my fifth now, wife." He pounded harder. "I hope you have not been too inconvenienced. I have a reputation to uphold, you know!" He laughed as he continued his thrusts. "I must say, your body is most amazing. I love you so much, Elizabeth."

Elizabeth replied, "I love you both so much. I give you all of my body. Oh, it feels so good!" He continued his thrusts until Elizabeth cried out and he released again.

"I have never known such pleasure, Elizabeth, and we will certainly give you time to revive after being such brutes last night. Thank you for being my wife. Thank you, Darcy, for sharing her fully with me. It means the world to be her true husband." Richard lay next to her and fell asleep again.

They spent the next two weeks in such an activity, even if not as fervently as the first night. Whether in the bedroom or study or library, anywhere the door could be locked, they were closeted in for hours on end to make love to their wife. By the end of the fortnight, they were convinced that they had filled her with enough seed to get her with child.

Chapter 38

"Lord Matlock! There has been an accident!" The servant rushed in and informed the party in the drawing room.

The Darcys and Richard had been visiting Lord and Lady Matlock to celebrate Richard's parents' fortieth wedding anniversary and they had had a grand dinner the night before and most everyone had awakened later than usual and were taking tea together when they received the news.

Elizabeth had been nauseous for a fortnight and guessed she was with child. Darcy and Richard had both assumed it quickly but since it was only two months along, it was not shared with anyone else. They were thrilled to expect their sixth child together and Darcy stayed in bed with Elizabeth to care for her while Richard had left for his morning ride.

Being at Matlock, they could not sleep together in the same bed and Richard was absolutely frustrated. He had missed being intimate with his dearest wife for two full weeks and they were to stay yet another week. Although he enjoyed seeing his family again and spending time with his brother and baby sister, he missed the tranquillity and privacy of Pemberley and was eager to return home.

Richard was not only frustrated physically, he was also mentally restless. Not only was his beloved wife out of his reach, his valet Garrison had blocked yet another young lady from entering his bedroom for a compromise last night. Knowing that he was still one of the most elite and desirable bachelors of all, women continued to flock to his side for his attentions and threw themselves at him. He gave no acknowledgement to these ladies, whether widowed or young or wealthy, and yet this was the fifth one to attempt to sneak into his room. All he had wanted was to lay with his beloved Elizabeth in his arms but he was lonely and miserable. He had slept awfully without his dearest wife by his side for so long.

His horse, Cyrus, had been left at Pemberley to stud a mare and although Darcy had offered Xerxes, Richard opted to break in one of his father's new stallions this morning to ride out alone.

It had rained moderately during the night and the grounds were still soggy, but Richard, in his frustrations, rode the untamed horse quite roughly and when he tried to jump over a small hedge, the horse panicked and stopped dead-cold, throwing off its rider.

The servants who were working the fields early saw the accident and ran to assist, finding the Honourable Richard Fitzwilliam bleeding from the front of his head and unconscious, but alive.

Lady Matlock screamed and Elizabeth fainted when they saw Richard's limp body being carried in by several men. Darcy caught his wife in his arms and laid her on the couch while Lord Matlock barked orders for the surgeon to be fetched.

~*~

Richard awoke with a serious headache and moaned loudly. *My head is killing me! What in the world did I do?*

He heard Garrison's voice. "Master Fitzwilliam, sir, are you well?"

Richard groaned again. "Garrison, hell! My head is throbbing. I feel as if a damn elephant is sitting on my head. How many bloody drinks did I have last night?" He slowly opened his eyes and saw his attendant of many years staring bewildered.

He looked around the room and saw his old bedroom. Richard continued, "I am at my parents' house? How the hell did I get here? Why am I not at Darcy's in London? What in damnation am I doing at Matlock?"

Garrison swallowed, "Um, sir, it was your parents' anniversary three nights ago. You have been here for over two weeks."

Richard covered his eyes with his arm as he groaned. "Oh, I forgot. Their thirtieth anniversary. That is right. Damn, my head. I just want a good fuck. I feel like my cock is going to pop and I need a good woman to set me right. How long has it been since I had a whore? Go find me a brunette, Garrison. With big teats! You know what I like." He did not hear Garrison gasp.

"Pardon me, sir. I will return shortly, sir. I will bring you some elixirs for your headache." Garrison quickly ran out of Richard's room and knocked on Darcy's door.

Darcy saw the flustered valet and invited him into his rooms immediately.

"Any word on Richard's condition, Garrison? What has happened?" Darcy asked.

Garrison, who was usually unflappable, spoke rushedly. "Sir, he... he believes it is ten years ago. He... he is asking for a... whor... prostitute. He spoke as if he were still a colonel and I do not think remembers Mrs. Darcy... He spoke as his previous ways, using language that I have not heard in years, sir. Mr. Darcy, he does not remember the past ten years. He thinks he is at his parents' home for their *thirtieth* anniversary!"

Darcy paled. "What?! How is that possible? I suppose with his head injury, he might be amnesiac but to have lost so much time! Elizabeth will be devastated." He paced. "Garrison, have someone fetch the doctor and share what you have learned, and I will go see him now. Lord, help us. Ten years..." He sighed.

Garrison bowed and left immediately. Darcy put on his coat and straightened his clothing. He had been napping with Elizabeth, who was still asleep, as she had been crying copiously for the past two days and had been inconsolable. As Richard's cousin's wife, she had not been allowed to see him in his state and had been devastated that she could not care for her other husband here at Matlock.

Darcy looked at Elizabeth and thought, *She might just have one husband from now on. If Richard completely forgets Elizabeth, I wonder if she can carry on, with him only as a rakish cousin. He was a completely different man ten years ago. She will be so heartbroken.*

Darcy entered Richard's room without knocking. He sighed as he saw Richard lying down in bed, frantically masturbating under the sheets and just finding his release, grunting quite loudly. Darcy quietly closed the door but loud enough for Richard to hear it.

"Oh, damn it, Darcy! You should have knocked." Richard smirked. "I feel like I have not fucked in ages and could not wait for a woman. I desperately need a good whore or two. How have you been? I have not seen you in a while, have I? I am a bit confused on how I got here but I must have had too much to drink last night. I had not been this hung-over since I woke up with that wench and vowed to quit drinking so much, remember? That slut with the big chest who was married and I had to run for my life from her husband?" He laughed. He stopped, seeing that Darcy was not laughing with him. "What is the matter? Why do you look as if someone died? Why do you look so damn old today?" he asked.

Darcy sat on a chair next to his bed and sighed. "Oh, Richard... You were not drinking, brother. You had an accident. You were riding on Uncle's new horse and was thrown off."

Richard scoffed. "Ridiculous! I have not been thrown off a fucking horse since I was thirteen! When I made Wickham shit in his pants, remember? Me, thrown off a horse!" He laughed. He sat up in bed, though, and rubbed his forehead. He felt the bandage on his head. "Hell! Did I really fall off a horse? I do not remember a thing. Who cut off my bloody hair?" He felt the rest of his head and found his hair short all over.

Darcy spoke softly, "You have been unconscious for two days. Richard, I have to tell you something else. It is not your parents' thirtieth anniversary but rather their... *fortieth...*" Seeing Richard's face in confusion, he added, "It appears you have lost ten years of your memory, brother. Many great changes happened in the past ten years." *Damn it! He needs to know the truth but I cannot tell him all.* "I am married and have five children." *Our wife, our children!*

"TEN YEARS?!" Richard boomed. "It is impossible! How can I forget TEN fucking years of my life, Darcy? TEN?!" Richard was quiet for several minutes. "You have FIVE children? Damn! Who the hell did you marry? Some blonde goddess? I hope she was not after your money. I am glad you finally settled down with your perfect woman. I know you were waiting a long time. Five children... damn, she must be fine for you to bed her so often." He sighed. "I feel like shit, cousin. Help me get up. I need to move around. I feel restless."

Darcy helped Richard sit up more and swung his legs over the bed. Richard was dizzy but what he was hearing from his ever-honest cousin was incredible and did not know what to think. He grabbed the washcloth that Garrison had left for him and began to wipe his face and neck.

While he washed, there was a knock at the door and he allowed entrance.

The doctor, along with Lord and Lady Matlock, entered. Hearing that Richard had lost his memory for ten years, they were in shock, but nonetheless gladdened to hear that their favourite son was awake and talking.

The doctor examined him and declared that other than his memory, Richard appeared to be physically healthy and that he would have to move slower and rest frequently for several weeks. He would have a small scar on the top of his forehead but everything else appeared well. Lady Matlock cried when the doctor advised them that his memory might or might not return and all they could do was to wait and see. After finishing his examination, the doctor bowed to the party and departed.

Lady Matlock hugged her son, "Oh, Richard, I am glad you are well, my son. I love you so much. We have been praying for you for two days straight and God answered us. Everyone will be so thrilled to see you well now. What would you like to eat? What can I do to make you happy, child?"

"Mother, I am seven and twen... No, seven and *thirty* years old. Damn, I am so old now." He looked in the looking glass that Darcy had handed him earlier, "I am no longer a child." He smiled. "Thank you, mother. I love you, too. Perhaps if you recall some of my favourite meals, you can send a plate up for me? I am famished." Richard kissed his mother on her cheek.

"But of course, my dear. Oh, we should have Lizzy visit. Seeing some old faces might help you remember and Iris and Georgiana are here with their husbands as well. They will all be so happy to see you!" Lady Matlock stood and smiled while Lord Matlock hugged his son and they both left to spread the news.

"Iris and Georgiana are both married? Blasted! Why can I not remember any of this? And who the hell is Lizzy?" Richard grunted.

"*Damn it, Richard!*" Darcy whispered under his breath. He took a deep breath and after calming, he continued. "Yes, your sister and mine are both married and have children. Lizzy is... She is our... she is my wife. I know you will love her." *You love her, Richard. You just have to remember. She will be so devastated.* "I have been married for eight years, Richard. She is the love of my life and I hope you will be kind to her."

Richard beamed. "Congratulations, Darcy. I know you have been waiting for someone for a very long time. Lizzy must be a remarkable lady to have captured you. Go, go and get her now. I want to meet your wife right now."

Darcy smiled for the first time since entering Richard's room. "Yes, she is amazing and I will tell her you are awake now. Rest, Richard. Your meal will be here shortly and I will return with my wife."

Richard remained sitting on his bed while Garrison helped him change his shirt and clean up. He did not wish to lie down again and although his head throbbed in pain, there was something that was nagging in his mind that made him more frustrated than ever.

I cannot believe I do not remember ten years of my life. I feel as if this is a terrible dream and I will awake from it any moment now. Wife... Darcy has a wife. Damn lucky bastard. I want a wife. Wait, I have a wife. Why do I have a wife? How do I have a wife? Mother mentioned nothing about a wife but I know I have a wife. Do I not?

He saw his hands and saw his signet ring on his left pinkie. *Why do I have a signet ring? And what is this ring?* He pulled off his wedding band on his right ring finger. He could tell that he must have worn this ring all the time by the tan line on his finger and how snugly it fit. He looked at it carefully as he attempted to recall where the ring was from. He felt very connected to this ring. He saw the engraving inside the ring with a simple 'E' inside. *Is this from a woman? Why is this ring so sentimental to me? Is 'E' my beloved?* He had flashes of laying over a petite brunette and although her face was blurry, he could smell her scent and recalled loving her. His heart began to burn to touch this woman of his dreams and he knew it must be his wife. He could not imagine making love so passionately to anyone else but a woman who was his wife. He felt such desire and love for this woman that he had never felt before. *She cannot be real. I am not married. If I had a wife, where is she?*

~*~

Darcy entered his room and saw that Elizabeth was finishing her dressing. *Oh, my love.*

Elizabeth excitedly ran to his side with a smile. "I heard; I heard he is awake. Everyone is talking about it and Hannah heard from Wilkins who heard from Garrison that he is awake. Is he well? Does he wish to see me now?" She eagerly asked with brightness in her eyes.

Darcy's heart broke for her. He knew she would be distressed with Richard's memory loss and that she had loved the man dearly. Elizabeth loved both men deeply and having such a loving soul, she held nothing back when she made love to them and was fiercely protective of them both.

Darcy finally spoke, "My love, Richard is awake. The doctor said that he will need to take it easy but physically, he is well and he is determined to leave his room today after eating. Elizabeth, my love, I have some... I have to tell you that he wishes to see you..." Elizabeth smiled radiantly, "but he does not... he does not remember the past ten years of his life." He saw Elizabeth gasp and her eyes opened widely in surprise. "He still believes he is a poor colonel but he is starting to accept that he does not remember. He is frustrated but is trying to learn and adjust quickly. He does not remember life with us together at all."

Elizabeth immediately cried. Darcy held her as she sobbed in his arms. After several long minutes, she finally calmed enough to speak.

"I feel as if you are telling me that my husband has died and my heart aches, but I must accept it. He is alive and healthy and recovering, and he will be well. I love you so much, Fitzwilliam. You know I love Richard dearly and I am saddened that he will not remember his children." She rubbed her abdomen, "This child inside me may never know his father," tears rolled down, "but I can only pray that either his memory will return or we will live our lives as best as we can without him. Perhaps seeing me, seeing the children, his home at Pemberley once again will help. I wish to see him. Let us go to him right now. I love you, Fitzwilliam. Thank you for always remembering me. I hope you never forget me."

"Never. I know that if my brain should be addled, I will still have you in my heart forever, my love. My soul knows you and we are forever connected." He kissed her tenderly. "I thank God for you every day, Mrs. Darcy."

Elizabeth straightened herself and stood, gathering her courage. "Well, Mr. Darcy, let us see this cousin of ours and perhaps we can fix him." She smiled.

Nervous but eager, she and Darcy knocked on Richard's door and entered.

Richard was alone now and had been contemplating all the questions that were rising in his head and most importantly, who the woman of his memory was. It could not be a dream, as he could feel her body touching his and her breath on his face. He could recall feeling such passion, holding her in his arms and making love to her, hearing her moans in his ear as he joined her soul. The memory was so vivid, it had to be real. He only wished he could see her face clearly.

Richard gasped when Elizabeth entered. His heart beat wildly as their eyes met. *She is the most beautiful woman I have ever seen. She could be the woman from my dreams but she is Darcy's wife. I could never impose on my dearest cousin's wife, could I?* He stood to greet her. He could not stop staring at her and felt his heart lurch, his fingers itching to touch her.

Elizabeth smiled softly. He was exactly as when she had first met him many years ago. She had not known then, but he had told her that he fell in love with her at first sight and she could see that it was the same reaction as when she first met him at Darcy House. She curtsied quickly and kept her eyes on him with hope for some recognition.

"You are Lizzy?" Richard finally asked. She nodded. He kept staring at her and did not turn his eyes from her. "It is very nice to meet you, Lizzy, although I understand it is not the first time we are meeting. Darce, since when did you like brunettes?"

Darcy laughed. They had had several conversations after his engagement about his preferences. "Yes, she is my perfect woman and my soulmate."

Richard thought, *Mine, too! She is incredible. Her eyes capture my heart and all I want to do is make her happy. But she looks sad. Why do I feel like I know her expressions so intimately? I feel happy and alive when she looks at me. I want to touch her and hold her.*

Elizabeth was torn. Her heart broke that Richard did not know her and had called her 'Lizzy' as he had done during the first few months of their acquaintance. She did not realise until now how each time he called 'Elizabeth' had truly meant that he loved her, as he had confessed on Xerxes all those years ago.

"It is wonderful to see you recovering. I... We were all very worried for you." Elizabeth finally spoke.

Richard stood nervously as Elizabeth walked closer to him. He reached for her left hand and kissed it, never losing his sight of her. He inhaled her scent and knew he was home. He could not help himself as he drew closer and kissed her cheek, wishing nothing more than to throw her onto his bed to ravage her. He asked again, "You are Lizzy?"

Elizabeth's eyes pooled with tears, "I am Mrs. Fitzwilliam... Darcy..." she replied, as she had teased him for years that she was not only Mrs. Darcy, but also Mrs. Fitzwilliam. Seeing the blank look on his face, she cried out, "I cannot..." and she ran out the door in tears.

Richard plopped down to sit on his bed. *I am certain I have been intimate with her. Have I been sleeping with Darcy's wife? Blasted cad I am. She is everything I want in a woman and she is Darcy's wife and my body knows her. Does Darcy know? How could I have been bedding my cousin's wife? I want her. I desire her more than everything I ever wanted in my life. Damn it to hell!*

Richard looked up and saw that Darcy was standing still, appearing grim. *He probably wants to beat me to a pulp.* He rubbed his left side of the jaw as he recalled being punched. *I am so confused.*

"Darcy, I... Am I good... *friends* with Lizzy? I feel... close to her." Richard asked timidly.

Darcy let out a laugh in relief. *Perhaps he does remember her a little. I hope so. I truly pray his memory returns soon.* "Yes, Richard. You two are very good friends. I hope your memories will return; so much has happened and I wish I could tell you everything. Richard, you and El..."

Just then, there was another knock at the door and Richard's meal was being delivered. Lady Matlock entered again and wished to sit with Richard.

"I will go check on my wife. Please excuse me." Darcy bowed and left.

As Richard ate, Lady Matlock filled him in on the main events of the past ten years and Richard sat awestruck that he was the master of Rosings, and that both Anne and Lady Catherine had died, and that he was permanently living with the Darcys.

I must have slept with Lizzy after living with them. How could I have done that to Darcy? Does Darcy know? How could I be so dishonourable? He is so protective of his own, there is no way he knows if he is still so friendly with me. Lizzy must be a harlot and I must have seduced her.

But he thought longer, *Lizzy is not a harlot; she could not be. She is perfection itself and Darcy would have never married anyone unworthy. It cannot be her. I think I love her but she cannot be the woman of my dreams. It must be a dream. Maybe I am in love with her and have fantasised it all, but it felt so real. I have never felt such a pull for anyone before. Who is my wife? I know I have a wife.*

"Mother, my memory is still gone but I am getting a few flashes and I recall a big black horse, I remember kicking Wickham, and some bits of seeing twin babies. Can you tell me... do I have a wife and children? Do I have a fiancée or is there a lady that I have been courting?" He shyly asked.

Lady Matlock smiled. "The twins are Bennet and Richie, Darcy and Lizzy's firstborns. You saved Darcy and Lizzy from Wickham's attack and you had vowed to stay with them to protect them yourself ever since. You seemed to desire a wife for a while after Darcy married but you quickly told me to cease my machinations for attaching you to someone and that you have been quite content with your lot, you have told me numerous times. You have been working hard with Darcy and you are godfather to all five of their children."

She smiled broadly, "You told me you have never been happier and I had never seen you so well, only three evenings ago. You have not shared with me about courting anyone and I certainly hope you would have told me if you are engaged, Richard." She laughed. "I do not know if you have someone. Darcy would know; you share everything with him. I hope you do not have a secret wife locked away in the country somewhere! God forbid, if you had illegitimate children out there, I would have an apoplexy. You have been an upstanding gentleman all these years and I trust you."

Richard frowned as his mother spoke of illegitimate children. *Something about having a bastard. I do not have one, even though I thought I might at one time. Damn it! I wish I could remember. Who is the woman of my memories?*

She wiped his mouth after he was done with his meal. She saw that he was drowsy and after helping him back into bed, she kissed his forehead. "Now, get some rest. I hope to see you downstairs for dinner tonight in a few hours. Everyone has been thrilled that you are recovering and cannot wait to see you."

Chapter 39

Richard looked around and smiled broadly as his family cheered for his recovery in the drawing room. He had slept through dinner but felt well enough to join them afterwards. All of the celebrating visitors had left after his injury and he was surrounded by those who loved him. Knowing that his memory was still missing, everyone tried to keep their inquiries simple and spoke of genial topics to not create more confusion or frustrations. Richard felt awkward wearing a gentleman's jacket instead of his redcoat and had bemoaned that he was a little thicker around the middle but was glad that it was not as awful as his brother's midsection. *Albert is so bloody fat and looks ancient! I remember his wife; she is the quiet one and I know she liked me first but she preferred to be titled. They have two children. And Darcy, FIVE! I will see the children tomorrow. Perhaps I will remember something by then.*

He observed everyone carefully. He was very pleased to meet Iris' and Georgiana's husbands. He was told Georgiana was now a Chatsworth and another memory flashed in his mind. *Lady Isabelle. Something about her and me. Damn it, did I sleep with her, too? She is too young. No, she is Georgiana's age. But she does not do anything for me. Blasted! I cannot remember anything else.*

He watched his parents and siblings. They were older but happy. His father kissed his mother's hand and Richard smiled seeing the affection. He also watched Georgiana and her husband; they were beaming as her husband was rubbing her stomach and he guessed that Georgiana was expecting again. Richard smiled in pride as he saw his baby cousin so grown up.

Richard rubbed his waistcoat pocket as he recalled always doing so out of habit. It felt like something was missing. Garrison had asked if he wanted his 'usual' items, but being at his parents' home, he had declined to have anything tonight since he felt tired and did not wish to carry any extra weight. He touched his coat pocket and wondered where his book was. *What book? I know I carry a book with me always but I do not remember why. I have a watch as well, do I not? Why do I feel like I am missing something important?* He looked at his handkerchief. *Who embroidered my initials for me? I would only let a wife do this for me. Why am I comforted seeing the lavender sprigs here? Lizzy smelled like lavender. I want her. I need her.*

He slowly lifted his eyes to watch Darcy and Lizzy. Darcy was smiling and speaking jovially with Georgiana and appeared as cheerful as the others, but when he looked at Lizzy, he saw that she appeared exhausted and depressed. She had a soft smile on her face but he knew, he just knew, that it was a façade and she was unhappy. *Lizzy... I do not recognise the name. She cannot be the woman of my dreams... But she has to be. My heart has never been touched like this and I feel as if my soul is craving her. I need to be near her, I need to touch her. Damn it. What the hell is wrong with me and why can I not remember?*

Then he met her eyes. She looked straight at him and he felt his whole body burn. *My wife! She is MY wife! She belongs to me and I cannot live without her.* He had visions of kissing her and holding her tightly in his arms. He could not stop staring at her and her beautiful green eyes stared back as if to pierce his soul.

He saw her fidget and rub her fingers, and when she lifted her left hand off her right, he saw it then. He saw his grandmother's ring on her slim finger. *The ring! There is no way my grandmother's ring is on her finger if she is not mine. I would never have given it to anyone who did not have my whole heart. I must find out! I need to talk to her!*

Richard stood abruptly, knocking his teacup to the floor and startling his mother next to him.

Lady Matlock yelled out in concern, "Richard! Are you well?"

Richard took a breath. "I am well, mother. I am... I am tired and wish to rest. Darcy, could you help me? And Cousin Lizzy, could you come with us?" He asked quietly.

Lady Matlock replied as she smiled, "Go and rest, Richard. I am certain a full night's sleep will set everything to right." She patted his shoulder and kissed his cheek.

Darcy and Elizabeth both stood up. They all bowed and wished everyone good night and headed for Richard's rooms.

Richard walked ahead, attempting to control his passions as well as organise his thoughts in his mind. *How do I ask if something happened with Lizzy and myself with Darcy here? How do I get her alone so I can ask? I need her. I need to touch her and hold her and make her mine. How long have I been... How could I be so dishonourable to bed my cousin's wife?*

He recalled clearly now, as he remembered the woman of his dreams and her face became clearer. It was his cousin's wife that he saw now, seeing her brilliant green eyes gazing at him and hearing her melodious laughter, her soft nude body under him as he kissed her face and breasts, and he remembered making love to her again and again. Visions of her loving him flooded his mind and he could not remain standing.

Darcy caught Richard as he was falling onto his knees. "Brother, what is the matter? Is it your head? Shall I call for a doctor?"

Richard shook his head as if to tear away the memory of this woman in his mind and shut his eyes tightly. He could not breathe. His head was piercing and it felt like it would split in two.

Then he smelled her scent.

The soft fragrance of lavender calmed him as he felt Darcy stand him up on one side with Lizzy on the other to walk him to his rooms. He stood and walked slowly, keeping his eyes closed and leaning towards Lizzy's hair to breathe in her intoxicating scent. His body was on fire where she touched him around his waist with her arm and her head on his shoulder.

Once they entered his bedroom, Richard stood on his own strength and slowly opened his eyes, still holding onto his cousin's wife while lifting his arm away from Darcy. It

436

felt so right to hold her in his embrace. He looked down and saw her tears flowing out and he finally released her shoulders and wiped her damp cheek with his thumb. *I love her. I do not remember but I know I am completely and wholeheartedly in love with her. My wife. Wait, she is carrying my child! She is my wife and is pregnant with my child. How is this possible?*

Elizabeth quietly whispered. "Oh, Richard, how could you forget me?" She stepped back and looked at Darcy with tears running down her face.

Richard stood frozen, hearing his name from her lips, as he had allowed no one to call him so intimately other than his immediate family.

"Fitzwilliam, I cannot... How do I...?" She sobbed.

Darcy flew to her side and hugged her. "Oh, Elizabeth..."

ELIZABETH! Richard's mind virtually exploded hearing his beloved's name. *My Elizabeth! My wife!*

His head was pounding worse than before now and he groaned loudly as he fell to the ground. He held his head between his hands as memories came back flooding in. Flashes of Elizabeth in his arms on Xerxes, Elizabeth with the twins bundled up in bed, her sitting on his lap to make love to him, kissing her after Amelia's birth, making her his wife after years of loving her. All of his memories came back all at the same time and then everything went black.

~*~

Richard was startled awake when he heard the tray cart roll into his rooms. He jumped to sit up in bed. His mouth was dry and his head ached, although not as severely as before.

Lady Matlock cheered. "Richard! You are awake!" She handed him a glass of water, seeing that he could not speak. "You had us so worried, child!"

"Mother, mother, I am fine. Where is Darcy? Where is Elizabeth?" He hurriedly spoke after swallowing. He remembered everything. He remembered his precious wife and her tears while he had forgotten her. He needed to see her. He needed to hold her. "GARRISON!" he yelled.

Lady Matlock tried to calm him. "I do not know where they are."

Richard panicked. *Have they left me? I need her. I need her right now. My precious wife; how could I have forgotten her? I need her more than anything in my life.*

Seeing the frightened look on her favourite son's face, Lady Matlock reached over and held her son's cheeks. "I think Darcy wanted to take Lizzy for a stroll in the gardens. I had to force Lizzy to take a break and go outside since she adamantly refused to leave your side for hours. They had been sitting here all night and morning and she finally agreed for some fresh air with Darcy. They had not left your side since last night when you collapsed. They were so worried for you and I know she was distraught that you did not remember her after all you have been through together. She adores you and you have been like a brother to her from the beginning. Do you remember anything?"

Garrison walked in. Richard barked, "I need to wash up and I need my coat. Hurry, man! Quickly!"

He looked at his mother and kissed her cheek. "I remember everything, mother. I need some fresh air as well. Everything is well. Everything will be well." Seeing her full smile, he kissed her cheek again. "Thank you, mother. Thank you for taking care of me and for allowing Darcy and Elizabeth to take care of me. I am loved and everything will be well."

"I am relieved, Richard. I should have allowed Lizzy to care for you from the beginning. You needed to see Darcy and Lizzy to recover quickly since they have been vital to your life for so many years. I will let Garrison work on you. I am going to tell your father the good news and we will see you downstairs soon?" Lady Matlock kissed his forehead and departed.

As soon as Garrison was done, Richard flew out of doors. He fingered his pocket watch and felt for his poetry volume that he had carried for the past eight years. *How could I forget? My mind might have forgotten but my heart always remembered. I need to find her. I need to hold her.* His head was still thumping but not as much as his heart. He knew Elizabeth had loved a particular garden path and hurried towards it.

Not seeing or hearing anything near the path, he did not know what to do. He thought of yelling out her name but not knowing if anyone else was nearby or the servants thinking he was completely mad, he walked over to a small grove where several hedges made a great hideaway for privacy, when he heard her.

Richard heard her crying, "What if he never remembers us? Our lives together? Our children?"

He ran faster and as soon as he turned the hedgerow and saw her, he yelled, "ELIZABETH!"

He ran to her and lifted her as he embraced her and kissed her. She immediately wrapped her arms around his neck as he drew her tightly against his body and plunged his tongue into her mouth. He kissed her with as much ardour as his body could express. After releasing her for breath, he continued to hold her firmly as he turned to Darcy. He shook his hand with Darcy behind Elizabeth's back and saw his cousin's broad smile.

"I am so sorry. I cannot believe I forgot ten years of my life. But my heart, my soul never forgot. As soon as I saw you, I knew you were mine, Elizabeth. I knew I loved you but I could not fathom seducing my cousin's wife. I was torn that I was a rake or that I had importuned you but when Darcy spoke your name last night, I remembered it all. My Elizabeth, my wife. My heart never forgot you. I remembered you are carrying my child. I remember everything. I am so sorry, so very sorry, my love, my dearest wife, my Elizabeth." He continued his words of love as she cried.

"It is well. Everything is right now." Elizabeth finally calmed. "I missed you so much and these past four days have been the most awful days of my life, Richard, but I am glad you are back with us. I am glad we will be a family again."

Richard caressed her cheek gently. "You never lost me. Even without knowing the situation, I knew I loved you. I knew you were my wife and my heart was yours." Smiling, he looked at Darcy. "I could not understand how I could betray my dearest cousin and I thought I had seduced you somehow but I saw the ring on your finger and knew I must have been in love with you. Everyone had called you 'Lizzy' and I could not understand what was happening but when Darcy called you 'Elizabeth', everything came back." He kissed her lips gently, "Thank you for staying with me last night. Mother told me that you and Darcy had not left my side. I love you so much. I am sorry I forgot and made you so miserable these past four days."

Elizabeth smiled, "You have returned to me. That is all that matters. I love you, Richard Fitzwilliam. I am so glad you have returned to us."

Darcy embraced his cousin as well and patted his back. "I am so glad, brother. Elizabeth needed both of her husbands and I needed my dear brother returned to me as well. The children will be happy to see you again. They have been asking for you."

"Thank you, Darcy. Thank you for sharing your life with me. Thank you for Elizabeth." Richard was teary. "I cannot imagine my life without you both and I was miserable believing that I was alone and unmarried. All I wanted to do was to make love to Elizabeth and I could not understand my body's reaction to being near her." He turned to Elizabeth again. "I love you, Mrs. Fitzwilliam. I love you with every breath in my body and even when I could not remember, my soul was searching for you and I could never forget you. I will love you until my last breath, Elizabeth. Please forgive me."

"I love you so much. I wish we were back at Pemberley. We were to leave tomorrow but with your injury, I do not know what to do. I need you back in our bed, Richard." Elizabeth whispered the last part.

Richard walked her over against the tall hedge and lifted up his beloved against Darcy's embrace, "Darcy, I need her now. This all began because I needed her and I rode that blasted animal that threw me instead." He pulled up her skirts and fondled her breast with one hand as he glided his erection into her womanhood. "I love you so much, Elizabeth. I missed being inside you for far too long." He thrust hastily into her and released with a quiet grunt in a few minutes. He glowed in bliss as he watched his dear cousin kiss her lips while he straightened his clothing.

"I missed you so much. I know we were a bit loud but it was so necessary. We should have done this last week instead of insisting on maintaining propriety. I wish to go home tomorrow. I need to get back in our bed and I promise to love you properly as soon as we have some privacy. I love you, Mrs. Fitzwilliam. Thank you, Darcy." Richard kissed her fondly again before returning indoors to see the rest of his family.

~*~

The merry group celebrated Richard's health with all the children in attendance this time and his family was tremendously relieved that Richard's memory returned. Richard laughed and smiled, seeing his children and hugging all of them several times and holding Madeline, the youngest baby on his lap. He was most content to know that he was not alone and that he was so dearly loved by Elizabeth and Darcy and all of the children.

The children were enthralled to have their *papa* back and they had fought over who could sit next to him. His heart melted seeing Amelia's beautiful face. *My daughter. My own daughter and another on the way. All five of our children are so precious to me, all thanks to my Elizabeth, my wife.*

All of the family members knew of the close friendship between Richard and Elizabeth and believed their relationship to be like brother and sister. No one outside of his immediate family ever called Richard by his given name, as he never allowed the intimacy, but for Elizabeth to have called him by his name from the beginning of their acquaintance had shown their close bond, which only grew over the years. Even the viscountess, after almost eleven years of marriage, still called him 'Colonel'.

They saw the two tease each other and laugh together and get along quite famously every time they were together, and Richard had always treated Elizabeth affectionately and protectively from the start, as he did with Iris and Georgiana. And it was quite obvious to everyone that after years of living together, Richard absolutely adored Elizabeth and loved all the Darcys very much.

Although Lady Matlock wished for her favourite son to stay with her a little longer, she understood the importance of getting back to the regular schedule of his life. She did wonder if there was a woman that Richard was seeing and knowing that he was a confirmed bachelor for life, she guessed that he must have a mistress, as it appeared his questions during his memory loss were around a woman of his memories. She sighed, knowing that both of her sons must have mistresses but recalling how her husband once was, she was resigned that it was the way of society and prayed that there were not too many illegitimate grandchildren. With the promise to see each other at Pemberley in two months, they parted company with full smiles.

The Darcys and Richard made love several times on the two-hour carriage ride and as soon as they returned home and saw to the children's well-being, they retired to their bedroom to love each other and were not seen for three full days.

After Garrison filled him in on the initial memory loss and what he was like, including his foul language and manners, Richard gave Garrison a large bonus and gifted Elizabeth with several presents, from flowers to books to yet another new carriage.

Chapter 40

"Papa?"

"Yes, Amelia?" Richard answered.

"Why do we have two papas? Bennet and Richie call you 'godfather' sometimes or 'papa' and you and Papa both answer us. Michael likes to call you 'goodpapa' but we just all call you 'papa'. Are you both our fathers?" She asked.

"I love you and all the Darcys very much. I watched you and loved you since birth and your mama has me and your papa to take care of her always so you and your brothers always grew up calling me 'papa'. I love you all like your papa loves you. Do you not wish to call me 'papa'?" Richard asked with a smile. *She was always the inquisitive one. My daughter.*

"No, I like having two papas. All my friends have only one and they get jealous. I heard some of my friends' mamas talking about you being so 'dashing'. What is that?" She innocently asked.

Richard laughed loudly. "I think it means they think I am handsome. Do you think me handsome?"

"Oh, yes, papa. You and Papa are the handsomest! Do you think my brothers are handsome?"

"Yes, absolutely. Your brothers are the handsomest boys in the world and you and your sister are the prettiest girls in the world." Richard confidently answered.

Amelia giggled. "Madeline is only two and I am five so I am prettier!"

"Oh, Amelia, beauty is not just on the outside and on the inside as well. Remember, you must be generous, like your mama, who is the most beautiful woman in the world to your papas, and never brag. I know you are beautiful but you will learn so much more to be a proper young lady and mama will teach you to be beautiful on the inside, understand? I love you, princess. Let me give your sister a kiss and I need to check on your mama." Richard kissed her forehead and kissed Madeline Grace's as well, before leaving them with their nannies.

He walked to the sitting room and peeked his head into Darcy's room. "Darcy, I am back. I was checking on the girls and they are well. Any progress?"

"I believe we are close. It has been a long day but she is still smiling. Why do you not see her for a moment? She will be happy to see your face." Darcy replied.

Richard stepped in and found Elizabeth in the middle of the bed. He walked over and kissed her forehead tenderly. "Elizabeth, you look remarkably well for having been in labour for the past five hours. Baby number six must be a good baby." He smiled.

"Oh, Richard, I am just tired but I think this baby is ready to come out soon. The girls were so much easier and I forgot how much work this is. Are the children well?" Elizabeth asked.

"Bennet and Richie are teaching Michael how to feed the foals and Amelia and Madeline are with their nannies. They are well and looking forward to meeting the newest Darcy. Is there anything else I can do for you?" Richard rubbed her hand as she grunted through another labour pain.

"Mrs. Meyers has been marvellous. I am so glad you delivered all my children, Mrs. Meyers." Elizabeth smiled. "I will be well. Thank you for checking on the children for me. I was concerned since I had not seen them for so long. I will see you soon, Richard." She breathed out and groaned another pain.

"Be well, Elizabeth." Richard stepped out to the familiar seat next to the door in the sitting room where he stayed through every birth since Michael.

Soon enough, a cry was heard and Darcy popped his head out in a few minutes. "It is a boy. We have a boy!" Darcy rushed back in. Seconds later, he jumped back out. "Elizabeth is well. She wants to know, Edward or Henry?"

Richard grinned. "Edward Richard Darcy." They hugged each other and Darcy ran back to Elizabeth's side.

He could hear Darcy shouting, "Edward Richard Darcy!" and he smiled broadly. *My son. My own flesh and blood.*

After Madeline was born, Darcy had gifted him with the second greatest treasure he could bestow, by allowing him to release inside Elizabeth consistently for two months while Darcy released outside. Darcy ensured that Richard's seed would impregnate Elizabeth and they had known, with full certainty, that this child was Richard's issue. A boy would have Richard as a middle name and a daughter would be named Rachel, as close to Richard as possible.

My son. Even when I could not remember, I knew she was carrying my child. Elizabeth is my heart and I belong to her fully. Even when my brain was addled, my heart and soul knew my beloved. He was extremely proud of his dearest wife.

As soon as the room was cleaned, Richard ran in to meet his own son. Edward's eyes were blue like his and he was beautiful. Even though his own, he loved all their children together and he vowed to be the best father to this beautiful boy as he had done with all five other children. He kissed Elizabeth soundly. "Thank you for making me a father again, Elizabeth. I love you so much." Turning to Darcy, he shook his hand. "Thank you, Darcy. Our boy is beautiful, like his fathers!"

They laughed and took turns holding the baby. Soon, all the other five children entered the room and rushed over to the bed to ogle at the new baby. The girls immediately fell in love and the boys were excited to have another brother to play with. Now, the teams would be even.

Darcy looked at his family and thanked God for their ever-growing family. Having grown up almost completely alone, he proudly looked at every one of them and loved the rowdy, noisy children who would laugh and fight and cry. He looked at Richard who had been their protector and best friend and knew that he had made the best choice to allow him to love Elizabeth.

Darcy looked at Elizabeth. The love of his life. The one that made everything possible. She captured his heart the first moment he saw her and he had never looked at another. She had brought him the joy and peace that he never thought possible and had so many fall in love with her. She had brought him their twins, Richard's unconditional love, and their beautiful children who radiated joy. She was the glue that held everything together, the foundation that made everything stand strong. *My love, my wife.*

Darcy leaned in and kissed Elizabeth passionately. "Thank you for being my wife, Elizabeth. I love you more than anything else in the world."

Elizabeth beamed. She kissed his cheek and whispered, "I love you, Fitzwilliam."

Richard kissed her lips lightly. She leaned over and kissed his cheek and whispered, "I love you, Richard."

Suddenly, Michael screamed, "EWWWWWW! He is wet!" The other boys and both girls jumped off the bed and laughed loudly.

Richard stood, "I will take Edward to the nurse. I need to have a talk with this young man." He winked.

"All right, children. Back to the nursery with you. Bennet, Richie, please take charge." Darcy commanded.

Bennet bowed, "Yes, papa. Come, Madeline. I will carry you, baby sister."

Richie smiled, "Yes, papa. Come, Amelia. You can hold my hand and Michael's."

"Our children are so wonderful, Fitzwilliam. I hope to have more. I want to have a full dozen, my love." Elizabeth hugged her husband.

"One baby at a time, my love. I am certain Richard and I can make it happen." Darcy chuckled.

"I love you. Thank you for allowing Richard to love me. My life is complete with the three of us and our children. I never imagined such happiness." Elizabeth sighed.

"Rest, my love. I know you will be out of bed tomorrow but rest for today. We must ensure your body recovers fully so you can have another baby when you are ready." Darcy smiled.

When Richard returned, Elizabeth was asleep. He lay down with her and watched her sleep. He whispered to Darcy who was on the other side, "Have you known such happiness, Darce? I have not."

"That is what Elizabeth said and I agree with you both. We are most blessed. Most blessed indeed." Darcy replied before falling asleep himself.

Richard leaned closer and kissed Elizabeth's lips. She kept her eyes closed but touched his face and whispered, "Richard."

Richard whispered, "I love you, Elizabeth. My love, my wife." And he closed his eyes to rest as well.

Epilogue

Elizabeth was indeed fruitful. The trio continued their fierce lovemaking and had three more children together: two daughters, Marianne Susan and Rachel Julia, and another son Alexander Henry.

Elizabeth was distraught after learning that she would bear no more after their last son, but with Darcy and Richard's help, she understood that she was blessed more than any other woman and rallied on. They continued to love each other deeply and frequently, no one else ever wiser on the on-goings of their nightly bedroom activities.

Richard believed that Amelia, Edward, and Rachel were his issue and Darcy had agreed that it was most likely, since they knew Edward was Richard's for certain, and the three looked more similar to each other than the others. It mattered not, though, since both men loved all the children the same and was grateful to have Elizabeth be their mother. They laughed quietly when Richard's mother commented that Michael, who was certainly Darcy's, took after the Fitzwilliam family the most.

Lady Matlock was very excited to see the family grow, as Elizabeth gave birth to so many children, as well as Georgiana, who had three sons and two daughters. Viscount Fitzwilliam had one son and his wife gave birth to another daughter three years later, although the Viscount did produce three other illegitimate children through his several mistresses. Richard confided in his mother that his life was full and could not be more content and that he had no illegitimate children nor was he dallying with loose women. His mother was pleased to hear that her favourite son was a stand-up gentleman, even if he was a confirmed bachelor for life. He had given so much to raise his status and reputation and she was immensely proud of him.

~*~

Jane and Charles Bingley were very happy with their two children, Betty and William, and felt very blessed to have resuscitated their marriage after their spectacular failure in the beginning. Bingley's income never returned to his 5,000 a year but he was able to invest and work hard to raise it to 4,500 a year and the Bingleys were content in their lot, working hard but making their marriage and family a priority.

Charles had discovered Caroline's son three years after her death when his solicitor was reviewing all of her possessions and documents. There was a journal that an assistant was reviewing to see if there were any secret properties that she might have owned. Mr. Henderson reported to Bingley that Caroline had placed her son in an orphanage in Portugal and that her diary indicated her son was the issue of one of three men that she had been sleeping with around the same time.

Bingley and Jane were disgusted and shocked but could not fathom leaving a family member to the whims of an orphanage, so they hired Mr. O'Connor to travel to Portugal to retrieve their nephew.

Mr. O'Connor returned with the four-year old boy with bright red hair and Jane immediately fell in love with the boy's green eyes. Mr. O'Connor also reported that although Caroline Bingley might not have paid attention, his investigation showed that there could be only one father, according to the child's eye colouring and due to the other two men being known for their infertility. Charlie was the illegitimate child of Lord Beresford's second son and once Mr. Beresford was made aware of his bastard, he sent £2,000 in restitution.

Charlie Bingley spent his days learning about land management from his Uncle Bingley and passing many of his happiest days in Derbyshire with the Darcys until he met a woman in the north that had the same hair colouring as himself and fell in love at first sight. He proposed to his beloved after a month of courting, and his uncle and aunt, the Bingleys, sat in silence when he brought his betrothed to meet his family in Hertfordshire. Darcy had written to him and advised him to tell Charlie the truth, as he did not feel it was his place to tell Charlie of his fiancée's origins.

Charles Bingley knew that the truth must be told when he saw the determination of the young couple in love to be married and reluctantly revealed to the couple that Charlie's fiancée was his own illegitimate child, Wendolyn Wickham, and that they were cousins. Mrs. Wickham had remarried but had not changed Wendolyn's name and although they would rarely meet, Charles and Jane were determined to be civil with the former Miss Sarah Fleming and to accept Charlie and Wendolyn's marriage. Jane was distraught for a couple of days but realised that it was so long ago and that she had fully forgiven her husband of the infraction which he had committed before meeting her. She felt some satisfaction meeting the former Mrs. Wickham, now Mrs. Wilson, and seeing that although she might have been a beauty at one time, her husband's former lover was now very plump after birthing seven more children.

Three months later, Wendolyn Wickham became Wendolyn Bingley, the name that was rightfully hers now.

~*~

Mary and Reverent Bertram had the greatest number of children. Mr. Bennet always laughed that the parson took being fruitful and multiplying too seriously after their tenth child was born. Richard, in his infinite kindness, ensured that each child had a trust set up with £1,000 each, using the court settlement from Maria Bertram's dowry, and Darcy and Elizabeth contributed another £1,000 each to their nephews and nieces.

Kitty Goulding was very happy with her simple marriage. She only had two sons but was pleased with her husband's skills in bed and Mr. Goulding was grateful for his brother Darcy and cousin Fitzwilliam in educating him on how to please his wife and they lived quietly in Meryton all of their lives.

Lydia and Lieutenant Denny were the most spirited of the Bennet daughters' marriages. Lydia delivered a large daughter, less than six months after the wedding, and even when the truth of the pre-wedding conception embarrassed her parents, she never batted an eye and immediately bore another child, eleven months after the first child was born. She birthed another daughter and yelled at her mother to 'shut it' when Mrs. Bennet bemoaned that her favourite daughter had birthed only daughters when her other four daughters had sons during the first or second births.

Lydia continued to be fiery and opinionated but her husband was at her beck and call, and by the time Lydia gave birth to her fifth daughter in five years, Mrs. Bennet had given up all hopes of seeing a grandson from Lydia. It was not until after Mrs. Bennet's death that Lydia had her seventh child, who was finally a son. The Darcys ensured that her children would be looked after as well, as they set up a trust for all of their nieces and nephews from all four sisters.

Mr. Bennet lived happily with Mrs. Bennet for years until Mrs. Bennet passed from a lingering illness after Samuel turned ten years old. Mr. Bennet was distraught to lose his companion of so many years but knew that she was at a better place. He poured his love into Samuel, teaching him about philosophy and estate management with Darcy and Fitzwilliam's help and was content to live out the rest of his life, visiting his daughters and taking care of his beloved son.

~*~

Darcy and Richard's income was tremendous. When they were not making love to their wife, they worked hard to grow their income and to provide for their numerous tenants and investments and everything they touched turned to gold. Eventually, the railroad investment as well as several others paid off in returns never expected and they were able to provide five incredible estates for their five sons as well as the extra properties already in ownership. They were also able to save enough funds to provide £100,000 each for their four daughters and made sure that an iron-clause was attached, that suitors had to pass a list of stringent tasks to be able to access their dowries, and their daughters would always have full control of their monies.

~*~

After the peace was finalised in the Continent, the loving family travelled to the continent and visited many places. Both husbands looked adoringly at Elizabeth who was enraptured by everything she saw. They vowed to do everything in their power to show her new places and give every gift she desired.

The very large family, including their children and governesses and nannies, saw amazing places and learned of important history, as well as continue to bond with each other throughout their travels as well as home. The Darcy Family was heralded as one of the most important families in history and was known for their dedication to each other.

When Richard Fitzwilliam finally published a book of his memoirs of his time during the war, no one questioned his valour and dedication to the Darcy Family, understanding the commitment he had made to his closest family, and even when the Darcy children called him 'papa' instead of 'godfather', people understood that he was part of the Darcy clan and never questioned his honour.

Elizabeth, Darcy, and Richard lived together for many wonderful decades, resolute to love each other as fully as possible, never taking each other for granted and happily knowing that their love was true and honourable.

The End

Printed in Great Britain
by Amazon

66795652R00265